Worldwide Praise for the Erotica of John Patrick and STARbooks!

"This writing is what being brave is all about. It brings up the kinds of things that are usually kept so private that you think you're the only one who experiences them."
— *Gay Times, London*

"'Barely Legal' is a great potpourri... and the coverboy is gorgeous!"
— *Ian Young, Torso magazine*

"A huge collection of highly erotic, short and steamy one-handed tales. Perfect bedtime reading, though you probably won't get much sleep! Prepare to be shocked! Highly recommended!"
— *Vulcan magazine*

"Tantalizing tales of porn stars, hustlers, and other lost boys...John Patrick set the pace with 'Angel!'"
- *The Weekly News, Miami*

"...Some readers may find some of the scenes too explicit; others will enjoy the sudden, graphic sensations each page brings. Each of these romans á clef is written with sustained intensity. 'Angel' offers a strange, often poetic vision of sexual obsession. I recommend it to you."
- *Nouveau Midwest*

"Self-absorbed, sexually-addicted bombshell Stacy flounced onto the scene in 'Angel' and here he is again, engaged in further, distinctly 'non-literary' adventures...lots of action!"
- *Prinz Eisenherz Book Review, Germany*

"'Angel' is mouthwatering and enticing..."
- *Rouge Magazine, London*

"'Superstars' is a fast read...if you'd like a nice round of fireworks before the Fourth, read this aloud at your next church picnic..."
- *Welcomat, Philadelphia*

"For those who share Mr. Patrick's appreciation for cute young men, 'Legends' is a delightfully readable book...I am a fan of John Patrick's...His writing is clear and straight-forward and should be better known in the gay community."
- Ian Young, Torso Magazine

"'BOY TOY' is splendid..."
– J.C., Illinois

"...'Billy & David' is frank, intelligent, disarming. Few books approach the government's failure to respond to crisis in such a realistic, powerful manner."
- RG Magazine, Montreal, Canada

"...Touching and gallant in its concern for the sexually addicted, 'Angel' becomes a wonderfully seductive investigation of the mysterious disparity between lust and passion, obsession and desire."
-Lambda Book Report

"Each page of John Patrick's 'Angel' was like a sponge and I was slowly sucked into the works. 'The Kid' had the same effect on me and now 'What Went Wrong?' has blown me away!"
-P. K. New York

"John Patrick has one of the best jobs a gay male writer could have. In his fiction, he tells tales of rampant sexuality. His non-fiction involves first person explorations of adult male video stars. Talk about choice assignments!"
-Southern Exposure

"The title for 'Boys of Spring' is taken from a poem by Dylan Thomas, so you can count on high caliber imagery throughout."
- Walter Vatter, Editor, A Different Light Review

"'Boys of Spring' is Patrick's latest piece of erotic imagination in overdrive!"
-Zipperstore, London

*Book of the Month Selections in Europe and the U.K.
And Featured By A Different Light,
Lambda Rising and GR, Australia
And Available at Fine Booksellers Everywhere*

MAD ABOUT THE BOYS

A New Collection of Erotic Tales
Edited By
JOHN PATRICK

Plus
Two Complete Novels
YOUNG & WILLING
By John C. Douglas
and
MAD ABOUT THE BOY
By John Patrick

STARbooks Press
Sarasota, FL

Books by John Patrick

Non-Fiction
A Charmed Life: Vince Cobretti
Lowe Down: Tim Lowe
The Best of the Superstars 1990
The Best of the Superstars 1991
The Best of the Superstars 1992
The Best of the Superstars 1993
The Best of the Superstars 1994
The Best of the Superstars 1995
The Best of the Superstars 1996
What Went Wrong?
When Boys Are Bad
& Sex Goes Wrong
Legends: The World's Sexiest
Men, Vols. 1 & 2
Legends (Third Edition)
Tarnished Angels (Ed.)

Fiction
Billy & David: A Deadly Minuet
The Bigger They Are...
The Younger They Are...
The Harder They Are...
Angel: The Complete Trilogy
Angel II: Stacy's Story
Angel: The Complete Quintet
A Natural Beauty (Editor)
The Kid (with Joe Leslie)
HUGE (Editor)
Strip: He Danced Alone
The Boys of Spring
Big Boys/Little Lies (Editor)
Boy Toy
Seduced (Editor)
Insatiable/Unforgettable (Editor)
Heartthrobs
Runaways/Kid Stuff (Editor)
Dangerous Boys/Rent Boys (Editor)
Barely Legal (Editor)
Country Boys/City Boys (Editor)
My Three Boys (Editor)
Mad About the Boys (Editor)
Lover Boys (Editor)
In the BOY ZONE (Editor)
Boys of the Night (Editor)
Secret Passions (Editor)

Entire Contents Copyrighted © 1995 by John Patrick, Sarasota, FL. All rights reserved. No part of this book may be reproduced or transmitted in any form by any means, electronic or mechanical, including photocopying, recording, or any information storage and retrieval system, without expressed written consent from the publisher. Every effort has been made to credit copyrighted material. The author and the publisher regret any omissions and will correct them in future editions. Note: While the words "boy," "girl," "young man," "youngster," "gal," "kid," "student," "guy," "son," "youth," "fella," and other such terms are occasionally used in text, this work is generally about persons who are at least 18 years of age.

First Edition Published in the U.S. in March 1996
Second Edition Published in the U.S. in December 1996
Library of Congress Card Catalogue No. 95-072419
ISBN No. 1-877978-78-7

Contents

Introduction:
SOMEONE IS WATCHING
John Patrick

VOYEUR
Edmund Miller

THE GREAT MAN'S BOY
John Patrick

ALMOST ANONYMOUS
John Patrick

THE BET
Matthew Rettenmund

DUTCH TREAT
Ray Burrell

SHORTS WEATHER
Al Lone

EXPLORING SAM
David Patrick Beavers

BROTHER FLESH
John Terron

ROUGH-BOY
Ian Stewart

A PERFECT SUMMER
Leo Cardini

TOBY
Andrew Richardson

TONIO JOE
Richie Brooks

14
Thom Nickels

A TRUCKER'S BOYS
Frank Brooks

DESERT STEAM
David Patrick Beavers

THE RENDEZVOUS
Jarred Goodall

THE MUMMY
L. Amore

PRACTICE PONY
David Laurents

ROMANCING THE BONE
Griff Davis

BROTHERS
Ken Anderson

PLEASE, TEACH ME MORE
Bert McKenzie

JOHNNY: OUT OF HIDING
Thomas C. Humphrey

EDDIE'S AUDITION
Peter Z. Pan

THE BLACKGUARD
William Cozad

NIGHT TRAIN
Edmund Miller

THIEF OF NIGHT'S BOUNTY
L. Amore

MILK RUN
Christopher Thomas

A CIRCLE OF A THOUSAND BOYS
Antler

LOVE IN THE BOOKSTORE
Ken Anderson

YOUNG & WILLING
by John C. Douglas

MAD ABOUT THE BOY
by John Patrick

Editor's Note

Most of the stories appearing in this book take place prior to the years of The Plague; the editor and each of the authors represented herein advocate the practice of safe sex at all times.

And, because these stories trespass the boundaries of fiction and non-fiction, to respect the privacy of those involved, we've changed all of the names and other identifying details.

INTRODUCTION: SOMEONE IS WATCHING

John Patrick

Just as I happened to look out the window of my hotel room, the slim, bare-chested youth, wearing Levis that bulged admirably at the crotch, walked over to the television in his little apartment across the way. His incredibly youthful beauty beckoned me to linger a little longer. Suddenly he walked away from the TV and out of sight, and the lights went out. I was about to turn away, thinking the boy had gone to bed, when I noticed a flicker down there. The TV was still on. I stayed, hoping the boy would return.

After an interminable amount of time, or so it had seemed, the boy reappeared – and in the dim light I could tell he was now wearing nothing at all. As he slipped a cassette into the VCR on top of the TV, my eyes became riveted on the magnificently rounded twin mounds of his buttocks. Then he went to the couch across the room, his generous cock flopping between his legs. In full view of the window, he stretched out and began to watch TV. His hand aimlessly stroked his forelock, scratched his cheek, brushed a bare nipple, then began to slowly stroke his cock. As it hardened, I stroked my own erection and watched in perverse fascination as he proceeded to get himself off...

The youth, by failing to close his blinds, became an unwitting exhibitionist, and I, through an idle glance out my window, just as unwittingly became a Peeping Tom, the colloquial expression for the more clinical word *voyeur*. *Webster's Deluxe Unabridged Dictionary* defines *voyeurism* as "a perversion in which sexual gratification is obtained by looking at sexual objects or scenes," and a voyeur as "a person given to voyeurism; a Peeping Tom." Voyeur comes from the French verb *voir*, to see. Benjamin Karpman, in his book *The Sexual Offender And His Offenses* uses the term *scoptophilia* interchangeably with *voyeurism* and defines it as "Excessive interest in looking at genitalia, sex acts, etc. as a sexual stimulus. (It) is a socially illegal act motivated by the desire to see the unclothed or partially unclothed sexual object."

Troy McKenzie in *Stallion* magazine said, "To be publicly labeled a Voyeur or Peeping Tom carries a social stigma with it, a stigma of being degenerate, unclean. People who realize too late that they have been the unwitting object of a voyeur sometimes experience emotional upheaval, most generally fear, anger, or both.

Since the Sexual Revolution of the '60s, Troy claims, voyeurism has found wider acceptability. But to fully understand this, we must define and categorize the types of voyeurism. In *Masturbation: The Art of Self Enjoyment*, J.L. Kullinger divides voyeurism into three categories, or "states." The first state is the man who enjoys going to strip shows, or seeing boys in tight shorts on the street or in Speedos at the beach. Almost *all* men fall into this category, he says. The second state includes a *majority* of men, says Kullinger. These are the men who enjoy erotic and/or sexually explicit films and stage shows, or enjoy watching one or more persons engaged in sexual activity. The third, and often pathological category, according to Kullinger, is the Peeping Tom. In this category, he places those men who must watch individuals who never know they are being watched. He considers the first two categories to be generally harmless ones, and implies that the third is a different story.

C.P. Oberndorf put it more succinctly in his book *Voyeurism As A Crime;* he states that it "is a crime only when the observed has not given consent. The emphasis of law is based upon the right to privacy of the person observed. Satisfaction arises from seeing when not being seen."

"However," McKenzie says, "voyeuristic encouragement surrounds us. We see it in television and print ads, movies, situation comedies, soap operas, books, suggestive clothing, photography – you name it, and it's there. It always has been, but with mass marketing in all phases of life, it's more overtly apparent, making it easier to step over that boundary separating the 'normal' person from the voyeur.

"Even the third state – the Peeping Tom category – has achieved a certain amount of acceptability not previously afforded it."

And as more and more is being written about voyeurism, we find there are no age restrictions on Peeping Tomism. In *Dream Boy* by Jim Grimsley, young Nathan becomes infatuated with his neighbor, Roy:

"His bedroom in the new house seems airy and spacious after the smaller rooms he has occupied before. Large windows face the Connelly house over the high privet. A figure in the upstairs window above the hedge draws Nathan's eye.

"Roy stands there. Maybe that is his bedroom, where the pale curtains fall against his shoulder. He has stripped off the dirty T-shirt and leans against the window frame. He has a smile on his face and a self-conscious look in his eye, as if he knows someone is watching. The curled arm is posed above his head. He moves away from the window after a while. But Nathan goes on waiting in case he comes back.

"Roy has been watching this same way for a while. In the beginning Nathan thought he was imagining things. The first morning he rode the school bus, he thought it was unusual to find Roy studying him from the rearview mirror. They had barely said good morning when Nathan climbed onto the bus the first time, and yet here was Roy watching.

"...Nathan watches Roy, the curve of his shoulders and the column of his neck. Roy steers the bus neatly on its tangled route. ...During the course of the ride, he works himself gradually forward, empty seat by empty seat, confident of eventual success since he will be riding to the last stop. Roy, efficient, steers from one dirt driveway to the other, and the orange bus discharges its passengers in clusters of neat frocks and clean blue jeans.

"...Now that the moment has come, Nathan sits, stupefied. He gauges the few remaining empty seats between him and Roy. Roy glances at him in the surveillance mirror. Finally he says, 'Why don't you come up here?'

"The question echoes. Nathan moves behind the driver's seat. A slight flush of color rises from Roy's collar. Nathan leans against the metal bar behind Roy's seat and hangs there, chin to seat back. The orange bus lumbers down the dirt road.

"The feeling is restful. They can be quiet together. Nathan is glad, and wishes Poke's Road were longer.

"...Later, standing at his bedroom window, Nathan watches Roy moving from barn to shed, shirt unbuttoned, sleeves rolled above his elbows, flesh bright as if the glow from a bonfire is radiating outward through his torso and limbs. He is cleaning the barn, stacking rusted gas cans and boxes in the back of the pickup truck, forking soiled hay into damp piles. He moves effortlessly from task to task as if he is never tired. The sight of him is like a current of cool water to Nathan.

"...It is a new feeling, not like friendship. Not like anything.

"...After a while Nathan retreats from the window, lying across the bed scribbling idly at homework. He wants supper to be over. The arithmetic figures waver meaninglessly on the pages of his text. When he tries to concentrate, the word problems make periodic sense. He reads one long paragraph, considers it, realizes he has remembered nothing he has read, then finally stands, pacing to the window and drawing the curtain carefully back.

"Roy stands below. He is waiting near the hedge as if he has called Nathan. He carries a wooden crate full of Mason jars with dusty, cobweb-covered lids. Nathan parts the curtains slowly. Roy waves hello without fear or surprise. Nathan fights the impulse to turn away, to pretend he has come to the window for some other reason than to look at Roy. Roy's gentle smile disturbs Nathan deeply. It is as if he knows what Nathan is thinking and feeling. He sets the crate on the back porch and turns. He heads back to the barn for more jars. Nathan goes on watching as long as there is light."

In his semi-autobiographical novel *Boy Culture*, Matthew Rettenmund says, "I don't have a good working relationship with the power of sex. I have had to deal with disproportionate attraction all my life. High school was one long exercise in unrequited attraction. I would spy a guy with some particularly enticing feature (legs so effortlessly powerful they floored me, a hairy thigh in summer shorts exposed accidentally, a shitty grin) and would go on for weeks trying to convince myself he wanted me, too. And the girls who liked me! Many of them had dated the studs in our class, but seemed to like me if I made them laugh or carried on a conversation with them. Maybe I should have become a sense-of-humor call boy, or marketed my 'We talked for *hours!*' skills."

Upper class folks who can afford it are often voyeurs, often preferring it to actual fucking. In *Genius and Lust*, Joseph Morella tells this tale about Cole Porter and his pals: "In Harlem black people and white people were more segregated than in Paris except in one arena: sex. New York in the Roaring

Twenties had brothels for men who wanted women and for men like Cole Porter. One of these houses in Harlem specialized in young black males. Both Cole and Monty Woolley shopped there. So did Jack Wilson.

"The pimp Clint Moore 'dealt' in mahogany merchandise. His house in Harlem was fully and richly furnished in this wood and with the mahogany male beauties who serviced the rich homosexuals who frequented the place. It was an exclusive and expensive club comparable to the fabled houses of female prostitution in old New Orleans. Nude black men mingled with the elegantly dressed famous and wealthy males who came to spend the evening. The only attire allowed the prostitutes were white terry cloth robes. Boys in training acted as servants, and guests could watch sexual training sessions through peepholes as older prostitutes taught newer ones the ropes.

"Cole was one of the regular and favored customers drinking and dining with Moore, along with Woolley and Lorenz Hart. Cole became friends with Clint Moore. In later years Moore would sometimes send one of the prostitutes to deliver a fake package to Cole's penthouse at the Waldorf. (This was in the 1930's when his legs had been crippled and he had lost the ability to go out in public without help.) The location of Moore's house was a closely guarded secret. Cole would go there and spend the night steeped in fantasies. Never mind that many of the boys available were fifteen years old, or that the actual 'employees' of the place led lives of virtual slavery and degradation. In those days the social consciousness was different; the idea that rich people could buy anything they wanted was a time-honored tradition."

And speaking of rich people, while making "The Wiz" in New York, the young Michael Jackson didn't indulge in the drugs offered him at Studio 54 but he did derive some voyeuristic pleasure from watching patrons turn on in other ways. Truman Capote remembered watching Michael stare intently as a man and woman engaged in a sexual act in the shadows. "We were all so used to that sort of thing," Capote said, "and I sort of expected him to be absolutely shocked. But he seemed to be studying them like they were mating panda bears in the zoo."

"Everybody who enjoys pornography is a voyeur," John

Preston said. "When we read an erotic story, a major part of the turn-on is being able to 'watch' the characters' sexual exploits. On another level, we are turned on by the sense that we are glimpsing into the author's inner fantasy life.

"...When we come across the rare account that we know is in fact true, a real insider's account, the voyeuristic thrill is electrifying. These 'behind the scenes' reports titillate because they speak the unspeakable, expose that which is meant to remain concealed."

Even porn stars enjoy the kick. In his infamous interview with Dave Kinnick, blond-haired, blue-eyed babe Claude Jourdan reveals that when he was eighteen and at college, a girlfriend pointed out that a guy was after him. "So one night the guy threw a party, and I went. After all the guests left, he said, 'Do you want to stay over?' I said, 'Sure. I'm drunk.' He lay down on the settee to sleep, and I was a bit nervous. His parents were upstairs, and we were downstairs. Typical first-time story, I guess. I already knew I was probably attracted to men, but I wasn't sure because I hadn't had sex with a girl yet. And I knew he was a fag.

"We had a discussion while training about some guys on the team. We were on the gymnastics team. He'd say, 'Look at this guy!' and act excited and watch me to see my reaction. Well, there we were on the settee, and he started kissing me. I said, 'Excuse me. I would like not to kiss you. I'm not used to kissing a man.' I still laugh about that because if some guy told me that now, I'd tell him to fuck off. He was really patient because he said, 'OK, that's fine,' and he started kissing my body and stuff, and then at one point he went right down there and put his mouth there and I went 'Oh, my God!' This guy knew how to suck! That was my first sex; I got sucked. For me it was more of a looking thing – voyeurism. I was afraid to touch him. I definitely didn't suck him."

But doing nothing at all can be painful – especially for a voyeur. "Fantasy Fights 2" is being sold as a sex-wrestling bout between two of the most solid muscleboys in the business, Tom Katt and Scott Randsome. But this is not a wrestling video; it's all about exhibitionism. Joe McKenna in *Inches* remarks, "Both of these heavy-duty body-builders are primo exhibitionists, cocksure physical show-offs of the highest order. They know you're looking at them, and they move like they care. But if it's really wrestling you're looking for, then this video isn't for you. It starts slowly. At first, you notice how fakey the fighting is, but then you begin to see that the only thing either guy cares about is watching himself in the mirrors that line one side of the wrestling ring. Randsome in particular keeps getting Katt into a hold, then whirling him around so they both can see their own reflections as their muscles strain against each other. Then you realize – it's actually a posing match, not a fight, and that's ultimately what makes it hot. These boys are both thoroughly into the image of themselves. Anyway, once Randsome works himself into a lather over himself, it becomes clear that he's the sure winner. Katt's preening, posing nature is no match for Randsome's, and he quickly submits to the superior Adonis. That's when they get down to some fantastic exhibitionistic fucking, with dominant Randsome getting Katt down on the mat naked and pounding the dark stud's ass with his cock. And needless to say, Randsome can't help himself – he turns around to watch himself ploughing Katt in the mirror. That was my favorite moment in the video.

"All too quickly, Randsome proceeds to stand over Katt and stroke himself until he shoots. The unexpectedly cool thing about this sequence is that Katt is on his belly so *he can't see it*! That's what I call real domination – straddle a naked guy, pump your muscles up, show off your hard, stiff prong and stroke it fast, but don't let him watch! Make him eat the floor instead!"

Yes, as we have so often heard, it's all in the mind. Indeed, in *The Erotic Mind*, Dr. Jack Morin discusses this in great detail. Our favorite among the case histories is the story of Carlos, who had always admired from afar the popular guys, especially the handsome jocks with muscular builds, the ones who exuded confidence and bravado. "His admiration for them increased in direct proportion to his self-hatred. Placing them high on a pedestal, he gazed at them with a mixture of awe, envy, desire, and resentment – for being so much better than he, and sometimes for teasing him ruthlessly. His fondest, seemingly impossible, dream was that one of them would befriend him and they would have sex. His eroticism was taking shape with him cast as unworthy outsider.

"Then one day after school Carlos, 15, was the last one in the gym after a long swim. Suddenly, in walked Drew, one of the guys he admired most, a star of the swimming team who had rarely so much as acknowledged Carlos's existence. This time he greeted Carlos with a smile and bantered with him playfully in the shower. As they talked, Carlos was transfixed by the strength and beauty of Drew's body. He tried to act casual in spite of having a full erection, a fact that Drew commented on with none of the derision Carlos expected. Their conversation turned to girls, to sex, and to feeling horny.

"As they dried off, Drew motioned toward the towel room door. Inside he reclined on a pile of damp towels, his penis now fully erect. He let Carlos rub and lick him everywhere. Reveling in the taste and feel of Drew's genitals, Carlos brought him to orgasm while masturbating himself. 'You're a great cocksucker,' said Drew, 'do it again' – an order Carlos eagerly obeyed.

"Afterward they dressed silently and left. Except for two other chance encounters, Drew continued to ignore Carlos most of the time. Carlos spent countless hours, however, waiting for opportunities to be alone with Drew. With great enthusiasm Carlos told me, 'I'd never felt so alive, so *accepted*.'

"The next year Carlos and his family moved to California. As a kid he had concluded, with the encouragement of his negative mother and racist community, that Hispanics were inferior. Now he saw plenty who were thriving, some of whom became role models for the success and self-respect he craved. Similarly, he met gays who celebrated their sexuality and formed the intimate, romantic bonds that he had always assumed were available only to straights. Gingerly, he began to come out of the closet.

"Paradoxically, as his self-esteem increased, his voyeurism became more obsessive. Whereas he used to cower in the shadows, now he became bolder, taking more risks, almost demanding to be noticed. And so when the complaints came, he was certainly devastated but also gratified to have finally become sufficiently visible to upset someone – especially the men to whom he mercilessly compared himself.

"Compulsive voyeurism, like other paraphilias, is relatively rare. Yet it's important to keep in mind that millions of men and women are regularly stimulated in nonobsessive ways by the very things that excited Carlos. Who hasn't been titillated by catching a glimpse of someone undressing or overhearing a sexual discussion or encounter? Most of us are also familiar with the bittersweet thrill of feeling inferior to those who most strongly attract us. And men and women of all sexual orientations, especially males in their teens and twenties, can identify with Carlos's sexual preoccupation and constant quest for visual stimulation.

"Carlos's eroticism was problematic because his negative core beliefs required that he stay in an inferior position. Yet within the self-defeating framework of his mind, Carlos used virtually every known source of arousal, including all four cornerstones of eroticism. The chasm between Carlos and the men he worshipped unleashed a flood of yearning. At the same time, a furtive sense of naughtiness permeated every scene, highlighted by the everpresent risk of discovery and punishment.

"The entire drama was further energized by a push-pull dance of power. On one hand, Carlos was clearly submissive to the men whose very existence seemed to mock him. Yet following the lead of his masturbation fantasies, primordial images of aggression and conquest helped him turn the tables. If the attention and reciprocation he craved weren't freely given he would steal them with stealth and cunning. He stalked the men he envied as prey, using them without their consent as pawns in his psychodrama. Finally, a forceful undercurrent of ambivalence toward everyone – himself as well as the men who simultaneously excited and demeaned him – added yet another dimension to an already explosive concoction.

"The entire scene was infused with plentiful and intense emotions. Some were positive, such as the genuine admiration and appreciation he felt toward the men who represented his ideals of masculinity. Negative emotions included resentment, hostility, fear, guilt, and shame. As Carlos explored his eroticism more deeply, he discovered that revenge was a particularly gratifying aphrodisiac. It was both frightening and exciting to be spotted by the men he stalked. Only if they knew what he was doing could they be made to squirm, as other men in the past had made him squirm. He savored the notion that they felt humiliated when Carlos used them as pawns in his sexual games.

"One thing Carlos's eroticism did *not* allow was the reciprocation of love and affection. He was trapped in the same bind as everyone whose eroticism is built on a foundation of self-hate: anybody who might be attracted to him was, by definition, excluded from the ranks of the desirable. Only those who reinforced his self-contempt were worthy objects of desire.

"Gradually, Carlos discovered why increasing self-esteem was making his voyeurism even more obsessive and problematic. His movement toward self-acceptance was threatening to unravel the central purpose of his eroticism: to turn the trauma of self-hate into the triumph of sexual excitement. He was torn about how to respond.

"Anyone whose eroticism is founded on antiself core beliefs and who later develops more self-loving attitudes and behaviors will eventually face an erotic crisis similar to Carlos's. *Webster's* defines 'crisis' as 'a time of great danger or trouble, whose outcome decides whether possible bad consequences will follow.' An erotic crisis is launched by the realization that the requirements of self-esteem and the lure of firmly established sexual patterns have become incompatible.

"For some this realization is gradual, beginning as a vague hunch that cherished turn-ons are somehow working against them, a hunch that builds until it demands attention. Often an erotic crisis grows out of a crisis of another kind, as it did for Carlos when he was threatened with expulsion for his voyeuristic activities. No matter how it begins, every erotic crisis ultimately reaches a point at which painful truths must be confronted and life-changing decisions contemplated. No one chooses such a crisis. Many will do almost anything to avoid it. And rarely, if ever, is any obvious solution in sight. It is indeed a time of great trouble.

"But an erotic crisis is often a sign that significant growth is under way. Some people unexpectedly stumble into erotic crises while working on problems that seem far removed from sex. Perhaps they are making strides toward greater confidence and self-affirmation when, much to their consternation, their progress inexplicably stalls.

"Caught on the horns of a self-hating dilemma, Carlos had

learned in early adolescence to use inferiority as an aphrodisiac. Once he confronted how his behavior magnetically drew him to idealized but unreachable men and dangerous situations, he faced many choices. For him, a major step was to disengage from locker room spying and venture into gay sex clubs, a world of consensual sex that sometimes leads to dates and occasionally even relationships.

"Some people may have trouble seeing how engaging in casual sex could be a sign of growth, but for Carlos it was. He had a strict safe sex policy so he could explore his sexuality without life-threatening consequences. I remember his delight at spending hours with men who were as enthusiastic as he. Of course, the men whom he considered most perfectly masculine and frustratingly aloof invariably attracted him most. But there were other men who pursued him, a totally new experience he didn't know how to handle. Though it wasn't easy, he coaxed himself into not turning away. He knew that learning to accept positive attention was the only alternative to the searing pain of constant rejection. Whenever Carlos was in emotional turmoil, however, his masturbation fantasies reverted to voyeurism. He noticed that his self-esteem took a nose-dive as he worshipped the objects of his desire. As a result of this awareness, he began to wonder what would happen if he were to celebrate his appreciation of the male form, to feel enriched by a man's beauty rather than demeaned by it. This became the central question of his therapy and his life.

"Gradually, Carlos experimented – in both fantasy and behavior – with positioning himself more favorably in relation to men he admired. His initial discovery probably won't surprise you: inferiority was sexier. Equality, however, was infinitely more gratifying. The only people who can fully comprehend this distinction are those who know firsthand the intensity of eroticized self-hatred.

"Carlos eventually began dating, cultivated the necessary social skills, and learned to avoid interpreting each man's reaction to him as a referendum on his worth. Eventually, he moved in with a guy who was handsome and affectionate but not as irresistible as the fantasy guys he continued to stalk in his imagination. This man wanted to love him, and Carlos's greatest achievement was the decision to receive that affection."

VOYEUR

Edmund Miller

Creeping to the window
shrouded in the artificial night
of all indoors,
I spy the little boy next door
angling on the sofa
in his underdrawers, there
before him his hated brother,
the bigger boy next door,
equally next to naked,
flailing his arms in exercise
fore and aft and checking
periodically his chest
for the tell-tale swollen
bruises of success.

THE GREAT MAN'S BOY

John Patrick

He was the perfect boy for The Great Man: A truly graceful specimen of a boy. He had long, golden hair that fell in rings and spirals around his shoulders. His eyes were lapis and his skin so fair it was nearly transparent. To my mind, he was beautiful beyond words.

I suspected the boy was asked to stay at The Great Man's mansion because he was great in bed. The Great Man was, doubtless, great as well. Although we had exchanged little more than perfunctory nods as he drove by my house in his dark blue Rolls, I knew much about The Great Man. I knew from his appearances on television he had a marvelous vocabulary, a vivid imagination, and a body that was remarkably well preserved. I knew from magazine articles that he had once been a minor film actor who had taken a percentage on a film rather than salary and the silly comedy had made millions. As his looks began to fade, he retired to sell real estate and become a multi-millionaire. I began renting his films; yes, in his prime, I would have been terribly attracted to him.

After the boy was ensconced at the house, I began to imagine them in bed. The boy's tidy limbs would be uncharacteristically askew, his neat torso flattened by The Great Man's greatness. Being accustomed to the superior position, The Great Man would probably splay his hands on the mattress, rising above the boy, his elbows a mighty lever. I pictured The Great Man poised above his young whore, looking down upon him with the kind of serene tolerance only great men can give.

I sensed The Great Man, his amusement great, answered everything the boy asked him with, "Oh?" or "Hmmm." After all, The Great Man had been a pretty fair actor.

For weeks I noticed only the presence or absence of cars in the driveway, lights in the windows. I never saw the boy. Perhaps, I wondered, was the Great Man into S&M and kept him tied up? Whatever, I hoped the kid knew somehow he wasn't entirely alone while I was next door.

It seemed to me that something was bound to change over there. I mean, how could such happiness continue unabated for long? I awaited signals of distress, sounds of despair. But there was nothing. Spring came and the remains of the garden bloomed and tangled and wilted right on schedule. The Great Man came and went, staying home no more than a day or two between trips.

And the lights would go off at three, then two, and I soothed myself with this sign that the boy was handling being with the Great Man a little better. By the time summer was fully upon us, I'd sometimes see his windows dark as early as midnight.

Nothing was really different otherwise. Except now that the weather was nice, I finally saw the kid in the yard. And when he saw me he acknowledged my presence with a nod. As time passed, I managed to find excuses to engage him in conversation. Occasionally I called him "son," but mostly I managed to avoid calling him anything. Just looking at him in his little yellow Speedo as he cleaned the pool gave me a hard-on and I had to keep my moments with him brief.

When the weather got really warm, the boy spent hours outdoors, sitting in the sun beside the pool, sometimes with a magazine, a look of pure absorption on his face. The cat, Dickens, would slither under the plastic slats of his chaise and lie there in the shade, panting. Without looking up from the page, the boy would reach down and pat whatever part of him was handy.

The boy almost always took the cat with him when he went out in the car The Great Man bought him shortly after they'd been together four months. It was a red Mustang convertible. On those rare occasions when the poor cat was left behind, he would collapse in the driveway to wait. No matter how long the boy was gone, his eyes wouldn't leave the direction in which he'd vanished.

Waiting for someone to come home was something I could relate to. Even now, around dusk, I still catch myself listening for the garage door to open and ex-lover Ben to drive in and turn the engine off.

Much as I missed Ben, though, the days didn't feel too big for the things I had to fill them with. There are all sorts of possibilities. And if I couldn't always account for my time, it was only because I kept too busy to worry much about it. Yet, I was never too busy not to think about my new neighbor. In fact, paying attention to the boy made me more mindful of time. The days of June and July seemed unbearably slow and heavy as I imagined how they weighed on him being alone so much of the time. He made me glad I was there. I invited him over and at first he refused, but eventually he relented. We would sit on the terrace and talk. He had a beer while I drank my martini. The cat would follow him over and eventually I was serving him some milk in a dish.

It saddened me to see the boy get up and go home, especially when so little seemed to be calling him back to that huge, cluttered house. By then, the evenings The Great Man made it home were rare. But the boy never let on, and neither did I. Around four-thirty, five o'clock, he'd say, "I better start dinner." I'd detain him briefly with pointless observations, another beer, but eventually he always slipped away. Those nights, after he'd been here, seemed longer than others. I hated to admit it but I was growing fond of him. *Terribly* fond. I longed to tell him that even though he had a lover, he could love other men. But I think too much, Ben always said. It made the advertising business hard on me and forced me into semi-retirement. And besides, I reasoned, if I had been remotely attractive to the boy, having a lover already wouldn't have stopped him.

Although the boy talked little about himself – in fact, talked very little period – I had pieced together quite a life for him from the tidbits he had thrown out. I knew he'd been active since he was 13 and his last real job was stripping in a bar, which is where the Great Man met him. I never imagined that I would actually make it with him, but I did. It happened one full moon night in early August. It was so warm that I went out and sat by the pool in the breeze for a few minutes before bedtime.

I heard footsteps, so soft I thought a thief was sneaking around my place. I tried not to sound alarmed. "Who's there?"

"John?" His voice was thin, startled.

"Hey."

He slipped from the darkness, wearing little white shorts,

and sat down on the chaise beside me.

"Dickens died this morning. Or during the night, I guess."

I just looked at him.

"He was awfully old," he said.

"I know. I'm sorry."

"I just wanted you to know."

"Thank you."

"Well...it's late." He started to get up.

I thought about reaching for his hand. But I remembered if you have to think about touching someone, then it probably isn't the right thing to do. But I did manage to say, "Hold your horses."

"Yeah?" He stood.

"Look, tonight you shouldn't be alone." I stood.

"Well – "

I couldn't help myself, I wrapped my arms around his tiny waist. He didn't pull away. I crushed him to my body in one long, slow, sloppy kiss.

Now he recoiled from my embrace. Concern that it would be over in a matter of minutes surfaced over my desire. I didn't want our sex to be a series of fumbling grunts and embarrassed apologies after I sucked his cock in the moonlight.

"Uhh, I don't know about this," he pleaded.

"I'm sorry," I said.

Then he chuckled and began kissing me with a passion I would never have guessed he possessed. His tongue surged deeply into my mouth. His teeth gently bit into my lower lip. With a wild and urgent need his hands gripped my body, molding himself to me. My breath became harsh and rasping in my throat, as he clutched my hips to his.

I led him up the stairs to the bedroom. Silently, he eased me to the edge of the bed, lightly forcing my shoulders down with just the merest touch of his fingertips, till I was sitting facing him.

Posing in front of me, he slowly removed his shorts. I tried to reach for the cock when it was revealed, but he spun away from my grasp. His eyes met mine, with a silent message. But I was too intent on his body to continue to look him in the eyes.

Moving towards me, he reached for my hand. I gave it to

him, trancelike, totally mesmerized by his movements. Taking my hand, he put it on the shaft of his erection. I groaned with the excruciating excitement that raced through my body. I thought it was the most beautiful penis I had ever seen, absolutely perfect in every way. He was more than worthy of the Great Man's love – of any man's.

Suddenly he pulled away. I was dumbstruck and pained. He moved behind me and his hands glided over my shoulders and unbuttoned my shirt. He pressed his naked body on my back in a catlike motion as his hot probing tongue licked my neck and earlobes.

"Please," I said in a strangled voice, "I can't hold off much longer."

"Sssh," he whispered, "we have all night."

Finally he removed my shirt and reached down to my shorts and opened them. While exposing my erection, he kissed me with promises of ecstasy. His tongue rolled in and out of my mouth, while his teeth gently chewed and bit as he sucked my lower lip into his mouth. Again, I groaned and reached for him, again he resisted my grasp.

Sliding down along my legs he tugged my shorts off, purposely grazing my legs with his incredible pecs. He lightly stroked my cock.

"Please – I want you..." I begged.

"Oh, it's so big and thick," he said in awe as he gripped the shaft tightly in his hand. "I'm going to love having you fucking me." He blew a stream of hot breath on the throbbing head.

Instead of feeling shy and insecure about my nudity, I felt bold and brazen. Thank goodness I began going to the gym when Ben moved out.

I gritted my teeth, but a small droplet of semen leaked out. It glistened in the light. The boy bent over and gently rubbed it off.

A deep low growl forced itself out of my mouth. "Fuck, I want you," I said in an agonized voice. "I've never wanted anyone the way I want you."

He delicately placed both his hands on my chest and pushed till I was lying on my back. Slithering, he crawled up the length of my body. My eyes were fastened on him as he positioned himself over me. I pointed to the nightstand.

He reached behind me and took a lubricated condom from the drawer.

"Please, hurry," I begged.

He quietly tore the package and carefully took the condom between his fingers. Then he slowly rolled it over my erection, his palm and fingers caressing the shaft. I groaned. The warmth of his hand and his skilled fingers sent a jolt of pleasure through my genitals.

Very gradually and deliberately, he straddled me. My cock slid into him. I was enveloped in heat and softness. He sat atop my hips, melding himself into me.

He straightened his back and locked his legs around me. Then he forced his inner muscles to tighten and contract on my throbbing erection.

"Yes!" I screamed out loud. My hands shot out and clutched his hips to mine. The tremors of my ejaculation jerked my body in a spasm of sublime release. My own buttocks tightened as I thrust deeply inside the boy, filling him. Within seconds I was completely spent. He lay next to me.

Coming down, I realized he hadn't climaxed, and I felt guilty. "I'm sorry," I said quietly. "I tried to make it last, but you had me so excited I couldn't control myself."

Gently stroking my cock, he removed the wrinkled condom. His lips caressed my shaft lovingly. I raised my head so I could watch as he slid the shaft in and out of his mouth, enjoying the sight and the sensation equally.

He got on all fours over me. Holding his lips around the base of my stiffening member, he began to stroke me. He synchronized the rhythm of his mouth and hands to the semi bump-and-grind dance he began performing with his ass, which I saw reflected in the mirrored closet. I could almost hear the music.

He cupped my balls, kneading them between his long, graceful fingers. My penis immediately responded and I yearned to enter him again, but he wouldn't remove his mouth, nipping, sucking, and tongue-whipping the head of my cock till I was once again in a frenzy of excitement.

"Please! I can't take it... !" I warned him. It seemed as if he was on fire, blazing, out of control. His hands cupped my ass, coaxing me deeper, slapping my gut against his face. I felt saliva dripping on my balls. I tried to slow him down; I brought my hands around his pretty neck. I felt his muscles flex and shift as he started to suck the very life out my prick. The intense pressure and release took me by surprise. I groaned and buckled as I erupted, spurting my juices in exuberance and sublime satisfaction.

He lay quietly next to me, then began running his hand along the curly black hairs on my chest. They were beaded with sweat droplets, catching the light like tiny prisms.

He jumped up and began to dance for me, his erection bobbing wildly. My eyes were riveted on the lovely cock. He caressed it, knowing that with each movement he seemed to be inviting my touch, my kisses.

Seductively, he ran his finger over one nipple and then the other, until they practically begged for suckling. Then he licked his own finger slowly, sucking it in his mouth as if it were my cock.

Watching me, smiling devilishly, he moved closer. I sank to my knees in front of him, buried my face in his crotch. As I sucked and kissed, he put his arms around my neck. He drew my face up and kissed me with a passion that almost singed my lips. He kept drawing me up, into his arms. Soon his prick connected with mine; our bellies crushed our cocks, trapping them. Then we started humping and I sank down, my tongue lapping his sweat. I backed off for a moment to look at it again, that magnificent boycock, jutting, bouncing, leaking precum. I began licking, greedy, knowing his proclivity for moving away.

But he seemed to want it now and simply thrust his hips forward, driving into me with an urgency that excited me further. My tongue traced the pulsing veins, coaxing precum from the slit. It was as if I had never tasted a cock before – sweet and salty at the same time, the fine hairs catching in my teeth as I took it down to the pubic hairs. As I nipped at it, his breathing became ragged and the tool became even harder. Sweat dripped off of him as the cock swelled and the flood began. His body stiffened. He whimpered, soft, low. I jerked the erection from my mouth and squeezed it, watching the cum spurt from the head, drop on my chest, my shoulders.

He stepped back slightly and smiled, his fingers rubbing the jism into my skin. Now I went briefly mad, lunging for him, taking the throbbing cock into my mouth once again, sucking it. In no time his cock head, swollen, was battering at my throat, his smooth thighs squeezing the breath out of me. His soft hands crushed my shoulders as I traced the contours of his cock with my tongue. His fingers curled urgently against my neck and he began another orgasm. My mouth filled and overflowed, yet he still kept on, until at last he was finished, telling me with a final thrust of his hips. I rose up and began to kiss his belly. I worked my way up his torso to his mouth and, slow and easy, we kissed.

I went to the bathroom and got a damp cloth and a towel. He was tugging on his shorts when I returned to the bedroom and I knelt down and wiped him clean, then tucked his cock and balls away, but not before giving them a farewell kiss. He ruffed my graying hair and chuckled.

I followed him down the stairs and out the back door. As he made his way across the yard, he called out something to me. I couldn't tell whether it was goodnight or goodbye.

The lights were on over there until two-thirty. Not just in the master bedroom but all through the house. By three I was feeling kind of panicky. I got up, went to the window in front and peered out. He had pulled his car out of the garage and turned on the floodlights. I stood at the window for a long time, watching him bring out suitcases, boxes, a pile of pictures in frames. Finally, he came out carrying nothing but a pair of sneakers. He tossed them in the passenger seat. Then he disappeared. The outdoor lights flicked off, then all the lights downstairs.

I got back into bed, propping my pillows so I could see the bedroom windows. When the last corner of the house disappeared in darkness, I scooted down into the bed, pulled up the sheet, and finally fell asleep.

It was still early yet when I woke up in the morning, but his car was already gone.

. . .

The Great Man came home tonight. I saw him pull into the driveway around supper time.

Now it's after one o'clock in the morning, and the bedroom

light's still on over there. I can't go to sleep for thinking, thinking about the boy, wondering where he might have gone. I hope wherever he's headed, it's to a place where things belong to him.

And I'm thinking about Dickens, too, silly as it sounds. In some way the cat dying had something to do with everything that changed, finally, over there. Like all such relationships, eventually, it just snaps. Maybe I had a hand in that. I suddenly feel guilty about fucking the boy.

I wish I could get to sleep. But with that light burning over there, I can't help wondering what The Great Man is thinking. If he's got any idea what he's lost.

I'd have guessed it would make me glad, seeing him the one left high and dry. But no, now I almost wish I knew the poor man so I could stop by in the morning and make sure he's all right. Maybe put an arm around him. Or something.

ALMOST ANONYMOUS
The Further Adventures of The Saint

John Patrick

"A color is almost never seen as it really is."
- *Joseph Albers, Bauhaus theorist*

    The first thing Lars noticed about Detroit was the smell. Almost as soon as he stepped out onto the curb at the airport to catch a cab, he thought he smelled a fire. Back home in Sweden he associated this smell with autumn, and the first fires of winter, the smoke puffing out of chimneys. But here it was midsummer, and he couldn't see anything burning.
    On the way into the city from the airport, with the windows of the cab rolled down and the hot air blowing in his face, he asked the driver about the smell.
    "Cars," the driver said.
    Lars, who spoke very precise school English, thought that perhaps he hadn't made himself understood. "No," he said. "I am sorry. I mean the burning smell. What is it?"
    "Cars. They make cars here." The driver glanced in the rearview mirror. "Hey, where you from?"
    "Sweden."
    The driver nodded, and the cab took a sharp right turn off the freeway and entered the Detroit city limits. Through the left window Lars saw a huge electric billboard. In hundreds of small incandescent bulbs, which went on and off from left to right, was the slogan: "It's today's CHEVROLET!" The driver pointed with his left hand toward another electronic signboard, this one with a small windowless factory at its base. It advertised tires. When he gestured, the cab wobbled on the pot-holed roadway. "Cars and everything that goes in 'em. There's always a fire somewhere."
    "But I don't see any fires," Lars said.
    "That's right."
    Lars sat back, feeling somehow defeated again by the American idiom. He had spent the past month with his Aunt Ingrid at Bear Lake, where she always spent her summers since

coming to America many years before. Lars had looked forward to this vacation more than any other because he was curious about America, attracted by its disorderliness. Disorder, of which there was very little in Sweden, seemed incredibly sexy to him. He was intrigued most of all by the disorder in America about sexuality. Before he left the country he hoped to sleep with a very disorderly American in a very disorderly American bed. That was his ambition, why he decided to take an extra day in Detroit. He wondered if the experience would have any distinction so he might be able to go home and tell his friends about it.

In his hotel room, he changed into his best jeans, a light cotton shirt his aunt had bought for him, and a pair of running shoes. In the mirror, he thought he looked relaxed and handsome. The tan he had acquired from a month at the lake agreed with him. His vanity amused him, but he felt lucky to look the way he did, especially if he was going to meet a disorderly American. Back out on the sidewalk, he asked the doorman which direction he would recommend for a walk.

The doorman, who had curly gray hair and sagging pouches under his eyes, removed his cap and rubbed his forehead. He did not look back at Lars. "You want my recommendation? Don't walk anywhere. Just stay inside and watch TV." The doorman stared at a fire hydrant as he spoke.

"What about running?"

The doorman suddenly glanced at Lars, sizing him up. "You might be okay, if you run fast enough," he chuckled. "But to be safe, just stay inside."

"Is there a park here?"

"Sure, there's parks. Lotsa parks. What're you plannin' to do?"

Lars shrugged. "See the sights."

"You're seein' 'em," the doorman laughed. "Buy some postcards. Look, if you wanted sights, you shoulda gone to California – "

Lars thought that perhaps he had misunderstood again and had the doorman hail him a cab.

"Where to?" the driver asked.

"The park."

"*The* park?" The driver peered at Lars through the rearview mirror. "Which park?"

"Any park."

The driver nodded as if he understood, and maybe he did, because he deposited Lars at edge of Palmer Park, six miles north of downtown, near what passes for a gay ghetto in The Motor City.

Lars sauntered about for awhile along the trails that wound through the bushes. He passed a few men. He found he liked the way Americans walked, with a purpose in their step, as if, having no particular goal, they still had an unconscious urgency to get somewhere.

At dusk, the light had a bluish-gold quality and the place looked like almost any city park to him, placid and decorative, a bit hushed. Lars didn't know what he was looking for but he sensed, sooner or later, he would find it. After about a half an hour, he passed a slender youth wearing white running shorts and a pale blue tank top. Leaning lazily against a tree, the boy, Lars decided, had just the right faraway look, just the right disorder about him. Lars thought he recognized this look. It meant that the boy was in a kind of suspension, between engagements. Lars put himself in his line of sight and said, in his heaviest accent, "A nice evening!"

The boy looked at him. "What did you say?"

"I said the evening is beautiful." He tried to sound as foreign as he could, the way Germans who visisted Sweden always did. "I am a visitor here," he added quickly, "and not familiar with any of this." He motioned his arm to indicate the park.

"Not familiar?" the boy chuckled. "Not familiar with what?"

"Well, with this park. With the sky here. The people."

"Parks are the same everywhere," the boy said, leaning his hip against the tree. He looked at Lars with a vague interest. "And the sky is the same. Only the people are different."

"Yes? How?"

"Where you from?"

As Lars explained, the boy looked past him, toward the entrance to the park. "Okay," the boy said when Lars was finished. "But why are you *here*?"

"I came to see my aunt," he said. "Now I'm sightseeing."

"*Sightseeing?*" the boy laughed out loud, and Lars saw him arch his back and thrust out his pelvis. The gigantic bulge at his crotch seemed to flare in front of him. The boy's body had distinct athletic lines. "No one sightsees here. Didn't anyone tell you?"

"Yes. The doorman at the hotel. He told me not to come."

"But you did. How did you get here?"

"I came by taxi."

"You're joking," he said. Then he reached out and put his hand momentatily on Lars's shoulder. "You took a taxi to this park? How do you expect to get back to your hotel?"

"I suppose," he shrugged, "I will get another taxi."

"Oh no you won't," the boy said, and Lars felt himself pleased that things were working out so well. He noticed the boy's eyes: blue, or maybe green. They kept changing. Whatever their color, they sparkled brilliantly. Fireflies danced around them. No one had ever mentioned fireflies in Detroit. Night was coming on. He gazed up at the sky. Same stars, same moon as in Sweden.

"You're here *alone?*" the boy asked. "In America? In this city?"

"Yes," he said. "Why not?"

"People shouldn't be left alone in this country, and especially in Detroit," he said, leaning toward him with a kind of vehemence. "They shouldn't have left you here. It can get kind of weird, what happens to people. Didn't they tell you?"

"No, certainly not."

"Well, they should have."

"Who do you mean?" he asked. "You said, 'they.' Who is 'they'?"

"Any 'they' at all," he said. "Your guardians."

"I don't have any guardians."

The boy sighed. "All right. Come on. Follow me." He broke into a run. For a moment Lars thought that he was running away from him, then realized that he was expected to run with him, that perhaps it was what people did now in America, instead of holding hands, to get acquainted. He sprinted up next to him, and as he ran, the boy asked him, "Who are you?"

Being careful not to tire – the boy wouldn't like it if his

endurance was poor – Lars told him his name, his interests, and he patched together a narrative about his mother, father, two sisters and his Aunt Ingrid. He told him that his aunt was eccentric and broke china by throwing it on the floor on Fridays, which she called "the devil's day."

"Years ago, they would have branded her a witch," Lars said. "But she isn't a witch. She's just moody."

He watched the boy's reactions and noticed that he didn't seem too interested in his family, or any sort of background.

"Do you run a lot back home in Sweden?" the boy asked. "You look as if you're in pretty good shape."

He admitted that, yes, he ran, but that people in Sweden didn't run as often as they did in America.

"You look a little like that tennis star, that Swede," he said. "By the way, I'm Terry." Still running, he held out his hand and, still running, Lars shook it. "Which god do you believe in?'

"Excuse me?" Lars asked.

"Which god?" Terry asked. "Which god do you think is in control?"

"I had not thought about it."

"You'd better," he chuckled, "because one of 'em is." He stopped suddenly and put his hands on his hips and walked in a small circle. Terry put his hand to his neck and took his pulse, timing it on his wristwatch. Then he placed his fingers on Lars's neck and took his pulse. "One hundred fourteen," he said. "Pretty good."

Again Terry walked away from him and again Lars found himself following him, this time toward the parking lot. In the growing darkness he noticed other men, standing around, watching the boy intently, this American with such beautiful strawberry blond hair, dressed in a skimpy running outfit, now soaked with sweat.

When Lars caught up with him, Terry was unlocking the door of a blue Chevrolet which was rusting badly. Terry slipped inside the car and reached across to unlock the passenger side. When Lars got in – he hadn't been invited to get in, but he thought it was all right – he sat down on several audio cassette cases. He picked them out from underneath his ass and tried to read their labels. Debussy, Bach, an original cast recording of

"Annie." The boy was taking off his running shoes.

"Where are we going?" Lars asked. He glanced down at Terry's bare foot on the accelerator.

Terry didn't answer him. He put the car into reverse. "Tomorrow" came blasting out of the speakers.

"Wait a minute," he said. "Stop this car."

Terry put on the brake, slammed the gear into park. "Now what?"

"I just want to look at you for a minute," Lars said.

"Okay, look." He turned on the interior light and kept his face turned so that Lars was looking at his profile. No matter what the light, Lars found Terry perfectly lovely. On the stereo, the little girl was singing "...the sun'll come out tomorrow."

"Are we going to do things?" Lars asked, touching Terry's thigh.

"Of course," Terry chuckled, shifting into drive. "Strangers should always do things."

On the way to the hotel, Lars thought it strange that he saw almost no one downtown. For some reason it was empty of shoppers, strollers, or pedestrians of any kind.

"I'm going to tell you some things you should know," Terry said.

Lars settled back. He was used to this kind of talk: everyone, everywhere, liked to reveal intimate details. It was an international convention.

They were slowing for a red light. "God is love," Terry said, downshifting, his bare left foot on the clutch. "In the world we have left, only love matters. Do you understand?"

"Yes." Lars nodded. He was beginning to feel very comfortable with this stranger. "So is that what you do, make love for a living?" He thought perhaps that was it, that he would be asked to pay. He was willing to do so.

"No, I do what everyone does. There is only one thing I do that is special."

"What is that?" he asked.

"I don't make any plans," he said. "No plans at all."

"That's not so unusual. Many people don't like to make – "

"It doesn't have anything to do with liking or not liking. It's just my, uh, religion."

"Of course," Lars said. He had heard of American cult religions but thought they were all in California. He didn't mind this talk of religion. It was like talk of the sunset or childhood; it kept things going.

"Have you been listening to me?"

"Of course I have been listening."

"Good, because I won't sleep with you unless you listen to me," he said. "It's the one thing I care about, that people listen. It's so damn rare, listening I mean." He turned to look at him. "Lars," he said, "what do you pray to?"

He laughed. "I don't."

"Okay, then, what do you plan for?"

"A few things," he said.

"Like what?"

"My dinner every night. Studying for my examinations. Meeting my friends after school."

"Do you let accidents happen?"

"Not if I can help it."

"You should. Things reveal themselves in accidents."

"Are there many people like you in America?" Lars asked.

"What do you think? Do you think there are many people like me?"

Lars looked again at his face, taken over by the darkness in the car but dimly lit by the dashboard lights and the oncoming of traffic. The boy was truly extraordinary, Lars decided. "Not very many," he said.

"Any of us in Sweden?"

"I don't think so. I've never met anyone like you. I've never *heard* about anyone like you. They didn't tell us in Sweden about pretty American boys who listen to Debussy in their rusty automobiles and who believe in accidents."

Terry chuckled and ran his hand up Lars's thigh. Lars felt heady, like he was tripping on a drug of some kind. It was all happening so fast; he could hardly believe his luck.

As they passed the doorman, he nodded, rubbing his chin. Lars introduced Terry and said that he was very friendly and wanted to show him, a foreigner, the sights. The doorman laughed.

Lars unlocked the door of the room and stepped inside. The room was reduced to an eerie grayish blur of odd shapes and forms. Terry went to the bathroom. Lars looked out the window at the street lights. They had an amber glow, the color of gemstones. This city, this American city, was unlike anything he had ever seen. A downtown emptied of people; a river with huge ships going by silently; a park with nothing but men...and one strange, beautiful boy, who was now taking a shower in his bathroom..

He wanted to open the hotel window to smell the air, but the casement frames were welded shut. He turned on the radio that was built into the television. Some light jazz was playing. Perfect, Lars thought. Some music was slow enough to dance to, in the slow way he wanted to dance right now, at this moment. Terry came from the bathroom, showered, scrubbed, a towel around his waist. Lars took his hand; it felt bony and muscular; physically, he was direct and immediate. When they held each other tightly and swayed together to the music, Lars began to feel as if he had known Terry for a long time and was related to him in some obscure way. Suddenly he asked him, "Why are you so interested in me?"

"Interested?" Terry laughed, and his long hair shook in quick thick waves. "Well, all right. I have an interest. I like it that you're a foreigner and that you take cabs to the park. I like the way you look. You're kind of cute. And the other thing is, your soul is so raw and new, Lars. It's like an oyster."

"What? My soul?"

"Yeah, your soul. I can almost see it."

"Where is it?"

Terry leaned forward, friendly and sexual and now slightly elegant. "You want me to show you?"

"Yes," Lars said. "Sure."

"It's in two places," he said. "One part is up here." He released his hand and put his thumb on his forehead. "And the other part is down here." He touched him in the middle of his stomach. "Right there. And they're connected."

"What are they like?" he asked, playing along.

"Yours? Raw and shiny, just like I said."

"And what about *your* soul?" he asked.

"My soul is radioactive," Terry laughed. "It's like plutonium. Don't say you weren't warned."

Lars thought that this was another American idiom he hadn't

heard before, and he decided not to spoil things by asking him about it. In Sweden, people didn't talk much about the soul, at least not relative to oysters or plutonium.

He drew Terry to him and kissed him. His breath was layered with toothpaste, mouthwash. Immediately he felt an unusual physical sensation inside his skin, like something heating up on a frypan.

Lars heard a siren go by on the street outside and drew back. He wondered whether they should talk some more – share a few more verbal intimacies – to be really civilized about this and decided, no, it was not necessary, not when strangers make love, as they do, sometimes, in strange cities, far away from home.

Terry began undressing Lars. The towel slipped off Terry's waist and Lars noticed that his cock, by the light coming in the window from the street, was as big and beautiful as he hoped it would be.

When Lars was naked, his cock throbbing, Terry took him in his arms again. Terry's skin felt vaguely electrical to Lars. They stood in the middle of the hotel room, arms around each other, swaying, and Lars knew, in his arousal, that something odd was about to occur: he had no words for it in either his own language or in English.

They moved over and under each other, changing positions, both lively and attentive, and at first he thought it would be just the usual fun, this time with an almost anonymous but incredibly friendly American boy.

Feeling bold, Lars slid a finger into the slipperiness between the lips of Terry's anus and this started his heart racing. Terry began whimpering pleasure and relief in every breath. And the fleshy place behind his knuckle moved into him, pressing. Terry gasped. The finger teased him awhile, then was removed. The moist finger traced a line to his throat, to his chin, lower lip, and he took the finger into his mouth, in his teeth, and the touch of his tongue made Lars laugh.

Tasting himself on Lars's fingertip, Terry begged, "Fuck me." Lars' feet were planted firmly apart as he got behind him and slid his cock into him, Terry bent at the waist. His hands on Terry's hips, holding him still, sometimes moving him, his cock growing larger inside of him. When Lars was close to coming, Terry tightened around him, bringing on a new sensation.

For Lars, his own orgasm never mattered much; he wanted his partner to come first, that was triumph enough for him. He pulled back, slid out from Terry, his cock glistening in the somber light. Terry stood. Lars turned him and they kissed, two hard cocks pressed between two hard bellies. Lars's hands explored the sweaty surface of Terry's back, lean and tough, and down to his ass as he sunk to his knees and Terry's penis pointed the way up his body; then he took it in his hand, pulled his head back and filled his mouth with it. He concentrated with animal-like preoccupation on the head of his cock, his head moving in a trancelike motion and his hand following, slipping easily along the moist length of it.

He pulled back suddenly and he stood again, rubbing the length of his body against the length of his clean wet cock and Terry ran his tongue up under his lips. Lars lifted him, a hand under each spread thigh, and slid him down onto him, and carried him like that, high, Terry's hands on his shoulders, his mouth at Lars's neck, to the bed.

Terry unlocked his ankles and lowered his legs as Lars pushed him back on the bed. Lars put one knee on the bed, then the other, straddling him, taking his own straining erection in his hand. Fist around his cock, he lowered himself over Terry and entered him again, his hands landing deep in the mattress on either side of Terry's head, his blond hair falling into Terry's face, strands of it sticking to the sweat on his brow. He lifted himself deep into him, opening his eyes and smiling down at him. Terry pulled Lars to him and rolled over on top of him, sinking his cock back into his ass. Lars kissed his pecs, massaged his nipples, one after the other, between the tip of his tongue and the roof of his mouth. Down his flat belly. Terry began quivering now, gasping, his body writhing. Terry was coming so close now, and Lars grinned there between his legs, playing with his erection. Nothing would please him more than every day bringing Terry to orgasm, grasping him by the soul and guiding him to ecstasy. Terry moved slowly up and laid his body down with care along the length of Lars. Now Lars plunged his cock as deep as it would go, and Terry tightened himself around him. His eyes were closed tight; he was holding the feeling with all his might. It was just the beginning.

Terry came liberally, smoothly with a fast, hot breath, an incredible contracting of every muscle in his long, shining body. Lars kept moving in ever-easier smooth strokes and began to come as well, his face in Terry's hair. After his orgasm, he moved slowly, tenderly, still inside of Terry, kissing his lips and his closed eyelids.

Later, resting with him, Lars's hands on Terry's smooth back, Lars felt a wave of happiness; he felt another wave of glorious color traveling through his body, surging from his forehead down to his stomach. It was like he was having another orgasm. It took him over again, and then a third time, with such force that he almost sat up.

"What is it?" Terry asked.

"I don't know. It is like colors were moving through my body."

"Oh, that?" He smiled at him in the dark. "It's your soul, Lars. That's all. That's all it is. Never felt it before, huh?"

"I must be crazy," he said.

Terry put his hand up into his hair. "Call it anything you want to. Didn't you feel it before? Our souls were joined together."

"You're crazy," he said. "You are a crazy boy."

"Oh yeah?" he whispered. "Is that what you think? Watch. Watch what happens now. You think this is all physical. Guess what, you're the crazy one. Just watch."

Terry went to work on him, has hands gliding over him. At first it was pleasurable, but he began to get nervous when he realized Terry was about to fuck him. He had never let anyone fuck him before. As Terry entered him and moved over him, it became a succession of waves that had specific colorations, even when Terry turned him and Lars got on top. Incredibly, with Terry's eight-inch cock buried in him, he had never felt such pleasure.

"Who are you?" he said. "Who in the world *are* you?"

"I warned you."

Lars put his hands on Terry's. "This is not love, but it – "

"Of course not," Terry said. "It's something else. Do you know the word? Do you know the word for something that opens your soul at once? Just like that?" He snapped his fingers on the pillow. His tongue was touching his ear. "Do you?" The words were almost inaudible.

"No, but I think you're wonderful," he said. Keeping Terry's cock in his ass, he reached down and embraced him.

In the morning, Lars watched as Terry dressed. His eyes hurt from sleeplessness.

"I have to run," Terry said. "I'm already late." He looked at Lars naked on the bed, tangled in the sheets. "You're a lovely lover," he said. "I like your body very much."

"What are we going to do?" Lars moaned.

"We? There is no 'we,' Lars. There's you and then there's me. We're not a couple."

"But after last night – "

"Look, I'm going to work. I've got so much to do. And you're going back to Sweden."

"Oh please, Terry – "

"I don't believe this," he said.

"What?"

"You think you're in love, don't you?"

"No," he said. "Not exactly." He waited. "Oh, I don't know."

"I get the point," Terry said. "Well, you'd better get used to it. Welcome to America. We're not always good at love but we are good at sex."

"Let me buy you breakfast."

"No, I must go."

"Please – "

"All right, but hurry."

Lars stood up and took Terry in his arms. With a sense of shock and desperation, he felt himself becoming aroused. Terry kissed him, and his lips tasted strangely sweet.

"You feel like a drug to me," Lars said, massaging Terry's groin.

"Hurry," Terry begged, pulling away.

Lars went to the bathroom. He looked in the mirror; he wanted evidence but didn't know for what. He looked, to himself, like a slightly different version of what he had been only a day before. In the mirror his face had a puffy look and a passive expression, as if he had been assaulted during the night.

A few minutes later, in the hotel's coffee shop, Lars asked Terry about his plans for the day.

"No plans," he said. "Didn't I tell you?"

"I am not sure I understand."

"We don't do all that much explaining. I've told you *everything* about me. We're just supposed to be enjoying ourselves. Nobody has to explain. That's freedom, Lars. Never telling why."   As Terry finished his eggs and bacon, he glanced out the window. His eyes widened, as if he had seen an accident, or as if he felt one was about to happen. "Excuse me," he said, pushing his plate away. "I'll just be a minute."

Lars finished his breakfast, lingered over his coffee. He looked at his watch. Ten minutes had gone by since Terry had left. Lars knew without thinking about it that Terry wasn't coming back.

He put a ten-dollar bill on the table and left the restaurant, jogged into the parking structure where Terry had left the car. Although he wasn't particularly surprised to see the car wasn't there, he sat down on the concrete and felt the floor of the structure shaking. He ran his hands through his hair, where Terry had grabbed at it during his orgasm. He waited as long as he could stand to do so, then returned to his room.

In the shower, Lars realized that he had forgotten to ask for Terry's address or phone number.

– *Terry first appeared to a mortal in "The Saint," a story in "Runaways/Kid Stuff."*

THE BET

Matthew Rettenmund

I never lose a bet.

That's why it surprised me when Red bet me he could shoot more hoops in a minute than me. Not to mention the fact that everyone knows I'm a better shot by a mile.

Red and I were up at the school after hours, not too long before the janitors show up to shoo stragglers out of the gym before they locked up. It was just us two, a strange combination since we never were the best of buddies, and both of us usually shot hoops after school with other guys on the team, never each other. But it was the middle of the week, nobody else really hanging around, so we just started hanging and shooting some balls and shootin' the shit.

Red's good-looking. Yeah, I like guys. I like guys quite a bit, actually, though I don't let that get around much, not around here anyway, not yet. When I graduate it's gonna be a different story. It's gonna be me and some cute blonde guy riding around the country, fucking like dogs.

But a guy's gotta do something to pass the time before fulfilling his life's dream. And there's a hell of a lotta worse ways to kill time than Red.

Red isn't a redhead, more like a strawberry blond, though it's hard to tell anymore now that he's shaved it so close to his head. But the hairs on his legs are red and his eyebrows are, too, so I guess that's where he gets his name. He's a short guy, about five-seven, but stocky enough to wrestle me and win for three years straight all through middle school. Yeah, I guess I've always carried that grudge against him. Maybe that's one reason I was so eager to take his bet, show him up.

"Hey," he said cockily, his arms across his broad chest. He was wearing a perforated tank top with a double zero on it and loose shorts cut from an old pair of sweats. I was distracted, checking him out, so I almost didn't catch what he was saying at first. "Hey, wanna bet?"

"What?" I asked, shifting my weight casually. I'm over 6' on a bad day, not built like Van Damme or Stallone, but I've been working on my arms and I like to think I'm in good shape. I don't think I'm the handsomest guy around, but I've got a good enough face to keep my telephone ringing. Girls, unfortunately. But if that's any sign, I thought I was good enough looking to bag Red if he was baggable by any guy at all.

"I'm on a roll," he grinned, swishing another basket. He was, too. "So let's say we bet I can make more baskets than you in a minute. What say?"

"Okay," I agreed, "But there's no sense in betting just for fun. What's the scoop?"

He must've had this planned, because he spit out this really elaborate bet too quick for it to be off the top of his head. "Well, if you win, I will kiss your ass. Literally, man. That's how sure I am I'm going to win this."

This, I thought, was a wet dream come true. I asked what was obvious, just to make him say it. "And if *I* win?"

"You'll kiss mine," he replied with a straight face.

The idea of a guy offering to kiss your ass is pretty sexy anyway, but to me the other option is even hotter. Maybe I'm a little kinky. I know a lot of people think guys doing guys is completely disgusting, and would die if they had to think about a guy actually wanting to lick another guy's asshole, but everyone has their own little buttons they like pushed, I guess. And eating ass is mine.

I don't get many chances to screw guys in the first place, much less lick their assholes. I've only had two guys before, one being this weird older kid who was sort of a foster kid who lived at home with us a few years back, and the other being a second cousin at our family reunion. I only got to lick the weird guy's ass, though, and then only because he made me. I didn't think I'd like it, but I was dead wrong. There's something really sexy about it, especially when the other guy's into it, too. It doesn't taste bad or smell bad one bit. It tastes really sweet and the smell is incredible, real musky. Yeah, there's nothing I love more than shoving my tongue up a guy's butt, and I thought I definitely had a primo shot with old Red.

"You're on," I said firmly.

Twenty shots later, he had a big head start. I was going to have to push it to sink twenty shots in a minute, what with having to shag the damned ball and shoot at the same time. I swished the first one to get off to a terrific start, and the rate I was going, I could see Red getting a little nervous. Or was he? I kept thinking how bad I wanted to beat this little punk after all those years of being screwed to the mat in wrestling, then suddenly I remembered that in order to kiss his ass, I had to lose. Talk about dilemmas. Shit! I missed three shots just worrying about it, and at the last second, I had to sink a shot just to tie him. I gave it the perfect arch and left my hand in the air where it released the ball, holding it perfectly steady like some sort of radar guidance system. If we tied, maybe we both got to kiss each other's asses? I mean *had* to, right?

The ball bounced high off the basket, then rolled lazily around the rim for two or three revolutions, trying to decide if it wanted to sink or swim. I changed my mind; I didn't mind losing after all. I wanted to lose. I wanted to kiss that sweet ass.

Plunk, the ball fell over the rim. Me: 19. Him: 20.

Red let out a whoop and paraded around with the retrieved ball. "You gotta kiss my ass, buddy! You made the bet!"

I was deadly calm. "I'm ready. But let's do it in the locker room. At least give me that much, in case somebody sees."

He seemed a little shocked I was really going to go through with it, but he agreed it was fair to do it in private. He strutted in front of me, wiggling his ass and showing it off, stopping to bend over and tie his shoe as some kind of joke. Oh, yeah, almost forgot – I was supposed to dread this. I smacked his ass hard and walked past him into the locker room, my mouth watering.

Inside, he didn't waste much time. We straddled the bench, me behind him sitting down, him in front of me standing up. He leaned forward with his strong arms straight out, palms flat against the wall.

"Okay," he said, suddenly a little nervous, "Go to it, stud."

The "stud" part was a little intriguing. Not unusual, but not what I expected right then. I was raging, my boner barely inside my gym shorts, and I worried he'd spot it, get wise, and take off. But something inside my head told me he knew the score, and he wanted it just as bad as I did. I pulled his sweatshorts down real slowly, letting his fat, bubblebutt pop out inch by inch. God, it's a great ass, a big, solid, meaty ass with little red wiry hairs all up the crack. I pulled his shorts all the way to his knees, where they were stretched about an inch above the bench.

"Hey, man, no need to pull my pants down," he said.

"No prob," I said, "I want to do this up right if I'm gonna lose a bet."

He was wearing a jockstrap, which I love because they frame an ass so well, push it out even more. I leaned forward and grabbed his cheeks really hard, two handsful with my fingers under the sexy white straps.

"Hey!" he said, surprised, but he stayed still.

I leaned forward and gave his left cheek a big wet kiss, smacking it loudly and doing it hard enough to taste his salty skin and get a whiff of his funky jock ass. Then, I did it to his right cheek.

"Okay, okay," he said, "You proved your point. You're a good man to live up to your debts..." But he stayed still.

I leaned forward and kissed his crack, which is weird since a crack isn't really a thing, it's more like a space. But it must really give you a hint about how good the rest can feel, because Red changed his tune right away.

"Man," he moaned, "That's fucking hot!"

I ran my tongue up his sweaty crack, then worked it about a half-inch in and dragged it back down. Damn, it tasted great, felt great with all those curly hairs tickling my tongue. Red spread his legs more and pushed back against my face, burying me in his beautiful butt. I licked the inside of each cheek like a champ, cleaned them out real good, rubbing my cheeks into the musky sweaty spit-soaked crack until I felt high on the scent. I whipped out my boner and stroked it hard; this was too intense to be long and slow and leisurely, I was going to have to go for a fast, hot wad or no wad at all.

"Yeah, french my ass, lick my ass, I love it..." Red kept saying how great it felt, kept moving back against me more and more, loving the attention.

Then I flickered my tongue on his puckerhole and he went nuts, really got into it, reached back around and grabbed a handful of my hair and pulled my head in as tight against him as it would go. I could hardly breathe, and all around my face was hot, wet ass. I shoved my tongue up his asshole as far as it would go, felt him working my tongue with his muscle and letting me eat him out deep and rough.

"Oh, man, shit, yeah! Do it do it do it, eat me! Lick my asshole!"

He was rubbing his jock with his free hand, his chest against the wall supporting his weight. His other hand kept my head in place, but I wasn't going anywhere except straight to heaven.

I couldn't take it. I blew my wad with my tongue up Red's asshole, come shooting on to the back of his leg, just before I felt his ass tighten up for his own nut. He got really quiet when he was coming, just gasping for air and trying not to yell out.

I sank back on the bench, playing with the come in my pubic hair, one hand still raised against his incredible ass. On impulse, and because the Devil made me do it, I shoved my middle finger up him as far as it could go, and from his sharp intake of breath, he enjoyed it.

"Fuck," Red said, finally pulling up his pants and turning around to look at me, which he could barely do. "That was awesome. I mean *weird*, but fucking awesome. Do you do that a lot, or...?"

"Never," I said, "But anytime you're into it...or anything else..."

He laughed and blushed and kept trying not to look me in the eye. "SH – yeah, sure. I mean, yeah. Cool."

We cleaned up, joking about what our coach would do if he found come all over his locker room, then we took off on our separate ways.

That was yesterday, and I'm betting it won't be long before I hear from old Red. Not long at all.

DUTCH TREAT

Ray Burrell

Andrew was sitting at a table in the hotel dining room in Amsterdam, waiting for his meal, and writing a letter to his wife.

Dear Margaret,
 I went to the ballet the other night. It was excellent. They really applaud here in Amsterdam, twelve curtain calls for the ballet, a modern one, called "Monument to a Young Boy." Tickets are very reasonable.

A shadow fell across the table. He looked up, expecting his traditional Dutch meal of chops and potatoes. Instead, a man who looked vaguely familiar was standing there with a friendly look on his face.

"Aren't you the chap I sat beside at the ballet last night?" he asked.

"Yes," said Andrew. So that's where he had seen this man before. The fellow had caught his eye in passing, because he had a young face beneath prematurely gray hair. Andrew guessed that he was about forty years old, about the age of his son back home.

"I am Cornelius Kaan," said the man with the young face.

Andrew got up and offered him his hand. "Why don't you sit down? I've just ordered dinner. Do you want to join me?"

When traveling alone, or when thrust into a group of strangers, Andrew found that it was necessary to talk to people and strike up acquaintances, otherwise you were too much alone with your own company and thoughts. Ever since his days in the Canadian Navy just after the Second World War, he had tried to be friendly and outgoing.

Cornelius pulled out a chair and sat down.

Andrew was aware that several patrons of the restaurant were looking at them. In the few seconds it took for Cornelius to be seated, Andrew's mind flashed back to an incident a few weeks earlier in London. At a production of *Joseph and His Amazing Technicolor Dreamcoat*, a young Australian man approached him during the intermission and asked if he would like to go for a coffee after the play. Andrew had gone, but in the cafe had become aware of a woman at a nearby table, glancing at them and whispering to her husband:

"There's an old gay man picking up a young boy," she murmured.

Andrew was disconcerted.

"It was a beautiful surprise meeting you at the play tonight," the youth said. Eventually, seeing no invitation forthcoming from Andrew, the boy said, "Oh, I've got to run to catch the tube out to where my aunt lives."

Andrew had thought about writing to Margaret about the incident, but felt embarrassed doing so. Thinking it over, perhaps it was a bit flattering to have been approached at his age. *Maybe*, he thought, *I look younger than my sixty-five years*.

Now, in Holland, the man at his table was looking at him intently.

"Where are you from?" Cornelius asked. "Are you an American?"

"Canadian," Andrew said. "Years ago, during the Liberation of Holland, some of my friends from high school — older boys — were killed. I was visiting relatives in England, and I thought since I'd come this far, I might as well cross the Channel and visit their graves, and see something of the rest of Europe while I could."

Back in the Navy, a couple of guys were caught in a sexual act. Someone had blown the whistle on them. Andrew had been surprised, never imagining that there was anything going on. In those days people were much more innocent. It was assumed that all men were attracted to women.

The two men were dishonorably discharged. In the years since then, Andrew had tried to keep up with the times, but still, he had been surprised on his travels to find himself the object of attention from men. He didn't welcome it, but he saw no reason to be horrified, or paranoid, either. All his life, he supposed, he'd had opportunities for same-sex encounters, but he'd remained oblivious to them, never feeling any urges in that direction. Now, on his own in Europe, he wasn't planning to experiment. However, he didn't see why others' assumptions, and the fear of idle gossip, should prevent his talking to someone who seemed sociable.

Cornelius spoke English with a slight accent. He explained that learning languages was compulsory in school and that he could speak five.

When the waiter appeared with Andrew's meal, Cornelius ordered the same.

"Do you mind if I order wine?" he asked

He chose an eight-year-old Medoc, insisting that he should pay for it. Andrew agreed, wondering if he should. He suspected it was an expensive wine by Dutch standards. Could Cornelius afford it?

He began to talk to Andrew about his wine cellar and then about his family. He said his people had lived in the northern part of Holland since the sixteen-hundreds and his mother still lived in the old family farmhouse. Cornelius worked for the City of Amsterdam writing brochures on the City's attractions and forthcoming events. Andrew explained that he had taken early retirement from his job and was free to travel.

They talked for an hour or so. When the check came, Cornelius paid for the wine as he had promised.

"Would you like to come to my place and have a glass of wine?" he inquired. "I live on the ground floor of a house in Helmersstraat not far from here. I'd like you to see my new CD player."

From his tone, Andrew knew he was proud of it. He had no qualms about going with Cornelius. Their dinner conversation had not touched on anything sexual. He looked forward to visiting a Dutch home. On the walk over he was surprised when Cornelius grabbed his hand.

"I wouldn't want any harm to come to you," he said. "Around here, tourists are accosted by thieves."

When they reached a large old house, Cornelius led Andrew into the foyer.

"Come and meet Mr. Koster, my landlord," he said.

In the living room an elderly man, very unsteady on his feet, rose as they entered. He peered at Andrew over his glasses.

"Cornelius doesn't often bring people home," he said.

Andrew admired the three large oil paintings in the room, and the old man seemed pleased, explaining that they had been done by his nephew.

Then Cornelius invited Andrew into his room, apologizing for its untidiness. The bed was unmade and clothing lay strewn all over the floor. He was surprised at the mess, as Cornelius looked neat and well-groomed. The man cleared a chair for him and they listened to CDs over several glasses of wine.

As Cornelius got up to change a disk, Andrew noticed that he moved slowly. He studied him while the younger man wasn't looking. Was there something the matter with him? Andrew remembered one of his children's friends back home who had been on some kind of medication, some tranquilizer or other which had slowed his reactions.

Poor boy, he thought, looking at Cornelius, who told him more about his life. His father was dead.

"My brother runs the farm for my mother," he said. "After she dies, it is to be sold and the proceeds divided between my brother and myself. I would like my share now so that I can buy a house in Italy. I speak Italian. Very well, I think."

Andrew remarked that Italy sounded exotic to him. But then, a farm in Holland sounded like a rare and unusual treat, conjuring up images of wooden shoes and windmills.

"I imagine it's quite different from the farms in Canada," Cornelius said. "Would you like to visit? I usually go there every second weekend to visit my mother."

"Fine!" He would have to write and tell Margaret that he was actually going to have an opportunity to visit with real Dutch people in their home.

"We'll meet tomorrow night to make our plans," Cornelius said. "I'd like to invite you to dinner."

"Thank you," Andrew replied. "That would be great."

Finally he decided it was time to get back to his hotel.

"That area is dangerous," Cornelius told him. "Never go walking alone through the park at night. Keep to well-lit streets. In fact, I think I should walk back with you."

Walking through the park, Andrew noticed a number of people lying on the grass, embracing, sitting on benches, and standing in the shadows beneath the trees or by the kiosks. From what he had seen of Amsterdam, it certainly seemed more liberated than Kingston, where he lived. He guessed he was old, but some of what he saw was disturbing.

"I know what it's like to be afraid of the world," Cornelius said, walking protectively close to him. "I was in a mental hospital for two years because of my fears. Only lately have I been able to talk about it."

Andrew felt more disturbed and was glad to say goodbye to Cornelius at his hotel. That night he worried. His new acquaintance did not seem at all threatening, but there was always the danger of getting mixed up with a psychopath. Maybe he only needed some normal human contact in order to feel at home in society again.

He went to Cornelius's place for dinner the following evening, and late that night he wrote about the visit to Margaret.

I don't know what to make of this fellow. He seems nice enough, despite his problems, and it's lonely in another country with no one to talk to. You should have come with me.

Cornelius invited me to dinner at his house at 10:30 p.m. The Dutch eat much later than we. He kept on saying, "only fifteen minutes, my dear boy, and everything will be ready." If he placed the glasses and the candles once, he moved them fifteen times. He was exasperatingly slow. We finally started eating at a quarter to one, after he brought the steak in to show me three times. I left as soon as I decently could, about two-thirty in the morning, and he again walked me back to the hotel. He seems a kind person, and I am looking forward to my visit to his mother's farm next weekend.

The evening before they were due to set off for the north of Holland to Cornelius's mother's home, they dined at a restaurant across from the hotel - Andrew's treat. There, he saw Cornelius do something peculiar, which worried him. He thought of it as the "wine ceremony."

Cornelius first rose from his chair with the waiter hovering nearby. He held the bottle up to the light for one or two minutes, turning it around slowly. Then he sat down, watched as the bottle was uncorked and cupped his hands around it, sniffing it for another minute. Then he tasted it, rolling it around in his mouth. Andrew found it embarrassing to watch. After swallowing, Cornelius announced, loudly, to the whole restaurant:

"A very fine quality, very fine."

Every eye was on their table. Andrew wanted to crawl under

it. He supposed he was a typical reserved Canadian, but he hated being the focus of attention, especially when the wine turned out to be not all that special.

Cornelius told him that he had chosen some special wines to take to his mother's house.

"I hope you didn't do it on my account," Andrew said. "I really prefer a very dry white wine."

Cornelius looked wounded. "My dear boy. I thought you liked all kinds of wine."

"I'm sure I'll like something you chose. One thing further. Do you mind if I leave my other suitcase at your landlord's place, so I won't have to pay to keep it at the hotel?"

"Of course not. That will be fine."

After having a traditional Dutch breakfast of cold cuts, rolls, cheese and coffee at his hotel, Andrew took a streetcar to the Central Station. Cornelius was late. They had agreed to meet at 8:00. He searched the concourse. The 8:30 express left. No Cornelius.

"Good morning, dear boy," Andrew heard behind him.

He turned and immediately noticed Cornelius's black eye. "What happened?" he asked.

"On my way back home from your hotel last night, I was accosted by a gang. They demanded that I give them my money. I wasn't about to turn over my wallet containing our cash for the trip. When one of them jumped on my back I fought him off. After me warning you about not walking through Vondel Park at night, to think that I, a native of the country, was attacked."

Cornelius told the story with great excitement. Something about the tale worried Andrew. When his children were young they sometimes made up elaborate stories. Cornelius's tale did not quite ring true.

"Maybe we shouldn't go to visit your mother," he said.

"She's expecting us," the man answered. "I've already telephoned her to say we'll be late. We must hurry now, or we'll miss the next train.

Andrew refrained from pointing out that they had missed two trains already.

He enjoyed the trip. Through the window he observed the Dutch countryside, flat, with irrigation ditches. He noticed splashes of daffodils, bent flat by the howling northwest wind. When they arrived at the station about noon, Cornelius's brother was there to meet them. He was older and wore heavy boots caked with mud, and overalls underneath a heavy coat.

Cornelius's mother was a small women with a round face and blue eyes. Andrew thought she looked flushed and worried, until he realized she had a naturally reddish complexion. In halting English, she welcomed Andrew to her home, saying that she hoped he would enjoy his visit.

She's worried about something, he thought, seeing her exchange glances with her older son. Was his visit an imposition?

After eating such a large breakfast he was not ready to eat the large noon meal that Cornelius's mother served. There was a large dish of kale mixed with mashed potatoes, a platter of European sausages, and a mixture of potatoes and carrots. For dessert there was fruit and cheese. He praised the food and the old woman smiled. Then she suggested that Cornelius take him upstairs and show him where he was to sleep.

Andrew found the room interesting. The windows were very clean and had a lace valance running across the top, but no blinds. *I guess out here in the country you don't have to worry about anyone looking in,* he thought. *I suppose when I undress I could go over to the bed.* That was recessed Dutch fashion, almost into the wall, with curtains which could be drawn for privacy. The room was overheated and a bit stuffy. He noticed the adjoining door. It would not lead to the outside, but to Cornelius' room. He threw open the window, breathing in the fresh country air. The wind had stopped. He unpacked.

Unsure what to do next, he tapped on the adjoining door. Receiving no response, he opened it wide and saw Cornelius lying on the bed, completely naked, his face turned away. Andrew froze. He sensed that Cornelius was awake. Then the man turned his head in Andrew's direction, smiled at him, and beckoned him to enter.

Andrew stepped back, closed the door, and sat on his own bed. He carefully went over the events of his friendship with Cornelius. He supposed he was naive, but he had never suspected that the man wanted anything more than friendship. Or was he misinterpreting something? Maybe it was common practice to take a nude nap after dinner. Or maybe Cornelius's nakedness was a sign of his mental problems. Maybe the smile had not contained an invitation at all; maybe it was all in his own mind.

Suddenly a memory came back to him. What had he been -- fourteen, fifteen, that night he'd been invited over to his friend George's house. In the middle of the night he'd been awakened by the sensation of someone working hands under his pajamas. The touch had made him uncomfortable. Opening his eyes, he had found George close beside him.

"What are you doing!" he'd demanded.

"You know," George whispered.

"Lay off." Andrew had drawn the covers around himself like a mummy. "Don't crowd me. Move over to your side of the bed."

George had done so, and that had been the end of the incident.

Now, he felt uncomfortable being upstairs. He would go down and strike up a conversation with the mother or brother. On the turn of the stairs, he overheard people talking in the kitchen. He had only a limited understanding of Dutch, but what was being said didn't require fluency.

"I don't like it," the brother said.

"I don't either," the mother replied, "but we don't want Cornelius to be sick again. Maybe this is what he needs."

"This man is too old for him," the brother said.

Andrew stood at the turn of the stairs for a moment, not knowing what to do. Should he go back to his Amsterdam hotel, or stay for the weekend? Just then the mother came out of the kitchen, crossing the hall to the dining room with a tray of puddings. She looked up and saw Andrew there.

"Is your room all right?" she asked.

"I think you've made a mistake about me," he told her. "Or maybe I'm the one who misunderstood. I think I should go back to Amsterdam."

The mother looked flustered. "Go back? But you only just got here."

"I think maybe I should, if your son will drive me to the

station. Everyone has the wrong idea."

The mother smiled. "Why don't you come and have some more coffee?"

Andrew sat across from her. Cornelius's brother stood by the door, wanting to go back to his work, but also wanting to hear what was said. Taking out his wallet, Andrew showed the mother a picture of his wife and children.

"I came to Europe to visit the Allied cemeteries," he explained. "I'm here for that and to see the country, not for any other reason." He told her how Cornelius had made his acquaintance. "I never had any erotic interest in him," he assured her. "I was just pleased to meet a native of the country who could show me a side of Dutch life not seen by the average tourist."

"Cornelius could do that," said his brother, chuckling as he went out the door.

"I meant this farm!" Andrew protested.

"Pay no attention to him," the mother said, pouring more coffee. "We've been so worried about Cornelius. He seemed like a normal average boy, even a talented boy, until he reached adolescence and then he became troubled. Maybe it would have been different if he'd had a father. I was pregnant with Cornelius when his father was killed in an automobile accident."

"I've enjoyed his company," Andrew said. "I want you to know that it has been on a strictly social basis. I had been looking forward to some sightseeing with him. But I don't know now."

"I don't see any problem with that," the mother said, "but you may have to make things clear to him."

Andrew got up and said he would like to go for a walk. He went down a roadway and looked across the flat green field where a herd of Holsteins was pasturing. Some of the cows were lying down, a sure indication of rain.

Should he catch the train back to Amsterdam and never see Cornelius again? He was cross at himself for not picking up on the many details that might have tipped him off on intentions. There was the living arrangement with the older man, the time Cornelius grasped his hand on the walk back to the hotel. He was horrified to think that he might have misled the man in some way. But no. He hadn't done anything; in looking for a companion Cornelius possibly would have sought out any reasonable looking man who was alone.

There was no good reason to be offended or to feel threatened. He knew he was not interested in Cornelius other than as a friend. All he needed to do was tell Cornelius that, and then perhaps they could continue being casual companions and see the sights of Holland together. There was no need to be afraid of what people would say, because no one knew him here. As long as he knew what his preferences were and what the limits were, that was all that mattered.

Poor Cornelius. Undoubtedly he had met with rejection many times. Perhaps he was searching for a father figure. It was one possibility, in view of the fact that his father was dead, that he lived with a very old man, and that he had hit on Andrew. Surely, as his mother had implied, he should be looking for someone his own age.

Cornelius had many good qualities...

Then he heard the sound of footsteps on the gravel and turned. Cornelius, fully clothed again, was coming toward him.

"I didn't know you were married," he began, his eyes blazing. 'Why didn't you tell me sooner?"

"I thought I had," said Andrew. "Maybe I didn't mention Margaret and the children. We've been married so long that I take it for granted. Didn't you see my ring?"

"I didn't realize what it signified," Cornelius said in an injured tone. "If I'd known earlier that you were married, I wouldn't have invited you to my home."

"Well, I'm sorry. I didn't purposely try to mislead you. I assumed you knew."

Slowly the anger went out of the man's eyes. "I've made mistakes like this before," he said in a low voice.

Andrew had been wondering about that, but decided not to mention it.

"My mother told me you were thinking of going back to Amsterdam. Please don't do that. There's no need. If you stay for the weekend I can show you around the farm and the village, and you can tell me about Canada and your family. We can listen to some Bach if you want."

Andrew stayed for the weekend. On the Sunday night, at the station, Cornelius's mother and brother saw them off. Although there was a stiff westerly wind, it was not too cold. Clouds moved quickly across the sky. He looked up at the cloudscape as it changed from light to dark gray. The blue patches had disappeared. He buttoned his trench coat as a precaution against the rain he was sure would start at any moment. He nudged Cornelius and pointed to the sky.

"This is the kind of Dutch sky that I see in many paintings," he remarked.

When they arrived back in Amsterdam, Andrew picked up his bag at Cornelius' landlord's house and the two of them went back to the hotel. He had checked out for the weekend but planned to stay there again until his return home.

At the desk, he asked if they had a room available, while Cornelius waited some distance away with the bag. The clerk gave Andrew the register to sign, handed him his key, and then, with a glance in Cornelius's direction, he said in a low voice, "I'm sorry, but we can't allow his sort in here. This is a respectable hotel."

"I want a room for myself only," Andrew said. "He isn't coming up."

He was angry at the clerk for his insinuation. Poor Cornelius, was he really so obvious? Then it occurred to him that Cornelius had probably been around this hotel before with someone else. Fighting back his feelings of disgust and concern, he took his bags up to his room, then rejoined Cornelius.

During his last week in Holland, Cornelius showed him a little more of the countryside. They went to a village near the Belgian-Dutch-German border, where they toured the town and the cemetery. Cornelius led him over to see a particular tombstone.

"One of the favorite sons of the village lies buried here and you can see the special care that people give his grave," he remarked.

Andrew noticed with interest a picture of the young man under a plastic oval. His steel helmet lay on the cement in front of the tombstone. There were fresh flowers in a vase. The dates indicated that the boy had died at eighteen. He noted the unique features of the grave but wondered why it was so special to Cornelius.

"Was he a relative of yours?" he asked.

Cornelius shook his head. Andrew knew he couldn't have been a friend; he had died before Cornelius was born.

"He was a friend of my parents," Cornelius said. "My mother had relatives in this village and she took me to see it. It made quite an impression on me and I wanted to share it with you."

They had dinner together the night before Andrew left to go back to Canada. When he mentioned that he would be back in a year or so, Cornelius remarked:

"I have a feeling that this might be my last year."

Andrew didn't know what to reply. An alarmist might think he was talking about AIDS, but Andrew was afraid he was talking about suicide. A cynic might say it was a last-minute attempt to manipulate Andrew's feelings and nudge the relationship in the direction Cornelius had wanted it to take. But Andrew didn't think so. The poor fellow was depressed.

"I hope not," he said aloud. "I hope to see you again on my next trip to Holland."

"No one else has said that to me," Cornelius said in a choked voice. "No one else has ever returned."

"Well, I intend to," Andrew said. "Now that I'm retired, I see no reason not to come back to Europe as finances permit. Next time I may bring Margaret with me."

Cornelius nodded quite calmly.

Back at home, Andrew occasionally mentioned meeting Cornelius. "It must have been interesting," said his friends from the church, "to meet a real Dutch person and be invited to his home. What an unusual experience with another culture!"

If you only knew, Andrew thought.

Sometimes he wondered about Cornelius's interest in that unusual gravestone in the village near the Belgian border. In time he arrived at what he thought was an explanation. The young soldier who had died had been loved by all the people in his village; even years after his death his memory remained vivid in his community. Poor Cornelius, with his need for affection and his psychological problems. He wanted to be like that young soldier.

The following year he unexpectedly went to Holland again, as he was doing some contract work for the Canadian government. He took along some CDs, classics that Cornelius wanted but couldn't afford. The man was still alive, much the same as before. They did some sight seeing and Andrew was relieved that Cornelius felt that friendship was enough.

"Good luck with your life," Cornelius said, when he saw Andrew off at the airport. "One of these years I may be going to Italy, and if I do, I'll let you know my new address."

"Great," Andrew said. He hoped Cornelius would achieve this dream, and maybe find a nice Italian boy to settle down with.

SHORTS WEATHER

Al Lone

I didn't know exactly what to expect when a consulting contract took me to Florida for a couple of months in the summer, but I soon found living in all that heat does have its compensations, not the least of which is that the boys wear skimpy shorts and little else.

After settling into my little rented house, I soon discovered that every afternoon around three-thirty a gaggle of boys were using the driveway of the house across the street to prepare their newspapers for delivery. Efficiency-expert that I am, it became obvious to me the job took considerably more time than it should have what with all the horsing around they did.

After observing them in their briefest of attire for a couple of days, I made a determined effort to ignore them. As much as admired the scenery, I felt it wasn't healthy for my soul to yield to temptation. Still, I would occasionally have to leave the house to visit the plant I was studying and one day I returned just as the boys were finishing, heading off on their bikes to make their deliveries. The tallest, handsomest member of the group smiled and waved to me as I approached him and slowed down. Another boy shouted to him, "Hey, Darren!" but he didn't turn away; he kept his eyes locked on mine. I blinked and my eyes fell to his crotch, a marvel in his cut-offs.

He snickered, "You should take a picture – it lasts longer." The twinkle in his eye and his lop-sided grin told me the ice had been broken and I covered my momentary embarrassment by stopping the car and asking if he could set me up for delivery of the paper. "Sure. Deliver it myself," he said, pedalling away.

I had noticed it was Darren who would most often be the one to start nut-grabbing one of his buddies and who seemed just a little too interested in physical contact. I also noticed a funny thing: Darren would deliberately wait until all of his other papers were delivered before tossing mine on the stoop.

August came in like gangbusters, with the thermometer

pushing 95 by five in the afternoon when Darren usually got around to me. One day, I took a break from my computer and went to the door, anticipating a view of him as he pedalled down the street. But instead, he was off his bike, coming up the walk. He wore only a pair of skimpy yellow nylon shorts. He had no paper for me. He apologized; they had shorted him, for which he said he was sorry, and I could call the office and they would bring one out.

"Oh, that's okay," I said.

"Boy, could I use a Coke," he said, wiping the sweat from his brow with the back of his hand.

"Come in," I said.

He looked about the room. "You stayin' here alone?"

"Yes."

"Thought so."

"Thought so?"

"First day I saw you I thought you might live alone."

"Oh, why?"

"The way you looked at me." He grinned. "I've seen that look before."

"Oh?"

"Yeah, I've had guys look at me like that lots of times."

"And what did you do about it?"

"Nothin'." His hand moved down, caressing his ribbed abdomen and coming to rest on the elastic band of his running shorts, tantalizing me. "Not that I didn't want to, but you gotta be careful around here."

"Yes, I've seen that."

"Yeah, I'd have stopped in sooner but Billy – ",

"The kid across the street?"

"Yeah. Well, he's got a big mouth, if you know what I mean."

"And if he saw you here – "

"Yeah. He's already suspicious of why I said I was gonna deliver your paper myself."

"Here, here's your Coke." My hand trembled slightly as I filled his glass and Coke was dripping from it as I handed it to him.

"Thanks."

"So where's Billy now?"

"He's gone with his folks in their RV. They'll be gone for the rest of summer."

Silently blessing dear Billy and his family, I put the cap back on the Coke bottle and put it in the refrigerator. Easing the door shut, I watched Darren gulp the cola. "Sure is hot," I said, referring to the weather as well as my young visitor.

As he kept on drinking, I decided he'd need a refill and brought out the bottle again. "Here, why don't you just finish this whole thing."

"You got anything stronger?"

"Stronger?"

"Yeah, I like it with some rum in it. You got any rum?"

"Vodka," I said, opening the cabinet above the refrigerator where I kept the liquor. "Just vodka. No rum. Anyway, you're too young to be drinking."

"I've been drinkin' since I was twelve. Not a lot, just enough."

"Just enough to what?" I asked, finding it impossible to keep my eyes off where his hand had strayed. It seemed he had developed an erection just talking about drinking. Or teasing me. Or both.

"Yeah, you know, to relax me."

"Yes, by the look of it, you *do* need to relax."

"So do you."

"Oh?" I asked, closing the cupboard and turning to face him directly.

"Oh, yeah," he said, groping me.

He quickly had my cock exposed.

"Take it easy," I winced as he tried to separate my dick from the rest of me.

"Oh, yeah," he said, bending over without hesitation to put out his tongue and licked all around the head of my swelling erection. Before long, he had it all down his throat and was sucking intensely. I stroked his cock as I watched him. What he lacked in expertise he made up for eagerness and cum was quickly spurting from my cock. He pulled it from his mouth to watch it splash on the floor.

"Oh, yeah," he said, over and over, as the last of my cum was squeezed out.

"Well, I gotta go," he said. "Thanks for the Coke."

"But – "

"I'll be back," he said, the twinkle returning to his eyes.

And he was. The next day I managed to get him into the bedroom. He sat on the edge of the bed and I kneeled between his thighs. Slowly I pulled off his cut-offs. His tender cock, hard and throbbing, blossomed before my eyes. Between licks on his cockhead, I said, "Don't think I'm unhappy with you or anything stupid like that, but I am wondering just why it is that you want to be with me like this. How come you wouldn't rather be with someone your own age?"

"Hell, no. I tried it with a Chinese kid last year, an exchange student. He wanted me somethin' fierce, but there were a couple of things wrong with it."

"Oh?"

"Yeah, for one thing, I want a man's cock. Big like yours."

"You're as big as I am," I said, lifting his cock, admiring it.

"Maybe."

"No maybe about it; it's a *big* dick!"

I began sucking it in earnest, but Darren had other ideas. As he stood up, I did too but he pushed me flat on my back. Spinning quickly around, he put one slim knee beside each of my shoulders and leaned over to slide his mouth over my now rampant erection, stopping only long enough to tell me to do him at the same time. As I rubbed my hands over his smooth limbs, hard buns and slim, supple back, my elation was almost beyond belief.

Without warning, he yanked his cock from my mouth and sat up with his thighs now grasping my head. "I want to try somethin' else now. Roll over." I hesitated and he roughly pushed me over. "You got any Vaseline?" he asked. "Oh, never mind. I saw some in the bathroom before."

With that he sprang off the bed and jumped quickly to the bathroom and back before I could even turn back over. Then, laying his full length on my back he pushed his cock into my quivering hole. "Neat!" he said after pumping furiously for a couple of minutes. "Now it's your turn."

My turn? I blinked. While I've never been much interested in being a bottom myself, I was willing to accept my fate. Rolling off me, he was soon offering his delicious buttocks to me, even pulling on his cheeks to give me full access.

Looking back over his shoulder, he said, "Well, what're you waitin' for?"

I shook my head. As I carefully began to invade his willing body he giggled and reached back to check on my progress. "God, I love it. Stick it in all the way."

I did as I was told, began pumping, slowly, savoring the tightness of him, when Darren, not known for his patience in our short-lived affair, soon wriggled out from under me and began to stroke my cock. "That was nice, but I really want to suck it some more." He wiped it off and then put his mouth where his interest lay, taking my cock down as far as he could, wrapping his hand around it after each down stroke to determine how close he was to getting me off. It didn't take him long.

"How was that?" he grinned, my cum dribbling from his lips.

Panting, I said, "You know how it was, you little devil."

I reached for his cock, but he sprang away. Quickly tugging on his shorts, he said, "I'll be back."

And he was, every two or three days. It seemed as if he only wanted to suck my dick, and with that I was content; pleasing him pleased me more than any words could express.

Our affair went on for a couple more weeks until my job was complete. On our last afternoon together, after I broke the news, I finally summoned the courage to ask him if I could suck him to orgasm.

He agreed, but first he wanted to suck me for awhile. He got between my thighs on the bed and worked me over until I was close. Then he straddled my chest and brought his cock to my mouth. Precum drooled from his man-sized tool and I stuck my tongue out, and licked it clean. I braced my hands on the hard cheeks of his ass and began lapping all along the veiny surface of his bloated cock shaft. He had a slightly raunchy, sweaty taste that kept my cock hard. I tongued his balls, popping one of the big orbs into my mouth. I sucked hard, loving the way the muscles in his ass flexed and knotted when I stretched his ball cord tight. I worked the balls over separately, then stuffed them both in my mouth.

He groaned when I finally let go and went to work on the big, spongy cockhead, lapping up the sticky stream of lube that continued to ooze out of him. His prick jerked up, and I had to put both hands around it to hold it steady. I took a deep breath, swallowed him to the hilt, and started sucking. His knob eased past my tonsils, cutting off my air supply. I moved my lips up and down his shaft, increasing my speed as his breath started getting louder and rougher. I slipped my hand up between his legs and tickled his big balls and his whole body shuddered. Cum gushed into my mouth, flooding over my tongue and squirting down my throat. Frantically I sucked and swallowed, not wanting to lose even one sweet drop of him. As I pulled back, letting his cock drop from my mouth, I leaned back and licked my lips. "Oh, Darren," I moaned, stroking my cock. I gazed at his semi-hard cock as I jerked myself off. Just as I began to shoot, he lifted up and brought his mouth over my erupting prick. He caught most of my jism in his mouth. Licking his lips, he chuckled as he mimicked me, "Oh, Al."

I longed to take him into my arms and smother him with kisses but he bounced off the bed and, reaching for his shorts, said, "Gotta go."

The next day I delayed my departure until the very last minute, when I finally saw him pedalling down the street. He stopped beside the car and I rolled down the window.

"I'm gonna miss you, man," he said, shaking my hand.

"I'll never forget this," I said.

He held on to my hand until the last possible moment.

As I turned the corner, I looked in my rear-view mirror to catch my last glimpse of his infectious smile – and his glorious basket in his incredibly tight yellow shorts.

EXPLORING SAM

David Patrick Beavers

Sam scraped the grungy, greasy rungs of the grill with the wire brush. Particles of blackened gunk disappeared in yellow-blue flare-ups of gas flames that singed his arms and made his face drip with sweat. But, he was used to it. He'd been working in his uncle's diner since he was fourteen, starting out as a work permit-carrying bus boy, then finally ascending to the Kingdom of Short Order Cook.

He threw the brush into the plastic barrel holding all the other ancient cleaning implements, then went to the sink to scrub his hands and face. No amount of soap seemed to clean away the smell of grease, though. Nor the redness in his face. But, this would all change soon, he thought. Three and a half years in this sweat box earned him a handsome stash of cash to begin a new life for himself. Midnight was closing in and so was his eighteenth birthday. Official freedom came at 12:17 a.m. Freedom to choose a life for himself unencumbered by restrictions imposed by the townsmen, by his family, by his friends.

Friends. Pseudo-friends, really. People who called themselves friends merely because he'd known most of them his entire life.

"Hey, Sammy, you done?!" Ellen asked as she dumped a bus tray onto the drain board of the huge, stainless steel sink.

"Done? I've been done for the last three years," Sam said sourly.

"Yer too green to be singin' the I'm too-through-blues, boy," she said as she rinsed her hands.

"I'm green, all right."

"Pooh pooh on that, doll," she said as she wadded up her apron and dried her hands with it. "Green's good, 'cause green's eager." She slipped into her coat and gathered up her purse from beneath a counter. "An' you'll be legal tender by the time you get up." She pulled out a bent envelope and handed it to him.

Sam blushed slightly as he opened it. A cheeky birthday

card. It made him laugh. "Thanks."

Ellen handed him a twenty. "Not much of a gift, but it's better than a six-pack of Jockeys. 'Sides, I work in this hash emporium, too, so you know the rules of finance."

"Why do you continue to work here?" he asked. "You've been here as long as I can remember."

"After fourteen years, I can do this job sleepwalking," she said. "Anyways, it's either here or the cannery. At least here I can get my meals free, ya know?"

Sam just smiled and nodded. "Yeah, Uncle Frank's leftovers."

"Beats a kick in the ass," she said. "I'll lock up the front on my way out."

"I'll get it," Sam said.

"You sure?"

"Yeah," said Sam. "See you day after tomorrow."

"Have a happy birthday, Sammy," she said as she left.

"Thanks!" Sam sighed as he pulled the keys from his pocket and locked the side exit. He left the kitchen and went out to the counter area. Ellen always left the area gleaming. Save for the formica, vinyl and stainless steel being worn, everything looked good. Real good. Especially for being forty-one years old. He went to the front door and locked it, then slipped the keys into his pocket.

"Well," he said to himself. "Happy birthday to me."

He went behind the counter again, pulled out his rucksack and went into the bathroom to change out of his grimy work clothes.

It used to make him apprehensive to remain in the diner alone, but as time went on, he began to find it calming. At times he'd look at the framed photos that dotted the wall. Pictures of the diner's first owner, some guy named Nathan and his family, then his uncle's photo, and pictures of various quasi-historical days in the diner's history. There weren't that many pictures, really, but he liked them none-the-less. He was in one old shot. A faded color photo, slightly grainy from being blown up, was of his uncle Frank when he purchased the diner from Nathan some twelve years ago. There was Nathan and Frank, his own mom and dad and him, Ellen, and Nathan's family. Sam remembered Nathan's wife's name being Valerie. There were two girls, Karen and Janice, who were in high school at the time, and Nathan's son, Lucas. He remembered Lucas very well. He was in college at the time and had come home for the event. Sam recalled spending the whole day with Lucas, being his tag-along little buddy. Lucas, with his lithe body and dark brown hair cut short and neat at the sides, but with long bangs that he kept sweeping aside. He had a rosy brown complexion and bright blue eyes. Happy eyes that smiled even when his face seemed sullen.

Sam stared at the picture of the group. There he was, standing in front of Lucas, his smiling buddy's hands planted firmly on his little shoulders. Lucas in that short sleeved button down of green plaid madras, with those fitted khakis and topsiders. He looked as much the college boy then as any college boy before him. The family moved away from town a few years after his uncle bought the diner. He never saw Lucas again. But Sam still had Lucas' sunglasses. Ray Bans of black plastic and deep green lenses. Lucas had given them to him that day. Sort of a parting present.

Sam pulled himself away from the photo and went into the bathroom to change. He ran hot water in the sink as he shucked his dingy kitchen whites. His skin still felt a bit slimy and faintly perfumed by cooking odors. He dug out his shaving kit from the rucksack and set out his toiletries as well as a wash cloth and a hand towel. As he scrubbed himself down with the make-shift sponge bath, he studied his reflection. The tow head he'd been in childhood was gone. His hair had turned a pale, pale brown bleached a golden wheat atop his crown. The streaks of blond looked odd, he thought. Stick straight hair, cut much like Lucas' hair had been cut, complete with the forelock that forever slipped down over his eyes. Hazel eyes. More brown than anything else, though. He thought they looked weak. They didn't have the intensity that Lucas' eyes had. His arms and face were a bit ruddy from sun and broiler flames. Darker than the rest of his body. He stared at the reflection of his torso. Formless, he thought. He should have taken more of an interest in gym class. He liked the weight room and swimming in the school's pool, but free time for students' use was limited. The school blocked off most of the weight room's open afternoon hours for the athletes to use the equipment undisturbed by anyone else. He always thought that unfair, but that's the way it was. At least he was thin, but a bit soft. His shoulders were square but spare in meaty bulk. Bulk he wanted. Bulk he fantasized about. He'd always thought he'd be a big man like his dad by the time he turned eighteen, rather than still looking like a neophyte freshman, fresh from a junior high sock-hop.

Sam sighed slightly as he glanced at his watch. He watched the second hand sweep around ticking off another twenty seconds.

It was 11:59. Eighteen more minutes until he was an adult. Less than a minute and it would be another Saturday. Saturday in June and his graduation a week behind him. The school superintendent officiated the proceedings, handing out diplomas to giddy kids. A diploma that was nothing more than a ribbon-wrapped, rolled-up piece of parchment that was printed with a message that read the student's real diploma would be mailed to their home address within four weeks. An absent diploma and a watch ticking away some concept of time were abstracts of his passage into manhood. He shook off the thought as he slipped his clothes from the rucksack and dressed. A short-sleeved, green-and-blue-plaid madras button-down, generic khakis, white socks and tennis shoes. He gave himself a quick once over in the mirror, gathered up his gear, then headed out of the restroom.

He locked up the diner completely, then went and climbed into his car. He sat there, key inserted in the ignition, body buckled into place and wondered what he was going to do. He'd told his parents he was spending the night with friends. No names were given as none were needed. He'd never lied to his parents before as he'd never done anything wrong, never done anything out of the ordinary, never done anything, really, at all. He'd always gone out with his group - Tina, Ramon, Mandy, Drew and Faith. All good kids. All the children of his parents' friends. All responsible young people. His parents trusted him to do what he "knew was right."

If he was so right, he thought, then why did he feel so wrong? Wrong for having dreams about Lucas. Wrong for never really dating a girl. Wrong for trying to fantasize about having sex with some leggy, buxom centerfold model in

Penthouse only to have her turn into a him halfway through a masturbatory frenzy.

He didn't want to be right at that moment. He wanted to be wrong.

He reached into the back seat and snagged his rucksack. He turned on the interior light and dug through his junk to the bottom of the sack, fishing for the small scrap of newsprint he'd stowed away. Trembling fingers found the flimsy piece of paper. It was crumpled and folded like a forgotten note tucked in a back pocket for a hundred weeks and a day. He smoothed it out and squinted at the ad from a four-page newsletter he'd happened upon last Christmas at the only adult bookstore in the entire county. He, Ramon and Drew had been cruising the touristy old-town section of the neighboring township of Zyante. The town had been a sleepy little hamlet tucked away in the northernmost section of the county. An ink speck of a burg that no one from the area ever went to. For almost a century, Zyante had existed as little more than a couple of buildings and a gas station with a zip code. Eclectic people started moving into the town in the mid-seventies, though. The sleepy hollow became a miniature mecca for an earthy-crunchy crowd. The old town section was renovated. New buildings were constructed with turn-of-the-century detail. Building design codes were suddenly enforced. New apartments, condos and homes popped up among the sequoias and eucalyptus like toadstools, each new structure conforming to some sort of Craftsman or Victorian architectural aesthetic. It was pretty. Quaint. Even the adult bookstore blended in with the rest of the town. And because this store was so innocuous, he and his friends stumbled into it quiet by accident. The clerk, a young guy, didn't seem to care that they all were young, that they all looked too young to be in there. The newsletters were in a stack outside the store. He picked one up by chance and, as he flipped the paper open, his heart skipped a thousand beats as he saw the advertisement for The Dragon Moon. The county's only gay bar-slash-club. They were advertising their annual Christmas soiree.

Over the ensuing months, he drove by the club almost every weekend, nervously glancing at the people patronizing the place. He chiefly saw men either coming or going, or just lingering outside. A few women made their way in and out, but Sam rarely saw them. His eyes were fixated on the men. He tried to recognize faces, but none were ever familiar to him. He wasn't old enough to drink, so the thought of entering the bar scared the crap out of him. Still, he could linger around the place. Observe the patrons while getting coffee and a doughnut at The DoNut Hut across the street from the club.

He stuffed the scrap back into his rucksack, turned off the interior light, then revved the engine and began his drive out of the diner's parking lot, around the streets, then onto the short length of highway that led to the private enclave of men.

The drive seemed to take forever. What he knew were mere minutes rolled by like hours as he watched the burn of headlights bore through blackness. A free hand pressed the illumination button on his watch. 12:14. He released the button, and focused on the road again, thinking that he might count in his mind the remaining minutes until he transformed magically into some legal man. A legal man. What's a legal man? Why was 12:16 any different than 12:17? One minute? The barrier between "yes" and "no."

Sam squinted to catch sight of a quickly passing exit sign. Within a minute, he turned off the highway and followed the exit down to a two-lane street flanked by tall eucalyptus trees. His stomach twinged involuntarily as he crossed the pavement and accelerated up Zyante Creek Road - a once upon a time pothole pitted gravel and dirt road that was now a smooth-as-glass, four-lane ride to the community.

He sped along, only slowing down twice when the headlights of oncoming cars seared his retinas. Before long, he crested the top of the mountain and was swallowed into the buildings of the downtown area. He slowed down to get his bearings, then parked his car a short block away from The DoNut Hut. Sam was uneasy, yet his need to explore his innate feelings prodded him from the car and onto the sidewalk. With rucksack in tow, he hunkered into himself and slowly walked toward a fruitful, yet safe, haven.

He could hear the music that leeched out from the walls of The Dragon Moon, the muted tones in syncopation with the beat - beat - beat of his own heart pumping gallons of adrenaline into his system. Erasure, he thought. One of their newer songs. His eyes broke free from the sight of concrete treadmilling beneath his feet to capture a glance at the club. A few men lingered by the closed door, smiling and talking. The door suddenly flew open as two young men blasted out, their arms snaked about each other's shoulder. Clean-cut men in denim and leather jackets. They exchanged a quick kiss as they hurried up the street to a pick-up. One let the other into the truck, then jogged around to the driver's side and climbed in as well. With a blast of blue exhaust, they were gone.

Sam's heart pounded fiercely for an instant, leaving his cheeks flushed red and hot. He was already upon the doughnut shop. He stared blankly at its glass and wood door; at the stenciled sign that read "Open 24 Hours." A young lady and young man were seated in one of the two small booths, embroiled in some intimate conversation. The counterman, a gentleman that Sam assessed to be near his own age, was seated on a stool near the coffee machine, with the receiver of the wall phone pressed to his ear.

Sam steeled himself and entered. As he approached the counter, the young clerk pivoted around, smiling at Sam as he indicated that he would be right there. He told his caller to wait, then bounced over to the counter.

"Hi!"

Sam suddenly wanted to run. "Hi..."

"Haven't seen you before."

"I don't get up here much," said Sam. "Can I get a glazed and... a large coffee, please."

"Partyin'?" asked the clerk as he adroitly whipped up Sam's order.

"Was..." Sam lied. "But it was lame, ya know?"

"Outsiders'll be here in droves in a week or so," said the clerk. "That'll be two-thirteen."

Sam fished some wadded up ones from his pocket and peeled off three. "Outsiders?"

"Touristas, ya know?" said the clerk as he plopped the change square into Sam's palm.

Sam felt the young man's finger tips linger upon his hand for a scant couple of seconds. "I know," he said as he pulled his hand away and stuffed the coins into his pocket. "We get' em, too, down in the flats. Not as many, though."

"Oughta come up here more often," the clerk said with a smile.

Sam let a nervous grin escape. He nodded to the phone. "Your call?"

"Oh!" The clerk hopped back to the receiver. "Thanks!"

Sam nodded again as the young man slipped back into chat mode. He picked up his coffee and doughnut and took a seat at a small table by the window that was as far from the couple in the booth as possible.

He dug a tattered note book and pen from his rucksack and made himself look busy. The pages of the spiral bound book were covered with scribbled notes that were nothing more than fleeting thoughts - thoughts that meant nothing to him once they were put down on paper. Thoughts that were whizzing through his mind at that moment as he stared out the window at the club across the street. Thoughts that were convoluted. Thoughts that were too embarrassing to write.

Sam sighed softly to himself as he blew on the hot coffee. The three men lingering in front of The Dragon Moon finally separated. Two went to their nearby car while the third man ventured back into the club. Sam caught a brief glimpse of a pulsing strobe light pinpointing fuzzy forms on what he suspected was the dance floor. He had another three years to wait before he could venture into that club to experience the radiant bath of male energy washing over every molecule of his body. How could he wait that long, he thought. Without any indication, the clerk suddenly pulled up a chair and dropped in on Sam.

"Cruisy club," he said to Sam.

"Is it?" Sam asked innocently.

"Yeah. I'm Randy."

"Sam," said Sam.

"Like Sam I Am?" Randy grinned.

"I do like green eggs and ham," said Sam.

Randy chuckled. "You oughta check it out."

"Right," said Sam. "I'm not twenty-one."

"You eighteen?" he asked.

"Yeah," said Sam. He was, just barely.

"Then you're in," said Randy. "They card ya at the door. Under legal, they stamp yer hand with one of those international symbols for *no*. Ya know, the slashed circle thing. Those old enough get a plastic bracelet."

"Yer kidding," said Sam.

"Naw! They got one of those kind of licenses."

"How?"

Randy shrugged. "Dunno," he said. "Maybe they paid someone off. Ya know?"

"You go there?" Sam asked.

"Sometimes," Randy said. "I'm usually workin' graveyard here, though. It's kinda po-dunk. Mostly older dudes. Over twenty-five is too old fer me. But, it can be cool."

"I dunno..." Sam said as he sipped the coffee. "Don't know anyone."

"You shy or somethin'?" Randy asked with a laugh.

"I feel weird in crowds," Sam admitted.

"Gotta get over that, dude," Randy said. "Go check it out. You don't like it, a double dose of doughnuts an' coffee are on me. Besides, they'll be closing in about an hour, anyhow."

Sam was both suddenly excited and suddenly paralyzed. "I... I... " he stammered.

"Go for it," Randy said. "We need an infusion of new blood around here. Pretty, young blood at that. At least 'til the touristas come."

"New, young blood comes here in droves?" Sam asked.

Randy nodded. "Mostly guys from the city. It's only a two hour drive for them to come up here. Lots of pretty boys, too. From the University."

"How old are you?"

"Me?" Randy ginned. "I'm twenty-eight."

"Shit," said Sam. "You look like you're my age."

"Flattery'll get you more than a couple of doughnut cockrings, my boy." Sam felt a rush of heat course through him as his face and ears burned crimson. Randy laughed. "Geez, you're a greenhorn, aren't you?"

"A bit green, yes," Sam said flatly. "Everyone's gotta start from ground zero."

Randy picked up the doughnut. "Go on. This'll keep."

It was almost like a dare to Sam. Yet, it wasn't. He looked out the window again, this time to see a foursome of hunky men slip into the club. He slowly packed away his pen and note book. "I'll probably be back in five minutes, ya know."

"I'll still be here, doughnuts awaiting," said Randy. He escorted Sam to the door. "I'll be watching from my perch."

Sam felt Randy's encouraging push-off, literally pushing him out the door. Now he knew what baby birds felt like when their mothers shove them out of the nest to test their wings for the first time. It's either fly, or land with a splat on the ground.

As he stepped off the curb, he glanced back. Randy was sitting at his table, sipping his coffee and waving him on. Sam took a deep breath, then hurried across the street and went straight for the club's door. As he gripped the handle, he felt his cock begin to swell. He took another deep breath, then yanked the door open and stepped inside a world throbbing with an old disco beat, the song thumping in his ears.

A lumberjack of a man with a square jaw, wide face and dark hair, cocked a curious brow at Sam. Sam suddenly felt as if he was eight years old and standing before the villainous principal. The man suddenly softened with a smile. Sam's swelling member twitched his attraction.

"You're blushing," the doorman said.

"I know," Sam replied.

"That either means you're underage or a rookie," said the doorman.

Sam was a flurry of clumsy motion as he fished out his wallet and pulled out his driver license for the doorman. "Is there a cover charge, or something?" Sam asked.

The doorman scrutinized the license under the brightness of an intense flashlight. "Sorry," said the doorman.

"Sorry?"

"You have to be at least eighteen," said the doorman.

"I am," Sam said.

The doorman recalculated the math on a note pad. "Huh..." he muttered with a bit of surprise. "But! Your birthday's tomorrow."

"It's today," Sam said. "It's after midnight."

The doorman got the biggest, shit-eatin' grin. "God damn, boy! Happy birthday!" He grabbed Sam's hand and stamped it with the slashed circle stamp. "They'll be doing last-call in about a half-hour." He handed Sam a florescent green coupon that was good for one birthday drink. "Take this to the bartender," he said. "Juice, soda, or types of water won't get ya ripped, but you'll keep a level head."

"Thanks," Sam said.

"Gotta check your pack, though," said the doorman.

Sam handed him the rucksack. The doorman barely bothered to look inside it, then handed it back to Sam. Sam nodded his appreciation, smiled, then stepped through the wide archway into a completely new world.

The strobe light suddenly came alive again, throwing Sam's sight and mind into a state of confusion. He felt disoriented as he tried to locate the bar. There, to his right, he saw it. Hand to the wall, he scooted around bodies he could barely see and made his way to the end of the bar.

As the song crescendoed, the strobe was suddenly replaced with a burst of brilliant light that blinked like a supernova, illuminating the entire club for just an instant. A nanosecond later, the soft lighting resumed, bathing the dancers with an aureate warmth; a vitality foreign to Sam that made them all seem bigger than life.

"What'll it be?!"

The voice startled Sam. As he whipped around, he found himself almost nose to nose with the bartender. Sam's gut sank with an icy chill as his cock shot rigid. He lost his voice for a second as he stepped back and thrust out his arm at this man, offering him the brightly colored coupon. The bartender had to tug the slip of paper from Sam's clenched fist. The bartender smiled as he glanced at the coupon.

Sam whipped his hand back to his side, inadvertently slamming his knuckles against the edge of the counter in the process.

The bartender winced at the cracking sound. Sam silently gasped his pain as he shook his wounded hand. The bartender leaned over the counter and grabbed Sam's hand. "Lemme see!" Sam said nothing as this man gently splayed his throbbing fingers and inspected the injury. "Ow ow ow!" said the bartender as he grabbed a wet towel and dabbed drops of blood from the scrapped knuckles. He set the towel aside, then scooped up a small handful of crushed ice from the bar well and slathered its coldness over Sam's hand.

Sam felt none of this man's nursing actions. He heard none

of his empathetic sounds. He could only see at that moment. He could see the man's bright blue eyes. Downcast, attendant to his numb hand, this man's eyes were captivating.

"Feel better?" the man said as he lifted his head and looked directly at Sam.

The words slipped slowly into Sam's mind, bringing him back into beta consciousness. "Yeah..." Sam croaked. He awkwardly tried to lay his good hand upon his injured one, but instead of his own hand, he felt his open palm blanket the hard, strong hand of this stranger. The alien flesh startled him, but before he could jerk his good hand away, the man stacked his remaining hand atop Sam's.

Sam glanced down at the four-tier hand sandwich on the bar. He let a nervous chuckle escape. "I'm such an idiot," he said apologetically. "Thanks."

"No one's an idiot on his birthday." The bartender patted Sam's hand as he freed himself to wipe up the melting ice. He pitched the towel below the bar.

"Yo! Ryan!" boomed a voice.

The bartender whipped around, away from Sam. Sam saw three men and two women waving money at the bartender. One guy drummed his fists on the bar.

"A little service over here, please!" barked a tall, skinny guy with poindexter glasses and greasy, thinning hair.

Sam felt a surge of anger bristle through him as the gaggle of rum-drunk geeks giggled like snot-nosed children and pounded on the bar, chanting the name "Ryan" over and over and over, demanding the bartender's attention. His bartender. Ryan.

Ryan stepped away from Sam, summoned by the call. But, as he moved toward the insufferable fivesome, he pirouetted, shooting back to Sam a devilish grin and a playful wink. The slight signal diffused Sam's anger and for the first time Sam saw beyond Ryan's eyes. He saw the man.

Thick, black hair, as shiny as new patent leather, swept back over the crown of his head, dusting the collar of his navy blue shirt of soft, brushed cotton that moved and stretched like skin over his sturdy, broad shoulders and wide, strong back. Billowing shirt tails curtained his ass and crotch, but Sam could see clearly the meaty thighs that fit snugly against well worn denim. He moved fluidly, Sam noted, as he served up the idiotic quints. He had a somewhat narrow face, with a squared, strong jaw and straight, sharp nose that loosely resembled a perfect four in profile. A thin upper lip rested comfortably upon its full lower mate. And when he smiled, his tanned, olive skin set off the polish of his milk-white teeth.

Sam's erect prick ached dully, wanting immediate attention. Knees slightly bent, he shifted his hips toward the bar, trying to conceal his tenting, khaki-clad crotch. His bruised hand slipped down to his groin, the heel of his palm pressing hard into his crotch and sliding over and down his rigid shaft, trying to shift his member back into place.

He wasn't sure he could stand this anymore. His cock was refusing to willingly deflate. It had a mind of its own, choosing to strain uncontrollably and snake its way out through the right leg hole of his briefs. Annoyed and embarrassed, Sam glanced all around, fearful of prying eyes, as he slipped his wounded hand down his pants and quickly untrapped his wayward cock. This innocent tug on his meat almost made him shoot a burning load. As he whipped his hand out of his pants, his scabbing knuckles caught the waistband of his shorts and he inadvertently set them bleeding again. Fist went to mouth where he reflexively licked the wound.

Ryan suddenly reappeared before him and slapped down a drink on the counter. "Here..." he said. "Give this a try."

Sam smiled again as he lifted the glass and sucked down a bit of clear liquid through a black, plastic straw. His mouth and throat tingled as a somewhat pepperminty flavor washed down into him. He quietly smacked his lips, then sipped again. "I like it."

"Good," Ryan said as he quickly scanned the club. He turned back to Sam. "So, Mr. Birthday, what's your name?"

"Sam."

"I'm Ryan."

"I know," Sam said sheepishly. "Heard them call you."

"That's why I think that we should all just be called numbers. You know, instead of them bleating out my name like that, they'd be calling 'Five!' 'Yo, Five! Service, please!' Now that would be perfectly anonymous."

"I'd choose Nine for a number-name," said Sam.

"I like that one," Ryan said. He glanced at his watch and

scanned the room again.

"Looking for someone particular?" Sam asked.

"Yeah," said Ryan. "The bartender I'm covering for. His name's Carlos. Had to run his sister up to the airport, so I said I'd stay until he got back."

"Maybe he's stuck in traffic," Sam suggested.

"Thought that, but her flight was at nine-thirty," Ryan said. "The ride up there from here, at worst, and I mean almost not moving at all, takes a maximum of two hours."

"I hate closin' up," Sam said.

"Where?"

"I work in my uncle's diner," said Sam. "Nightshift, mostly."

"Ah, so you wanted to get an early jump on your birthday?" Ryan asked.

Sam shrugged. "Something like that." Sam caught sight of tall, Hispanic man enter the bar area.

"Ryan!" he called.

"Well, the prodigal son returns!" Ryan said.

"Sorry, man." Carlos dove straight into his clean-up routine. "Long story. I'll fill you in later."

Ryan grabbed a rather large beer stein from the register area, then set it down beside Sam's drink. "Quittin' time!"

Sam sucked down the rest of his drink with amazing speed. The peppermint rush was a bit overwhelming. He watched while Ryan washed his hands in the sink, then snagged a jacket from a cupboard below the bar. He gave Carlos a pat on the ass, then exited the bar area. He thought for a second that his man was disappearing on him, then he looked at the stein. He lifted the pewter lid just a bit and found it to be stuffed with money. Tip money. Ryan had left it there in his care.

He waited patiently until Ryan returned. "What's in the mug?" Sam asked.

Ryan lifted the lid. "Tips. You gonna head home now?"

"No," Sam said.

"You want to... hang?" Ryan asked.

"With you?"

Ryan's smile faltered slightly. "I guess..."

Sam let a broad, but embarrassingly eager smile, light up his face. "Sure! Um, I gotta make a stop at the doughnut place across the street."

"Ah! You know Randy?" he asked Sam as his hand clamped down playfully at the nap of Sam's neck.

"Yeah." Sam almost collapsed under Ryan's firm touch. He grabbed his rucksack, casually holding it at hip's heighth, to hopefully conceal his straining hard-on. He led the way as they left the club.

Out the door, across the street, then into The DoNut Hut. Randy smiled wryly as the two approached the counter. "Well," Randy said. "Two large black coffees and two raised glaze. To go, no doubt."

"That'll do just fine," Ryan said.

"You got it," said Randy as he slipped Sam a conspiratorial wink.

Without much fuss or small talk, Randy served up their order, then Ryan and Sam decided that Sam should follow Ryan to his house. It was a short, short drive, but the longest drive Sam felt he'd ever made. The whole while, he wanted to free his cock and pump it hard to quell the pulsing ache in his groin.

Ryan's house was a small, well-maintained, Craftsman bungalow with a neat patch of a yard, that was flanked all around by sequoias and pines. The living room was rather large. Comfortable furnishings invited one to park it on the oversized sofa and remain forever watching the trees grow beyond the panes of window glass while the cheery hearth burned sweet-smelling fir.

It was on the oversized sofa that Sam took his seat, while Ryan talked loudly from the adjacent kitchen. Small talk, mostly, about how long he'd been there and why he'd given up a lucrative career as a line producer for the movieland moguls down in Hollywood to become one of two partners in The Dragon Moon. He finished up his tale as he returned to the living room with the two cups of coffee poured into mugs and the two doughnuts sitting on a small plate. He set the refreshments down on the coffee table, then slipped onto the floor, very near to Sam.

"I nuked the coffee a bit," Ryan said.

Sam took a mug and sipped. It was just a bit too hot for his taste. "I don't know that I'd give up a real career in a city to hide away in the sticks."

"Your tastes and perceptions will change as you get older," Ryan said. "Different things become important."

"Do you have a boyfriend?" Sam asked quietly.

"He stayed back in L.A.," Ryan said. "He gave me an ultimatum. Us in the city, or just me in the sticks."

"How old was he?" Sam asked.

Ryan lit a cigarette. Inhaled deeply, then got up and expelled nicotine exhaust as he opened a window and turned on a couple of air filters. "Thirty-five," Ryan said. He returned to his seat on the floor, set his smoke in the ashtray, then unlaced and removed his worn boots. "Great guy, but he has a real paranoia of the sticks. Thinks everyone up in the mountains is a survivalist Nazi."

Sam wanted to get down on the floor with Ryan. To nuzzle against him. To rub his tired feet. But, he was afraid to move beyond the space he'd assigned to himself. "There aren't any gays down in the flats."

"Yeah, there are," Ryan said with a smile as he leaned his head back onto the sofa cushion and stared up at Sam. "You just haven't met them. Yet."

"You gonna introduce me around?"

"Is that what you want?" Ryan asked. "My birthday present to you?"

"Maybe," said Sam. "How old are you?"

"Forty-three," he said.

"I hope I can look as good when I'm your age" Sam said. His fingers took on a life of there own, gently tracing two faint lines along Ryan's forehead.

Ryan closed his eyes, relishing Sam's gentle touch. "And you are, what? Just eighteen? That makes me twenty-five years older than you, Sam."

"So?"

"So? So you've got a whole lifetime of choices to make and people to meet still ahead of you."

"Maybe," said Sam as his fingers stroked Ryan's hair.

"Well, birthday boy, what would you like to do?" Ryan asked. "We could drive up into the city for a very early breakfast at an all-night diner. We could hit an after-hours club that's excitingly illegal and underground. We could hit the twenty-four hour convenience stores and shop for strange, little gifties? We could...."

Sam lay his hand over Ryan's mouth. "I've never had sex with a man," he confessed. "But I don't know any guys who'd want to sleep with me." He watched Ryan's bright blue eyes grow wide with surprise. He started to remove his hand from this man's mouth, but Ryan took firm hold of his wrist.

Ryan teasingly licked the flat of Sam's palm, then, one by one, he sucked Sam's fingers, then thumb. When he let the boy's hand go free, he quickly killed his cigarette, moved the coffee table away, then removed Sam's shoes and socks.

Sam's entirety was in such overload that the second Ryan's warm, moist lips wrapped around his toes, his cock involuntarily spasmed and shot a heavy, wet load in his briefs. Sam suddenly flushed red as soon as his cock spewed. He wanted to scream his frustration, but any sound was sucked back into him as Ryan massaged and tongue-bathed his feet. The sensation of touch was so intense for him that his cock strained and swelled longer and thicker than it had ever done before. He just groaned and closed his eyes and allowed himself to feel the pleasure; to feel his legs being lifted and his body turned lengthwise onto the sofa.

Sam could sense Ryan all around him as the man moved to remove his shirt and pants. He listened quietly as the sounds of Ryan, stripping down, filtered into his ears and fed the imagery of his unfolding fantasy. Sam was again scared to open his eyes again. He didn't want the spell of the moment broken. But when he heard no more, when he felt no more, he forced his eyes to open slightly.

There, in a fuzzy aura, he saw an expanse of marvelous male flesh exposed. Ryan was kneeling beside him, staring at him. His man's massive chest and thick, muscular arms: his beautiful face, framed by a black mane, hovered over him. A mat of silky black hair covered wide, squared pecs, then overflowed onto his stomach and shoulders. Sam's hand pressed against the fuzzy hardness. A layer of wool atop concrete. He found thick, nubby nipples erect at attention. He squeezed one gently, then kneaded the meat all around as he sat up, gracefully pivoting his form to catch his kneeling man between scissoring legs.

Ryan pressed his face against Sam's delicate chest, then ran his broad, wet, rough tongue over the youth's velvety pec until he found Sam's soft, pinkish tit. His thick fingers gently pinched a plump protrusion of breast meat that his lips clamped down upon to suckle.

Sam folded over his man, his fingers raking over the flesh of Ryan's back, scratching him hard. He felt Ryan's teeth bite down on his tit in response. Sam's body trembled as an icy chill shot up his spine. His legs reflexively lifted and wrapped themselves tightly about Ryan's waist. He felt Ryan's head lift and he looked down into those brilliant blue eyes. Sam's hesitant lips found Ryan's eager mouth, running wet with wanting. Sam drank greedily the secretions of mucilage that kept him fused to his man.

Ryan abruptly broke free and slammed his face into Sam's shorts. The thin, faded cotton ripped like tissue paper as his teeth tugged and tore through the cloth barrier between his hungry mouth and his lad's tender meat. Fingers felt the wet spot of thick, gloppy cum matting fine pubic hair to flesh. Ryan gripped the briefs adroitly and ripped them through and through.

Sam succumbed to this aggressive attack and flopped back onto the sofa. His hips shifted slightly as he felt and heard the bulk of his briefs being ripped away from the waistband. In an instant, the barrier was gone and his cock slapped up high and hard against Ryan's sweating face. His hands clamped down on his man's head, gripping reins of thick black hair, and he watched himself pull Ryan's eager mouth along, all around his cock and swollen balls, to the puddle of sticky cum. He wanted to watch his man use tongue and teeth and lips to clean away his mess. Ryan didn't disappoint him. His tongue swabbed and bathed, while teeth combed hair and lips vacuumed away all that was there.

Then Sam watched Ryan's nose slip down below his balls and push into the split of his ass. Forceful hands and arms beneath his lower back jacked his pelvis up and he felt all of Ryan's hot, wet face press into his crack, spreading his ass open wide. Sam tensed up sharply, suddenly afraid and embarrassed as he felt the gentle wind of Ryan inhaling the smell of his asshole. Then he heard that deep, throaty growl slip from his man. Sam started to move, then an unexpected, numbing ripple of pleasure coursed boldly through him as he felt for the first time a man's tongue slip around and into his tight asshole.

Ryan forced his long tongue up into his boy, savoring the headiness of the virgin hole, loving the feel of the lad's sphincter loosing, then clamping down tightly around his snaking tongue. He cleaned his lad up all around his ass. He could hear Sam's pleased, responsive breathing - deep sucks of air – growling gasps – and his torso twisting slightly, side to side as he tried to shimmy his pelvis to bear down hard on Ryan's inviting mouth.

Ryan reluctantly left his delicacy behind to attend to the needs of his young man's loose, fleshy balls and that long, slightly swayed staff of flawless, velvety skin that was his lad's cock. He tongue-washed his boy's scrotum with slow, deliberate ease, allowing each testicle to loll on his tongue, then slip between his lips to suckle on each tasty orb.

Sam was slipping headlong into a vortex of surging pleasure. He could think of nothing beyond the feel of his man's attentive mouth sucking and licking and probing his most private areas; this feel that made his mouth and tongue twist and twitch in like, wanting to do as he was being done to.

He reached out blindly for Ryan's head, grabbing fistfuls of thick locks, and tried to lead his man up onto him. He wanted to feel the crush of hairy, muscled weight smother him. But Ryan wouldn't be dissuaded from his feast at that moment. His man's head rose up only far enough to wrap around, then swallow whole, Sam's rigid cock. As Ryan pressed his face down into the soft of Sam's groin, Sam writhed sharply from the intense, burning pleasure of the tight, slick, hotness of his man's throat contracting all around the tip of his prick, tickling his glans with a succession of gentle squeezes.

Sam ran his hands wildly over his chest, tugging fistfuls of his own flesh, pinching his nipples hard as he felt that boiling churn in his groin. He could feel the cum rising slowly, so slowly from his retracting balls. Then he thought he felt his man's tongue again, slipping up into his ass. But it couldn't be his tongue, Sam flashed in his mind. Ryan's tongue was helping hold his cock hostage deep in Ryan's throat. The image of a slim finger shot through Sam's mind as he suddenly became aware of Ryan's finger. His pinky. Pressing up in him...

Sam trembled with a violent shiver as Ryan pressed his prostate. That simple touch of the switch sent a tankard-load of cum shooting through his shaft and spewing deep, deep into Ryan's bowels.

Ryan continued his probing massage of Sam's prostate as he bobbed up and down feverishly on the sleek, young cock, milking every last drop of sticky, sweet juice from within. It had been so long since he'd tasted anything so wonderfully pure; since he'd really tasted anything at all. Like a greedy kid at the bottom of the milkshake glass, he kept sucking and sucking hoping to find some small reserve well.

Sam breathed evenly, but heavily, spent by the intensity of his first real orgasm. He felt warm and sticky and savored that feeling. Once again, Sam tried to dislodge his man from his groin and to guide him up onto him, but Ryan refused to let Sam's cock slip free from his mouth. He continued his slow massage of Sam's prostate, his slow sucking of Sam's still rigid cock, as his one free hand began to massage all around the soft tissue of his lower abdomen and groin. Sam gave in. He closed his eyes and relaxed, letting Ryan do his thing. It all felt good, for a time, then Ryan's fingers glossed over the area of Sam's bladder. Sam suddenly felt that nagging pressure within him. He started to shift to sit up, but Ryan's firm hand and crisp eyes suggested he keep his seat. Sam was going to speak, then Ryan's palm pressed down around Sam's bladder again. Sam winced slightly. Ryan's eyes smiled. He firmly massaged all around Sam's tender bladder.

"Easy..." Sam finally whispered. "I gotta pee..."

Ryan slammed his face down hard into Sam's groin, then pressed down even harder on the lad's bladder. Sam felt an involuntary spurt of piss blast from his stiff cock and splash down Ryan's throat. Sam burned red with embarrassment as Ryan finally let Sam's cock to free with a slurpy-lip pop.

"So," Ryan said as he licked his lips. "You can piss with a hard-on."

"I didn't mean to, but..."

Ryan cut him off. "You liked pissing in my mouth, didn't you."

Sam stared into his man's bright, devilish eyes. "You wanted me to."

Ryan licked his young man's pretty prick again, then pulled his finger from the lad's ass and sucked on it slowly. "There's a lot I want to do. Teach you the paths of young sex and man sex."

Ryan stood up and, for the first time, Sam saw all of his man – naked, thick musculature dusted with a webbing of black hair. A pouch of loose, shaved flesh, held huge, heavy balls, and his long cock, thick and meaty, stood up strong and hard. Sam sat up and wrapped both hands about the base of Ryan's equipment, gathering all of him up in a bouquet of flesh of pale olive and redness.

Sam nuzzled his man's offerings, feeling the satin texture of his skin, gently licking the thick veins in his shaft and the wrinkled folds of his scrotum. He pressed his face hard into his man's groin, sucking in the musky scent of sweat and the faint, sharp bite of urine-clouded cologne. He felt Ryan's hands tenderly stroke his face and hair. Sam's mouth ran wet as he nimbly slipped back the sheath of foreskin covering his man's thick, squared glans. All slick and shiny and purply-red his hammerhead was. The slit in the tip was wide and Sam imagined the sensation of gallons of jism spitting out from it, all over his face and form. Without reservation, Sam wrapped his spit-slicked lips over the hammerhead glans, sucking on the huge knob like it was a jawbreaker. The salty taste was delicious to him. He slipped further down his man's thick, burning shaft to savor his flavor even more.

Ryan's strong legs buckled slightly as he watched his boy explore his cock with lips and tongue as soft and pliant as oiled kid leather. He strained to keep from shooting a load right then and there, but the urge to cum became critically intense. He eased Sam away, then grabbed the young man's hand and escorted him out of the living room.

They went into the bathroom and Sam was surprised by the rather spacious accommodations as they stepped into the tub. Sam thought they were going to shower, but, instead, Ryan got on his knees and sucked Sam's prick to full attention. He then let a wad of spit slip from between his lips into the palm of his hand. He reached around to his ass and smeared the mucous over and up into his hairy asshole.

As he stood up and turned around, he reached behind him

to grip Sam's prick, then he pressed his twitching, slick hole against the head of Sam's dick and pushed himself back.

Sam gasped sharply as he felt himself slip up deep into Ryan's ass. He gripped his man's meaty, hairy cheeks and squeezed them hard, then he wrapped his arms around his waist and held him tight.

Ryan craned his face around and found Sam's mouth as eager for attention as his own. As they chewed tongues and lips, Sam slowly pumped Ryan's ass while he stroked his thick tool.

"You ready to do something different?" Ryan whispered.

"Sure..."

"Relax, Sam..." said Ryan softly. "Just relax those hips and remember your bladder."

"What?" said asked.

"You still gotta piss, baby boy, don't you?"

"Yeah..." Sam whispered.

"It's all right, Sammy... You'll see..."

Sam stopped all activity. He closed his eyes and let his mind go blank. Within seconds he felt his urine streaming freely. Up his man's ass. As Ryan moaned, Sam held fast to him. Chest to back, they pressed deeply into one another.

Then Ryan pulled away suddenly and whipped around on his knees to catch the remaining blasts of piss that Sam expelled. The wetness saturated his fur, rinsed out his mouth and glistened his skin. When the last golden drop dripped freely, Ryan stood up and hugged Sam hard. Sam was excited by the slick feel of Ryan's piss soaked flesh and hair. It made him even hornier.

Ryan pulled away again. He turned on the faucets, letting the water warm up. "You start showering while I dispose of your deposit in me." He stepped out of the tub and drew the shower curtain closed.

"Did that hurt?" Sam asked.

"No..." Ryan said softly. "I want to be clean for you."

Sam heard the toilet seat slap down on the commode. He heard the seat creak slightly as Ryan sat down. Sam turned the handle and started the shower blasting, drowning out any other immediate sounds.

Within a few minutes, the shower curtain parted and Ryan stepped into the tub. Sam drew his man close to him, beneath the beating spray of water. He ran the cake of soap over Ryan's chest, then stomach, watching the suds bubble up and rinse away. Then he slipped the soap around and kneaded a frothy lather over his man's fuzzy ass.

"I love the way you feel," Sam said shyly.

"You're a beautiful young man, Sam," Ryan said with a smile. "And tonight's your night to explore."

"I thought we just did that," Sam grinned.

"We just scratched the surface of sex," Ryan said. "There's better than that we've still to delve into."

"What?"

"Making love."

BROTHER FLESH

John Terron

Jamie had his eye on his older brother, Vic, for a long time, or rather, he had his eye on the bulge in his brother's trousers. He longed to stroke that appetizing shape and feel what was inside the pants. He could imagine the shaft and balls, loose in the underpants, and he fantasized playing with his hand down there, rearranging the organs, slowly, under his manipulations making the cock grow thick.

Vic wore his cock on the right and Jamie, copying his hero, arranged his own in the same way. Depending on the cut of the trousers and whether Vic wore Jockeys or boxers, Jamie could make out the state of the shaft: thick and floppy in hot weather and, on cold days, poking forwards against the fly. The seam of a pair of tight trousers pulled up in the crotch, balls on one side, thick tube on the other. A more classic pair had the whole handful hanging down the leg of the trousers, revealing the attractive, soft curves of maleness nesting there. Vic in swimming trunks, his sinewy body exposed, his equipment clearly outlined, gave Jamie an erection on the spot. Jamie masturbated over a photograph taken of Vic on the beach, sporting an obvious boner in his trunks and smiling sheepishly at the camera.

Sometimes Jamie at least had a glimpse of that cock, like when they were having a pee in the cinema. He noticed Vic's technique of pulling back the foreskin, peeing, shaking himself and then pushing the skin back over the head with any stray drops. He copied this, too, from that day on. They had separate bedrooms, but Jamie often had to move in with Vic when guests came to stay with the family. Vic was much older and usually came home late from his dates when Jamie, who was still in school, would already be in bed, even asleep. Whenever he could he would have a peek through half-closed lids as Vic was undressing for bed, as the underpants slid off that delicious ass, perhaps catch sight of the balls dangling between Vic's legs as he put on his pajamas. But Vic always had his back turned, frustratingly, and in the mornings he jumped out of bed to make a lightning change from pajamas into underpants.

But these mere glimpses didn't satisfy Jamie. He wanted to see that prick *properly*, the trousers down, the cock and balls framed by the crotch hair and strong thighs. And, more than seeing, he wanted to *touch*. He wanted to handle it when soft and thick, when hard and pulsing. He concocted all sorts of lecherous schemes: to spill coffee on Vic's lap and help wipe the fly (but he may just get a clout on the ear); to hide Vic's pajamas, provoke a rough and tumble and cock-grabbing with his naked brother; to give Vic a massage, first the back, pulling down his pants and then: THE FRONT! He rejected these masturbatory fantasies. His lust for Vic's body was rampant, but he was scared to make a wrong move. He knew that, first of all, he had to break the ice. He had to get Vic to be more open, to allow himself, at least, to be *seen* naked.

On a Friday afternoon, the two of them went in their father's car to fetch their aunt coming to visit for the weekend. Jamie prepared a story in advance about swimming in the river with his classmates, that the others swam bare-ass but that he didn't want to take off his clothes.

"Why?" Vic asked.

"I'm shy, just like you."

"Me? I'm not shy."

Jamie had carefully planned this opening: "Well, I'm your brother and I've never seen you bare-ass."

"Come on!"

"Never completely."

Vic laughed, teasing, "I see you having a good look when I get ready for bed!"

"You never show anything, anyhow."

"I used to swim bare-ass, too, you know. And I walk round like that in my room. All the time."

"Not when I'm there."

Vic quickly changed the subject: "I take this turn to the right, don't I?"

But Jamie wouldn't allow him to escape: "Okay, I dare you to walk around bare-ass in your room, in front of me."

"Okay."

"In front of me?" Jamie insisted, courageously.

"Why not?"

"Tonight?"

"Sure."

Jamie felt a stirring in his groin. Things were moving well. He ventured further: "You should see some of those guys at the river. Enormous things between their legs."

"Who's got the biggest?"

"Freddy."

"Ah! Like his brother, John."

"How do you know?"

"I've seen John, many times. He loves showing off his cock."

It thrilled him that Vic used the word "cock."

"If I had a monster cock like Freddy's I wouldn't be shy showing it off either."

"You think you're small?"

"Yeah, small compared to Freddy."

"It's natural. He's older 'n you."

"No, we're the same age."

Vic laughed. "Don't worry so much about it. Your's will grow as your body grows."

"You've got a big one? As big as John's?" Jamie hoped he didn't overstep the bounds.

"What the hell," Vic said, giving his brother a sidelong glance. "You've seen my cock. It's normal size, I suppose. Big enough when hard." He broke off the conversation. "We're arriving. There she is waiting at the front door as usual."

Jamie had an embarrassing time concealing his hard-on as he got out of the car, but, boy, was he looking forward to the evening!

He was sitting in bed, reading, when Vic came in. He put his book down to watch Vic stripping, watching openly after their talk in the car. Vic started to do his usual quick-change act. Jamie arrested him just as he was about to step into his pajama trousers. "I thought you said you were going to walk around bare-ass?"

Vic looked over his shoulder at Jamie and burst out laughing. He pulled off his T-shirt and strutted around, naked, his hand covering his cock.

"Cheat! I can't see anything."

"Okay, boy, you wanna see my cock? You see better like this?" Vic came to stand right next to his brother's bed, hands on hips, thrusting his prick forwards, making a joke of the situation.

"Wow!"

"How's that for a cock?" he gave it a pull downwards.

"Wow! Super," Jamie groaned. His beautiful brother, his hero, was at last vulnerably naked in front of him. He savored the moment, admiring the body, feasting his eyes on the shape of the soft cock hanging invitingly in front of him.

"Well, let's see yours, then," Vic said.

"No," Jamie said, blushing.

Vic wouldn't accept that. He pushed the covers down, opened Jamie's pajamas. Jamie's stiffening tool bounced into view.

"Well," Vic said, staring at it.

Jamie scrambled to his knees onto the bed, body square-on to Vic's, and displayed himself, his cock almost touching Vic's. Forcing himself to keep calm, he casually slid his hand around Vic's cock. "God, it's heavy," he moaned, weighing it in his palm.

"You're not so small as you made out," Vic said, reaching down to take Jamie's prick in his hand and giving it a squeeze. "Christ! You're rock-hard!" He let go and started to pull away, but Jamie curled his fingers round his brother's cock, holding him captive. Vic tugged at his hand, but Jamie hung on, kneading the swelling flesh.

"Let go," Vic commanded, finally getting his well-fondled prick free. He grabbed his pajamas and was in bed like a flash, and turned off the light.

Jamie felt elated. He revelled in the pleasure of Vic's body, of holding his cock in his hand. And he had felt Vic getting hard as he rubbed it. Uncontestable. He fabricated randy follow-ups: long, hot sex sessions between them. As soon as he heard Vic's light snoring, he started pumping himself. He fantasized them wanking each other and in next to no time he spurted his cum, letting out loud grunts.

He suddenly became aware that Vic was awake. At first he panicked that he had been overheard wanking himself, then he thought perhaps it might have turned Vic on, might tempt him to follow suit. He pretended to doze off quickly, not even wiping the spunk off his stomach, but kept a close watch on the bed across from his.

After a long wait, even in the dim light he could see that Vic was indeed giving himself a good wanking, jerky breaths and all. Stopping for a moment to check whether Jamie was asleep, he whispered, "Jamie?" then lifted his hips, pushed his pajamas down, spread his thighs and started up again in earnest.

Jamie could visualize that cock now bursting hard and Vic's strong hand encasing it. He could almost see the swollen head, the generous foreskin sliding up and down. And all thanks to his provocation! And then Vic was pumping harder, breathing in gasps, working up to an orgasm.

"Vic," Jamie whispered.

"Fuck!" Vic grunted, stopping abruptly, turning on his side, away from Jamie.

"I'm sorry," Jamie said, but no reply came. "Don't stop because of me." Still there was no response, no movement. "Vic?"

"Fuck it, then!" Vic turned brusquely onto his back. His hands went down between his legs again.

Jamie sat up to see better as Vic began to fondle his throbbing meat. "Ah... Ah..." He was doing himself with delicious slowness, savoring each long stroke. "Ah... Ah..."

"Oh, yeah, Vic."

"Ah... Ah..." He threw off the bedclothes, and pushed his pelvis up in the air. "Ah... Aaah..." He began to shoot in long spurts, his body in spasms of ecstasy.

"Wow!" Jamie murmured.

Vic slowly sank back down, totally spent. It took him long to recover his regular breathing. Suddenly he put on the light. Jamie stared wide-eyed at the powerful prick, more than doubled in size, lying on the stomach, dripping with cum. Vic took some tissues from a box next to his bed and began wiping himself. His body jerked once more as he milked the shaft empty and pulled the hood over the flared head.

"You want a tissue?"

"You heard me, then?"

"Of course I heard you. It's you that set me off." He pulled up his pajamas.

"It's gone dry on my skin."

"Well, then, night-night." Vic put out his hand and they clasped hands between the beds, Vic's hand still sticky with his cum. Jamie unconsciously brought his hand to his lips and licked, tasting the family spunk on his fingers.

"Thanks, Vic."

"That's okay." The two brothers looked at each other for a long moment. Vic put out the light, again, and was asleep in minutes. Jamie was wide-awake, jubilant with his evening of success.

Jamie now wanted to see how far he could go with Vic. The next evening, Saturday, he hid Vic's pajamas, forcing Vic to search for it clad only in his tank-top, ass bare, his cock dangling between his bare thighs.

"My pajamas! You little shit! Where are they?" Vic pulled the covers off Jamie and started to roughen him up. Jamie promptly grabbed him between his legs.

"Hey, watch it!" he shouted, trying pull away, but Jamie held firm. He pulled Vic off balance and on top of himself, his other hand clutching Vic's ass.

"Hands off." But he couldn't loosen the grip and retaliated by grabbing Jamie between the legs, too.

"Christ! Little bugger is hard again!"

"You, too."

"No, I'm not." Vic got his cock free, shook Jamie, "My pajamas!"

"You *are* getting stiff!" He had his hand, quick as lightning, round the shaft again. "God, it's enormous."

"Let go of my cock..." Vic broke loose, got up from the bed. Now his cock was no longer hanging straight down, but raised at a rakish angle.

"Where are my pajamas?" He hauled Jamie out of the bed, onto the floor.

Jamie clasped Vic round his legs and got hold of the slab yet once more. "Just look at the size of it," Jamie gushed, roughly forcing the skin back.

Vic looked down and knew he was lost. It was true: his cock *was* hard and growing. Not as big as John's, but plenty big enough. And now with the air hitting the head, it grew even more. He loved his cock like this, lusciously big before a complete hard-on, and seeing another guy holding it for him made him horny. Jamie sensed Vic's resistance melting away and started pulling him off in the way he had seen Vic do himself the night before, with long, solid strokes. He licked his hand and wetted the shaft and head. He got the cock bursting hard into a glorious male aggressiveness.

"Oh, Vic!" Jamie cried, savoring the feel of his brother's flesh.

"Jamie-boy!"

Vic gave himself voluptuously, completely. With his thrusts, fucking into the hand, he set the rhythm slow. He wanted this to last.

Jamie got up from the floor, pajamas at his ankles and put their pricks together. He delighted in the feel of Vic's hardness against his own, the heat of it. He jerked both their cocks and Vic clutched Jamie's ass. Now his thrusts demanded a faster stroking to intensify his pleasure, and he quickly erupted, followed immediately by his partner.

Holding each other they collapsed onto the bed, front-- to-front, rubbing their cum-smeared pricks together.

Vic had implicated himself to the hilt. Jamie no longer had to hide that he had his eye on him, or his eye on that gorgeous bulge, or that he wished to seduce him, and seduce him again and again.

Before lunch on Sunday, he made it obvious to Vic that he was looking at his packet at every available opportunity, that he was hot for him, wanting his cock. And Vic understood, perfectly.

And so, at long last, that afternoon, Jamie could play with his brother's body in the way he had often fantasized.

They were lounging in deck-chairs in the garden. Vic was asleep, spread-out defenselessly on his back, his body an invitation to a man's hand. Jamie leaned over him and caressed his shoulders, his chest and his waist, but careful not to wake the beautiful owner. He explored Vic's legs, his thighs right up to his balls, cupping them lovingly, then onto the curve of the cock, outlined in the loose linen trousers. He felt a quivering of the weapon and took great pleasure in stroking the object of his desire. It began to thicken under his hand into a lazy tumescence, to lengthen and swell down the leg of the trousers.

Vic sighed with deep pleasure in his slumber, his handsome face relaxed, his lips half-open. He drowsily opened his eyes and realizing that it was Jamie and not only a sensuous dream, smiled into his eyes.

He suddenly sat up in consternation, "Where's Mum and Dad?"

"They've taken auntie out in the car."

He relaxed again, opening his legs as Jamie pushed him back into the chair. He tugged at the material of his pants to make more room for Jamie to play with his cock, to move it around freely inside the trousers, to slip it out of the fly of his boxers. Jamie manipulated the foreskin. He rolled it over the ridge of the head and rubbed the sensitive underside of the cock.

"If you continue, you'll make me come inside my pants," Vic murmured.

"I'd love you to." He wanked Vic through the thin cloth, his fist round the truncheon.

"It'll make a mess," Vic said, but at the same time offering himself to the intimacy of the hand round him. He squeezed Jamie's fore-arm, signalling his pleasure. His own hand began to wander, searching. For the first time he showed desire to feel his brother, too. His hand sought the boy's weapon. Found it, held it, inexpertly, at first, after a while starting to fondle.

"Oh, Vic!"

Now, they were indeed equal partners. And both in ecstasy.

Then, much too soon: "Oh, God! Get it out, quick!" But it was already too late: Vic's trousers blossomed with an abundant wetness.

Just at that moment they heard a car pulling into the driveway, rudely interrupting their idyllic moment. They had to cope, and fast, with the changing of Vic's trousers, but now *both* of them were looking forward to the evening.

ROUGH-BOY

Ian Stewart

Finally, on a Sunday unencumbered of the weekend's madness, Ravel – a man, really, but boyish, wide-eyed – is lying mostly naked; black jeans and clanking belt buckle down at his knees; gritty boots still on, staring flat at the ceiling, from a mattress-less bed of black, streaked plywood. This plywood bed, with a rack of many hangers holding only two shirts underneath, fills at chest-height all of the tiny cube-proportioned room, but for a sideways space, the shelves where he'd tossed socks and underwear, black T-shirts. He found an eroticism in having dark cotton underwear out in the open, manly, on the shelves, alongside woolly thick work socks, and under the naked light his tumescent dick still drools clear on his belly, sticky in his cock-hair.

Yesterday's dirty socks on the black plywood are his cum rag. His mind flashes caution for jock-itch, when you shoot onto your socks, rather'n having a towel, or sheets you wash, to jerk-off in.

It's the daytime - late afternoon - but no sun gets here, down the lightwell, only the noise of talking neighbors; Elvis Costello; brushing teeth and flushing toilets. But Ravel is always a fool for romance; the romance of living manly: his own little rathole in the city. And a giant stretch, torso-naked and drooling-dicked, on the hard plywood, exhaling a big sigh off a solid wank. Suddenly, unexpectedly, his body tightens, locked in mid-writhe. "Listen, I can't talk about it anymore. I can maybe give you a call during the week. We can go for a drink. That's all I can do. I've got things to do. I gotta go." Edward, at his work, is panicking over the phone.

Unbidden, unexpected, tears well up in Ravel's eyes. Flat on the sofa at Powell's uptown apartment, his voice goes very soft, plaintive.

"Okay, I'm sorry Eddie . . . I thought when we'd planned on this, it'd been too much for you: too much an' too fast . . ." A deep breath, and now he knows he's launching into saying all the wrong things, and he can't stop it, ". . . but, like, I really like you a lot, Eddie . . . (another deep breath) . . . and, like (quavering) I think of you as someone very special, Ed as boyfriend material ... (faster now; a flood of messages) and I know that absolutely freaks you out, and it's the wrong thing to say, and it's not like I'd plan to move in with you or anything. But it's like I really really just want to sleep with you tonight: to hold onto you like you'd said; and it's not even as if I'll throw you some big bone or something: I'm just up here at Powell's, and you know it's such a fucking haul for me to get up to the fucking East Side; and I just wanted to be with you tonight; for us to hold onto each other in bed; to have my arms around you– "

"Listen, I've gotta go. I've got things to do. Like I said; we can mebbe call. I like you fine, Rav. I like to spend time wit' you. We can get together in the week . . . we can go for a drink. I've got work tomorrow. Maybe Wednesday. It's not a good time right now." Edward's voice rises, like a child's. edged and higher. A thick Brooklyn tang to it, invisible most times, comes through more and more. "I'm sorry, maybe we's shouldn't be seein' each other Ravel. I tries not t' lead youse on . . ."

"Hey, this is just so stupid, Edward. But fuck. We're both big men, here. Just give me a call sometime, okay? Really, I'm sorry this all got going too fast for you; but, like, get it together Edward. For fuck's sake, all I want to do is fuckin' sleep with you. It would've been nice, is all: a nice bed to sleep in, together."

"Okay. Another time. An' please call. G'bye."

Ravel puts the phone down with a "fuck."

He sits up.

"Hey, Evie," he says to the sleeping cat, the only living object in the room. He falls flat, face up, on the soft bed. But the ceiling offering no cues, he jumps up, agitated, and lights a smoke. He strides to the bathroom, for a long and angry piss.

And the moon still shines on taxicabs yellow, honking bumper to bumper, and lovers in the park, on a shot Saturday night; and silver, reflected, over the cool East River, hangs heavy and pregnant; an orb to seeing.

Chilly. Nighttime. Ravel takes sidestreets to the video-booths.

He's thinking about how this is Alf's neighborhood, and with a curse is already upon the restaurant, before he pivots and marches back the way he'd come, not keen now to bump into a former roommate.

He passes a ton of kids out in front of the porn store, takes the door and marches straight in. He goes to the counter for tokens, but then, nodding to the counter-guy, he steps to the racks first to sniff out what's happening. It's been awhile since he's done this.

And some hick is here, with some dorky guy, crazy enough to bring a girl to a porn store, as some kind of a turn-on thing. The woman, who looks like a nutcase, is stepping into the booths' hallway, and making stupid comments. Even in her noisy chatter, the dim imagination of her comments, she's intuiting only the half of it.

The token-guy sits in a chair, ignoring everyone over the interval of her presence: getting a chance to read over this temporary halting of the continuous, ferocious, 24-hour male prowling.

The woman shuffles about here and there, yammering. Ravel pulls out video titles; looks over lurid covers; spotting for kink; for uncut cocks. He's happy to be ignoring the noisome chick: to have cut quick onto casual.

She will leave. And meantime, a doctor-looking guy cruises him down two aisles. Then an African-American man shows a title to a friend, beside him. A Rough-boy, big, unshaven, ballcap, nods a Lothario sneer to Ravel, and steps behind the entry to buy a fistful of tokens from the disturbed token-guy.

The woman lingers at the front of the store, calling after her dork boyfriend: "Did you get everything, did you get everything?" Soon her aggravating voice disappears into the night.

Stepping into a booth, Ravel plunks one token into the videoscreen and punches fast the green button. Breath held, the glassed-in partition grinds up on Rough-boy, alongside. The sturdy boy's powerful arm slides down the heavy brass zipper on ratshit jeans. A thick heavy hand pulls out a long uncut cock. Ravel mouths soft at the grate, "I'll come around."

With straight porn flashing the video screen - some luscious blonde red-lipped babe sucking off two happy dark men's thick, held-together dicks - Rough-boy flips around his baseball-cap visor, and gorfs deep down Rav's thick, savory dick. Rav pulls ball-cap hard against him, and bucks slowly into the man's mouth, his fist. Not deep enough, but good, very good. The television blonde chick is licking a dark uncut dick - and loving it – the steel-hard smiling man's obvious enjoyment, and suddenly Rav's pressing hard on the ballcap and Rough-boy is taking his load, gulping - all of it - and pumping Rav's cock fist-sure for more. Rav holds his hard dick in Rough-boy's mouth, and slides trembling in and out, the guy's tongue running 'round his sperm and drool while he jerks his own dick, half-hearted; a few pulls. Then leaning back to a dark corner, he sighs and softly spits up Rav's cum.

Rav tosses his head and snorts back a noseful of snot. He paws the grey ribbed undershirt, sucking in man-scent, and the unshaven face he wants to run his thick tongue over.

"Take care," he grunts instead, pressing his shoulder, strong, to ribbed-cotton chest.

"Yeah," the guy nods.

As Rav pulls his sweatshirt off the hook, Rough-boy his coat off the door, the blonde chick is still greedily sucking dick, now to tinny music.

A guy in the hall passes Rav a cigarette, for free.

And, the moon still up, a half-ball, not circle or crescent, Rav pisses into the river, hanging his dick through the chainlink, casual-like, leaning up on the fencetop, overlooking the black swell.

Later, the guy at the deli gives Rav a break on the price of a beer.

"You from Germany?" he asks, while Rav's digging the change out.

"Hey, Jim," Rav calls, quickly jumping up from the plywood at his roommate's coming in.

"Yo." Jim sticks his head 'round the room's curtain. Rav casually fastens his belt.

"How's yer evening, Jim?"

"Quiet."

They talk out the events of their day; Jimbo's Saturday score with sexy Terry; Rav's latest panicked let-down in the ever-running Ravel and Edward show. But the whole time, Rav is flashing - and can't get off it - on his first big love, for Michael: when he had his motorcycle, and in the mountains they'd slept together in the same sleeping-bag; huddled, bony skinny naked boys-bodies, staring wide-eyed; up where fiercely-defined against the black trees, a moonless night, the velour blanket of chilly northern California stars clutched to grasp down and yank and pull and rip their very souls out of their helpless mouths. Of making love to Michael, fucking his butt, a newly-discovered treat, and just feeling waves and waves of love for this man, and that feeling of loving this man so much making him come explosive and all warmth deep inside him.

"Yep," says Jim, "Romance. Just somethin' invented by the Disney company."

The buzzer from downstairs sounds. So grand a statement, so gravely delivered, and Jim right away has to exit, behind the heavy black room curtain.

"Yeah, well, hide all the fuckin' razors, Jimmy," Rav calls after him,

"I'm gonna give that... that... fuckin' bastard Edward a call. Don't be sick if you overhear it; it won't be pretty."

Two rings, and hoping for the answering machine.

"Oh... hey, Edward."

"Hey, Rav. I'm so glad you called." Happy. This opens the floodgates.

"Yeah, well, I'm still really fuckin' pissed-off at you, asshole. But fuck man, I been thinking you hadn't called, and I wasn't wantin' to lose your friendship, pal, so I thought I better call."

"Well, great. I'm happy you called, Ravel."

"Yeah, well. I was thinking what happened there, Edward; I was going through a lot this week, and so guess that's why I wanted so much to connect with you. I'm a total fool for wanting to be holding another man when I'm stressed-out. But it's better now, and I'm getting a lot more squared-away, and I just wanted to connect with you, and see how you were doin'; if you were mad at me, 'cause I've sure been pissed-off at you ..."

"Yeah."

"Yeah... yeah, but I still want to take you in my arms..."

"Yeah! That'd be great," says Edward, very upbeat. "We

should do it."

And the moon just keeps right on shining, and the autumn leaves are turning. Roommate Jim, stepped out with his new lover Terry, walking briskly crosstown, continues the gritty upbraid he'd launched into on the course of the evening's events:
"You know, I just keep telling the women at work that these idiot men they get involved with are going to hunt out exactly what it is the girls want to hear, and they're going to entirely feed them exactly that, until they get what they want..."
"Which is?" Terry questions.
"Well, yeah .. into their box, of course," says Jim, looking askance, "and not because of anything, either: no good or bad motives; but just because that's the way it works."
"Oh," says Terry, frowning at the passing sidewalk cracks.

A PERFECT SUMMER

Leo Cardini

Now listen up. This is a course in creative writing. So don't you think you could have come up with a more original first assignment than "What I Did Last Summer"? Like: "What I did last summer that I didn't tell anyone about." Or: "What I did last summer that night I was so horny I thought I was going to scream." Besides, as it turns out, you know perfectly well what I did this past summer. Were you surprised today when you saw me walk into your classroom? I mean, how often does it happen on the first day of the fall semester at the University of Vermont that a professor discovers one of his students was a bartender at The Gay Escapade? And, in fact, the very bartender that he tried to pick up on more than one occasion during the past summer. It's not that I wasn't interested in you. Actually, I'm a real sucker for tall blond men with broad shoulders and narrow waists. That night in June when I first saw you and those three turn-on friends of yours enter The Gay Escapade, I was so stunned by your appearance as I watched you approach the bar that for a moment everyone else faded into the background.

Today in class you were talking about a writer exercising his power of observation. Well, how's this? That first night I saw you walk into The Gay Escapade, I was absolutely awed by your presence. About six-foot-two, right? You were wearing your soft, blond hair down to your shoulders in back. It was parted in the middle and you shook your head whenever it had edged too far over your forehead. I'll bet you're unaware of that half the time you do it. You had on a loose-fitting, short-sleeved, white cotton shirt that dramatically emphasized your deep tan. It was unbuttoned halfway down your chest, revealing the curly blond hair that lightly covers your pecs and forms a slightly denser forest between them, narrowing down to a thin line that descends to your navel. And although I couldn't see its final progression below your navel, I have thought about it on more than one occasion as I lie cock-hard in bed. You were wearing tight, faded Levi's that hugged your narrow waist and bulged at your crotch, particularly on the left, where the greater part of your soft cock rested. And when you turned to talk with your friends, I noticed how your two firm asscheeks tortured the seat of your Levi's, forcing the denim to edge up into your asscrack, displaying the tantalizing curvature of your ass. When you came over and ordered drinks and I got a closer look at you, I noticed your deep blue eyes, your dimpled chin, and the circular gold earring in your right ear. But, most of all, I noticed the air of cool confidence you exuded. You were such a turn-on that I wanted to reach across the bar and run one hand through the hair on your chest while leaning forward far enough for my mouth to reach one of your nipples.

But, instead, all I could do was say, "Hi. What can I get you?" and restrain myself as you returned my smile and ordered drinks in that measured, baritone voice of yours. And now for an exercise in imagination. You see, a lot of people think it's glamorous to be bartender in a gay bar. Fact of the matter is, it's just another job, and sometimes it's boring as hell. So when someone like you walks in, my mind reels with all kinds of thoughts. Well, as I turned to mix your drinks, I thought, "He's just too perfect to be true, like he just walked off a movie screen. Yeah, that's it. He's 'The Hunk From Outer Space.' His mission, to observe homosexual behavior on the planet Earth. Disguised as the Hollywood version of the typically gay American male, he has chosen Burlington, Vermont, as the locale in which to conduct his investigations." While I was mixing your drinks, I could feel that your gaze had never left me. With your alien eyes that have investigative powers we earthlings do not possess, you quickly scanned all five feet and eleven inches of me, sizing me up and storing away in your mind my background and the story of my life. You noted Italian ancestry, resulting in smooth, dark skin and wavy black hair. I could practically feel your eyes as they moved onto my back, probing through my T-shirt, examining my wide shoulders, and then slowly descending to my thirty-one-inch waist. How warm my asscheeks felt when you scrutinized them, perusing every square inch of their terrain. And then when you beamed into my asshole and gathered up an intoxicating collage of impressions of all the cocks that have visited there, giving and receiving so much pleasure, I wanted to give you a condom right then and there and say, "Go ahead! Right here, right now!"

When I turned towards you with your drinks, I could feel your eyes on my chest, commanding my nipples into instant hardness and teasing them better than any massage of thumb and index finger could ever do. I felt you examine my torso, registering how religiously I work out four times a week so I could have the body I look for in other men. And when your eyes burned into the crotch of my 501's! How discreet of you not to get me any harder than I was, but instead to use those extraordinary mental abilities of yours to create a holograph of my erect cock that was visible for your examination only. I could feel you as you began at my balls, large and tight in my brownish, furrowed ballsac, lightly sprinkled with black bristly hairs. You worked your way up my thick, smooth, nine-inch cock that stands straight up when hard, like it's trying to kiss my navel, incessantly twitching like an impatient child. You examined the finer, paler skin just below my cockhead, reminding you that you have never fully comprehended why some men - like me - are cut, while others are not. And when you finally reached my flaring, pink-brown cockhead, dwelling on that sensitive spot just under my piss slit, I could feel the pre-cum beginning to ooze out, dampening the front of my lo-rise Jockey shorts. I tell you, being probed like that, it was very difficult for me to maintain my bartenderly composure and not spill a drop of liquid in the four glasses I was carrying. When I finally made it back to you with your drinks and you paid for them, I noticed how large and manicure-perfect your hands were.

Maybe it sounds kinky, but I really get turned on by over-sized hands. Oh, yes, you really gave me a thorough checking out. I felt it on every inch of my body, making me ache for a repeat examination. But there were other customers waiting for service and my cock-stirring, nipple-hardening indulgence in the fantasy of "The Hunk From Outer Space" had to be put on hold. So why didn't I ever accept your offers to join you when I got off work? You're probably not aware that, quite by coincidence, I'm sure, you only asked me on nights when the weather forecast predicted warm and sunny weather on the next day. You see, when I say you know what

I did last summer, that's only partially true. You know only what I did during the nights. But the days...well that leads me to the story I want to tell you about in this assignment.

. . .

One afternoon in early June, I was bored and didn't have anything to do, so I drove over to that abandoned, water-filled quarry deep in the woods just four or five miles outside of Plainfield. You know, the one where all the Goddard College students go to swim and sunbathe in the nude. I'd like to sound really hip and tell you it's because I'm a nudist at heart. But the truth is I was hoping there might be some really hot-looking guys there. Well, when I reached the end of the narrow dirt road that abruptly stops a five-minute walk from the quarry, there were no cars around, so I knew I was alone. I parked, stripped, tossed my clothes into the back seat of the car, and headed down the scarcely visible path through the woods that leads to the quarry. I tell you, every time I go there, when I first take off my clothes and step bare-assed into the woods, I feel like I've just stepped out of one reality - pale and bland in comparison - into a fuller, more idyllic one. It's like all my hang-ups and hassles are left behind, and this delicious, sensual feeling washes over me. My body gets so sensitive to the soft touch of air all over it that I usually get a hard-on I have to distract myself to lose before anyone sees it. But on that day I figured, "What the hell? There's no one here but me." So I gave my stiff prick full freedom to bounce up and down in front of me, playing a game of tug-of-war with gravity, as I made my way to the quarry. Every time I emerge from the woods into the shock of sunlight shining down on the quarry, I never fail to be astonished by its beauty. Who would ever expect to find an abandoned, water-filled quarry cut into the side of a mountain in the middle of the woods? Its deep, placid water glistened in the sunlight, and the large slabs of granite that bordered it radiated a languid, seductive warmth. Well, the first thing I did was to dive right in. But the water was chillier than I expected, so I didn't stay in any longer than it took to swim the length of the quarry and back. I emerged invigorated, but shivering and covered with goose bumps. I settled down on a large, flat slab of granite. The mellow warmth of the sun-soaked rock against my backside, and the more intense heat from the sun above soon lulled me to sleep. I don't know how long I slept, but I'm sure it couldn't have been for very long. When I awoke, even before I opened my eyes, I could sense I was no longer alone. Turning my head to the left and squinting against the sunlight, I saw there was someone standing on the same slab of granite about two yards away from me. He was looking at me with unfeigned interest. Out of the corners of my eyes I could see that my cock had reached semi-erection in my sleep, which it often does. But strangely, I felt no need to try to conceal it. In many ways this stranger looked like what I'd imagine you to have looked like about twenty years ago, if I'm correct in assuming you're now in your late thirties. He was about six feet tall, he had this glorious head of blond hair spilling across his forehead, and although he wasn't as broad-chested as you, he had smooth, lean muscles, a gym tight abdomen, a narrow waist, and a runner's legs. He was more cute than handsome, with large blue eyes, sensual lips that were slightly parted, revealing the impossible whiteness of his teeth, and a half-smile on his face that inched up further along his right cheek than his left as he stared at me with seemingly innocent curiosity. He stood there with his legs slightly spread apart. The "o" of his left thumb and index finger encircled the rim of his cockhead, the other three fingers shading it from my view, as he absentmindedly pulled his long, soft cock slightly to the left. It reminded me of the way little boys sometimes hold their teddy bears carelessly by their side when they're pre-occupied, dangling it by one of its arms. He didn't have much hair on his chest - just a light sprinkling on his pecs, and a slightly thicker growth between them that narrowed down to a thin line that descended to his navel, and then below to a surprisingly ample forest of bristly pubic hair. Longer strands of blond hair escaped from his armpits, promising similarly ample growths. I longed to explore them with my tongue, lapping the boysweat from under his arms. As I leaned over onto my left elbow and shaded my eyes with my free hand, this Cupid by the quarry smiled all the wider and asked, "Like some blueberries?"

"What?" I mean, this isn't a common occurrence in my life;

being awakened while sunbathing in the nude to gorgeous young boys offering me blueberries.

"I said, would you like some blueberries? I know where there's lots of them."

Sometimes you don't question the strange gifts life brings you. So, with cock-hardening interest, I said, "Sure," aware that I was staring at his crotch, and that he could see that I was. In response, the little showoff took his hand off his cock and it flopped long and heavy in front of him, soft and cut with a slightly oversized, purple-pink cockhead.

After allowing me a few seconds to savor his presence, he said "C'mon then," and nodded in the direction of the woods. While I got up to follow, he walked towards the trees, looked back at me with an enticing smile on his face to make sure I was following him, and then silently led me into the woods. The sun fell through the trees in random, ever-shifting patches, the birds racketed above us, ceaseless in their activity, and the brown carpet of last year's leaves crunched beneath our bare feet as I followed this kid, watching the play of his muscles as he dodged low-hanging branches from above and prickly undergrowth from below. And his asscheeks! Oh, the way they repositioned with every step! I just wanted to reach out and feel the light fuzz of blond hair that covered them.

When we emerged into a large, open space, he turned to me. His eyes immediately went to my cock. With absolutely no embarrassment, he just smiled and said softly, "Wow." Then he pointed several yards off. "See?"

Blueberry bushes. Lots of them, yielding a plentiful crop. He went over to them, got down on his haunches and started picking. He looked up at me for a second, smiled again, and turned back to his picking. I willingly joined him.

Picking blueberries on my haunches next to this young kid who had unexpectedly entered my life, I could feel his palpable proximity on every inch of my skin. I was very aware of my nudity, of my hard, sensitive nipples, of the way my asscheeks were slightly stretched apart by the position I was in, and of the heaviness of my cock and balls as they hung down between my legs. When I had amassed a small pile of berries in my left hand, he turned to me. Our faces couldn't have been more than two feet apart. For the first time I noticed how very remarkably deep blue his eyes were and how his unblemished face and serene expression made him look like he had never suffered a moment of unpleasantness or anxiety in his entire life.

Looking me in the eyes, he said, "Here. Let me show you something." He turned until he was facing me, and then he fell forward onto his knees. "Make a fist."

I looked at him, puzzled.

"Get 'em all crushed up in your hand."

I did, feeling the juice burst out of the berries.

"Now open it again."

He leaned over, stuck his tongue out and slowly licked some of the mashed berries out of my hand. Then I felt his warm, wet tongue and lips sensual against my palm as he maneuvered the rest of the sweet pulp into his mouth. And all this time his eyes never left mine. I felt like I was falling into them, plunging into his very being. When he had consumed the berries, he took each finger into his mouth, one at a time, and sucked it clean. I could feel my cock stiffening, ascending to its full nine inches like it couldn't resist a closer view of what was going on. When he was finished with my hand and sat up again, he studied my hard-on, looked into my eyes again, and smiled mischievously like we were partners in some deliciously wicked little act. Then he made a fist around his own handful of blueberries, opened it up again, and silently offered it to me. I held his hand in both of mine and accepted the offered fruit. I could see his own cock hardening as I licked the berries out of his palm. I felt like I had stepped into another world. I mean, what route had I travelled to arrive naked in the middle of the Vermont woods with this also-nude young stranger, licking crushed blueberries out of his hand? By the time I was done, I could no longer contain my curiosity. "Who are you?"

"Wes. Wesley Barton."

Like that really explained a lot.

"And what's your name?" he asked.

"Danny D'Amato."

"Hi, Danny."

"Do you live around here?"

"No, I'm just up for the summer. My uncle and his lover live nearby - just outside of Groton."

"Uh-huh?" I coaxed as I settled onto my knees in front of

him, my legs slightly spread apart. Wes inched forward until our knees touched and we sat there facing each other. "You really want to hear about me?" he asked.

"Sure do," I replied, absolutely intrigued.

"Well, I've always been very close to my uncle. Ian. That's his name. And to his lover. He's just like an uncle to me, too.

"Not that they ever came out and told me they were lovers. And my family...well, to them it was always, 'Your Uncle Ian and his famous Hollywood friend,' like that somehow explained it all away. But I knew what they really meant.

"Well, I think all my life I knew I was gay, too, but it wasn't until last summer that I talked to them about it. They were really, you know, supportive. They answered a lot of questions I had. And they lectured me about safe sex and about never, never having sex with an adult because of all the trouble you could get someone in, even though I was going to be eighteen in January.

"Then, that winter when Uncle Ian came to visit for Christmas, he told me that he and Todd..."

"Todd?"

"His lover. His 'famous Hollywood friend.'"

"Not Todd Skyler!"

"Yeah. Isn't that something!"

"The 'Son of Schwartzenegger' is your uncle's lover?"

"Oh, how he hates that nickname! And you know that columnist who gave it to him? Well, one night Todd saw him in a gay bar, and boy what a story that is!"

Well, as an aspiring writer, I'm always on the lookout for a good story, and I was all ears. However...

"So anyhow, Uncle Ian said he and Todd had been thinking about me and that if I liked, after I graduated that spring, I could spend the summer with them, and they would see to my sexual education.

"My father hit the roof when I asked if I could. Of course, I didn't tell him about the sex or anything. Then there were all these phone calls between him and Ian, and all these private conversations between him and my mother. But they finally said 'okay.' I guess they figured if I was gay I was gay and there was nothing they could do about it. And I know they really respect Uncle Ian. And I know they're really impressed that his lover's a Hollywood star.

"Well, what a summer it's been! And I thought gay sex was just about sucking and fucking."

"It's like every day I learn something new about sex. They have this wonderful old house in the middle of nowhere way off the road. And they have all kinds of friends who come up to visit. Gay friends, a lot of them actors and other Hollywood people that Todd works with. And I get to have sex with them, too, if I want to, though I usually end up sleeping with Todd and Ian."

"So what are you doing here?"

Wes gave me a mischievous smile and continued.

"Well, you see, I was a bad boy yesterday, and that's how it all began." You could hear it in his voice and read it in his smile that he was savoring the thought of what a bad boy he'd been.

"What'd you do?"

"It wasn't just me. These two guys - Kurt and Jaimie - they've been staying with us, until this morning. Kurt's in his late thirties, but Jaimie's just a little bit older than me. He's Kurt's slaveboy. Do you know what that is?"

"Yes, I think so."

"Well, it was the two of us who got into trouble together, but that's another story. Anyhow, for punishment we were sent to bed early, but we were sent to bed together so it wasn't really much of a punishment. Oh, and before that Jaimie also got a spanking, bare-assed in front of all of us. I think he liked it, though, because...but that's another story, too." This kid was a modern-day Scherazade.

"So, anyhow, this is what happened this morning..."

- - -

When I woke up, Jaimie was still sleeping, so I put on a tee shirt, which is the way I like to walk around in the morning. I got myself a mug of coffee from the kitchen and stepped out onto the deck. Todd was already there. The remains of his pancake breakfast were on the deck table and he was sitting in the sun in his favorite cedar wood chair wearing nothing but a pair of maroon silk boxer shorts. After we exchanged "good mornings," I put my coffee mug down on the table and rubbed the sleep out of my eyes while I stretched my body awake. I know I'm a tease when I do this, but I also know Todd loves it, so I took my time and pretended I was totally unaware my cock was waggling between my legs while I was doing it. When I'd finished stretching, I took another sip of coffee and looked over at Todd. He was sitting back in his chair with his legs spread apart, and his cock was rising out of the front opening of his boxer shorts. He's cut and he's got this real fat cockhead - like an over-sized mushroom - and this nice thick, smooth cock that when it gets hard sticks out straight as can be, which always fascinates me because of the way mine curves up, like yours. Well, about four inches of it is sticking out of his shorts and he's sitting there grinning at me. "Missed you last night, Wes. Have a good time?"

"Sure did, Uncle Todd."

That's when I learned about the blueberries. What happened was that Todd kept grinning at me in that way that meant he was thinking about sex. I could feel my cock stiffen at the very thought of what might be going on in his mind. "See that bowl of blueberries on the table?"

"Yeah."

"Take a handful and close your fist around them."

So I did.

"Now come over here, Wes."

I stood in front of him.

"Uh-huh, that's it. Now open your fist"

Then he started to lick them out of my hand. It felt kinda ticklish at first, but it was exciting feeling his tongue and lips on my hand while I looked down and watched him slowly stroking his cock to full erection. My cock got stiff in no time, like the palm of my hand was transmitting to my cock all the sensations it was receiving from Todd's tongue. That's what I mean about sex being more than just fucking and sucking. Well, when he was finished licking my hand, he looked at my hard-on real close up, contemplating it while he continued to stroke his cock. He looked up at me and smiled again. Then he leaned over to the table for the bottle of maple syrup on it and poured some out into the palm of his right hand. Then he took his hand and smeared the syrup all over my cock. Did that ever feel good! And Todd's got these really fantastic hands. He's so powerful and muscular, but he's the gentlest guy you'll ever meet. So while he wrapped his fist around my cock, all shiny wet and slippery with syrup, and stroked up and down on it, I squirmed and pulled my tee shirt off. As I was pulling it over my head, Todd put some more maple syrup in his hand and then reached for my balls and covered them with it also. I looked down and watched. His hand felt so good the way he was stroking my balls, jostling them around in my ballsac, that my cock kept twitching in front of him. And he just watched it, like he was amused by the way he'd got it performing for him. Kinda like a puppeteer manipulating a puppet, you know?

Then he looked up at me again and took his syrup-covered hand and moved it up to my mouth. I licked it off. Boy, was it sweet! I licked first along his palm. And then I took his fingers into my mouth, one at a time. This wasn't the first time I've sucked on his fingers. They're large and strong and I guess maybe I'm developing a finger fetish. Isn't that kinky? Well, when I finished licking the syrup off his fingers he said, "Spread your legs apart a little more." I did, and while he was still staring at my dick twitching in front of him, he slipped his boxer shorts off. He was fully hard. You should see his cock. It's a good ten inches. Really. Oh, and he has this great bush of silky, brown pubic hair. And these two big, practically hairless balls in a ballsac the size of a baseball, except now they were trying to press out on either side of his cock because they were being crushed against the seat of the chair. Well, he leaned forward, stuck out his tongue and started licking my balls. He always does this real carefully; not great, big slurps, but just the tip of his tongue travelling very, very slowly over each of my balls so I can feel every detail. It was heaven. Then he gently sucked one ball into his mouth. Then the other. When he had them both in, he looked up at me. I could see his face beyond my twitching cock as he started flicking his tongue all over my balls, every once and a while giving my ballsac a playful tug that would pull my cock down until it was almost horizontal in front of me. I took my left hand and ran it through his soft, brown hair. He loves that when guys do that to him. He closed his eyes and he had this real blissful look on his face while he continued to work on my balls.

Isn't that something? When you see him in the movies he's always playing these he-man types who'd as soon kill you as look at you. But in his private life he likes nothing more than to treat a man's body like he was worshipping it. You should just see the expression that comes over his face. And yet, he's so sure of what he's doing it makes him seem like more of a man when he's, like, sucking on someone's balls than when he's doing all those violent things in the movies. Anyhow, there I was running my hand through his hair when I heard someone come out the kitchen door. It was Jaimie, wearing nothing but a pair of lo-rise briefs. When he saw what was going on, he stopped where he was. You could tell he didn't know whether or not he was intruding. But Uncle Todd waved him over.

When Jaimie was standing next to me, on my left, Todd asked him, "Wouldn't you be more comfortable without those briefs on?" He gave Todd this mischievous smile and took them off. His long, pale brown cock and two low-hanging balls flopped down below his bush of dark brown pubic hair. Jaimie lives in California and you can tell from his tan line that he spends a lot of time at the beach. And that what he wears is really just a posing strap that doesn't do much of anything but enclose his cock and balls, which must be quite a task, considering their size. "Why don't you offer him some blueberries, Wes?"

So I squished a bunch of them in my hand, and held it up to his mouth. He needed no prompting to lap them out of my hand. While he was doing this, I massaged the back of his neck, like I was petting a dog. Todd reached for the maple syrup again and got Jaimie's cock and balls covered with it, too. Soon Jaimie's cock was hard also, sticking out and twitching in front of Todd's face as Todd stroked his balls. Jaimie shaves his balls and they're as smooth as silk. I think I'd like to try that someday.

When Jaimie had finished lapping my hand, he got down on his knees in front of Todd and lapped all the maple syrup off of Todd's hand while Todd took my cock in his mouth and moved up and down on it with long, slow suckstrokes, licking the maple syrup off it, ever so careful not to get me so excited that I would come too soon, which I always have to watch out for. Once Jaimie was done with Todd's hand, he stood up again. Todd slowly licked the syrup off Jaimie's balls, the way he had done with me. Jaimie just stood there with his hands clasped behind his back and his eyes closed, like a patient, accepting slave. When Todd had licked them clean of the maple syrup, he silently positioned us so we stood next to each other in front of him. He moved back and forth between our cocks, taking one in his mouth and slowly working on it, and then the other. Jaimie and I turned our faces towards each other and kissed with open mouths while Todd continued to work on our cocks. I took my right hand and ran it across his chest, feeling the stab of his erect nipples as it brushed passed them. He inhaled and thrust out his chest. I knew from last night this meant he wanted me to play with his nipples, so I took his left nub between my thumb and forefinger and squeezed it hard, pulling it out as far as it would go. He forcefully sucked my tongue into his mouth as he welcomed the pain. Then I worked on his right nipple, this time sucking his tongue into my mouth.

Just then, Uncle Ian came out onto the deck. Jaimie and I looked over at him. He stood there naked, his broad-chested, narrow-waisted body on full display. You should see my Uncle Ian. He may be almost forty years old, but, like Todd, he's really conscientious about keeping his body in shape. He smiled at us while he put his free hand on his half-hard cock, absentmindedly yanking on it as he watched us resume our activities. After a few moments he moved over to us, got down on his haunches beside Jaimie, and watched close up as Todd continued to take turns sucking us off. I had taken my hands off Jaimie's chest, and he was now fingering my nipples. He did it very lightly, though, since he knew I couldn't tolerate the rougher treatment that he begs for. My left hand moved behind him and I ran it across his smooth, nicely rounded ass, feeling how solid and practically hairless it is. Then I slipped my hand between his asscheeks. They're so firm, I really had to struggle to get in there. I pulled my hand out again, stuck my middle finger into my mouth, got it nice and wet, and worked my hand back in between his asscheeks. I was having trouble managing to get my finger up his asshole, but Uncle Ian moved behind Jaimie, got down on his knees, and pulled his asscheeks apart. While Uncle Ian watched, I teased the rim of Jaimie's hole a bit, first brushing against it with my fingers, and then tugging at a few of the hairs that surround it. Finally, I wet my

could go, he got up and moved to one of the chairs about five yards away so he could watch us from the side. He leaned forward, resting his right forearm on his thigh, slowly stroking his cock with his free hand. I placed my hands on Jaimie's hips and snuggled my cock in between his asscheeks. Once I could feel it at the entrance to his asshole, I shoved it in about an inch. It slid in easily, and Jaimie let out a low moan. I continued to slide the rest of my cock into him at an even pace until my hips were pressing against his asscheeks and I could go no further, even though I tried very hard to. Then I just stood there, feeling my cock in his ass, my hands on his hips and my body pressed against his asscheeks. I just wanted to fully appreciate the moment. I looked over in front of Jaimie and there was Todd, his eyes still closed and one hand still stroking his dick while he moved his mouth steadily up and down Jaimie's cockshaft like he had all the time in the world. I looked to my left and there was Uncle Ian watching us, stroking his own cock. When he saw me look at him, he smiled and winked at me. It's a strange feeling having your uncle watch you at a moment like that. I could practically feel his attention wash over my body, making me feel even hornier than I was, if that was possible. But Jaimie was getting impatient to be fucked and he bumped his ass against me to urge in into action. I moved my cock slowly in and out of him several times while I figured out just how to position myself behind him. When I found exactly where to plant my feet, I moved my hands up to Jaimie's nipples and pinched their hard little nubs while I suddenly rammed my cock all the way up his ass. "Oh!"

His chest heaved with pleasure.

I pulled my cock almost all the way out of him and quickly shoved it up his ass again. Another "Oh!" and another heave of his chest.

Soon I was shoving my cock in and out of him with a regular ramming motion. But I was doing it with such force - the way I knew he liked it - that I had to remove my fingers from his nipples and place my hands on his hips again so I wouldn't lose my balance. Every time I shoved my cock up his ass, his body bumped forward and his cock slid right down Todd's throat. Todd had his lips firmly wrapped around Jaimie's cock, welcoming it into his mouth with every push forward, burying his nose in Jaimie's pubic hairs. He was still stroking his own cock, but now he was also fondling Jaimie's balls with his other hand. Soon we were working together like we were some sort of sex machine. I could hear Jaimie's short, urgent "Ohs," and I could hear my own "Ahs" every time I shoved my cock up his ass, our sounds as regular as our motion. And all this time, Uncle Ian just sat there stroking his cock as he looked on, witnessing my cock ramming into Jaimie's ass, forcing Jaimie's cock deep down Todd's throat. We kept up like this until it felt like we no longer had control over ourselves. It was like we had become slaves to our own desires. Well, we were getting sweaty and short of breath, and I had finally reached the point that I knew I was going to come. I could tell Jaimie and Todd were too, and that we'd all be able to come at the same time. I manage to force out the words, "Jaimie! Shoot it all over his chest!" Todd really likes this. In fact, he told me that once he had six guys - three of them stunt men - jack off all over his chest and shoulders at the same time. And then they cleaned the final drops of cum from their cocks by rubbing it into his hair. Anyhow, I could feel the cum churning up behind my balls. I held onto Jaimie all the more securely to steady myself, and the cum exploded out of my cock. With every cockthrust up his ass I could feel more cum spurting out. The pleasure was so intense it spread like wildfire throughout my body and I could feel my legs shaking like they were about to give way. At the same time, Jaimie pulled his cock out of Todd's mouth and shot spurt after spurt of cum all over Todd's massive pecs. Todd in turn jacked his cum off in a series of milky-white pools between Jaimie's legs, sort of like he was making an offering at a shrine. When we'd finally milked all the cum out of our cocks, it was like someone had turned off our sex machine engine. We gradually wound down until we finally came to a stop and recaptured our breaths. I looked over at Uncle Ian. His cock was now half-hard and his cum was all over the deck for several feet in front of him. When he saw me looking at him, he winked at me again, and gave his cock a long, slow stroke, urging the final few drops of cum out of it. Then we all heard someone in the kitchen doorway let out a prolonged, ascending "Ahhh!"

    We all turned, and there was Kurt, a naked Hercules holding

his hard, fat cock in one hand while the other played with one of his nipples. And just as we turned to him, the cum shot out of his cock. You should have seen it. I didn't think anyone's cum could shoot out so high in the air. Or so far. I tell you, by the time he was done, between Kurt, Uncle Ian and Todd, the deck was a mess of cum. Well, Jaimie and Kurt left this morning, and that was too bad, because I really enjoyed their company, especially Jaimie's. You know, he's my age, but he knows so much more about sex than I do, and I was really curious about what it would be like to be a slaveboy. Like, I was thinking, supposing if Jaimie and I were slaveboys together, serving the same master. After they left, Uncle Ian and Todd had a serious talk with me. They told me Jaimie and I were really irresponsible taking the car out and go riding around bare-assed, especially since we didn't even take our clothes with us. That's what we did that got us in so much trouble. I knew it was wrong at the time, but Jaimie talked me into it, which is no excuse, I know, but he made it so tempting. Like the way it's always so irresistible to try to get away with things in school. You know, it's you versus the adults, and you want to see if you can put one over on them. Uncle Ian and Todd understood all this, and they told me that seeing me and Jaimie together they'd realized I really should be spending some time with guys my own age. They said the one thing they can't give me - sexually speaking - is the fun of sharing something new and surprising, since practically nothing's new to them any more. And they said that's really a pleasure I should have before it passes me by. So they told me I could take one of the cars over here. And they hoped I'd meet someone nearer my own age. And wasn't I lucky! As soon as I got here, there you were, sleeping in the sun, like you'd been placed there as a present for me. Uncle Todd's always said I was born under a lucky star. Maybe he's right.

. . .

By now we both had hard-ons sticking up between our legs. I couldn't resist reaching over and wrapping my fist around Wes's thick log of a cock, feeling its surprising warmth. Wes let out a soft, prolonged "Ohh," and I could tell from the way he stretched his torso that the sensation of my fist clenching his young, overly-sensitive cock was spreading throughout his body. Wes leaned forward with his hands on my thighs and kissed me very gently on the lips. "I think Todd and Ian are right. I can't tell you what a wonderful summer I've been having with them, but there's something about being with guys around my own age. Like Jaimie. You can just tell how excited he is about learning what it's like to be a slaveboy. And he's always getting into trouble, you know, but you can just tell it's because he wants to see what new punishment Kurt will surprise him with.

"And you! Well, I knew you were surprised when you woke up and saw me standing there looking at you and admiring your body. And later when I lapped the blueberries out of your hand. Now, Ian and Todd would've loved that, but it wouldn't have surprise them the way it did you."

He kissed me again, except this time his tongue slid between my lips. His tongue met mine and they playfully sparred with each other within the wetness of our mouths. When he withdrew his tongue he kissed me again, this time on the chin. He descended my throat with his delicate kisses, taking his time, like he was worshipping me. I closed my eyes and tilted my face towards the sun to make my throat all the more accessible. I felt the slow journey of his kisses below my throat, onto my chest, making their way between my pecs, descending to my abdomen. When he reached my navel, he let his tongue linger in it, lazily swirling round and round.

I opened my eyes and looked down at him just as his lips tried to continue their journey below my navel. But my cock was in the way, sticking straight up, hard and throbbing, begging for his attention. He stared at it like a little boy intrigued with a new toy, and then he looked up at me and smiled. I'm sure he could read the urgent, heavy-lidded look on my face that my cock was going wild for his touch. Without breaking eye contact, he moved his mouth close to my cock, stuck out his tongue and delicately teased my piss slit. Pinpricks of pleasure shot throughout my entire body.

"Ohh, Wes. You do that so well!"

He pulled his tongue back into his mouth and smiled up at me in pleased acknowledgement of my praise. His tongue-teasing had set my cock twitching out of control, pleading for more of his attention. I placed my hands on the ground behind me so I could thrust my hips slightly forward. My cock moved several inches closer to his face. Wes moved his mouth onto me. When his lips were wrapped around my dick just below the ridge of my cockhead, his tongue continued to tease my piss slit, the intense, localized pleasure of it spreading throughout my body. When the pleasure was almost too much to bear, he removed his mouth. "Did you like that?" he asked, betraying a certain amount of adolescent uncertainty about his abilities.

"Mmm."

"Uncle Ian and Uncle Todd have taught me a lot this summer."

"You're very lucky to have them."

"I know. Every night in bed with them, once we're finally resting and I feel the warmth of their bodies under the covers as they're falling asleep, I think just that. Sometimes just lying there between them makes me horny all over again and I have to jack off. I used to try to hide it from them, but that's really impossible, you know, and they said just go ahead and do it if I want to. Usually Todd then slips one hand over my inner thigh and keeps it there until I've finally jacked off, and that's a real turn-on."

Wes leaned forward again, reached under my ballsac with his right hand, cupping it, and then bent forward until his mouth was on my cock again. He very slowly descended the length of my cockshaft until his nose was buried in my pubic hair. He let out a muffled gag and I knew that for all his carefulness he had taken too much of me down his throat too soon. I placed my hands on either side of his head and pulled him off until I was sure that what he had of me in his mouth was manageable. He remained there, acclimating himself to the length of my cock while his fingers stroked my ballsac. Then he held firmly onto my ballsac and slowly moved up and down my cock with suckstrokes that were so smooth and deliberate that I had to toss my head back and forth to work off the excess of pleasure he was lavishing on me. Soon, I was on the verge of coming.

"No, wait," I said, placing my hands on either side of his head and lifting him off my cock. Wes read my mind as I started to reposition myself. In no time we were side-by-side each other in sixty-nine position. Seeing his magnificent cock close up like this, twitching repeatedly like a rebellious slave fighting against the domination of gravity, I could make out the network of blue veins that meandered along the underside of his cockshaft. And below, I observed his ample ballsac, pinkish brown and covered with bristly blond hairs. I stuck out my tongue and started to lick his balls.

"Ahh. That drives me absolutely crazy!"

Then I felt his own tongue on my balls.

It seemed like a blissful eternity that we stayed there licking each other's balls. When I had his thoroughly wet, I moved underneath them and lightly bit into him. "Ah! No one's ever done that to me before!"

I can't tell you how good I felt knowing that Ian and Todd weren't the only ones who could show him something new. I took the swollen ripeness under his balls gently between my teeth and licked the length of it. Wes followed suit, a quick study who soon had me going wild with pleasure. I returned to his balls and coaxed the wonderful fullness of his ballsac into my mouth, giving it a thorough tonguing, occasionally tugging on it, playfully urging his cock away from his navel. Finally I could resist no longer and I took his cock in my mouth, lingering on his purple-pink cockhead before sliding down his thick cock until my nose was pressed against his balls, smelling my saliva all over them with each inhalation. I felt Wes copy my efforts, and we rested there each fully in the other's mouth. Finally, we began working on each other's cocks with long, slow suckstrokes. Soon, we were wonderfully lost in this world of just the two of us, naked beside a patch of blueberry bushes in the middle of Vermont woodland. The rest of the world became inconsequential and faded away. All that mattered was the moment, blissfully lost in the crotch of this boy who was equally lost in my own. Eventually, Wes withdrew from my cock, leaned up on his elbow and asked in a thick voice, "Would you like to fuck me?"

I leaned up also and looked at him, surprised.

But as if he could read my mind, he said, "It's alright. I've got condoms in the car." I responded with a wide grin. Wordlessly we got up and headed for the car. If we had walked directly and without pause it probably wouldn't have taken us more than five or ten minutes. But instead we slowly meandered towards the car; hand-in-hand, hands around each other's waists, hands patting each other's ass. And we paused frequently to embrace and kiss. And once, when Wes was leaning against a beech tree I took the opportunity to tongue his nipples. "You can bite them," he said. "But not too hard."

That was all the invitation I needed.

When we finally arrived at his car, he pulled a condom out of the glove compartment, grabbed my hand, and said, "C'mon. I want to show you something."

"What?"

"Just c'mon, okay?"

"Sure."

He led me back to the quarry. There were now four or five people there - most likely students from Goddard College. He led me to the far side of the quarry where its border ascended about fifty yards straight up into the mountain it was cut out of, and we followed a steeply rising path that led us a third of the way around the mountain. We emerged onto a small, grassy plateau that couldn't have been more than ten yards long and five yards wide. On three sides it rose practically straight up, covered with hardy, stubborn vegetation. But the outermost side looked onto a breathtaking, panoramic view of miles and miles of gently rolling Vermont countryside, the lush carpet of greenery obscuring the small towns nestled in it. He walked over to the ledge, shaded his eyes with one hand and looked out. I joined him. He took my free hand in his and we stood there surveying this idyllic scene. "Uncle Ian once spent an entire summer camping out up here, right on this very plateau. He was going to Goddard then. He never wore a stitch of clothing the whole time. And he had a boyfriend who stayed with him here and they spent all their time, day in and day out, making love all over the place. Isn't that something?" He sat down on the grass and leaned back, resting on his elbows, legs apart and knees raised. "Imagine how many times my Uncle Ian and his boyfriend fucked each other right here." His cock was growing hard again.

I stood between his spread-apart legs, looking down at him. I took my cock, which was already half-hard again, and gave it a few slow strokes. Wes watched in smiling fascination while stroking his own cock. When I was fully hard, Wes got up on his knees in front of me, unwrapped the condom and carefully unrolled it over my dick. "You have to get me all wet inside first, okay?"

"My pleasure!"

He turned over and crouched down with his legs spread apart. I got down on my knees behind him, looking at those two smooth, lightly haired, twin mounds of boy butt. I spread his asscheeks apart and peered at the pink pucker of his asshole and the sparse hairs that were privileged to encircle it. His hole twitched in anticipation. As I massaged his asscheeks, slowly inching my thumbs towards his expectant asshole, Wes rested the weight of his upper body on one forearm so he could stroke his cock with his free hand. His ballsac slowly moved forwards and back in response to his jackoff strokes, looking like an irresistible piece of exotic, ripe fruit. In my Garden of Eden this would have been the fruit of temptation. My thumbs finally reached his hole. I withdrew my left thumb, stuck it in my mouth to get it all wet, and slowly maneuvered it into his asshole. Wes started to moan softly while my thumb worked its way in until it could go no further. I felt around inside, slowly stretching and relaxing his hole. I withdrew my thumb, and was about to press the tip of my dick into him when he said, "No. Wait a minute." He turned around.

"I want to see you when you fuck me. Is that okay?"

"That's more than okay," I said grinning.

He got on his back, and pulled his legs up and apart. I took them from behind the knees and gradually pushed them back. "Don't worry. I'm pretty limber."

Soon I had his legs stretched back until they were almost on either side of his head. I pressed the tip of my cock against his asshole.

"Oh!"

He reached for his cock and made a fist around it.

I gave a slight push forward and my cockhead easily entered his asshole. His mouth opened, this time in a silent "Oh!" as he suddenly gave his cock four or five fast strokes. And then I slowly and steadily pushed my cock into him. His eyes widened as they stared into mine, silently encouraging my entry. When I was all the way in and I could feel my abdomen press against his butt, Wes smiled. "Oh, you don't know what it feels like to have you inside me like this. But go slowly at first, okay? I'm still kinda new at this."

"You let me know just what you want."

I had withdrawn until only my cockhead rested inside him. My cock then slowly made its way into his butthole again. From there on in, there was no need for him to tell me what to do. Our eyes rarely broke contact and I could read in the expression on his face exactly what he wanted. I moved in and out of him at a slow, steady pace while he stroked his cockshaft with his fist. Gradually, I accelerated my fuckstrokes. His open-mouthed face was strained with pleasure as his widening eyes begged me to continue. Our breathing became heavy, audible and urgent. It reached the point I could feel the cum about to explode out of me and I could feel my mouth opening wide in a silent, repetitive "Ahh!"

Wes quickened his cockstrokes. Our breathing got louder and shorter, and in one energetic burst of activity we both came. I felt like my reservoir of cum was endless as spurt after spurt of it blasted waves of pleasure along my cock and under my balls, spreading with lightening-fire intensity throughout my entire body.

At the same time, a loud, prolonged "Ohh!" issued from Wes's mouth as his cock exploded with an abundant outpour of cum that landed all over his chest in a series of milky-white pools. Underneath his ballsac I could see his ripe, swollen cumswell contract with each spurt as his body jerked in response to the intensity of each new discharge. When we finally came to rest and caught our breaths, I withdrew my still-swollen, half-hard cock from his asshole. I lowered his legs and removed the condom. When I was done, I reclined beside him balancing myself on one elbow, admiring him as he rested with his eyes closed and his cock in his hand. I leaned over and we kissed a lush, lazy, after-sex kiss.

I ran my fingers through his hair, looking down at his sweet, mischievous face as he opened his eyes and squinted against the sun to return my gaze. After a moment he said, "Whew! Let's go back to the quarry so I can clean off. Okay?"

"Sure."

I could tell by the position of the sun it was getting to be late afternoon. "But I'll have to leave afterwards - to go to work."
"You do?"
He sounded so disappointed.
"'Fraid so."
"Wanna meet again tomorrow? Uncle Ian's bringing some friends from Boston out to some of the local bars. But I'm too young to go with them, and Todd hates bars. Once anyone recognizes him, he can't have any more fun because everyone's trying to impress him. So he said he had something very special in mind for me tonight. I could tell you all about it tomorrow." While he was saying this, he was absentmindedly fingering my left nipple. It remained hard and sensitive to his touch, and if nothing else encouraged me to agree, it was the gentle coaxing of his inquisitive fingers.
"Sure," I said as I placed my free hand on his right inner thigh, feeling his warmth, "I'd very much like to hear. About the same time - more or less?"
"Okay."
Hand in hand we slowly walked back to the quarry to clean off, returning to our cars shortly afterwards. We dressed and hugged and kissed goodbye, prolonging the moment. The boy who had so turned me on nude all afternoon was still now giving me a hard-on as I felt his body pressing against mine through our tee-shirts and worn Levi's.
I returned the next day. Wes was there ahead of me, waiting. We ascended to the privacy of the plateau where twenty years ago Ian had spend the summer with a boyfriend. He told me all about the night before with Todd, and then we spent the rest of the afternoon lazily making love. So on every fine weather day this summer I met Wes at the quarry and he'd tell me about his adventures with his Uncle Ian, Todd, and all their friends.
And what stories they were!
I heard about the night Jaimie encouraged Wes to spank him bare-bottomed in back of the barn.
I heard about all those toys Steve brought Wes from the Pleasure Chest down in New York City. I heard about the Kirby twins. And so many more stories. But most frequently, I heard about Ian and Todd, their genuine affection for him, and their

careful initiation of Wes into gay sex in all its variety. So that's why whenever you came into The Gay Escapade with your stunning friends I refused your offers to join you after I got off-duty. I was always eager to get home and rest up for an early start on the next day. Well, Wes has gone off to his freshman year in college, and it's getting a little too chilly to go to the quarry anymore.

So ends a perfect summer. Being a transfer student, I hadn't even bothered to look at your name on my class schedule, since it wouldn't have meant anything to me. But when I walked into your classroom today and recognized you as the man who tried to pick me up on more than one occasion this summer, I immediately looked at my schedule. You can imagine my surprise when I read your name: Professor Ian Barton. And then it dawned on me: you were at The Gay Escapade only on nights that Wes said his uncle was showing visiting friends the local gay bars. So now you know all about what I did last summer, not just the nights.
And, as you can see, I know all about what you did, also.
The only mystery that remains is, what are you doing this Saturday night?

TOBY

Andrew Richardson

As I ambled along in the heat, nearing the cooler air of the river in the valley of the Yorkshire Dales, I approached the footpath and one of the busier routes through the scenery.

The immediate shores of the river were beginning to look dried and cracked as the low water retreated. Farther along, some guys were paddling through the river and kicking water up over each other. I wished I was with those fellas getting a good soaking and cooling off. I could feel my balls were getting sticky with sweat and as I strode along, I had to shuffle my hand down there to hold the weight up for a second and reposition them in my favourite tight shorts which held my balls tight and squeezed my hard arse cheeks together.

I could feel the heat of the rays behind me – my legs were beginning to burn though my neck was protected by the large straw hat I was wearing. The more I thought about it, the more I wanted to be in the water to cool off, but I was only half a mile from the woods now.

The footpath branched several ways at the edge of the woods – and I was tempted to cut over to the Johnsons' place just to see Toby. He was my age but had already left school and was working the family farm now. Toby had been the object of many of my fantasies, with his jet-black hair and broad shoulders I could hardly stop thinking about him some days. Thinking about the strong red nipples he had – the way he massaged his chest after a football match. In fact I hadn't seen him for a few months since we had bumped into each other in a pub at Christmas time. Perhaps later, I might call in on him and see if he fancied a pint.

Into the woods and into the cooler shade, it felt good to be stretching my legs after the lazy and sultry morning in bed. I had managed three consecutive wanks that morning and then one in the shower a little later. My testicles were filling up nicely with this walk though and I was pleased that I had emptied them so friskily earlier on.

I left the trail of other walkers and took the much quieter and less trodden route throughout the woods. The small group of people ahead of me were, I realised, the folks I had seen in the water half an hour before. They were looking at a map and obviously were aware that as well as the shallow tourist route, there was also a slightly steeper path to take which involved a tiny bit of easy climbing – though none of it was at all dangerous. This was my favourite route and so I followed the five lads up through the trees to where the secondary path began. Not sure if any of them were aware of being followed, I paused when they stopped to take a piss in the undergrowth. As I was kneeling down out of their immediate view, one guy took his relief right in front of me and his stream of urine surged onto the leaves of the bush next to me. As soon as I could move quietly, I put my solid cock back into my shorts – it had sprung out down my leg as soon as I had seen the slender length of that man's cock. I toyed with the idea of staying right there and stroking my veiny shaft to a climax, but realized I might be in for some more sights with these lads.

The guys were as fit as anything on a football field and I was itching to see more of them as the moments passed. The chap pissing next to me was humming away and beyond him, I was lucky to witness another lad unfasten his shorts and loose his hold on them as they tumbled to his ankles. Full and muscular and smooth, his ass cheeks clenched tight as he finished watering the plants. Then as my hand subconsciously pressed my cock head, he bent fully forward to pick his shorts up, his bare ass flesh parted and a shaft of sunlight gloriously hit his pucker like my cock gliding all over the illuminated entrance.

They were soon finished and set off again with me following. Hungry to keep an eye on the pairs of thick thighs and wet tee-shirts clinging to muscular arms and erect nipples, I adjusted my strong erection and caught the men up just as they were approaching the rising rock face.

I made a point of keeping my distance and not talking to the men – somehow I felt that to speak might break the spell I had over them, that they were all going to feature in a fantasy of mine later that night, especially the chap whose arse I had already been made privy to. Behind him on the climb up, I was able to gaze into his deep arse crack; his buttocks were as divine in the flesh as they looked covered in brief red shorts.

As the sun blazed down and the sweat gathered on my brow, the lads maintained a steady pace which I was easily able to keep up with. As I panted in extreme randiness, they grunted and sighed from mild activity and the warmth. It was hardly a strenuous climb and involved only a little stretching and grabbing the rock surface. Finding nooks to lodge feet into was no problem and before long I was close up behind the men who were nearing the top of the 40-meter climb. Occasionally I would look behind me to admire the view into the valley – hillocks and fields of rich green sloping down to a blue river which flattened into a broad and shallow stream. The rich foliage of the tree tops gathered below us, shading the damp, cooler air. Most of the time, though, I was busy looking at their moist arm pits and straining muscles. Their tanned legs, heavy walking boots and thick, woolen socks comforting sweaty feet that I wanted to lick all over. Occasional splashes of dried mud splattered their legs.

The treat of the climb came right at the top of the slope when one almighty stride was needed to hoist yourself onto the grassy ledge. Most people might struggle a little and need a helping hand – athletic or tall folks could straddle their legs up the last bulk of rock and this is where I almost lost my grip. The rest of the group had scaled the hill without a problem and my man was almost there. Just finding his grip and positioning himself correctly, he had his right foot resting on a natural peg of rock and shifted his left leg up to another peg to raise himself. I gleefully watched his musculature in motion and the tight fitting fabric of his shorts, when suddenly as his leg rested, his balls bulged out down the side of his thigh and hung within my grasp. Hairy, yet with a taut and tanned sack, my cock was dancing as my eyes traced the skin seam on the underside of his scrotum. The man foisted himself up and forward and appeared quite unaware of the whole incident.

I left the gang of lads admiring the scenery from this higher view and began wending my way in the direction of home and again, past the Johnsons' land – which I was never a trespasser on. Once I had reached the farmyard I was disappointed to note that all the vehicles were out of the garages which was a sure sign that nobody would be in. A quick snoop around the place, though, made me realize that since the cows were in the milking shed there must be somebody at home.

I checked the other animal barns out. The pigs seemed well enough fed. Then I meandered into the bullock enclosure. Those animals always had me awe-struck since I was a kid. Especially when they were randy – geez, the size of some of those guys. Huge black cocks swaying down like pendulums, frothing cum out everywhere.

I hoped Toby was around, another fucking stallion – all I needed after the stunning men previously was the more stunning view of Toby and his black, short hair. His broad shoulders, and his square jawed, full lip face. Hoping he too had a huge, thick cock which frothed gallons of semen.

Other than the cows, the place seemed deserted. I milled around and looked into the other barns near the house, mindlessly strumming away at my erection through the pockets of my shorts. All looked perfectly well but there was no sign of life. Even the pigs looked OK and they had fresh food. Obviously the family only recently had left and were due back soon. Instantly, I decided to kill the time in my usual way and dashed into the hay barn to get my shorts down and my cock out for some action. The thought had me raring to go before I could fantasize one cock in my mouth, another up my ass, mine in another ass whilst I fondled the balls I had been only half a meter from on the steep rock.

Inside the hay barn was cool yet musty. I took my hat off and brushed my hand through my hot and damp locks. The dry and baled winter feed was piled to the roof and trails of straw padded the ground. Sneaking into a cosy, unravelled bundle of hay, I had no qualms about dropping my drawers and freeing my hard prick. I pulled my shorts down to let my rigid phallus dart free and sank my bare cheeks into the cool soft hay. I gave my cock, red with veins, a quick rub to loosen its clammy stickiness. Knees parted, I then unfastened my walking boots and peeled my think wooly socks off – sniffing the sweaty aroma whilst scrunching my toes into the hay. Boy, my hand felt good gripping my shaft like a vice and squeezing it until the veins bulged to near bursting. My cock head plopped out of my foreskin and I dragged the flesh down my shaft so I could spit onto my helmet and rub the raw glans.

Like a cat padding its resting spot, I shuffled the hay under my ass and bulked it up to feel it rubbing my naked backside. I raised an arm and smelt the damp sweat of my underarm hair, turning myself on more. I was so proud of my thick and hefty length, and I liked to press it against my inner leg to feel the curious heat. With one hand I took hold of it at the base, and with my other hand I began one more pleasurable session of masturbation.

My hands glistened in the light as my spittle drooled from my mouth onto them. Greasing my piston up, I gently gasped just as my imagination led my tongue into the piss-hole of one of the walkers. Slowly masturbating in the barn was blissful. I even decided that I would come onto the hay, not my face – in the sure knowledge that Toby would be touching this hay and might feel a strand of it coated in my own seed. This excited me further as I imagined my face being splattered with semen from the walkers, I knew I too was going to release my load forth.

"Oh yeah," I groaned as my fingers clenched my cockhead. "Ohh," as my thumb rotated around the rim. I tugged my balls down and again felt their aching weight of semen ready to be spurted out. Faster and faster. I got really worked up and jigged my bum up and down onto the stack of hay – my ring twitching and throbbing to be filled.

Suddenly and from nowhere, I felt water splashing onto my face and over my hair. Caught out, I quickly hid my cock down in the hay and looked around to see where the water might be coming from. My heart pounding, I heard nothing at all.

Looking up I saw the hose releasing its spray – Toby's thick naked thighs, his sculptured arms and chest and his enormous weapon – he relaxed further and looked right down at me as his stream of piss showered onto my head.

Toby leapt down from the top of the stack utterly in the nude apart from tough boots and thick socks. He was laughing at his brilliant aim. His cock was a fat and long sausage which sprang to glorious life.

"Toby," I said, a little embarrassed at the situation and the bobbing prick between my legs. "Wha....wher...."

He was looking right into my eyes and stood before me with his arms folded, allowing his own cock to harden grandly. It glistened with the moisture still remaining on his bell end.

"Do you know," he interrupted, "ever since I saw you tossing off in here, it's where I spend half of my time shooting off."

He'd seen me before!

"I knew you were a filthy little arse lover when you got the handle of that hammer up you," he nodded towards the tools and workbench. I blushed slightly remembering the time I slavered all over the sledge hammer handle and sat my rump down onto it – spasmodically jerking away at the sheer fat thrill of knowing Toby's hands might have just used it or might use it next. And loving the hard wooden shaft filling my guts.

I was just nodding and gawking at him – almost a silhouette in the shaft of light coming through the barn door. Toby stepped towards me. "I'd never have known how fucking good it felt if I hadn't tried it myself after you'd finished with it."

My cock strained upward, crushing against my stomach. Toby prowled forward and pawed his way up my hairy legs, my inner thighs. I grabbed his shoulders and pulled him up to me, touching his chest, pulling at his pert nipples and holding him everywhere. He fell on top of me and as our lips sank together, our chests met and our cocks jerked between our bodies pressed together. Toby looked down into my face and kissing me full on the lips as he gently ground his pelvis into mine, lubing our cocks up with the musty piss still on my skin.

I moved back as Toby slid between my legs and eagerly shoved my knees in the air. Fingering my butt hole with one hand and jerking off with the other, I rested my feet on his shoulders with my knees around my head. The thick saliva drooling from his mouth poured onto my cock and balls and mixed with the day's sweat which I helped rub into my crack. As I relaxed more and saw the desperation in Toby's face, I parted my ass wide and Toby's direct aim slid up my throbbing chute.

"Oh. Oh. Ooh, ah....," the searing pain of his phallus was fantastic. Toby collapsed his body onto mine and worked his groin up and down until I was slack enough for him to work up a fast and furious fucking rhythm.

His lips on mine. His dark hair dripping sweat. He shoved my arms over my head and crooked his neck to lick my damp pits – chew on my hot and hard nipples. I was panting and grunting as his cock ploughed it's way through my fertile innards and my legs now rested comfortably on his shoulders. In a swift and easy move, I heaved forward, pushing Toby up and as the very tip of his prick loitered at my sphincter, he tumbled back and I sat down onto his cock, from the thick base where his pubic hair was sodden with my ass juice and sweat, to the red hot helmet, as hard as iron. His bar of manhood was ramming my ass into a fucking orbit.

As I sat and pounded my rectum onto his cock, Toby had my snake in a vice grip and was stretching my cock skin tight down my shaft. Holding my foreskin back, he drew his rough and callused hands over my cock head and almost had me coming. I was bucking away faster and faster on his pole up my rectum and simply rested my hands on the hard muscular mounds of his chest. As I raised up farther to feel the ride of his cock longer, Toby doubled the rhythm and raised his pelvis up. We were working harder and harder – Toby and me sweating in the dusty barn, surrounded with hay – harder and harder to stem the flood of cum for as long as possible and reach a higher climax. Oh, the ridges of his member. Oh, the thick base, the fat shaft, the bulbous end. He was groaning. "Oh, oh, your ass. Oh, your...oh, your smooth ass. I can... Oh, yeah ride me...."

His thighs were opened like frogs' legs, but closed together tight lifting his egg sized balls up to feel on my ass cheeks. Hands on my prick clenched harder into a rapid and furious blur. Toby's head arched back and his eyes rolled upwards.

"Oh! Oh! Arghhh." Down down down onto his cock. "Oh fucking hell." Spurting onto his chest, his face, his hair and his mouth – I dumped my spectacular orgasm all over him. Smearing my come into his skin, I gingerly raised my throbbing sore ass off the rock-hard prick. As it flipped out of my hole, as it splattered against his stomach, a huge glob of Toby's come slid out of my fudge-soft hole down my sweaty legs.

Less than half an hour later I had Toby bent forward over a big square bale of hay giving his perfectly smooth, rounded arse a decent rimming. Then, holding onto his sturdy shoulders, pressing his face into the hay and gripping his big balls hard, I was soon fucking his brains out.

TONIO JOE

Richie Brooks

A strike by some stevedores in Sydney, a three-day delay in Tahiti after the ship had run onto a reef just outside the harbor, then a long wait in the line for the Panama Canal. It was obvious that there would have to be a change in the itinerary. The announcement came as we glided through the still waters of the lakes that make up the bulk of the Canal: the ship would not have time to visit Miami as scheduled, but would call in Kingston for a few hours instead.

Many of the passengers voiced their disappointment, but I was delighted. I was looking forward to visiting the island again after an absence of ten years. It had always been my favorite Caribbean island when I was working on the old S.S. Golfito, as she plowed back and forth across the Atlantic on the Banana Run; dropping passengers first at Kingston, then round to Bowden and Port Antonio to load up bananas in the refrigerated holds, before calling in at Kingston again for more passengers; a round trip of about twenty-eight days, which I really enjoyed; the Golfito was a happy ship.

Danny Wilson had become my bunk-mate by then. And this stud was a stunner: six feet tall, lean and muscular, inheriting his good looks and dark, silky skin from his Jamaican father. Although born in Jamaica, Danny had been brought up in Newcastle on Tyne and had a real "geordie" accent.

Danny was openly bisexual, and I shared his bunk two or three nights a week, but in port he would invariably pick up a B-girl, just to prove to his mates on the deck that he was just as much a red-blooded man as they were. This arrangement suited me fine, leaving me free to pursue other interests when ashore, although in Kingston I would often accompany him to visit some of his many relatives, who lived mostly in French Town. We would sit there half the night drinking with them in the local Bar, before wandering back to the ship to the chorus of frogs and the chirruping of the cicadas; a magic time, where I had been made to feel so welcome and accepted as one of them, because I was Danny's friend.

But Port Antonio was my real favorite port of call. It was set on the far side of a beautiful circular palm-fringed lagoon, with a small island at the entrance and lush mountains in the background. We would glide in there to the shouts of the children as they waved to us from the many beaches all around.

The town was about half a mile from the jetty where we had to take on the bananas, and right on the outskirts of it was the Princess Bar, well known to all seamen; the first, and for many often the only, bar they visited.

It was a long, low structure; in one half was the actual bar with a few tables and chairs, a Wurlitzer jukebox and a small dance floor, and you had to go around the back to enter the other half, which consisted of half a dozen cubicles, which had a bed, a washbowl on a stand, a chair, and a curtain to pull across for privacy; primitive but adequate for the purpose for which they were designed.

The girls were young, pretty and friendly, and they would socialize freely in the Bar, irrespective of whether one required their services or not, and that also applied to the rent boys who dropped in from time to time, looking for a free beer or two.

The first time we called in "Tonio," as the locals called it, Danny took me straight to the Princess and, after he had bought me a drink, disappeared with one of the girls, first making clear to the others that I wasn't interested in them, so that I wouldn't be pestered. While I was sitting there, tapping my feet to the Reggae music that the jukebox belted out continuously, I suddenly felt two strong arms wind themselves around me from behind, then a voice with a chuckle in it whispered softly in my ear, "Hey man, you wanna buy me a beer?" He was a good-looking Jamaican guy and he slid onto the stool next to mine, fixing me with a cheeky grin. He was small and slim, a teenager, with black crinkly hair, a wide generous mouth, and sexy brown eyes that twinkled all the time. He wore a pair of faded cut-off cotton jeans and a threadbare T-shirt with a picture of the lagoon and the word TONIO printed under it.

He offered his hand and said, "Me name Joe, but everybody call me Tonio Joe," pointing to his shirt, and grinning broadly. He shook my hand with a firm grip.

"I'm Richie."

"I know," he told me with a mischievous twinkle. "Danny tell me, he say to look after you, and maybe you buy me beers," then added casually, "Danny me cousin."

"Is that so?" I was feeling a bit miffed that not only had Danny deserted me, but had sent a complete stranger to keep an eye on me, which is what I suspected. But Joe was an attractive boy with the natural inborn friendliness that all Jamaicans seem to have, and I warmed to him right away, even though I also suspected that he wasn't Danny's cousin at all. There again, Danny had so many relatives on the island, that it could well have been so.

After the third beer, and an entertaining potted history of the island from Joe, he looked at me shrewdly for a moment, then asked casually, "So how about it, man, you wanna come back to my room?"

I had suspected all along that he was rent, now I knew for certain, but he was so attractive that I cast aside any doubts and nodded. We drank up quickly, and tried to leave the bar as unobtrusively as possible, but not quite making it. A chorus of cat-calls from some of my shipmates and the bar-girls followed us as we went out the door.

His room was in a shack down by the beach, which he shared with two other guys. "But dey not come back for a long time, dey working de bars in town," he reassured me. He began undulating his slim body sensually, moving up close, finally taking my head in his hands, and pressing his mouth firmly on mine. His long, moist tongue forced its way through my lips and played tag with my own as he pressed his body even closer. His hands now began running up and down my back, over my buttocks, seeking, caressing, his crotch pressed so close to mine that I could feel his hardness.

Swiftly and expertly, he undid the buttons and removed my shirt. He now transferred his questing mouth to my neck and throat, along my shoulders and upper arms, then my nipples; teasing with his tongue until they stood up firm and proud, causing thrills of excitement to run up and down my spine.

Sinking down on his knees, he undid my belt and slowly pulled down the zip of my jeans. Together with my briefs, he tugged them downwards until they fell around my ankles.

By now I had a firm erection, and after running his hand gently up and down it for a few seconds, he began to do the same with his tongue; more shivers tingling up my spine as he finally took it in his mouth and began to suck, his hands once again caressing my buttocks. One stiff finger found its way inside me and gave me such a sensuous finger fuck that I came halfway down his throat before I could warn him, but he swallowed without protest.

Then it was my turn. I sank down on my knees and pulled down his baggy cotton jeans, marvelling at the long slim cock that sprang out of them. I took it in my mouth hungrily while I caressed his beautifully rounded and muscular buttocks, my own forefinger seeking its way up between them.

But after a couple of minutes, he withdrew his cock, and whispered in my ear, "Let's go on the bed, man, I wanna fuck your arse, o.k.?"

We lay on the mattress, me face down, and after taking a big jar of petroleum jelly from the bedside table, he knelt astride me, those hard buttocks resting on the backs of my thighs as he started to gently grease me up, first with one finger, then two, and finally three. Before he eased himself forward, he said, with a chuckle, "Now you gonna get the real thing, man." Then he thrust that long, hard cock way up inside me, pausing for a moment while he spread his body along mine, then started to fuck me with long slow strokes, which gradually quickened as his strong arms gripped me tight. His labored breath was hot on my neck as he reached his climax, biting into my skin with that last deep final thrust. His cum spurted high up inside me as he almost crushed the breath out of me.

His body grew limp and heavy as he relaxed and lay atop me, nuzzling my cheek. "How about dat, man, you like me fucking?"

"Yeah, you're the best, Joe."

"Better than me cousin Danny?" he asked slyly, and I had to admit that he was. Although Danny was clearly no amateur, especially when he was in a randy mood, Joe was much more loving, seeming to enjoy the kissing and cuddling just as much as the raw sex.

Suddenly, he rolled over onto his stomach and said, "Your turn now, man."

As I knelt astride him and greased him up, my cock was hard and rampant again. I thrust it in.

It seemed I couldn't fuck him hard enough. "Do it harder, man, give me all you got!" he kept begging.

And, of course, I did my best.

We fucked each other again during the next couple of hours, and when I finally called a halt and said I had to be getting back to the ship, Joe said, "I walk back dere with you, dere are some muggers waiting for seamen walking back to the ship on dere own, but I protect you."

As we walked down the path to where it joined the road, he pointed out a couple of shadowy figures lurking near the little bridge, calling out to them in the local patois, and getting an answer back, then he told me, "Dey not bother us, dey know me, we o.k."

After that night, whenever we docked in Port Antonio – and however much he was tempted by other guys from the ship, some of them, hungry for that cock, upping the asking price of his services by twenty five percent – he'd turn them all down, staying close to my side in the bar. He would then escort me back to the ship after another night of sex in his shack. Whenever I thought of Jamaica, I could still hear the chorus of frogs; the chirruping of the cicadas; almost smell the mimosa; and feel Joe's cock deep inside me. It was a magic time in my life.

But that was ten years ago, and as I hurried down the gangway, I wondered if the island had changed much in my absence.

Most of the passengers were going on a hastily arranged coach trip to Shaw Falls, but I declined, having seen it before. Instead I got a car and asked the driver to drop me off at the Straw Market down by the fisherman's harbor, and was pleased to see that the little bar was still there in the corner; it had been our first and last call when we docked in Kingston.

I had toyed with the idea of going over to Port Antonio on the other side of the island, but Jamaican buses are not renowned for punctuality, and a taxi would have been too expensive, and not much quicker. Rather, I settled down in the bar for awhile, intending to do some shopping later.

It was a warm day; a small group of musicians were lazily

playing Ska as only Jamaicans can, and I was so engrossed in the music that I failed to notice a boy with rasta dreadlocks walk into the bar. Sensing that I was being watched, I looked up to meet his quizzical gaze, his mouth widening into a broad grin as he said, "Hey, man, I know your face."

I realized that it was Tonio Joe himself, now smartly dressed in fawn Chinos and a dusky pink shirt, the cheeky mischievous twinkle still in his eyes.

We gave each other an affectionate bear hug, and after I had bought him a beer, I asked, "What you doing in Kingston, Joe, Tonio not good enough for you now?"

He grimaced, looked around carefully to make sure we weren't being overheard, then replied sheepishly, "We have to leave Tonio damn quick last year".

"How come?"

"Me beat up tourist. He no wanna pay me, now de fuzz in Tonio after me arse."

I lifted up my hands in mock horror, and after wagging a finger at him, said, "Naughty boy, now you can never go back to Tonio."

He shrugged, then said airily, "I no mind, I do all right here, man. Me make more money than in Tonio. Me girlfriend too, she have good job here. Kingston good for me".

I told him I was pleased for him, and after we had chatted about old times for a while, I asked, "Seen anything of Danny lately?"

"I hear sometime that he married now, but I not sure."

When I told him that I had seen neither tip nor tail of Danny since he had so mysteriously disappeared, he got quite indignant, "That Danny he no good. You were good friend for him, he ought not treat you like that."

Than glancing at his watch, he asked, "How long you in Kingston, man?".

"Just a few hours. The ship sails at five-thirty, I have to be aboard by five".

"We still got four hours. You wanna rent me?"

I pretended to mull it over, but he wasn't fooled, so I asked him slyly, "Do I get a discount for old times' sake?"

This time he pretended to think it over. "Tell you what man, I give you all afternoon for price of a short time."

"Think you can stand the pace? You are ten years older now."

"We both ten years older, but buy me another beer, an I show you."

He had a neat clean room not far from the bar, and immediately we started to undress each other, then kissed, our hands roaming lovingly over each other's back and buttocks.

Eventually guiding me over to the bed, he said with a wicked grin, "What's your favorite flavor man, strawberry, raspberry, or chocolate?"

"Chocolate, I guess."

He laughed heartily, then jumped up and went to the fridge. He selected a chocolate yogurt from a box of assorted ones, and bringing it over, he said, "Now we have a real good sixty-niner, you dig?"

He proceeded to smear a generous helping of the yogurt all around my cock and balls and between the cheeks of my arse, then handed it over for me to do the same to him.

I could barely wait to lick off all that chocolate flavored goo. In fact we both practically ate each other, sliding our eager tongues into every little nook and cranny to lap up every last morsel.

Then, still using the yogurt, he fucked me lying on my back, my buttocks propped up with a pillow, his strong arms wound around me. He plastered my mouth and face with yogurt as he kissed me and nuzzled my ears, the two of us giggling like naughty schoolboys having a first fumble behind the bike-shed.

It was a magical afternoon, each of us enjoying our bodies to the fullest. He came to the ship with me and we said our sad goodbyes at the gangway, Joe saying fiercely, "You not take so damn long to come back again, you hear man?"

"If I get the chance, Joe, you know I'll be back, but I can't promise. Who knows what tomorrow will bring?"

"You'll be back, man, you'll see. An you know where to find me."

And then he was gone. But it was nice to know that, sometimes, you can go home again.

14

Thom Nickels

The new security guards at Temple University's campus in downtown Philadelphia are a mean-spirited bunch. As a unit, they fit in with the conservative trend now flooding the nation. This is discouraging, to say the least. Still, I've done all I can to protect the freedom and privacy of the once-active men's room on Temple's 14th floor. For many years this bathroom was a haven for students and professors, as well as walk-ins from the street who knew the spot as a juice-flowing mecca of hot sex and endless surprises.

The last time I was kicked out of Temple 14, I telephoned the director of the downtown campus and complained that guards were going around checking under the stalls. "Not only that," I stated, "they're timing how long people stay in the bathroom. If they feel someone is staying beyond the time it takes for a bowel movement, they start pounding on stall doors."

The director didn't think the guards' behavior was reminiscent of Nazi Germany, nor did she think that pounding on stall doors was excessive.

"We've been having problems with this bathroom for years," she said. "People have been having sex on 14 and interfering with the running of the university. Public sex is disgusting behavior. University administrators use this bathroom and are constantly running into people having sex. We're at the end of our rope."

It's no surprise that the director, a matron in her fifties, found tearoom sex disgusting. How could somebody like that understand the ways of men? Some women – most women – just don't get it when it comes to casual sex. They think that love and sex should always be like a romance novel.

"Look," I told her, "I was in a stall minding my own business. Next to me was a student. He had a lot of stuff with him. Backpack. Books. He even had a spare jacket draped over his backpack. At one point he leaned over to change his shoes. I happened to be leaning forward going through my backpack, when a guard walked in and happened to see a part of my body hanging down close to his right foot. The guard thought we were having sex, and started pounding on our doors. He chased us both out of the bathroom and followed us into the elevator. He was still screaming at us when we reached the lobby. The lobby was filled with people, but this didn't stop him from shouting as we left the building. The experience was very humiliating."

My reasoning fell on deaf ears. She was obsessed with how disgusting public sex was and how it had to stop.

I was not lying when I told her I was not having sex. The truth is, I was sucking a foot. But sucking a foot is not sex per se. True, the foot belonged to a handsome 22-year-old student with hairy legs and a beautiful eight-inch cock, but I never touched his cock. I never felt his ass. So how did I wind up sucking a foot in a cocksucking haven? Well, I was cruising 14 when I noticed a student in big size 12 sneakers in the stall beside me. The student started tapping his right foot. I tapped back, even though I was cautious about a businessman one stall away who wasn't doing anything, not even tapping his foot, but sitting quietly taking a shit and pretending to read the *Wall Street Journal*. I pegged this guy as a cockteaser, though in retrospect I bet he was a spy for Temple administration who beeped the guard when he saw what was happening next to him. Of course, he could have also been one of those closeted executives who nurse their bowel movements but periodically tap their foot in response to another guy's tap but never go beyond that to actual contact. Philadelphia lawyers are famous for this sort of behavior (they like to wear fancy, tasseled shoes), as are compulsive masturbators, who like jerking off as guys beg them to do something more. These cockteasers are immune to notes (on toilet paper), or invitations to stick their cock under the stall. To me, these guys are "the enemy"; on more than one occasion I've rolled up balls of toilet paper and bombarded their side of the stall in fun-warfare. Most of the time they take the hint and leave. This frees the stalls for students, who are usually not so anal.

I started pressing my fingers on the kid's sneakers, massaging his feet until he began to moan. He extended his right leg under the partition, whereupon I got on my knees and took off his right sneaker. I loved the look and smell of his clean white socks as I pressed and caressed his toes and the balls of what promised to be a most handsome foot.

I removed his sock, ran my hands up and down the finely sculpted shaft, then sucked each of his toes. It was a fine foot with vibrant, healthy looking toes and a smooth underside. It smelled of musky flesh and sneaker manliness. As I caressed and sucked, he moaned some more (I guessed he was masturbating at the same time), extending his leg farther in my direction as my tongue excited the web of nerve endings – a process which always produces a hard-on of unusual intensity (just ask your local reflexologist what the right foot massage can do for your sex life).

Feet are like that. Too many men forget the feet during love but treat them as useless appendages. A thorough foot massage (and suck) can produce one of the most thrilling orgasms known to man. I was getting into his foot when the bathroom door opened. Neither of us had time to jump back when someone shouted, "Okay, get out of here right now. Buckle up and come out. Both of you!" Whoever it was banged on both our stall doors. The kid left first, though not without a lecture from the guard: "Don't ever come back here!" he shouted.

I was next. The fuming guard was one of those haywire heterosexual types who use any "legal" excuse to verbally bash gay men. Silently lurking behind his enraged "Why can't you get a motel for that shit?" was a "You goddamn fucking faggots – you shouldn't even be having sex at all." Usually I respond when spoken to or challenged in this way, but this time I followed the student's example and said nothing as I walked to the elevator.

The student was in the elevator when I got on. He was tall, maybe six-one, and wore a baseball cap. I thought we were alone but suddenly the guard slipped in behind me, still ranting and raving. I dreaded what was coming: we had 14 floors to travel with this hetero maniac.

As the student stared at the buttons on the elevator panel and I focused on the elevator doors, the guard kept up his tirade: "Why can't you get a motel room for that? Don't let me see you here again!" I suppose he was angry because we weren't answering him or looking him in the eye. Also, by not looking at him or responding in any way, we were telling him that he didn't exist. "The next time I see you in here, I'll have you arrested," he shouted.

Arrested for what, I thought, sucking a foot? I resisted the temptation to say anything, although my temper was boiling over.

When we reached the lobby, any chance of a quiet exit was nixed when the guard spotted a crony and announced that we were banned from the building forever. I didn't turn around, though I could feel him pointing in my direction as I also felt the stares from people waiting for elevators – other students, professors, administrators – even other cruisers headed for the 14th floor.

I haven't been back to 14 since because I'm playing a waiting game. In time, things change, guards are fired or transferred. Sometimes they even forget faces. But the time-off has given me a chance to think about my favorite 14 experiences, of all the people I fondled, jerked off, sent notes to, or hissed at. To be honest, I was spending too much time on 14 and was getting worried that I had a sex addiction problem, even though I usually read in the stalls and otherwise used my time constructively.

Temple 14 had four stalls facing a row of urinals, a sink and a mirror. My favorite stall was the next from the last. These were the farthest from the door, and consequently, the safest. I'd go in the mid-afternoon, around 2, and sit till 4. Sometimes I went at night, since the place was open till 10.

The nice thing about 14 was that it rarely got so crowded that contact became impossible. When too many guys showed up, the energy was scattered. This meant that somebody you liked was afraid to do something because there were too many people cruising. Urinal cruisers were the worst because they never sat in stalls (or stuck their cocks under the partition) but exhibited themselves at the urinal. These flashing exhibitionists created havoc: guys who'd normally stick their cocks under the stall would become immobilized because the exhibitionists kept walking around and making everybody nervous. Most flashers were not interested in actual touching or sucking but in boring group j.o. scenes. They wanted everybody to open their doors and form a circle jerk. Circle jerks did nothing but result in big piles of sperm in the middle of the floor for the Temple administrators to step in.

Flasher arrogance irked me: these were not shy men at all but jaded public-sexers who'd peek through stall cracks, going from one stall to the next, unconcerned that the person inside may have been in the thick of sex with somebody else. These were the hijackers of tricks, ruining everything with their desire for orgies – orgies that were almost always interrupted when somebody new walked into the bathroom.

When this happened, they'd all buckle up and rush into the stalls or pretend they were urinating. When the coast was clear, they'd begin the process all over again, get interrupted once more, though maybe one person might manage to have an orgasm. Frustrated, the orgy participants would go away unsatisfied. How much more sensible it would have been if they had just entered a stall and engaged in uninterrupted one-on-one sex under the partition. It's much harder to see kneeling legs and feet under stalls than foolish frolic in the open air.

I wrote this sign on the wall above the urinals: NO URINAL CRUISING – DO IT IN THE STALLS! But even this didn't deter the bar-clone queens who'd visit from the prissy bars, guys into cosmetic perfection who checked out each of their prospective tricks with magnifying glasses and telescopes. These prima donnas spent more time analyzing people than just enjoying themselves, and very often they went away unhappy (and unfulfilled) because their constant comparisons wasted time. In a public bathroom, the idea is not to waste time, but to seize the day and do it quickly.

One of my most memorable conquests was an Italian night student, maybe 19. When he came into the stall beside mine I noticed his torn sneakers and frayed trousers. "An impoverished lad," I told myself, "who spent all his money on books and tuition." I only saw his face (ruggedly handsome, with thick brown hair) once or twice, and even then only briefly as I was on my way to the stalls. I pegged him as straight trade who loved to be sucked or jerked off. He had an eight-inch cock which angled to the left; when he stuck it under the partition it swung like a pendulum. I met him for the first time when he came in after a late class and immediately began to tap his foot.

In no time, he was kneeling on the floor, his cock bobbing upwards (a cock ascending a staircase), shooting straight across my stall onto the other wall, splattering my shoes with delicious-looking ooze.

He turned out to be a regular contact I'd meet every now and then, though always by accident. We never talked, though I'd always recognize his old shoes and frayed clothing. He disappeared when the semester was over, though there were plenty of other students to take his place.

There was a Greek Catholic boy from Athens, as tall, lean and handsome as a stick of beef jerky. His penis was not memorable but he had a peachy ass. Thank God he wasn't into shaving his ass or balls because he had wonderful downy pubic hair. I first jerked him off in the downstairs bathroom, a less popular tearoom than 14 but more private because there were only two stalls. He came in long spidery lines after a few jerks and pulls: as he came he let out a soft moan. I saw him soon after this and wrote him a note (the bathroom being too crowded for contact), asking him if he wanted to go home with me. He didn't say yes or no, but waited for me in the lobby of the building. I took him back to my apartment where I sucked him off in a condom.

My competition in all of this was a downtown office worker who'd arrive everyday at 4. I nicknamed him "Green" because he always wore drab green clothing and dark green shoes. Green was note-happy and wasted no time tapping his foot and slipping guys notes. Without exception, they read: "Let my skilled hands massage your cock to a wonderful orgasm." Green meant this too. His exhaustless, talented hands always knew the right spot to touch (and when). So many people change rhythm or slow down or give up when they're jerking somebody off, but Green kept up a steady pace (no matter how long it took you to come), inserting the fingers of his free hand under your balls and pressing or light-tapping the correct nerve endings so that when you came, you had to control yourself not to shout out.

Green was so good that I often let him do me, even though my specialty was his specialty. When I went to 14, I wanted to pump as many student cocks as I could. I wanted to see a wide variety of orgasm styles, some shooting up, some shooting straight across, some shooting in slow thick slides, like volcano lava. I was also after a good foot to suck, especially big feet, size 11 and up. I let Green do me only after I had one or two students. Then I'd kneel down and pretend I was the sexy student getting done by me, getting off by imagining this was how the student felt as I jerked him off. When I didn't want Green, I wouldn't respond to his foot tapping or notes. Sometimes I sent him a note which said: "I just got here myself. I want to meet a student. Maybe later." Green, always a gentleman, never hogged stall space but at that point he'd get up and check out the downstairs bathroom. On slow nights he'd come back, and there we would be again, the two of us waiting for the same thing. But Green would always leave first.

I felt sorry for Green, an unfair emotion because he was doing nothing I wasn't doing. I don't know why, but I imagined he had a dreary sex-addicted life and lived in a (sex saturated) one-room apartment, his solitary shuffling back and forth to 14 the only exciting thing he had to look forward to. I imagined he lived for sex.

But I also hung around 14 for hours, and yes, I hated myself for all the time I spent sniffing student farts and bowel movement flushes. Jerking one student off was never enough. It was like eating one delicious chocolate chip cookie – one always had to have another. This scoreboard mentality meant that sometimes I'd jerk off four or five students per session, sometimes getting on my knees and licking their balls as they cried out or thrust their loins against the shaky partitions. Sometimes their cries were so loud I was afraid they'd be overheard by (high heel wearing) Temple administration secretaries walking the halls.

Many students who visited 14 were just coming out or getting used to the idea of "public sex." Some, very young and new at the game, knelt down so far away from you, you could barely touch their cock. I guessed they were afraid of oral-genital contact in the age of AIDS. Or perhaps they did not want to be tagged as a "homosexual," thinking that a no-touch session would qualify as anxiety-free sex play. I coached two students through this awkward stage, one a lithe blond freshman with sleek limbs, a boy resembling many of the teenage stars on TV's mindless sitcoms, so cute, so hot, so ready to kneel down and point his sturdy cock towards the Big Release. The first time, he wouldn't let me touch him at all. I had to reach under the partition with my arms, rub his legs and stroke his cock while he sat back on the toilet. All that stretching worked my muscles and my nerves. He eventually came high into the air and I saw his semen fall to the floor in an umbrella-like splatter. I mourned his exit, wishing that I had given him my telephone number, and fantasized about him for weeks.

When he showed up again, a couple weeks later, I motioned for him to kneel down. I did what Green did and wrote him a note: "Kneel down this time – don't waste it. You can jerk off at home!"

Well, he did a tentative kneel-down, so I only half leaned over in his direction, expecting another arm-wrenching experience when, to my surprise, he finally stuck his cock all the way under.

How can I describe the look of that perfect member? It was as only a teenager's cock can be: so stiff it could have hammered a nail. It was also crowned with drops of white pearl, late boyload's eager nectar. I was so excited I couldn't decide what to do to him first. Should I suck him all the way? Should I jerk him fast for fear somebody might enter and I'd never get the chance to do it again? Should I invite him home so I could savor every ounce of the experience? Should I suck him off in a condom and then contemplate his bubbly for days afterward (a dark perversion, to be sure)?

But this was 14 – hesitate and you're lost!

While the debate raged in my mind, he shot his spunk across the floor and all over my black shoes.

The person I jerked off most was the boy without arms. He was about 20, thin, maybe Irish. Usually he wore clogs, so I could always tell it was him. He had small feet, and once he was in his stall he'd tap his foot without any fanfare or checking underneath to see who was beside him. I realized that for him, coming to Temple 14 must have been therapeutic since he could not masturbate himself and really needed a helping hand. That he was appreciative of my helping hands I have no doubt, at least judging by his excitement level and the size of his loads.

His cock was excellent as cocks go. He had a beautifully shaped purplish head and a long, thick shaft. The skin was smooth and very fair.

Usually he'd come after forty or fifty whacks – he never had trouble cumming, as did so many Philadelphia lawyers – and he was brave enough to stick his cock under the partition when other men were in the room.

My nickname for him was Torso Good Luck because after a session with him, I seemed to have good luck meeting as many students as I wished.

Now that I'm banned from 14 I often think of Torso and wonder how he's getting along. Although he's cute, I know the bar-clone types aren't helping him out much (since the only thing they want is perfection), so I wish I could be of service to him again, and I plan to, of course, in time, when the guard forgets my face and the hatred in his soul has boiled down to a resigned grumble.

A TRUCKER'S BOYS

Frank Brooks

They say the trucker's life is a hard one, and they're right. I've been a trucker for 25 years, since I was 25 years old myself, and I can't remember a time on the road that my uncut ten inches of trucker meat wasn't hard as bone from sundown to sunup to sundown. There's something about the hum and vibration of a diesel engine and the freedom of rolling down the road that acts as a perpetual aphrodisiac. The roads are crammed with the horny.

Right now I'm not on the road, but being shown to my hotel room in a quiet town in the Caribbean. I always spend my winters somewhere in the South where the trade winds blow. I own my own diesel cab and decided long ago that keeping it running 24 hours a day, everyday, during a northern winter isn't my idea of fun. So, I park the truck on November first of each year and take a five-month vacation, always to someplace warm and balmy – and someplace where young men like the one showing me into my room just now are plentiful.

After 25 years on the road I've become an expert at reading people, and from the moment Angel here picked up my bags and said, "This way, Senor," and gave me that look, I knew he would offer me any service I wanted.

Angel is a slender boy with shiny black hair and skin like satin. He can hardly lift my bags, crammed as they are with several thick notebooks, my "trucker's logbooks," journals of my days on the road, which I never tire of reading during my long winters under the palms. By the time we get to my room, Angel's pretty face is misted with sweat.

He sets down my bags and says, "Welcome to paradise, Senor," and opens the curtains on a view of the bay and its beaches. "If I may be of any further service, do not hesitate--"

He lets out a giggle as I pull him against me and kiss him, then sighs and lets his tongue slide into my mouth. I suck his tongue, taste his copious flow of saliva, and thrust my own tongue into his mouth. Sucking my tongue, he presses his hardon against me. I press my hardon against his and we rub them against each other through our pants. I could easily come this way, but I want to feel him against me naked.

"Let's take off our clothes," I say.

Naked, I sit on the couch and spread my legs. My ten inches throb against my hairy belly. Angel, his young cock pointing ceilingward, drops to his knees between my legs and starts nuzzling and kissing my balls and cock, marveling at how big they are. His own cock measures six inches at the most. It throbs and twitches, its foreskin completely retracted in his excitement, lubricant oozing from his pisshole as he services me.

I've always enjoyed the sight of a kid going bonkers over the size of my cock. Over my 25 years on the road, I've seen thousands of guys on their knees in front of me, many of them young hitchhikers, going ape-shit over my trucker's dick. They've all had different faces and different features, but behind the mask they're all the same kid, hypnotized by my ten inches of vein-bulging, uncut man-meat.

Angel uses two hands to jerk me off as he licks and smooches up and down. He manipulates my foreskin expertly, making my pisshole gape and bubble lubricant, which he gobbles up as it leaks down my knob and shaft. Thrills shoot all the way to my toes as he swallows my dickhead, slides his lips down the shaft, buffs the rear of my knob with his wet tongue. His raisin eyes gaze up at me as he sucks, his cute face so stuffed with cock that he looks as if he's trying to swallow a cobra.

"That's it, baby," I say, stroking his head.

He caresses my sweaty balls, slides his hand between my legs, wiggles a finger between my asscheeks and sticks it up my asshole. I see stars, and with a grunt I ejaculate all over Angel's face as he jacks me. After that long plane ride I've stored up quite a load and the kid laughs as my hot spurts rain onto his face and chest in thick, juicy splashes. What leaks down my shaft slicks his jerking hands.

When I finish, Angel smiles at me and slicks his own cock with my cum. "Would you like to fuck me, Senor?" he says, working his rampant teenaged meat. I reach into the pocket of my discarded pants and extract a rubber, a supply of which I keep always on hand, just as I do pocket change. In seconds

I've rolled it down the length of my ten inches. I've done this so many times I could do it in my sleep.

Angel hops onto the couch, straddles my lap, and lowers his ass onto my sheathed cock. His hot asshole engulfs my knob, then every inch of my shaft. Though extremely tight, his asshole takes my cock so smoothly and easily that I know Angel's a pro at this, that he keeps his anal canal well-lubricated at all times for the convenience and pleasure of any male guests who might want to enter his incredible young asshole. He's so tight and hot that I feel as if I'm not even wearing a rubber.

"Senor, it is so large!" he pants, his arms around my neck, his silky body squirming against me. "Oh Senor!" He bounces on my lap, corkscrewing his asshole up and down my cock.

"Baby, you're something else," I say.

He kisses me, sticking his tongue in my mouth, fucking his cum-greased cock against my belly as he rides me. The rhythmic, squishy noises of my cock plunging in his asshole excites us both. I grab his rotating ass and knead the smooth cheeks.

"Senor!" he gasps, his eyes rolling back. His body shudders and jism spurts from his cock, creaming my abdomen. His asshole grips with each explosive spasm. The aroma of his spunk fills the air. "Oh Senor!" he cries.

Ramming upward into his spasming asshole, I grunt like a bull and explode. "Ahhh!" I bellow, letting my loins buck, letting my jism flow.

"Oh yesss, Senor!" Angel licks my nose as I fuck bullets of spunk into the rubber inside him. When I'm finished, he laughs and slides off me. "Thank you, Senor."

After licking his own spunk off my hairy belly, he dresses. "If I may be of further service, Senor, at any time, please send for me. I am your dutiful servant and will do my best to please you."

I tip him ten dollars. He thanks me effusively and leaves.

I unpack my bags. Still naked, the smell of teenaged Angel all over me, I recline on the couch to peruse one of my logbooks, selected at random. The logbook is dated 1973, over twenty years ago. As I begin to read, my cock swells, stretching to its full length, and I stroke it, slowly working the foreskin up and down.

1 April 73: 4 AM. On the road again after winter in Jamaica. Nice vacation, but too long out of the saddle, without the old diesel humming between my legs. Balmy breezes and spice-scented boys are fine for awhile, but after awhile life down there gets overly sweet and I start craving the dirt and noise of the road – and sex smelling of motor grease.

6:30 AM. Roaring hardon, which I need serviced. Conveniently, I'm passing by Red River where I know I can get it taken care of. Whenever I pass through town I stop to see Dan, 45, and his teenaged lover, Paul, size queens who are always thrilled to see me and my ten inches.

Dan, half-asleep, answers the door in his bathrobe, which is tented out with a hardon. "For christsake, trucker, can't you call ahead and let us know you're coming? What the hell time is it, anyway?"

"Time for some fun," I say, and reach inside his bathrobe to squeeze his hardon.

He catches his breath sharply, sighs, and pulls me into the house. In the bedroom Paul is sleeping uncovered and stark-naked on the bed, a big hardon throbbing against his belly. I strip, Dan drops his robe, and we join Paul on the bed. Paul's young cock looks so inviting that I lift it off his belly and go down on it immediately.

Paul moans, arching up, and his eyes open. "Man, suck that fuckin' – " But he notices I'm not his lover. "What the – "

I smile at him as best I can with my mouth full of stiff young cock. He recognizes me then and presses down on my head. "Suck that big hog, trucker."

As I suck Paul, Dan goes down on me and shoves his own cock into Paul's mouth. We've got a sucking threeway going, and the air fills with the sounds of smacking lips, moaning, and with the smell of three hot male bodies. Spit runs down the cockshafts and balls. We play with each other's nuts and probe each other's assholes with stiff fingers.

Paul is the first to go into a humping frenzy and to spurt his load. He groans, his mouth stuffed with his lover's cock as I jack his hot jism onto my face and chest. Suddenly, Dan explodes in Paul's face, and Dan's frantic cock-sucking as he writhes in orgasmic ecstasy brings my own pleasure to a head. Dan is still moaning with his own orgasm as I fuck his pumping hand and cream his face and chest. The air is heavy with the sweet aroma of three freshly shot loads of man-juice.

Dan brews some coffee and we all have a cup while I tell them about the boys of Jamaica, all three of us working our cocks as we sip the brew. Dan and Paul resolve to vacation in the Caribbean soon. Once we're all good and stiff again, we return to the bedroom where I relax, hands behind my head, and let the two lovers service my rigid dick.

They're nuts about my sliding foreskin, and I have to tell them every so often to slow down their licking and jacking and sucking so I won't blow my load too quick. They decide to give me a thorough tongue-bath, and in unison they lick my entire body from toes to nipples to armpits. As they lap at me, they jerk their stiff prongs, which drip lubricant in their excitement. When I finally come, spurting high into the air as both of them jack me off, they add their own loads to mine, spurting all over my stomach. The cum runs down my sides in sticky rivulets and each man laps up his own cum.

11 AM. I'm passing through corn country on an old highway off the Interstate. Nothing but corn in every direction and the smell of it gets me half drunk. I pull into a wayside reststop with outhouses. The place looks dead. No cars with their horny drivers waiting for me, so I'm disappointed, but I can at least take a piss and read the new graffiti that's been scrawled since I last stopped here a year ago.

Surprise! Sitting on the outhouse stool, a wooden bench with a hole cut in its top, is a long-haired blond boy, a freckle-nosed farm kid, barefoot and shirtless, jeans down around his ankles. His right hand hides his cock, which is shoved down out of sight into the stool hole. I say hello and haul out my heavy slab of man-meat, half hard. There's no stall separating stool from piss-trough, so I have to stand right in front of him, in profile, to piss into the trough. Out of the corner of my eye I watch his mouth drop open and his eyes bug out at the sight of my cock.

"Shouldn't you be in school?" I ask.

"Not anymore," he says. "I'm graduated."

I give my heavy cock a shake and swing towards him. He swallows and looks like he's going to fall off the stool in his excitement. My cock swells to a full erection, foreskin retracting halfway off the knob, which is purple and moist.

"Like it?" I ask.

"Yeah," he says, his mouth open, his tongue hanging out.

With a smile, I slide my cock into his face, shoving it down his throat until I have to ease back before he chokes. His spit trickles down my cock-shaft and balls. His jaws look like they're going to dislocate. With a growl, he starts to suck. He lifts his own stiff cock out of the stool hole and pounds it.

"Nice job," I say, fucking his mouth. "You're a damned good cocksucker. I bet you sit here all day, sucking one dick after another. But I bet you don't suck many of 'em this big."

"Mmmm!" he growls, his blond head bobbing, his long hair swinging along his cheeks. His freckles dance as his nostrils sniff the scent of my groin and sweaty balls.

Few sights turn me on more than that of my veiny dick buried in a cute young face. I grab the kid's head and start fucking in earnest. He's able to take more of my cock now, and I fuck it to the hilt into his mouth and down his throat, swinging my heavy balls against his chin. He moans and sucks, jerking off in a frenzy.

His blue eyes cross and roll back. His bare toes clutch at the rough floorboards and suddenly he's shooting farmboy spunk all over my boots and the legs of my jeans. The smell of his fresh jism – corn-scented, I swear – brings my excitement to a head. I yank my cock out of his mouth, grab it, and pump fat wads of man-spunk all over his flushed, delirious young face.

"The mess you've made!" I say at last, looking down at my jeans and boots.

With a shy smile the red-faced teenager, his face and chest running with trickles of my melting jizz-wads, crouches at my feet and licks his cum off my boots and jeans. His own jeans have slipped off entirely and he's stark-naked, his bare ass wiggling in the air. My cock swells with fresh blood at the sight of his willowy young body and I fist myself.

"You like to get fucked, honey?"

"Oh man, yeah!" he says.

I pull him up and wrap my arms around his hot, naked body and kiss him deeply. His mouth tastes of corn. His tongue darts between my lips. As we're kissing I take a rubber out of one of my pockets and a tube of K-Y out of another. The teenager insists on rolling the rubber down my shaft himself, and his hands shake. In fact, he's shaking all over.

The rubber fits so tight on my cock that it's almost not there. I coat my sheathed fucker with the lubricant and rub some between the boy's tight asscheeks. He bends over, braces his hands on the top of the stool bench, and turns up his young ass. I grab his ass, pry apart the cheeks with my thumbs, and brand his brownish-pink pucker with my red-hot dickhead. The kid moans, wiggles his ass, and pounds his meat. As I lean into him, his tight pucker opens and my dickhead lodges in his gaping, vise-tight anus. The kid pants like a woman in labor.

"Stick it in!" he moans. "All the way!"

Clutching his hips, I thrust forward and sink my cock in to the hilt. He's so tight I almost come instantly.

"Fuck me!" he gasps. "Fuck me!"

I'm afraid I'll split him in half, but he wiggles his ass and begs for it so pleadingly that I start ramming, hardly able to control my thrusts. He whines like a tomcat and pounds his boy-meat. My loins smack his upturned ass. His slick, hard-gripping asshole sends such pleasure through my dick that after a few-dozen thrusts it's all over for me. The spunk uncoils in my nuts, my cock flexes so hard that the kid lifts up on his tiptoes, and I grunt like a bull, hugging the boy's tight loins and exploding into the ballooning tip of the condom.

"Feels so damn good!" the kid pants, and his loins start to jerk and his own jism to fly. Hot spurts splash against the stool bench and the boy howls in ecstasy. The small outhouse fills with the smell of teen spunk.

4 PM. Where has the afternoon gone? I've been in such a blissed-out daze since fucking that skinny-assed farm-kid that I've driven a few hundred miles without noticing what scenery has gone by. Damn, he was hot! And so fucking tight! I'm tempted to turn right around and go back to him for a fresh fuck. He'll probaby be there till midnight, sucking hard dick and turning up his ass for whatever truckers or traveling salesmen that come along.

I squeeze my 30-year-old dick in my jeans and force myself to drive on. Sometimes this being horny all the time can get to be a hassle. I wonder if my cock is ever going to stop torturing me with its need. Sometimes I think I ought to give up sex for a while – for a month say, or for a week, or at least for a day – and see what it's like. No time like the present: I hereby resolve to have no sex for the next 24 hours. What's 24 hours! Piece of cake.

5 PM. I pick up a young hitchhiker: A barefoot, shirtless hippie with a backpack. Sandy-colored hair to his shoulders, held in place with a leather headband. A tall, broad-shouldered, youngster with smooth, well-developed pecs.
"I fuck chicks," he tells me when he catches me eyeing by reflex the over-sized bulge in his jeans.
"Good for you," I say, reminding myself of my vow and relieved to be riding with a straight kid who won't come on to me.

6 PM: The hitchhiker has been talking nonstop for the last hour about all the chicks he's screwed and his hand keeps rubbing the bulge in his jeans, which has swelled to mammoth proportions. I'm hard as a rock myself, despite myself, although I'm trying to ignore the sex-throb in my cock.
"I think I'll haul out the old joystick and relieve some tension – " the kid says, "if you don't mind. All this rapping we've been doing about nympho chicks is giving me blue balls."
"Sure," I say. "Go ahead." I resolve not even to watch.
He pushes his jeans to his knees, sighs as his cock springs free, and he starts to pound it. The smell of his cock and balls fills the cab. Suddenly I'm looking at his cock without even intending to. It's huge, nearly as large as my own, and sticking up out of such skinny loins it looks almost unreal. Suddenly I'm pulling the truck off the road. I'll go without sex some other time, I decide – like tomorrow.
"What's up, man?" the kid says, his hand jerking away.
"Looks like you are," I say. "And so am I. So let's slip back into the back and take care of ourselves. I can't drive anymore in this condition."
The kid puts up token resistance to the idea, but I persuade him to come in back, and after a little more persuasion I get

him to strip. He keeps saying that he wishes some chick were here so he could slide his "joystick" up her.

He sits on the cot, his back resting against the wall, his legs spread, his hand jerking. The smell of his young balls and armpits fills the cubicle. He looks wide-eyed at my cock when I pull it out of my jeans. When I kneel in front of him, between his legs, he asks me what I'm doing.

"Close your eyes and pretend I'm a chick," I say, pushing his thighs wider apart. The scent of his nuts makes me woozy. I kiss his nuts and start tonguing them and under them and all around them.

"Shit, man," he says. "I mean, fuck – I mean, I don't think you should – " His voice trails off and he beats his cock faster.

"Stop pumping so hard," I say. "Relax and enjoy it."

He closes his eyes. I lift his legs so he can rest his feet on my shoulders and I can better nuzzle and lick under his balls and get at his ass. There's nothing like the smell and taste of young ass to get me higher than a kite. He presses down on my shoulders with his feet and lifts his ass even higher so I can lick and suck his sweaty crack and wiggle my tongue up his butt.

"Oh wow!" He pounds his meat frantically. "Lick it out!"

My own cock-beating matches the rhythm of his. I'm getting close, and I can sense that he is, so I slip my tongue out of his asshole and take his cock away from him. I hold it vertical in front of my nose, sniffing it.

"Beautiful meat!" I say, squeezing the huge young fuck-tool, testing its hardness and hotness and silky smoothness with my fingertips. I kiss and nibble it from balls to pisshole. His lubricant tastes like warm sap and I milk out as much as I can and gobble it up.

The kid is squirming, his toes working with sensation. "You're driving me nuts, man. For christsake, go down on it!"

I swallow his cock to the balls and feel the belly of it pulsing in my throat. My nose presses to his silky-haired groin and my chin rubs his smooth-skinned balls. I suck rhythmically and bob my head, rotating my wet tongue against the back of his cockhead and shaft. My lips smack and my spit runs down his balls. As I suck him, my right hand pounds my own lube-dripping cock.

"Yeah!" the kid moans. "Oh, yeah!" His balls swell. He

twists his head from side to side. I shove my left hand under his balls and stick a finger up his asshole. As I jab his prostate, he starts to jerk, so I take his cock from my mouth and punk it. "Uhhhh!" he grunts, his cock going off like a fuckin' Old Faithful, spurting hot spunk all over both of us.

Pumping his spasming dick, ramming my finger in and out of his hard-squeezing asshole, I shoot spunk all over the floor. It feels so good I nearly pass out. To hell with resolutions! I decide. I can live with this.

. . .

Lying here on the couch in my hotel room in the Caribbean, stroking my cock as I read my logbook, I'm about to shoot off on my stomach. I release my cock so I won't come yet and let it throb and jump, the tip of it pecking at my navel. I skim a few more pages of the log, ahead through the rest of that April day twenty years ago, and have only to read a few words of each entry to bring all of it back in vivid detail.

When I start reading about the kid at the Bluesville truck stop, whom I joined in his toilet stall for an hour one afternoon and watched suck off a dozen men through the gloryhole, I put the logbook down before I shoot off spontaneously and I phone the hotel desk and ask them to send up Angel. My cock is painfully hard and standing straight up, dancing like a cobra, and the eyes of the young bellhop zero in on it as he enters my room and sees me standing there naked.

He approaches me, smiling. "May I be of service, Senor?"

He's not Angel, I realize, but a look-alike of Angel. "Where's Angel?" I ask.

"Senor, Angel is occupied at this moment with another guest. I am Raoul. Angel has told me all about you, Senor." He begins to undress.

Incredibly, naked, he's even sexier than Angel. His golden-brown skin is incredibly smooth. Without touching himself, he wiggles his uncut seven inches at me. Pre-cum oozes from his pisshole.

And then he smiles and asks the most foolish question I have ever heard, "Would you like to fuck me, Senor?"

DESERT STEAM

David Patrick Beavers

The Carabella engine whined shrilly. Dust and desert sand caught up in a raging current of air blasted his cheeks and neck as he sped along his impromptu motocross course. Ron loved the feel of the heat, the vibration of the bike, the free-form flying over dunes and ledges and rocks of the Mojave. He was running free, speeding with abandon, celebrating his matriculation from the bowels of bucolic, public school hell and passage into the realm of citiscaped university life come August.

As he blasted up a soft, steeply graded incline, the rosy hues of sunset expanded before him like an outpouring of watercolors bleeding into infinity. More throttle. Faster. Faster. His speed. His heart. The incline of sandy soil disappeared suddenly. Ron felt himself soaring, body and bike momentarily weightless, flying up, then arcing, then gravity caused his stomach to drop as flesh and metal descended smoothly like an incoming jet for a landing.

Ron pulled up on the handle bars, setting the rear tire down first, then letting the front end connect to land. He didn't see the pick-up and the tent that were in his path, or the guys that scrambled out of his way as he touched down. His reflexes were quick. He skidded out, dropping himself and the bike just flush with the pick-up.

Hot metal pinned his left leg as his body slammed down on the hard ground. The cloud of dust shrouded him, the dry dirt clogging his nose and stinging his throat. He didn't see them, but felt arms and hands dragging him out from under his motorcycle, then letting him down gently. His helmet came off, releasing a miniature flood of sweat that ran down his forehead, stinging his eyes.

"You okay?" Ron heard the voice, but could only cough a response. The man spoke again. "Get some water!"

Ron tried to sit up, but strong arms held him fast. He coughed again, then squinted to see clearly. Just as his sight was coming back, he felt the steady splashing of tepid water over his face. He sat up sharply, shaking the wetness off. As he coughed again, a plastic jug of water was stuck in his face. He grabbed it and drank down mouthfuls before coming up for air.

Brilliant green eyes were staring straight into his. Large and soulful, filled with concern and curiosity. He blinked hard to diffuse the remaining fogginess. The guy looked young. A raccoon's mask of clean, pale flesh contrasted sharply with the grimy, sunburned face. Greasy, dark blond hair was thick and short. The guy grinned. Chapped, full lips, the lower one split a bit, curtained a bright, but snaggle-toothed smile.

"You okay?" he asked.

Ron slowly moved himself. Nothing broken. Nothing felt sprained. "Just bruised," he answered.

The strong arms behind him gripped him under his arms and hoisted him to his feet. Ron turned around. The other guy was taller than him. Broader. Beefy. Long, thick black hair and penetrating black eyes set off his ruddy brown skin. The guy grinned as he patted Ron on the back.

"Birds have feathers," he said. "Only fools in leather try to fly."

"Hell of a landing, though," the blond said.

Ron coughed slightly, then cleared his throat. "Been riding out here for years. Never known anyone to park down here."

"We're tourists," the blond said. "From Yuma."

"Well," said Ron. "Glad I didn't spoil the trip by plowing through your pick-up."

The dark fellow righted Ron's bike, parking it in its landing spot. "The truck would've survived better than you, I think."

"I'm Paul," said the blond. "That's Yazi."

"Yazi?"

The big guy grinned. "Ignacio Yazi. You walk through life with a name like Ignacio, you'll prefer being called Yazi."

Ron grinned. "Ron."

"This is an old bike," said Yazi as he inspected it closely.

"Used to be my mom's."

"Yer mom's?"

"She'n my dad used to ride motocross back in the '70's. Nothing competitive. He had a Suzuki."

"A one-twenty-five?" Paul asked.

Ron nodded to the bike. "Yeah, and noisy as hell."

"Mexican bike," said Yazi.

Ron nodded to their stripped down, modified bikes. "Kawasaki?"

Paul nodded. "Customized. Illegal. Just for dirt."

"Just ridin' through the desert?" Ron asked.

"You could say that," Paul said. "We're slowly makin' our way out to the coast."

"L.A. or San Diego?"

"Santa Barbara," said Yazi.

"We've been accepted at the U.C.," said Paul. "We're gonna hit the campus tour to see if we really wanna go there."

"I'm heading to USC," said Ron.

"Good school," said Yazi. "Your bike looks okay."

Ron unzipped his leather jacket, a real motorcycle jacket he'd inherited from his dad. His t-shirt was saturated. The air hitting the fabric chilled him, making his nipples rise erect. He crouched by his bike and gave it a once over. The old thing was indestructible, he thought. "Sturdy machine," he said pridefully.

"True," said Yazi.

Paul studied young Ron. He figured him to be about five-ten, just a couple of inches taller than himself. He could make out the lean, lanky form beneath the sweat soaked t-shirt. A form he liked. Shaggy, honey-hued hair, greasy with sweat, hung like wilted vines, framing his face. Angular. Wide. Strong jaw and a lopsided grin. Fine skin, pale around goggle marked eyes -gold flecked, hazel eyes with a mischievous spark. His cheeks were tanned, almost sunburned. Paul liked the package. He cleared his throat. "What're you gonna study?"

Ron had to think for a moment. "Urban planning, I think," he said. "I think it'd be interesting to design a city."

"Cool," said Yazi.

"What about you guys?"

"Silver-smithing," Yazi said.

"His family's in jewelry," Paul added. "He's great at other stuff, though. See?" He pulled a pendant out from beneath his sweat shirt.

As Ron stepped closer to Paul to inspect the trinket, he heard Yazi groan. The pendant was a rather handsome gargoyle with very pronounced genitalia. "Funky," said Ron as his thumb lingered a moment stroking the exaggerated penis.

"I call him Dick P. Phallus," said Paul. "The patron saint of *getting it*."

"Hey, with all the feminists' goddess stuff these days, I'd say he's quite necessary," Ron said with a smile.

"You guys wanna ride before it gets too dark?" Yazi asked.

"It's already dark," Paul said.

"There's a great gorge 'bout a half mile from here," Ron offered. "Old river bed that floods once or twice a year when the rains come."

"I might be a bit reckless, but I ain't dumb," said Paul. "Don't want to be caught off-guard when the lights go out."

"So, we'll ride it in the morning," said Yazi.

"I should get back home," said Ron. "My folks are pretty loose, but if I'm a no-show, they'll have the Rat Patrol out here searching for my carcass."

Paul walked over to the pick-up, reached into the cab and fished out a cellular phone. He tossed it to Ron. "Call'em."

Ron hesitated for a second, then dialed. Through the crackling static, he got clearance from his father. He tossed the phone back to Paul. "Done."

"No grilling?" Yazi asked.

"I'm eighteen," said Ron. "Besides, my dad was eighteen once. He remembers."

"Cool." Yazi flipped down the tailgate on the pick-up, hoisted the cooler from the bed and carried it to the center of their campsite.

Ron was intrigued by the ease with which Yazi handled the cooler. It was big and full of cans, bottles and icy water. Yazi popped a can of soda, held it high and guzzled it down. His body was thick. Solid, Ron thought. His long hair made him look feral. Raw masculinity. Ron felt the sudden, icy contraction in his gut. Flesh to cotton to leather, his cock slowly swelled. He discreetly shifted his weight, then snagged a dripping can for himself. Right fingers pried the tiny lever, letting the fizzy-popping bleed out slowly as his left hand backcombed the tangle of locks from his forehead. He felt grungy. He bent down at the cooler again, splashing a couple of handfuls of water on his face.

"You want a towel?" Paul asked.

Before he could answer, Paul pulled a wrinkled beach towel from a rucksack and pitched it to him. Ron wiped his face. "Thanks."

"We usually boil some water," said Yazi. "Sponge baths."

"It's getting kinda cold for that," said Ron.

Yazi shrugged. "Cold's good. Burns fat." He grabbed a shovel from the shadows beside the tent, then started digging a hole near the cooler. "Sleeping bags for sleep. 'Til then, a plain, old campfire."

"Come on." Paul tagged Ron. "Let's see if we can scrounge up some rocks an'... whatever'll burn."

"Got a flashlight?"

"Lanterns. In the tent."

Ron followed Paul to the opening of the tent. A big, well-worn green thing. As Paul pressed inside, Ron caught a glimpse of their quarters. Roomy for two. A bit of a fit for three. Unzipped sleeping bags and thermal blankets carpeted the flooring, which was nothing more than thick canvas. Overstuffed, nylon gym bags were parked in one corner.

Paul emerged with two large battery-run lanterns. He handed one to Ron. "We recharged them at our last campsite."

"There's an arroyo back the way I came," said Ron. "A few dried up branches from rain wash up north. Not much else, but there are rocks."

Paul handed him an empty, ratty-looking canvas field pack, then slung another, worse-looking one over his own shoulder. "We don't need a lot," he said. "Just enough. Are we gonna walk or ride?"

"Conserve gas for the morning," said Ron. "It's not that far."

They tossed their good-byes to Yazi who was piling sandy dirt around the hole he was digging. Ron felt a bit apprehensive as he led the way to the arroyo. They had to climb the incline to the precipice. Not a bad climb, but one that inspired their sweat glands to work.

"How far?" Paul asked.

"Maybe a ten... fifteen minute walk," Ron said. They pressed on.

As they walked, Paul hooked his lantern to his belt. "I like those leathers."

"My dad gave 'em to me. He quit riding about ten years ago."

"How come?"

"Got tired of it."

"My dad was into horses."

"That's fun. Higher maintenance, though."

"Yazi's folks have a stable back in Yuma."

"How old is he?" Ron asked.

"Nineteen."

"You guys been friends a long time?"

"Ten years," said Paul. "He was the only kid who'd talk to me when we moved to Arizona."

"From where?"

"St. Louis."

"Is he Mexican?"

"Navajo," said Paul. "Mostly. He's got gringo blood in him, too, but he doesn't lay claim to it."

"How come?"

Paul shrugged. "Doesn't want to."

"He's a big fellow?"

Paul inadvertently let a laugh slip. "That he is, all right."

"What is he? Six-two?"

"Almost six-three," said Paul. "People used to call us Mutt'n Jeff."

"What do they call you now?"

"Not much since we're bailing town."

Ron understood well that notion. He was bailing town, too. Small town life. Small town minds. Small town gossip. "It's good to start new, ya know?"

Paul scoffed. "What the fuck's new?"

"Whaddaya mean?"

"Never mind," Paul sighed.

They walked the rest of the way in silence. Ron almost said something more a couple of times, but decided against prodding the issue. "It's over there," he said as he pointed. Paul caught sight of the arroyo and nodded. Ron let him get a few paces ahead. While Paul may have fallen into a somewhat sullen mood, Ron enjoyed this new mini-adventure. He'd started out that morning to go riding for a few hours, then to putt back home to a shower, a meal, then to bed. At eighteen, he really didn't have a life. Not there. As soon as he had begun writing to colleges in his junior year of high school, he started detaching from everything and everyone around, wanting any break he made to be a clean break. He still had a few friends - Cheryl and Callie and Cain. The girls didn't much care for dirt biking. Cain was into his car and nothing else. Cain. His only male friend. They were both loners, of sorts, choosing minimal to no company at all. Cain was coarse. A trucker's mouth and rocker's mentality in a preppie, corpsman form. Cain who was anti-authority, anti-rebellion, anti-anything and everything that groups of people strove to be. It was Cain who introduced him to sex. They were fourteen. Freshmen. Cain found a book about boys and sex, written by Ph.D.-crowned clinicians, that defined all sorts of tumultuous adolescent emotions; that defined the things boys that age do. One reference was to circle jerks. The doctors wrote the book stated that circle jerks were rather common. Cain used the good doctors' credentials to validate the action, then he coerced Ron into experimenting with him. It didn't take much to convince Ron. He'd always found himself oddly attracted to his friend. Cain, with his buzzed, dark brown hair, his deep brown eyes, and his absolutely ghostly white skin. They found that their hard cocks were the same size. Cain's balls hung low, though. Low and heavy. He had only a whisper of pubic hair, unlike Ron, who's crotch was a nest of light brown eiderdown that bled down his thighs, then calves; that crept in secret up the crack of his ass.

They had, at first, simply manipulated each other's cocks, masturbating slowly until their loads spat out onto the ground or the garage floor or onto Cain's bedroom carpet. Ron was content with their playing, unaware of the pleasures of alternate courses of action. It was Cain who led them, though.

Cain's parents had gone to Bakersfield for a long weekend, leaving Cain in the care of his sister, Joyce, who was all of eighteen at the time and completely into partying. Joyce bailed before their parents' car had rounded the first corner. Cain had called him to come over. Ron threw some clothes into an backpack and almost ran all the way over.

Cain had a couple of old copies of *Playgirl* that he'd pilfered from his sister. He was on the bed, in shorts and nothing else, leafing through the pages when Ron showed up. Ron set himself down on the bed and scanned the pictures of hunky, naked men, flexing and posing into many women's fantasies. They discussed bodies and muscles and what makes a man a man for hours, utilizing the photos to define what each thought was perfect. Through the course of this dialogue, Ron's coat, then shoes, then socks, then shirt somehow slipped off his body, piece by piece, until he was just in his jeans, lying next to Cain in nothing more than his threadbare shorts.

Cain simply removed the remainder of his clothes, letting his rising cock snake up to full attention against his belly. Ron wanted another session. Another mutual stroking of dicks. He slipped off his jeans and shorts, his own cock already rigid and twitching. It felt the same, yet different to him. They'd never before been completely nude or on a bed during one of their sessions. He and Cain had very similar bodies. Slim and lean, almost verging on skinny. But Cain was talcum white and nearly hairless. The faint tuft around his groin and under his arms, then only a shadow of hair on his calves and shins. Hair as fine as a newborn's, only raven black. His own flesh was ruddier, with an abundance of adolescent hair covering his lower half. His pinched, oval nipples, stood out like drops of chocolate, unlike Cain's. Cain's nipples were almost perfect circles of pinkish skin, so pale as to be nearly indistinguishable from the rest of his chest.

They lay there for some time, stroking, massaging each others' cocks. Ron was feeling the familiar pleasure slowly spreading through him. Then Cain gripped his cock hard at the base and tugged it. Ron flinched slightly. Before he could utter a protest, he watched as Cain slipped down and wrapped his dripping lips over the head. It was like an icy burn piercing his crotch that made his whole body tremble. Then Cain slowly slid down the entire shaft, a hot jelly glide, swallowing him whole. Ron's stomach contracted sharply, painfully, as his thighs tensed and his ass cheeks clenched hard. His prick was the slide and Cain's mouth the whistle, drawing up then going down, up and down his cock until he exploded. Ron winced as he shot his jism, thinking instantly that Cain would be repelled and angry, but Cain slammed his face into Ron's crotch, sucking up and drinking down all the thick, sloppy cum. Ron felt completely spent, his whole body ten times heavier, twenty times more relaxed than he'd ever been. Cain grinned and told him that was just Step One. From there....

"This is it?" Paul asked.

Ron carefully tugged at his crotch, shifting his straining prick. "See? There's a piece of an old desert pine."

They climbed down the incline into the gorge. Rocks of almost fired-clay hardness were abundant. Paul shucked his pack and started loading it with rocks. "Get some wood for kindling."

Having nothing more than his bare hands and rocks to work with, Ron broke up and tore away bits and pieces of the long dead tree, haphazardly filling his pack. They worked in silence, only commenting now and then on their faint fears of unfriendly snakes and scorpions, then ascended the incline again, each well-weighed down with the bulk of their haul and sweating more than before. The quickly setting sun nudged them to hasten along.

"These things must multiply like tribbles," Paul said, referring to his heavy pack.

"Do we really need this many?"

"Cook'em in the fire and they hold their heat," said Paul. "Gets goddamned cold out here at night."

"Too bad there's not showers out here in bum fuck USA."

"We got some squirt bottles."

"Sponge baths..." said Ron.

"Hey, it's better than nothing." Paul grinned. "Think about how those old cowboys felt."

"And smelt."

"Take a bath twice a year an' head into town to the saloon an' the whore house."

"I guess those ladies didn't smell much better."

Paul let out a vicious whistle. "Skanky!"

"I guess a fuck was a fuck, though," said Ron.

"They must've been used to the stink, screwin' each other on those lonely nights out on the plains."

"You really think they fucked around?"

"They do it in prison now, even with conjugal visits," said Paul. "A hole's a hole, ya know?"

Ron liked that sentiment, though he kept it to himself. He wondered what Paul smelled like right then, all freshly sweaty and grungy with the wear and tear of travel. Sponge baths are adequate, sometimes. More thorough washing is most often warranted, though. A washing Ron thought he wouldn't mind doing.

They talked about their bikes, grunted under the strain of their packs, then talked more about living in the desert, dirt bike riding, and college. When they arrived at their campsite, Yazi already had the nucleus of a fire burning in the hole. But Yazi wasn't around. Paul dumped out the rocks near the campfire, then pulled Ron's pack from him and emptied its contents onto his pile. He started stoking the fire, placing rocks around the fire and in the fire. Ron got on all fours and pitched in, following Paul's leads.

"Good, scouts!" Yazi bellowed with a belch.

Ron looked up. Yazi was standing buck naked, save for thongs on his feet, a towel around his neck and a bucket in his hand. Ron's cock flared instantly. The true feral man. Tall, beefy, smooth... He looked massive. His cock looked massive. Ron had never seen a cock like Yazi's in person. Long, thick, uncut and flapping loose between his thighs. Ron's immediate thought was how big did it get?

Ron felt eyes on him. He glanced to the side, catching sight of Paul fixated on him and smiling slightly. Paul stood up, shucking his jacket and sweatshirt. Mr. Dick P. Phallus swung heavily, to and fro, between his hairy, cut pecs. "Tub time," he said to Ron.

Yazi went over to a tarpaulin spread out neatly just in front of the entrance of the tent. He stepped out of his thongs, carefully stepping into the center of the ground cover. Ron watched Paul strip down completely in the dirt, then just as carefully step onto the tarp. Paul was almost as beefed up as Yazi, though his musculature belied the countless hours of gym work he'd done to cut and define those plains and hills of sculpted definition. The fire bathed them with amber light, making their oily, sweaty forms glisten. An almost surreal image, Ron thought as he squinted to better see them there. Yazi was young. Skin like burnished copper. Shadow and light created the illusion of an animated, polished statue come to life. And Paul, a yellow-red glow of the essence of boy to man transition. Downy hair carpeted his chest. Tapered down to his groin, plump with its sweet meats already straining to rise up. Thick thighs and a full, round ass hosted a forest of golden strands that reflected, shrouding him in aureate light.

Ron's parched mouth suddenly flooded with a wash of wanting. Wanting to be there with them. Reticence kept him glued to the ground. Yazi crouched before the bucket, his pendulous cock and scrotum hanging low, almost grazing the canvas. He wrung out a sponge again and again, while Paul stretched a long, labored stretch up to the sky. His form relaxed. His hands skied down his chest to the soft, furry expanse below his stomach. Fingers gently traced his dick, the mere touch sending it shooting out erect and ready. First Yazi, then Paul glanced over to him.

"If you're gonna sleep in our tent, you gotta get washed," Paul said. With that, Yazi slowly stood up, his dick swelling fatter still as Paul turned around and offered up his back. Yazi slowly swabbed the sponge over his friend's shoulders, all around the nape of his neck, then down his spine to that full, fuzzy ass.

Ron unconsciously slipped back down to the ground, sitting with his arms wrapped around bent knees. Fingers automatically loosened the laces and unfastened the buckles of his heavy boots as he watched Yazi gently run the sponge down Paul's inner thighs, down his calves, as his other arm slid around Paul's hips, holding him fast. Yazi pressed his face into the small of Paul's back, licking it slowly. Ron's unconscious mind became alive and he cleanly removed his boots, his socks, his leathers, most everything, until all that covered his flesh were sweat-soaked shorts. His cock was rigid, seeking escape through the leg hole of his underwear. He squeezed his glans, trying to stave off his impending explosion. He wanted to get up. To join them.

Yazi pulled Paul into him, pressing the furry ass into his chest. He blindly dunked the sponge into the bucket again, then ran it over his own stomach and thighs. He knew Ron was scared, but that he was also wanting to join them there on the tarp. He let himself slip down, his tongue wiping a trail of slick saliva down Paul's spine to the top of his ass. He decided to tease, to coax Ron from his solitary seat. Yazi pulled his head back, tossing back a tangle of black locks. He smiled a taunting smile at Ron, then slammed his face into the crack of Paul's ass, nuzzling the sweat slicked flesh and hair, inhaling deeply the husky, funky scent. His tongue plowed down the dirty valley as Paul groaned and parted his legs further, bringing himself lower, exposing himself fully. Yazi's fingers pulled Paul's ass cheeks apart and he ground his face into the puckered sweetness. The tip of his tongue connected with the ridges of Paul's hole, then burrowed its way inside. He felt Paul's hands clumsily clasp his head, encouraging him to eat.

Paul let out a low, sensual moan as he felt Yazi's hot, wet tongue snake up inside him. His own tongue reflexively stretched from between his lips as he turned his face toward Ron. He smiled. He nodded to the left-out boy.

Every molecule in Ron's body was zinging. He wanted to feel these men he watched. He wanted to taste them. He wanted to know what they knew. He slowly rose on wobbly legs, gathered up his clothes, then slowly approached the two guys. Paul watched him come, encouraging him with a lustful expression. Ron dropped his clothes on the pile of Paul's at the edge of the tarpaulin, then stood there, nervously shaking. Paul extended his hand just as Yazi's finger pressed his prostate. Ron saw a glimpse of euphoria shoot across Paul's face. He took Paul's hand and stepped onto the tarp.

Paul bent further at the waist, his fingers catching the waistband of Ron's shorts. He dragged them down Ron's legs as he himself bent further down, wanting, needing Yazi's tongue, his thick fingers up his ass. Hands at ankles. Ron stepped out of the shorts. Paul gripped Ron's ankles hard, then slowly started climbing back up. Up to meet Ron's stiff, perfect prick with ravenous lips. He swallowed Ron whole. Ron's knees almost gave way. He folded himself over Paul's back just as Yazi's face slipped up from the depth's of Paul's heady crack. Yazi clasped Ron's head hard, yanking the apprehensive lips to his own.

A salty, hot mouth of watery spit entreated Ron's tongue to probe deep inside the Navajo god. The taste was a sublime intoxicant for Ron. Teeth chewed lips as tongues entwined as wetness flooded down scraping chins, the sensation shooting through Ron down to his cock - stuffed down the tight, slick sheath of Paul's burning throat. Suction cup intensity of Paul's undulating mouth milked Ron furiously. Ron's stomach contracted sharply as his legs went jelly. He panted hard down Yazi's throat, stifling grunts of his rapidly rising ecstasy. His soaking tongue slipped from the Navajo's mouth and painted up his cheek as he caught scent of the lingering sweet smell of Paul's cozy ass perfuming Yazi's face and hair.

Paul squeezed Ron's little boy ass hard as he slammed the succulent shaft down his throat again. He felt the hot burn of fresh, creamy jism spit out, flooding his mouth, coating his tongue and teeth. He swallowed and sucked, swallowed and sucked an incredible outpouring of juice.

Ron nearly collapsed, but Paul and Yazi braced him. Paul slowly stood, then pressed his lips to Ron's receptive mouth. He let a lingering puddle of cum slide from his tongue to Ron's. Ron swallowed his own cum eagerly for the very first time. They parted with a couple of friendly pecks. Paul gripped first Ron's cock, then Yazi's, then led them into the tent.

Ron's flaccidity was short-lived. Paul's touch revived his prick, which engorged even more, stretching his skin so taut it felt like it was going to split. Paul let them both go, then fumbled through soft piles of bedding and cloth for another, smaller lantern. He turned it on, then fished out from somewhere a few small pillows. He flopped down on his back, spread his legs high and wide, holding them fixed with his hands.

"Hungry?" he said to Ron.

Ron stood transfixed, staring at the hairy split and the ruddy, puckered opening. Yazi let a low laugh slip as he stretched out, perpendicular, beneath Paul's splayed legs. He wedged the right side of his hip under Paul's hips, supporting Paul's offering. His own straining cock, a good nine inches of fleshy meat, pressed sideways into Paul's asscheeks. The T intersection of light and dark was a human hot dog - Yazi's meat nesting between Paul's buns.

Both men leaned back as Ron kneeled down beside them. Ron pressed his face into their sandwiched flesh, inhaling deeply their acrid, heady, sweet, sweet smells. He let his hands come to rest atop their stomachs, independently feeling the tautness, the fleshiness that made them separate yet the same. Paul's skin felt like plush-covered leather. Masculine. Animal.

Yazi, though had flesh like tightly woven silk. Feminine in its supple smoothness, yet dense muscles were unyielding to his probing hand. Ron's member strained further. He slowly licked the length of the ass-clenched cock, wetting it profusely, loving the salty taste. His lips slipped over the fat head, pushing back plump foreskin, until the meaty mushroom popped free to rest on his tongue.

Yazi felt the tickle of spit trickling down his shaft - hot cooling cool, teasing him. His body tensed in response. Hips arced up slowly, pressing his cock a little deeper into Ron's runny mouth, rubbing firmly against Paul's sphincter. Paul groaned softly, clamping his ass cheeks hard to grip the prized dick.

Ron held fast to Yazi's cock, swallowing another inch or so until his nose pressed into ass meat. He sucked gently, all the while swirling his tongue around the swollen glans. Then he let it slip from his mouth and let his eager, exploring tongue plow down the furry furrow to the tight hole. He wanted in. He pushed his tongue into the orifice, tasting its delicate offering, feeling its constricted softness. He become instantly addicted to this dish. He pushed his face into Paul's fuckhole, hungrily stabbing it with his tongue, sucking on its muscle, wanting to drill way up inside or to slurp it inside out. His gorging was abated by the heavy thump, thump, thumping of Yazi's fleshy log bouncing off his cheek. Ron gripped the prick hard and coated it with a mouthful of spit, then he peeled back the juicy prepuce and pressed the head against the saliva-soaked fuckhole. Yazi responded by slowly forcing his length into Paul's twitching entryway. Ron pressed his drooling tongue against the union of the two, feeling, tasting, both ass and cock as his slick spittle dripped, greasing the way. Tongue to ass to cock. Paul succumbed easily to the pleasure that fueled Yazi's desire. Long, slow pumping picked up speed as bronzed, piston hips accelerated, pummeling ass cheeks and face cheeks sandwiched between. Ron remained fixed on feeding on flesh, reeling in intoxicant scents, revelling in the suffocating feel of his face pinned between men. The moans of one led to the panting of three as Yazi strained a stifled choke and yanked his throbbing prick free. It slapped hard against Ron's nose as globs of jism sprayed his face. Ron caught the cock and jammed its erupting head between his lips as he rammed his finger deep inside the tight, mushy bowels, finger fucking the eager ass while swallowing down expulsions of cum.

The two men collapsed, breathing hard, while Ron gently licked them clean. Yazi let out a throaty purr, then pulled Ron between them.

The two sandwiched their new friend between their bodies, their fingers and arms and tongues and lips slowly massaging and nibbling their prey's tender flesh. Static, bristling, tingling explosions rippled through Ron's entire core as his balls contracted and his cock expanded painfully.

The guys intuitively sensed the quickening climax. In an instant, Ron felt Paul's rough face and cat-like tongue spreading his ass, drilling into his hole while Yazi's burning hot mouth swallowed him down. A thick, long tongue made Ron all lickerish and beyond control. His well was sprung. His cum felt like a scalding of oil-drenched feathers shooting through his shaft. His hips bucked sharply, thrusting his entirety down his Navajo's throat. Yazi sucked hard, extracting every thick drop and swallowing it down. Ron felt his bristling body tingle then go numb as he fell back spent. Their tongues and lips fused to his own. Three hungry, silent voices savoring the moment, lulling them to sleep.

Ron awoke some time later. The two men entwined with him, their bodies warmed by a tangle of bedding. Ron could feel each of their hearts, independent, yet beating as one. He welcomed the lamplit dimness. A fichu of security, of clarity.

He didn't want the morning to come.

THE RENDEZVOUS

Jarred Goodall

Gerald glanced at his watch. He didn't need to, really, because he'd peeked at it only a few minutes before. He'd set its beeper alarm for four o'clock. Sure enough, it was only 3:55.

The boys were probably meeting now, coming from their separate schools: the tall blond boy with long '60s-style hair and red bandana, and his shorter friend whose dark hair was drawn back into a ponytail.

They'd both be ready for the rendezvous, desperate for it, in fact, adolescent testosterone rampaging through them like grassfire in the May drought. And he would be ready for them, too, beer in one hand and his binocs...

Good lord, his binoculars! They were in the glove compartment of his car. He sprang to his feet – and gave a gasp as his cock, trapped down a pantleg, kinked to the angle of agony. He fell back on the couch, quickly rearranged things and then was off, out of the apartment, down the elevator, into the garage, came back up with binocs in hand, wristwatch squeaking as he locked the door behind him. Out on the balcony at last, he dropped to his knees among the plants and brought the binocs up to his eyes.

And there they were, just crawling through the hole in the shrubbery and entering their garden of delights. Blond Bandana-Boy shrugged off his backpack. Ponytail opened it and brought out the familiar tan blanket (how sperm-stained and crusted it must be – what a shame his binocs weren't more powerful!) and spread it on the grass.

They lost no time, now. Off came their T-shirts, down came their Levis. Ponytail had a nice summer tan; Bandana-Boy had only a few freckles across his broad shoulders – curse of being very fair. They sat on the blanket to get rid of shoes and socks and work their legs out of fashionably hugging denim. Then Ponytail took Bandana-Boy into a wrestler's hug, Shakespeare's "beast with two backs," the two of them rolling about cheek to cheek but not kissing, chins locked at the join of neck and shoulder.

After a minute of this, they broke apart, whipped off their skivvies, firmly up-cocked. Bandana-boy stretched out on his back. Ponytail bent over Bandana-Boy's waist and went to work on his impressive cock with fingers and lips and tongue. Bandana-Boy's eyes were closed, his mouth slightly open, chest heaving. Whenever Ponytail activated some particularly sensitive nerve, Bandana-Boy's forehead and eyelashes would twitch as if in pain.

Suddenly Bandana-Boy sat up and pushed Ponytail's head and hands away. Bandana-Boy hung there panting, between heaven and earth, as it were, for a moment, beaded with sweat. Then he urged Ponytail around so Ponytail was half-lying, half-crouching on knees and elbows above him in the 69-position. Cocks were directed with nervous fingers towards mouths. Lips engulfed them, pouting out like doughnuts.

From his position half-hidden on the balcony, Gerald had a clear view of Ponytail's up-angled buttocks tucking in, rolling back up, repeating, repeating, slowly, nervously. In its crease the anus winked, virginly pink and still quite innocent of fringe hair. Bandana-Boy moved his hand, cupped one thrusting buttock-cheek, explored with his middle finger, touched target, pushed, entered two knuckles deep.

The motions accelerated, became frantic, then the two boys froze in catatonic rictus. This was their timed culmination; a matched peak obviously coordinated through ample experience with the counterpoint of each other's responses. The whole episode had lasted barely a minute and a half.

Ponytail rolled away and stretched out on his back, lazy, dreaming, fulfilled. They were talking, now, absently, every so often swatting away flies attracted to the after-leak oozing out of their cocks.

Fifteen minutes later they climbed to their feet, dressed, stowed blanket in backpack and crept away through the bushes.

Teeth brushed, cheeks razored and redolent of an expensive after-shave, Gerald settled on a bench not far from where the boys would be entering the park. At his age he couldn't wear kids' clothes any longer: he'd retired his last jeans several years ago. Instead, he wore a pair of neatly pressed tan slacks, an expensive grey turtle-neck shirt and nicely shined loafers. It was quarter to four on a cloudless May afternoon and for some reason the park was almost deserted.

It was a momentous decision he had made. On the one hand, it would be a kindness to warn the boys: if *he* could spy on them with a pair of bird-watcher's binocs, then so could countless other cliff-dwellers whose windows overlooked the park. On the other hand, it was risky. High school boys lived in their own teenage world and reacted with suspicion, if not hostility, to any strange adult trying to enter it.

He looked up, and there they were, walking rather quickly towards the thicket which fringed their place of assignation. "Boys," he said, "may I speak to you for a moment?" The gambit had begun.

They stopped and looked at him curiously. Ponytail nodded a Yes.

"I wouldn't do that," Gerald said.

"I'm sorry?" Bandana-Boy was polite but cool.

"Go into the bushes. It's a lousy spot for that sort of thing."

Jaws dropped. They caught each others' eyes. Pupils dilated. After a moment, Ponytail turned to Bandana-Boy. "I don't know what this guy's talking about, do you?"

"Look around you." Gerald pointed. "I live there, on the sixth floor. Believe me, yesterday afternoon, and a whole lot of other times, I had a real good view of what you fellows got up to."

Bandana-Boy's rather prominent adam's apple moved up and down with a gulp. "You did?"

"My binoculars helped."

Ponytail came out of shock with a snort. "Jesus, this guy's a pervert!"

"Now if that isn't the pot calling..."

But Ponytail's outrage only grew. "Christ, he gets off spying on people making out."

"Wait, wait." Bandana-Boy's adam's apple was working over-time, now. "Mister, what're you going to do?"

"Danny, he's been spying on us through a pair of fucking spy-glasses. Let's split."

So Bandana-Boy was called Danny, a nice name, in fact a favorite name of Gerald's ever since the sixth grade when he used to jerk off with Danny Moore. Now this Danny,

Bandana-Boy, was holding his eye, ignoring Ponytail. "Are you going to turn us in to the cops?"

"Do I look like that kind of man?"

"I don't know what kind of man you are. We don't even know you... sir."

"Gerald. Call me Gerald. And I'm telling you never to use that spot again."

"Mister," said Ponytail, "what we do and where we do it ain't no business of yours."

"That's a shame, because I was going to offer a better place, and one that's far more comfortable into the bargain."

"Yeah, like where?"

Gerald turned and once again pointed to the front window of his apartment on the sixth floor.

It had worked, after some ten minutes of arguing and persuading. Now the two boys were sitting rather stiffly side by side on his living room couch, each with a Coke in hand. Danny – Bandana-Boy – was into ecology, it seemed: saving whales, eagles, redwoods and the ozone zone. "But obviously not sperm," Gerald couldn't help cracking, which did nothing to put the boy at his ease.

Ponytail was named Jorge Millikens, sprig of an upwardly mobile family of mixed ethnic stock. He liked surfing and about any sport that happened to be going on at the time but was less enthusiastic about school work on which he got a lot of help from Danny.

The cola disappeared rapidly, not so the boys' plainly visible erections. Gerald took pity on their plight. "Well, we can talk more later. Meanwhile, here are a few house rules."

Which were no shoes on the bed – all clothes had to come off, and that included dirty socks. He didn't care about sperm and sweat and a little drool on the sheets and pillows....

"You got *two* pillows?" Danny asked.

"Yes, it's a big bed – you'll see.... but if you plow any furrows..."

"Huh?"

"Ass-fuck, breezebrain," Jorge explained.

"Oh."

"...you must let me know so I can put something down."

"We don't do that," Danny said firmly.

He led the two boys to his bedroom and nodded towards his bed with the covers thrown back: an inviting expanse of tight-stretched white bottom sheet.

"There's your playing field. It should be a lot better than that old brown blanket, right? Well... I'll leave you two alone. Enjoy."

When he came in a half-hour later, after knocking, with a coffee pot and condiments and three cups and a plate of warm, sticky breakfast rolls, they were sitting up in bed with a sheet modestly pulled over their laps. Jorge had released his hair from the pony-tail elastic and it spread out over the pillow he was leaning against in a big dark cloud.

"Time out," Gerald said. "Time to refresh and nourish and replenish lost body fluids."

"Sir," said Danny, "it's rather queer for a man to be talking that way all the time. You shouldn't do it."

"Why on earth not?"

"Danny's a very proper guy," Jorge explained. "He doesn't even talk dirty at school."

"He's the sort of boy you have to watch out for," Gerald said -- it was obviously time for some fence-mending. "While the big-mouths are busy bragging, the quiet ones like Danny are having all the fun."

A shy smile crossed Danny mouth before it closed around a semi-detached nebular arm of hot coffee roll.

An hour later, they emerged from the bedroom, dressed, hair once again tamed by pony-tail elastic and red bandana, looking friendly, handsome and relaxed.

"Tomorrow, same time, same place?" Gerald asked.

They nodded and grinned. "Yeah," said Danny, "if you don't mind."

"Don't mind at all. And let me know if you have other preferences for snacks."

That night Gerald revelled, even orgied, on the lightly sperm-sprinkled sheet and pillows smelling ever so slightly of face sweat, hair and adolescent saliva redolent of coffee and breakfast roll.

The next afternoon they were back, feeling much more at home. Danny confided he loved more than anything else in the world ("Even more than sex," Jorge interjected and was told by Danny to shut up) chocolate cake with chocolate frosting washed down by cold, white milk. Jorge liked fruit juice -- "Any kind of fruit, except the two-legged kind -- oh, sorry!"

They disappeared into the bedroom. There was the usual pause for snacks and to recharge batteries and then Gerald once again regretfully closed the door upon them. Hadn't he perhaps traded down in moving the boys' assignations to his apartment? Now they writhed, sucked, rolled about and cuddled sight unseen: all he got erotically out of their visits was his subsequent rut upon their body-scent-impregnated sheets.

Right or wrong, wise or stupid, the boys now became part of his stable daily routine. They would arrive every weekday around four; they would be gone by five-thirty, leaving behind nothing but their scent in the air and certain traces of body fluids on the bed. Saturdays and Sundays he didn't see them, for they always seemed to be engulfed in family plans.

"You got a whole lot of paintings of guys," Danny said one day as the boys were preparing to depart.

"That's right."

"I guess a man wouldn't buy them unless he was interested in guys himself."

"I *told* you," said Jorge.

All Gerald could do was shrug.

The next afternoon when Gerald came into the bedroom with snacks, Jorge asked him right out, "Sir, what do *you* get out of letting us come here to make out?"

Danny turned bright red with embarrassment. And Gerald found his own face heating up. "I... well, I hate to see kids get in trouble. I..."

"You really were perving on us through your binoculars, weren't you?" Jorge went on. "That's kind of nice, in a way, I mean, once you get over the shock – someone turning on seeing you turning on to someone you turn on to. And you've been so nice to us, you're such a nice old guy. Danny and I've talked it over, and we'd be real willing to have you join us in bed -- after snacks. Isn't that right, Danny?"

Danny was almost beet red, but he nodded.

This was more than Gerald had dared hope for. Of course, he had entertained fantasies of drilling holes through the closet door and installing a remote video camera trained on the bed so that a little later he could lie on that same bed and jerk off to the sight of their coupling. He'd had wilder and more juvenile fantasies of wartime rescues, nursing a wounded Danny back to health in an abandoned bunker, adopting Jorge and enlarging his tastes until the boy was an avid concert-goer. What he'd never imagined was being invited to participate in their love-making in such a simple, prosaic fashion.

Jorge shoved down the sheet, fisted a rubbery, extended cock. "Come on, sir, join us. See, this old boy is already rising to the occasion, and I'll bet Danny's is, too."

After that, Gerald's days were full of almost agonizing anticipation, intensified ten-fold when the boys walked alone into the bedroom – "Because," as Danny blushingly explained the next day, "you know, well, like, the first time's gotta be for us."

But what followed, after chocolate cake and juice, was worth every minute of the wait: the ecstasy of being clasped between the boys' smooth bodies, young and warm, savoring the smell of their schoolday sweat, their hair, their cheeks, the taste of their mouths (each so different: Danny's still redolent of chocolate, Jorge's of apple or orange or grape).

And then their cocks would be rising from the ashes of the day's first or even second ejaculations, no longer penis-scented because both had just been sucked clean – soaring cocks, vital cocks, slicked with spit, one fringed with dark, coarse hair, the other growing from a lighter, softer, blonder bush, now rubbing over his nostrils and teasing his lips – and entering!

He would feel his own cock being sucked deep into the back of Danny's or Jorge's throat, passion rising to unbearable heights until his semen erupted like molten silver, determined to pulverize everything that stood in its way, until at last the shuddering transport would be over, leaving him in a heavy sweat (these were still hot spring days), gasping to catch his breath. Now, with Jorge and Danny flanking him, they would dreamily rub off against him for the last time, splashing his hips, first on one side and then the other.

There were variations, of course. "I want to kiss ol' Danny Boy here while you suck him off, okay?" And when he laid Danny's somewhat flattened tool on top of his tongue, he could feel in its erectile rigidity, glans swelling to the bursting point, the extra voltage Jorge was kissing into Danny's mouth.

Some days he would give Jorge's dark cock a nice slow B-J while Danny, squatting astride Jorge's chest, fed his tool into Jorge's mouth. Other times the boys would languidly kiss, rubbing spit-wet faces slowly against each other while Gerald, crouching at the foot of the bed, would lean between their unclasped loins and engulf the penis first of one boy and then the other.

Summer came. The school year ended. Danny and his family would soon be leaving in their camper for a trip through the northern Rockies.

"I'll miss you – and this!" Gerald said, lying between the two boys after completing a rather athletic *sex-a-trois*.

Danny, as often happened when the sex was all over and it was very hot in the room, looked tired and slightly depressed. "Me, too," he said. "Four weeks in that dumb camper sleeping only six feet from your Mom and Pop!"

"Come on, Danny, you never jerk off by yourself anyhow," Jorge teased.

"Shut up."

Jorge got to his feet, stretched and, still naked, peered out the window. Something attracted his attention. "Gerald, where'd you put your spy-glasses?"

"I don't know. Since you boys have been coming here I haven't thought about them much."

"Well, where *are* they?"

"In that top bureau drawer, I think."

Jorge opened the drawer, fumbled, drew out the binocs, went back to the window and put them to his eyes. "Un huh! Just as I thought. Danny, come here."

"Why should I?"

"Then, Gerald, come and look. This is something more for you anyhow. There. You play your cards right, you might not have such a dry summer after all."

Gerald got up and took the binocs from Jorge and trained

them down into the boys' old bush-rimmed rendezvous place in the park. And, sure enough, two boys were there, this time a red-head and a *cafe-au-lait* black, both a bit smaller than Jorge and Danny, stripping off their clothes, kneeling, confronting one another with up-thrust, dancing cocks, giggling at the naughtiness and deliciousness of what they were about to do.

THE MUMMY
or I'LL BE DAMNED

L. Amore

I stopped at the post office box on my way to work. Yet another invitation to yet another White Party as the only piece of mail in the box. This White Party was to be held at, appropriately enough, the Black Hole. I crammed the invitation in the pocket of my pants and hurried out the door.

On the way to work, stuck in traffic on the Q-bridge, my mind wandered to the last White Party I'd been to. All or most of the men dancing in white briefs, jockstraps and less. My hand instantly went to my swelling cock, massaging it through my dress pants. The urge to pull it out and do a more thorough job passed as a truck came up to my left and the passenger looked down and saw me kneading my crotch. He elbowed his buddy who was driving and then they were both looking out of the passenger side window.

Just as the driver, who actually wasn't that bad to look at, started to blow me a kiss, the traffic picked up and I was on my way again and at work ten minutes later.

Raymond, the hunky marketing manager whom I'd had the hots for since he started working at the pharmacuetical company about a month before, happened to pass my desk just as I was marking my calendar. "Good morning," he said in that deep, superstud voice of his.

"Morning," I said.

He smiled as I wadded up the invitation and tossed it in the wastebasket. I looked over my shoulder to see his incredible ass as he walked away: two perfect bubbles that were beautifully encased in his navy linen dress pants. You could almost see the rippling butt muscles through the thin fabric as he swaggered down the corridor. *Someday*, I vowed.

As the week passed, I received three calls from friends who wanted to know if I was going to the party and which train I was going to catch into the city. Then Jesse called, asking the usual question, "Do you want some E?"

"Does the Pope shit in the woods?" I replied.

He laughed. "The usual?"

"Actually... make it three."

"Will do. See you at ten." And he hung up.

My door bell rang at quarter of ten. It was Jesse and his friend Christian.

"I've got your Tic Tacs, baby."

He handed me a Tic Tac container with three pills in it and I handed him the seventy-five dollars for my little treasure. At first glance they looked like the one and a half calorie breath mint everyone knew and loved, but with closer inspection they definitely were not. Just small, unmarked white gelatin capsules.

"Cool Beans." And we were off.

There was a large crowd outside of the club. The group consisted mostly of beautiful men, with a scattering of drag queens. The men in all shapes and colors. Inner City's "Follow Your Heart" was pounding at so loud a volume that the ground was actually shaking. Some of the boys in line just couldn't wait – and were dancing in the street. Waiting to get in was a longer period of time than it seemed, but I wasn't complaining. The sights around me more than occupied my mind and in case I'd missed something, Jesse was there to nudge me and point. "Look at that one," he would say. Then his eyes would catch another. "Oh my god!"

"Calm down," I told him, just barely able to control myself, so I couldn't blame him at all. It was going to be a very good night.

The air on the dance floor was close with warmth and the smell of sweating bodies. Walking through I kept inhaling large gulps of the mansmell that permeated the club.

I'd already lost Jesse and Christian, but forgot all about looking for them when a man wrapped up like a mummy walked past me. All the man had on was mummy wrap. The cloth looked very absorbent, kind of like thick cheesecloth or heavy gauze.

It was a good look for him. Large gaping holes were everywhere, showing off exactly what he wanted shown off. Most of his abdomen was showing, from his right nipple all the way down to the top of his pubic hair patch, which seemed to be the only hair on his torso. The ripped muscles bulging and flexing and very defined, being totally devoid of hair. But the piece of anatomy that drew the eye was his enormous totally erect cock that was wrapped in the same white strips as the rest of him. A small gap of pink flesh showed through. Probably to show everyone that it was really his cock and not a piece of flesh colored dildo. I looked down as he walked by me. He stopped, leaned back and pushed his hips forward in a gesture that told me to 'reach out and touch him', so I did. It was definitely him! I could almost feel it throb under the cloth. He reached out and grabbed my own hardening dick clad in ripped white denim shorts. I groaned, swooned and he walked away without a word.

"Oh my God!" It was Jesse. I didn't have to find him, he found me. "I don't have to ask you if you saw that one. You felt him! Mmm-mmm."

All I could manage was, "I need a drink".

The drinks were light, but all the better because you're really not supposed to drink much when you take a hit of Ecstasy. Something about counteracting the effects. I'd taken my 'tic tac' a half an hour previously, so I had about another half hour before I started to feel the effects.

The music was truly brilliant, amazing: DJ, actually DJs, two beautiful Hispanic men dressed in nothing but white jockstraps and suspenders, churned out the best house and techno music I'd heard in ages.

The Mummy seemed to be everywhere, his penis always in some state of erection, never totally flaccid. I'd almost thought he was following me at one point. Maybe there were two of them. No, I'd only seen one at a time, so that couldn't be. It would have been nice, but improbable.

The first Ecstasy rush started to hit when the music stopped for a second. Sade's smoky voice filled the club, and a moment later the house beats accompanied her voice perfectly. I could feel the sweat start to come, as it always does when you do a hit of E. Your limbs feel lighter and you get a blast of energy from nowhere. Everyone around you becomes your best buddy, and all your problems, no matter how big, fade to nothing. The most important thing is the music, the camaraderie of the people around you and the dancing.

Before I even realized I was dancing I found myself in the heavy sweating throng of people on the lit floor. The strobe lights striking everyone in poses again and again in a stop start intensity that was a little disconcerting if you paid to much attention to it.

Before me there was a couple; one dressed in a vest and thin white rayon pajama pants, the sweat making them cling to his nakedness underneath, the other in just classic white briefs. They too were obviously on Ecstasy, clinging to each other and gyrating seductively to the heavy synthetic bass line. While grinding their bodies and dancing they suddenly seemed aware of their surroundings and looked up to find me staring at them. They both smiled in unison and gestured for me to come over to them. I probably wouldn't have if I wasn't high, but I thought what the hell. They both opened up their arms and invited me into their private little dance troop. Four hands were on me before I knew what was happening. The smiles on their faces were blinding. They both had blue eyes, blond hair and killer bodies. I couldn't believe my luck. Their names were Kairn and Kraig and they were brothers! Or so they said, but after they told me this I tore my eyes from their bodies and looked at their faces again, and they did resemble each other! I thought to myself if only I could get them and the Mummy, I'd never have to make another diary entry again.

I enjoyed their warm sweaty hands on my body. One caressing my legs, one my chest and nipples, respectively. I was never able to get an erection right off when I was doing E, and any other time I probably would have cum right then, but now on the drug, I just felt the pleasurable sensations of being touched and a sweet affection for both of them. The song mixed into another one, 2 Unlimited I think, and I decided to get another drink and to search out Jesse and Christian. The brothers looked sad when I took my leave, but when I looked back they were all smiles again.

Drink in hand, I found both of them feeling up this tall mustachioed Italian guy. It seemed as though he was straight, meaning not on anything, definitely not E. The hard-on he had in his tight white jeans was huge! Amazing. I'm sure that Jesse's and Christian's hands on his crotch were the cause of it. They both saw me at the same time and took their hands off the Italian stud's dick. I smiled and they lost the guilty expressions on their faces. Why they were there in the first place, I didn't know. They introduced me to Pasquale. Pasquale offered his hand to me. I took it to shake. Pasquale had another idea. As he took my hand, he placed it on his tumescent organ. The thing felt like a foot length of PVC pipe. You know the kind of thick plastic tubing that people use for piping in their bathrooms and under sinks? It was that hard too!

"Well, hello Pasquale," I shouted over the music. He didn't say a word, just kept running my hand up and down his cock.

"It's nice to meet you, too," I smiled at Pasquale and looked over at Jesse and Christian with raised eyebrows to say 'can you'? And just as I took my hand off of Pasquale's hard-on, and 2 Unlimited turned into Janet Jackson's 'Throb', Pasquale grabbed me by the shoulders, forced me against the bar that he was previously leaning on, and gave me the kiss of my life. His tongue invaded my mouth, taking a swipe over my own tongue and the roof of my mouth. I almost gagged on his spit. This was too much, and even with the E coursing through my veins, I felt my dick stir and start to swell. My tongue dueled his with equal vigor.

"Mmmm, you go girl," I heard Jesse's voice respond behind me and Christian gave a little laugh. I pulled myself away and told Pasquale I had to go. He didn't respond at all, just stared off into the crowd.

I changed my mind about him not being on anything. He had to be on *something*, or I had just met a person who had just enough intelligence to draw breath and take up space. Jesse said, "Well, the white parties don't attract the neurosurgeons of the gay community."

"Well, if you like 'em stupid, he's perfect. Not like those guys you take home and fuck and they talk and talk and talk. Until you finally have to ask 'em, 'Don't you have a cigarette to smoke or something'? Although, I did have this one guy who wouldn't shut up so I had to stick my dick in his mouth again just so he would. It wasn't a bad blow job. As Bette Midler once said 'I don't have to be well informed, just well endowed." The boys chuckled and we went off arms locked, looking like some perverse vision of gay "Charlie's Angels" all in white.

Jesse, as always, was the one who kept track of the time. Not because we had to go at a certain time, but because he wanted everyone's 'E' high to last so no one would crash. He always looked at his watch, not saying anything but giving us this wicked grin. We all 'popped' and downed our drinks.

Things were heating up on the dance floor, well, everywhere for that matter. Occasionally you would walk by a discarded heap of clothes, and more than occasionally you would come upon people getting blown - with someone before them on their knees going at the task before them with seldom-seen gusto - or fucked - bent over in a dark corner, moaning loudly, but little of it was heard over the loud crashing music.

And if you ever got to be a Superstar,
With aeroplanes and works of art,
You'd still be hanging round the singles bar,
Cos, that's the way you really are,
You must have simple stuff inside your head,
Dragging your body from bed to bed,
Now you want to be back in my arms,
Well I'm not falling for your charms,
Please, stop, kicking my heart around...

When Dead Or Alive came blasting from the giant speakers, everyone rushed to the dance floor, dropping most of their clothes on the way. Caught up in the throng, I felt someone put their hand between my cheeks, and they weren't touching my nose either. I turned around and saw that it was the Mummy. Looking down I saw that his cock was again full mast. I didn't need an invitation this time. I touched it, grabbing a firm handful. The gap of exposed flesh was now about three inches of the base of his shaft. The heat emanating from his member was intense. It was like touching a fever victim. I kept walking to the dance floor leading him by his cock.

The heat was sweltering. Mr. Mummy spread his legs and started to grind against me so that his cock was nestled between my thighs. A gentle stroking that drove me wild and also made the bandages loosen and more of his cock appear. My own started to thicken, the blood coming into it seemed to rush through my ears.

The bandages on his face were also coming undone a little.

And for the first time I looked at his countenance. There was a familiarity to his visage, and I found myself staring at him, perplexed and slightly annoyed that I couldn't put my finger on this feeling of recognition. The eyes. I know that I'd seen those eyes before. But my concentration went as Mr. Mummy started to unwrap some more gauze revealing more delectable tidbits of his torso. His nipples, a tawny color, not pink against his pale flesh, were the size of half dollars. Quite large, but this was always a fetish of mine. I bent down to take one in my mouth, feeling it harden instantly. I thought I heard a moan but that I'm sure was my imagination because you wouldn't have been able to hear someone screaming over the pounding of the music.

I looked down and the moment I was waiting for finally came. The gauze finally came off the head of his cock. It gave a whole new meaning to cheesecloth. He was uncut, fully erect and he still had a nice bit of overhang. I felt like breaking into my version of "These Are A Few Of My Favorite Things," but just decided to bend over and stick my tongue in his very ample pee slit. With my mouth on his head, and him gyrating to the music, his whole glans popped into my mouth seconds later. I tongued the spongy foreskin, lightly chewing on it, while somehow still dancing.

I tore myself away and realized that an appreciative crowd had gathered around us. From behind I felt a hand caressing the crack of my ass. The damp denim sticking to the hair there. I turned my head to see who was administering this helping hand and I saw Kairn, with Kraig standing right beside him with the same shit-eating grin. Kraig's hands were tightly gripping my shoulders from behind.

Mr. Mummy unbuttoned my shorts with one yank of my fly. I didn't normally wear button fly anything but, such is fate. My cock leapt free more than half hard and turgid. It flopped on the Mummy's tongue. More of the bandages were off, revealing his face further. It seemed more familiar to me now, but still I couldn't place it. I gave myself over to the mouth on my cock, warm wet and engulfing. It was expert to say the least. The sheath that enveloped me, came and went with the rhythm of the music... and the hand on my ass... and the strong hands kneading my shoulders.

I looked down and really couldn't believe my luck. Gorgeous blond brothers on either side in back and the fascinating man of the hour, Mr. Mummy. I've always had an aversion to hoods, ski masks or anything that covered the face, but this was somehow hitting a nerve. It had more intrigue, like a Mardi Gras masquerade. There was nothing sinister about it. But this could also have been the E.

My head spun around taking in the lights and the crowd. Pasquale, the Italian stud, was standing three feet away. He was just staring at the four of us. Not dancing, or moving at all, just massaging his cock through the worn denim he was wearing. I looked up. His eyes met mine and he just gave me a cold stare. Nothing more. But his hand was busy stroking his massive rod.

Kairn's finger found the bud of my ass. On the drug, I was so relaxed that I thought my ass would engulf his finger in a second. Sit on a fire hydrant even, with nary an ouch. His fingers deftly and gently probed my hole. Despite myself I felt my body instinctively backing up against his hand, only to be drawn forward again by the now intense sucking of my cock. Kraig's fingers were tweaking hard at my nipples and rubbing the underside of my pecs. When I threw my head back, totally oblivious to the world, lost in a state of pure sensuality, our Italian Stallion came over to administer the deepest French kiss I'd ever experienced. *So* continental... I liked that. I chuckled to myself, not that any of them would have noticed anyway.

I finally opened my eyes and the actuality of seeing firsthand what was going on, being done to me, sent me over the edge. They all had their cocks out, Mr. Mummy's cock bandages were all off now and I saw that just one piece of gauze was dangling from where it was tied to his engorged dick and scrotum. His cock really was massive. The red monster was waving around menacingly, the blue veins sticking out almost to bursting point.

I reached down to grasp him behind the head. More bandage slipped off. The hair was light brown, thick and soft to my touch. His forehead and eyebrows were visible now. More recollection bubbled to my brain but still nothing clicked.

Italoman grunted a couple of times and dropped a load on the dance floor, before walking away, his massive dick still the dance floor, before walking away, his massive dick still hanging out of his open fly. Just goes to show you, big dick doesn't always mean big load. Kraig and Kairn were beside me going at one another with equal ardor. Their cocks meshed together between their sweat-soaked bodies. I'd never seen two brothers together, but seeing them swapping spit and numerous other things, I made a mental note to watch "Brothers Should Do It" again when I got home. They were in their own little world and I was in mine, so I decided to get back to it.

I pulled Mr. Mummy up from his squatting position and had the most desirous urge to kiss him. He'd lost most all bandage coverage by this point so I reached up to his head and started rolling off what was covering his face. It didn't strike me at first, even after all his glorious visage was uncovered, then it hit me.

"I'll be damned!"

His shit-eating grin revealed the pearly whites I'd seen at work every day for the past six months. It was Raymond. Straight Raymond. Straight Raymond had just given me the sucking of my life and now it was time to suck his face then return the favor.

I grabbed the dangling gauze and pulled him to me. His breath hot and pleasant against my mouth. My tongue slowly licked his lower lip as I felt all the exposed parts of his flesh stick to my naked torso. He tasted good and as I bent down to bite his right nipple I got a whiff of his armpit. I almost fell to the floor in a puddle of cum right there. (Brown paper packages tied up in string, sweaty smelly armpits, these are a few of my favorite things.)

Breaking me out of my reverie of sucking pits, he slapped my stomach with his cock and pushed me lower. The scent down there wasn't bad either and I attacked his organ with a lusty gusto that escapes my memory. His cock was exquisite. Just thick enough to cause my jaw to ache and long enough to go past the base of my throat and not gag. Although this might have been the drug working on my gag reflex, but I wasn't complaining. I just made a feast of the meal offered to me.

I pulled myself off his rod and dragged him to a more inconspicuous corner. He seemed to be reading my mind because, as if by magic, suddenly a condom was in his hand. He ripped it with his teeth and had it on in no more than five seconds. I braced myself against the wall and he entered me easily and with no preliminaries. He push his head in and I backed up against him so he filled me totally. There was no pain thanks to the E and I wanted him to pound me as hard as he wanted. And that's just what he did. I had to grip the wall so as not to become part of it. My cock straining with want was pressed between it and the buttons of my fly. So much for the inconspicuous corner. We had drawn a crowd again. I looked back and saw that most of them were gyrating to the music, their bare, hard cocks in their hands. A look of desire and envy on each of their faces until they discovered the men around them and started to get acquainted.

God, I thought, had I ever been fucked so well? I reached between the wall and my body to grab my dick but his hand beat me there. It was rough against the tender skin, but it was expert in its manipulations. He increased his strokes to my ass and I knew he was ready to cum. He fucked me so hard that the hand on my penis caused me pain with each thrust as I was slammed to the wall again and again. His guttural moan in my ear started my own orgasm. I pulled back and watched each dollop of my cum hit the wall, cling for a second and start to drip down making glossy rivulets against the matte finish. There were hoots and catcalls from the crowd but they barely registered. After what seemed like an extra-long lunch hour there was no more semen to come out of me. The scent of it hit my nostrils and my legs went weak. I had to lean on the wall so as not to fall.

Raymond was hugging me. I felt the sweat dripping off both our bodies, much colder when it hit my calves. He pulled his still-hard dick out and I felt like I'd lost my best friend. This might also have been me coming down from my second hit but he turned me around and kissed me. All was well again.

I was totally enraptured with him as he led me to the bar. I was in a catatonic state following behind him, my hand in his, watching his partially exposed ass flex with each stride he took.

"Scared a' you honey." It was Jesse's voice coming from behind me. "It's the man who tamed the Mummy." He just kept walking, which at that moment I was grateful for.

I opened my mouth to ask Raymond a question, still in awe that he was actually in front of me, but realized it wouldn't be of any use with the music that loud. He ushered me to the dance floor and we spent the next four hours getting to know each other with no words spoken.

And I never did take that last Tic Tac.

PRACTICE PONY

David Laurents

I couldn't stop thinking about the sign I'd torn down from the post office door:

PUT A BEAST BETWEEN YOUR LEGS!
JOIN THE POLO TEAM.
INTRODUCTORY MEETING
TONIGHT AT 9

I had ripped the notice off the door and stuck it in my back pocket, then began rushing across campus. Oh, I thought, to be astride a horse again, to feel withers pressing up against my asshole, rubbing back and forth! I was getting so hard I was sure that everyone walking past must notice my erection, and I swung my books loosely in front of my crotch, feeling like I was in high school again.

I'd grown up on horseback, riding competitively in dressage and hunterchases until I hit high school and decided it wasn't masculine enough. Even then, I knew I was gay, but I was afraid people would find out. In high school, it's just not accepted. So I did everything I could to pretend I wasn't. In college, things were different, but I still wasn't comfortable being completely out. There were these football players who lived on my floor, whom I had to share a bathroom with, and I was afraid of what they might do to me if they knew I was gay and thought I'd been watching them in the showers all this time, desiring them.

But the idea of polo was sexy – and somehow extremely masculine. Despite the wording of their sign: Put a beast between your legs. Did they know what that sounded like? Could they mean... I was afraid to finish the thought, lest I jinx myself. I glanced at my watch, then thrust my hand into my pocket. Just eleven hours until I can find out, I told myself, hopefully, as I squeezed my hard cock in my jeans and walked into my anthro class.

I'd gone to the meeting for the Equestrian Club during the first few weeks of my freshman year, but when I walked into a room full of about thirty women I just pretended I had stumbled into the wrong meeting and fled. My heart had pounded in my chest as I hurried back to Old Campus and my dorm; no way was I going to be the only boy on an all-women team! That would've been like running through the streets shouting, "I'm a faggot! I'm a faggot!," and I wasn't ready for that. I'm still not, although I'm much farther out of the closet than I was last year.

I didn't think the Polo Team would be anything like the Equestrian Team. It didn't seem like a women's thing, so I was surprised to see four or five girls in the Davenport Lounge when I walked in a little before 9 p.m. But there were also a dozen guys sitting about, half of them in riding pants or chaps and boots. There was one man – young, but not a boy like most of the people present – who seemed to dominate the whole room. His skin spoke of some exotic clime: Brazil or Argentina, some place Latin, some place where heat and passion were a way of life. He had liquid black eyes and lips that curled in a small pout when he stopped talking. Obviously tall, even though he was sitting on a couch, his long legs were casually spread wide.

I quickly looked away. Great first impression, Glenn, I berated myself, drooling all over the men. But as I scanned the room and my eyes fell on him again, as he talked with a group of three very frosh-looking guys in jeans who stood facing him, I knew that I'd be joining the team if he was on it.

I struck up a conversation with someone I recognized from one of my Poli Sci classes, and after a moment Mr. Drop Dead Gorgeous stood up and called the room to order. He was even more attractive when standing, I thought, as my eyes traveled up and down his tall frame. The bulge in his crotch seemed even more enormous below his thin waist.

Turns out he wasn't just on the team, he was Captain. Which meant I'd suddenly developed a new hobby.

The smell of shavings always brings back the memory of the first time I'd sucked another man's cock: the hot summer afternoon one of the stablehands took me into one of the back stalls and dropped his pants. I'd been so enthralled by that huge, veined piece of flesh that swelled between his legs. It reeked of his sweat as I knelt down to examine it more closely. The whole barn reeked of strong scents: cedar from the shavings, the stale bite of the horse's urine, steaming mounds of manure baking in the heat. Precum was leaking from the tip, and I reached out to wipe it away; my fingers burned as they brushed against the swollen, throbbing glans, but rather than pulling back I grabbed hold of his cock in my fist. It was easily twice as thick as my own, I thought, and half again as long. I'd hardly imagined cocks could be that size. "Suck on it," the stablehand commanded, pulling my head towards his crotch. There was no way I could take it, I thought, but as I opened my mouth to protest his cock pushed in and –

I shifted uncomfortably in my jeans, suddenly very aware of my surroundings in the Armory. My cock was stiff as a polo mallet, and feeling far too confined in the Jockey shorts I was wearing for a change. I'd want the support, I knew, once I was on horseback; I hadn't made allowances for getting such a raging hard-on. And staring at the Captain's tight ass in his riding chaps as we followed him to the arena wasn't helping it go away!

There were eleven of us left who'd been interested enough, after listening to the requirements for being on the team, and the commitment we'd have to make if we joined, who were now about to try getting up on horseback. Many had never ridden before, so it was a chance for them to see what it was like, to get used to being astride a living creature. There were only four horses saddled up in the arena, so we took turns getting on and walking around. To keep us humble, if simply staying astride wasn't battle enough we had to walk forward and try to hit a ball. It was hard enough just holding onto the mallet – I rode English, but you had to keep the reins bunched in one hand and neck rein like in Western styles, so that your right hand was free to hold the mallet. And when I tried to hit the ball! It looked so easy when the team did it, but I must've missed by four feet.

I kept guiding my horse around, in tight circles, again and again, trying to hit that damned ball. But I never did. The mallet struck too high or too low or too far to one side. I was really impressing the Captain like this, I told myself each time, trying hard to fight the blush of shame and embarrassment that colored my cheeks.

To my surprise, as I dismounted, the Captain said, "You've got a good seat and you ride well. But you can't hit the ball for shit. Meet me in the practice room at the gym at 6:30."

My heart was beating so hard and loud I couldn't hear my own reply. I must've mumbled something. He hadn't offered anyone else a private lesson, so he must actually see something in me. My cock felt pinched in my Jockey shorts again. I wanted to climb up into the hayloft and jerk off, but I didn't know how to get up there yet. I went into the bathroom, instead. My hand was covered with grime and horsehair but I didn't care; I ran my hand up the inside of my thigh, rubbing the side of my swollen cock which had poked free from the confines of my briefs. I wondered how soon he'd show up; did I have time to go jerk off which would let me concentrate on the lesson at hand? But even if there was time, where? I looked over my shoulder at the tiny window in the door. Even though not many people came all the way down to the end of the corridor, it would be just my luck that someone would.

I dismounted and walked over to the wall to select a mallet. I would practice my swing, to take my mind off my aching cock. If I didn't lose this erection by the time the Captain showed up there'd be no way he couldn't notice it. I chose the longest mallet and climbed back on the wooden horse. I stood up in the stirrups like they'd shown us yesterday and took a swing at an imaginary ball. The mallet cracked against the side of the horse and I winced at the sound. I was glad no one was there to hear that, and also that I wasn't on a real horse! I took another swing and this time managed to avoid hitting the horse, although I still couldn't keep the mallet directed where I wanted it.

Again and again I swung, trying to get accustomed to the heavy weight of that long stick, and its arc as it traveled towards the imaginary ball.

"Your mallet is too long."

I was on the follow-through of a swing and I almost swung myself right over the side of the horse I was so startled by his voice.

I turned around. My heart was beating so fast as I stared at him; he was so damned hot! He was a tall shadow in the dusty light; dark hair, dark skin, and those liquid dark eyes.

So much for having forgotten my erection, I thought, as I twisted back to resume my proper seat and break eye contact.

"I hadn't realized you were there," I muttered.

He walked towards me; I could feel his presence behind me, just beside the horse. He exuded tremendous energy, something sensual that sent an electrical charge through my body. My swollen cock thumped against my leg each time he spoke, vibrating to the timbre of his voice.

"I told you six-thirty. And that was ten minutes ago."

My eyes flicked to meet his; he'd been watching me for ten minutes! I couldn't read anything from his expression, so I looked away, down at my hands in my lap, the reins bunched between them and the mallet jutting off to one side like a giant erection. I let the tip of the mallet dip; it helped to hide my real erection.

He took hold of the mallet and handed me another one. "This is a better size for you." The new stick was half a foot shorter. I leaned over the side of the horse to try and touch the floor, and almost slid off I had to stretch so far.

He laughed, a short, quiet burst of sound. "Much better." I turned to look at him, and he met my stare; I couldn't read him at all, which is part of what I found so sexy about him; he was a cipher.

"You've got to stand up in your seat when you swing."

He offered no more explanation, so I went ahead and tried it, assuming that's what he wanted me to do. I stood up and leaned forward to take a swing. It was much easier to keep the head of the mallet focused where I wanted it to go. I wasn't entirely convinced it was the size of the mallet, however, except the fact that the shorter mallet was as a consequence lighter. I'd just spent a good twenty minutes swinging that first mallet, so I felt some of my skill had simply been my own practice.

I took another swing with the new mallet, and then another. He didn't say anything, just watched me from beneath those dark, brooding eyes. I kept practicing. Occasionally he would comment, in the form of an instruction. "Slow down the swing."

"Lift your arm higher."

"Take off your jeans."

I looked at him, surprised. Had I heard him correctly? My heart was beating so fast I could almost hear it rev; I could hear nothing else. At last, this was the moment I'd been hoping for! Then, why was I hesitating?

I dismounted and looked up at him. He hadn't moved. He was watching me, casually, almost disinterestedly, waiting. But he was watching me.

I stripped down for him, peeling off my chaps slowly, giving him a bit of a show. I undid the buttons of my jeans and remembered suddenly that I'd shaved off all my pubic hair the previous week. What would he think? I worried, as I stripped off my underwear with my pants. As I bent over to step out of each leg my erection was pointing straight at him, so hard it was throbbing like a discotheque. I couldn't believe what I was doing; this was a public gym! What if someone walked past and looked in? But right then, I couldn't care about anything but him and what he wanted from me.

Naked from the waist down, I climbed back atop of the practice horse and stood up in the stirrups, my ass up in the air as it had been when he asked me to take off my pants. My sphincter twitched, anticipating the feel of him sliding into me. I thought of him using his crop as a dildo, thrusting the long black leather whip into me. A bead of pre-cum dripped onto the saddle.

Pain flashed across my buttcheeks!

I spun around, almost falling to the floor before I realized where I was and caught my balance in the stirrups. I sat down and gripped with my knees to keep my seat in the saddle. My ass bumped against the leather, a strip of heat-pain.

He'd whipped me!

"I didn't tell you to take your chaps off," he said.

I dismounted again. He was standing much nearer to me this time, I could feel the closeness of his body making my own respond so strongly. He saw all of me, naked, before him, so obviously desiring him, but he made no move toward me. I had to wonder what he planned to do with me, or to me. Whatever it was, my body wanted it, and was ready for him.

I bent down to pick up my chaps and couldn't help looking

at his basket, which always bulged so prominently I couldn't even tell if he was hard now or not. I climbed back into my leathers, pulling them over my legs. My ass and cock were left bare, and it felt as if a sudden draft snuck through the tiny window, deliciously cold and making me even harder.

I climbed back onto the practice horse and resumed my position in the stirrups, leaning forward over the neck, my ass thrust into the air.

He tapped the inside of my leg with the crop and I tried not to flinch. Slowly, he tapped his way up my inner thigh, sending goosebumps across my skin.

He tapped my balls, on either side, making them swing.

He didn't say anything.

Suddenly the crop was gone. I wanted to turn around and see what he was doing, but I stayed where I was. I strained to hear what he was doing, listening for a rustle of fabric, a footstep, anything, but there was no sound of any sort – I couldn't even hear if he was in the room with me.

There was a rush of movement behind me, and I sat down – right onto his cock. I cried out, unprepared for this impaling; heat flared through my gut. I hadn't even heard him move, not to unzip his pants, or unroll the condom he was wearing, nothing. His cock was long and thin, like his body; it seemed I could feel it inside me, well above my navel.

"Grip with your knees."

I did so, pulling myself up off his cock a few inches. I held there a moment, and then he stood up in the stirrups to slide into me once more, pushing me forward with a grunt. I leaned into the wooded neck before me, wrapped myself around it and held on for dear life. He laced his fingers through my hair and jerked my head aside, so his hot mouth could more easily find mine and forced it open. My jaw ached as his long tongue snaked its way down my throat as he reached under my shirt and seized a nipple between his thumb and forefinger.

I arched my back with the sudden pain. He thrust into me grinding forward. My cock slapped painfully against the polished wood. I reached down and grabbed the reins; I looped the leather cords over my balls so every forward thrust made them tug my cock.

His breath was hot in my ear, pulsing rapidly in horse-like

bursts from his nostrils. I couldn't hold back; I'd been so excited thinking about him for so long, I shot my load onto the horse's neck letting it ooze down the length of the wood. He didn't stop thrusting into me, riding my ass relentlessly, thrusting into me deeper and deeper. My insides felt like they were being torn apart. But he didn't stop, and soon my cock grew hard again with his filling me up.

At last he too came, crying out in a short bark as his body spasmed, then silence. His long cock was still within me, holding me up.

He dismounted, and I slid down against the wooden horse. My ass burned; it twitched against the smooth polished wood. I collapsed against the wooden neck, my cock slicked by my own cum as it slid between my stomach and the wood.

"You've got a good seat," he said, "but you've still got to practice your swing."

ROMANCING THE BONE

Griff Davis

I have spent the better part of my thirty-odd years in pursuit of straight-boy dick, or so it would seem. Now, you've gotta understand that I didn't always look like this. When I was 19, I was a tall, 140-pound, blue-eyed blond with a ready smile, fairly big dick and, most importantly, an eagerness to please.

For instance, one night after getting off work at the music store at University Square Mall, I happened to notice a youth sitting forlornly on the curb by the back entrance with a duffel bag next to him. I zipped over in my 240Z and rolled down the window. I asked him if he was okay. Yeah, he said, he was just waiting for his folks.

"How long you gotta wait?"

"An hour maybe. They got held up."

"Then why don't you get out of the heat?" It was August and even at 9:30 p.m. it was still eighty humid degrees.

At first he was reluctant but I pushed open the door, letting the cold air blast in his face. I slipped a ZZ Top tape in the stereo. The whole car began to vibrate. He shrugged and, wiping the sweat from his forehead, eased himself into the bucket seat.

Still, he held onto the door slightly ajar. We grooved on the music for awhile and exchanged a few pleasantries. He was dressed in a cut-off T-shirt that exposed his hard, hairless stomach, tight denim shorts, and high-top sneakers. He was perfect – without question the cutest young towhead I'd seen in months. In fact, we could easily have been mistaken for brothers.

Finally I asked him if he was hungry. He said he was but he'd spent all his money on games at the mall.

"No problem," I said.

He agreed to go to McDonald's with me, located on the perimeter of the mall's parking lot, and he put his duffel bag behind his seat.

Over hamburgers, I began to share some of my adventures with girls. Over the years I'd managed to fashion a few brief encounters, coupled with a vivid imagination, into a set series of stories that, if true, would have put me in a league with Aly Khan. He was fascinated by my explicit details, offering that he'd come "awful close" to getting some pussy but that was about it.

On the way out of the McDonald's lot, I turned right instead of left and headed for the part of the mall lot that was obscured by trees.

Previous experience had taught me this was an ideal spot to get into some heavy discussions about sex, which is what I proceeded to do once we had parked.

The back entrance was a hundred yards directly in front of us so we could "keep an eye out" for his folks. I explained being parked right at the entrance might cause the security force to worry.

As we sat in the car finishing our Cokes, I went on with my tales of nimble young pussy. As had been the case in the restaurant, the boy, who said his name was Ken, began sprouting a considerable bulge in the crotch of his jeans. I began rubbing my own crotch, saying, "Shit, man, just thinkin' about it gets me hard."

He nodded his head. I reached over and stroked his bulge. "Yeah, I guess so," I said. He brushed my hand away but left his right where mine had been.

I went back to rubbing my swelling cock and finally just unzipped my jeans and took it out. "Oh, that's better," I said.

Eyes bulging, he stared at it, gulped, then looked away.

"Oh, yeah," I said, "when a chick puts her mouth there, god, I get off in nothin' flat. You ever had a real good blowjob?"

"I've come close," he offered, returning his gaze to my throbbing erection.

"Hey, man there's nothin' like it. But most chicks don't know how to do it. They're all teeth."

"Oh?"

Feeling incredibly bold now, I went for it, plunging my hand in his groin, unzipping his jeans and whipping out his boner so fast he didn't have time to protest. "Oh, yeah," I said, "any chick'd love this one."

"You think so?"

"Yeah, this is hot dick, man." I stroked it to full hardness and let it wave in front of him. It was cut, thick, maybe seven inches in length.

"It's not as big as yours," he said, reaching over and taking mine in his hand.

"You're still growin', man," I chuckled, remembering how often I'd used these lines and they always worked.

He sat up and watched my stroking of his cock. Pre-cum formed on the head.

"You say chicks don't know how?"

"Most of 'em," I replied, bringing my mouth over it. "Most of 'em do this – " And I proceeded to nearly bite a piece of it off.

"Eee-ooow," he cried.

"Yeah. Now this is the way, man." As I gave it a good bath with my tongue, then began lovingly nibbling on the head, his hold on my prick intensified. I thought I would come myself from the pressure, but I concentrated on sucking him.

Finally, when I could feel he was nearly ready, I took my mouth from his cock and said, "You wanna try?"

Gasping, he nodded. I lifted up my ass so that he could dive down and put it in his mouth. He was so eager I began to understand that he'd probably been waiting to do this for years.

He licked and nibbled and finally settled in to sucking it the way I had demonstrated.

Only a few moments passed before I was so hot I couldn't hold back and groaned, "Oh, I'm gonna shoot, man."

He didn't lift his head; he stayed right on it, taking the full load down his throat.

"Oh, goddam," I groaned.

"Was that okay?" he asked, lifting his head, cum dribbling from his lips.

"Yeah, man. But you didn't have to swallow it."

"I thought that's what you did."

"Well, yeah, but not always."

"Oh."

Pre-cum was oozing from his prick again and I pushed him back against the door and went down on him once more.

I pressed my thumb against the muscles beneath Ken's hairless scrotum and continued to suck until he was tingling.

He shot in seconds.

I pulled my mouth off it and stroked it while the blast slammed into my face and hair.

"Oh god," he moaned over and over, shaking as if he were having a fit.

"There, see, it's nice to just watch it go off sometimes."

"Oh, yeah," he cried, pushing my head back down in his crotch.

I slipped the sopping prick back into my mouth. It began to harden almost instantly, but then he squealed, "Oh, no, there's my folks."

I looked up over the dash to see a late-model Oldsmobile stop in front of the back entrance. We hurriedly stuffed our cocks back into our jeans and, wiping the cum from my face and hair with a tissue from the box I kept under the front seat, I turned on the ignition. "We should continue your lessons tomorrow."

"Okay."

As I steered the car, I fished through the console for my pad and pen, then realized my last conquest had "appropriated" the pen.

"Nuts," I muttered.

"What?" Ken croaked. He was shaking, obviously fearful of what to expect when we got to the Oldsmobile.

"Oh, I was gonna write down my phone number for you but my pen's gone. Do you think you can remember my number?"

"Sure," he said, growing more visibly anxious with each passing second.

I told him the number and made him repeat it. By that time we were at the Oldsmobile. He flung open the door, reached behind the seat for his duffle bag, then managed a smile. He repeated the phone number and slammed the door.

I nodded at the man behind the wheel of the Oldsmobile, then slowly made my way to the intersection. I turned left; so did the Oldsmobile. I deliberately let them pass me and waved at Ken as they did.

All the way down University Drive, Ken's pretty young face was framed in the back window of his folks' car, illuminated by my headlights. He was grinning from ear to ear.

Sadly, Ken never called me, and in the three more months I worked at the mall, I never saw him there again.

Oh, and the day after my rendezvous with Ken, I ordered some cards with my name and phone number imprinted on them. I learned one thing, if you're going to be "romancing the bone," you gotta be prepared.

To be continued.

BROTHERS

Ken Anderson

"He who wishes more is poor."
– *Seneca*

They were poor, but rich – rich in the fewness of their wants, as the saying goes, their mother, Dixie, raising them on welfare checks and the right amount of insurance left by the father, Cal. They were three years apart – Mat twelve, Willie nine – and so Willie was not as tall as his brother or as rugged of frame. Willie took a paper route, and Mat mowed lawns or cleaned gutters, whatever odd job came up. They could get by very well on the welfare checks, and since it didn't take much to lead a comfortable life in the late Fifties, they never felt deprived or pressed to work.

A fire took the family album. So Willie didn't have the slightest idea what his father had looked like. Mat, however, believed that he could remember him, a tall, gaunt, shadowy figure. At times, his dad's little setbacks seemed more than a story.

The pecan tree Cal had planted in the back yard, the sons were told, had just started bearing when lightning struck it. Though he and Dixie never had a car, the house did have a garage, which Dixie used as a wash shed, putting in beside it a sunny bed of black-eyed Susans. Behind it grew a big fig tree, and Cal had fenced the area as a yard for his beagle, which he took squirrel hunting. But someone, a neighbor, for no reason at all, at least none Dixie could think of, had poisoned the dog. And then there was the ill-fated garden, neat rows of tomatoes, beans, and beets, all washed away when the drainage ditch flooded.

When Cal died, his parents asked if he could be buried in the family cemetery three states over, and Dixie consented, leaving the boys with not even a handy grave to visit. The largest piece of physical evidence of his existence was the remains of a swing between two cedars in the front yard, two uprights and a crossbeam painted white. The swing itself had long since vanished, and the frame looked like an entrance to something, but the two brothers could not quite figure out what.

There was, oddly enough, one old, faded, daguerreotype-looking snapshot of Dixie dating back to a trip to the Ozarks before she married. She was sitting on a rock, her legs crossed at the ankles, her hands folded on her knees. Leaning forward, she seemed to be displaying the large cloth rose on her hat. Her pretty face caught some light among the shadows. She looked young, smug.

Mat and Willie did not look like Dixie. They shared each other's features, what must've been their father's good looks. There were differences, of course. Mat was blondish, Willie brunet, a darker version of his brother with an olive complexion and wavy, dark-brown hair.

Yet for the most part, they were a mirror, an echo, of each other, right down to their pleasant tone of voice. Though slow, even calculated in their movements, they possessed strong physiques and could spring into confident, vigorous action on the field. Both had the creamy skin of youth and thick, glossy hair slicked back with a fragrant tonic. When they were shy, their cheeks colored a faint rose, and all anyone had to do was glance at the healthy glow of their smiles, and he or she could tell that they were obviously very happy together. The homespun cut of their lives suited them well.

Mat was tall, lean, and fair with straight, streaked hair weaving back over his ears. His face was bold with a broad forehead, deep-set, slate-blue eyes, and a long, blunt nose. He had a strong jaw, already sprinkled with light stubble, and large, pink, eloquent lips usually drawn back just enough to suggest a pensive smile. Because of his bemused expression, he always seemed pleased with, yet somewhat puzzled by, everything.

Like his brother, Willie was long, lean, and remarkably serene for someone as young. To enhance the resemblance, he aped his brother's poses and glances so that in time they seemed inseparable in the least detail of their stance and moods. They had a way of staring at the ground when troubled or embarrassed, of glancing from under their eyebrows, hands in pockets, when amused or receptive, of crimping the forehead, hands clasped behind their backs, when surprised or skeptical. They even had their own way of touching their lips thoughtfully, the left hand on the hip, or, a jacket slung over a shoulder, looking to the right or left with sadness, scorn, or desire.

The pose Willie copied the most was keeping his hands in his pockets. The gesture seemed to indicate that he was faithfully waiting for someone, usually Mat. As always, whatever Mat wanted was fine with him. Even his happiest moments, though, were even quieter, more philosophical than Mat's. He'd clasp his hands in front of his chest, curving his lips in a big, flower-like grin.

They not only looked alike and acted alike in many ways. Of necessity, they also shared a certain simplicity of taste in clothes, with Willie wearing Mat's somewhat frayed, yet fastidiously clean hand-me-downs. Mat really only had one decent outfit to wear on special occasions – a pair of dark-blue, wide-wale corduroy pants with a matching dark-blue, oversized cotton shirt so old, to tell the truth, he'd slip it on gingerly. On the rare occasions when he did try to dress up, he always buttoned the shirt to the neck, a habit which he thought not only looked good, but also gentlemanly. But his favorite item was a generous melton jacket that had belonged to his dad. He wore it with a wool scarf and, glancing up mischievously, felt very grown up. Of course, to roust about in, he had his favorite pair of faded jeans and a big, loose T-shirt.

Willie didn't like dressing up any more than Mat did, but what he felt most comfortable in when he did, though the outfit was humble enough, was a cuffed jersey, a brown cardigan, and a pair of flat-front cotton trousers. His narrow alligator belt, like Mat's jacket, had belonged to his dad. When he did wear a shirt, he'd button it at the neck, like Mat, and for cold weather, he had a roomy sweater which his mother had patched in the elbows. The boys each owned a pair of lace shoes, which they polished often, repairing them for years.

At about the same time, it occurred to them that they were, in fact, brothers, two sprouts from the same seed, and because each identified physically with the other, he identified with him mentally and emotionally as well, treating him as he would himself, with consideration. They were unusually aware of each other's thoughts and feelings, fears and thrills, their internal bleeding, as it were, as well as the moments of great joy when their oneness healed. In short, they felt drawn to each other. They felt a growing love, but did not know why, not quite, giving themselves up to the feeling because, whatever its source, the love itself, as all love was, was good.

At school once, a bully slugged Willie, knocking him to the ground, then dared him to get up, rearing over him defiantly like the statue of the horse in Mat and Willie's bedroom. In a daze, Willie touched his upper lip, then stared at the blood on his fingertips. From nowhere, Mat appeared, like a great shadow, scaring the thug. Willie had never seen such fierce lightning flash from his brother's eyes.

Since Willie was mature for his age, he and Mat shared certain close friends, handsome, moody boys like themselves. Oscar was a powerful Nordic type with fair skin, a scruffy hat, and hair like spun gold. He was also, as Mat put it, big on the vine, which no one could help but notice – he could hardly hide it – and he was both proud of and embarrassed by the endowment. He played trumpet in the school band and could be heard murdering scales over and over again in the evening.

Brett was a freckled, square-faced, Irish youth who liked baseball better than anything, despite the fact he'd walked behind the batter one day and the boy had hit him, full swing, knocking him out. The knot on his head was as big as a baseball.

But for some reason, Mat and Willie felt closest to Drew, a slim, brooding, droop-shouldered boy with long, flaxen hair. Dixie had a reputation for being weird, but fun, on coffee, but Drew's mother was really crazy, yelling at him and hitting him all the time, and so he never had much to say, following them around like a lonesome, tuck-tail dog. He was partially deaf, often misunderstanding them, and, because he'd broken his leg falling from a tree, walked with a slight limp. Though the gang might make fun of him at times, they defended him from other kids and, otherwise, were kind to a fault.

When younger, they all liked to play in the drainage ditch behind Mat and Willie's house. Sudsy with Duz, it ran through a thick canebrake, which they pretended was a jungle. Since he had the best physique, Oscar always got to play Tarzan, King of the Jungle, beating his chest and yodeling "A-E-O" in a secret code. The others echoed in turn.

The canes concealed a clearing, which they used as a den, lying about in the leaves, and once, with the birds flitting and twittering among the stalks of bamboo, they talked about the future. Oscar wanted to be a jazz musician, Brett a baseball player, of course, and Drew a doctor, he guessed.

"I want to cure my momma," he joked, sullen.

Mat didn't know, but when Oscar asked Willie what he wanted to be, he surprised everyone by saying, "Mat's brother."

On Halloween the boys used the garage, Dixie's wash shed, as a Spook House, charging kids a penny, but they had to be under nine. Under the roof was a platform, a sort of half-completed ceiling, from which certain amazing effects could be achieved. Pieces of cardboard flapped through the air. A table rose. A voice from the dark foretold.

Strangely enough, when older, none of the boys had the slightest desire to drink or smoke cigarets. Cokes and candy bars were the worst of their vices. At home, they did chores and homework, and on weekends they still liked hanging around together, playing football or baseball at school or on the weedy field behind the abandoned church. Sometimes they could all be seen riding their bikes in a row over to the willow-lined river. The neighborhood was bounded to the south by railroad tracks, to the west by the school, to the north by the refinery, and to the east by a highway. In one direction, the road led toward the river – in the other, downtown. For all of their youth, the boys wouldn't roam much farther.

All of their homes were modest enough, but they met at Mat and Willie's more, mainly because they had more fun there, playing in the garage and out back. But what the brothers liked about the house most, other than the relative privacy of the back bedroom, had nothing to do with the others. The house was graced with two big porches, front and back, where they could sit at night with Dixie, talking and taking the air. On the front porch sprawled a metal couch and chairs, and Willie as a child had played with his Lincoln Logs among them, clasping his hands with delight at the cabins he built. The floor was made of clay tiles which looked like a scattered puzzle. The back porch was screened, and when the bugs were bad or a good thunderstorm approached, they'd all roost there, watching the sky twinkle or crack and roar with tremendous fireworks.

Mat and Willie's room was messy but comfortable, furnished in a heavy, yet light-colored maple which gave the room a warm, bright look, all that a pair of growing boys could want – sturdy twin beds, a chest of drawers, a dresser with a mirror. A couple of tables with lamps and chairs served as desks for schoolwork. On Willie's table, there was a bronze statue of a cowboy on a bucking bronco, a copy of a Remington. Amid his books, papers, and pencils lay scattered several pocket knives, tiny stereopticons with their goofy school pictures, and a colorful clutter of bubble-gum wrappers. Often a filmy glass, a saucer with cake crumbs, and a smudged fork teetered on a corner of Mat's desk. Throw rugs splotched the hardwood floor, serving as soft stepping stones on cold mornings.

A little wood box sat at the back of Willie's table, and when Willie was out, sometimes Mat would stand, his hands in his pockets, peering into its jumble as if into his brother's meek soul. There were Willie's favorite marbles; a wrestling medal with a blue ribbon that Mat had given him; four gold studs, some collar stays, and an old signet ring of their father; various worn-looking cufflinks and a tie pin from when they had gone to Sunday school; a little green scarab with mysterious Egyptian markings (as a girl Dixie had visited a museum in Chicago); small, handsome, broken stones; safety pins and needles; watch entrails; pennies which Willie, on impulse, had cut and twisted into odd shapes.

The room was at the end of the hall, on the other side of the bath from their mother's, so that they could talk late at night, even cut up and laugh, without waking her. Besides, they knew she wouldn't mind. They understood how hard it was raising them alone and treated her so well she'd never have thought of complaining about their youthful exuberance, let alone entering without knocking and calling out. To say the least, she respected their privacy. She knew that boys had secrets.

Besides the privacy, one of the most distinctive features of the room was the virtual scent box of intimate, adolescent smells-- a potpourri of odors from the mussed sheets, their jeans and T-shirts draped on chairs, the tumble of their boots and athletic shoes on the floor of the closet. Sometimes the room smelled of balsam and glue from model planes. Sometimes they'd leave out the wax polish and shoe brush, and the curtains breathed a musty odor which reminded Willie of gourds.

The coziest places in the room, of course, were the beds, where at night, within reach of each other, Mat and Willie usually slept soundly. There were no headboards, and during the day, they'd prop against the wall, reading a book, making a model, or just listening to records – the wrinkled, yellow wallpaper, with its faded cowboy pattern, dark with the stains of their oily hair tonic.

When little, Willie would sometimes climb into his brother's bed at night, slipping beside him under the sheet. During cold snaps, the floor furnace in the hall breathed forth a swaying ghost, visible waves of heat, and Willie would fly across the gulf between the beds, curling into the crook of Mat's arm. The Tooth Fairy also worried him a lot. Willie had pictured her as a cripple crawling out of the floor to grab his feet. Finally, Mat had to explain that it was he himself who left the quarter.

When older, Willie frequented Mat's bed for other reasons perhaps not all that different, though the bed was certainly too narrow for them. Sometimes, though his covers were toasty warm, they could not match the smoldering fire of Mat's body. The room stood at the northwest corner of the house, taking the brunt of winter, and on nights when gusts moaned at the screens, he'd go to him, and Mat would take him in, his arms stretched out to him, or, sound asleep, simply move over. Once Willie woke from a bizarre dream to find himself embraced by Mat like a lover as Mat slept, snoring lightly. In the dream, the rearing bronze horse, a hundred times bigger, had kicked him in the face, flipping his head onto Mat's pillow.

But the worst nights were those when he'd wake terribly afraid, even then, of life without Mat. It was on those nights, with the shadows flitting like bats just beneath the ceiling, that he'd hold his brother tight, longing for some emotional guarantee from him, some ironclad insurance policy against the great loneliness of life.

At an early age, Willie had become very aware of his own mortality. Drew, the timid one, had drowned one Christmas, taking a shortcut across a frozen lake. They had all been skating at a farmer's pond, all, that is, except Willie. He had no skates, but enjoyed watching Mat and the others. Hands in his pockets, he stamped for warmth, smiling.

Without talking, the others would glide around the pond, scarring the ice, making a grating sound incredibly clear in the silence. The brown reeds drooped, laden with snow, and the sun had begun to slip behind a row of glistening trees. As it grew dark, Willie helped Mat off with the skates and on with his brogans, lacing one up as Mat laced the other. Then they all headed home, except Drew, who, because of a joke about his long hair, veered off alone. The stars blinked on, and a covy of quail startled Willie, bursting from the tall grass near his foot.

Later that night the police knocked, and the next day they found him. Willie imagined the shattered mirror of the ice, Drew's eyes, agates of fear, his flaxen hair billowing in the murky water. Where Drew had been, only a vague, unremarked mist.

Willie's own brush with death was a groggy bout with pneumonia. He got chills, though buried under blankets, and his teeth chattered. The room spun, and though he wasn't rolling off the bed, sometimes he felt as if he were. During the worst of the delirium, he dreamed about riding up and down on the macabre horses of a silent merry-go-round.

By chance, Brett had been the spark that lit his interest in sex, but what small amount Willie knew about it he, of course, had learned mainly from his brother. In class, Brett had passed a smeary sketch of someone who, though Willie had never seen a naked girl, he knew could not be anatomically correct, and his teacher, a mousy spinster, had crumpled it, glaring at him. Later, Willie would see a word painted in white on a rusty barrel behind the auditorium, and the next morning, as Mat was shaving, he asked him about it. Mat smiled, then squeezed his Jockey shorts.

"It means sticking *this* in someone."

"In someone," Willie murmured. "Where?"

"In someone's ass."

Something Willie had never thought of. But a strange thrill shot through his body, a feeling akin to what he felt whenever he saw Mat's grownup member dangling from his pants or Oscar's huge one or even the callow birds of the other boys. When Mat left, Willie stood on the side of the tub, gazing into the basin mirror, staring at his fledgling privates, then, spreading his cheeks, the pink bud of his anus. He tried to imagine Mat in there or Oscar or the Italian barber to whom Mat took him.

Willie liked getting his hair cut, though he knew most kids hated it. The barber was young and lean with slicked-back hair and a jaw shaved smooth, though dark with beard, and close, he smelled of a sweet, yet masculine, cologne. He had a cool but tender way of touching Willie to turn his head, to tilt it down or up or slightly to the side, and to Willie, his voice was a marvelous male music.

The shears would whirr, the scissors snip, and Willie would shyly peek at himself and the barber in the endlessly receding perspective of the big, round mirrors on the walls – Willie in the chair with a bride-white bib and the barber very suave behind him, scissors and comb poised. Willie recognized the same strong attraction, the same strange exhiliration he felt for Mat. When his elbow touched the barber's thigh, sometimes his crotch, the impulse always was to reach out and hold him.

Willie never felt that way about girls. He and Mat had double-dated to Mat's junior high school prom, but the date didn't work out well as far as Willie was concerned. They'd bought their dates corsages, clumps of yellow mums, but even though Willie couldn't dance very well, his date, Billie Jean, was worse, clumsily stepping on his toes. Once at a party, everyone played spin-the-bottle, and when Mat twirled the coke bottle, it eventually pointed to a girl named Barbara. Instead of just kissing her, Mat looked as if he were trying to eat her face, and Willie wondered what the hell was going on.

One day Willie asked, and since they were brothers, Mat showed him how to masturbate. A couple of nights later, Mat fell asleep aroused, and Willie approached him, taking him in his hand. And so playing with each other became a natural part of their growing up together, a wonderful secret they, blushing, shared with no one, for they knew almost instinctively that their stolen moments of pleasure – a pleasure sweeter than Dixie's meringue – was also a great taboo.

At first, Mat had experienced a few qualms about his feelings, satisfying himself in the bathroom, eventually responding humbly to Willie's, if not his own, tender needs. Then he and

Willie took full advantage of the immediate gratification each offered, exploring each other, giving and taking glowing moments of pleasure.

Willie had a mole about the size of a penny on his right buttock, and once when they cuddled, Mat's front to Willie's back, Mat made fun of it, drawing a circle around it with his finger. When he tentatively, mischievously cupped Willie's cheek, Willie's cock popped up, hard.

One night Willie woke to find his cock stiff in Mat's hand. They were embraced like spoons, and Mat had reached around him girding him, to play with his cock. Mat's cock prodded his cheeks, but since the position felt good, Willie let him, and as Mat quietly pumped him, poking the tight knot of his anus again and again, they came at the same time.

About the fifth time Matt dry-humped him, the knot slipped, and Mat's cock slid all the way up Willie's ass. Mat carefully rolled him onto his stomach, then held him in a full nelson. The submission implied in his positions excited Willie since he trusted his brother and his trust allowed him to try new thrills. As Mat's cock rubbed Willie's prostate, Willie's cock dry-fucked the sheet, shooting at the same time. And so all of the sensual joys became a natural part of their growing up together.

If fucking him didn't bring Willie off, Mat would turn him on his side and, with his cock stuck in his ass, jerk him off firmly, yet gently, working him like a control stick, guiding him through ecstatic clouds to the sun.

Sometimes satisfying Willie would excite Mat all over again, and he'd have to have him twice, their arms and legs lashed together like vines. Willie gladly obliged, relaxing and enjoying the deep, soothing strokes, their feelings gathering and flowing together, one.

Sometimes Mat would suck the head of Willie's cock as he jerked him off, and almost immediately Willie would shoot a string of sweet, milky come in his mouth. Since Mat wanted to make sure he pleased his brother, he soon learned how to take him deep in his throat and satisfy him there, his lips clasped tightly and affectionately around the base of his shaft, like Willie's ass around his. He'd hold him in his mouth for a long time, savoring the musky smells, his nose pressed into the nest of soft hair. Afterward, they'd smile blissful, grateful smiles,

smiles beautiful as Dixie's black-eyed Susans, then snuggle, drifting into a mutually mellow sleep.

Once they fell asleep embraced like spoons in Willie's bed, and Dixie, having called out, entered the room, but since she was an innocent woman, thought nothing of the gentle, peaceful scene. She was proud of how Mat loved and protected Willie. After all, there were only the three of them, and Mat was the man of the house. It was obvious that Willie adored his brother, and she attributed their perfect manners to the great harmony between them.

In high school, the good-natured Oscar replaced Drew as their best friend. Blonder than Mat, he wore an old homburg all the time, his golden locks flaming from the sides. They undressed and showered together in gym, and he stood out like a stallion in the herd of lanky boys. Sometimes at the river, they stripped and dove in, horsing around until all of them showed admirable erections. Blackberry bushes lined one bank, and Willie remembered vividly the red nicks, like little roses, on Oscar's thigh as, muscles flexing, he reached among the brambles. Willie and Mat glanced at each other, then continued picking and eating handfuls of the ripe, purple fruit. Nude, scratched, their mouths and hands stained, they looked like fierce, but happy aborigines.

Sometimes Oscar would stay over, having dinner, then sleeping with them in their room, taking Willie's bed. He thought nothing of walking in on them in the bathroom and peeing, his heavy, thick-veined member casually lolling from the wisps of hair on his groin. And while one of them bathed, he could sit on the side of the tub, talking endlessly about band practice or loose girls or geometry homework.

One night as a thunderstorm raged, Oscar woke and, turning, studied Mat and Willie as they lay embraced asleep. As long as he'd known them, he could hardly help noticing how well they worked together, as a team, though hardly aware they were working at all, whether folding papers on the front porch, fixing a bike in the yard, or running an end-around, and in public, they'd never been evasive about their great affection for each other-- in fact, open and honest. And so deep in his heart, Oscar, too, wished he had a brother, especially one as good and true as Mat. He envied the way Mat turned down his little brother's collar or bought him a chocolate ice cream or the way Willie bucked up his big brother when he'd failed a test, paying his way to "Wagonmaster" or "The Searchers" or some other western at the matinee.

What Oscar didn't know, of course, was the precise effect he had on them. Willie flipped the downs at scrimmages, shifting the sideline markers with the plays. Pitted against Oscar, Mat would tackle him, crushing him as they groaned and laughed on the ground, and sometimes after football practice, or when the two or three had tangled, wrestling in the gym or ducking each other in the cool river, Mat would take Willie long, yet even more tenderly that night, imagining that Oscar lay beneath him.

Willie, of course, knew who he was when Mat would arouse, then ravish him, caressing his face and kissing him fondly when they came, and yet Mat's exquisite tenderness always balanced out what Willie thought of as his brother's greater, more urgent needs. Besides, more than once as Mat labored above him, Willie saw Drew's dreamier eyes gazing down at him.

But Mat could tell, despite the way they horsed around, Oscar was simply not, and never would be, interested in him the way Willie was. To have broached the subject in deed or word would've mortified both. The attraction was strong, but he had Willie, and gradually he realized it was better not to see Oscar as much, especially in intimate circumstances. He'd only frustrate himself. Besides, Oscar's parents had the money to send him to the university, which was far away, and Mat knew that after graduation, they'd see each other, if at all, only three or four times a year.

So Oscar, or even the wistful memory of Drew, never challenged Mat and Willie's faith in each other. The brothers automatically sorted it from their fantasies, the gold from the gravel, as if fasting with Oscar whetted Mat's appetite for Willie, at times made him insatiable, or Willie's feelings for Drew could reveal themselves in loving Mat. Such friendships sweetened their lives.

So many new and complicated feelings, however, proved almost too much for Mat's already shaky high school career, though Willie, of course, helped him with his homework. Mat was not a very good student, not because he was actually dull, but because, having few aspirations, he never tried. Why should he struggle to reach some high goal when he could simply reach out to Willie and he'd come to him without a word? At first, he couldn't understand his brother's slavish devotion, but since he indulged in it, even wept over it – the grimace of grief hardly distinct from the rapt orgasmic grin – he finally quit wondering about it, accepting it for the mystery it was, love.

Willie, on the other hand, tried to learn as much as he could at school and generally succeeded, bringing home a decent report card. For him, there was no conflict between his desire for Mat and his need to excel, to rise above their modest beginning. Besides, he feared the hazards of life, the uncertainties of the future. Grades, a job, financial prospects – such practical considerations were a stay of some vague threat assembling on the horizon. He could imagine a life without Mat, yes, but a lonely one in which he'd have to survive as best he could, adjusting quickly to the curves life threw him, inventing ways to step from day to day.

One of the first curves life threw him came zipping past soon after Mat's graduation. One day Willie noticed Mat's class ring next to their dad's signet ring in the wooden box, and it was obvious from the angelic expression on Willie's face and the tenderness of his kiss that he regarded the ring as a solemn pledge. Then Mat got on at the refinery, as his father had, and moved out, taking a small, furnished apartment.

"I love you. You know that," Mat chuckled, open and honest as always. "More than anything else in the world. Even Mom," he added, ashamed. "But I'm grown-up! I want to live on my own. To, at least, try to fit in! You can understand that, can't you?"

"Sure," Willie said, hands in his pockets. "Who wants 'is kid brother hangin' around?"

"I feel chained to this – "

"Me?" Willie asked.

"Us!"

Since Mat had moved out, a curious pressure had been building in Willie's chest, a terrible feeling he feared would never go away. It grew and grew so that he believed, if he couldn't stop it, something awful would happen. He'd explode somehow. He'd shout and go mad. He wanted to turn it off, but didn't know how. If he could only sleep, he thought, he could block it out, at least for a while. He understood why people killed themselves.

"Mat, please," he asked. "You caught me off guard."

Mat touched his lips, his left hand on his hip. He looked as if he were peering at some wiggly snake in a well.

He'd gone on a few dates with a girl whose name was spelled Cel, pronounced Seal, short for Celia. She had a pretty, oval face, pearl earrings, which she wore all the time, as well as a grey ribbon she used to tie up her hair. They'd sit in the balcony of the movie theater, and he'd kiss her neck, her face, her lips, slipping a hand under her brassiere to feel the full, soft flesh of her breasts, her firm nipples. He knew that he could never really care for her the way he did for Willie, but wanted to explore her, anyway, to see what she was like. He was happy with Willie, but sex was sex, or so he thought, and he toyed with the idea of one day settling down with her, or some woman, and raising a family.

He heated and served a couple of frozen dinners at his new place one night and afterward, on the couch, felt her thigh, then straining against her undergarments, the warm, gluey place he wished to pierce. But she wore a girdle, she said, not because she was fat – she wasn't – but because she didn't want to get pregnant.

At that point, Willie showed up, and Mat, of course, knew why, and that night Willie gave himself to his brother with a muscular ardor poor Cel had never dreamed of, reaching into the inmost depths of his soul to show Mat not only the blinding light of his love, but also an incomparable sensuality.

With more difficulty this time, Mat imagined Willie as someone else, Cel, trying to piece together like a puzzle the pale breasts, the welcome cleft, himself attached flush and secure within her. He took the intense pleasure Willie offered, but not in any thoughtless, mercenary, or cruel way. He loved his brother and, therefore, would never hurt him, and so he let him stay that night and the next and the next out of a compelling sympathy for him, telling Cel, the one other time he saw her, little of his reasons for breaking off. In reality, for Mat and Willie to have remained apart would have pained both unbearably. Nothing in life would ever match their rare bond.

"Sorry, Willie," Mat apologized, his forehead wrinkled, his hands behind his back.

"That's OK."

"Life's not gonna be easy," he explained, pacing, glancing over his shoulder. "Thought I could handle it better alone. You know, one less to worry about."

"Thought I'd be better off, didn't you?" Willie asked. "Weren't thinking of yourself at all."

"Don't worry about it, buddy."

"No harm done."

"Won't leave you again. I swear." Then he added, smiling sweetly, "Should've moved to another town, huh? Another state."

Willie stroked Mat's face, then said, "We ever gonna get a double bed?"

As it turned out, the flirtation with Cel only drew Mat and Willie closer. It was a test they'd passed, a pain soothed. Alone, they now had the leisure to experiment sexually and, though they explored D & S for a while, dominance and submission, never once violated the bond of trust between themselves whether in bed or in the matter of their great fidelity. Mat would tie up Willie with rope, at times even taping his mouth with a wide piece of adhesive, so that as he lay stripped and helpless on the floor, he became, as bound hostage, a stark image of his staunch devotion to Mat, and hooked inside him, Mat covered him with his fervor in return, folding him into himself in a fierce access of possession. Willie's ropes freed his love, kept him from holding back even if he'd wanted to. Mat's hands, through mastery of his instrument, achieved sublime effects.

At times, a kiss would do.

As a matter of course, Mat and Willie followed different lines of work. Willie went to a small college across town and became an elementary-school teacher, slowly building a secret investment in stocks and bonds. Sometimes he wondered if his job were a case of regression, a retreat from the world, but he was a good teacher, always patient and encouraging, and his students were fond of him. After a time, he became a teaching principal at the school and, when offered a job with the board of education, refused because he knew he'd be happier in the classroom and on the playground.

Mat was a welder at the refinery, then because of his dependability, a safety inspector. Management had rarely seen anyone so thorough and loyal, but when they offered him an office job, he, like Willie, balked. Early on, the two had more than enough money for some place better, but continued to live in the small apartment. Its intimacy nurtured their intimacy. Later, especially as Willie's portfolio appreciated, work was what they did to pass the time between what they really lived for, each other's arms.

Over the years, the one machine they'd become became even more finely tuned, gliding quietly through life, like the new cars they bought – Mat a Falcon and Willie a Corvair. In fact, the only real difference between them at home and in public was the extra physical bond they shared. Willie got home earlier than Mat and would prepare his meal and do his laundry just as Mat had for him when Dixie was sick or away. Mat, being the more mechanical of the two, looked after the cars. On weekends, they would work out together at home or hunt and fish, sometimes sleeping near the river or in a clearing under the stars. And it was only appropriate that their oneness at heart was reflected in their striking physical appearance. Mat grew more clean-cut, Willie more rugged, evening out, as they aged, the family resemblance.

Living in the same town with her, Mat and Willie naturally had kept in close contact with Dixie, who, with the boys out of the house, seemed pretty much at sea. At first, they'd suggested dating, but she wouldn't out of loyalty to Cal. So they paid her a visit from time to time, especially on holidays, when, instead of the usual red beans and rice, she served pot roast, rice and gravy, potato salad, and lemon meringue pie. Dixie would go to the hutch and bring out a soft, white tablecloth, then the china and silverware, but those formal moments had a way of spooking Willie. He felt more comfortable, as they all did, in the kitchen.

Then Dixie's mind began to go, Willie thought from all the loneliness, and on one of Mat's visits, it took her a second, when she opened the door and he held her, to recognize him.

Mat took most of the responsibility for checking on her. For some reason, Willie couldn't face her failing health without Mat by his side. She had acquired a few older friends, who were good for her, Willie knew, but they always depressed him, deriding or making much of their own sons, rattling on about a husband's death, a broken hip, a stolen purse. Dixie sipped Sanka now – doctor's orders – yet had taken up Lucky Strikes.

Occasionally, the brothers would stay overnight, making love in the back room with a sweet, wistful flair. At breakfast, Mat would read the newspaper aloud because Dixie was coming down with cataracts. A light frost had begun to steal across her eyes. To deepen Willie's depression, Dixie, smiling, would talk to him as if he were still fifteen, and sometimes she dreamily referred to Mat as Cal.

At night, she'd lock, then prop a chair against the door, then light a cigaret, blowing the smoke, Willie thought, as if to silhouette some familiar presence, perhaps Cal's. He didn't know, was afraid to ask. She'd leave on a lamp, check her keys, then, sheepish, forget where she was going. The precautions were simply the wise thing to do, and yet there was, curiously, always an easy air about her, as if she knew, despite the situation, some wonderful secret, some sure sign that all was basically well. Willie doubted how aware she was of her own plight.

On one visit, Willie couldn't sleep, and so he got up and sat in the window, nude, bathed in moonlight. He thought of the moon as an old freighter bound for some remote celestial port and wondered where he and Mat were going and for what purpose. Then he decided it didn't matter. Wherever they were going, they were going together. Then he noticed a wasp nest, like a grey flower, on the eaves. He picked up his watch and looked at it. A minute later, he picked it up, looking at it again. A few feet away, Mat snored lightly.

Though she protested, they bought Dixie a television, but overall the gift seemed only to hasten her decline. She'd sit, happy, staring at it all day, but at night she never sat on the porch or even looked outside. She'd lounge, drowsy, stretched out on the couch, or, drug dull, labor serenely from room to room till, fed and tired, she slept. Sometimes Willie would cry about her, but neither seemed willing to move back, nor did they think she wanted them to, though all she had to talk about was having raised them, the crowning achievement of her life.

Once on the way home from Dixie's, Mat stopped at a different filling station and realized that the raw-faced man who pumped his gas was drawn to him with the same deep, inexplicable longing as his brother's. Standing by the car, Mat stared at him unashamedly – the soiled uniform, the quizzical grimace in the glare, the way he solicitously leaned over the fender, as if his physical connection with the car were, in fact, a form of intimacy. He was not much older than Mat and wore a wedding band.

The man replaced the nozzle on the pump and the cap on the car as if in a daze, taking Mat's money with undue sadness. For a second, the two stood near each other quietly, the traffic raising a din around them.

Then the older man asked, "Check yer oil?"

"Sure," Mat responded.

The man wiped his fingers on a rag, then extended his hand. "Name's Mort."

"I'm Mat," he said, shaking hands.

They released each other's hand, and Mat gazed at the splotches of grease and oil on the pavement – his left hand in his pocket, his right feeling the soft pleats of his cotton trousers.

"Mat and Mort," the man pondered, straining to grin. "Drop by. I'll give 'er a good tuneup."

And Mat did drop by, but not for a tuneup. A week later, as Mort was closing up, Mat pulled up not to a pump or into the garage, but beside the men's room, and when Mort stepped inside, Mat followed, locking the door. As soon as the door closed, they were hidden in darkness, a quiet obscurity interrupted only by the sigh of close breathing, the occasional rasp of a car on the street. Though he couldn't see Mort, Mat could feel him, his body heat. He could smell the rank sweat of his fear, the traces of oil and gas on his clothes. Then tentatively, respectfully, a pair of hands began to fumble with Mat's belt buckle.

A month went by, and since Mort built homes as well, they met in an empty house, and Mat let him make love to him in the blue light streaming through a window. Strangely enough,

Mat most enjoyed their first tremulous moments together, the way the man unbuttoned Mat's shirt, then kissed his chest, his nipples, the chiseled dip of his groin as he knelt before him. For Mat knew that, despite the thrill, the brief slavery of the man's passion, or for that matter anyone else's, would never be as true and fine and as genuinely joyous as Willie's. Thinking of Willie, he wondered why he was standing there at all, his hands behind his back, peering at the tousled head.

Eventually, Mat reciprocated, and the tables turned so that soon Mat only made love to him. Yet the man's moodiness never went away no matter how long and hard Mat worked to please him, satisfying himself as he clasped the man's thigh, took the man's cock deep in his throat. Afterward, Mort would stand in the dark, shaking, a hand to his forehead, his pants around his ankles.

Sex with Mort was sadness – with Willie, bliss.

"What am I thinking of?" Mat wondered. "How could I hurt such a sweet boy?"

For that is how he always thought of Willie, as a boy.

Was he making him jealous to stoke the fire? Stoke, hell. Their love was a sea of flames.

Though Mat had not found Mort particularly attractive, he'd let him make love to him because, alone with him, he was aroused, as with Willie, by the magnitude of the man's desire. He'd returned the gesture because he felt guilty about using him. As with Cel, he knew that he could not really care for Mort, and whether Mat's lust was finally slaked or curbed by a sense of shame, he decided, without telling him, not to see Mort anymore, simply not showing up one night, though he felt sorry for him – he seemed so lonely – and wished him well.

"I'm not gonna see 'im anymore," he told Willie, chucking him on the shoulder.

Willie clasped his hands in front of his chest, smiling thoughtfully. Though aware of the affair from the beginning, he'd never changed one detail of their domestic tranquility, one dovelike moan of their love. He somehow knew unquestionably that their love was not only good and warm and precious as Cal's clothes, but also inevitable, no matter what anyone thought, even themselves. They were how love had come to each other. They had to love each other. All they had was to love each other. But that was enough.

Ten years went by like a week, and Dixie died from a stroke – all things considered, perfectly content with her life and the two fine sons she'd raised. With her death, Mat saw that he, too, was alone, something Willie had tried to explain all along. After the funeral, it was Willie, however, who begged Mat never to leave, but in his heart Mat knew he needed Willie just as much, if not more.

Another "week" went by, and their rapport refined itself, sifting itself more and more from the coarse chaff of the flesh, from the petty concerns of people, until they achieved as perfect a thing as can be in this world – perfect love.

Their bodies aged, but time didn't matter, a day, a year, since their hearts never changed, never grew older. Mat's mind clouded, but late at night as they lay together dreaming or in some quiet corner of the day as they sat and talked, the sun broke through, and Mat remembered, as Willie always had, their first few moments of sweet discovery. Again, he kissed the penny on Willie's cheek, God's penny. Again, he carefully rolled his brother onto his stomach. Again, he pressed his finger deep into the warm, moist seam....

Then it was as if the sun itself were a cloud drifting aside to reveal another sun a million times brighter, and Mat remembered even farther back in time. He and Willie were building a snowman in the front yard, a kind of makeshift father with button eyes, a carrot nose, and sticks.

Mat looked beyond that moment, even farther back in time. He stooped, peering under the house, where Willie was playing in the dirt with his colorful trucks and cars.

"But I am cleaned up," Willie said, smiling, yet concerned, and Mat woke, realizing he'd been dreaming again.

He also realized that, despite the different cut of it, he'd always felt very comfortable in his life and that, with loving care, his brother had in his as well. They'd struck a deal early on, and Mat had pretty much lived up to it – in some higher sense, adhered to it to a T.

The day after Mat's funeral, Willie bought a gun and that night, lying in bed, shot himself. He was wearing his father's belt and Mat's ring, of course, and he'd pinned Mat's athletic medal to his shirt, then left a note with strict instructions he was to be buried next to his brother. And a strange thing happened despite all the usual cross-purposes of the world – he was.

At night, Mat and Willie still turned to each other, and Dixie, just a few feet away, dreamed on innocently. But a change took place. Since their bodies were no longer in the way, the brothers' souls got mixed up when they made love, as souls will even among the living. Mat's soul would enter Willie's and Willie's would surround Mat's over and over till they both shone with a golden light. When Willie or Mat would return to his grave, he'd find he'd become more of the other, till at last they could not tell themselves apart, sleeping as one, embraced forever.

PLEASE, TEACH ME MORE

Bert McKenzie

My roommate volunteered to man the gay rap line. It was a worthwhile cause and I admired him for it. The rap line was a phone line that was staffed by volunteers and provided an information clearing house and volunteer counseling option for people who called in with questions about the gay community.

Callers were seeking information about bars, churches or events in our area, or calling to ask questions about a lifestyle they knew little about, or wanting to talk because they had just discovered their own sexuality, or uncovered that of someone close to them, be it a son or daughter, spouse or friend – even a parent.

Ben was a psych major at the local university, and thought he would be doing something very noble by working the rap line. Unfortunately, it didn't turn out that way. When a volunteer was selected, the phone was forwarded to his home number so he could take calls into the night without having to journey to an office. This ensured that there would be a number of volunteers and that they could use their own phones but with complete anonymity. Well, Ben used our phone in a way that was certainly not intended by the founders of the rap line. If he got a curious virgin on the line who thought he might be gay, Ben would arrange a meeting and used the rap line to get dates. When I found this out I made him quit the rap line by threatening to turn him in.

I found out the hard way, by coming home one night and catching him in the middle of a young man, still obviously in his teens. The frightened boy bolted and Ben confessed everything to me, making me promise not to tell on them. He was genuinely more concerned for the feelings of his young partner than for his own legal and ethical problems.

Ben knew my interest in young men. In fact, I often commented and lusted over cute boys, barely out of their teens, and some still in their teens. I was an admitted chicken hawk, but one that would never act on such impulses. I was very conscious of legal ramifications to such actions. Nevertheless, this didn't stop me from dreaming about nubile young boys, sucking and fucking with me. Ben and I had often talked about such things and commented on some street tough we might see walking down the boulevard in tight cut-offs and a baseball cap, but nothing more.

After I got Ben to agree to quit the rap line, he made me an offer. He asked me if I would be interested in talking to a young man about gay sexuality. The boy was only fifteen and needed to chat with someone. I felt this was a mistake because the local child welfare laws were very specific. Such action could be misinterpreted as child abuse. But Ben said this boy was the one to initiate the call, and he really needed someone to talk with. Despite my interest I was adamant in my refusal.

Ben didn't let it rest there. About a week later the phone rang, and when I answered it, a young voice asked for me by name. I was angry with Ben when I realized what he had done. He had given my name and phone number to Javier. I politely told the boy that I was not able to talk with him and hung up. Unfortunately, Javier was much harder to discourage. He called repeatedly and always asked to speak to me. Finally in desperation, I gave in, agreeing to just talk.

To start out with nothing sexual was said. We spoke about superficial likes and dislikes. He asked me to describe myself and I did as best I could without sounding too vain. I have a decent body from working out, long blond hair to my shoulders, and green eyes. He asked about my cock and I told him that I didn't feel comfortable talking about that. Javier surprised me by describing himself. He told me he was 5'5" tall, weighed about 115 pounds and had soft bronzed skin, dark brown hair and brown eyes. He said he had a thin but growing patch of pubic hair surrounding his cock which he had measured at six inches when it was hard. His penis was circumsized.

Again he asked me about my body. Did I have a hairy chest, arms, legs? I told him yes, I had light blond chest hair, and a fine coating of blond hair on my arms and legs. Javier asked about my crotch. Was I hairy down there? "Yes," I said. "I have a thick patch of blond hair completely covering my pubes and surrounding my dick."

"Are you circumsized?" he wanted to know.

"No," I told him and felt myself coloring in embarrassment at such a personal question.

"I've only seen one man's dick that wasn't circumsized," Javier admitted freely. "I saw the man in the locker room at the swimming pool. I wanted to look more, but he noticed me and called me a little fag. I would love to see an uncut penis up close. I would love to see how it works. Does the skin cover up the head all the time? Does it feel different?"

I explained as best I could about how things worked. I told him that the skin was loose enough to pull back out of the way. He said he really wished he could see it. Then my young friend had to go to supper. As I hung up I realized that I had a raging hardon. I had gotten really excited describing my prick and now I unzipped my pants, taking it out for a quick jerk off. As I was nearing my climax, Ben walked in the door and surprised us both. "Well," he said with a grin on his face. "I bet you were just talking to Javier."

"Fuck off," I replied, my face coloring a deep red.

"Love to," he retorted and unzipped his own jeans, pulling his long cock out and beginning to stroke it in my face. I leaned forward and sucked him to a quick climax, then yanked his jeans down to his ankles, spun him around and slid into his tight ass. My fucking was a bit violent, but I needed to cum quickly as well as relieve the emotional tension that had built up between us.

Two days later Javier called again and told me he was alone at home. His family had all gone off shopping and he managed to stay behind. As we chatted, he finally admitted to me that he had stripped his shorts off and was masturbating. I told him that I would be happy to talk with him another time, but he said, "No, I want to talk to you while I do it. I do it all the time and when I do I think about doing it with you."

"Javier, I'm too old for you," I explained. "You are under age, and I could get into serious trouble just talking to you about these things."

"No more trouble than you could if you and I were together and we were doing it to each other," he answered.

"Oh, yes, we could get in a lot more trouble doing that."

"Not if we were careful," he pleaded. "Not if I came over to your house where we could be alone together. I could see your uncut dick, and maybe you could let me feel it, let me try sucking on it. I've always wanted to suck on a dick ever since I heard about blow jobs."

"This isn't something we should talk about," I told him, but I had already pulled my cock out of my jeans.

"I'm rubbing my prick right now and it's all juicy," he said. "Are you rubbing yours?"

"Javier, I don't think..."

"Are you?"

"Yes," I admitted.

"Great! That makes me even harder." We continued to do our joint masturbation for a few minutes, then his breathing grew ragged and he began to moan. In seconds he was coming, and I matched him groan for groan as I unloaded at the same time.

What really surprised me the most was that after we climaxed together on the phone, I wasn't overcome with guilt. In fact, I felt relieved. I knew it was wrong, forbidden, taboo, but I had enjoyed it; I had enjoyed it a lot. Javier could sense the tone in my voice as we talked about the experience.

He asked me if I ever ate my cum. Did I run my fingers through it and then taste it. He told me he did this and he enjoyed the flavor. He really wanted to taste someone else. Then he asked me if we could meet.

This sent up the red flags. "Definitely not," I said firmly.

"Just to talk. I think of you as a good friend. I just want to meet my friend and just talk with him."

"Well..." My resolve was weakening.

"I will be at the baseball diamond in Central Park on Saturday."

Saturday morning as I drove to the park I realized how foolish this was. I had no idea how I would find him. His description could fit about any young Hispanic boy. But I pulled into the parking area, and knew him immediately. He was sitting alone on a big rock beside the drive. He must have recognized me as well, because no sooner had I stopped the car than he jumped up and came over to it. Without even an invitation he opened the passenger door and slid into the seat. "Let's go," he said. "I don't want any of my family to spot me getting into your car."

I was suddenly very nervous and asked if maybe he shouldn't get out. But he said, "Just drive, man," and I did. I drove out of the lot and headed for the bypass.

"Do you live close to the park?" I asked.

"Not real close, but my little sister often likes to follow me."

"Shit."

"Hey, don't sweat it. It's cool," he said. Then he sat back and looked at me, taking a really long look. "You know, you are really hotter than I imagined."

I blushed at the compliment, but managed to glance over at him, appreciating what I saw as well. Javier was young and beautiful. He was wearing baggy denim cut-offs, a loose fitting muscle shirt and sneakers. As we drove, he reached down, grabbed the hem of his shirt and slipped it off over his head. "What are you doing?" I asked, feeling nervous panic rising in my chest.

"Just getting comfortable. You know it's really hot out there. It feels good to have the air blowing on my skin." He reached up and rubbed his chest, wiping the little bit of sweat off that had given his sternum a glistening appearance. I watched as he rubbed his tits, small little brown circles with tiny points in the center. "I wish I had a hairy chest like yours," he said and reached over to feel the hair that was curling up out of the neck of my shirt.

"I don't think you should do that," I said, feeling my body responding.

"Oh, come on. I really want to see your chest. To feel it." Javier was now rubbing my chest, unbuttoning my shirt and playing with my nipples.

"Not while I'm driving," I ordered.

"Then this would be out of the question?" he asked as he dropped his hand to my lap and felt for my growing cock.

"Don't," I said and reached down to move his hand. He gripped my wrist and guided my hand to his chest, guiding me as he worked my fingers up to his tiny nipples.

"This is really not a good idea," I said as I pulled into the driveway. I realized that I had just come home, parking beside the house.

"Is this your place?" he asked and jumped out of the car, bounding up the porch steps to my door. I followed him like a lamb to the slaughter, unlocking the door and letting him step inside.

"It feels really good in here," Javier remarked as the air conditioned interior hit our hot bodies. "I bet it feels good on all of our skin," and he began to pull his pants down.

"Javier, don't do that," I said again, but I was gazing at his tender young body, my cock throbbing in my pants.

"But I want to," he said as he dropped to his knees in front of me and tugged at my shorts, yanking then and my underwear down to my ankles. My cock bounced up into his face. "Cool! Now I get to see what an uncut dick really looks like. Wow, it's so big. Are all uncut dicks this big?" He gently wrapped his hand around my prick and pulled back, sliding the foreskin off and revealing the pink head with a drop of precum poised at the tip.

I groaned in answer to his question, then looked down to see him stick out his tongue and lick the sparkling drop from my piss slit. "Mmmmm," he breathed. "That tastes good. Kind of like salted almonds. I want some more." Javier placed his lips against my cock head and sucked.

I couldn't help myself. It was so good and so hot seeing this young, nubile boy kneeling at my feet, his lips planted firmly on my penis. I pushed forward and my dick began to slide into his mouth. The boy tried to push back, but lust overcame me and I grabbed his head, sliding my fingers into his black, curly locks and pushed into him.

My cock filled his young teenage mouth and caused him to gag. As he did, his teeth nicked my sensitive shaft and I grunted, pulling back. "Watch those teeth," I ordered. "Try to keep them out of the way and just use your lips and tongue on my cock." He obeyed and I pushed in again, this time getting my shaft all the way into him, pressing back into his throat. The boy swallowed in reflex and his tonsils massaged my dick head, causing me intense pleasure. I pulled back and let him breathe, then pushed in again, beginning to pick up a rapid fucking motion.

Javier was a natural born cocksucker. He quickly caught on to the movement, bobbing his head in time to my thrusts, and flicking my cock with his tongue. The sound of his slurping only added to the intensity of my fucking and in no time at all

Javier's eyes grew wide, and I thought he must be in incredible pain, but he took only a moment to slide further down on my prick, then a wide grin spread across his face. "I don't believe this," he whispered. "I don't believe I am here and I am sitting on your cock. I don't believe you have it up inside me."

To convince him I pushed up with my hips and he gasped for a moment. "This is just what I was my sister Rosalie was doing with her boyfriend," he cried,, bouncing up and down on my hard prick.

His tight virginal butt quickly massaged my cock to climax and in no time at all I was unloading my cum up his guts. He fell off me and lay beside me, my hot sperm slowly oozing out of his abused asshole. "Thank you," he said.

"Thank you," I replied.

In a few minutes, Javier jumped off the bed and dashed out to the living room. I followed him only to find him pulling on his pants and shirt. "I gotta go," he said, a bit too quickly.

"Okay," I agreed and dressed, fishing in my pocket for the car keys. We headed back downtown in silence. I didn't know what to say; I wondered if he was happy, upset or what.

Finally he said, "Stop here," and jumped out of the car in front of an ugly grey apartment building.

"Is this where you live?" I asked.

"No," he replied with a big grin. "This is where my sister's boyfriend lives. He said if I ever got my ass broken in proper he was willing to fuck me, but he doesn't do virgins. Now I can have sex with him whenever I want."

I was crushed. Javier was just using me so he could steal his sister's bisexual boyfriend. After our one encounter he never called again. I should have been relieved that he didn't try to blackmail me because of his age. I saw him many years later after he had graduated from high school and taken a job as a foreman on a construction team. He had aged well and became quite successful at his career, and told me he now had a wife and three kids. When I asked about sex he laughed it off and said, "All kids go through that phase. Your trouble is you fags never outgrow it."

Javier may be right. But I hope to never outgrow the joy of gay sex.

JOHNNY: OUT OF HIDING

Thomas C. Humphrey

Johnny and I undressed in his parents' cabin on the lake and ran bare-assed down the moonlit grassy slope to the water. We paused on the boat dock for a lingering kiss, and my cock immediately sprang to life, even though he had given me a superbly slow and loving blow job only a couple of hours earlier. We were in the third week of a strangely satisfying one-sided relationship in which he could not get enough of my cock and I could not be sated by him.

As his tongue probed for my tonsils, he cautiously maneuvered me to the edge of the dock, abruptly broke our embrace, and gave me a quick shove. I balanced precariously and then pitched over backward into the surprisingly cool water. When I surfaced, Johnny was laughing with boyish glee, bent over and slapping both knees.

"That ought to calm that thing between your legs down for awhile," he said. "I want to swim, not be poked to death."

"Oh, yeah? Well, just for that, it's off limits for three days. Don't touch; don't even look," I threatened.

"Bet I can make you change your mind," he said.

He jumped feet first into the chest-deep water, moved in front of me, submerged, and took my withering pole into his mouth. Predictably, it immediately rose to its full rigid length under the skilled attack of his tongue. Just as I was beginning to wonder how long he could stay on it without breathing, he poked his head out of the water.

"Want me to leave it alone?" he teased.

"No," I admitted.

"Some willpower you've got," he said, swimming away. "But you'll just have to wait; I'm not in the mood."

It had been that way the entire three weeks. Around me, Johnny was a fun-loving, trouble-free kid, completely enamored with me and almost obsessively addicted to my cock and the idea of servicing it, without expecting, or even permitting, any reciprocation beyond our sometimes prolonged foreplay.

Just out of high school, he had a summer to kill before

escaping from our small Georgia town into the big city and the liberating environment of college, and he was doing his damndest to squeeze as much pleasure as possible out of life. From my friend Bill, through whom I had met Johnny, and from Johnny himself during quiet times after sex, I knew that he was much more complex than this surface persona indicated.

His last year had been pure hell for him. The younger of two sons in a solidly middle class family with deep roots in the community, he was earmarked for law school and a career in politics. His brother, Wade, a college sophomore, already was being groomed for the medical profession. However, family plans for Johnny had suffered a major setback the previous fall when his mother had snooped through his room and uncovered some very explicit letters from a kid he had had a hot affair with at camp that summer and had planned to visit during winter vacation.

Johnny's mother and father set out to "bring him to his senses." But first, they exposed the other kid to his parents by sending them copies of the letters and accusing him of corrupting their son. In several brutal family discussions, some including his brother, they tried to extract confessions of sexual involvement with other local kids. Despite his refusal to implicate anyone else, Johnny was forced to give up many of his close male friends and had to account for his whereabouts almost every minute of the day; his mother would ride around town at night, checking to see if his car was where he said he would be. She also orchestrated a whirl of social events to see that he dated girls almost every weekend.

Although on the surface he docilely complied with his parents' wishes, Johnny secretly defied them at every turn, taking great pleasure in outsmarting them and in promiscuously seeking out as many sex partners as he could seduce in our little town. He even latched onto a lesbian girlfriend, and they became each other's cover. Supposedly on a date with her, Johnny would drive her and her lover to the theater, leave his car parked outside, and ride off for sex with some guy while the girls enjoyed the movie. He almost dared his parents to catch him in his deceptions.

If I had known all of this that first night, I probably would have run from Johnny, but by the time I pieced together his circumstances, I was as hooked on our relationship as he was. After a stint in the Army, I was living with my parents for the summer while waiting for an out-of-state job to open up, and I was having my own problems coping with the stifling atmosphere of my hometown.

As a teenager, I had played football, guzzled my share of beer, bedded a few girls, and fooled around with several of my buddies – mostly with our pants around our ankles in a cramped car seat on some lonely country road, the kind of emotionless animal-need sex you engage in but don't talk about afterward. Despite a few eye-opening experiences in the Army, at twenty-two, I was still about as sexually repressed as I had been in high school. Johnny's playful, affectionate, and worshipful behavior toward me, and his completely unselfish willingness to satisfy my every desire was a refreshingly liberating experience.

Before I met him, I had fought against boredom and attempted to suppress my sexual need by spending most of my time in our town's only game room, shooting pool and playing video games, usually with my old high school buddy, Bill, who had gone to work in Johnny's dad's electrical contracting business after high school. Bill and I had done a little playing around together when we were younger, but Blll, who had always been completely selfish in our sex play, had now outgrown such "kid stuff" and had built quite a reputation around town as a super stud and even had a couple of married women on the string.

It wasn't long before Bill mentioned Johnny to me as a faggot kid who couldn't get enough of his cock. He took great pride in having the boss's son give him regular blow jobs in the warehouse on company time. Then he told me Johnny was interested in meeting me and offered to set it up. I didn't say yea or nay, but the next night Johnny showed up at the game room, and Bill introduced us. I recalled having seen him a couple of times before, and he did not interest me any more this time than he had then.

Johnny wasn't a particularly attractlve kid. He was tall and rawboned, with a rather nondescript flat, square face and straight dirty-blond hair. He had no effeminate mannerisms, but his movements were clumsy and graceless. He stood around for awhile making small talk, but I pretty well ignored him as I concentrated on shooting pool. I did not even know when he left the game room.

As I was driving home, I noticed a car tailing me, making every turn I made. On a dark residential street, its lights began blinking in some kind of code. I pulled to the curb and Johnny drove up beside me.

"Come on and ride around with me awhile," he said, flashing a beautiful smile.

Earlier, Johnny had done nothing to titillate my desire, but now he piqued my interest because, like the storied mountain, he was there – and because any alternative was preferable to another solitary jack-off in my lonely bed. Without thinking, I killed my car engine and crawled in beside him. Immediately, his hand groped for my crotch.

"Where can we go?" I asked hoarsely. I was no longer familiar with relatively safe parking spots.

"How about my house?" he said.

"Is that safe?"

"Yeah," he assured me. "My folks will be at a party until two o'clock, and my brother's out somewhere getting drunk."

"Okay," I agreed. By that time, he was opening my fly, and I was thinking only with my dick.

In his bedroom, with a dim light on, he slowly undressed me and had me sprawl on my back. For the next ten minutes, without either of us saying a word, he gently ran his hands all over my body and kissed and licked every square inch of it. He spent another five minutes squeezing and kneading my marginally bigger than average cock, gazing at it adoringly, as if in a near-trance, before he finally took it in his mouth. Immediately, I knew I was in the hands of a pro who loved his work. For what seemed like thirty minutes, he kept me on the brink of explosion with techniques I had never before experienced, sensing time after time at the exact last moment when to ease off to avert my orgasm. By the time he finally permitted my cock to geyser interminably in his mouth, I was clutching and grasping at him desperately and begging him for release.

Although I was totally worn out by the time he removed his mouth from my flaccid cock, I felt that I should at least try to give him a comparable experience. But when I reached for his dick, he shoved my hand away. "Uh-uh," he said. "Just rest awhile. Then I want you to fuck me."

"*What?*"

"You heard me."

And so fuck him I did, twice before our night ended, and it was like nothing I had ever experienced before. Johnny got us in every position he could think of – standing, kneeling, squatting – and we fucked all over the room – in the bed, on the floor, on top of the dresser, and even in the bathtub. Throughout our long, exhausting session, he squirmed and wriggled and gyrated and contracted muscles I didn't know existed, moaning and whimpering and nibbling and begging for more all the time, until he had milked me completely dry. We finally staggered out of his house just minutes before his parents were expected home.

After that first night, neither one of us could get enough of the other. We managed to get together every day, sometimes twice a day. We spent a good bit of time plotting and scheming and arranging our meetings, which sometimes were quickies in a service station restroom or out in the middle of a peach orchard, and at other times were extended sessions at his house, dangerous as that was, or at their lakefront cabin.

I had never known the blissfully vitalizing effect of regular, totally uninhibited sex such as Johnny offered, and I entered into it wholeheartedly, even somewhat blindly, and took what I knew were foolish risks almost daily in order to be with him. For his part, I think he reveled in having run across such an insatiable and enthusiastic partner. He concentrated on me full time and cut himself off from all the other guys he had been servicing. Bill even half-seriously complained that I had stolen Johnny from him.

When he didn't have my dick in his mouth, Johnny and I did a lot of talking and developed a genuine friendship. I knew all along that my interest was not much deeper than sex, but I did quickly come to care for him, though not in a way that even approached loving him. At times, I suspected that he was in love with me, but he never expressed it in words. What he did express was the desire to escape our hometown and his parents' restrictions and demands and to be able to live free of the pressures of deceit and subterfuge by which he had survived the previous several months. When he found out that I would be moving out of state about the time he went off to college, he even fantasized about running away to live with me, and we did talk seriously about him visiting me when he was in college and out from under the watchful eye of his mother.

But except on rare occasions, our conversation seldom was serious. Johnny was a fun-loving, life-affirming kid with a terrific sense of humor, and we mostly laughed and teased and played and attempted to suck the marrow out of life together without analyzing it too deeply.

Our best times were at the lake cabin. Johnny's father and brother worked all day, and two or three afternoons a week his mother was obligated to attend some social function or another. His parents almost never came to the lake at night, and he and Wade had an understanding that if they arrived at the cabin and saw the other's car, they would respect each other's privacy and go somewhere else. This meant that several afternoons and nights every week Johnny and I could spend hours alone and unhurried. It was so idyllic that we completely relaxed and let down our guard.

This particular night, after he had teased me into an erection and then swum away, we wrestled and dunked and groped and kissed for a long time before crawling onto the dock and settling into some serious sex. He had my dick throbbing and my balls aching as he excruciatingly teased me toward orgasm. Suddenly, the darkness was cut through by the sweeping glare of headlights as a car circled among the pines and stopped in front of the cabin.

"Oh, shit, it's Wade!" Johnny said. "He knows he's not supposed to stop when I'm here."

My cock shriveled and my heart raced. Talk about vulnerability! There I was, stark-assed naked on the dock with my clothes completely out of reach in the cabin. I was stranded miles from town without my car, without even a towel to drape around me. I silently cursed myself for my stupidity.

We hunkered down and prayed that Wade would drive off, but this hope was short-lived as we heard car doors slamming and the raucous drunken talk of several people, including at least one woman.

"Goddamn it! They're drunk and planning a gang bang," Johnny said. "Wade's done it before and tried to get me to join them. That bastard! Why'd he have to do it tonight?"

"What are we going to do?" I fretted.

"I don't know. They're liable to be here most of the night."

"Yeah. And they just might decide to go swimming. Then what the fuck do we do, hide out under the dock?" I fumed.

"I could go get our clothes," Johnny said, "but I can't just walk in naked." He searched around in the bottom of the boat and finally turned up an oily, ragged towel which had been used to clean the motor.

He wrapped the towel around himself and screwed up his courage. "I'll go in and throw your clothes out the window. Then I'll dress and meet you at the first turn down the road," he said.

I waited for him to go inside and then crouched beneath the bedroom window, feeling as exposed as if I had been on Main Street at high noon. Time seemed suspended as I waited forever for him to come to the window. Then the bedroom door opened, bathing me with light, but Johnny did not appear above me. I could hear a jumble of voices, but nothing distinct, until Johnny yelled out, "Get away from me, you fat bitch!" and everybody laughed. A few moments later, there was a loud crash and the sounds of a scuffle.

"You goddamned cocksucking faggot! I'm ashamed to be your brother," a drunken voice yelled out. Then there was another loud crash and a cacophony of excited voices.

I huddled completely helpless under the window, afraid that Johnny was going to get his ass beat without me being able to do anything about it. But then he spoke in the hardest, most forceful voice I'd ever heard him use. "Back off, you fucking redneck drunks," he said. "I'm going in for my clothes, and I'll kill any bastard who touches me."

The window above my head opened, and, at last, Johnny leaned out to drop me my clothes. I hurriedly dressed and dodged through the pines to the road. In a few moments, Johnny's car whirled out of the driveway and careened recklessly toward me. He screeched to a halt beside me and barely gave me time to get in before he scratched off and sped down the narrow lane like a madman. He was wearing only his jeans, and he was trembling violently and babbling incoherently.

"Whoa! Slow down," I cautioned, laying my hand on his shoulder.

My touch calmed him and he got the car under control. "Pull over and stop," I said.

With the engine running and the headlights on, Johnny threw the car in park and collapsed into my arms, where he clutched at me and sobbed uncontrollably. I held him tightly and kept whispering, "It's all right; everything's all right," until he finally regained control of himself, choked back his tears, and took several deep breaths.

"Tell me what happened," I urged when he lifted his head off my chest.

"That bastard! That goddamn bastard!" he spat out.

"Tell me," I insisted.

"They had a whore – a big fat, ugly whore," he said. "She was naked and totally gross. Wade wanted me to fuck her, and when I refused, he and Allen grabbed me, and Wade ripped off my towel. And that bitch came over saying she'd make a man out of me. She started slobbering all over me and rubbing her fat tits against me. I wanted to puke. Then she got on her knees and started sucking my dick."

"And what happened?" I encouraged when he paused.

"I kicked her over the coffee table and Wade grabbed me and called me a faggot. I knocked the shit out of him. I probably broke his nose. Blood spurted everywhere. I hope I killed the bastard!"

"Oh, hell," I said, "there'll be trouble in Georgia!"

"I don't care," he said. "What's my fucking brother gonna do about it? He can't tell Mom and Dad, or his ass is in a crack. But I don't care anyway. I don't give a shit about anything. I just want to get the hell away from this stinking town and my whole stinking family. I'm not even going to college; I'll move to Atlanta and get a job. I just don't care anymore!"

I pulled him back against my chest and wrapped my arms around him and just held him. I felt totally ineffectual. "It'll be all right," I told him. "You'll be out of here pretty soon. It'll be all right."

"No, it won't," he said. "It'll never be all right as long as

I'm in this town and around my family. I've got to get away and live my life, and now's as good a time as any."

I knew he was serious, and not just reacting to the moment. "Think it over for a few days," I advised. "You can stand it a few more days. Then if you think leaving is your best move, you can live with me. Things'll work out."

His face brightened. "You mean it? You want us to live together after you start your job?" he asked.

Without having given it any thought, suddenly I knew that was what I wanted. "I mean it," I said.

He grabbed me in a bear hug that quickly turned into an embrace. "I'd like that," he said softly.

He lay quietly in my arms for awhile, and then he reached for my cock. "We've got some unfinished business," he said.

"Not here," I said. "Somebody might come by."

"I wish everybody in town would come by. I'm not going to hide anymore," he said, loosening my belt.

I reached to turn off the engine, but left the headlights on. I leaned my head against the passenger window and raised my hips for him to slide my jeans down. As his warm lips encircled my throbbing cock, I, too, wished the whole town would parade by to witness. I did not want to hide anymore either.

EDDIE'S AUDITION

Peter Z. Pan

"I don't need a lot; Only what I got.
Plus a tube of greasepaint and a follow-spot."
— Sondheim

Why aren't greenroom's ever really green? the boy thought, staring at the peach wallpaper. *Why does "five minutes, señor" always turn into fifteen minutes because the ham ahead of you just has to squeeze out two encores before finally leaving the stage?* He looked around the room. The Spanish chatter sounded almost foreign to him, like chicken clucking. He had been away so long.

But these weren't normal chickens. No, they were the *creme de la creme* of show biz fowl. And he was right smack in the middle of the prestigious hen house.

But why?! He wasn't in their league. Did he deserve to be there — *again*? He really didn't know. He only knew he was sick to his stomach and his hands were shaking so badly, he couldn't even hold a cup of water without spilling some all over his costume. He wanted out of there. Oh, he wanted out of there badly. He wanted to rip off the tight show clothes that bound him, change back into his comfortable sweatpants, T-shirt, and Reeboks, and get the hell out of there. Run the hell out of there, as a matter of fact, past his shiny stretch-limo, through the crowded streets of Mexico City to the sea, where he would swim across the Gulf back home to Florida. The idea was very appealing. Hell, the idea was almost unbearable to resist.

Yet deep inside, he knew he couldn't do it. He had invested so much time and energy into this, his "big comeback," that now he just had to go through with it. After all, getting on that show hadn't been easy. In fact, it had been a big coup for his agent. This was the big break he'd been waiting for. His debut as a solo artist.

Siempre En Domingo was the premiere variety show of all Latin America. Though the new album was a modest success, his performance that night would make or break his solo career – and he knew it. He knew it all too well. He had to go out there and not just be *good*, but blow them away. He had to prove to the world – and mostly to himself – that he wasn't a has-been ex-child-star from a "manufactured" teenybopper group. That he was a *real* singer with *real* talent. And that he didn't need his four little sidekicks to back him up.

But he *did* need them. He never needed them more in his life. Not so much their bodies out on the stage with him, as their moral support. Looking around at all the famous faces in that room, he never felt more alone, more inadequate. Sure they smiled back at him when their eyes met, yet they weren't real smiles. They were as fake as the people who donned them: envious, back-stabbing egomaniacs who wouldn't think twice about cutting your throat to advance their precious careers. He couldn't remember how many times he'd met stars who seemed so nice on TV but were really bastards and bitches in person. He had been a fan of so many of them – almost worshipping the ground they walked on, in some cases – only to be crushed upon meeting them. Behind all the smiles in that room, he knew there was an underlying feeling of scorn and competitiveness. They didn't wish him well. In all actuality, they hoped he would fail miserably so *they* would be the hit of the show. God forbid he stole that dear spotlight away from them. He needed sincere moral support at that moment, and those phony smiles just weren't doing it.

He longed for Carlito, Rico – even Chico. Most of all, he longed for his beloved Juanie. Sweet, benevolent Juanie. He would know the right things to say to calm his nerves. Best of all, Juanie would hold him. He would hold him that dread moment before stepping out on the stage – when your heart jumps to your throat, almost choking you. Oh, how he wished his Juanie were there.

One of the assistant stage managers again came in the room. "Cinco minutos, Señor," said the bald, little man wearing the headset to the boy. Tito Puente was in the middle of his second encore and this time the stage manager really did mean "five minutes."

The boy stood, only to find his knees were made of rubber. The stench of caviar, champagne, and cheese that permeated the room suddenly kicked him in the stomach, making him almost vomit on Maria Conchita Alonso. Paul Rodriguez shook one of his clammy hands and told him to break a leg, while the voluptuous Xuxa patted him on the back with one hand as she pinched his ass with the other.

He followed the stage manager to the wings, all the time searching for the nearest exit, just in case he built up enough courage to make a run for it. Then as he approached the enormous stage, a tidal wave of total recall struck and enveloped him, almost knocking him over with its awesome magnitude. It all came back to him then: the first time they did the show; all the concerts; the screaming fans stampeding the stage and ripping at his clothes; the horny groupies; the drugs; and, oh yes, the hot nasty sex. More than four years had passed – almost five – yet he suddenly remembered all of it as if it were yesterday.

When he went from poor, Cuban refugee Eduardo José Pacheco to EDDIE, singing star of Los Muchachos. And it had all begun that fateful day he came across that newspaper ad. The ad that changed his humdrum life forever.

OPEN CALL
INTERNATIONAL TALENT SEARCH
FOR BOYS 12 TO 15
TO JOIN LATIN POP SENSATION **LOS MUCHACHOS**
No experience necessary, but some singing & dance training is preferred. Boys must be cute, speak Spanish, and look good in tight clothes.
BE A TEEN IDOL AND SEE THE WORLD!
Auditions will be held at ll a.m., Saturday, June 4th. Gusman Center, 175 East Flagler Street, Downtown Miami.

"That's tomorrow!" Eddie exclaimed to himself, alarmed and excited at the same time. His big brown eyes were glued to the ad in front of him.

It was in the Entertainment Section of *The Miami Herald*, sandwiched between *Friday The 13TH VII: The New Blood* – its "*4th* Smash Week" according to the giant letters underneath the hockey mask and knife – and *Salsa: The Motion Picture*. "It's Hot," the promo line added. He was supposed to be looking through the Help Wanted Section, of course. That was the only reason his mother had seen fit to spend an entire quarter on the paper.

Money was very tight and every penny counted. That quarter could have easily bought a package of Campbell's Ramen Noodle Soup; they were four for a dollar at the neighborhood Sedanos' Supermarket. It wasn't exactly nutritious, the poor-man's soup, but those thick noodles and chicken-flavored broth could sure fill you up on nights there was nothing else in the kitchen cupboard or in the refrigerator, except for a can of generic cat food. The worst part was, they didn't own a cat. The no-frills feline cuisine was there for an emergency. Luckily, they had never been that hungry, though many a time they had come close. Too close.

Eddie's mother did her best to provide for herself and her only son, her only living family. She broke her back everyday waitressing at Los Cubanitos Restaurant in Little Havana. But a waitress only earns so much...especially at a dump like Los Cubanitos. And her drinking didn't help things either.

She started hitting the bottle back in Cuba after Eddie's father was executed for attempting to organize a coup against the Castro regime. Eddie was only ten months old. Five years later, Maria Pacheco and her young son made it to America as part of the infamous Mariel Boat Lift: a flotilla of hundreds of private vessels that carried refugees from Mariel, Cuba to Key West in the spring of 1980. They were hungry, thirsty, and frightened; but they were *libre* – free. They had made it.

Now, eight years later, they were just barely making it. Eddie's mother was drinking more and more and they had less and less every day. She went from one abusive boyfriend to another, searching for love and security, ending up with heartache and unpaid long-distance phone bills instead. Some of the men were nice enough, yet most of them were violent freeloaders who drank more than his mother. She had a knack for picking losers, Eddie always thought. Except for his father, of course. Eddie idolized him, though he didn't remember him, really. Yet he was proud to have the blood of a brave revolutionary running through his veins. Eddie could have been the son of Cuba's first democratic president this century. Instead, he was stigmatized as a dread *Marielita:* the popular

Miamian word for Cuban trash.

He had to help his mother make ends meet, thus he had been looking for a summer job that Friday afternoon. But he could never pick up a newspaper without looking through the entertainment section first. He'd always dreamt of some day being in show business. In his fantasies – and there were a lot of them – it was his way out of the Cuban ghetto he and his mother were forced to live in. And why not? After all, show business *was* in his blood.

His father had been a somewhat famous stage actor in Cuba before he got involved with politics. That's how he'd met his mother; she was a dancer in a show he was starring in. That would explain why Eddie always had this basic, instinctual need to perform. He just loved being in front of a crowd, entertaining. And since his mother had taught him to sing and dance before he could walk almost, the boy was quite good. Though he only got a chance to show it off at school talent shows and on slow nights at Los Cubanitos when – accompanied by his mother on the guitar – he would make the patrons cry with old songs from the homeland. He and his mother would make out like bandits in tips on those nights. "No one tips better than an old, crying Cuban yearning for home," Maria used to say jokingly. When she joked and didn't have a hangover, that is.

"Los Muchachos," Eddie whispered, brushing the long strands of auburn hair out of his eyes. He remembered seeing them on all the Spanish variety shows his mother watched in between "novellas." He wasn't really a fan of their music – he preferred real dance music as opposed to the pop bubble gum stuff Los Muchachos did – and he'd always thought they looked a bit tacky in their matching polyester costumes; yet for some reason, he could never take his eyes off the boys when he'd walk by the TV and they happened to be on. He even secretly wished he could afford to buy concert tickets when he found out they were performing that weekend at the Gusman Center. He quite honestly didn't know what it was about them that fascinated him so. Was it their music? Was it the synchronized choreography? Was it their cute, little...?

Whatever it was, he was embarrassed by it. After all, Los Muchachos' only fans where horny teenaged girls – everybody knew that – *not* boys. It was sissy stuff. And he was no sissy. Not the son of a revolutionary!

What he *was* was excited at the thought of actually being a Muchacho, being famous, being rich, performing in front of millions. The images racing through his mind were intoxicating, filling him with a strange, warm sensation that made his small body tingle and his peter stand. But ever since he started getting hair down there, the darn thing would stand at the drop of a hat. And at the most inopportune of times, such as in the church confessional at the sound of Father Garcia's husky voice, and in the school shower room after gym class. It was like it had a mind of its own. It was embarrassing.

Eddie wanted to run into the living room and show his mother the audition ad. She had just gotten home from work and would soon take her first drink of the day. This would lead to the nightly drunken stupors he had reluctantly learned to live with. The boy wanted to get his mother while she was still coherent – God knows he sure as hell avoided her when she was sauced – yet he certainly couldn't parade into the living room with his underpants a small, white tent.

He had two options: either think of something really gross to make the bulge subside, or do what he learned by spying on one of his mother's boyfriends five years back while she was at work. The latter somehow seemed a more pleasant option. It always did. Ever since he copied what his "Stepfather of the Month" was doing on the couch that morning he had the flu and was forced to stay home from school. He had just stood behind the man, imitating his every move, his every jerk. He couldn't however copy the man's spectacular finale not for four more years that is. He'd never forget the first time it happened. It was quite a pleasant surprise, the new sensations, poor Michael Jackson's face dripping wet on the Thriller poster over his bed, all of it. It's one of those things guys always remember. Like your first car.

Eddie put a chair up against his bedroom door. He then lay back in bed – on his old "Return of the Jedi" bedspread, soiled from the many times before – and pulled down his Fruit of the Looms. It was up all right, at twelve o'clock on the dot. The boy spit into his left palm – he was a "lefty" – and closed his eyes, letting his wet hand wander down his burning body to his crotch. A bit of his spittle dripped upon his milky, upper thighs as he grabbed hold of his young erection. A droplet then trickled between his plump fleecy legs, landing just beneath his tender butt cheeks and tickling him.

Around him, the faces of his favorite stars looked down at him from the many posters on the walls – not passing judgment, but enjoying this sacred, little boy ritual they had the privilege to witness with bated breath. The half-naked River Phoenix rooted on his every jerk while Billy Idol's girlish eyes feasted upon his slender form, perhaps wanting, yearning to stroke his flaming loins.

The room smelled of a boy's room: of dirty socks that should have been picked up days ago and put into the hamper; of boy white-honey – a lush nectar – leaking slightly from his little boy peter; of boy sweat, tangy yet sweet, like the aroma of a fine liqueur.

Usually, he would have thought of the dirty pictures in the *Hustler* he'd found in the back alley behind Los Cubanitos. His mother had unfortunately come across it while cleaning his room and – like any good Catholic mother – had thrown it away. But not before he'd memorized every single dirty photo in the magazine. This was normally the mental masturbatory material he would use to get off. This time, however, he didn't seem to need it. For reasons beyond his comprehension, just the mental pictures of him with Los Muchachos – singing and dancing and showering after a concert, soaping each...

That was enough for him to make Michael Jackson's face wet again. But the gloved-one was used to a young boy's gooey seed dripping from his chin, wasn't he?

Eddie was able to reach his mother before the first drink. She was so excited by the whole idea, she didn't even take one swig of vodka, her poison of choice as Eddie thought of it, that entire night. Instead, she helped her son prepare an audition.

"I seen dos boys perform a million time," she told him in her broken English, which she now spoke as much as possible for the practice, "and dey got nothing on jew, baby." Her face then filled with pride. "Jew have real talent. Pacheco Family talent. It's in jour yenes!"

Maria and her son worked into the night, perfecting every last bit of his audition routine. It was like she was going to try-out right along with him, she was that excited. Maybe she felt it was her last shot at stardom. That if she couldn't make it in show business herself because of all the unfair obstacles life threw in her path, then maybe her only child would make it – and that would be just as gratifying. Eddie didn't know why she seemed so happy, so thrilled. All he knew was that he felt closer to his mother that night than ever before. It was grand – while it lasted.

The place was buzzing with excitement as over two hundred boys and their stage-mothers crammed the Gusman Center lobby that hot June day. A majority of them looked Hispanic, although there where a few gringos, blacks, and Asians scattered in the crowd.

Most of the boys wore T-shirts with sweat pants or shorts. Some even wore tights. The sissy ones, Eddie thought. Not him, though. He looked bad and he knew it. Tight jeans, shredded in all the right places, hugged his shapely, round ass. Tired old motorcycle boots from the thrift shop, that still looked kind of hip in an ominous sort of way, gave him the air of a gorgeous young Brando in one of those awful biker flicks. A black bandanna wrapped around his forehead kept his long, lustrous mane of auburn hair off his badboy face. And the *piece de resistance*: no T-shirt. Instead a black, leather jacket one of his stepfathers had left behind covered the nakedness of his smooth, slender torso. *Bad!*

All the boys had numbers pinned to their shirts, Eddie to his jacket. He was number sixty-nine. An effeminate little man was handing out printed sheets of paper to the boys. When he came to Eddie, his beady eyes lingered on the boy's ass after giving him his copy.

Eddie and Maria quickly devoured the sheet, as did everyone else in the lobby. It read:

LOS MUCHACHOS RULES
  1. To be in Los Muchachos, a boy must be at least twelve years of age, good-looking, and speak fluent Spanish.
  2. A Muchacho must be a talented singer and dancer, dedicated to performing.
  3. Muchachos must be healthy, for they rehearse all the time when they're not performing; they must study hard and get good grades – a private tutor goes along on the tour so that the boys can keep up

with their classes; they must not have bad habits, like cigarette-smoking or taking drugs; and they must get along well with others.

4. A member of Los Muchachos must *leave* the group before his sixteenth birthday, or if his singing voice changes, or he gets too tall.

THE HISTORY OF LOS MUCHACHOS

In 1979, Luis Miguel Martinez, an ex-dancer himself, got the idea to form a singing & dancing group that would perform in Spanish to audiences in Puerto Rico. He had no idea that MUCHACHOMANIA would soon sweep over the world when he recruited the original five talented boys. They worked incredibly hard on weekends and after school every single day. After long hours of repeating lyrics and dance steps, the boys began appearing in public on weekends. They'd perform to prerecorded music, so they didn't have to learn to play any instruments. In a year's time, the five dark-haired boys, dressed in identical outfits, became so popular that they began to travel – not only around their native Puerto Rico, but all over Latin America, performing for a growing multitude of fans. Then in 1981, Los Muchachos invaded America much like The Beatles did before them, making millions of new screaming, young fans.

Nine years and thirteen different boys later, Los Muchachos are a hit all over the world, where many of their chart-topping albums have gone gold and platinum. They tour year round, have starred in two hit movies in Latin America, and their weekly TV show out of Puerto Rico is seen all over the globe.

And the legend continues – *with you*.

After waiting a couple of hours behind the closed lobby doors for the first three groups of twenty boys to audition, Eddie was finally on stage, but with nineteen other boys. They stood shoulder to shoulder upstage, filling the length of the platform, numbers sixty-one thru sixty-eight to Eddie's right, numbers seventy through eighty to Eddie's left.

Downcenter on the apron facing them, stood the man. Above him, the tiny specks of light on the high ceiling over the house looked like stars in the night sky. Except for a young boy in the darkness of the third row, this man seemed to be the only one who would be watching their audition. Eddie felt relieved at that. He really didn't know what to expect and upon seeing over four hundred people waiting in the lobby, a dread fear hit him that they would all be sitting in the auditorium – evaluating his audition. That had sent a cold chill down his spine that almost made him wet his pants. Now as he looked out into the empty house, he felt relieved. It wouldn't be that bad after all.

"Welcome, gentlemen," said the man with a thick Spanish accent. "I am Luis Miguel Martinez. I'm the creator, manager, producer, and choreographer of Los Muchachos." He spoke in a no-nonsense tone that filled Eddie with fear again.

Luis Miguel was a tall, muscular man with a slim dancer's build and long brown hair he wore in a ponytail. He was slightly effeminate, yet came across exceedingly assertive and domineering, like a gay drill sergeant. He wore no shirt – just black tights and dance shoes – showing off the well-defined pectorals, biceps, and triceps hidden underneath a forest of thick body hair. Though quite handsome, he looked ragged, with dark circles under his eyes. Eyes which were an odd shade of green that seemed out of place against his dark complexion and Spanish features.

But wait, they were green contacts over black eyes, weren't they? Eddie couldn't tell. His gaze kept leaving the man's eyes and focusing on his bulging crotch. He didn't seem to be wearing any underwear, his big basket just protruded through his tights like two baseballs squeezed into a marble bag. His huge shaft appeared carefully positioned so as to come down his pants leg in front of his right thigh.

Eddie tried not to stare at it, but he couldn't help it. Just as he couldn't help the shifting in his jeans. He of course felt guilty, as he usually did when aroused by a man. Then a horrid thought slapped him in the face: *How the hell are you gonna dance with a fuckin' boner?!* Sweat was now pouring from every pore of his small body.

"For the first time ever, we are casting outside of Puerto Rico," Luis Miguel continued. "We are hoping that hiring a boy from America will broaden our appeal here in the States. Pedrito Rodriguez, who has been a Muchacho for four years now, will be turning sixteen next year, and maybe one of you will take his place."

They're only replacing one of them! thought Eddie, quite incensed. He was suddenly struck by the harsh realization that there was no way he would be picked over two hundred other boys. He didn't have a snowball's chance in hell. He felt stupid for even being there and wanted desperately to go home. Yet the erection remained.

"Okay boys, spread out," directed Luis Miguel. "It's time for you young studs to show me what you've got! Make me excided!" This sounded like a half-cheer and half-order, dripping with sexual overtones.

The man then walked the boys through complicated dance steps, repeating: "one, two, three, four, five, six, seven, eight," in time to a dance beat.

Eddie found the routine exceedingly easy. He had it down pat the first time through. Just as his insecurities were about to whisper in his ear that he was doing it all wrong, Eddie looked around at the other boys. It was the third and last time the choreographer was going over the steps and most of them were still tripping over their own feet. A powerful locomotive with boxcars chock-full of self-confidence suddenly struck him with a fury, bringing a cocky smile to his angelic face. It quickly became abundantly clear to him that he could dance circles around these boys. They looked like clumsy hippos in an old cartoon next to him. Maybe he *would* be picked after all!

The Muchachos hit, "Motorbike Daydreams" blasted through the boom box speakers at Luis Miguel's feet. The music didn't seem to help though, the other boys still appeared zombies next to Eddie. Not that they weren't good dancers; except for one hopeless case, they all had the steps down. It was their delivery that paled in comparison. He simply blew them off the stage.

A bright light, a magical presence, emanated from Eddie, filling the stage with a thermanuclear glow. His lithe young body oozed of sensuality as it gyrated to the passionate Spanish rhythm. He appeared to fly through the air, flinging his limber limbs and landing effortlessly. He contorted his body like a seductive serpent, making every move his own. Especially the deep pelvic thrusts and a slow, erotic belly dance that was as hypnotic as watching a long, wiggling cobra coming out of a basket. He had become one with the music: a hot-blooded Santeria priest from the islands, *his* islands, possessed by a hedonistic demon and dancing around a campfire in a forbidden, carnal ritual. His pubescent loins hot and his rock-hard six inches wanting to burst through his button fly.

Towards the end, some of the boys just stopped dancing to

look at him go. But Eddie was in a trance of sorts, oblivious to everything but the music.

Luis Miguel turned off the tape, bringing Eddie back to reality. He suddenly became aware that everyone was staring at him. Some of the boys looked at him in awe, some in defeat, but most in envy, their lips curling up to form a sneer. Luis Miguel's eyes drank Eddie in, as if all he wanted to do was lick his sweaty body with a moist, hot tongue – tasting the burning droplets of sweat that trickled from his face onto his naked, velvety chest and pink, hard nipples. The intensity of Luis Miguel's stare made Eddie feel quite uncomfortable, if not confused.

"Thank you, men, that was..." Luis Miguel finally said, searching for the proper word, finally giving up and settling for, "exhilarating." He took a deep breath and continued. "Number seventy-four and..." his stare was now ripping every stitch of clothes off Eddie's succulent body, "...oh yes, number sixty-nine. You two boys stay." His voice then turned cold and callous. "The rest of you may go. Thank you for coming." In other words: fuck off; don't call us, we'll call you; welcome to the cruel cold world of real live showbiz, kiddies; and by the way, fuck off.

Disappointment engulfed the stage like flames in a dry forest. Eddie wanted to feel bad for the eighteen boys who were walking off, their dreams crushed. But he was too excited to feel much of anything except total euphoria.

Next came the singing part of the audition for number seventy-four – a gorgeous specimen of Latino boyhood, about fifteen – and number sixty-nine. Seventy-four sang a cappella some obscure Spanish song Eddie had never heard before. Eddie didn't much care for the song, but he did care for the tall boy's singing voice, not to mention the rest of him.

Eddie performed Michael Jackson's "Bad" along with the audio tape he'd brought. He miraculously recreated every dance move Jackson did in the video to the last detail. His clear, crisp voice filled the theatre – a delicate, yet loud, high flute with perfect-pitch – effortlessly drowning out Jackson's shrills. Midway through the song, in the dance break, he instinctively stripped off his jacket, somehow knowing Luis Miguel would enjoy it. His well-defined young torso glistened with perspiration.

He was *bad*!

Luis Miguel asked Eddie and Seventy-four to return the next day for a "callback" at noon, right before the matinee show. He tried to maintain a poker face, only telling Eddie that he was quite good for an amateur. But Eddie could see the man was impressed with his talent. Very impressed.

That night Eddie and his mother were too excited to sleep, so they stayed up talking all night like friends at a slumber party. Again she didn't have a single drink all night.

Morning finally came and Eddie took the number eleven bus over the First Street bridge to Downtown Miami. Maria had to work that afternoon so Eddie had to go alone. He had of course promised to call her immediately if he was picked. Or, as she put it, *when* he was picked.

Eddie came in the backstage door just as he was told. The queeny little man with the beady eyes was there to let him in. He told Eddie that Mr. Martinez was conducting the callbacks in the main dressing room at the end of the hall. He then patted the boy's behind to start him walking in the right direction. Eddie felt violated by the man's touch, but was too nervous to think about it twice.

Around him, the place was a three-ring circus as people dashed past him preparing for the matinee show. He was quite overwhelmed by the sheer magnitude of the cavernous structure. He was also about to puke his brains out. As he got closer and closer to the dressing room door, his stomach sank deeper and deeper. It was the longest walk of his life and he was about to toss his cookies. Luckily, he saw the men's room out of the corner of his eye, making a run for it before making a mess on the floor. He got to the toilet just in time to deposit his breakfast.

As he knelt there hugging the porcelain bowl, he heard similar spewing noises coming from the next stall.

"Do you use your index finger or your middle one?" asked a young, impetuous voice with a Spanish accent.

Eddie stepped out of the stall to investigate its origin. The door to the adjacent stall was now cracked open, allowing Eddie to peer in. A slender boy about his age was kneeling next to the bowl. He wore only a short kimono that just barely covered his petite buttocks.

The pretty stranger repeated his strange question. Then, after wiping his mouth with his sleeve, he added: "I prefer the middle finger myself." With that, he stood with the grace of a ballet dancer and flushed the toilet with a flourish. He seemed to possess both male and female characteristics. This confused and intrigued Eddie simultaneously.

Eddie immediately recognized him but couldn't quite place him. He looked *so* familiar: the shiny brown hair in a dutch-boy cut, the thick pouty lips, the contrast of his incandescent green eyes to his dark complexion, everything! "Do I know you?"

"Hi, Eddie," said the boy with a friendly smile. "I'm Juanie Santos from Los Muchachos."

Of course! He'd seen him a zillion times on TV. "How did you know my name?"

"I saw you audition yesterday. Boy, you were hot!"

Eddie was struck by a revelation of sorts. "You were the boy in the third row."

"That was me." His gaze had now wandered to Eddie's crotch. "I couldn't take my eyes off you. Nobody could."

"Thanks," said Eddie awkwardly, not knowing exactly how to take a compliment.

"I see you and me have something in common, man."

"What do you mean?"

"We make ourselves puke to stay skinny. It's the only way I can fit into those tight costumes."

Eddie had heard of girls doing that, but never *boys*. "I didn't make myself throw up!" he stated rather indignantly. "I'm just real nervous."

"Don't worry," said Juanie in a comforting tone. "Just do whatever Luis Miguel says and it'll be over before you know it. I usually help with initiation, but you're much too special to share. I'd rather wait till I can have you one on one, man." He then coyly winked at Eddie. "*Bienvenido a Los Muchachos*, Eddie." Juanie pecked him on the lips and darted out of the mens room before Eddie could react.

Eddie could not process the overwhelming influx of homoerotic data, a multitude of emotions foreign to him, that deluged his mind at that moment. *My God! A boy just kissed me! Not just any boy, but Juanie Santos! Is he a faggot? I got a boner! Does that make me a faggot?! He had such a nice ass! Why did this have to happen now?! And what did he mean by "initiation"?!*

Eddie looked like a zombie as he walked to the main dressing room. He was about to knock, when the door swung open and the boy who was number seventy-four from the audition ran out, pulling his pants up. A leather-clad Luis Miguel stood in the doorway holding a bullwhip.

"Dammit, boys, you know better than to leave the door unlocked!" A chorus of youthful voices begged his forgiveness from inside. "Well, he obviously didn't have what it takes to be a Muchacho." Luis Miguel looked at Eddie's stupefied face. "What the fuck are you looking at?! You're late!"

The musclebound man effortlessly pulled the boy into the room, quickly locking the door behind him. "Welcome to showbiz, *muchacho!*"

The horny groupies, the drugs and, oh yes, the hot nasty sex. It had been fun while it lasted – almost two years. Until that fateful night in 1990 when they were busted at Miami International Airport for drug trafficking. That was the downfall of Los Muchachos. But not of Eddie Pacheco. His star may have gone supernova, yet deep in his heart he knew it would someday shine once more.

Like the voice of God, if God were Latino, the announcer's booming baritone filled the auditorium, bringing Eddie back to reality. *"Y ahora damas y caballero, ex-Muchacho, Eddie Paaacheco!"*

The crowd roared when Eddie walked onto the stage. And when the follow-spot hit him, he knew he was home again.

THE BLACKGUARD

William Cozad

"Blackguard: a scoundrel; one who uses foul or abusive language." - Webster's New World Dictionary

I had to pass the glassed-in security office to get to the men's room at the department store. The toilet was at the rear, up a flight of stairs. You'd think the closeness of the security office would be a deterrent to cruising the tea room, but it wasn't. This place was one of the busiest such places in town. While I never considered myself a tea room aficionado, I knew you took your tricks where you found them, and this night I was horny as hell. Climbing the stairs, I thought about the last time I'd scored in this toilet. There was someone in one of the stalls and I peeked through the door crack. A twentyish blond hunk was sitting on the throne, masturbating. Wasting no time, I entered the next stall, bent down, and looked up underneath. I asked him if he needed some relief and he responded by kneeling on the tile floor and presenting me with his long, thin, uncut prick. A pretty cock on a hairy, studly blond. It only took a few slides on his hard throbber before he blew and, since it was nearing closing time, he took off soon after. I licked my lips and headed home too.

This time, as I passed the office, I noticed a large, thirtyish black man with a shaved head, seated at the panel of television monitors. He was in uniform: a navy blue shirt with a company logo shoulder patch, and navy slacks. He glanced up and I smiled at him. I'm normally not attracted to black guys but he was *gorgeous*.

I continued to the john, thinking about that black guard. He shaved his head like a pro athlete – that was what made him look so incredibly virile. And show me a man in uniform, any uniform, and I'm putty in his hands. Maybe it's a throwback to when I was fourteen and fifteen and started picking up servicemen.

I was inside the men's room, taking a leak, when I heard the door open. I was surprised to see the black guard walk up to the urinal next to mine. He reeled out his cock and there were no divider shields, so I got a good look at it. And what a beauty it was – fat black shaft with a pink, circumcised head. My jaw dropped as I gawked at his awesome dick.

He splashed golden piss into the bowl, then shook off the drops. He started stroking his meat, which grew quickly, until I realized I was staring at an engorged ten inches. He waved it in my direction.

"Like it, eh?" he asked.

"Oh, yeah. You've got a beautiful piece of meat."

"Go on, touch it."

I hesitated. Maybe he was a decoy and would bust me. Maybe he was a crazy. I'd recently read that there were a million and a half security guards in the U.S. Some states didn't run background checks, they just gave them a badge and sent them to work.

But I couldn't stop myself. In a trance-like state, I reached over and felt his now throbbing cock.

"Wanna suck on it, don't you?"

"Oh, yes," I gushed. "It would be an honor and a privilege."

I knelt on the floor. He pulled me back to my feet.

"What's wrong?"

"Gotta secure this place. I don't want no interruptions. I work here, you know."

I watched while he stuffed his dick back into his pants. He got the "Closed for Cleaning" sign out of the closet and locked the door from the inside. He leaned against the door and rubbed the bulge in his pants. "Okay, kid, do your thing," he barked.

Kneeling on the tile floor again, I rubbed my face against his gabardine uniform pants and nibbled at his boner.

"Take it out," he demanded.

Unzipping his fly, I freed his monster meat and bobbed it up and down.

"Whatcha waitin' for?" he snarled.

Holding his thick dick by the base, I swabbed the bulbous crown. I could feel the heat of his throbbing boner.

"Put it in your mouth."

I'd sucked all kinds, but never a black one. I had to stretch my lips to fit them around it.

"Oh yeah, suck it. Suck that big motherfucker."

I managed to swallow about half of the shaft before I gagged. But I was really hungry for that piece of dark meat. I only let it slip out for a moment to catch my breath.

"Jack it while you suck it. Never found me a bitch who could swallow the whole thing. I thought maybe a 'mo could, with all your experience."

"I can do it," I bragged.

But I took my sweet time. His big balls were beauties as well, and I paused to lap at his wrinkled sac.

"Yeah, suck my balls. That makes me hot."

It wasn't easy to fit those monster low-hangers into my mouth, but I managed to get them both in and hummed away on them.

"Oh, Christ, yes. Suck my nuts. They're boilin'."

I swished his bull-balls around for a while, then returned to the task of sucking that dick. Burying my face in his kinky pubes, I drew in his funky man scent. My own cock was hanging out of my pants, hard and throbbing.

"Oh, yeah, kid, suck it. Suck my big black dick."

With renewed gusto, I gobbled up the guard's cock, managing to take it all the way down and deep-throat it.

"Oh, yeah, you did it, you little shit. Yeah, suck it. Keep suckin' it."

I jerked my prick in the same rhythm that I sucked on his tube steak.

"Take it all again. Oh, yeah, that's it."

I could have choked to death but I didn't care. I loved the feel of my throat being stuffed with his dick.

Apparently my slow suck wasn't doing it for the security guard. He clasped my head and furiously mouth-fucked me. I kept beating my meat while he pumped his prick down my throat. His cock kept getting harder and harder. I knew he was about to explode.

"Cumming, cocksucker! Shooting my load in your motherfuckin' mouth!"

I felt him spurt his wad down my gullet and concentrated on siphoning the jizz from those big bull balls. I could take care of myself later. The guard helped me up to my feet.

I couldn't stop myself. Reaching over, I grabbed his cum-slick softening cock.

"Want some more, don't you?"

My jaws were sore but I wasn't about to turn him down. It looked like he had a double load in his nuts.

"You know, I've never had any white boy butt before."

Next thing I knew he had my jeans and shorts down, and I was bent over the porcelain urinal. Looking over my shoulder, I realized what was about to happen. I wanted it, that's the truth, but I couldn't help wondering if I could take a dick that big.

"No, I can't. I don't get screwed."

"Sure you do. All 'mos take it up the ass."

"Not me."

He stood behind me and slapped it against my ass.

"No, don't," I protested.

"All bitches love my big dick. I can last a long time screwing."

"Please don't."

"Once I get goin' you'll love it."

I continued to watch over my shoulder while he sucked on his fuck finger, making it slick with spit, then inserted it up my hole.

Trying to act chaste, I lost it when I felt him finger-fuck my butthole.

"It's tight. But I can take care of that and stretch it."

"No, I don't want it. Let me go. I'll scream for help."

"I'll gag you with my dick."

I was just playing with him, teasing him. But I was worried. Maybe he'd force it in and really hurt me.

He fingered my hole, loosening me up while he jacked his dick, pressing it against my butt.

"Got a lily-white ass that was made for fuckin'. Made to take my fuckin' big black dick."

He took his finger out and started to slap my ass.

"Stop, you're hurting me. Damn!"

"Just gettin' you all warmed up, little boy."

"No, don't. This has gone far enough."

"Okay, wimp. I thought you were man enough to take it."

"I can't – not without a rubber."

"Okay. I can handle that." He grinned and pulled one of

those jumbo condoms out of his pocket. He tore it open and slid the latex down the shaft.

"You're gonna want all of it. I was right about you. The way you smiled at me with that lusty look in your eye, I knew this was my lucky day, that I'd found a white 'mo to service my big black dick."

I spit in my hand and stuck a gob in my crack. I never thought I'd be so wanton. But I wanted this stud more than I'd wanted anyone in years. I clutched the cold white urinal as he rubbed his stiff, condomed cock in my crevice. "Fuck my crack," I begged. Reaching behind me, I spread my asscheeks as wide as I could.

The guard pressed his prick right into my assring. I don't even remember the last time I'd been opened up so wide. The pain of penetration made me gasp, brought tears to my eyes.

I bucked back and he rammed his meat up my hole. I knew it was in all the way because I could feel his wiry pubes. I clutched his uniformed legs, feeling the muscular thighs, and gulped for breath.

"Fuck me. I want it. Oh, I need it *real* bad."

"I know, boy, I know!" He held onto my waist while he thrust into my hole. He pumped slow and deep at first then harder and faster. I felt his big bull balls slapping against my cheeks. Despite what he said, that he could last and last, he came right away.

"Get ready. I'm gonna blast my big load up your pretty white butt. And you're gonna take it! Take it all!"

Despite the jumbo rubber, I felt the fiery sperm when it spewed into my bowels.

"Please," I screamed, "stay inside me. Don't pull out yet!"

While he rotated his hips and moved his softening prick around in my butthole, I beat my meat for all I was worth. My asshole was on fire and stuffed with black dick.

"I'm coming! I'm coming with your big black dick up my ass!" I roared, and let go with gobs of frothy jizz which landed in the urinal and dripped down the shiny porcelain.

When the guard pulled his cock out, I suddenly felt abandoned, vacant. I'd never been stretched that much in my life.

I flushed the urinal and the guard peeled off his rubber and flushed it to oblivion.

As I hoisted my shorts and jeans, he stuffed that incredible black snake back into his uniform trousers.

"I'd better get back to my panel," he said. "Shit, the store was probably robbed blind while I was fuckin' around on company time. Good thing the sergeant is off today or I'd get canned for leavin' my post."

"I'm glad he was off," I chuckled.

He smiled as he unlocked the door and checked to see if the coast was clear. He ushered me out. "Speakin' of gettin' off, I get off at midnight," he said, winking at me. "Do you know where the employee entrance is?"

"I'll find it," I said, shaking with anticipation. "God, I'll find it!"

THIEF OF NIGHT'S BOUNTY

L. Amore

*"Your soul is back from the confines of my prison
Prisoner of a sky of lazy paths of flight
Where so calmly in the hollow of a poem
Under the sky of my hand had slept one thief's night."*
 - *Jean Genet*

    The breeze did nothing to quell the heat in the room. The room was hot, as it usually is in New Orleans in September. He sat in the wicker chair looking up to the ceiling. The salmon paint peeling away in various spots to give way to the puce-colored plaster beneath it. The look of elegant decay. He found it disconcerting now that he'd actually paid someone to do this. He thought to himself that he could have just had it painted, waited a couple of years and let the heat and humidity do it's magic. The results would have been the same. Too late now.

    The shutters were locked and the slats open to allow in what little breeze there was coming off the river. He loved New Orleans, and in a couple of months when it started to cool and the rainy season came he would love it even more. It was raining now. The slow steady warm rain he always connected with the city. Through the slats, amidst the dark of the mist and the verdant shining foliage, he could see a lit window of the house behind his, past the almost unbelievable length of the garden that was his backyard. The lit window a shining beacon above and behind the explosion of color that was the bougainvillea clinging to the intricate wrought iron fence in vivid purple and orange bursts.

    The mood of faded glory, ruined finery, accompanied his mood perfectly. He didn't know why he'd come back to New Orleans. The house had been closed for two years, all the furniture shrouded with white covers. It felt right to be back. Just right.

    His memories of New Orleans were good ones. The Mardi Gras floats and the parties at the bars afterward. God the parties afterward. He smiled to himself. The dark backrooms. The time he had shot, with deadly accuracy, the lighted neon necklace from his neck to the erect penis of an anonymous man being fucked on a pool table twenty feet away. The banana trees that even without fruit had leaves that you thought would pop from just the slightest touch. The bougainvillea in all their ruby shades, lighting every nighttime corner if graced with even the slightest illumination from any street light. The night's bounty. The night that only New Orleans could countenance. Elegance and decay.

Out of the corner of his eye he saw a movement in the lighted window across the back yard. It was a second floor window, floor to ceiling, that opened onto a side porch, high enough that the view wasn't spoiled by the jungle below. He quickly dimmed the lights and squinted through the slats. Rain hit the open slats and lightly sprayed his face. He saw that it was a man as he came into view again. He was walking around in what looked to him as boxer shorts, but he was too far away to tell. Suddenly remembering his binoculars, he almost had to tear himself away from the window. The second he did guilt settled on him and he was surprised by his feelings of want. Wanting to see this man. Stealing. Stealing what?

Dusk hit the light in the window. He looked again; it was very dark. Now the decision was made for him. There would be nothing to look at. His head leaned on the shutter, the rain still hitting his moist visage, as he felt almost vexed that there was no more. Suddenly the light flooded the rift to someone else that the window so generously offered. The light was different now. Amber imbued with lightning flashes of pure white. He had the television on now and it looked as if he was standing watching just a few feet away.

Whether it was his mind playing tricks on him or the actuality of what his hand was massaging he couldn't see from the distance. All he knew was that he hadn't been as exited in forever and he wanted more.

He tore himself from the window and ran to get his binoculars. He hadn't used them in years and any other time it probably would have taken him a week to find them, but all his senses were heightened by lust. He found them in less a minute. The thief was back at the scene of the crime .

Glorious. It seemed as though he were in the room with him. All the dark wood, clearly visible now, framed the man who was leaning on the back of a sofa watching television.

And what a man. Sandy brown hair topped off a profile God bestowed to only a lucky few. The stalwart torso seemed to hold it's bulk with a reverence, like the devout clutching their religion. His thighs like the Italianate pillars flanking the window, framing a view to what had the possibilities of paradise. His thick arm ended with the hand that was rubbing the sandy locks. Each ripple of muscular lat stirred as his hand moved over his head and the back of his neck. There was a definite swelling in the crotch of his boxers. His other hand came to grip the corpulent node straining his shorts.

Weak with excitement, he felt the stirring in his own loins. Unlike what he'd felt in a long time, this weakness in the thighs along with the guilty pleasure of having it at someone else's expense. Stealing. Stealing what? Stealing someone's intimate moment they had no intention of sharing. Taking pleasure from someone oblivious to knowing they were giving it. There was a power dynamic involved that put a gloss on the skein of desire that wouldn't be there in any other situation.

The binoculars were shaking and he rested them against the moist wood as he rid himself of his pants. They fell in a damp puddle of cotton as his cock was freed to ride the humid air. The breeze was still coming from the river yet it went unfelt as the heat now was internal. The shirt ended up with the pants before they were both kicked across the room. Disorientation reared it's head before he was able to focus the lenses to the window again. He was lost.

His boxer shorts were gone now. The hand that cupped his bulge now enwrapped his overweight sex, which was almost hard. The motion of his fist soon brought this gargantuan organ to full tumescence. The man's soul snatched with each glance through the binoculars. Each second was owning him, each minute was etched in memory to have him forever. Stealing the night's bounty. More bounty then city itself could ever offer, moist, verdant and decadent as it was. This was pure. decadence. Afforded to the few who would dare catch a glimpse.

His own hand worked his straining penis. The other grasped the binoculars with a fierceness that was one part desire to keep the scene in view, and the other not to drop them and finish the job quickly. The view was all profile. Exultant sexual profile. There he was. The sweat that was running down his arms and thighs was the same glistening the torso of the man in his lenses. He thanked God that he'd bought the expensive binoculars, the ones that gave him this vision. A thief of sex.

The man in the window leaned back further against the chair and spread his legs. Through the binoculars he could see the blond fur that started at the man's ankles and traveled up in varying thickness. Each movement was languid and sensual. It was almost as though he were putting on a show. The man's face turned to the window and he got scared that he saw him. His face exquisite, thick arched eyebrows, mustache and goatee, great cheekbones. His eyes seemed to be searching in the darkness. He rationalized that it would be impossible with the dim lighting in the room and the distance, to be seen.

As soon as he calmed the man grabbed his cock at the base and shook it. It was monstrous. Eleven inches if one inch. He turned back to the television. His hand went to the head of his penis working it like he was turning a door knob. It moved down the shaft until it rested on it's base. He gave it another shake and it seemed through the binoculars that it got harder and took an even sharper upward angle.

The whole time, the one free hand of the thief worked his own tool. He had come close to climax three times but stopped just in time to let it continue. He wanted release when it came to the desire of his objectification.

His desire was now pulling on his nipples. He raised the binoculars to see the hard buds, as big as pencil erasers and surrounded by golden down. His excitement brought the lenses back down to his cock. His hand was off his member, but quickly came back to it. More spit. The man's hand glided up and down and he thought of what he wouldn't do to be kneeling between those wide spread legs.

He adjusted the sight and visually closed in on the hand and cock. The hand working over every delicious inch, every vein creating a bold blue lace covering the shaft. The movements got quicker and he knew the man was nearing the end, stroking his cock with insistent purpose. He widened his view slightly and saw the man's pecs bulging with exertion, his upper chest and neck red with effort. His head was thrown back, all the cords in his neck standing out. His discharge arched high, wet and out of view, which was a good four feet away. The geyser was unending. Stream after stream of come exploded from his red, engorged cock. Finally it ebbed enough to where it's landing could be seen in the confines of the window. The man was massaging his furry chest as he neared the end of his orgasm. His body wracked with spasms of pleasure.

With the binoculars still locked into place pleasure was taken again. Drenching the window and the wall beneath it until he was spent. He stood feeling the weakness that comes after.

A strong breeze hit, rattling the slats of the shutter, cooling his drenched torso. The light across the way went out. He finally lowered the binoculars feeling a tight pain in his arm he hadn't noticed before. He was left with the sultry night scents of New Orleans. A smile came to his lips. He turned back around seeing all the draped furniture, like amorphic ghosts littering the rooms. He decided to stay for awhile.

NIGHT TRAIN

Edmund Miller

It was the end of a long day, but at least I had missed the rush-hour crowds. By 7:50 in the evening you can always find a place to sit down, by 9:20 you can get a whole seat to yourself, and by 1:20 a.m.—when I was finally getting out of the city—there were only eight or ten other people in the car. As I entered, I instinctively headed toward one of those out-of-the-way end sections.

There I locked eyes with him right away. He was in a triple seat, and he had the whole thing to himself. So I took the double across the aisle. He glanced out the window as I fumbled among my papers for something to do. So what if he wasn't interested: I was just window shopping. As I figured it, at least we were together.

The final "All aboard" was called, the buzzer sounded, and the train lurched out of Penn Station. While we waited for the conductor to make his way into our little corner of the world, I gave the guy the twice-over. Barely legal, he had large dark eyes and neatly trimmed dark hair. And he was a golden tan all over. His skimpy attire consisted of a tank top, sneakers, and a pair of cut-offs. The muscles of his chest were straining the tank top just about to the limit. He stared straight ahead, paying no attention to me as I rummaged in my briefcase, losing my heart and my cool.

After the conductor took his ticket and looked at my monthly pass, I settled in for some serious surreptitious viewing. And, wouldn't you know it, the guy played right into my hands by raising one leg up on the seat in comfortable abandon. His cut-offs revealed what he had on underneath: very white Jockey briefs. With the unself-consciousness of youth, he chose this moment to stretch and expose himself even more. It really was an all-over tan, I learned—with him in this position, I could see a good distance up his legs beyond the cut-offs, which he neglected to pull back into place. While he had his arms up to stretch (incidentally revealing just a little pale fuzz on his belly), he took a sniff at his armpit. He looked up at me—or through me—and then took another sniff before turning to stare out the window into the night.

Then the train hit Woodside, and the conductor walked the length of it for a second time, once again looking at tickets. Having been told by the conductor to take his foot off the seat, the guy slouched down with his knee up on the back of the seat in front of him, leaving himself—if anything—even more exposed to my scrutiny than before. We were going to be alone for twenty minutes; the conductor wouldn't be walking the length of the whole train again before we reached Great Neck.

So there I was, my indiscreet eyes glued to him and my tongue hanging (figuratively) out. There he was, his eyes searching the darkness outside the window and his hands looking for something to do. And then they found it. I was sure at first that it was no more than just some unself-conscious fiddling as he reached inside his cut-offs and adjusted his crotch. But then after a few minutes I caught his eyes mirrored in the blackness of the window. He knew I was watching him all right, the little tease. And he started kneading himself through his cut-offs. I shut my eyes for a second to make sure it was all real. Indeed it was. At least, when I opened my eyes again what he was doing was running his index finger inside the elastic of his briefs—they were, after all, getting a little constricted. Then he whipped his finger under his dick and gave it a quick flip so that it would have more room to grow. He ran his hand over the tautness which strained at his briefs, then lifted the elastic with his finger, giving me my first glimpse of the dick itself.

I sat up in my seat and scanned the car. Someone was dozing just two seats away, but I seemed to be the only one paying any attention. As I shifted in my seat, the guy slipped the elastic down over the whole length of his dick. For a moment it bobbed in the air like a tree about to be felled. It was the same lush gold color as his skin: he seemed not to have any tan lines at all. Then he freed his balls as well. These were like robin's eggs, a delicate translucent handful beside the giant dick with veins visibly throbbing by this time. But his delicate balls seemed to serve his purpose well enough. He put his hand underneath to free them completely, then cupped them alternately in his fingers as if debating the merits of two indistinguishable plums at a fruit stand.

The train pulled into Murray Hill, and somebody got on. But the new passenger went into the other part of the car. The guy ran a finger slowly up the length of his dick and glanced down to watch it vibrate in response. When the conductor opened the door to come through to collect the ticket of the new passenger, the guy quickly shifted his leg and brought his arm down to provide a temporary screen. But a few seconds later, he was back in business.

This time he ran his hand under his dick, palm down, as if displaying a piece of goods in an expensive jewelry shop. He still had not turned to look at me, but he no longer pretended to be looking out the window into the darkness. He was giving me an occasional glance—but very shyly and tentatively considering the circumstances.

I thought it looked like a good time to do something to get me more actively involved in what was happening, so the next time he glanced my way I cocked a thumb toward the little restroom just behind us. He looked around to see where I meant, then tidied himself up in the minimal way necessary for the change of location. I heaved all my papers into my briefcase and made for the rest room as fast as I could without disturbing the dozer. The guy followed right behind me.

As soon as we were inside, he stood up on the metal platform that encloses the toilet, threw his head back, and closed his eyes. He left it to me to lower his cut-offs and free his engorged dick from its prison of cotton briefs. This last operation was a little tricky since the briefs were stretched just about to their limit by this time. He winced when I accidentally let the elastic snap back just after I had exposed the head. Then again perhaps it wasn't an accident. To some extent I think maybe I wanted to see whether I could get him to lend me a hand or at least say a few words of encouragement. But he did neither. Of course, he had to hold on to keep his balance in the moving train, but I thought he might at least have opened his eyes. Still, you don't look a gift horse in the mouth—so to speak.

I played with the dick, straining to get my hands around it. I also toyed with his balls because I knew he would like that. I soon got him so impatient that, with one hand, he applied a little light pressure on the top of my head, indicating that he wanted me to suck some dick. I was not unwilling to go down on him, but naturally I wanted to savor every sensation of the unexpected opportunity. I started by licking the shaft. With so much surface to cover, it took me a fair amount of time just to get the thing properly slick. As I did so I slipped his cut-offs and briefs further down his legs and made him take them off entirely. I wanted to see what I was working on. However, he wouldn't let me take off his tank top; he even pushed my hand away when I tried to massage his tits.

So instead I started to work on his balls very seriously. This was all he needed to get his lube juice flowing, and when the shaft of his dick was all slick with it, I ran my tongue around the glans a bit but held tight for a minute, resisting his thrusts just to prolong the moment. Then when I could tell he was nearly desperate for me to get on with it, I took a firm hold on his hard hairless backside and started rubbing it and spreading his cheeks apart. When I knew he could stand the waiting no longer, I took the whole dick down my throat with a single gulp. I deep-throated him for a couple of thrusts as I twisted his ball sac. He grunted ecstatically.

When he was just about to shoot, I went all the way down on him. His hard young dick lurched forward, driven by his upper body. I thought for a minute there that he was going to puncture my esophagus. As he scrambled to regain his balance, I rammed two fingers up his asshole and spread them wide. He started convulsing in my mouth and didn't let up for a whole minute.

When he stopped shooting, he made a few half-hearted swipes at my hand—still firmly in place up his ass. But the train lurched, and he had to stop trying to dislodge my resident fingers—otherwise he would have lost his balance. I popped in another finger just for good measure as I began the delicate work of licking his shaft of his dick clean. I kept at this for a while, gently massaging with my fingers the whole time.

Finally I noticed that the train had become surprisingly still. I pulled my fingers out of their cozy nook and peered out the window. Sure enough: we were at the Port Washington terminus.

As I turned back around to make the appropriate comments about the end of the line, I saw the door to the little rest room swing shut. The guy was gone. Worse than that—my destination had been Great Neck. I had overshot my station.

Later, taking the milk train back from Port Washington to Great Neck, I had to keep rubbing my eyes to stay awake. I certainly did not want to overshoot twice in the same night.

MILK RUN

Christopher Thomas

Here one seeks paradise
in a tight pair of faded jeans,
random fuzz on the chins of the young,
the haughty armpits
of the perfectly built.
It's a place to go down with slow kisses.

One seeks magic in the gaze
of the green and gangly,
the gentle swelling
when one finds the sweet gender
bulging below the belt
like a corn dog on a stick.

One circles the block,
an endless seeker of nirvana,
the groins of heaven,
the oral auras,
the lush appendages
of them that suck the divine sword.

A CIRCLE OF A THOUSAND BOYS

Antler

What is it about sucking while being sucked
    that is so beautiful?
The pleasure of getting your cock sucked
    while sucking a cock
      knowing everything your cock feels
      the cock you're sucking feels also...
A circle of a thousand boys sucking each other's cocks
    at the same time...
A circle of a hundred boys sucking each other's cocks
    at the same time...
A circle of ten boys sucking each other's cocks
    at the same time...
A man sucking a young man sucking a boy...
The one being sucked by the one being sucked
Sees how the increasing joy his friend feels being blown
    is translated into his own sucking passion...
Sees the two cocks sucked at the same time...
The cock of the third completely visible,
    throbbing by itself, bright
    and lubricant-jeweled...
If the three are delirious enough
    perhaps it will come
    without even being
    touched...

LOVE IN THE BOOKSTORE

Ken Anderson

After dark
whenever the urge arises
like a troubled spirit
I visit the bookstore. I cross
into the other realm
of night. I step
inside a haunted house
where men, like zombies, wait
or walk. Some carry their eyes
like eggs. Some play a secret game
in corners. And then
there are the sorry
and the few
who follow men
as if they follow love
into a movie stall.

One steps
inside a stall
where a young man slumps
against the wall – his blond hair blue
in the light. They dog-fuck
till the manager knocks
and the bottom drops a quarter
in the slot. The top holds on
to his partner's sides, bumping his butt
the way
he bumps
a sensitive pinball machine.

You wallowed
in my crotch, and I, in turn,
would blow your smoldering embers
to a fire. We found each other's awkward lust
no less erotic

than the silent film
where graceful jocks performed.
Then a fierce hunger drove us on
to mouth each other's mouth
and hold each other tight
like buoys. Above
the sighs
and whispers, yes, the murmurs
and the moans – the radio sang
its simple carnal song. If only
for a minute, something else
could happen, there – while all
around us
in the stalls
the strangers stripped
and fucked.

Young & Willing

A Novel by
JOHN C. DOUGLAS

STARbooks Press
Sarasota, FL

I love sex. I'm the first to admit it
but it has afforded me much pleasure
living in Nashville writing books ab
business. In 1979, I was in the middle of
book ever when my lover of two years up

To pull myself together, and finish the b
needed to get away, to return to a place wh
comfortable once, a sleepy little town in Florida
Georgia border. It was my hometown and in thos
some reason, I, a precocious teenager, tended to
around almost every corner. I was happy to discover
hadn't changed much.

Foreward

It's caused me a lot of grief as well. Years ago, I was ...out the country music ...my most challenging ...and left me. ...ook, I decided I ...ere I felt truly ...just over the ...e days, for ...find sex ...things

One

I was surprised that Mrs. Lonas didn't hear her son's sharp cries of pleasure, or the squeaking of the bed as his muscular young body writhed, bucked and quivered beneath my savage hunching.

It would have made little difference to either of us, for the union of our aroused bodies produced an ecstacy that rendered us oblivious to everything but the increasingly delightful fusion and friction of responsive flesh.

Randy Lonas was no novice, and he had welcomed my initial advances with an undisguised eagerness which I recognized as that mysterious chemistry which attracts two males in a way no straight can understand.

Young Randy's body might well have been sculpted by a highly talented and imaginative pederast. His skin was flawless and sun-bronzed over the rippling muscles, the face was a handsome blend of youthful innocence and ageless sensuality. It flickered in the long-lashed green eyes, and betrayed itself in the suggestive curve of the full, ripe lips.

The boy's hair was a cap of tight blond curls which accented his appeal to my own bisexual nature, and I wasted no time in determining this lovely creature's true inclination. The first time we were alone, I slid my hips down in the chair and angled my thighs to give him a good view of my bulging crotch.

Randy did not try to disguise his stare, and the green eyes narrowed in speculative interest.

"I hope you don't mind sharing your bathroom," I said innocently. "I'm pretty easy to get along with."

His eyes were still on my basket as he answered, "I don't mind. In fact, I wouldn't mind sharing my bedroom. Sometimes I get kinda lonesome."

"Same here," I nodded. "The trouble is that some people can't understand that." I paused. "I like to sleep in the raw, Randy. Will that bother you?"

He wagged his head. "I do that, too. It's okay."

I waited until he raised his eyes to meet mine. Then, "I believe we understand each other. Don't you think so, Randy?"

The tip of a pink tongue teased his upper lip, and his

response was a near whisper. "Oh, god! I hope so! I hope I'm not wrong in what I'm thinking."

"No, you're not wrong," I assured him, deliberately cupping my bulging basket and sitting straight again as I heard his mother's footsteps. "We're thinking the same thing!"

The house I was born in was now a rooming house, run by Mrs. Lonas, who offered board as well. At first, I wasn't sure I wanted to stay there, but once I took a good look at Randy, I would have paid ten times what she asked for the privilege.

Just two hours after our conversation, I was on the boy and in him, my cock filling and stretching his hot ass as I worked it deeper and deeper into the convulsing channel of responsive tissue.

Randy was on his back, knees drawn high and wide to elevate that perfectly curved bottom. I had lubricated my huge prick before mounting him, and I had at least half of the nine inches inside his anus before I lowered my chest onto his, and covered those soft lips in a long and tongue-swirling kiss.

By the time I came up for air, the youngster had seven inches of cock in his asshole, and I could tell by his muffled whimpering that he had never taken more than that.

"Oh, Christ!" he groaned, his arms embracing me, and his legs climbing higher to scissor my waist. "You've got a big dick!"

I kissed him again, driving my cock deeper.

"And you've got a tight ass!" I grunted. "Damn, baby! If I stayed around you very long, I'd fuck myself to death! You are one beautiful boy!"

"Is my ass really good?" he demanded, flexing his rectum about my throbbing prick. "I want to make it real good for you, man! I want it to be the best you ever had! I've never been fucked by a famous person before."

"Shit!" I grinned down at him. "I'm not famous. Just a half-assed writer with a few successes."

"But you know all those famous people – "

"I don't know them. I have interviewed them. There's a big difference."

"Did you fuck any of 'em?"

I licked those delicious lips and rolled my belly against his pulsating dick where it lay trapped between us. "No, but I want to give *you* the best fuck you've ever had so when *you're* famous you can tell an interviewer like me all about it!" He cried out at the exquisite frictioning of his anus as I pulled my dick back through the slippery grip and eased it in again, the flared knob massaging his prostate through the intestinal wall. His ass twisted and jerked to increase the delightful sensation.

Still giving him only a part of my cock, I slid it in and out, working my knees alongside his grinding hips. Straightening my upper body, I gripped his ankles and spread his legs farther apart.

His fingers clawed at the rumpled sheet. "Oh, god!" he panted. "I can't wait, Jeff! I'm gonna come!"

He hadn't touched his own dick, but that organ was rearing up and jerking over his belly each time I drove into his ass. Unlike most guys, who beat off while they're being balled, Randy was getting his pleasure only from having his colon packed.

"Shoot it!" I groaned, fucking him with short strokes that concentrated on that responsive prostate. I covered his mouth with mine, muffling his cries, as his asshole convulsed, and between our bellies, his cock jerked and spurted in an explosive orgasm, the hot sticky semen making our flesh squish exitingly as I humped him through the ecstatic release.

"I'm sorry, Jeff!" he whimpered. "It felt so good that I couldn't hold back!"

"Don't apologize, kid," I said, increasing the speed of my strokes as I fucked him. "Just work that ass for me. I'm gonna screw you till you can't walk!"

It took some time to work the head of my prick past the point where the boy's asshole had been stretched by the other dicks he had welcomed during the past three years. But, when I had forced the last two inches into his convulsing intestine, he began grinding his hips with renewed and even greater pleasure.

Only then did I fuck the lad with the practiced skill of a veteran, varying the position, depth and speed of my thrusts as I kissed those sweet lips and gave him my tongue to suck, knowing that later he would suck my dick with even more passionate eagerness.

Drawing my cock almost out of his squirming anus, I fucked

him with short rapid strokes. Then, as his hips climbed receptively, I plunged my prick to the hilt in that hot juicy channel, grinding my pubic hair against his balls, and massaging his dick with my belly, the area already lubricated with his own come.

That's an advantage of having a big cock. You can lean forward enough to swap kisses without having to pull out of your partner's ass. And once you've slid up into his tail, pulling out is the last thing you want to do.

For several minutes, I fucked him with full-length strokes that made him whimper.

Finally, he panted, "You really know how to fuck!" He wanted to say more, but I suddenly altered my stroke to a short deep jabbing that made him grunt each time my prick rammed its big head into that newly explored area of his gut. His arms and legs embraced my hunching body as I feasted on his delicious mouth and fucked that hot spasming asshole.

He couldn't tell me that he was about to come again. He didn't have to. The savage writhing of his hips, the rhythmic contractions of his rectum, and the hot jerking of his trapped cock told me all I needed to know.

I began running my tongue in and out of his mouth, still fucking his ass with those deep short strokes that enabled me to keep my belly pressed against his dick as it spilled its second load between us.

"Nobody's ever made me come twice like that!" he gasped as I let him rest for a few moments. He kissed me with a fierce tenderness. "I think I love you, Jeff!"

"Better wait to decide that," I warned, "until I'm through fucking you. Are you ready for a load of come in that ass?"

"Jesus! Yes!" he cried, squeezing his rectal muscles about my cock. "I want your come! Fuck me, Jeff! Fuck my ass! Fuck it hard!"

Until then, I had been experimenting and preparing the lad for the next several minutes. In doing so, I had loosened his asshole just enough to permit those anal muscles to really work on my prick, and the channel was now slick and juicy, its walls coated with a mixture of my own pre-ejaculate and the natural oil of his intestine. It was just like I wanted it for the ecstatic gallop down the home stretch.

"Pull your legs up higher, Randy, and work that ass for me. I'm not gonna stop again."

That's when the noise really began, for I was fucking his ass with bed-jarring thrusts, and he cried out each time my big cock drove up into his belly. And, in addition to his cries and whimpers, and the rhythmic squeaking of the bed, we could hear the wet squishing of my prick as it pistoned, full-length, in and out of his bouncing, twisting asshole.

I knew that we were making too much noise, but I no longer cared. Our mouths were fused, tongues probing, and I was getting one of the best pieces of ass I had ever had.

Every stroke sent thrills back through my throbbing prick and into my swinging balls as I fucked Randy harder and faster.

Inside, his asshole was chewing, sucking and churning about my driving cock, and it was feeling more wonderful with every thrust.

I tried to cram even my balls into that juicy anus as the first ecstatic jolt of my orgasm convulsed my naked body.

"UNNNGGGHHH!" Randy cried, for my come was spurting deeper than any he had ever felt before, and he yelped again with each powerful volley of the thick cream far up in his wildly churning rectum.

The anal muscles milked my jetting cock, and his ass bucked and writhed to friction the convulsing channel about my prick. The boy had just been fucked by the biggest cock he had ever taken; he had been screwed longer than ever before; and he had already experienced two gut-wrenching orgasms.

Now, as his asshole accepted the greatest single load of come it had ever received, and he felt it much deeper and hotter than ever before, the youngster came again, actually screaming in unbearable ecstasy while his prick jerked, throbbed and exploded between us.

When I could control my own passion, I hissed, "Your mother will hear us, Randy!"

Panting, his ass still grinding about my cock, he gasped, "She knows! It's okay! She knows! . . . Oh, god! . . . It's so fucking good!"

It was later, while he lay panting in my arms, that he explained. Mrs. Lonas knew her son was gay, and she accepted it. Aware of my books, she had concluded that I would welcome the opportunity to enjoy Randy's young body, and that he, in turn, would appreciate the experience of an older man.

"Some of your books are really wild, Jeff." He was still breathing hard from our strenuous workout. His cheek rested on my bare chest, and his fingers toyed with my balls as we talked.

"Which ones do you like the most?" I asked, running my own fingers through those thick curls. He responded by licking my left nipple and squeezing my semi-erect cock.

"The ones about gays, naturally," he replied. "I get horny when I read one of them."

"Have you ever fucked a girl, Randy?" I said. "As handsome as you are, you could have your pick."

"Yeah," he agreed. "They come on pretty strong. But I don't fool around with them very much. Once in a while, I ball one, especially if she lets me screw her ass. That way, I can pretend she's a boy. But what I really dig is a dick! I can't help it. That's just the way I am."

"Show me how much you like my dick," I whispered, pushing the boy's head down toward my cock, its swelling shaft held in his curled fingers.

Eagerly, his mouth found the velvet knob and slipped over it like a warm, wet glove, his tongue caressing and circling.

Slowly, almost lazily, the youngster began sucking, his lips sliding up and down the column, his saliva bathing it as he nursed, his beardless cheeks hollowing with each delightful tug.

As the pleasure mounted, I began working my hips in rhythm with Randy's oral strokes, pushing upward as his head descended, and retreating as his lips slid up the throbbing prick.

"Goddamn, baby!" I gasped. "You are good!"

He gave a little nasal murmur in recognition of my praise, and as if seeking to prove his ability, he drew back until only the meaty head of my cock was held captive in his mouth. Then, sucking with quick pulls, he flicked his tongue back and forth across the sensitive tip, while his hands worked between my thighs, gently manipulating my balls and teasing my anus.

He seemed to sense my wish, for his lips suddenly pulled free, and he buried his face between my legs, his tongue licking my balls. Tenderly, lovingly, and one at a time, he sucked the oyster-like orbs into his mouth, rolling them about and moaning with anticipation, knowing that his prize would be their creamy content.

For a moment, I thought he would stop at that point, for some males are reluctant to do what Randy did then. With a soft exclamation of passion, he used his hands to elevate my thighs, positioning my anus for his probing tongue.

"Jesus!" I groaned as the hot wetness invaded the delicate circle, stiffening to bore through the anal sphincter and wriggle up into the responsive channel.

"UNNNGGGHHH!" I cried, as Randy's lips shaped their softness about my rectum and, with his tongue buried deep, he began sucking.

I don't think anyone would deny that what we were doing was perverse, wicked, unnatural, and immoral. It was also almost unbearably delightful because it was so wrong.

We were sampling the forbidden fruit, enjoying a pleasure that we are told is not to be experienced. For myself, I was on the edge of orgasm, as Randy's tongue fucked me, and his greedy lips sucked and caressed the nerve-laced circlet. As for the boy, his nasal moans and whimpers told me that he was beyond rapture, beyond ecstacy. He was intoxicated with the sheer enormity of our shared wickedness, as was I.

Panting, and almost sobbing, I cried, "Get back on that cock, Randy! I'm almost there!"

There was a wet, slurping sound as he pulled his tongue out of my asshole and raised his head just far enough to take my prick in his mouth again, swallowing the head as he slid his lips down to the thick base. His throat contracted and quivered, sending thrills back through the swollen shaft to my seething balls.

His head bobbed, that sucking mouth fucking my prick by shaping a tunnel between tongue and palate. I grabbed his blond curls and thrust upward, ramming my cock deep with every stroke. And the youngster took it with moans of eagerness, his nursing more avid as he sensed my approaching orgasm.

Some men and boys suck for the simple pleasure of sucking a dick, and accept the orgasm only because it brings their partner extreme pleasure. Randy was sucking me for that, but it was eminently obvious that the boy wanted my come.

His own hips were jerking, down there between my legs, and I didn't have to see it to know that his prick was about to erupt, triggered by my impending finale.

"Oh, Randy!" I panted, my voice weak, for all my energy was being expended by my driving hips, shoving my cock in and out of his hungry throat.

The release was almost painful in its intensity. The come surged up through the throbbing shaft and spurted against his writhing tongue. He gave a nasal sound, almost like a whinny, an expression of ecstatic fulfillment, as he took my sperm with noisy and repeated swallowing.

My ejaculation was both forceful and prolonged, the ropy semen jetting into Randy's mouth in what threatened to be endless volleys.

Much later, he admitted that he had never received such a load, requiring him to gulp at least a dozen times to make certain he had it all. Even then, his lips and tongue continued their ministration, draining my balls of the last delicious drop, then holding my cock in his mouth and gently caressing it with his tongue as my passion subsided.

Moving up in the bed, he lay beside me, one slender leg draped over my thigh, his hand cradling my nuts, his warm, soft lips nibbling at my cheek.

"I love your cock, Jeff!" he whispered. "And I love your come!"

I turned my head to taste myself on his mouth. "You're gonna get plenty of both," I promised.

Two

Over the next five days, I fucked the pretty youngster in every position we could assume, and he sucked my prick repeatedly, drawing semen from my balls when I was convinced they were empty. Between that talented mouth and the hot, slippery suction of his tight ass, I could not get enough of him.

Mrs. Lonas pretended innocence, but expressed deli[ght] her son seemed happy with my companionship. I bega[n] on my book, and Randy left me alone for most of the d[ay]... hours. But, each night found me in Randy's room or him in mine.

Then, on Friday afternoon, Mrs. Lonas announced that she was going to visit her sister in Jackson, about two hundred miles away.

"She and Randy don't like each other," she confided. "But I don't like to leave him alone . Now that you're here, I feel he'll be all right."

I couldn't imagine the two of us doing anything we hadn't already done several times, so I agreed that I would keep an eye on the boy.

She planned to take a plane Saturday morning, and on Friday night, Randy came up with a pleasant surprise. He had told me of four boys who shared his propensity for a male sex partner, and with whom he had enjoyed several uninhibited couplings.

"You met Duane Eastman," he reminded me. "He came by yesterday, remember?"

It was not difficult to summon up an image of a slender, dark-haired beauty in a pair of denim cutoffs that displayed a pair of mouthwatering legs, a promising basket, and a deliciously curved ass.

"What about him?" I asked.

"Did you think he was attractive?" Randy asked. When I hesitated, he added, "Go on, Jeff. I won't be jealous."

"Yeah," I agreed. "I thought he was pretty."

"Would you like to fuck him?"

I'm not easily shocked, but Randy's question rattled me. If I said no, he'd think I was lying, and he'd be right. If I said yes, he's probably wonder why I wasn't satisfied with all the sex he was giving me.

"Why would I want to fuck him?" I played it safe.

"Because he's never had a dick up his ass, and he wants you to break him in. You and me."

"Both of us?" I asked, arching one eyebrow. "Why not you? You guys are buddies. How come you haven't already screwed him?"

"He wouldn't let me," Randy admitted. "Anyway, I'm not

that crazy about pitching. I love to play catcher."

"Yeah," I grinned. "I'll vouch for that."

"We've sucked each other off. But he's always stopped anybody who tried to fuck him. Now, he's changed his mind."

"Has he ever fucked you?"

"No," he answered. "I've tried to get him to."

"You said that he wants both of us."

"He wants you to screw him. I'll get him ready for that big dick."

"Baby," I assured him, "if anybody can get his ass ready, you're the one."

Randy grinned, licking his lips. "You really liked it when I sucked your ass, didn't you, Jeff?"

"Fucking right! First time I've ever been screwed by a tongue." It wasn't, really. But I didn't have to let him know that.

"Maybe I'll do it while you're fucking Duane," he teased.

We played it cool that night. For the first time since I moved in, I didn't ball Randy, and he didn't go down on me. He did rub his prick against mine as we kissed, but we agreed that it would make the session with Duane a lot hotter if we waited.

We drove Mrs. Lonas to the airport, and watched until the plane disappeared in the thin clouds. Then, admittedly excited, we returned to the house, where Duane was to meet us within the hour.

It's funny how knowing that you're going to fuck a boy makes him more attractive. In Duane's case, that was hard to do, for he was already girlishly pretty, with a luscious body, and a full, sensuous mouth. His dark hair was long, with a natural wave, and there was just a hint of the feminine in his voice and actions.

When Randy led him into the living room where I was seated, I stood up, and Duane almost held out his hand in greeting.

"Come here," I smiled, holding out both arms. "Let's do this right."

Five feet, eight inches of boy-flesh pressed itself against me, and his hips moved provocatively when he felt the hardness of my prick against his belly. My hands cupped his firm ass cheeks, kneading them through the cutoffs, and his lips parted eagerly for my probing tongue.

"Damn!" Randy exclaimed, watching our exchange. "You guys don't waste any time!"

Minutes later, the three of us were naked, and on the bed in Randy's room, Duane back in my arms, and Randy leaning over us, kissing our cheeks as we sucked each other's tongue in a wild and wet series of kisses.

"Let me have that big dick, Jeff!" Duane hissed, freeing his lips and beginning to slide down toward his goal.

I rolled onto my back and spread my legs, grunting with pleasure as the boy's mouth engulfed my cock, his tongue dancing about the head as he began sucking.

Randy waited until Duane positioned himself between my legs, on his knees, with that cute ass rearing up in the air.

Then, Randy moved to kneel behind the lad, bending to press his lips into the cleft of Duane's buttocks.

"UMMMMPHHH!" was the sound Duane made, still working on my prick, as Randy gave him the same treatment he had given me that first wonderful night. The youngster did his best to swallow my cock, his lips sliding all the way to the wrist-thick base and back to the flared rim of the glans, his tongue dancing and licking to add to my intense pleasure.

There was no need for words; our bodies were speaking a language older than any other, and each of us was lost in a whirlpool of physical delight, existing for the moment only to enjoy our connected flesh.

It was Duane who released my dick to cry, "Now, Jeff! Now!"

I didn't have to ask him what he meant. Nor did Randy, who pulled his mouth away from the boy's ass so Duane could roll onto his back, drawing his knees up to his chest and spreading them far apart.

Eagerly, I mounted the aroused youngster, and I felt Randy's hand seize my cock and guide it into position, the tip pressing the now-slippery circle of Duane's virgin anus.

Not content with merely placing it there, Randy began rubbing the slitted knob against the delicate orifice, making Duane's hips grind reponsively as he felt the alien caress.

"Do you want it, Duane?" My voice was husky.

It isn't every day that I get to take a teenager's cherry. I was horny, and my prick felt like a hot poker.

"Yessss!" the boy hissed, his hips pushing upward, the movement forcing the head of my cock into the hot embrace of his asshole.

"UUHHHH!" he bleated, unable to retreat, yet trying half-heartedly to escape the punishing invasion. "IT HURTS!"

"Easy, baby!" I soothed him, adding another inch of dick. "Just relax! It'll start feeling good in a minute!"

That's when I felt Randy's tongue begin lapping the crack of my ass. I moved my knees a little farther apart, widening the crevice for his oral assault, and I forced another inch of cock into Duane's rectum.

"OH, GOD!" he cried. "IT HURTS!"

"Just a little more, Duane!" I urged, adding yet another inch to the delightful penetration. I was in far enough to begin that ball-tingling in-and-out motion, but I froze in position when I felt Randy's tongue lick across the curve of my balls.

His fingers gently lifted the scrotum, giving his mouth access to the juncture of my prick and Duane's ass. With four inches inside the boy, there was still plenty of dick left for Randy to feast on, and he began coating the column with his saliva, making it easier for me to invade Duane's tight little butt.

I pulled back, letting the flared rim of my cockhead tug at the youngster's anal sphincter, making him cry out again, his hips jerking and his rectal muscles spasming. It was incredibly good, and it felt even better when I pushed it up into his ass again, a little deeper than before. He yelped again, but not as loudly, and he moaned when I drew my dick almost out and began fucking him with shallow strokes, driving just deep enough to massage his prostate with the head of my dong.

"Oh, Jeff! . . . Oh! . . . Oh! . . . Uh! . . . Uh!"

The cries were completely different now, for the friction of my prick in that sensitive channel was beginning to create the pleasure he had anticipated.

"Yeah, Duane!" I grunted, my hips rising and falling above his grinding hips. "You like that dick, don't you?"

"It still hurts! But it feels good, too!"

Randy was adding the wetness, and my cock was spilling little spurts of seminal fluid into Duane's tail, making the corridor slick, and letting me drive still deeper.

Randy gave my balls a wet kiss, and glued his lips to my asshole, spearing me with that stiffened tongue. The intensity of the sensation made me ram my prick almost to the balls in Duane's bottom, and he gave a choked cry of pain-pleasure at the sudden filling.

Pulling back, I could feel the rectal tissues clinging to my prick, and Randy's mouth kept its seal on my ass, his tongue stabbing in again, my balls pressing the boy's back, all nine inches of prick inside him.

Duane realized that he had accepted the full length of my cock, and his asshole relaxed enough to let me slide in and out with delicious thrusts, burying the pulsating knob deep in his intestine again and again.

Randy managed to follow the rise and fall of my hips, and his greedy mouth provided an added dimension to the thrill of fucking Duane. Beneath me, Duane was panting and moaning, grunting each time my cock bored into his spasming hole, stretching and filling it, then tugging it outward as I drew my dick almost out, only to jam it in again.

"Good, boy? You like that, boy?" I panted, my hands gripping his shoulders for leverage as I fucked him.

"God, yes!" he groaned. "It's wonderful! It still hurts, but I don't care! Fuck me, Jeff! Fuck my ass! Fuck me hard!"

I don't know how Randy managed to hang on, for my hips were pounding, my prick sliding in and out, full length, and the boy's ass was twisting and hunching to add even more frictioning to our joined flesh.

"I'm gonna come, Jeff!" Duane's fingers clawed at my waist, his legs flailing the air on either side of my driving hips.

"So am I, baby!" I grunted, fucking him still harder. "Right in your sweet ass!"

Duane's orgasm struck first, the contractions echoing in his colon, which tightened about my cock with each spurt of his semen. The come jetted up over his belly and his chest, the initial glob of cream splatting on his chin.

The increased tightness of his hot ass sent a thrilling signal through my prick and my balls released the flood of ropy sperm, spraying the youngster's intestinal sleeve with its soothing wetness.

"UHHHHHH! . . . UHHHHH!" he cried, his body writhing

and his asshole grinding about my cock.

In my own ass, Randy's tongue worked in a demanding circle, suddenly withdrawing. I felt the boy scramble into position behind me, and his dick nuzzled my well-licked anus.

His hands gripped my hips and, with a cry of rapture, he drove his cock up into my asshole, all the way, his balls pressing warmly against mine, holding the shaft buried as it jerked and swelled, shooting his own load up into my belly.

For a long time, we refused to move, for both Randy's cock and mine were still hard, and Duane made no move to make me pull out of his still-spasming rectum.

Randy's dick felt good, lodged in my asshole, and I wondered why I hadn't had the youngster screw me earlier. It would have been even better if he had had time to drive it in and out a few times.

Finally, giving Duane a long, juicy kiss, I pulled my prick out of his well-filled anus, and felt Randy's cock slip out of mine.

Leaving the two boys on the bed, I headed for the shower, returning to find Randy finishing the job of licking the come off of Duane's belly and chest. It was a natural thing, then, for him to take the youngster's prick in his mouth, and begin sucking it.

Watching Randy's lips slide up and down that rearing cock gave me a brand new erection, and Duane eagerly opened his mouth when I straddled his chest and offered it to him.

It was one of those times when I wanted to have my dick sucked, but I didn't want to come. Evidently, Duane was in the same mood, for he admitted later that he did not give Randy his load. Sometimes, it is enough just to feel a guy's mouth working on your cock, and his tongue dancing and playing about the knob. Reaching an orgasm brings all that to a temporary end, and it's nice to delay the conclusion, and just enjoy being nursed.

It was decided that we would go out to eat, Duane remarking that he knew what he wanted for dessert, and giving my prick a loving squeeze for emphasis. Randy agreed that Cream de la Jeff was really tasty.

I tossed Randy the keys to my car and the three of us piled into the front seat, laughing and talking as we headed for a restaurant Duane said was famous for its steaks.

It was dimly lighted, giving us the opportunity to do a little feeling of each other under the table as we studied the menus by candlelight.

The cute waitress took our orders, and both Randy and Duane flirted with her outrageously. Since both boys were extremely attractive, the girl responded in a most positive manner, rubbing her big tits against their shoulders at every opportunity.

"Would you like to fuck her?" I asked the two, when she had retreated.

"Sure," Randy grinned, "if I could suck your dick while I screwed her."

"I'd like to have Jeff's cock in my ass," Duane observed, "while I fucked her. I like pussy, but I love dick!"

"Hey!" Randy exclaimed. "Look who's here." He nodded toward a nearby table, where three people were dining. "That's Tim Goodson and his parents."

I almost did a double take, for if Randy hadn't given his name, I would have thought Tim Goodson was a girl. An exquisitely beautiful girl.

Long brown curls fell shoulder-length about a lovely face, with long-lashed eyes, dainty nose, and full, sexy lips. I couldn't see much of his body, but with a face like that, the boy would have to have a luscious figure.

In spite of the fact that I had spent the afternoon with two avid youngsters working on my cock, that organ began a determined swelling and stiffening.

"I believe Jeff likes what he sees," Duane said impishly.

"That's virgin territory," Randy said, shaking his head. "Tim likes to play, but he never has gone all the way."

"What do you mean?" I demanded.

"I mean," Randy said, "that he'll let a guy kiss him and feel him up. But when you try to open his fly, or get him to open yours, he backs off. He says he just likes the loving part. He's a fucking tease, just like some girls."

"Yeah," Duane chimed in. "He's got me all hot like that, and then said he wouldn't do it."

Randy frowned across the table at me. "Think you could make him, Jeff? Hell, if anybody could, it'd be you. I don't think he could turn down a cock like yours." It was at that moment the boy at the other table looked over and directly into my eyes. Something almost electric flashed between us, and a surge of heat washed through my belly and into my hardening prick.

The youngster's eyes widened, and I knew that he was feeling the same thing I was feeling. A blush spread over his girlish features, the pinkness visible even in the dim light.

"Looks like you've got a fan, Jeff," Duane drawled.

Still staring at the boy, I said, "How old is he?"

"Eighteen." It was Randy who answered. "Looks more like fifteen!"

"Looks like a girl," Duane inserted. "Hell, he's prettier than most girls."

I didn't respond. From almost thirty feet away, I was drowning in those soft brown eyes, and imagining the taste of that sensuous mouth.

My survey was interrupted by the waitress, who placed our steaks on the table, managed a few tit massages, and wiggled off, leaving the two boys a big smile.

I ate, but the food received little of my attention. Each time I looked across at the Goodson table, the youngster was staring at me, a strange expression on that lovely face.

"You've got him hooked, Jeff," Randy chuckled. "All you got to do is reel him in."

"Using your pole for bait!" Duane laughed. "You sure hooked me with it! My ass will be sore for a month!"

"Bullshit!" Randy told him. "If we were at home, you'd let Jeff screw you right now!"

"Sure, I would!" Duane nodded. "But my ass is still sore!"

I indicated the Goodson table with a gesture. "Are you sure that's a boy?"

"If you mean have I seen his dick," Randy said, "the answer is no."

"I got a quick feel of it," Duane admitted, "before he made me stop. I was gonna suck it, but he wouldn't even let me play with it."

The Goodson family was preparing to leave, and for the first time, the boy seemed to recognize Randy and Duane. He spoke to his mother and father, then walked over to our table, his brown eyes fastened on my face. My own gaze drank in that superb body, its curves accentuated by a knit shirt, and a pair of ultra-tight levis. The legs were fantastic, and the bulge of his basket was surprisingly large. Unless he was wearing padding, he was quite definitely male.

"Hi, guys!" he said, his voice a sultry sound that I could feel in my balls. "Who's your friend?"

"This is Jeff Archer," Randy introduced me. "He's staying with Mom and me. Jeff, this is Tim."

Warm, soft fingers gripped mine, squeezing just enough to make my prick try to leap out of my trousers. The full lips curved, moist and inviting.

"I guess you saw me staring at you," he admitted, his eyes holding my gaze, and his hand still on mine. "I apologize."

"For what? I was staring, too. You're a beautiful creature, Tim."

"You're makin' me blush," the boy murmured. "But, thank you."

"Why don't you drop by the house, Tim?" Randy suggested. "Mom's not there. We could all have a drink and you and Jeff could get better acquainted."

Tim looked at me. "Is it okay?" he asked in that soft voice.

I squeezed his hand before releasing it. His parents were getting impatient. "The only problem is that I may not let you leave," I smiled.

His tongue caressed his upper lip as he answered, "Maybe I won't want to leave."

"Jesus!" Duane exclaimed. "You guys are getting me horny!"

"You're always horny," Tim said, goodnaturedly. To Randy he said, "Are you guys going straight home after you eat?"

"Yeah," Randy said. "How about an hour from now?"

"Okay." He smiled at me. "See you, Jeff."

"You bet," I smiled back. My prick went wild as I watched that exquisite ass move beneath the denim as he walked away, his slender hips swaying more than was necessary.

"Goddamn!" Randy hissed. "You've got our little virgin all steamed up!"

"If he does the usual," Duane warned, "he'll make you think he's gonna let you do anything you want. Then, he'll start backing up."

"I'd like to be behind him when he backs up," Randy observed. "That's a beautiful ass."

"You know," I grinned. "You two are cock crazy."

"You'd better believe it!" Randy laughed.

"Guilty, your honor!" Duane admitted.

Three

Back at the house, Randy changed the linen on the bed in his room, while Duane checked the liquor cabinet and the icemaker.

"When Tim gets here," Randy told me, "Duane and I will leave you two alone, so you can get him in your room."

"Where will you be?"

"We'll use my room," He gave me a little smile. "I'm not jealous, Jeff. But I do envy Tim. I wish you had been the first one to do it to me. Duane was lucky, too."

"What makes you so sure Tim will let me fuck him?"

"All I know is that he's crazy if he doesn't."

I felt like a kid on his first date when the door chimes announced Tim's arrival. Randy let him in, and led him into the living room where Duane and I waited.

In the brighter light, the youngster was more beautiful than ever, his flawless skin almost radiant. Those inviting lips were moist and red as they smiled at me.

"Hello again, Jeff," he said warmly, extending his hand. This time I took it in both of mine, and he moved closer, his eyes searching mine.

"Hello, Tim," I answered, pulling him still closer. He did not resist, but let his slender body curve against mine, his hips pressing that well-filled basket against my own pronounced bulge. When I released his hand, his arms went about my neck.

"Jesus!" Randy shouted. "Let's get out of here, Duane! I think these two want to be alone."

"You got it!" Duane agreed. "Don't you all do anything we wouldn't!"

Both Tim and I ignored the teasing, but we waited until the boys closed the door of the bedroom behind them before our mouths fused in a tongue swirling kiss that I felt all the way to my toes.

I wanted to run my hands over that deliciously curved ass, but I hesitated. Instead, I gripped his narrow waist and pulled his yielding hips still harder against mine, letting him feel the throbbing of my fierce erection.

His arms tightened about my neck, and his lips worked feverishly as his tongue twisted and probed, dancing in concert with mine.

"Let's sit down on the sofa, Tim," I whispered, and he let me guide him, as we lowered our hips onto the soft cushions.

Eagerly, he came into my arms again, his lips parting for yet another ball tingling kiss. As our tongues fenced, I reached for one of his hands and pulled it down to my knee, turning it until his fingers were gripping my lower thigh. Slowly, I urged his hand upward along my leg, higher and higher, parting my thighs so he would have plenty of room.

Suddenly, he resisted my gentle tug. Against my lips, he whispered, "No, Jeff!"

"No what, Tim?" I asked innocently.

"Don't try to make me touch you down there," he said. "Just kiss me. I want to be loved, Jeff."

"That's the way people make love,," I reminded the boy. "Making love is more than just kissing."

"You can touch me anywhere but there," he promised, "and I'll touch you anywhere you want except there."

"Can we take off our shirts?" I asked, brushing my lips against his.

"I guess so," he said, hesitatingly. But he sat quietly as I tugged the tail of his shirt out of the Levis, and up over his head. He ran his fingers through his wavy hair, tossing his head to force a stray lock back from his pretty face.

"You've got a beautiful body, Tim," I told him, taking off my own shirt and baring my pectorals, the nipples stiff with excitement. Tim's eyes stared at them.

"So have you, Jeff," he said in a husky voice. "Looking at you makes me feel all funny."

Leaning toward him, I slipped one arm about his waist, and lowered my head to where I could fasten my mouth on one of his dainty nipples. He gasped as I lashed it with my tongue and sucked it into a strutted hardness.

"Ohhhh!" he cried in that soft voice. "That feels good!"

While my mouth teased his breast, I moved my hand up between his denim encased thighs, gently squeezing the firm flesh. Just before my fingers touched the outline of his balls, Tim grabbed my wrist.

"No!" he exclaimed. "I told you not to touch me there!"

"Sorry," I apologized, my lips moving against his tasty nipple. "It's just that you turn me on, Tim."

"You turn me on, too, Jeff," he countered, running his fingers through my hair. "Can I kiss you like you're kissing me?"

"Yes," I agreed, "if you'll do something for me."

"What?" he demanded.

"I've already said that I wouldn't touch you down there," I indicated his crotch with a nod. "But, I would like to touch your legs without those damned pants."

"You want me to take them off?"

"Would you?"

"Will you take yours off?"

For an answer, I sat up on the sofa and unfastened my belt. Unzipping my fly, I slid my trousers down and kicked them off. All I had on were my shorts and socks. I had stepped out of my slippers when we first sat down.

The youngster's eyes roamed up and down my bare thighs, lingering on the pronounced protrusion in the front of my shorts. He began unfastening his levis, and I sank to my knees on the rug, turning to face him.

"Let me help, Tim," I said, catching his waistband on either side of those slender hips, and tugging the pants down over those breathtaking thighs. "God! You've got pretty legs!" I tossed the levis aside and, still on my knees, placed my hands on his thighs, urging them apart. Before he could object, I dipped my head and pressed my open mouth against the inner curve of his left thigh, working my tongue against the smooth skin. I felt his muscles tense, and he gave a long sigh of pleasure, his fingers tangling in my hair.

Only inches from my caressing lips, his shorts swelled with a promising erection, and I could feel its heat against my cheek. I worked my lips still closer, and Tim's hands tightened, holding me back.

"You promised!" he whispered.

"Okay!" I said huskily. I raised my head and bypassed that gorgeous basket to fasten my mouth on his firm belly, just above the waistband of his jockey shorts. My tongue licked eagerly, and my chin brushed the swell of his dick.

Quickly, I murmured, "Sorry! I didn't mean to do that!"

"I guess it's okay," he said, his voice a little thick, "if I've got my shorts on."

What I did then can only be called nuzzling. Lowering my face to a level with his outlined cock and balls, I opened my mouth wide and let my hot breath bathe them through the thin shorts. Feather light, I brushed my parted lips against the straining fabric.

"Oh, Jesus!" he gasped, his thighs clamping my shoulders and quivering. "That feels so wonderful!"

"Want me to do it again?"

"Yesssss!"

This time, I added a little pressure, opening my mouth even wider, until my lips could actually capture the curve of his swollen cock through the shorts. I nibbled gently, working my way down toward those tender balls, tracing them with my mouth. My hands were on the boy's hips, and I could feel his urge to thrust them upward.

He surprised me with his sudden exclamation. "Let me do you like that!"

"Are you sure?" I asked, raising my face to look up at him.

"Yes," he said, licking his lips. "I'm sure. Just don't try to make me do anything else."

"Promise," I said, getting to my feet and sinking onto the sofa beside him, pulling the youngster into my arms for a long, delightful kiss.

His hand was on my thigh, the fingers working just below my balls, and when he pulled his lips from mine, he bent over my lap.

The first thing I felt was his warm, moist breath, bathing my cock and making it push upward against the restraining shorts. Then, to my intense delight, his lips lightly touched the bulging outline, moving along the swollen length from down around my balls, up to the delicate vee just below the knob.

"Oh, baby!" I groaned. "That feels good!"

His words were little gusts of wet heat on my dick, as he whispered, "I like it, too, Jeff!"

"Think about how much better it would be," I said, "if we didn't have these damned shorts on!"

He hesitated, his mouth hovering over my basket. Then, with a groan of surrender, he nodded, his own hands tugging at the waistband of my shorts. My cock sprang up against my belly as he pulled the shorts down and I kicked them aside. He stood up just long enough to remove his own shorts, and I stared hungrily at his stiff, young dick.

He sank down beside me and bent over my lap again, this time, his parted lips pressing eagerly against the head of my prick. I felt his wet tongue gather the pearl of jism that had formed there, and he made a little moaning sound as he tasted cock for the first time, his swallowing audible, as the mixture of seminal fluid and saliva slid down his throat.

"Let's get on the bed," I whispered, bending over the youngster's head as he nuzzled my cock. "I want to kiss you like that."

His breath fanned my prick. "We shouldn't be doing this!"

"Don't you like it?" I asked gently, my lips brushing his silky smooth shoulder.

"Yes! But it's wrong!"

"Come on," I urged. "I want to taste you."

Reluctantly, he raised his head and I drew his soft lips to mine, my tongue sliding into that delicious young mouth and tasting the tartness of my own cock. His arms went about my neck and his whole body shivered with response as we kissed.

There was no resistance when I stood, pulling him to his feet and leading him into the bedroom. Willingly, he let me lower him onto the bed, and I sank down beside him, pulling that naked body against me and running my hands over his deliciously curved bottom.

He shivered with excitement when I kissed my way down to his dainty nipples, gently nibbling each one and caressing it with my wet tongue. As I sucked his tits, I twisted about until we were head to toe, and his mouth began imitating mine as he licked my chest.

My tongue slid down over his smooth belly and dipped into

his navel, and his mouth fastened on mine, his own tongue working hungrily. Our hands were busy, playing along the curves of thighs and hips, caressing and kneading buttocks, and dipping into the cleft between them.

Then, with a groan of surrender, the boy's head moved lower, and his lips found my cock, claiming the swollen knob and drawing it into his wet, hungry mouth. His tongue danced wildly about the slitted tip, and his fingers clutched my ass cheeks to pull me even closer as he took my prick far back in his oral embrace.

I took a moment to savor the delightful sensation, letting him begin that spine tingling nursing, before I took his dick between my lips and did to him what he was already doing to me.

It was obvious that the youngster had wanted this for a long time, for he moaned as he sucked, and he repeatedly drew my cock deep, taking the head far down his spasming throat.

We both spilled occasional jets of pre-cum, and mingled it with our saliva, relishing the tart salinity and musk of the seminal fluids.

Hips pumping, and mouths sucking, we climbed the mountain of ecstacy together, our bodies trembling with the shared pleasure and expectation of the approaching orgasms.

I shifted one hand to fondle his balls as I felt his prick swell and jerk in my mouth, and I felt his fingers tease my puckered anus.

My cock throbbed and my hips gyrated as my semen surged though the swollen shaft and into the boy's throat. At almost the same moment, I received the first delicious spurt of his own cum, and I swallowed it with grunts of enjoyment, just as he was gulping my creamy offering.

It was his first experience, but he was not about to let it end. His lips tightened about my prick, and his tongue fluttered hopefully about the tip, trying to draw one more drop from the tiny eyes. He moaned with desire, and his dick moved in my oral grip, echoing his lust.

I pulled my lips up and off of his dick, letting it press against my cheek as I began licking his almost hairless balls. My tongue slid lower, and I lifted his leg so I could work my way past the sac, teasing that delicate area between it and his virgin anus.

He was sucking my cock again, nursing it with hungry tugs,

and I was stroking it in and out of his slurping mouth, my excitement mounting as my tongue zeroed in on his tiny asshole, flicking and probing in a way that made his hips writhe with lust.

I coated his anus with my saliva, working my stiffened tongue into the tight opening, leaving it slick and ready for what I planned.

The boy knew what that was. He moaned softly, still sucking, and I felt his sphincter spasm as he anticipated the feel of my cock sliding up into his belly.

His oral efforts were pulling me toward another orgasm, and I wanted to drop this load in his cute little tail. I forced my dick out of his mouth, and quickly reversed my position, rolling the boy onto his back and pulling his slender legs up and apart, fitting my hips between them.

"Put it in for me," I whispered, and the youngster reached down to guide the head of my prick until it was pressed against that hot circle of striated membrane.

His girlish face stared up at me, his eyes wide in anticipation, and his full lips parted to show those perfect teeth and that nervously flicking tongue.

"Go slow, Jeff!" he breathed, his hips quivering as I added pressure to the contact of cock and anus. "Please!"

"Relax," I urged the youngster. "Just let me get it in."

Most boys automatically tighten their sphincter when they feel that first hard dick about to penetrate their virgin bottom, and it's almost impossible to just go limp and let the cock slide in. It's only after some experience that one can do that. However, a few youngsters instinctively know that the way to open up for easy penetration is to try to fart. It's also the way to tell one what to do in order to get into that waiting channel.

I didn't have to tell Tim anything. As I increased the downward pressure of my hips, I felt that little circlet soften and yield, and the slippery wetness slid onto my cock, fitting itself about the invading glans like a hot, slick glove.

"OHHHHH!" he cried, his features contorting as he strained to accept the prick. "OH, GOD, JEFF!"

"Easy, baby!" I encouraged the trembling boy. "It's going in. Just keep it relaxed for me."

"I'm trying!" he panted. I could feel his rectal muscles

tighten and relax about my cock as he fought the urge to try to force the shaft out of his colon.

The head of my dick rubbed past his outlined prostate, and he gave a bleat of unprecedented pleasure, his whole body shaking as the thrills shot through his pelvis.

"That's just a sample, Tim," I whispered, halting my intrusion long enough to work the knob back and forth against his prostate, making him cry out in delight. "Like that?"

"YESSSS!" he keened, his fingers clawing at my waist. "DO IT TO ME, JEFF!"

I pulled back until only the swollen head remained inside his sphincteral ring, and his hips arched upward, seeking to retain the hot hardness that was filling and stretching his young asshole.

Slowly, savoring the feel of that slick, convulsing corridor, I slid my prick into him again, deeper than before, beginning a measured stroking that sent it in and out like a piston in a well-lubricated cylinder.

Tim's cock was hard, arching up over his belly, and it jerked with each thrust, and his hips pushed upward, working that hungry asshole farther onto my shaft with every entry.

"Good, Tim?" I gasped, my hips driving as I hilted myself again and again in the boy's spasming ass.

"GOD, YES!" His own hips ground and pumped responsively. "FUCK ME, JEFF! . . . FUCK ME HARD!"

That's when you throw the book away, when your partner tells you to do it hard. That's when you head for the finish line at a dead gallop, letting those surges of ecstacy build and spread from your balls to the head of your prick, knowing that you can't stop until you shoot your load into his hungry ass.

Sometimes, if you're lucky, the short rows can last a long time, and just keep getting better and better. That's how it was with Tim and me.

Still hunching my cock in and out with little short strokes I bent forward over the boy's body until I covered his parted lips with mine and our tongues fought a love-duel in his delicious mouth.

Tim's orgasm preceded mine by one powerful spasm, and I felt it through the intestinal wall. The sudden tightening and pulsation sent a wave of pleasure back through my dick and into my tense balls, triggering my own release.

Tim cried out as he felt my cum spurting deep in his ass, and his hips jerked and quivered, his prick jetting his creamy semen up against my belly and over his own heaving chest.

The echoes of his passion made it feel as if his asshole was sucking and milking my cock, the rectal muscles clamping about the shaft in a rippling movement that was enhanced by his grinding hips.

Keeping my prick hilted in his ass, I pushed my upper body back until I could stare down into the youngster's pretty face. His features were flushed, and he was panting, that pink tongue darting across the sweet curve of his full lips.

"Wow," he exclaimed breathlessly. "I had no idea it would be so wonderful!"

In answer, I let him feel my weight, my mouth seeking his in yet another long and uninhibited kiss.

Four

It was almost one o'clock when Tim finally insisted that he had to go home, but it was obvious that he didn't really want to. The boy had enjoyed a taste of the fruit he would savor for the rest of his life, and he wasn't anxious to leave his first cock.

"I could suck you all night, Jeff," he purred, licking my balls as he crouched between my wide-spread legs. "Why didn't I do this a long time ago? I've never liked girls, and the only sex I've had was jerking off."

I ran my fingers through his soft hair. "Now that you know how good it is," I said, "how about having some fun with Randy and Duane?"

"Will you stay with me?" he asked, looking up into my eyes. "I think I'd like it. But I'd feel better if you were there, Jeff."

"You've got it," I promised. "How about Friday night?"

He blushed. In spite of all that we had just done, the boy actually blushed. "Will you fuck me again?"

"Damn right!" I grinned, urging him up and on top of me, to where I could pull his soft lips down to mine. "I'll pump that hot little ass all you want, Tim!"

His mouth covered mine, and we exchanged another of those torrid kisses before I let him roll off and sit up on the edge of the bed. His young body was a work of erotic art as he turned to look down at me over one shoulder.

"You know," he admitted in a soft voice. "I've wanted to do this since I was eleven years old. But I was always too scared. I think maybe I didn't want to find out how I really feel about things. I was afraid of what people would say if they found out."

"Times are changing, Tim. We've still got a long way to go, but most people are a little more understanding than they were a few years ago."

"Yeah," he agreed. "My mom knows how I feel, but the old man'd have me seeing a shrink if he found out. He thinks all gays should be shot."

"Give him time. Maybe he'll come around one of these days. It took my parents a while to accept some of my writing. And even longer to accept what I am."

He grinned, running his tongue over those generous lips.

"You do write some pretty hot stuff, Jeff. That's why I was so attracted to you. I figured you'd know how to break me in the best way."

I sat up and pulled him into my arms, turning him about so that our mouths were almost touching.

"Did I pass the test?"

"Better than I ever dreamed possible," he answered, parting his lips for my kiss.

When we finally separated, he said, "Let me slip out without seeing Randy and Duane. Okay? You can get things all set for Friday night. Is about seven o'clock all right?"

"Perfect. Can you spend the night?"

"Yeah," he agreed. "I'll work it out with my parents. They like Randy and his mom. I don't have to tell them Duane's gonna be here. They're pretty sure he's gay."

I kissed him again at the front door, and stood watching as his car drove away. Tim Goodson had just given me some of the best sex I had ever enjoyed, and the next session promised to be even better.

Shutting the front door, I walked down the hall to the closed door of Randy's room, grinning as I heard the unmistakable sounds of two mouths greedily working on two stiff cocks.

I was tempted to join them, but Tim had drained my balls, at least temporarily, and I proceeded to my own room, inhaling the heady scent of our prolonged coupling.

With a contented sigh, I sprawled across the rumpled bed.

I was asleep in minutes.

The smell of bacon and fresh coffee roused me, and the radio clock on the bedside table read 8:40. Climbing to my feet, I let a stinging shower clear the fog from my brain, and I grinned as I recalled the events of the previous night.

Tim Goodson was a treasure, and I wanted a lot more of his firm young body. Having all three boys available was more than I could have hoped for.

I was spending several hours each day on my new book, and enjoying Randy almost every night. Now, I had two more eager partners for fun and games.

Randy and Duane were in the kitchen, Randy at the stove, and Duane setting the table for three when I joined them.

"You look like the cat that ate the canary," Randy said teasingly. "Was the canary named Tim?"

"I'm a gentleman." I pretended to be offended. "I do not eat and tell."

Duane snorted. "I told you he'd do it! You had him hooked from the time you two met at the restaurant. Damn! I wish I could have seen that."

"So do I," Randy added. "Tim is a real beauty."

"You'll both get your chance Friday night," I said. "He's decided to let you guys have a little."

"You're kidding!" exclaimed Duane. "How did you arrange that?"

"Trade secret. The same way I talked you into letting me sample that tail."

Duane was pouring my coffee, and he leaned over to offer me a quick kiss. "I couldn't resist that big dick," he murmured. "Thanks for showing me what I've been missing, Jeff."

I gave his ass a squeeze, and Randy flashed a broad grin of understanding. I had been a little afraid that Randy might not want to share me with his friends, but the lad was showing a remarkable maturity.

Over bacon and eggs - Randy was an excellent cook - we discussed our plans for the day. I was running behind schedule with my book, having planned a minimum of five pages a day. So, I would be on the word processor for several hours.

"I'm going over to Duane's house," Randy told me. "He's got a new computer, and some really cool games."

"And I'll slave over a hot keyboard," I said, "while you guys have fun."

"That's the penalty for being grown up," Duane ventured. "Two more years, and my folks will kick me out if I don't go to college."

"Don't you plan on going?" I knew that Randy was headed for State University in the fall.

"Maybe," the boy sighed. "It's either that or get a job."

"You've got a good head, Duane," I assured him. "Use it."

Randy grinned. "He *gives* good head, too."

The two youngsters cleaned up the kitchen while I enjoyed a third cup of coffee. Each of them gave me a disturbing hug before leaving for Duane's house, and I entered my own room to face a blank computer screen.

An hour later, the phone rang, and I hurried down the hall to the living room. It was Mrs. Lonas. Her sister, she told me excitedly, had been involved in a car wreck, and had broken her right leg in two places.

"I simply must stay here," she explained, "and look after her two children. Her husband is a complete idiot, you know. He couldn't possibly cope with the situation. Tell Randy that I'll call him tonight. I do apologize, Mr. Archer, for my absence."

"Nonsense," I said firmly. "Randy and I will be just fine. You stay as long as you want to. And I hope your sister gets better very soon."

"Oh, you are a dear!" she trilled. "I'm so happy you're there to keep an eye on Randy. You know how young boys are."

It didn't seem wise to answer that, so I changed the subject, and assured her that Randy would be waiting on her call.

There were no more interruptions, and I got in five hours of writing before Randy returned. I told him about his mother's call, then I suggested that we eat out that evening and the youngster quickly agreed.

"Let's catch a movie," he said. "There's a good one at the Strand."

"The Strand's still in business? God, the movies I saw there!"

"Now it's only a buck."

"Deal," I agreed. "Hey, you feel like Mexican?"

He arched one eyebrow exaggeratedly. "You know I like anything hot!" Then he added, "Mom'll call early. We can leave right after that."

Mrs. Lonas called at six-thirty, and Randy was smiling when he came into my room after talking with his mother.

"I don't like Aunt Louise," he admitted. "But I wouldn't wish her a busted leg. Still, I'm glad we've got the place to ourselves for a while."

"What's with you and this aunt?"

"It's about her daughter," the boy shrugged.

"You put the make on her?"

"Hell, no! It was the other way around. Aunt Louise wanted me to play up to her, and I can't stand the girl."

"How old is she?"

"Not old enough," was his quick reply. "Even if she was, I wouldn't fool with her. She's the type that would get you in trouble real quick! She'd screw anything that had a dick on it! I guess that's one reason Mom is staying. Aunt Louise has trouble with the kids when she's got both legs. They'd give her fits now."

"Your Mom's a nice lady, Randy," I said. "I don't want to pry, but what happened between her and your father?"

"My Dad is gay," he said easily. "Mom didn't know that until they had been married a couple of years, and I was about eight months old. She kicked him out, but then she went to a psychiatrist for a while, and she changed her opinion about gays in general. That's why she accepts me without any fuss."

"Do you think it's genetic?" I queried.

"Being gay?" he frowned. "Maybe, in some cases. I've read a lot about it. The only thing the experts agree on is that it comes with the body. It's just the way you are."

"What about bisexuals?" I pushed.

He arched one brow again, a cute habit in a boy as handsome as Randy. "Maybe it's like some people have a little, and some have a lot. I've been with a few girls. But they just don't turn me on, you know?"

"Think you'll ever get married, Randy?"

He hesitated. "I might. But I'd want the girl to know all about me. I guess it'd be nice to have kids someday. Hell! I don't know. I hate to have to hide the way I feel about things."

"I know. But it's like civil rights. It just takes time for people to come around."

"Yeah," he shrugged again. "I guess I ought to be glad that Mom understands."

We ate at The Hot Place, a small restaurant on the west side of town. Run by some recently naturalized Mexicans, the food was excellent, and after the first few bites our scalps were perspiring.

"That's the real test of spicy dishes," I said, as we enjoyed our suffering. "If your scalp sweats, it's hot enough."

The Strand was only a block away, so we left the car in the restaurant's parking area, and walked to the movie. The first evening showing was about to begin when we found seats about halfway down and on the aisle. The old place had seen better days but the buck admission had practically filled the house.

Arnold was showing muscles and mangling the language with his usual charm, and we settled back to watch the bad guys get creamed.

Within moments, Randy's hand was in my lap, but only searching for my fingers. Like two kids, we held hands throughout the film. If it hadn't been so crowded, I knew he would have gone down on me.

But after the movie, as we walked back to the car, he said, "Tonight I feel like cuddling. I don't know why – "

"I think I'd like that, Randy. I think I'd like that a lot."

I let the car idle as I turned to examine his pretty face in the light from the dash. His eyes returned my gaze with a new note of seriousness.

"Yeah," I said, "tonight we'll just cuddle up a storm."

We had a drink when we reached the house, bourbon on the rocks, and sat talking about inconsequential things until almost midnight. Then, choosing my room, we stripped to the buff and crawled onto the bed, the boy's head resting on my arm, and one slender, satin-smooth thigh draped over mine.

We kissed, gently and lovingly, our tongues playing about without becoming the tools of passion they usually were.

"I love being with you," Randy whispered. "It feels so good like this."

"I'm glad," I told him. "I feel the same way."

We slept in each other's arms, our bodies pressed together without the hungry searching that precedes sex. We were acutely aware of our maleness. But it was comforting, and our sleep was kind.

George Masters, my agent and mentor, called the following day to ask how the book was progressing. I was not his most productive client, but we enjoyed a special rapport. As he put it: "You didn't buy my yacht, Jeff, but you've furnished a lot of fuel for it."

We chatted for a while, and I promised again that the book would be finished by late June. At his insistance, I gave him enough of my research to work up a teaser for promotional use, and he made a few suggestions about who I could call to check information.

Duane decided not to come back until Friday, and Randy and I continued our self-enforced celibacy, sleeping with arms and legs entwined, but limiting our erotic caresses to kisses and occasional fondling.

Subconsciously, I suppose, we were saving ourselves for Tim's visit, and on Thursday afternoon, the boy called.

"I'm excited, Jeff," he confessed, "and scared, too. All this is new to me. I've dreamed of it for years, but this is real."

"We can call it off, Tim. You don't have to do anything you don't want to."

"I want to!" he exclaimed. "God, yes! I've wanted to since you showed me how wonderful it is. It's just . . . I guess I'm a little shy. I don't know how to approach Randy and Duane."

"Don't worry about them," I said. "It will all fall into place when we're together."

"Is it all right if I say that I like you a whole lot?"

"Sure." I put a smile into my voice. "And I like you a lot, Tim. You are one beautiful person."

"Know what?" he whispered. "You're giving me a hardon!"

"Save it," I laughed. "I'll take care of it tomorrow night.

And you can take care of mine."

"Oh, I will," he promised. "Anyway you want it."

Mrs. Lonas called again that evening, while Randy and I were watching television. They talked for several minutes, and Randy repeated his mother's hello to me before hanging up the phone.

By mutual agreement, we slept in our own rooms that night, but it took me a while to get to sleep. Just thinking about the youngster only a few yards away kept me with a semi-hard until slumber claimed me.

I arose before Randy on Friday morning, and had breakfast almost ready when he joined me in the kitchen. It seemed perfectly natural to take the boy in my arms and kiss those soft, moist lips, feeling his slender hips stir against mine as he responded with familiar passion.

"Looking forward to tonight?" I asked later, holding my coffee cup up to savor the fragrance of the rich brew.

"Damn right!" he said. "I've wanted to make it with Tim for a long time. Are you sure he's willing to do this?"

"As sure as I can be," was my reply. "Let's just say that I'll be very surprised if he doesn't go through with it."

Duane arrived at six, and he and Randy followed my instruction in preparing a pitcher of drinks. Seven-Up, lemon juice, sugar, and a healthy amount of vodka. Add ice cubes and enjoy.

"Hey!" exclaimed Duane, sampling the result. "This is all right."

"Just take it easy," I warned. "That stuff can sneak up on you."

We toyed with one small drink each, sitting at the kitchen table, until the doorbell rang, announcing Tim's arrival. He was five minutes early. Randy welcomed him in, and he greeted Duane and me with a faint blush.

I wanted to embrace him, but decided against it when I saw his nervousness. Instead, I motioned to the fourth chair and invited him to sit down.

Randy poured Tim a drink, and refilled our glasses, more generously this time. Before he could claim his seat, I waved one hand.

"Randy," I said. "Get a deck of cards. Let's have a little

fun."

Duane gave me a curious frown. "I've got fifty cents on me, Jeff. If this is for cash, include me out."

Tim made no comment as Randy opened a cabinet door and withdrew a small box. He tossed it onto the table, and I opened it, pulling out the almost new cards.

"Strip poker!" Tim said with a grin.

"My god!" was Duane's comment. "That's for kids!"

"It depends," I announced, "on how you play it. In this case, the rules are a little different. First of all, is everybody willing to play?"

They exchanged glances, and all three heads nodded. I shuffled the cards and slid them across to Tim. "Cut?"

He licked those inviting lips as he lifted about half the deck and placed it beside the remainder. "How do we play?"

"Is everyone familiar with the rules of poker?" I asked, and again I got three nods.

"Okay. We're playing draw poker, no wild cards, usual rules. Only we're betting clothing instead of money."

"That's strip poker!" This time, it was Randy who protested.

"But a different version," I said. "The stakes are higher. You can bet one sock, or just a shirt. That way, you end up naked after just a few hands. Of course, if you want to, you can lose purposely, and get out of your clothes right away."

"Then what?" Tim asked.

"Then we bet certain activities," I explained. "In reverse. If I bet a blowjob, for example, it means that if I win, you get to go down on me."

Tim's brow wrinkled in thought. "And if I bet a piece of tail, and win, you get to do it to me."

"Hey!" Duane cried. "I like this! But how do you determine who does the screwing?"

"The winner picks his partner," I said. "In other words, if you bet a piece of ass, and win, you get to pick whoever you want to screw you."

Randy said, "And if you win a blowjob, you're really picking out the guy you're gonna go down on."

"You've got it," I nodded. "Does everyone agree?"

Tim gave us all a sexy smile. "I should warn all of you that I play a mean hand of poker."

"You can beat me anytime," Duane said teasingly. "You know how I feel about you."

"Yeah," Randy added. "Me, too."

"The catch is," I reminded them, "you have to win to pick your partner."

"What if one guy keeps winning?" asked Randy.

"After two wins and collections," I answered, "the winner then can demand that any two players do whatever he wants them to do."

"You mean the other two have to just sit and watch?" was Duane's objection.

"Losers, weepers," I grinned. "Shall we play?"

There was no argument, and I dealt the cards, five apiece, and placed the deck on the table. I picked up my own hand.

Tim said, "Pass," in a quiet voice.

"Gentlemen," Randy announced, "get ready to drop your trousers."

"Bullshit!" said Duane. "I bet shirt, jeans, shoes and socks!"

He was seated on my right, and I gave him a questioning look. I held two kings, two aces, and a seven. I had a good chance at a full house.

"I'll see that," I said slowly, "and I'll raise you one undershirt."

On my left, Tim studied his hand and pursed those ripe lips in hesitation. "Call," he finally announced.

Randy, a little rattled by Duane's boldness, frowned for a moment. "Oh, hell! Call!"

Duane extracted one card from his hand, and placed in the center of the table. Randy asked for two, and I added my seven to the discards. Tim stood pat.

I distributed the cards and peeked at the one I had drawn. I now had three aces and a pair of kings. I felt safe.

From the look on Randy's face, he hadn't helped himself. Duane's expression was unreadable.

"You started this mess, Duane," I reminded him. "What do you do?"

"Shorts," he said. "That's all I have left. I'll bet my shorts."

"I'll see them," I said. "And then I'll see what's under them."

"That should be interesting," Tim murmured, causing both

Randy and Duane to give him a quick look. "Call."

"I can't raise," Randy complained. "All I can do is call."

"Show your hand, Duane," I told him.

He spread his cards on the table. Three jacks, ace high.

Randy put down two pairs, nines and sixes, and I laid down my aces and kings.

"Shit!" Duane exclaimed. "What did you draw"

"An ace," I grinned. "I guess this is my hand."

"Not quite," Tim corrected me. "I believe it's mine." He spread his five cards for our inspection.

"Jesus!" Randy cried. "Four whores!"

"Would you gentlemen like to pay off?" the youngster said with a teasing smile. "I love strip shows."

"Son of a bitch!" Duane snorted. "One fucking hand, and I lose my ass!"

"Wrong," I commented. "That's the next hand."

Tim sat there grinning as the two boys stood up and began shedding their clothes. I joined them, and we tossed our discarded duds onto the kitchen floor.

Tim's eyes explored our exposed cocks with a gleam of aroused hunger. All three of us sported semi-erections.

"Now what?" Randy demanded. "How do we get him undressed?"

"We keep playing," I said.

Duane curled his fingers about his dick as he said, "Now, I get it! This is where we bet our ass!"

"I warned you." Tim's smile broadened. "I'm pretty good at this."

We eased our bare bottoms down onto the chairs, and Tim gathered the cards, shuffling them with a surprising deftness. He dealt the hand quickly and expertly. I looked at my cards and tried to hide my elation. The youngster had given me a royal straight flush, ace high.

Evidently, the others had received good hands, for Randy was squirming with anticpation as the last cards fell, and Duane was staring at his cards with a look of disbelief.

"What can I bet?" Randy asked eagerly. He had shoved his cards together and was drumming them on the table. The nipples on his hairless chest were distended. Since I was quite familiar with the taste and feel of those dainty morsels, the sight sent a thrill through my belly.

"Depends on what you want," Tim replied, his eyes boldly exploring our bare upper bodies.

"Hell!" was Randy's rejoinder. "You know what I want. I've tried often enough."

"You have to say it," I reminded him, and Tim nodded his agreement.

"Okay, I'll bet you a first class blowjob!" He looked over at me. "Now, if I win, who blows who?"

"Does it really matter?" Duane laughed.

"The winner decides," I said. "The bet is what you do. The winner decides who does it."

"Got it!" Randy nodded. "One blowjob is the bet."

"I like this," Duane commented. "Even if you lose, you win." He looked at his cards. "I'll see your blowjob," he said, "and raise you one piece of ass."

I studied my hand for a moment. "I think I'll see you, but I don't believe I'll raise." I looked at Tim.

"I might as well lose my clothes," he said easily. "Will that cover the bet as it stands?"

I nodded, and the other two boys added agreement. "Do you want to raise?" I asked.

Tim let his full lower lip creep up over its mate in a cute pout. He shook his head. "Just call."

All three boys drew cards, while I stood pat, waiting until Tim had finished dealing.

I looked at Randy. "Want to bet?"

"Not with you looking like that."

"Duane?"

"I'll check," was his reply.

"So will I," I said. "Tim?"

"Call," was the boy's response.

Randy tucked his cards under his chin and let his eyes drift over our faces. "This is gonna be fun," he murmured.

Slowly, gloatingly, he spread his hand for us to see. He had an eight-high straight flush in clubs.

With a sigh of mock disgust, Duane showed a full house, jacks and queens. Tim solemnly laid down two pairs, nines and tens.

"It's my lucky day," I drawled, putting down my hand.

"Holy shit!" was Duane's reaction. followed by Randy's "Damn!" Tim just sat there with a little smile on that pretty face.

"Let's see what I won," I said. "First, all of your clothes, Tim. Then I have a blowjob and a piece of ass with each of you."

"And you get to decide who does what each time?" Duane asked.

"Right," I said. "And we start with Tim. Randy, if you'll fill our glasses, you two can see what you've wanted for so long."

Naked, and with his dick semi-erect, Randy circled the table, pouring the concoction we had prepared earlier. As he bent over my shoulder, I gave his cock a gentle squeeze.

Tim took a long sip of his drink before he stood up and began removing his clothes.

Five

Just watching Tim Goodson undress would have been reward enough for the evening, for the boy's body was a work of art, and he displayed a peculiar gracefulness as he stripped off the shirt, then stepped daintily out of his jeans and shorts.

His dick, not as big as mine, but larger than that of either Randy or Duane, was fully erect and heavily veined, swaying in its upward angle as the youngster moved.

Like mine, Tim's cock was uncut. But in its swelling, the foreskin pulled back from the plumlike head to reveal that tiny slit, and the pearl of seminal fluid that nestled there.

His shyness was gone, and in its place was an inviting boldness, accentuated by the way he deliberately worked those slender hips, then thrust them forward to make his cock slap up against his belly.

"My god!" Duane exclaimed in a hoarse voice. "You're gorgeous!"

"Edible!" was Randy's almost whispered comment. "Very, very edible!"

"I like what I see, too," Tim answered in a sultry voice. "I just wish I had tumbled sooner. It took Jeff to show me what I've been missing."

Duane gave me a warm smile. "Yeah, he taught me a few things, too."

"Before you make me blush," I said, standing up and revealing my throbbing erection, "let's adjourn to a more suitable room."

"Mom's room," Randy said. "She's got a king-sized bed, and I've got it all ready."

The four of us trooped down the hall, led by Randy, who reached back to take Tim's hand as they entered Mrs. Lonas's bedroom. The bed had been stripped down to a fitted white sheet, and the ceiling light had been turned low, yet it still gave sufficient light to let us examine each others' naked bodies at will.

"Lie down, Tim," I told the youngster, while Randy and Duane stood hesitantly beside the bed. Turning to them, I said, "For the moment, just watch."

Tim lowered his slender hips to the bed, then, urged by my hands on his shoulders, he lay back, his eyes fixed on my cock as I hovered over him. I used my knees to separate his, and leaned forward until my prick touched his, making it jerk upward. It rubbed hotly against mine, and our juices mingling.

"Oh, god!" the boy whispered. "I want you, Jeff!"

Supporting my upper body on extended arms, I let my weight down until my lips reached his, finding his sweet tongue waiting to fence with mine inside that delicious mouth.

I didn't linger there long. I kissed his chin, and as he arched his neck, I pressed my mouth to his graceful throat, moving downward to those perfect pectorals, and gluing my lips to first one nipple, then the other, savoring the way his hips writhed as I nibbled them with gentle bites.

"I can't stand this!" I heard Duane's husky complaint. "I gotta do something!"

I had reached Tim's flat-muscled belly, and was teasing it with my tongue. Now, I raised my head and pushed myself up until I was kneeling astride Tim's sleek thighs.

Looking back over my shoulder, I caught Duane's eyes and indicated what I wanted him to do. There was no doubt in my mind that it was exactly what he wanted, and he proved me right with a vigorous nod of his head.

Spreading my knees farther apart, I moved upward over the

naked Tim, deliberately letting my heavy balls drag against his belly, then his bare chest.

Behind me, Duane dropped to his knees beside the bed and began raining kisses on Tim's inner thighs. Tim's eyes squeezed shut and his lips drew tightly over his clenched teeth.

Knowing Randy's inclination, I didn't have to look to know that he was behind Duane, probably preparing the lad's ass for invasion. It was not what the game script called for, but it would involve all four of us, and I made no objection.

Again I shifted upward, and Tim opened his eyes to focus on my prick, its bulbous head only inches from his mouth. He ran his tongue around those full red lips, and his eyes almost crossed in concentration.

Duane was already nursing the boy's dick, so Tim was more than ready for mine. His mouth opened wider, and I lowered my hips to let the swollen knob slip between his lips, over his swirling tongue, to nudge the soft palate before sliding farther in.

"Ummmmm!" he moaned, beginning a hungry suction that sent thrills radiating back through the shaft, into my balls, and up into my belly.

Tim's hands had been at his side, his fingers clutching the sheet. Now, they gripped my buttocks, clutching them, and urging me to drive my cock farther into his hungry mouth.

I could feel his hips thrusting behind me, and knew that he was fucking his own dick into Duane's lips, even as I was feeding his. Duane was grunting as he sucked, for Randy had worked his dick into his young friend's asshole, and was beginning to hunch in and out in time with Duane's bobbing head.

I wanted to take it easy with Tim, for it was only his second encounter, but it was too good. Also, the fact that all four of us were connected magnified the pleasure of our union, and I could not halt my hips as they rose and fell, thrusting my engorged cock deeper and deeper into the youngster's throat.

Instinct and passion must have told him how to relax so that my dickhead could slip between his tonsils, for he gagged only once. Then, with his hands kneading and pulling at my ass cheeks, I fucked Tim's mouth with groans of pleasure, pulling back, now and then, to let his tongue punish the invading glans, bathing it in his warm saliva and spreading the occasional spill of seminal fluid over the slitted tip.

I felt his fingertip on my anus, and I pulled back until my prick slipped out of his mouth.

"Don't stop!" he hissed, his hands tugging me down.

"Wet your finger, Tim!" I exclaimed thickly. "Put it in my ass!"

Quickly, one hand moved between us, and then back to the cleft of my buttocks. As I reinserted my cock in the boy's mouth, I grunted with delight as his finger, slick with saliva, forced its way into my anus, wriggling as it slid up into the chute.

"I want your prick in there after while!" I panted, beginning the in and out motion again, and feeling him suck even more eagerly than before.

Behind me, Duane was making little slurping sounds as he worked on Tim's dick, and Randy was groaning with pleasure as he fucked faster and harder, pushing Duane's head forward with each thrust, making him take Tim's full eight inches with each bob of his head.

My balls slapped Tim's chin, and I could feel his nose in my pubic hair each time I drove into his mouth. His tongue pressed upward beneath my pistoning cock, fashioning a snug channel through which my prick rode, pulsating with the ever-increasing goodness.

"I'm gonna come!" was Randy's panted cry, and it spurred Duane to greater effort. The boy snorted with excitement as he swallowed and reswallowed Tim's throbbing dick.

Tim was moaning as I mouth-fucked him, the moaning interrupted each time my prick filled his convulsing throat.

I could tell that he was close to his own orgasm, and his passion ignited mine.

"Take it, Tim!" I panted, pulling back to let his tongue polish the head of my cock, caressing it until the shivers of pleasure became an earthquake of ecstacy that spread upward in liquid jolts as my come spurted into the youngster's willing mouth.

His gulping was audible, which increased my own orgasmic pleasure, and my hips quivered as Tim's mouth savored its reward, and his lips and tongue milked my cock for the last drop of semen.

I shifted my hips downward, my bottom pushing Duane's head away as he tried to drain still more from the boy's dick. I positioned myself above that young cock, and looked down into Tim's glazed eyes.

He stared back at me with a mixture of affection and lust, neither of us speaking as his finger deserted my ass to grip his still-hard prick and hold it in place.

Slowly, carefully, I pressed my anus down until I felt the hot tip of his dick send thrills through my colon. My hands rested, palms down, on his meaty pectorals. With a sigh, I slipped my asshole onto the pulsating hardness, impaling myself on the thick shaft.

"Oh, god, Jeff!" the boy breathed, his dick jerking and swelling as my intestinal sleeve slid down over it like a hot glove. "It feels so good!"

I twisted my hips as I forced my asshole farther onto his cock, gasping with effort, for he was filling the channel with that hot hardness, and I could feel its throbbing deep inside me.

Suddenly, Duane moved into view on the other side of the bed, settling his knees on either side of Tim's now-touseled head. He wrapped one hand about the base of his prick and squeezed.

"I didn't come when Randy fucked me, Jeff!" His voice was thick with desire. "Suck it for me!"

Screwing my anus about the root of Tim's big cock in complete acceptance of that beauty, I opened my mouth and leaned forward, claiming Duane's dick as I began working my hips up and down above Tim's.

The tart, slightly salty tang of Duane's pre-come sent a thrill down my throat, and the feel of Tim's cock became a constant pleasure as the swollen knob slid past my prostate again and again.

As I sucked him, Duane eased his hips downward until his balls pressed Tim's parted lips. Eagerly, the boy began licking them, opening his mouth wide to claim one at a time, rolling them about with his agile tongue.

I rode the youngster's prick with furious hunches, working my asshole up and down the slippery pole while I paid oral homage to Duane's delicious dick, letting him fuck it in and out of my mouth as he gripped my shoulders for leverage.

Tim's hips aided my effort, rising and falling in perfect rhythm with mine, assuring that each thrust drove his prick into me all the way to his balls.

"I'm gonna come, Jeff!" was Duane's breathless gasp, and I felt his prick swell and pulsate. I pulled my lips back until only the head was behind my teeth, and fluttered my tongue over the slippery knob, using the tip to tease that tiny slit. My cheeks hollowed with suction, and I heard Duane cry out just as the first jet of semen splatted against my palate.

At almost the same instant, I felt Tim's dick jerk and quiver inside me, and his warm wet come sprayed my thirsty intestine in powerful spurts.

I caught Duane's first volley with my tongue, and spread it over the satin smooth glans as the second surge erupted. I sucked thirstily, and the boy's hips thrust and trembled with the ecstacy of his release.

My hips writhed, screwing my ass about Tim's erupting cock, and he jabbed it deep as he filled the anal canal with his sperm, moaning and whimpering, even as he continued to lick Duane's exploding balls.

I waited until the tremors of Duane's orgasm had diminished before swallowing his load, my whole body trembling as the thick cream slid down my throat. Then, with lips and tongue, I milked the youngster's dick, sucking gently, but hard enough to coax out one final spill of come.

Beneath me, almost sobbing with the pleasure of his second release, Tim put one arm about my waist, while his free hand grabbed my cock. Soon he was caressing it with a feathery touch that made me grunt with pleasure.

While the three of us were engaged in that three-way union, Randy had contented himself with sitting beside us on the bed and merely stroking his swollen prick.

Now, he leaned over and planted a wet kiss on my right buttock, lingering to let his tongue tease the sensitive skin of my upper thigh.

Slowly, giving it a final lick that made him whimper, I released Duane's cock, and began lifting my hips, pulling my asshole up and off of Tim's prick. I deliberately flexed my anal muscles as my anus climbed the shaft, assuring that I stripped all of that creamy offering from the youthful hardness.

Only when my sphincter slipped over the flared rim of his dickhead did Tim uncurl his fingers from about my cock. Duane had backed away, and the boy could now stare up at me with those long-lashed eyes.

"Fantastic, Jeff!" he breathed. "I thought I'd never stop coming!"

"I loved it, too," I said, licking my lips. "Why don't you and Duane get a little better acquainted?"

Having the boy's thick eight-inch prick in my ass had taken me very close to another orgasm, but I had managed to hold back.

I wanted to give that next creamy load to Randy, for the kid had become very special to me, and he had been patient while Tim, Duane and I had enjoyed our romp.

When I swung my body off of Tim's slenderness, Duane dropped onto the bed beside him, and the two became locked in a feverish embrace, lips and hips fused in preparation for a more fulfilling union.

All four of us were lying crosswise on the big bed, and I rolled over into Randy's waiting arms, our mouths mating, and our tongues dueling in happy welcome.

His hands roamed over my back and my buttocks, urging me to press my engorged cock against his own swollen member. A wave of passion and simple affection washed through my belly, and I freed my lips for a moment.

"Suck my dick a little, Randy," I urged the excited boy. "Get it good and slick. Then, I want to fuck you!"

With a little groan of lust, the youngster slid down to where he could take my cock in that warm wet mouth, massage it with his tongue, and slide his lips up and down its wrist-thick hardness.

His fingers toyed with my balls as he sucked, and I gripped his blond curls as I thrust the head of my prick deep into his willing throat.

"Don't make me come!" I gasped, knowing that he would have welcomed my semen in his thirsty mouth, but determined to enjoy his tight young ass.

I forced his lips up and off of my cock as I told him, "Turn over, Randy, onto your belly. And spread those pretty legs."

Obedient to my instructions, he had left my prick wet and slick with his saliva, and it glistened in the soft light of the room as I knelt between his sleek thighs, my arms supporting my weight above his naked back.

Beside us, Tim was in the same position as Randy, and Duane was riding his writhing ass with steady thrusts, each of the boys moaning with pleasure as they fucked.

Tim's face was turned toward me, his pretty features distorted by passion, and he managed to give me a twisted grin as he saw what I was about to do.

Randy's cheek rested on the sheet, and he inched his way closer to Tim, managing to get close enough to brush his lips against the youngster's mouth, finding Tim's tongue ready for play.

Then, holding my prick with my left hand, and balancing on my right arm, I guided my cockhead between Randy's buttocks until the tip felt the hot circlet of his anus.

I had fucked the handsome youth at least a dozen times before, but for some reason, each time I mounted him was like the first time. The feel of that resistance as his sphincter barred my early pressure; the delightful tightness of his colon as my prick entered, and feeling the ring squeeze the intruding shaft just behind the corona of my glans were always new.

Then, the warm slippery embrace as his asshole swallowed my cock, the walls shuddering and undulating as the hardness frictioned their delicate membranes, sliding up into the boy's belly with a slow determined pressure.

The sudden jerk of Randy's hips told me when the head of my dick pressed his prostate through the intestinal sleeve, massaging that nutlike gland and sending pulsations of unique pleasure through his belly.

I savored each of those sensations as I entered the passionate youth, and began fucking his hungry, spasming ass, and Randy's hips responded with a cooperative grinding that worked his asshole wildly about my pistoning cock.

Duane was riding Tim with almost savage hunches, making the boy cry out again and again as the dick stroked in and out of his still tender tail. But the cries were those of excitement, accompanied by an occasional voiced urging for his rider to plunge deeper and harder.

Beneath me, Randy grunted with each thrust of my prick into his grinding ass, and his fingers clutched the sheet on either side of his blond head, scrabbling mindlessly as the pleasure intensified.

It isn't often that it happens, but it can and does now and then. Both Tim and Randy gasped their readiness at the same moment, spurring Duane and me to greater effort. The bed squeaked and rocked as our hips rose and fell, bellies pounding the firmly curved bottoms of our respective partners as our cocks drove in and out, frictioning, rubbing, filling and massaging the aroused channels of young flesh.

"Oh, god!" I heard Duane yelp, and recognized the strain of a beginning orgasm.

"Now, baby!" I panted into Randy's dainty ear, just before surrendering to the volcanic eruption of my own powerful come, ecstacy shuddering through my balls as they spilled their liquid fire through my driving cock and into the boy's convulsing ass.

The rhythmical spasming about my spurting prick was evidence of Randy's own orgasm, for his prostate's repeated contractions were echoed in that sucking corridor.

For a few delicious moments, I was blind and deaf to everything but the sheer pleasure of my release and Randy's thirsty acceptance.

We showered in pairs, Randy and I, and Tim and Duane. I would have bet that Tim and Duane did much the same as we. As the stinging warmth of the water enveloped us, we embraced with a new and more intimate sense, our hands and lips exploring more daringly and with even less inhibition.

"Having you here has meant a lot to me, Jeff," the youth said, his hand cupping my balls and my flaccid dick. "I can appreciate what I am, instead of trying to hide it."

I ran my fingers through the crease of that delightfully and firmly curved ass as I answered, "There are times, Randy, when you have to pretend. Someday it'll be different. It has to be. The world's changing, and societies have to change. That's what my book is all about. Until then, you have to enjoy moments like these and savor them."

"I'll remember tonight as long as I fuckin' live," he said, one arm drawing my head down to his, his lips parting as we shared a long and delicious kiss. "You're the only one who's ever made me come just from being screwed. I've always had to play with it, or have the other guy do it. You make me come by the way you fuck me."

"You know, you seem to get better every time we do it."

"I'm learning," he smiled, sticking his tongue out and sliding it across my lower lip. "You're a good teacher."

It was while we were toweling down that I made my suggestion: "Why don't you and Tim spend the rest of the night together? Duane can sleep with me."

"Sleep?" he repeated with a knowing grin.

"Some," I smiled back. "I won't guarantee how much."

We joined Tim and Duane in Mrs. Lonas's room. All of us had wrapped towels about our middles, and developed a weird sense of modesty. It was Tim who noticed this first.

"It's funny," he observed. "We have all kinds of sex with each other, then cover up like we were strangers."

"Post-coital embarrassment," I suggested. "It's normal. Let's have a drink in the kitchen, and we'll all get back to normal."

"Heaven forbid!" exclaimed Duane with an exaggerated mincing gesture, making all of us laugh.

"I wouldn't want to go back to just wondering what I am," said Tim, acting as bartender and filling our glasses before sitting down with us. We were positioned just as we were for the game.

"Neither would I," added Duane. "I was confused as hell til I was about fourteen."

"You guys know about me," Tim said. "I guess I knew what I wanted, but I wouldn't admit it."

"I knew when I was little," Randy supplied. "I was just a kid, but I was attracted to the older boys before I knew why I wanted them."

Looking at me with those big brown eyes, Tim asked, "How about you, Jeff?"

"I suppose I'm like a lot of guys," I admitted. "As far back as I can remember, I found myself interested in both boys and girls."

"I have trouble making out with a girl," Randy said. "I can, but it's not the same."

"Yeah," Duane nodded. "I have to pretend they're boys."

"I've tried to make it with girls," Tim told us. "I get hot when we kiss and feel around. But when we start to do it, I get as limp as a rag."

"Part of it," I commented, "is in your mind."

"That big cock of your's ain't just in my mind!" Randy exclaimed.

"Damn right!" Duane echoed. "A girl can't bruise your tonsils like that!"

"Or ram it up your ass til you think it's gonna come out of your mouth!" Randy laughed.

Tim smiled with us, then said, "I guess when I think of sex, I think of a prick. I didn't want to admit that until I made it with Jeff. I wanted to, but I kept trying to tell myself that it was wrong. My father goes on all the time about queers and faggots. He hates them. If he finds out how I really feel, he'll boot me out of the house.

"But Mom is different. I've talked with her about it, and she knows that we're all different, and that we can't help being whatever we are."

"Does she know that you've actually done it?" Randy asked.

Tim shook his head. "She suspects that I don't come over here just to watch television with you and Jeff. But she doesn't know about either of you."

He gave Duane a nod. "Dad is convinced that you're gay, and Mom suspects it. That's why I didn't tell them you would be here tonight. I'm sorry, Duane."

Duane shrugged a dismissal. "A lot of people think it. But only a few are sure."

Randy gave the boy a mock frown. "Do you mean to tell us that you'd suck a big, nasty prick?"

"Hell, no," was Duane's mild reply. "I'd wash the damned thing first!"

We chatted freely for as long as it took to finish the pitcher of drinks before I said, "It's late guys, and we all need to recharge our batteries. Tim, how about you sleeping with Randy in his room?"

"Sure," the boy said. He looked at Randy. "Okay with you?"

"Is the sun hot?" was Randy's grinning answer.

"I might get that way too," Tim grinned back.

"Does that mean I get to share your bed, Jeff?" asked Duane with a suggestive smile.

"Among other things," I said. "Do you mind?"

Duane looked around the table. "If I'm found in the morning, fucked to death, you know who to blame."

"And you're so young and pretty to go like that," Tim chuckled.

"Does anybody know a better way?" Randy demanded, standing up and pushing his chair back into place. "Come on, Tim, baby. I've got something to show you."

"I think I've seen it," the boy replied. "But I'd love a much closer look."

Duane rose and placed the back of one hand on his forehead in a pretended swoon. "Please, Jeff! Take me away from these perverts!"

I slipped an arm about his slender waist pulling him to me and toward my room. "Come, darling," I said teasingly. "I'll protect you from these horrible people."

He pressed one hip against mine and leaned his upper body away from me, batting his lashes mockingly. "I'll bet you're going to fuck me!" he exclaimed. "You old guys are all alike."

Several delightful and fascinating minutes later, I proved the youngster right.

Six

Randy and Tim prepared breakfast, letting Duane and me sleep an extra hour. The three boys made short work of the bacon and eggs, while I settled for toast and coffee, nursing a mild hangover from a heady mix of sex and booze.

Tim studied my face from across the table as he ate. In spite of my satiety, I found the boy extremely arousing. I suppose part of it was his seeming innocence, and the reminder that I had been his first sexual partner.

"Duane must have really worked you over, Jeff," he said jokingly. "You look tired."

"Better watch it!" I managed a smile. "I'm not too tired."

"Then," Duane interjected, "let's do it again tomorrow

night."

"Mercy!" I exclaimed, holding both palms up. "Have pity on an old man!"

"Old, my ass!" Duane protested. "You sure as hell weren't old last night!"

"Last night is what made me old," I laughed. "But I'll be my youthful self in a couple of months."

"What'll you guys bet," Duane said, "that he won't screw Randy tonight."

"God!" Randy sighed. "I hope so!"

"Hey!" Tim said when the laughter faded. "Anybody like spelunking?"

"You mean exploring holes?" Duane leered. "I love it!"

"Seriously," Tim insisted. "I know a couple of boys who love to search around in caves and caverns, and I've been with them on a couple of trips. We had a lot of fun."

"Are these boys gay?" Randy asked.

"I don't know. We've never talked about girls or sex."

"How can anyone live for a full hour," Duane puzzled, "without mentioning sex? It's inhuman!"

"You are warped!" Randy said jokingly. "There are other things in life than a stiff dick!"

"Yeah," Duane sighed. "But not as much fun."

"I've been in a few caves," I said. "It's fascinating to explore the different passageways, as long as you don't get lost."

"Would you all like to do that?" Tim inquired. "Say, on Sunday?"

"You mean with these guys you know?" Randy asked.

"Yeah," Tim answered. "I think they'd enjoy it. It's all they do."

"Jesus! That's tomorrow," Duane said. "Can we get ready in that little time?"

"All we need," I said, "are flashlights, batteries and water."

"And food," Randy added. "Plenty of food."

"We can always eat each other," Duane suggested, creating a chorus of groans.

"I could call Scott," Tim said, "and see if they want to go."

"Go where?" I wanted to know. "Is there a cave nearby?"

"Sorry," Tim said. "I should have explained. Scott and Chris have been after me for a long time to go to this place called Blevin's Hill. It's on property Chris's grandfather owns, and there's a cave that runs back in and under the hill. It's only about five miles outside town."

"Has it been explored?"

"Chris has been back about a mile or so," Tim answered. "But Scott has never seen it. We keep talking about it, but just never have gone."

"Is it safe?" Duane asked.

"Oh, yeah. It's solid rock, according to Chris."

"What about it?" I asked the others. "Want to go?"

Their response was positive, if not enthusiastic. and I told Tim to call his friend and make the arrangements. I suggested nine o'clock as a good starting time, and the boys agreed.

"We can go in my car," I added. "It's big enough for six people."

"Ummmm!" Duane smirked. "Cozy!"

"Chill out," I said casually. "Let's not make it hard for Tim."

"I'd sure love makin' it hard for Tim," he teased. "Okay. I'll be good." In a softer voice, he said, "But it sure as hell won't be easy."

The three of us stayed at the table while Tim went to the front room where the phone was. We discussed the little we knew about cave exploration, and discovered that Duane had never been in a cave. Randy had, but only a few times, and those were guided tours.

"We'll pair off," I told them, "so one of each couple will know the basics. In a cave that small, I doubt that you can get lost. If it was really big, you would have heard about it."

"Who's gonna supply the flashlights and stuff?" asked Randy. I assured them that I'd pick up all that we needed. I had learned my way around in the town, and knew the location of a promising sporting goods store.

Tim came back, his pretty face wearing a broad smile. "It's all set," he told us. "Chris was there when I called, and they're both excited about it."

"Golly, gee whiz, gosh and stuff!" Duane exclaimed. "We're all gonna crawl into a big hole in the ground! What's exciting about that?"

"Lighten up, for god's sake!" Randy said. "Let's have a little fun. It won't kill you to do something different once in a while."

"Okay! Okay! I'm just kidding!"

Tim's smile faded. "If you don't want to go, Duane," he said, "you don't have to."

"I'm going already! Think I'd let you three go without me being there to take care of you? Dauntless Duane will be there!"

"I'm sure we all feel much safer," I groaned. "How did you set it up?" I turned to Tim.

"Chris will meet Scott at his house, and they'll come over in Scott's car. Then, we'll leave from here. They'll get here about a quarter to nine."

"Good," I nodded. "Is that okay with you, Duane?"

"Sure," the boy agreed. "I'll be here at eight-thirty if you'll have breakfast ready."

Randy smiled. "Promise."

"Same here," Tim added. "Wish I could stay here all day. I like being with you guys."

"I think that goes for all of us," I said, and both Duane and Randy nodded eagerly. "I believe I could stand a few more nights like that one."

Randy and I watched from the front door as Tim and Duane piled into their cars and drove away. Then, closing the door, the boy came into my arms and pressed his firm curves against me, his hand groping between us for my crotch. His lips parted for my kiss.

"You know, Jeff," he said, holding his mouth close to mine. "I could fall in love with you mighty easy. I think I've been happier since you've been here than ever before."

"Easy, Randy," I said quietly, my fingers caressing the curve of his shapely ass. "Let's not complicate things. You have your whole life in front of you, and it's a big world."

"Don't worry," he said, squeezing my cock through my trousers, and tensing his buttocks under my fingers. "I'm not gonna get sloppy on you. It's just that I've never felt like this about anybody else."

His green eyes searched mine. "Have you ever loved another guy, Jeff?"

"That's hard to answer," I frowned. "How can you really

know when *like* becomes *love*? I've liked a couple of boys a lot. But I'm not sure it was love. I think when you fall in love, you want only that one person. So far, I can't say that I'd be satisfied that way."

I pulled him closer. "Think you'd be happy if you never made it with anyone other than me?"

He sucked in a deep breath, and worked his fingers beneath my balls. "When you put it like that," he smiled, "it does make you wonder. I do like the way you do it to me better than anyone else. Of course, I haven't had all that much."

"For the record," I said, "you are one hell of a lay."

He grinned happily. "And do I give good head?"

"Damn right!" I assured him. "Right up there with the best of them."

Randy did the cleaning chores, and I spent a couple of hours on my book, rewriting a chapter I wasn't too happy with. At twelve-thirty, we ate sandwiches and made up a list of the items we would need for the next day.

"Don't forget spare bulbs for the flashlights," Randy said. "I've read about people getting lost because a bulb burned out or got broken."

"Got it," I answered. "I think I'll pick up some stuff from the deli. Then we won't have to spend a lot of time fixing sandwiches."

"Suits me," he said. "Want to go anywhere tonight?"

"Not unless you've got plans. I'd as soon watch the tube and get some sleep."

"I want to run over to Terry Simpson's for a while. I promised I would."

"Have I met him?" I asked. Several boys had dropped by the house to see Randy, but I couldn't remember all of them. A few, like Duane, were extremely attractive, but I immediately forgot their names. All that remained was the memory of deliciously firm and delightfully curved young bodies, and promising baskets swelling those tight jeans or shorts.

"I don't think so," he frowned. "He hasn't been over for a while. I saw him at the supermarket the other day."

"I'll be back before you leave," I said. "Want me to bring back some dinner?"

"Pizza!" he exclaimed. "We've got beer. How about it?"

"With anchovies?"

"Sure," he nodded. "You like 'em?"

"Love 'em. I won't be gone long."

He followed me to the door and put his arms around me, lifting his lips for a kiss. Our bodies pressed and rubbed, and our tongues toyed with each other while our hips moved restlessly.

"Keep that up," I said into one dainty ear, "and I'll have you in the bedroom."

"I wouldn't put up much of a fight," he whispered. "I get hot just thinking about your big cock."

"Be a good boy, and I might give you a little."

Laughing at our exchange, we separated, and I made a show of adjusting my dick in my trousers before stepping out into the warm summer sun.

I gassed up across from the sporting goods store, then spent almost an hour selecting the items we had listed, and adding a few others.

A strong, but lightweight nylon rope, and several balls of twine seemed like good ideas. I also purchased a pack of large marking pens. I pushed the shopping cart up to the checkout counter, where the clerk, a blond in his early twenties, looked them over.

"You must be going out to Blevin's Hill," he commented, giving me a warm smile.

"Elementary, my dear Watson," I grinned back. "Ever been there?"

"Sure," he said. "But it was a long time ago. I was just a kid. That was before old man Lampley bought it and fenced it off. It used to belong to some lumber company, and us kids would explore the place. It's been fenced off for about five or six years."

He gave me a closer look. "Don't I know you?"

"I doubt it," I smiled. "I'm just here temporarily. My name's Jeff Archer."

His eyes widened. "The writer?"

I nodded, and he reached for my hand.

"Jesus! You? Here? I love your books, Mr. Archer! I've read every one of them. Jesus! It's really you!"

He was holding my hand with both of his, the fingers busy, as if to reassure himself that I was real.

"I'm here to get some writing done," I explained, beginning to like the sensation his touch was creating in my balls.

He was a handsome youth, and it was all too easy imagining how it would feel to make love to him. The counter was low, and the slacks he wore indicated a sizable weapon behind the fly.

"I'm Bill Newberry!" he told me, still giving my fingers a workout. "My god! Imagine meeting you in person!"

"It's my pleasure, Bill. Always glad to meet a fan."

"Oh, I'm a real fan of yours! I love the way you get right down to the nitty gritty with things."

"Uh . . . Could we get down to the nitty gritty with these things?" I suggested, careful not to offend him. Fans are a writer's second most valuable asset. The first is talent.

"Sure!" he exclaimed, finally letting go of my hand. "I just can't get over it. Really meeting you."

He began ringing up the items from my cart, still shaking his blond head in amazement.

"Can I tell you something, Mr. Archer?" he asked, his voice softening. "I mean personal like."

"Sure," I said. "Like what?"

"You know that picture of you they put on the cover of your books."

"Yeah," I grinned. "Makes me look like a movie star."

"Oh, you're a lot handsomer in person! God, yes! Well, sometimes, after I've been reading it, I turn the book over and look at your picture and . . . " His voice trailed off, and a blush suffused his handsome features.

I leaned over the counter, our faces almost touching, and he froze in position, his breath warm and sweet.

"You jerk off," I whispered.

His tongue slid out to touch his upper lip, curving wet and pink, sending me an unmistakable signal. "Yessssss!" he breathed. "Ohhhh, yessss!"

I straightened. "I'm flattered," I said, giving him a broad wink of understanding. "You, Bill, are a very good-lookin' man."

Still blushing, he began bagging my purchases, his eyes

darting now and then to my face. "Do you think so? You're not just saying that?"

Assuring him of my admiration, I paid cash and dodged his fingers when he returned my change. Inside, I was feeling proud that my detection system was still functional.

"Will I see you again while you're here?" he asked, his voice husky and hopeful. "I mean, will you be in again?"

"Who knows?" I said with a little smile. "You're a most interesting person."

He followed me to the door, his hands fluttering as if about to touch me, but never making contact. The look in those long lashed eyes was one of pleading.

"You *do* understand, don't you, Mr. Archer?" he asked, opening the door for me. My arms were full of packages. "You write about people like me all the time. You *know*, don't you?"

Instead of answering, I gave him a slow wink that made his whole body wiggle with excitement. He made no attempt to hide the significant and rapidly growing bulge in his summer slacks.

"Oh, yes!" he cried. "You know!"

"Maybe we'll meet again, Bill," I said, breaking eye contact with the excited youth. "Bill Newberry, right?"

He nodded eagerly. "Anytime!" he said breathlessly. "Anytime at all!"

I loaded the packages in the trunk of the car and, after making sure there were no police cars in sight, made a U-turn to park in front of the Brickfront Deli, next door to the gas station.

From a long refrigerated glass case, I chose a half dozen meats, pickles and salads. The bread I limited to white and rye. Then I sat back with a cup of coffee while the fat proprietor prepared the sandwiches and wrapped them for me.

Then I had him fix a couple of carryout dinners for Randy and me. The fat man said all that I had to do was pop the containers into the microwave for four minutes, and we'd have delicious meals. He patted his large belly for emphasis.

I stopped by Kroger's and picked up a case of bottled water and a case of cokes, wondering how we were going to lug all that stuff into the cave. But, there would be six of us, and we would leave some of it back at the entrance.

Randy was climbing into his car as I pulled up into the broad drive. He waited until our windows were even, and we both lowered them. The heat rolled in, battling the air conditioner.

"That cave air will feel good tomorrow," he said. "It's ninety-six degrees."

"Happens every summer," I laughed and looked at my watch. "What time will you be back?"

"A couple or three hours. About six or six-thirty."

"Have fun," I said, waiting til he pulled away to open the door.

Carrying my purchases in took two trips, and I made room in the fridge for the sandwiches and the two dinners. The other stuff I dumped on the floor in the den. We could sort it out when the boys arrived in the morning.

I built myself a tall bourbon and carried it into my room, turning on the computer and calling up the last thing I had written.

Sometimes, the muse just will not cooperate, and I finished the drink without adding a word to the screen. A full hour passed, and I hadn't managed a line.

I heard the newspaper strike the front porch, and went out to recover it, watching the newsboy extend one bare leg to balance his bike as he tossed a copy to the house next door.

He was wearing denim cutoffs and a thin knit shirt, displaying a marvelously tanned and shapely body that was inviting, desirable, undoubtedly delicious, and too damned young.

Going back inside, I killed the computer, went into the living room, and sat down in one of the easy chairs, scanning the front page of the paper.

There was nothing new. People were screwing each other, and Washington was screwing all of us. People were buying guns in greater and greater numbers, and trying to figure out ways to keep anyone else from buying one. It seemed that Americans were doing little but fucking, killing, robbing, and shooting up. Congress, as usual, led the pack.

I turned to the comics, chuckling at Dagwood's latest blunder, and was halfway down the page when the phone at my elbow rang.

"Hello," I said, wondering why Mrs. Lonas had never put

an extension in any of the other rooms

"Is this Jeff?" It was Randy's youthful voice.

"No," I drawled. "You've called the White House by mistake, and the president is busy."

He ignored my feeble humor. "Jeff, would you get sore if I stayed with Terry tonight? His folks won't be back till tomorrow, and he asked me to. I'll be back by seven in the morning." He paused. "Do you mind, Jeff?"

"Of course not," I lied. Subconsciously, I had been looking forward to the evening with Randy. But, I understood his request. "Have fun, and I'll see you in the morning."

"You sure you don't mind?"

"Like I told you, Randy," I assured the boy. "I'm gonna relax and watch television. You two have a ball. And don't tell me you and Terry don't plan on getting it on tonight."

There was a long silence. "I didn't plan it this way," he said. "Honest. But we got to fooling around . . . "

"And you both got hard, and you want to fuck each other," I finished for him. "Hell, Randy! That's no crime. Enjoy yourself. I thought I made it clear this afternoon that I don't want any reins on me, and I sure as hell won't put any on you. We're friends, and I love to make it with you. But I want you to do whatever you like."

"As long as you're not sore."

"I'm not sore," I said. "Have fun, and get here in time to cook breakfast."

That brought a half-hearted laugh. "I promise. Good night, Jeff."

I hung up the phone and sat staring at the paper, not really seeing it, for a long minute. Then I tossed it aside and reached for the telephone directory in a slot on the end table. In the yellow pages, I found the number for the sporting goods store, and punched it out on the phone's white buttons. It rang five times before a familiar voice answered.

"Is this Bill?" I asked, dropping my free hand down to cup my balls. "Bill Newberry?"

"Yes, it it."

"This is Jeff Archer," I told him. "I was in there a while ago."

"Oh, yes. How could I forget? Was there some problem,

Mr. Archer? If there is, I'm sure we can fix it."

"There is a problem, Bill," I said meaningfully. "but not with the purchases. It seems that you and I have some very important and unfinished business."

"Oh, my god!" he gasped. "Do you mean what I think you mean? I mean what I hope you mean!"

"Are you free tonight?"

"For you, Mr. Archer, anytime! Anytime at all!"

"I'm staying with a family here," I explained. "But they will all be gone tonight, and I'd like a little companionship. That is, if you're interested."

"Oh, my god! Yes! Am I ever!"

I gave him the address, asked if he had a car and when he got off work.

"At seven. I could be there by seven-fifteen."

"Don't rush," I told him. "Go home first, bathe and change clothes. Tell me, do you ever wear cutoffs?"

"Oh, yes! A lot. Want me to wear them tonight?"

"Would you? And do you have a knit shirt?"

"A pink one," he answered. "Will that do?"

"Perfect. Think you can find the house?"

"I know exactly where it is," he replied. "Oh, god! I'm so excited, Mr. Archer!"

"Do me another favor," I said. "Call me Jeff."

"Oh, god! Yes! Jeff! Jeff! I'll be there, Jeff. No later than eight o'clock. Okay?"

"Fine," I said. "Are you sure you want to do this?"

"Yes! Oh, god. yes!"

"See you at eight, Bill."

"Oh, god!" was the last thing I heard as I hung up the phone. Bill Newberry was ready for action, and I didn't plan to disappoint him.

I gave the bulge at my crotch another squeeze and went to the kitchen for more ice and more bourbon. It was shaping up to be a most interesting evening.

Seven

As Bill Newberry entered the living room, he looked about nervously. "I guess I'm early," he said quickly. "I sure didn't want to be late. Is it okay?"

"Relax," I said, shutting the door and leaning back against it, eyeing the boy up and down. He was wearing denim cutoffs, and a tee shirt that showed off his prominent pecs.

His thighs were gorgeous, and those hips were just the type to grind like crazy if I ever got my dick in his shapely ass," I thought we ought to get a little better acquainted, Bill," I said in a soft voice. Deliberately, I cupped my crotch and his eyes stared at the swelling there. He ran his tongue slowly around the oval of his full red lips. His hands pressed his thighs, toward the front, rubbing the rounded firmness.

"I'd like that, Jeff!" he answered, still watching my hand. "I kept thinking about you after you left today."

His blond hair was long and wavy, one strand falling down over his left eye. For the first time, I noticed that he was almost beardless. There was only a fine down on those soft cheeks, and I revised my estimate of his age downward.

I reached for him then, using both hands to grip his narrow waist, urging him toward me. He offered a slight resistance, and I tightened my grip, my fingers digging into the yielding waist, just above the low-slung cutoffs.

He let his hips press forward, and I felt his genitals against my swelling cock, his own dick beginning to stiffen as he leaned backward, increasing that delightful pressure, but keeping his upper body away from mine. His eyes searched mine and he wet those inviting lips.

"Do you know?" he asked softly, his arms reaching up to fasten graceful fingers on my shoulders. His hips stirred restlessly.

I didn't answer. Instead, using one hand at a time, I tugged his shirt out of the cutoffs, baring his waist, and digging the tips of my fingers into the tender flesh.

He winced, but his hips pressed harder, and a strange look entered the deep blue eyes. Holding his hips in place, I slid my hands around to cup his firm buttocks, kneading them with stronger motions.

He groaned with the sudden pain, and his eyes closed, his lips tight and his teeth clamped together.

"Oh, god! . . . Yeah!"

He wanted more of the pain, but I released him and stepped back, admiring that well-muscled and deliciously curved body.

"Let's have a drink, Bill," I suggested. "Let's not rush things."

He drew a shuddering breath and pressed his hands to his thighs again. "Whatever you want, Jeff," he said.

"Bourbon okay?" I asked, leading the way into the kitchen and plucking two glasses from the cabinet. Without waiting for a reply, I got ice cubes from the fridge and poured two generous slugs of whiskey, handing one to Bill.

He took it and raised it to his lips, his eyes on my face as he gulped down almost half the contents. He drew a long breath, watching me take a much smaller drink of the potent liquid.

"Mind if I call you Billy?" I asked.

"I like that better'n Bill," he answered. "That's what my folks call me."

He finished his drink in another long swallow, and set the glass on the table, moving closer to me. The front of his cutoffs were distended by an obvious erection, and his hands trembled as he placed one on my arm, and the other on my shoulder.

Without a word, I set my unfinished drink down beside his and pulled him into my arms. My lips covered his open mouth, and his tongue raced to meet mine, thrusting and curling in a wet delicious kiss. My fingers found his ass cheeks again, kneading and squeezing, and he gave a little nasal moan of pleasure as I tightened my grip on those rounded buttocks.

"Yeah!" he whispered fiercely. "Hurt me, stud! Hurt me!"

His bottom would be bruised tomorrow, but I was making him happy tonight. I had found his weakness, and discovered that I was enjoying giving him the treatment he desired.

Freeing one hand from his tensing ass, I reached up and wound his blond hair about my fingers, tugging his head back until his face was turned toward the ceiling. His eyes were shut tightly, his mouth open in a gasp of pleasure-pain.

"Put your hands between us!" I ordered, making my voice harsh. "Feel my cock!"

For emphasis, I pulled his hair even harder, and gripped his buttock more tightly. His face contorted, and I eased the pressure of my hips to let him insert his hands between our bodies. His fingers groped my crotch, curling warmly about the outline of my prick. His other hand eased between my legs, cupping the bulk of my balls.

"Tell me you want that big dick, Billy!" I hissed, and his fingers tightened their hold. "Tell me you want to suck it!"

"I . . . I . . . want to suck your prick!" he gasped. I yanked his hair again.

"Tell me you want it up your ass!"

His jaw worked in a chewing motion. "I do!" he cried. "I want you to fuck me! Hurt me, stud! . . . Hurt me!"

Still keeping my hold on his hair, and with his fingers still gripping my cock through my trousers, I forced the youth into the hall and down it to my room.

Once there, I released him. "Take off your clothes, Billy!" I ordered, and watched as he tugged the shirt over his head, then shoved the cutoffs down to reveal his small but fully erect cock.

"Now," I said, "undress me!"

"Oh, god!" he murmured, his fingers fumbling as he loosened my belt and slid the zipper of my fly down. He dropped to his knees before me while I unbuttoned my shirt and took it off.

He released the band of my slacks and slid them down, giving a gasp as my prick sprang up like a suddenly released spring.

"Oh, my god!" he cried, his eyes following the dick's waggling when I stepped out of my slacks and stood naked before him. "It's gorgeous, Jeff!"

He started to reach for me, but I grabbed his hair again, tugging him upward. Moaning, he climbed to his feet, and I released his hair, wrapping my arm about his waist. I used my free hand to pinch the distended brown nipples, twisting the tiny protrusions until his hips writhed, sliding his hard cock against mine.

"Yes!" he cried, and I could feel his prick jerking. "Punish me, Jeff! Make me your slave! Make me do things! Beat me! . . . Hurt me!"

The last thing I wanted to do was really hurt the youth. But his obvious need for pain could not be ignored. I moved my hand from his waist to the crack of that rounded ass, dipping my fingers into the warm cleft. My forefinger found his little anus, and I lightly scraped the striated circle with my nail.

"Oh, Jeff!" he groaned, as if realizing what I was about to do. "Oh, god!"

Slowly, enjoying the way his asshole clenched about it, I forced my finger up into the hot tight orifice, feeling his dick jerk against mine, the tip already slick with oozing seminal fluid.

The youth moaned, hips writhing, his hand working feverishly on my cock, working the foreskin up and down, rubbing the head over the knob of his own swollen organ. His other hand played with my scrotum, gently fondling the rolling glands in the their pliant sac.

My finger thrust deeper, twisting inside his asshole, rubbing that tender entrance and widening it. He cried out as I forced the insertion of a second digit, stretching the lips still farther.

"Nooo!" he choked out. "Please! . . . Please don't!"

Experience had taught me to ignore his protests. They were part of the game, and I had learned how to play it from several experts.

"Yes!" I said harshly, wiggling my two fingers in that spasming grip. "I'm gonna fuck you, Billy! I'm gonna fuck that tight little ass till you won't be able to sit down for a week! Turn around, kid, and bend over!"

His hand action had produced an oozing of jism from my cockhead, so that member was slick, and my fingers had drawn the intestinal oils from Billy's internal membranes. It would hurt him just enough to satisfy his needs, yet his asshole was now ready for penetration, and my prick was eager to slide up into his inviting tail.

Sobbing, he released my dick, and when I pulled my fingers out of his ass, he turned and bent over the end of the bed, spreading those shapely legs as I moved in behind him.

His whole body jerked when he felt the head of my cock press against his anus, and that sensitive circlet spasmed, its lips seeming to kiss the tip of my dick. We were in perfect position, I didn't have to touch my prick. All I had to do was hold Billy's hips and push my own hips forward.

"UUUUNNGGHH!" the boy half-screamed, his rectum yielding to the hardness. "OHHHH! . . .UNNNHHH! . . . OH, JEFF!"

"Does it hurt, Billy?" I grunted, rotating my hips as I forced my prick still deeper.

"YESSSS!" he cried, his legs trembling as my cock moved inward, stretching and filling his asshole. "DO IT! . . . HURT ME! . . . MAKE ME TAKE IT!"

It was my turn to go "UHHH!" as a sudden relaxation of his rectal muscles let my prick slide almost all the way in. The youngster's prostate was being pressed through the intestinal walls, and Billy Newberry was about to be thoroughly and expertly fucked,

My hips retreated, pulling my cock back through the straining tissues, threatening to turn his asshole inside out. Just when the head was about to pop out of the well-stretched anus, I rammed it in again, my balls pressing the warm perineal plane between his ass and his own nut sac,

I held my dick there, buried in the boy's asshole, letting the convulsions of that torrid channel work their magic on its inserted length.

"That's the way, Billy!" I grunted. "Chew on that prick!"

Billy's hips ground his bottom back against my pelvis, working the hungry rectum about my cock, his hands braced on the arm and back of the sofa.

Keeping my dick hilted in his ass, I reached around to grip his thrusting fuckpole, working my fingers up and down its throbbing length as I began a slow rhythmic hunching that slid my prick in and out of that spasming asshole.

"Am I hurting you, Billy?" I asked, leaning over the youth's arched back.

"Yessss!" he cried breathlessly. "And I love it!"

My hand motion matched the thrusts of my dick, pumping his swollen shaft in perfect harmony with the probes of my hardness in his intestinal corridor.

Each stroke drew the oily exudation from his tortured tissues, and my continued oozings of seminal fluid added to the lubrication of the tight passageway.

I was really fucking him by that time, my hips slamming against his buttocks with meaty thumps, and he was grunting with every thrust, but still pushing his bottom back to take my cock.

"You're killing me!" he cried, his head flung back and his neck turned, that handsome face looking back over one shoulder. "You're tearing my ass up!"

"And I'm gonna tear it up some more!" I panted. I made him gasp as I drew my cock out of his asshole and turned him around, pushing him down onto the cushions, lifting one slender leg and draping it over the back of the sofa.

Quickly, I knelt between those sleek thighs and lifted his other leg, spreading them to expose his reddened asshole. All I had to do was ease my hips forward, and my dick slid up into that torrid grip again.

"UUNNGGHH!" he bleated, for in this position I could drive deeper than before, and I fucked him with punishing thrusts that made him cry out with a mixture of pain and delight.

"RIP MY ASSHOLE, JEFF!" the boy screamed, his rectal muscles clenching and chewing on my driving cock. "HURT ME, LOVER! . . . FUCK ME TO DEATH!"

I learned a long time ago that one of the secrets of satisfying a masochist is by not giving him what he wants. Now that I had managed to get my entire prick into Billy's ass, he was enjoying the feel of that hot throbbing hardness sliding in and out, and it was time to stop.

"No way, kid!" I said in a harsh tone, pulling my hips back and dragging my cock out of his slippery anus with a slurping sound. "You like it too much! I'm gonna let you suck it for me!"

Before he could resist, I was straddling his hairless chest, and aiming my prick toward those inviting lips. He stared at it, wide-eyed and more excited than ever.

"No!" . . . he exclaimed. "It's been in my ass! . . . Don't!"

I rubbed the head across his mouth, and when he tried to turn his face away, I grabbed a handful of that blond hair and forced him back into position.

"Open your fucking mouth, Billy!" I ordered angrily. "I'm gonna stick my prick in it!"

"NOOOO! . . . UUMMMPPPHH!"

The last sound was his wet groan as the head of my cock slid between his lips, his teeth, over his tongue, past his soft palate, and between his tonsils. He gagged and swallowed, the throat tissues sliding and massaging my glans.

"Suck it, Billy!" I panted, beginning to hunch my dick in and out of the boy's mouth, my balls rapping his chin. "Suck my cock! . . . Eat that son of a bitch! Make me come!"

Suddenly, Billy's hands were clasping my ass, the fingers tight on the tensing cheeks, pulling me down with every thrust. I was fucking him in the mouth, and he was loving it!

I was no longer interested in playing games, pretending to hurt him. I wanted to come.

"Oh, shit!" I gasped, my hips hammering. "Take it, baby! Suck it harder!"

I pulled back to where the head was lodged just behind his lightly gripping teeth, and where his tongue could flutter and dance about the slitted tip, scooping up the little globs of pre-come and spreading them over the satin knob.

He grunted as the first spurt of semen splatted against his palate, and he nursed thirstily, his jaw working as he sucked. His fingers kneaded my ass cheeks, urging me to drive my prick deep in his throat. He swallowed noisily and greedily, gulping almost in time with the powerful volleys.

The orgasm was a long and powerful one, making it feel as if my balls were melting and surging up through my cock. My hips jerked and my thighs quivered with each blast of semen, and I worked my prick in and out of Billy's mouth until he had milked the last drop of cream from the throbbing shaft.

He tried to hold onto my prick when I pulled it from between his lips, but I withdrew it with a wet sucking sound. I stood up, staring down at the naked youngster.

"Turn over, Billy!" I barked. "I want some more of that ass!"

This time, there was no protest, no cry of pain, and no plea for punishment. With a sigh of anticipation, Billy rolled onto his belly and parted his thighs so I could kneel between them. Only when I pushed my still-hard cock back into his tender asshole did he finally gasp. But it was a gasp of pleasure.

Slipping my hands under his shoulders, I began fucking him with full-length strokes, slow and deliberate, frictioning every inch of his anal passageway with my sliding dick.

"Oh, shit!" he moaned. "It feels so fuckin' great, man!"

His hips began grinding, rotating that sweet ass as I screwed him, his asshole seeming to suck and squeeze my cock as I drove it in and out, my balls slapping his with every thrust.

I switched to a deep, short stroke, ramming the head of my dick far up in his belly, but pulling back just enough to let it massage his prostate.

"UNNHH! . . . UHHH! . . .UUHHH!" he panted, his asshole clenching. "I'M GONNA COME!"

Each spurt of his semen was accompanied by a powerful spasming of his rectal muscles about my cock, and I felt the delightful contractions of my balls as they shot their second load of thick cream into the excited youngster.

I was in no hurry to pull my prick out of his ass, and his body finally relaxed beneath me, his anal canal still gently squeezing my spent prick as I lay atop him.

"Like that?" I breathed into one ear, his blond hair tickling my lips.

"Oh, god, yes!" he exclaimed, almost sobbing. "It's the best I've ever had!"

"You're good, kid. Damn good," I said, gripping his upper arms for emphasis. My cock was still hard, and I wanted to fuck him again, perhaps letting him finish me off with that talented mouth. But I also wanted something else.

He gave a strangled cry when I pulled my cock out of his asshole, and climbed to my feet beside the sofa. He pushed himself to his knees, looking down at the smeared puddle of semen on the sofa seat.

"Jesus!" he said. "I've made a mess!"

"It can wait," I said, staring at his dick, its swollen length thrusting up from the dark blond curls, and lifting the walnut like balls.

"Sit down, Billy," I ordered, and the boy wiggled about to sit at one end of the sofa, avoiding the wetness of his earlier ejaculation.

He began a protest when I knelt before him and placed my hands on his knees, spreading them apart.

"Shut up!" I grated. "Just sit still!"

I leaned forward, my hands on his bare hips, and began licking his distended prick, running my tongue upward from the base to the inverted vee of the glans.

His body trembled and he moaned with each touch. With one hand, I gripped the root of his dick, and began licking almost savagely at the slitted head.

His cock was coated with his semen, and its tart taste filled my mouth and tingled in my throat. I opened my mouth and slipped my lips over the slippery knob of his cock, and took about half its length before I began sucking it with quick little tugs, still moving my tongue beneath it.

"UMMMMM!" he moaned, his hips pushing upward.

I brought my other hand into play between his thighs, my fingers teasing his balls. My head moved up and down, sliding my encircling lips about the pulsating hardness, claiming more and more of the youth's prick. I felt the slick head in my throat, and I relaxed the tissues, taking all of it as I buried my nose in Billy's thick pubic curls.

The boy was wild with pleasure and excitement, and his hips bounced as my head bobbed, my mouth fucking his dick faster and faster.

"I'M GONNA COME!" he panted, his hands darting to my head and the fingers lacing through my hair. "OH, GOD! . . . JEFFFFF!"

Passion spurred me to greater effort, and I sucked even harder as the thick cream shot into my mouth, its heady tartness seeming to spread through my entire body as I gulped it down and nursed his cock for still more of the ropy sperm.

I held him for several minutes, moving the head of his dick about in my mouth with gentle motions of my tongue, and Billy whimpered with the unexpected addition to his pleasure.

We showered together, fondling each other and exchanging long kisses under the stinging spray. Together, we cleaned the sofa cushion where Billy had ejaculated, and he apologized several times as we worked.

It was almost midnight when I escorted him to the door and let him give my cock one last feel, promising him that we would repeat the night's performance before I left the town.

He had already given me his phone number and his address. The boy roomed not far from the Lonases, and his family lived some fifty miles away.

"You read me like a book, Jeff," he admitted, his hand pressed to my crotch. "You seemed to know exactly what I wanted." He gave a little shiver as he added, "I love that big cock!"

"I'll give you some more of it," I assured the lad.

"Next time," he said, "I want you to tie me up and fuck me. Will you?"

"I've got several ideas about what we can do," I said. "Just take good care of that ass for me."

We kissed before I opened the door, then I stood on the porch as he drove away, flashing his lights as he backed out of the drive.

I checked the couch again, then fixed myself another drink, and sat in the kitchen, elbows on the table, as I sipped it, my cock stiffening as I recalled the previous four hours. Billy Newberry was a most interesting youngster, and I had every intention of enjoying that responsive body again, and very soon.

Setting the alarm for six-thirty, I undressed for the second time that night, and sprawled across the bed. I drifted off to sleep thinking about Billy's dick.

Eight

It was only six o'clock when Randy leaned over the bed and planted a wet kiss on my right nipple, leaving his lips there long enough to run his tongue about the responsive swelling until I was wide awake and reaching for his slender body.

"Did you miss me, Jeff"

I pulled him, fully clothed, on top of me, spreading my legs and pushing my growing erection against his own warm crotch.

"I had company," I admitted. "So, don't start apologizing for staying with your friend."

He moved his hips suggestively. "Anybody I know?"

I described Billy, and Randy nodded his head. "Yeah, I've seen him a couple of times. I don't blame you for having him over. He's a cute guy."

"Like I told you, Randy," I said, rolling him over to where I could straddle his hips. "It's a big world. Let's enjoy it."

I let my weight down on the boy, and covered his mouth with mine in a long and delicious kiss. Until that moment, I had been uncertain as to Randy's ability to adjust to my attitude. Now, I was convinced of his willingness to accept our relationship for what it really was.

I climbed to my feet, and he reached out to give my swollen cock a loving squeeze. I ran my fingers through his blond curls, and we shared a smile of understanding. Then, I headed for the shower, and Randy went into the kitchen to begin breakfast.

Duane arrived as we were having our first cup of coffee, explaining that he couldn't sleep. He settled his hips in one of the chairs and leaned over the table.

"What do you think about these boys Tim's bringing?"

Randy said, "We won't know til we meet them. Hey! All we're doing is exploring a cave."

"Yeah, maybe. But what if they're real cute?"

"Come on, Duane," I protested. "You can't have every cute guy you meet."

"Why not?" he leered, licking his lips, and drawing a laugh from Randy.

"Let's pretend we're all straight," Randy said, getting up to check on the bacon.

"Damn!" Duane exclaimed. "That smells good!"

The three of us demolished the bacon, eggs and toast, and enjoyed another cup of coffee before we checked over the equipment I had purchased.

We separated it into four piles. Each one contained two flashlights, spare batteries and bulbs, markers and twine. The food and the rope I placed with the other things.

"I thought about buying backpacks," I told the two boys. "But it seemed silly to do that for just one trip."

"Looks like you spent a small fortune," Randy noted.

"It's okay," Duane remarked teasingly. "He's a rich writer who can afford it."

"Right," Randy grinned. "And he'll probably make us all suck his dick to pay for it."

"Or vice versa!" said Duane.

"You know," I said with mock seriousness. "Until I came here, I was pure and innocent. You two have utterly destroyed my virtue."

"And I play tackle for the Giants!" Duane retorted. "I had a virgin ass til you showed up."

"Is that a complaint?" I asked.

"Hell, no!" he said. "But it's a fact!"

The exchange could have gone on indefinitely had it not been interrupted by the door chime. Randy answered it, and ushered the three boys into the kitchen. Tim gave us a broad smile and introduced his companions.

Chris Lampley was the older one, a blond, blue-eyed, faintly-pretty youth who gripped my hand with surprising strength.

But it was Scott Harper whose dark eyes drew mine with a look that sent a thrill racing through my belly.

Black hair fell in soft waves about perfect features, among which was a pair of full lush lips that curved in a smile as he acknowledged my attention.

"I read your last book. I'm a big fan of Minnie Pearl," he said. "It's a real pleasure to meet you in person."

I shrugged. "It's a living. I tried a few other things, but they were too much like work."

"Don't let him kid you," Scott said knowingly. "Writing is about the hardest work in the world."

"I'm taking up sports," Duane commented dryly. "All I

have to do is hit a ball with a stick, and they'll pay me five million a year."

"And I'm gonna be his manager," Randy nodded, "at fifteen percent."

"I'm waiting for another war," Tim put in. "Then I can rob a bank and blame it on stress."

"We'll all go to college," Scott said, "like good little boys, and then we'll work our butts off for the next fifty years."

"That," I laughed, "will never make the best seller list."

Chris had the most experience as a caver, and we let him explain what we should do when we arrived at Blevin's Hill.

We asked a few questions, and he answered with a reassuring ease. He looked at me.

"You want to pair us off?"

"I think we've agreed that one of each pair should have experience," I said. "How about you and Duane, Tim and Randy, and Scott and me?"

"Sounds good," Chris agreed. "Tim knows quite a bit. Does that suit everybody?"

There was chorus of assent, and we began lugging our stuff out to the car. When it was stowed in the trunk, we piled into the two big seats. Chris, Randy and Duane sat in the back, while Scott sat between Tim and me as I slid behind the wheel.

I was acutely aware of the boy's bare thigh against mine. We had all decided to wear shorts or cutoffs, although it was certain that the air in the cave would be quite cool.

Driving took most of my attention, but I managed an occasional glance at Scott's well-filled basket, and found myself wondering what his reaction would be to an obvious pass. Those sleek, perfectly rounded thighs were tempting, but I kept both hands on the wheel, and my eyes on the road most of the time.

"Turn right at the next road," said Chris from the back seat. "You'll have to stop and let me unlock the gate. Granddad wants to keep people out."

Leaning across Scott's lap, Tim said, "All our folks know where we are. If we're not back by six this evening, they'll come looking for us."

"That'll give us seven hours in there," I said. "That's plenty."

The dirt road curved through a patch of woods, and I halted the car at a sturdy wooden gate set in a barbed wire fence. Through a gap in the trees I could see Blevin's Hill, a steep and densely wooded mound about a hundred yards ahead.

The gate was secured with a chain and a heavy lock. Chris got out and undid the chain, swinging the gate open and closing it after I pulled the car through.

"The road runs right past the mouth of the cave," Chris informed us. "We can park there."

I had expected a large opening, but the entrance was surprisingly small. From the roadway, we climbed a grassy bank about ten feet, to where a rock ledge shaped a natural doorsill.

We transferred most of our equipment and supplies to the ledge, then divided up the items I had separated earlier.

Chris checked to make sure each of us had everything we needed.

"I'd suggest that we carry an extra bottle of water with us," he said. "Canteens would have helped, but we can always make out."

There was enough light from the entrance to see Duane's face, and I stepped on his toe when he started to make a comment. He stuck his tongue out at me. Then grinned.

Just inside the mouth of the cave was a large area about thirty by twenty feet, and some fifteen feet from the irregular floor to the rough rock of the ceiling. From this room, four passageways led off in different directions, all leading downward and under the hill.

"That opening on the left," Chris explained, "goes back only about a hundred feet, and then it dead ends. I've been back in the next two, but not in the one on the right. Duane and I will take that one."

"Are you sure it's safe?" Duane's voice betrayed his nervousness. He flicked his flashlight on and ran the beam over the shadowy opening.

"I'll lead the way," Chris told him. "Don't worry."

He shined his own flash toward the second entrance. "Scott, you're an old hand at this. You and Jeff try that one. It's a little rough in spots, but you can handle it."

"That leaves us with the third one," Tim said to Randy. To

Chris he said, "Anything we should look for?"

"Yeah. There's a rock face about a quarter mile in there. You won't need rope. But take it easy as you go up."

He checked the plastic bag holding the batteries, bulbs, twine, markers, and water. Bending, he picked up another bottle of water.

"Don't forget that extra water," He warned. "It's awkward to carry, but you'll be glad it's there before the day is over."

"Now," he said. "These three passageways come together in a big room about two miles in. The cave goes farther, but I've never been beyond that room. We'll meet there. That should take about two hours."

"Jesus!" Duane exclaimed. "Two hours to go two miles?"

"It's not an expressway," Chris replied. "You'll see what I mean when we get in there."

Duane stiffened and extended his arm in a silly salute.

"We who are about to go where no man has been stupid enough to go before will see you guys after while!"

Beside me, Scott Harper stifled an amused snort. "Your friend is quite a character," he said, just loud enough for me to hear.

"If you only knew," was my quiet rejoinder. "But, he's a lot of fun."

"I'll bet," he said. He led the way into the second slot-like opening, turning sideways to slip between the rock walls. I followed him, and we found ourselves in a passageway about four feet wide and eight feet high. Scott's light played over the distance to be swallowed up by the darkness.

"Looks clear," he said. "According to Chris, we won't have to crawl anywhere. That's why we wore shorts."

Trailing behind him, I said, "And I thought you just wanted to show off your pretty legs."

He stopped suddenly, and I almost bumped against him in the semi-darkness. The sounds of our four companions had faded after the first few steps, and we were completely alone.

"Was that a joke?" he asked. "Or did you mean it?"

He snapped his flashlight off, and let the blackness cloak us, but I could feel the warmth emanating from his body, and the clean youthful scent of him teased my nostrils.

"Both," I answered. "Was I out of line?"

"No," he said, turning the light on again and leading the way deeper into the cave. "It's just that every time I go into one of these, I get a strange feeling."

The corridor made a sharp left bend, and the floor began sloping downward. We moved forward another ten yards and emerged into a room some twenty feet square and much higher than the passageway. Several stalactites were suspended from the ceiling, and our lights picked out one giant stalagmite forming a column at the far end of the room.

"Beautiful," Scott said admiringly, turning to sweep the walls and ceiling with the beam.

"Yeah," I agreed. "They've been here a long time."

"Right. Makes you feel awfully small."

"Is that the feeling you were talking about?"

"No," he said hesitatingly, moving forward across the uneven floor. "That's different."

Now and then, I let my own light flash across the curve of his young ass, perfectly delineated by the tight cutoffs. The rounded cheeks were obviously firm, but they jiggled enticingly with each movement of his perfect thighs.

"Want to talk about it?"

"Maybe," he answered. "When we stop to rest."

Across the room, the passageway began again, and curved left some twenty yards later. This time, the downward slope was a little steeper, and Scott warned me to watch my footing. There was little debris on the stone and dirt floor, but here and there the rock protruded upward, and we stepped over these minor hindrances with ease.

Suddenly the path took a sharp upward curve, ending in a vertical wall about five feet high. Shining our lights over it, we could see that the path leveled out again, but was five feet higher.

"I guess we climb," I observed, half jokingly.

"I'll boost you up," Scott said. "Then you can pull me up."

"Why not let me give you a boost?" I countered, suddenly imagining that well-filled basket even with and close to my face. "I weigh a lot more than you."

Reaching up, he laid his flashlight and bag of supplies on the top of the wall. I put mine on the ground, with the beam directed toward the rock face. I made a cup of my linked hands and Scott placed his left foot in it, one hand resting lightly on my shoulder.

For a long moment we froze in that position, our bodies close enough to sense that unmistakable aura of personality that either repels or attracts at such a distance. In our case, the attraction was overwhelming.

Scott drew a long shuddering breath, seeming to fight for control of his emotions, while I hoped he would lose the battle.

Then, gracefully, and all too quickly, he swung his lithe body upward, and for one glorious instant the bulge of his prick and balls brushed my cheek.

He pulled himself onto the higher level, picked up his flashlight and looked about him. Putting it down again, he leaned over, braced those slender but muscular legs, and extended his right hand down to me.

I handed him my bag and light, then gripped his fingers, feeling his youthful strength as I climbed up to stand beside him.

"How far have we come?" I asked, lowering my voice. The rock walls reflected the sound and made even a whisper seem loud.

"Less than a mile, I'd guess. From what Chris told me, there's an underground stream about a half mile ahead. We can stop and rest a while there."

We heard the water long before we reached it. The passageway curved into a large cavernlike area and paralleled the swiftly flowing stream for some thirty feet.

The water came through its own opening in the rock, gurgled across the room and disappeared into another hole in the opposite wall. The path was some six feet wide beside the stream, and we dumped our bags and sat down, stretching our legs out and leaning back against the rock wall.

"Do you like spelunking, Scott?" I asked. We had switched off our lights, and let the darkness cloak us in its almost tangible embrace.

"I like the feeling it gives me," was his response. "Especially in the dark. I can be anything I want to be down here."

"Does that mean you're not happy with what you are?"

"Sometimes," he sighed. "Other times I wish I were

someone else."

"Like who?"

"You'll laugh at me."

"No, I won't. Promise."

"I'd like to be a girl," he said in a near whisper. "Isn't that crazy?"

"No," I answered, my own voice low. "A lot of men feel that way. And a lot of women wish they were men."

"I've told only one other person about that. He wouldn't even talk to me after that. I figured you'd understand, because of the way you write."

In the darkness, I reached out and laid my hand on his bare thigh, my fingers pressing reassuringly. His own hand covered it, urging it upward along the rounded sleekness.

"I understand," I whispered, spreading my fingers and cupping his balls and the gratifying swell of his cock.

I squeezed gently, and felt the tremor of desire course through his body. He turned toward me, his free hand reaching for my crotch, and our mouths met, open and thirsty.

It was easy to unfasten his cutoffs and work the zipper down as we kissed, and he adjusted his hips to aid my tugging until they were down about his knees.

I bent over the boy's middle, holding his prick in place as my lips found it and drew the delicious head into my mouth, my tongue swirling greedily about it, and pressing the tip against that delicate slit.

"Jeff!" he gasped, widening the angle of his thighs to let me fondle his balls. "Oh, Jeff!"

I pulled my mouth up and off his cock to lick my way down to where my tongue could caress those dainty orbs. I drew them, one at a time, between my lips, sucking and teasing.

"Let me do you!" he breathed, his fingers still holding the bulge of my dick through my shorts. "Let me suck your dick!"

The stone and dirt floor of a cave is not the ideal spot for sixty-nine. But we were so caught up in our passion that we did not notice the hardness of our makeshift bed. All that mattered was the hardness of the pricks that we claimed with wet, hungry mouths and flicking writhing tongues.

We had scooted down to where we could lie on our sides, facing each other, but reversed so that our lips could devour the succulent prizes that jutted out from our lower bellies.

Scott moaned as he sucked, a nasal whimper of delight as my cock spilled those little spurts of pre-come. The boy left no doubt of his eagerness to go all the way, and my own need was for the load of come that I could sense in those young balls.

Our hips thrust and gyrated, fucking our distended organs in and out of each other's mouth, slurping and grunting as the excitement and pleasure grew with each thrust.

Scott was well hung, and the head of his prick was pressing the back of my throat each time he rammed it in.

He was taking the full nine inches of my cock, and holding the head in his throat for deliciously long seconds, the warm wet tissues moving caressingly about it.

"Ummmm!" he gasped, his fingers clutching my ass cheeks, pulling me into that torrid suction. One of his fingers slipped into the crack of my ass and began teasing my anus.

I paid his tight asshole the same homage, fucking his mouth faster and harder as I felt the ecstatic surges that signaled the approach of my orgasm.

Scott was grunting each time I pulled my prick back to where his tongue could massage the head, and he nursed it with ever increasing greed.

As if controlled by some invisible force, we drove into the short rows together, our hips bucking and thrusting, and our mouths sucking with fierce tugs as our pricks jerked and spurted, spraying our palates with the ropy cream that we accepted with strangled cries of delight.

Jolt after jolt of sheer ecstacy thundered through my belly, and I knew from Scott's reaction that his orgasm was just as powerful as mine.

We swallowed the last drop of our ejaculate, lips milking and caressing as the passion subsided. Our fingers still clutched and held, keeping our dicks inserted long after the final surge of release.

Scott's lips slipped up my cock, releasing it, but remaining close enough to let me feel the wet warmth of his breath. "That was paradise, Jeff! . . . Sheer paradise!"

"Is that what you wanted, Scott?" I asked, letting his prick rest against my cheek.

"That," he said, "and a lot more." He adjusted his hips on

the rock. "Think how good it will be when we're more comfortable."

I worked my way around, careful to stay far away from the edge of the stream, and sampled those lush lips, tasting my own sperm as his tongue met mine.

"Have you ever been fucked, Scott?" I asked softly.

"No," he answered. "I've done what we did a few times. But it wasn't that good. This was heavenly." He paused, and then added, "I'll let you fuck me, Jeff."

"How about you fucking me?" I said, running my tongue over his parted lips.

"Christ, yes!" he groaned. "I did that to one boy, a long time ago."

"How long was 'a long time ago?'"

"I was twelve," he said. "That'd be seven years ago."

"And he didn't screw you?"

"He didn't want to. He just wanted me to fuck him."

"Don't you ever go out with girls?" I demanded.

"Sometimes," he said. "But I can't work up a hard with them. And I don't know any guys I can trust to tell them how I really feel."

"Not even Chris?"

"I've wanted to," he answered, his hands exploring my body, just as mine roamed over his firm hips and waist. "He's a good-looking guy. But I don't know how he'd react."

"I'd bet money that Duane sucks him off," I said.

"I've heard that Duane is gay," he replied, his hand finding my cock and toying with it. "How about Randy and Tim?"

"Let's just say that they like to play," I said. "If Duane gets Chris to come across, we could have a real blast."

"Jesus!" the boy exclaimed. "Six of us!"

"I'd settle for just you, Scott." I claimed his lips in another long kiss, then groped for one of the flashlights. I turned it on and we pulled our shorts into place and stood up. He pressed his body against mine once more, hands roaming over my ass cheeks as we kissed again.

"We'd better move on," he whispered. "But I'd love to let you fuck me right here."

"Let's get going," I warned, "before I do!"

We reclaimed our bags and flashlights, and entered the

passageway opposite the one through which we had entered. The floor began sloping downward again, but there were no obstacles, and we were able to maintain a brisk pace for several minutes.

Suddenly, Scott came to a halt in front of me, and I automatically threw my arm about his waist as I bumped into that firm young ass, the bulk of my cock pressing happily between his buttocks.

"Shhhh!" he hissed, turning off his light. "Listen!"

I strained my ears, but I also kept my hips jammed against him, my prick swelling as it absorbed the warmth of that inviting crevice. All I could hear was the ever-present roar of silence.

"What?" I whispered.

"I thought I heard something," he whispered back. "Sounded like a voice'"

"Maybe the others are just ahead."

He reached back to pull my hips closer as he said, "I don't think so. If I'm right, we're still about half a mile from the place where this all comes together."

"Hold it!" I grunted. "I heard it then!"

It was faint, but it was a human voice, and it was somewhere ahead of us. Scott pulled his hand away and tucked the flashlight beneath his arm. He shaped a trumpet with his palms.

"HELLO!" he shouted. "CAN YOU HEAR ME?"

The echoes rolled over us for several seconds. Then, very faintly, we heard it again.

"Somebody's in trouble!" Scott muttered. I stepped back and flicked my own light on. "Let's go!"

Hurrying now, we moved down the sloping passageway, our ears straining to hear something other than the sounds of our own progress.

Nine

We had traveled only a dozen yards when we heard it again, much more clearly. Our lights explored the walls and Scott gave a little cry of excitement.

"There!" he exclaimed, the beam of his flashlight centered on an opening in the wall just ahead and to our right. "It came from there!"

"Are you sure?" I hissed. "That's not the main passage."

We crept forward, ears tuned, to the small aperture. It was only a couple of feet wide and almost circular, and was only inches above the floor of the cave. We crouched down in front of it, listening, clicking our lights off as if to hear more clearly in the darkness.

"Help!" It was still faint, but the word was quite distinct. Scott's fingers curled about my wrist.

"That's Tim's voice!" he whispered hoarsely. Then, thrusting his head into the opening, he yelled. "Tim! Can you hear me?"

"Yes!" came the distant reply. "Help us!"

Scott flashed his light into the hole, turning wide-eyed to me. "It's almost too small to get through."

"We've got to try," I said. "We can always back out."

"Maybe we should go down the main passage."

I shook my head. "My guess is that they tried exploring some other way and ran into trouble."

"Okay," the boy said. "I'll go first. If I get stuck, you can pull me back."

He shouted again. "We're comin', Tim! Just hang on!" Working quickly, he tied the plastic bag with our equipment and water to one ankle. Then, kneeling, he inserted his head and shoulders into the narrow opening and wriggled out of sight. I dropped to my knees and, taking a deep breath, followed him, dragging my own supplies behind me.

There was just enough room to edge forward, using elbows and feet, but not enough to crawl on hands and knees. Now and then our backs scraped the rock ceiling, but Scott kept going, his flashlight playing ahead like a dancing flame, and I followed his flailing legs and that plastic bag.

"Tim!" he called, halting for a minute. I lay face down, one hand reaching forward to rest on his bare calf. "Can you hear me?"

"Yes!" The voice was clearer, and obviously closer. "We need help!"

"Hang on!" Scott yelled. "We're almost there!"

To me, he said, "There's got to be an opening up ahead. If there wasn't, we couldn't hear him that well."

"Let's go," I urged. "Maybe one of them is hurt."

"God! I hope not!"

We inched forward, the passageway narrowing and making our progress more difficult. Scott paused again, flashing his light ahead.

"I can see your light!" came Tim's excited cry. "It's coming through a hole about six feet up the wall!"

"How big is the hole?" Scott yelled. "Can we get through?"

There was a moment of silence. "I think so! It's pretty small!"

"Are you guys okay?"

"I am," was the shouted reply. "But Randy's in a hole."

"Damn!" Scott muttered. "How did that happen?"

"Guess we'll find out. Can we make it up there?"

"I'll try," he said, moving forward again, but more carefully. Again he reminded me, "If I get stuck, you can pull me back."

The only sound was that of our scrabbling for purchase on the rock. Then Scott grunted, "I can see it!"

"Is it big enough?" I asked. I was breathing hard from exertion. Dragging the bags with us was hard work.

"I can make it," he answered. "I'm not sure about you. Your shoulders are broader than mine."

"If you can get through," I said, "so can I."

"Tim!" Scott called. "Can you reach the hole?"

"Yes!" came the reply.

"I'm gonna need help getting down," the boy explained. "Come over where I can see you."

He worked his body forward, and I moved up to where I could see the opening beyond him.

"Yeah," Scott said. "I can see out now. It's a room, and a hole in the floor. Here's Tim."

"My god!" I heard Tim's voice. "Am I glad to see you!"

"Let me hand my stuff to you," Scott said. "Then, brace

yourself so I can use your shoulders to swing down on."

There was a lot of grunting and wiggling, but I coudn't see what was going on until Scott's hips and legs disappeared and I could move forward.

Looking out through the opening, I saw Scott and Tim leaning over the hole and shining their lights into it. Scott turned back to me.

"Can you get through, Jeff?"

"Yeah," I grunted, working the bag up alongside of me and pushing it toward the hole. "Take this crap, will you?"

Tim hurried over to catch the bag, and Scott took my flashlight.

"I'll have to put one arm through first," I told them. "My shoulders won't fit any other way."

It was a trick I had learned as a kid. By placing one arm at your side, and the other above your head, you could make your shoulders much more narrow.

"You two are gonna have to catch me," I warned. "I won't have but one hand to grip with."

"We'll do it," Tim said. They had placed two flashlights in position, and their young bodies were braced and ready.

It wasn't easy, for in the awkward position, it was difficult to move forward. I pushed with my toes, and wiggled my hips to work my head and shoulders through the opening. I had trouble at one point, for I was rubbing hard against the rock.

Then, suddenly, I was through, and my own weight was pulling my hips and legs forward and down. The boys' hands gripped me, easing me down and lowering my feet to the rocky floor.

For several seconds, we embraced, bodies clinging and arms tight. It wasn't sexual, but I was quite aware of their youth and maleness.

"What happened?" was Scott's first question.

"Randy wanted to explore a passageway we found," Tim said. "We followed it to this room, and saw this hole. Somebody had put a rope ladder down there, and Randy decided to climb down."

"Jesus!" Scott exclaimed. "Why didn't you stop him?"

"I tried," Tim insisted. "But I guess I didn't try hard enough."

"You mean he's down there?" I asked harshly.

"Yeah. He was almost down to where the hole curves, and the ladder broke. He yelled one time, then I didn't hear anything else. You can't see the bottom from up here."

"Christ! How long has he been down there?"

Tim looked at his watch. "About thirty minutes. It happened just before I heard you two."

"I'd have gone down after him," Tim explained. "But there's no place to tie the rope, and the ladder broke right at the top."

"I'll go down," Scott volunteered. "I just hope we've got enough rope."

I went over to the hole and shined my light down. The shaft went straight down for about fifteen feet, then curved until the rest of it was hidden from sight. Scott was opening our bags and tying the two ropes together. He seemed to know what he was doing, and since he was the smallest of the three of us, it made sense to let him climb into the shaft.

He dumped the contents of one bag onto the floor, and put batteries and bulbs into the sack. Then, he knotted it, and fastened one end of the rope about his waist, pulling it up until it was under his shoulders. With the loose end, he secured the bag and the flashlight.

"I'll see how badly he's hurt," he said. "It'll take both of you to pull him up."

"Jesus!" Tim said, his voice almost breaking. "He could be dead!"

Scott put his hand on the boy's shoulder. "Let's hope for the best!" He waited until both Tim and I took hold of the rope and drew it taut. Then, dropping to his knees, he lowered himself into the shaft. The two of us braced ourselves as we felt his weight.

The rock was smooth where the rope ran over the lip of the shaft, so there was little danger of the line fraying. Slowly, as Scott shouted guidance, we played out the rope, letting him slide down the vertical corridor.

"I'm at the bend!" he called. "Hold it! Let me see if I can spot him."

There was silence for a few seconds. Then, "No! I can see the bottom. But I don't see Randy!"

"Go on down!" I called back. "He could have rolled when

he fell. How does it look down there?"

"Just like up there!"

"God! I hope he's okay!" Tim breathed as we played out more line. Suddenly, the rope slackened.

"I'm down!" Scott shouted. "I see him!"

"How is he?" Tim asked, leaning over the hole as if he chould see past the curve of the shaft. "Is he hurt bad?"

"Hold on!" came the reply.

"I feel so fucking helpless!" Tim exclaimed. "I should have stopped him when he started down."

"Randy's not a child, Tim," I reminded him. "He just made a stupid choice."

From the shaft, Scott's voice called, "He's unconscious. But he's breathing okay, and his pulse is strong."

"Is anything broken?" I yelled down.

"I'm checking," was his reply. "I don't think so. Can you guys haul him up?"

"Sure," I said. "But we'll have to do it slowly."

"Give me some more slack!"

We lowered more of the rope and saw it jerk and weave as Scott fastened it about the unconscious Randy.

"Okay," came his cry. "Start pulling, and I'll guide him as far as I can."

Slowly and carefully, we pulled the boy up the shaft, pausing each time there was the slightest difference in his weight. It meant that he was caught on some projecting rock, and we had to lower him a little to let his body swing clear.

It took about fifteen heart-pounding minutes to get Randy up to where, with Tim holding the rope tight, I could lift him out of the shaft and stretch him out on the floor of the cave.

Tim unfastened the rope and tossed the end back into the shaft while I examined Randy. I ran my fingers through his blond hair and found a large bump on the back of his head.

Lifting his head slightly, I checked him more closely. The skin was unbroken. Pulling each eyelid up, I shined the light into his green eyes. The pupils dilated pefectly.

"Can you give me a hand?" Tim asked. "Let's get Scott up here."

Bringing Scott up was much easier, for he could bounce himself away from the walls. He was panting when I gripped his wrists and hauled him over the rim of the shaft.

Tim had removed his shirt and soaked it with water, and was applying it to Randy's face. The boy stirred, drew a shuddering breath, and gave a low moan.

I knelt beside him, opposite Tim, while Scott held the light centered on Randy's pale face.

"Easy, Randy!" I said encouragingly. "You're okay! Just take it easy!"

He moaned again, and his eyelids fluttered. Scott aimed the flashlight lower, and the boy opened his eyes. He moistened his lips.

"What . . . what happened?" he asked weakly. Tim lifted one of the water bottles to Randy's lips and let him take a long swallow.

"You fell," I said, leaning close so he could see my face. "The ladder broke."

"Stupid! . . . Stupid!" he said almost angrily.

"Yeah," I agreed. "It was. But you're okay. Just rest a while. You've been out for quite a while."

He moved restlessly, checking his arms and legs. "I don't think anything's broke." He winced. "My head hurts like hell!"

Scott dug in his bag and came up with a small plastic bottle. "I've got some asprin. Maybe that will help."

He shook four of them into his palm and placed them in Randy's mouth. Tim offered the water bottle again, and the boy swallowed.

"Is the passageway clear where you came in?" I asked.

"Yeah," Tim answered. "The main path is not far back. We never had to even bend over."

"Can you sit up?" I said to Randy.

"I . . . I think so." He stirred, and with our help sat up looked over at the hole. "Stupid!" he said again.

"Let's try standing," I suggested.

It took several minutes, but Randy was soon able to walk unaided, and insisted that he could make it back to the other passageway.

We gathered our gear and with Tim leading the way, we wended through the cave, exiting the passageway into a room larger than the one we had just left.

"This is where we went wrong," Tim pointed. "We should have gone straight through there." He indicated a large opening to our right. "But we thought we'd see where that hole led."

"You didn't," Randy protested. "I was the stupid ass who suggested exploring. Stupid! Stupid!"

"How's the head?" I asked.

"It still aches. But not as bad."

Single file, we entered the larger opening, and followed the passageway for some ten minutes before we heard voices ahead of us.

"Hello!" Tim called.

"Hello!" came Duane's bellow. "Where have you guys been?"

We emerged into a cavern-like room almost fifty feet long and twenty feet high. Chris and Duane had been sitting on a rock ledge, and they stood up as we filed into the room.

"Randy had a fall," Tim explained, giving the pair a full account of our activities. Chris insisted on examining Randy's head, and probing around the lump.

"OWWW!" Randy yelped. "Take it easy!"

"I want to make sure you didn't fracture your skull."

"I'm okay," Randy insisted. "Hey! I've been knocked out before."

"That's better than being knocked up!" Duane put in. "I may bring suit against Chris."

"What kind of suit?" Scott asked innocently.

"He raped me," Duane answered. "We stopped to rest, and he attacked me like some crazy animal!"

"Are you sure it wasn't the other way around?" said Tim.

"He's crazy!" Chris exclaimed. "Nuts!"

It was Randy who demanded, "Did you two make out?"

"Just once," Duane said.

Randy turned to Chris. "Did you?"

"Oh shit!" Chris exhaled noisily. "Okay! Yes! We did! He says you all do."

It was my turn. "Did you like it, Chris?" I asked.

"Hell, yes!" he blurted. "Who wouldn't?"

Scott moved closer to his friend. "Want to try it again?"

Chris deliberately shined his light on each of our faces, taking his time before answering.

"Damn right!" he said.

Randy said, "Let's get out of this fucking hole."

"I suggest we eat first," Chris said. "You may not feel all that tired, but moving around in here takes a lot of energy."

I stayed close to Randy, keeping an eye on him. But he seemed to be doing okay. Now and then, he rubbed the back of his head and winced. Nevertheless, he managed to eat three sandwiches as we demolished the food we had brought.

We took the path that Chris said was easiest back to the cave entrance, and Randy assured us that his headache had almost disappeared. He showed no evidence of concussion, and we loaded our gear into the trunk and climbed into the car.

"Do any of you have to be home tonight?" I asked, backing the car to turn it around.

"We have to let our folks know we're back from the cave," Chris answered. "And I'd like to bathe and change clothes. Why? What's up?"

"I think," Scott said, placing a warm hand on my thigh, and sliding it dangerously near my basket, "that we're going to have a party."

"Can I be the party?" Duane asked mincingly.

"Get in line," Randy said, and in the rear view mirror I saw his hand move to Chris's crotch. The boy spread his knees accommodatingly.

"Christ!" Chris sighed as Randy's fingers curled about his outlined cock. "What have I got myself into?"

"Me!" Duane exclaimed. "Have you forgotten already?"

Scott's fingers were bolder now, and I glanced over to see Tim's hand at work between Scott's rounded thighs.

I floored the accelerator.

Ten

As I pulled into the drive and parked beside Tim's Toyota and Duane's old Chevrolet, I looked over my shoulder at Randy. "You sure you're okay?"

"Positive," he nodded. "I was just knocked out. No big

deal."

"Let's leave the crap in the trunk," I suggested. "You can bathe here. In fact, we all could."

"If we're gonna be here late," Tim pointed out, "we'd all better go home and explain."

"We could be back here by eight," Chris said. "How does that sound?"

"We'll be here," Randy supplied. Then he got a laugh with "And if you're not here by eight, we'll start without you."

We had gotten out of the car and were standing in the drive. Scott gave my arm a squeeze.

"We've got some unfinished business, Jeff."

"Ready when you are," I grinned. "Maybe more so."

The trio climbed into Tim's car and backed out, Tim beeping his horn as they drove away. Randy unlocked the front door, and the three of us entered. Duane headed for the bathroom, and Randy turned to me.

"Did you and Scott get it on?" he asked.

I slipped an arm about his lithe waist and pulled his hips against mine, letting him feel my cock. His own arms went around me.

"Jealous?" I asked softly.

"A little," He admitted. "But that's silly."

"I was worried as hell about you," I told him. "I'm gonna want some more of this." I gripped his buttocks and pulled him closer.

"Any time you want it, Jeff," he said, parting his lips for my kiss. "Maybe I don't *love* you, you know, like that, but shit I do love that big dick."

"I'll settle for that." I let him try to swallow my tongue as my hands explored his firm young ass. The blow on the head hadn't diminished his responsiveness. Randy was ready for anything I wanted to do.

Duane came back from the bathroom and I suggested a drink before we showered. Randy insisted on pouring the bourbon, and we sat down at the table in the kitchen.

"So you got to Chris?" Randy said to Duane, causing the older boy to favor us with a broad smile.

"It didn't take much persuasion," he answered. "He's just like a lot of guys. He wants to do it, but he doesn't want anybody to know about it. His cock is almost as big as yours, Jeff."

"Which means you liked it," I commented.

"Damn right!" was the youth's response. "And I think he liked mine."

"You got him to go down on you?" Randy demanded.

"Like a starved calf!" Duane grinned. "It's funny how a guy will insist he wouldn't do that for anything, then try to swallow it when he finally breaks down."

"You know," I mused, swirling the bourbon and ice in my glass. "It looks like it's gonna be quite a night."

"Then, let's get ready," Randy said, finishing his drink. "I'm for the shower."

"Can I join you?" Duane asked, waggling his eyebrows.

"No way!" Randy replied. "Let's save it for later."

While Randy showered, Duane poured another drink for us, and he told me a little about himself.

"I knew I was gay," he said, "when I was about eight years old. My cousin Jerry was twelve, and we used to stop by his house after school. Both of his parents worked, so we had the house to ourselves.

"Jerry had some books showing men and women sucking and fucking, and he liked to look at them and jerk off. I didn't care about the pictures, but I got a funny feeling when I saw his dick get hard, and I wanted to feel it. Once I began playing with it, I wanted to suck it, and we went from there.

"I couldn't come, 'cause I was too little. But it sure felt good when he sucked my pecker."

"Didn't he ever try to screw you?" I asked.

"Yeah," he nodded. "But I was scared of that. I guess the other was enough for me till you changed my mind."

"Are you sorry?"

"Hell, no!" he answered quickly. "I think I like that better."

Randy rejoined us, having changed to a clean pair of cutoffs after his shower. He had donned a loosely knit shirt that hugged his pecs and outlined the nipples, and a pair of loafers.

"You can have the shower," he told Duane. "I put out a pair of my shorts for you. We're about the same size."

"Good," Duane grinned. "I like to get in your pants."

I left them alone, using my own bathroom and enjoying the

hot spray, letting it wash some of the earlier fatigue from my muscles. After toweling dry, I settled for a satin robe, and belted it about my waist. It promised to be an exciting evening, and I wanted to be ready for action.

I had been in the small town only six weeks, but they had been pleasant ones, and my young friends had made sure that my sex life was quite satisfactory. Now, with the addition of Scott and Chris, it was even more delightful.

My book was coming along nicely, and George was immensely pleased with the chapters I had sent him. All in all, it was a most rewarding summer. I realized my adorable Randy had been a godsend. The boy was more than willing for sex any time I wanted it, but he was also understanding when I decided to be alone. Even more important, he accepted the fact that I needed other bodies, just as I recognized his hunger for new flesh. I would hate to leave this place, but I could always visit from time to time, and I promised myself that I would do just that.

Duane was in the shower, and Randy was watching an old sitcom on cable when I strolled into the living room. He pointed to the coffee table, where a glass of bourbon and ice waited for me.

"Thought you could use it," he said. He was in the big recliner, his legs stretched out and relaxed on the extended footrest.

"Thanks," I said, taking the glass and dropping onto the sofa, recalling that it was exactly where I had screwed Billy Newberry only last night.

Duane hadn't bothered with a shirt. When he came back, all he was wearing was the pair of shorts Randy had loaned him.

Like me, the youngster was stripped for action. Now that he had finally let himself be fucked, it seemed he was eager to try it in every conceivable position. "Whatever feels good," he said.

Seeing us with the bourbon sent him back to the kitchen to refill his own glass, and he plopped down beside me on the sofa, deliberately pressing his thigh against mine.

"I like that robe," he said. "But I like you better without it."

"You're a sex fiend," Randy teased.

"Card carrying!" Duane nodded. He pressed my thigh more

firmly. "Would you like to be fiended?"

"Maybe later," I smiled. "When the others get here, we can have a gang fiend."

Randy pushed himself erect. "How are we gonna work this? Chris and Scott may be a little bashful."

"Let's play it by ear," I said. "Duane can guide Chris, and I'll take care of Scott. You and Tim can get it on."

"I'd like to make it with Scott," Randy admitted. "He's a knockout."

"Once we get rolling," I assured him, "I don't think he'd fight you off."

Our discussion was interrupted by the door chime, and Randy hauled himself up to answer it, ushering Tim into the room. The boy, like Randy and Duane, had opted for shorts, and the sight of those sleek thighs sent a rush of heat through my balls as I remembered just how good he had made it for me.

Randy fixed Tim a drink, and the four of us sat talking for a few minutes. It was obvious that we were all impatient to exchange more than mere words.

Chris and Scott arrived together, Chris explaining that he had swung by Scott's house and picked the younger boy up. Both of them were wearing cutoffs, and the sight of five pairs of muscular, yet slender male legs made my cock start doing exercises beneath my robe.

This time, Duane played host and we settled down, Chris, Duane, Scott and I on the sofa, Randy in the recliner, and Tim seated on the floor in front of him, each of us with a drink in hand.

Randy had straightened up in the recliner, which pulled the footrest back under the chair. That gave Tim room to lean back between Randy's knees, and drape his arms over the boy's thighs. When he tilted his head back, it rested against Randy's genitals, and he deliberately rubbed against them each time he took a sip of his bourbon.

Scott put his hand in my lap, giving a soft gasp as he felt the hardness of my prick through the robe. His fingers curled about it.

"I want that," he whispered, his dark eyes gleaming. He moved closer, ignoring the other two boys on the sofa. "I want you to fuck me, Jeff."

To my surprise, Chris was feeling up Duane, his hand busy between the youth's thighs, fingers working as the bulge of Duane's basket grew. Duane's legs parted, and his hips squirmed encouragingly.

Tim had turned halfway around, enabling him to fondle Randy's crotch, and as I watched with mounting excitement, he tugged the zipper of Randy's shorts down.

"Why don't we all get more comfortable?" I asked, reaching for the sash of my robe. "Let's stop pretending we don't know why we're here."

All five boys moved as if they had practiced the maneuver, shorts and cutoffs sliding down, and shirts lifting over touseled heads. Five naked bodies sported erections as they resumed their original positions, hands now gripping and squeezing the hardnesses they had created earlier.

Chris stared as I stood and shrugged out of my robe, revealing my own throbbing cock. He gave a low whistle of admiration.

"Jesus!" he exclaimed. "You are really hung!"

I nodded at his dick, which Duane held in his curled fingers. "That," I said, "is not exactly *small*."

Scott urged me down onto the sofa, and he bent over my lap, bypassing my prick to lick lovingly at my hairy balls.

Running my fingers through his long wavy hair, I spread my knees farther apart to give him greater access. I pushed my hips upward, encouraging the boy to slide his tongue beneath and behind the dangling sac, and felt the warm wet tip graze my anus.

Beside me, Chris had straddled Duane's thighs and was rubbing his distended cock against the boy's stiffened dick, their mouths fused and hands roaming in erotic exploration.

Tim and Randy had slipped to the carpet, Randy on his back and Tim astride his head, each greedily sucking on the other's swollen prick.

"UUNNHH!" came Chris's yelp as he forced his virgin anus onto Duane's dick. I spared them a quick look as the older boy's hips settled, driving his colon down about the meaty spear. Evidently they had used only saliva for a lubricant, and Chris was being initiated the hard way. But he was too horny to care.

Still groaning, he lowered himself all the way onto Duane's cock, grinding his hips to make sure he had every inch inside him.

Scott was busy with my balls again, his tongue lapping about the base of my prick while his hands gripped my upper thighs and hips. Ever so slowly and deliberately, he licked his way up the ventral ridge and on either side of the engorged shaft, coating it with saliva and moaning with ever-increasing passion as he neared the satiny knob.

Only hours before, the youth had enjoyed his first taste of my cock, and he was eager for a second helping. But no more eager than I was to supply the succulent feast. And, since his secret desire was to be treated like a girl, I would gladly show him that such treatment was unnecessary, and that being treated as a beautiful young boy could be far more delightful than his original fantasy.

Leaning forward, I whispered, "Get it real slick, kid."

It would be the same method Chris and Duane had used, and Chris was now riding like a demented jockey, his hips hunching as he forced his asshole up and down Duane's prick, their grunts and groans increasing my own excitement as Scott's lips finally slipped over the head of my cock.

On the carpet, Randy and Tim had changed position. Randy was still on his back, but his legs were drawn up until his knees touched his chest, while Tim knelt over him, inserting his dick in Randy's eager bottom. The shaft was slick with saliva from Randy's oral ministrations, and while Scott took my own cock deep in his throat, Tim drove his prick up into Randy's receptive asshole. He worked his knees forward, lifting the boy's hips so he could plunge to the balls in that torrid channel.

I knew first-hand just how good it felt to slide my cock into Randy Lonas, and it was obvious that Tim Goodson was enjoying the spasming orifice just as much. He gave a groan of ecstacy when Randy began grinding his hips to increase the friction in his well filled butt.

Scott was sucking my dick with instinctive skill, pulling his lips up the column until only the swollen glans was still captive in his mouth. He held it there while his cheeks hollowed, and his tongue savaged the knob, lashing and swirling to urge the seepage of jism from the tiny slit, and moaning as he tasted the musk laden juice.

Although he wanted the load of come he knew was waiting in my heavy balls, Scott had not forgotten our promises back in the cave. And I not only wanted that hot young ass, I needed it. But I also was enjoying the feel of his hungry mouth and that warm wet tongue that polished and caressed as he sucked.

Chris was bouncing on Duane's cock, his thighs tensing as he lifted his hips to drag that asshole almost off of the boy's dick. Then, each time he took it full length into his belly, he gave a grunt of pleasure. To me, one of two things was obvious. Either Chris had been fucked in the ass before, or he had discovered that having a big dick rammed up into his belly felt much better than he had expected. Either way, he was getting his kicks, and Duane was getting a very responsive piece of tail.

Now and then, I find myself able to enjoy sex for a long time before surrendering to the exquisite convulsions of orgasm. This promised to be one of those times, and even as Scott's lips and tongue coaxed me toward the finish line, I determined to make the most of the evening.

Gripping Scott's hair with both hands, I began aiding his bobbing head by thrusting my hips upward, driving my cock deep in the boy's throat, feeling the warm wetness encircle and convulse.

"Suck it, Scott!" I urged, a needless suggestion, since the youngster was nursing with almost painful tuggings. I let him slide his mouth up and down the shaft several times, then I would force his lips all the way to the root, burying the head in his throat and holding it there for as long as I dared before letting him come up for air.

Finally, I leaned forward to remind him again, "Leave it good and wet, Scott! I want some of that ass!"

The boy spilled his saliva over the head and the upper half of my nine inches, bathing it in the wetness until he decided it was ready.

Breathing hard and fast, he released me and stood up just long enough to spread his legs and place his knees on the sofa on either side of my hips. I scooted down on the seat to accommodate him, and reached down to grip my cock as he positioned himself to be fucked.

"I've been dreaming of this for years," he whispered,

lowering his hips just enough to press his hot little anus against the tip of my cock. "I've wanted to do it. But I was always too scared."

"Are you scared now, Scott?" I had my hands on his slender waist, ready to urge him down.

"Not any more!" he said, adding a little pressure, his eyes narrowing as he felt the hardness. "I *know* what I want!"

Scott added weight to the pressure, and I pushed my hips upward, feeling the hot tightness yield and fit itself about the tip of my cock.

The boy's eyes squeezed shut, and his full lips shaped a near snarl as he felt the swollen knob entering his asshole.

He sucked in a deep breath and held it, his naked body quivering in tense expectation.

"UUNNGGHH!" he bleated. His own weight had forced the sphincter over the head of my prick, and the flared rim of the glans had snapped through and into his colon.

"Relax, baby!" I grunted, my fingers gripping the firmness of his waist. "It's in!"

"God!" he gasped, his eyes opening to stare into mine, his anal muscles working like a hungry mouth, chewing the part of my cock that was inside him. "It's so damn big!"

"Does it hurt?" I raised my hips to slide farther into the inviting channel.

"It did," he said, "when it first went in. Just a little bit now."

"Want to stop?"

"No way!" His voice softened, and he slid another inch onto the pole. "I want that big thing!"

With the head and about an inch of the shaft inserted, I was able to begin that frictioning movement which is the very heart of fucking.

My hips thrust upward, driving my dick still deeper in Scott's ass, and I added a little screwing motion that made the head rub the walls of his intestine.

"JEFF!" he cried, his body arching, suspended by his hands on my shoulders, and his quivering thighs. "OHHHH!"

I could feel the throbbing knot of his prostate as the head of my prick slid past it, and I let my hips descend, drawing the cock back to rub that responsive area again.

It took all of two strokes for the youngster to get the idea. His lithe hips began a rise and fall of their own, sliding his clenching asshole up and down my prick, every slide claiming more of my throbbing pole.

Scott was being fucked for the first time, but his eagerness left no doubt that it was only the first of many couplings, for the boy obviously loved having his asshole packed with hard cock.

On the floor, Tim was pounding the meat to the groaning Randy, his shapely ass rising and falling as he drove in and out of his companion's elevated rear. Tim had reared back on his knees, and was holding Randy's ankles, keeping his slender legs spread and lifted, keeping that ass in perfect position.

Scott's hip motions were not the only thing shaking the sofa. Chris, who was riding Duane's prick in the same way Scott was riding mine, was slamming his ass down with each thrust, and grinding when the cock was fully buried in his tail. Like Scott, he had found the pleasure he had denied himself for so long, and he wanted every inch of the throbbing hardness that pierced his tingling ass.

The room was filled with the sounds of our hunching, writhing, thrusting bodies; flesh slapping flesh; the sexy slurping of stiff pricks sliding through spasming, slippery membranes, young voices whimpering, moaning, half-sobbing with the ever-mounting pleasure of gratification.

I tightened my grip on Scott's waist. "Lean back, Scott," I urged the excited boy. "I want some of that dick!"

He didn't want to stop fucking his ass on my cock, but he could not resist the potential of enjoying both acts at the same time.

He lowered his hips, taking me full length in his hot ass, and let his upper body bend back over my knees, his fingers holding my shoulders.

I bent forward, able to reach his rearing dick and slip my lips over the head of it. I fluttered my tongue over the tip, and sucked just enough to make his asshole spasm about my hilted cock.

"Don't make me come, Jeff!" the youngster hissed, his hips screwing and jerking. "I want it to last a long time!"

I didn't answer. I was too busy enjoying that delicious prick, tasting the tart saltiness of his jism as it spilled from the tiny slit and mingled with my saliva before I let it slide down my throat.

My cock throbbed and swelled inside the boy, and he began slowly fucking again, careful to keep his hunches short so as not to dislodge his dick from my nursing mouth.

On my right, I saw Duane staring at us, then imitating our action by reaching for Chris's big cock, and making the boy cry out with the suddenly increased pleasure.

On the carpet, Tim and Randy had reversed roles. Tim was on hands and knees, while Randy knelt behind him, driving his sizable prick in and out of Tim's willing bottom.

I deliberately pulled my mouth up and off of Scott's cock, ignoring his gasp of protest. I urged him to me, working my prick even deeper in his clenching tail.

"Let's switch, Scott," I told the panting boy. "You fuck me for a while."

Reluctantly, he raised his hips, dragging that hot asshole from about my dick, and gasping as the head snapped past his sphincter on the way out. He stood up, his legs trembling, and his prick thrusting out in readiness.

"Don't go away!" I said, climbing to my feet. "I'll be right back."

I padded down the hall to my room and opened the drawer of my nightstand, withdrawing a tube of lubricant I had used with Randy. My absence was no more than three minutes, but that was time enough for the action in the living room to alter considerably. Chris was now standing astride Tim's back while Randy's mouth worked on his dick. Behind Chris, Duane was rubbing the head of his cock in the crack of the boy's ass. Scott was standing to one side, watching the trio, and slowly stroking his own rearing prick.

I walked over to Duane and extended the tube of lubricant. He opened his palm and I squeezed a generous glob onto it, returning his grin while he smeared it over the head and shaft of his dick. Then he ran that same hand through the cleft of Chris's buttocks.

Chris was about to enjoy the second most pleasurable act possible. Randy would be sucking his prick, while Duane packed his asshole with hard, throbbing cock. I suddenly decided to give the youngster his ultimate baptism in ecstacy.

Handing the tube of lubricant to Scott, who immediately greased his dick, I added my own body to the foursome. All I had to do was spread my legs a little and straddle Randy's back. My cock was thrusting upward, and Chris, his face contorted with strain as Duane's prick forced its way into his asshole for the second time, looked down to see the inviting spear aimed for his parted lips.

Without hesitation, the youth leaned forward and slipped his mouth over the plumlike head of my cock, his tongue dancing and his cheeks hollowing in eager suction.

Behind me, Scott was pressing the knob of his dick between my buttocks, and I pushed my hips back to encourage him. I grunted as I felt the hot hardness penetrate my asshole, and with Scott's fingers gripping my hips, his prick drove up into my belly and began a delightful pistoning that massaged my prostate. At the same time, Chris was sucking noisily on my dick, while feeding his own cock into Randy's skillful mouth, and taking Duane's prick up his ass.

Of the six of us, Tim was the only one who was simply being fucked by Randy. But he was acutely aware of what the rest of us were doing. Randy was fucking Tim and sucking Chris's dick. Duane, of course, was pumping his cock in and out of Chris's bottom; Scott was fucking my ass, and I was being fucked and sucked, a most pleasant experience, excelled only by the ecstacy Chris was enjoying: a three-way hookup.

Although two of our party were relative newcomers to the world of male-male pleasure, and Tim was only a recent initiate, all six of us had cast aside our inhibitions and were bent on enjoying every possible position and orifice.

Scott, now experiencing the thrill of driving his prick up into a man's ass for the first time, was gasping as he pounded his meat into me. I could tell by the way his prick throbbed that he was not far from orgasm, and I grabbed Chris's blond hair and urged him to suck harder on my cock.

Since he was being sucked and fucked in addition to having my dick rammed down his throat, that youngster was quite willing to oblige.

I felt Scott's prick swell, and he drove it deep to deliver the first spurt of come far up in my belly. That rush of warm wetness inside me triggered my own release, and the goodness washed through my balls, channeling up the shaft of my cock and into Chris's waiting mouth.

He snorted with delight as the creamy liquid splattered his tongue, and he sucked with short, avid tugs that made my ass tighten about Scott's jetting prick, milking that member until I had received the last drop of his load.

Chris gulped down my offering, and teased me with that eager tongue until he was sure I was drained. It was then that Randy made a gurgling sound, for Chris was shooting his come into the boy's throat, a treat that made him loose his own load into Tim's asshole. At almost the same moment, Duane gave a sharp gasp, and Chris grunted, chewing more hungrily on my cock as Duane's semen spilled up into his intestine.

Since Tim was on the bottom of the pile, I couldn't tell whether or not he had achieved his orgasm. It was not until we untangled our limbs and bodies, pulling spent cocks from mouths and asses, that the youngster climbed to his knees and gripped his stiff dick.

"What about me?" he demanded, skinning his cock back and favoring us with a questioning look.

It was Scott who moved from behind me to drop onto hands and knees in front of Tim, his head bending and his full lips claiming Tim's rearing prick. Tim seized the youth's long hair and began hunching his dick in and out of Scott's mouth.

"Suck it, Scott!" he panted, his head thrown back and his hips working feverishly. "Suck that dick!"

For a boy who only that day had taken his first hesitant step on the road of forbidden pleasure, Scott showed a remarkable talent, and an even greater hunger. Clasping Tim's buttocks with both hands, he welcomed the full-length thrusts of Tim's cock, moaning with excitement.

Eleven

Fresh from our showers, we lounged in the chairs about the kitchen table, temporarily sated and sipping the drinks Randy made for us.

"Where do we sack out?" Duane asked, his eyes darting

about the table, exploring our naked chests. "I mean who sleeps with who?"

"Randy," I suggested. "Get a pen and a sheet of paper. Let's surprise ourselves."

When he brought them, I tore the sheet into six pieces and wrote our names on the slips, turning them over and moving them about.

"We draw," I said. "And if you draw your own name, you put it back."

Duane reached out and picked up one of the slips. He turned it over and gave a big grin. He looked across the table at Tim.

"Your ass is mine, buddy!"

Tim fluttered his long lashes in mockery. "After you eat me, you naughty man!"

Scott was next to draw, and his dark eyes found Randy's green ones. "You and me," he said softly.

"I guess that means I sleep with you, Jeff," Chris said, turning the last slips over. He ran his fingers through his blond hair and looked about at our five faces.

"You guys are all so great," he said quietly. "Oh, I knew what I wanted. But somebody had to make me admit it."

He looked straight at Duane and nodded. "You did that, old buddy. And I want to thank you. Hell! I thank all of you. For the first time in my life, I'm contented with myself."

"That goes for me, too," Scott added. "I've never been this happy."

"It gets better," Tim put in, "as you go along. I was just like you two till Jeff showed me what I was missing."

Chris stood up, adjusting the towel he had draped about his narrow hips. "Come on, Jeff. You can show me."

Randy climbed to his feet. "Duane," he said. "You and Tim sleep in Mom's room. Okay?"

"Sleep?" Duane leered. "With an ass like that in bed with me?"

"You're a bunch of sex fiends!" I teased, pushing my chair back. "Come on, Chris. I've got a couple of new books we can read til we get sleepy."

Their laughter followed us down the hall and into my room.

I shut the door and turned to see Chris drop the towel just before reaching for me.

My towel joined his on the floor, and our arms went about each other, bodies pressing and moving as his lips parted for my kiss, his tongue twisting and probing while his hands explored my ass cheeks. One finger dipped and found the sensitive circle of my anus, teasing it as he rubbed his swelling cock against my own stiffened dick.

His lips deserted mine, but just enough to whisper his need. "Can I do what I want to do, Jeff?"

I ran my hands up and down the curve of his naked back, over his firm buttocks and the slender waist, savoring the feel of that young body moving warmly against me.

"What do *you* want to do?"

His eyes closed, and his tongue slid around the oval of his lips, touching mine as it circled. My cock jerked with arousal.

"I can't tell you," he said hesitantly. "Just let me show you. Lie down on the bed, and spread your legs."

Freeing my arms and stepping back to where I could run my eyes over that slender young figure, I could think of nothing the boy could do that I wouldn't like. And if it was something so perverse that he wouldn't describe it, I had no doubt about my desire to share it.

I lay down on the bed, shifting myself to the middle, then parting my thighs until my heels reached the edges of the mattress on either side.

"God!" he exclaimed, moving to the foot of the bed and staring at my rearing prick and big balls. "That looks gorgeous!"

He placed a knee on the bed and curled the fingers of his right hand about his own distended cock, skinning it back and squeezing the meaty shaft.

"Pull your knees up, Jeff," he said in a husky voice. "Let me see your ass!"

Keeping my legs as far apart as I could, I drew them up until I could grasp my ankles and pull them even higher. I smiled up at the boy over the swollen head of my dick.

"See anything you like?" I asked softly.

"Yeah," he answered, his hand busy on his cock. "Everything."

"It's all yours, Chris," I breathed. "Do anything you want to, baby."

With a little sigh of surrender, the youngster placed his hands, palms down, on either side of my hips, first leaning, then lowering his body until he was lying where he could bury his face in my crotch.

I felt his warm wet tongue on my balls, licking and lifting, and the greater pleasure when he took the globes into his mouth, one at a time, gently sucking and rolling them about in their leathery sac.

"Don't stop, Chris!" I hissed encouragingly. I was pretty sure where he was headed, and I wanted to make sure he didn't back off. I pushed my hips higher.

"Oh, damn!" he gasped, his mouth reaching beneath my balls and that eager tongue lapping at the perineal area. "Oh, god, Jeff!"

"Get it, Chris!" I urged. "You know you want it!"

His hands suddenly gripped my hips, lifting them, and his parted lips found my anus, fastening their softness about it while his tongue stiffened and bored inward. I gave a sigh of pleasure when I felt the meaty spear penetrate me, forcing its warm wetness into the sensitive channel.

"I like that, Chris!" I whispered, using one hand to caress the boy's blond hair and pull his head closer. He drove that wriggling tongue farther up into my ass, and his lips fastened themselves more securely about the striated circle.

Then I felt the delightful suction as the youngster pulled the tender circlet into his mouth, and I gasped with delight when he began pushing that stiffened tongue in and out of my asshole.

Chris's oral attack on my anus told me he was ready for anything I might suggest, and that he was finally fulfilling his long-suppressed desires. I let my mind drift while my senses absorbed the thrills created by his probing tongue and nursing lips.

I was in no hurry to come, and I didn't particularly care what Chris and I did, so long as it meant that our bodies were connected in some erotic way. I had enjoyed several orgasms during the past twenty-four hours, so there was no rush for satisfaction. I could relax and let the eager fledgling experiment with his newly found courage; let him use my body as he pleased, and savor the excitement he displayed as he cast off his previous inhibitions and yielded to his basest desires.

Chris made little snuffling sounds as he sucked my ass, and his buttocks tensed and relaxed while his hips ground his prick against the curve of the mattress. The boy was hot, and probing my anus with his tongue was making him even more excited.

He pulled his mouth and tongue free, and raised his blond head, licking his lips as he stared up over my cock and into my face.

"Can I fuck you?" his voice was hoarse with passion, and his tongue flicked at my balls between his request and my name.

"Stick it in there, kid!" I answered, my own voice husky with lust. Duane was right. The boy's dick was almost as big as mine, and I was anxious to feel it frictioning my asshole. "Oh, yeah, fuck me good, baby!"

His face was flushed, and his well-formed pectorals heaved with rapid breathing. He pushed himself to his knees, then scooted them up alongside my raised hips, one hand guiding the stiff cock to its goal.

For a novice, he showed surprising skill in fitting the head of his prick into my anus. First, he jiggled the tip against the nerve-laced hole, sending tingles up into my belly as I anticipated his entering me. He pressed the meaty head against me, letting me feel the softness of the glans and the hardness that lay just beneath its smooth surface.

"God, put it in!" I urged, keeping my knees raised, and pushing my hips higher, pressing against that threatening lance.

Slowly, his eyes staring almost angrily down into mine, the youth pushed his prick-head into my ass, stretching the protesting sphincter until the flared rim snapped through and the cock was sliding up into my intestine, filling and massaging the membranous canal with its throbbing bulk.

I felt the pulsating head rub the thin barrier between it and my sensitive prostate, creating a spasm of excruciating pleasure that spread through my belly like a giant wave.

"Give me all of it, baby!" I gasped, and then cried out when Chris shoved the full eight inches up inside me, his pubic ridge pressing my balls while his hips circled to stir that big cock in the grip of my colon.

My fingers clutched the rumpled sheet on either side of my arched body, bracing myself for what promised to be one of the best fuckings I had ever received.

Keeping his prick hilted in my ass, he leaned back, his eyes drinking in the sight of our joined flesh, only the thick base of his cock visible below my taut hairy balls.

Slowly, continuing to stare downward, the youth drew his hips back, pulling his dick almost out of my anus, the rim of the head tugging at my sphincter after sliding luxuriously past my prostate again.

I consider myself fortunate in loving to be a bottom as well as a top, and relishing both receiving and giving when it comes to oral action. And at that moment, what I wanted most of all was to be thoroughly and deeply fucked by the handsome youngster whose cock was throbbing and swelling inside of me.

"Fuck me, Chris!" I grunted, flexing my anal muscles about his dick. "Fuck me good, baby!"

The kid could've made a fortune dancing, for he possessed that rare ability to thrust his hips forward and pull them back without moving the rest of his body. "Bumping" it's called, while the accompanying twist is labeled grinding.

That's what he did to me, ramming that big cock in, then pulling it almost out, the swollen knob rubbing my prostate in a rhythmical massage, while the shaft stroked every inch of my colon, from the anus to a point eight inches in, the point where I could feel that head slide and swell with each powerful thrust.

"Damn, Jeff!" the boy panted, his hips pounding my ass. "That feels good!"

"Get it, baby!" I grunted, surrendering to the pulses of rapture created by that plunging cock. "Fuck my ass!"

We were caught up for the moment in the simple act of fucking and being fucked. There was no thought of first entry, or of future orgasm. Only the overwhelming sensation of hot hardness sliding in and out of sensitive and slippery membranous embrace.

The sound of that pistoning was clearly audible. Chris had left a copious supply of saliva in my tail. To that had been added the exudation produced by the frictioning of his dick through the tender sleeve, and the occasional spillings of seminal fluid from the probing head. This juicy mixture was stirred by his thrusts, and produced a wet slurping sound each time his cock drove in or pulled out.

His delightful hunching slowed, and he buried his prick deep, his eyes searching mine. He licked those luscious lips and left them slick and inviting.

"Let me get it from behind," he said throatily.

He pulled his dick out of my ass, making a little sucking sound as the head popped out of the sphincteral grip. Before I could turn onto my belly, he leaned forward and slipped his mouth onto my cock, sliding his lips down the column until I felt his throat spasm about the head.

Slowly, sucking with quick tugs, he raised his head, and pulled his lips free, pausing to run his tongue over the slit of my glans.

"I just had to have a taste!" he said, moving to let me turn, then following me down and settling between my spread legs.

I grunted as his prick entered me again, and I groaned with the exquisite pleasure of having it bore up into my ass and begin that delightful stroking again.

He let his weight down onto my back, his hands slipping beneath my shoulders for leverage, and his agile hips pounding my upturned buttocks as he fucked me.

Once again, we yielded to the rapture of unbridled union, our senses magnifying every thrust and retreat, the feeling becoming so intense that it seemed every nerve in our bodies was responding to the frictioning of his prick in my asshole.

"It feels like it's sucking!" Chris panted, his lips just above my ear, his chest sliding against my naked back. "God! It feels good!"

"Keep fucking me!" I gasped, my hips writhing to add an extra force to the delicious frictioning. "God, I love that big cock!"

That's when he rammed it in until his balls were pressed against mine, and began screwing me with short savage jabs, keeping almost the full length inside me, but letting me feel it sliding just far enough to make me cry out with pleasure.

His breath fanned the back of my neck as he grunted, "I want you to fuck me a while!"

At that point, it really didn't matter whether I was fucking or being fucked. The only important thing was that we were using each other. Getting and giving were the same, for both acts brought ever-increasing delight to our pulsating pricks and hungry asses.

He withdrew his cock and flopped down onto the bed beside me, rolling onto his back and waiting, his prick rearing and glistening with the moisture of our union.

"Turn over, Chris," I told the boy. "And spread those pretty legs!"

He flashed me a smile before twisting into position, his perfectly rounded ass drawing me like an erotic magnet. My prick throbbed with excitement as I knelt between those shapely thighs, one hand steering my tool to press the tip against Chris's anus.

He gave a sharp cry as I pushed into him, feeling the resistance yield as he loosened the clenching sphincter and let me drive up into his ass until my balls were jammed against his, and nine inches of hard cock were buried in his gut.

I fucked him then, slowly at first, then faster as the goodness grew, and his slender hips responded with a grinding motion that screwed his asshole about my cock. I stroked in and out, full length, and Chris moaned with pleasure each time my prick slid up into his belly.

The ecstacy mounted, and I could tell from Chris's reaction that he was almost as close to orgasm as I was. But I didn't want to come. Not yet. Not until I had enjoyed that tight young ass a lot longer.

I rested my chest on his back, still hunching my hips over his rounded ass. The boy turned his head, those full lips reaching eagerly for mine, his delicious tongue ready for play as our mouths fused in a torrid kiss while I continued poling his squirming ass.

Minutes later, I drew my cock out of his asshole and urged him onto his back. Realizing what I intended, he shifted his naked body until he was lying diagonally across the mattress, permitting me to reverse my position and kneel astride his blond head. His arms went about my hips and pulled them down, his mouth opening for my prick and his tongue flickering about the head as he sucked it deep.

My own mouth found his rearing cock and claimed it in hungry suction, making his hips thrust upward to drive the shaft farther into my mouth. My own hips descended, sliding my prick between his lips and down his willing throat.

For the next several minutes we hunched and sucked like sex-crazed minks, our hips thrusting and our heads moving in any way that would ensure the deepest penetration of the two cocks.

His hands were fastened on my bouncing ass, pulling me down until my balls spread over his nose, and my pubic hair pressed his busy chin.

I was taking the full length of his dick when my head went down, and he rammed his hips upward for good measure. The pulse-pounding surges of pleasure were racing throughout our bodies, every nerve linking with those in our mouths and our dicks. It was as if the rest of the world had ceased to exist, and there was nothing but our mouths and our cocks, sucking and fucking with wet sounds that only added to our gut-wrenching pleasure.

Time did not exist, only the rise and fall of my hips and my head, fucking Chris's greedy mouth, and devouring his pulsating prick. We moaned between the vacuuming tugs of pursed lips and hollowed cheeks, and swallowed noisily when our mouths filled with the heady mixture of saliva and seminal fluid. My fingers dug at his ass cheeks, pulling his hips up as he was tugging mine down, each of us determined to claim the full length of the delicious pricks.

Ecstacy shot through my balls and my belly, spiraling into my cock and making it jerk and swell in the youngster's mouth. In spite of his inexperience, Chris recognized the signal, and his own dick began a powerful throbbing against my tongue.

We were coming, our senses wild with the almost unbearable sensation of release, and our semen spurting in copious jets to be claimed and swallowed with noisy gulps.

I didn't pull my prick out of Chris's mouth for several seconds after I had delivered the last drop of my seminal load, and he continued a gentle nursing, just as I did with his spent dick.

Finally, I lifted myself up and off the boy, turning about in the bed to cover his mouth with mine, savoring my own come on his moist lips and the tongue that met mine in a torrid kiss.

"I never dreamed it could be like this, Jeff," the youth

whispered, his lips moving against mine, and his hands exploring my body as though he had just found it. "It's wild!"

"Maybe that's why we like it so much," I said quietly. "We want to see just how far we can go."

"Oh, yeah," he sighed. "That big cock drives me crazy!"

"You're just horny, Chris," I assured him. "You'd feel the same way with Scott or Tim."

"Maybe," he shrugged, gently teasing my balls. "I know that I want a lot more of this."

He turned over then, pushing his firm, sweaty ass back against my cock, and, spoon fashion, we held each other as we drifted off to sleep.

Twelve

The boys left early Monday morning, Scott pulling me aside to tell me that he would call me to set up a meeting later in the week. I assured the youngster that we would definitely get together, and that I was as eager as he was to enjoy some time with just the two of us.

"Jesus!" Randy sighed, watching them out of sight. "What a weekend!"

"It was unusual, to say the least," I agreed. "But I'd say we accomplished a great deal."

"Scott is really hooked on you," the boy said. "He was still talking about you while I was screwing him."

"He'll get over it," I smiled. "It's just that I'm so naturally lovable."

"It's because you fuck so good!" Randy insisted. "I was hoping I'd draw your name last night."

"We'll have plenty of time together. I'll give you all the cock you can handle."

He reached down and gave my balls a gentle squeeze. "Want to start now?"

"Don't tempt me. I've got to catch up on my book. I'm two days behind."

"You write," he said. "I'll clean up the kitchen and Mom's room."

I put my hand on his blond curls and felt for the bump he got in the cave. He took advantage of our closeness to put his hand on my outlined cock.

"The swelling's gone down," I said. "That's good."

"Yours is still up," he grinned impishly. "That's **real** good."

"It'll keep," I said, pulling away from his groping fingers. "But my book won't wait."

I had been at the keyboard for about an hour when the phone rang, and I heard the vacuum cleaner cut off as Randy went to answer the call.

Minutes later, he stuck his curly head through the doorway and gave me a look of disgust. "That was Mom," he reported. "She wants me to bring her a list of stuff she needs. She thinks she may have to stay another month."

"That's a long way to drive," I commented. "Why not mail the stuff, or ship it?"

"She wants to see me." he shrugged. "Wants to make sure I'm okay."

"Are you gonna tell her about your accident?"

"Hell, no! She'd have a fit! And I won't tell her about last night, either." He smiled. "She knows that you and I get it on, and she likes you. But I don't think she'd want to hear that Tim and Duane used her bed."

"When are you going?" I asked. "And how long will you be gone?"

"She wants me to leave about noon. I can make it by about seven or eight tonight. But she'll make me stay over at least a day. I'll be back by Thursday. Maybe even Wednesday."

I offered to help him, but he assured me he could handle things better by himself, so I went back to the computer while he loaded the family car with Mrs. Lonas's selections.

We snacked for lunch, and Randy left at eleven-thirty, but not before embracing me, keading my crotch, and giving me a kiss that curled my toes with its tongue-probing lust.

"I want you to fuck me silly when I get back," he whispered, rubbing the bulge of his cock against mine, his arms tight about my neck. "Nobody here but just you and me. Okay?"

"You got it, Randy," I promised. "How about calling me while you're there?"

"Tonight," he said. "I'll call when I get there."

I went back to my writing, trying to ignore the hard his kiss had produced. In spite of all the sex I had enjoyed, I was still horny.

A little past four, the phone shrilled again, and I went into the front room to answer it.

"Jeff?" came Scott's sultry voice. "Hope I didn't disturb you." I felt my dick start swelling.

"You didn't," I said. "At least, not the way you mean."

"I'd like to see you," he said, his voice softening. "I mean, you know, somewhere where we could be alone. Maybe a motel."

"Why not here?" I said. "Randy's on his way to Jackson to see his mother."

"Honest?" he exclaimed. "Can I come over tonight?"

"Name your time and what you'd like."

I heard him take a deep breath. "You know what I want," he said. "How about eight o'clock?"

"Can you stay all night?"

"If you want me to? Do you?"

"Damn right," I said. "Don't you?"

"You know I do," he answered quickly. "See you at eight."

I hung the phone up and sat staring at it for several seconds, a plan shaping itself in my brain. After the events of the past day and night, I wanted something different. I checked the directory and called the sporting goods store where Billy worked.

His voice became excited when I identified myself, and he almost stuttered as he tried to tell me how much he had enjoyed Saturday night.

"I've got someone I want you to meet," I told the boy. "Can you come over about eight?"

"Oh, god! Yes! Is it okay? I mean, what about the others?"

I explained Randy's absence, and that the person I wanted him to meet would be a visitor. The youngster agreed to be there at eight, and without my asking added that he would do anything I wanted.

Scott rang the door chime at a quarter to eight, and could hardly wait until I closed the door to throw himself into my arms. His lips were soft and warm, and that agile tongue worked its magic on mine in a long and arousing kiss.

"I want you to do something for me, Scott," I explained, holding him with my hips pressing our cocks together, both of them swelling from the contact.

"Anything, Jeff."

I told him about Billy Newberry, and the boy's penchant for pain. "I don't want him really harmed," I said. "But I want you to make him do anything you think you might enjoy."

"What are you gonna be doing?" he demanded.

"Watching," I answered. "Just watching. Although I may have to join in if the action gets really hot. Then, when I send him home, I'll take you to bed and fuck your brains out."

"Now," he grinned, "you're talking! Are you sure he'll let me do it to him?"

"He wants to be dominated, Scott. That's how he gets his kicks. I'll make him let you do anything you want."

"And then," he said, "you'll do it to me. That's what I want, Jeff. Just you and me."

"Do this for me," I told him, "and we'll have a ball."

The youngster had worn my favorite outfit, a pair of those hip hugging cutoffs and a knit shirt, the same sort I had told Billy to wear. Just looking at him made my prick hard.

"Let's fix some drinks," I suggested, following Scott into the kitchen and watching the rise and fall of those cute ass cheeks, and the play of his thigh muscles. The kid had a deliciously curved body, and I found myself comparing him with the absent Randy. It would be a gift from heaven if I could keep both of them on hand at all times. I could just imagine sleeping between those shapely youngsters, reaching out to feel of them whenever I wished. I'd probably screw myself to death in short order.

Scott prepared three drinks, bourbon on the rocks, and we carried them back to the front room, placing them on the coffee table just as the door chimed.

"Just follow my lead," I told Scott when he shot me an anxious glance. He nodded nervously.

Bill Newberry was even more nervous, refusing to meet Scott's eyes for the first few minutes, but stealing quick glances at the youngster's exposed flesh even as I introduced the pair.

"Don't shake hands!" I said to Billy, making my voice harsh. "Do you think Scott's pretty?"

Billy took a longer look at the boy, shifting his feet on the carpet. The front of his own cutoffs bulged obscenely.

"Yeah," he nodded. "Real pretty."

"Then, feel of his dick."

"I can't do that!" he protested. "I don't know him."

Stepping close, I gripped one wrist and shoved it up behind his back, under his shoulder blades. Just hard enough to make him grunt.

"Don't argue!" I growled. "Grab a feel of that big dick!"

Billy's hand reached out, tentatively, his fingers groping for Scott's cock. The boy shifted his feet cooperatively, and let the hand fondle the bulge of his semi-erect cock.

"How does that feel?" I asked, leaning close to the boy's ear, my breath moving his blond hair. My own half-hard prick brushed the curve of his firm ass, and I deliberately jammed myself against it. I added pressure to his arm.

He gasped, and his fingers became more bold between Scott's legs. "It feels good!" he exclaimed. "Real good!"

Scott's hips were thrust forward, giving the boy's hand plenty of room to play.

"Now, Billy," I said, my lips almost touching his ear. "We are all going to take off our clothes. Understand?"

"Yes!" he breathed, trying to shove his hand farther under Scott's balls. I yanked him back, making him grunt.

"You don't do one fucking thing," I grated, "unless I tell you to! You got that?" I gave his arm a shove for emphasis.

"Got it," he groaned. "Don't hurt me!" He didn't mean it.

Scott stepped back, ignoring Billy's outstretched hand, and began removing his clothes, starting with the shirt, and leaving his long black hair touseled and somehow arousing.

Billy held his breath when Scott slipped his cutoffs down to reveal that swollen prick, jutting enticingly out from its dark nest, the head shiny and almost purple in its engorgement. A little tremor of lust ran through Billy's body, and I jammed my cock more tightly against his lush bottom.

"I'm turning you loose, Billy," I said. "And you're going to strip naked. Understand?"

"Yes!" he nodded, his eyes devouring Scott's dick. The youngster had demonstrated his love for cock during his Saturday night visit. Now, he was eager to taste that luscious prize that stood out in throbbing readiness, just out of his reach.

Releasing his arm, I stepped back and began stripping off my own clothes, while Billy took off his shirt, kicked off his sandals, then lowered his cutoffs, letting his prick flop up against his belly, then settle down at an upward angle, jerking now and then with his mounting excitement.

Scott's dark eyes were on my cock, and he licked his lips, with a slow sweep of that pink tongue, lifting his gaze to give me a knowing smile that made my balls tighten.

"Put one foot on the sofa, Scott," I said, cupping my balls and watching him lift one slender leg, his cock waggling with the movement.

To Billy, I said, "Down on your knees, cocksucker! Lick his balls!"

"Noooo!" the boy protested, already dropping to the carpet before the naked Scott. "Don't make me do that!"

I knelt behind him, reaching around his naked waist and catching his prominent nipples between thumbs and forefingers, pinching and twisting just hard enough to make him groan.

"Let's see some tongue action, bastard!" I ordered. My cock was pressed against his back, and I deliberately rolled it against the warm skin. "Lick his balls!"

Billy's hands went out to clasp Scott's thighs, and he leaned forward to run his tongue over the youngster's hairy sac, making Scott push his hips forward and his dick jerk with pleasure.

"Take your hands off of him!" I warned. "Take hold of your own cock! Just use your tongue on him! And let's see some real action!"

Billy's fingers found his own erection, one hand beneath his balls, the other gripping his dick. The boy's head moved to drag his wet tongue over Scott's sac, and Scott cooperated by thrusting his hips forward and spreading his thighs farther apart.

"Turn around, Scott," I instructed, "and bend over. Let's see how this little son of a bitch likes ass."

"No!" Billy wailed again, but I tightened my grip on his nipples, and when Scott presented that shapely bottom, the youngster's tongue dove into the cleft and began a furious licking.

"Don't fart around!" I told him in a hard voice. "Suck that asshole!"

I didn't have to add pressure to his tits. Billy's face burrowed against Scott's buttocks, and Scott gave a little gasp, letting me know without words that the talented tongue was wriggling into his anus.

"Suck it hard!" I demanded, working my hips to rub my cock over his arched back. I was tempted to force it into his ass, and knew that he would have welcomed it. But I was determined to save it for later that night, when Scott and I were alone.

Scott's head was thrown back, his eyes closed, and his lips parted in a half-snarl of pleasure, for Billy was sucking harder, and it was obvious that his tongue was plunging in and out of that spasming orifice.

"Turn around, Scott!" I said. "Let the poor bastard have a taste of that prick!"

I yanked Billy back, his hand working furiously on his own dick, and Scott twisted to present his rearing cock, its tiny eye already oozing a pearl of jism.

"Open your mouth!" I said to Billy. "Let Scott fuck it!"

I freed my left hand and grabbed a fistful of his blond hair, yanking his head back. His lips parted, shaping a wet oval into which Scott guided his cock, sliding it in until his balls were jammed against Billy's chin.

Scott didn't need any further instructions. His hips began a slow hunching that drove his prick in and out of the youngster's slurping mouth. Billy was sucking whenever the prick pulled out far enough to let him tug on it, but for the most part, he was doing just what I had requested, letting himself be fucked in the mouth.

The shrill of the telephone froze all three of us for an instant, Scott's cock buried in Billy's throat, and my hands gripping the boy's hair and his right nipple.

"Keep fucking him, Scott," I said. "I'll get that."

I stood up and took the three steps to the end table, plucking the phone from its cradle. "Lonas residence," I announced.

A soft voice almost whispered, "How would you like to have your dick sucked?"

"I see you made it okay," I answered, pretending to ignore the throaty question.

"Shit!" Randy said in his normal tone. "Thought I could fool you. Yeah. It was a drag, but I got here. Mom wants me to stay a couple of days. Do you mind?"

"Yes," I replied. "But I guess I can stand it. Is your cousin still trying to get in your pants?"

Just feet away, now that I wasn't coaching them, Scott was holding Billy's head, and Billy was gripping Scott's hunching hips. Scott was fucking the boy's mouth with mighty thrusts.

"Naw," Randy said. "She will, though, before I get away."

"Give your mother my regards," I told him after we had

chatted for a minute. "How's the head?"

Almost whispering, he said, "It'd feel better if it had your dick in it."

"Same here," I agreed. "Call me tomorrow night?"

Agreeing, and his tone altering, letting me know that someone had come into the room, the boy said goodbye, a wistful note in his voice.

I hung up the phone just as Scott hit the short rows, his ass cheeks tensing as he pumped his cock in and out of Billy's greedy mouth. Billy moaned as he sensed the approach of Scott's orgasm, and he sucked harder, his fingers clutching the boy's thrusting hips.

"Hold it!" I exclaimed, grabbing Billy's hair and pulling his head back from Scott's cock. Scott gave a groan of disappointment. He had been within just a stroke or two of coming.

Pushing Scott's foot from the couch, I lay down on it, my prick sticking up in the air. I nodded to Scott.

"Use your hand, Scott," I said, "and shoot your load onto my dick."

He frowned his curiosity, but stepped forward to stand over me, his curled fist working up and down his strutted cock. Billy was still on his knees, pumping his own tool, but staring at Scott's motions with hungry eyes.

"Damn!" Scott panted, his hand moving faster, the head of his prick almost touching mine. "I'm gonna shoot, Jeff!"

"Pour it on me, baby!" I urged, pushing my hips up, hoping that he would press the head of his cock against mine when he started coming.

The boy's hips jerked, and the white cream shot from the tip of his dick, splatting against mine and trickling down the shaft to my balls. Some of the semen sprayed onto my belly, but most of it found its target, leaving my cock coated with the ropy sperm.

Scott milked his prick, squeezing out the last drops and then rubbing the head against my belly with a sigh of satisfaction. He took a step backward, waiting for my next move.

"Okay, Billy," I told the kneeling youngster. "Take care of this mess!"

"What . . . What? . . . What do you mean?"

"Lick it up!" I told him. "Every fucking drop of it!"

Scott's slight frown disappeared, and he gave me a tight grin that Billy could not see. He dropped down behind the lad and repeated my trick with Billy's arm, making him cry out as he pushed it up under the youth's shoulder.

"You heard him!" he barked, urging Billy's head toward my belly. "Lick my come up!"

The boy's tongue flicked over my skin, gathering up the splatters of cream, drawing them into his mouth, then searching for more of the spilled semen. He lapped about the base of my cock, then upward, darting and caressing, capturing the rich liquid and swallowing it with noisy gulps.

"Get it all!" I grunted. His licking was making my cock jerk and swell, and I came close to popping my own load when he began running his tongue around the rim of my glans.

As a last resort, he slipped his lips about the head and sucked it for a moment before I reached down and yanked him away.

"Now," I told him. "Put your clothes on and get out of here!"

He offered no protest, avoiding our eyes until he was dressed. I steered him to the door, careful to stand where I couldn't be seen from outside.

"That was wonderful, Jeff!" Billy exclaimed, his hand on the doorknob. "I'll dream about that tonight. You really know how to get me hot."

"Next time," I said, "you can pretend to be a virgin, and I'll rape you."

"Oh, god! I'd love that!" he assured me. "Just say when you want me."

I eased him through the doorway and returned to the waiting Scott. The boy was all smiles.

"That was weird, Jeff," he said, shaking his head. "I've heard of people like that, but I've never met one before."

"It takes all kinds, Scott," I countered. "This way, we get a kick out of giving him **his** kicks."

"He sure knows how to give a blowjob," Scott observed.

"So do you, baby," I said, putting my arm about him and drawing his naked body against mine. He turned to face me, our cocks pressed together between our hips.

"Are you gonna fuck me?" the youngster asked in a soft voice, his eyes staring into mine, and those lush moist lips parted in invitation.

"Are you too sore?" I asked, fingers caressing his lower back and that delightfully curved ass.

"Not that sore!" he said quickly. "I want to feel your cock inside me, Jeff. I want you to fuck me slow and easy. Okay?"

"Any way you want it, Scott," I answered, covering his mouth with mine.

We showered together, resisting the urge to go beyond the tantalizing exchange of kisses and caresses as we luxuriated in the feel of the stinging spray on our naked bodies. Then, we toweled each other dry before hurrying back to my room and falling across the bed.

"Lie back," the boy whispered, his tongue flicking my ear, "and let me love you."

I spread my legs wide, and extended my arms to let my fingers grip the edges of the mattress, my eyes devouring the luscious curves of the aroused youngster.

He slid off the foot of the bed to lean over and kiss my left ankle, alternating between kissing and licking as his lips moved upward to my knee. There, he moved to the soft inner thigh, trailing the warm wetness up until his cheek brushed my balls.

Then, he switched to the other leg, beginning just above the knee, sending shivers of pleasure through my rearing cock as he licked toward my balls again.

This time, he seemed to ignore the thrusting shaft, and planted a moist kiss on my navel, spearing it with his stiffened tongue. He kissed up to my pectorals, eagerly sucking each nipple, and teasing it with hungry licking.

I wanted to push his head down to my prick, but I forced myself to relax and let the boy do it his way. The mere act of waiting added to my own arousal, and when Scott's mouth claimed the head of my dick, and that fluttering tongue began its dance of demand, I groaned aloud with gratification.

I had expected him to mouth-fuck me to a quick orgasm, for he was quivering with desire, and his breaths were short and audible as he sucked my engorged prick.

But Scott was doing just what he had promised. He was loving me. Not just sucking my cock, or trying to bring me off.

The youngster was savoring the mere act of holding my dick in his mouth; of running his tongue over the smooth surface of the swollen head; of sliding his lips down until the whole nine inches was hilted in his hot spasming throat; of knowing that he was bringing me the most intense pleasure, while satisfying his own desire to feel my hardness inside him.

His movements were slow and deliberate, and I surrendered to the almost lazy motions, moving my hips only when his mouth descended to swallow my cock, and I felt the delicious contraction as his throat muscles reacted to the erotic invasion. I had to thrust upward then, jamming my balls against his almost beardless chin.

It was more than I could bear. If he continued, I would come in that hungry mouth, and I wanted to spill my load in the youngster's tight little ass.

"Let me fuck you!" I panted, my hands clutching his long black hair, but not trying to pull his lips from my dick. It would be his decision.

Reluctantly, his lips slid up my cock and over the head, lingering to lick the oozing slit before he buried his face between my thighs and applied that agile tongue to my balls.

Between those wet caresses, he asked, "Can I suck you off later?"

"Baby," I told him, my voice hoarse with lust, "you can suck it all night after I fuck that sweet ass!"

He raised his head and crawled up onto the bed beside me, sliding that firm warm body against me until his mouth could reach my lips, and his hot throbbing cock was lodged with mine between our bellies.

The kiss was more than sex. It was companionship, love, sharing, and a deeper awareness that we both wanted the same thing, a mingling of our inner selves.

"God, Jeff!" the youngster moaned, his hips gyrating, and one thigh draped across mine. "I've never been so hot! I want that prick!"

"Get on your back, Scott!" I told him. When he rolled into position, and spread those fabulous legs, I reached down and drew them up, draping them over my shoulders as I setded my knees under his elevated hips.

His dark eyes smoldered with passion as he felt the head of

my prick nuzzle his anus. His long hair was splayed out on the pillow, framing that pretty face and making him seem far younger than his eighteen years. He licked those full red lips.

"Fuck me!" he hissed through clenched teeth. "Fuck my ass!"

My hips pushed forward just enough to force the tip of cock into his asshole, stretching the elastic lips and challenging the powerful sphincteral ring. I waited then, not trying to put it in, but savoring the feel of his hot anus pulsating and nibbling on my dick.

Scott's fingers scrabbled at the sheet on either side of his hips, and his thighs flexed and relaxed as he waited for me to penetrate his willing young ass. He moaned softly, his lips moving in a wordless plea. The boy wanted my dick inside him, wanted to feel it sliding up into him.

"God," he whispered, his voice at once both fierce and gentle. "It's so wonderful! . . . It's so fucking good!"

"Just relax, baby," I told the boy. "Let's take it real slow and easy."

"UUNNGGHH!" he grunted, for I forced the head of my prick through the sphincter and let it snap about the shaft just behind the flared rim, holding me like a lover's embrace as his anal muscles slowly relaxed and accepted the wrist thick invader.

I felt the tenseness fade, and the hot grip loosen about my cock just enough to permit the introduction of still more of that throbbing shaft.

Scott cried out again when I added another three inches to the insertion, but he was trying desperately to accommodate my dick. He had already experienced the sensation of having it thrusting in and out of his ass, and he knew what to expect, so he was no longer afraid. But his colon was probably still tender from Sunday night's activity, and it would take several minutes to bring him to that point where the discomfort would become insignificant.

"Can you take it, kid?"

The dark eyes answered me more clearly than words as the boy assured me that he was ready for all of my cock. His lashes waved encouragement and I added pressure to my hips, sliding my engorged member up into his ass until my pubic hair was pressed against his balls.

Almost motionless, except for the involuntary throbbing of my hilted prick, I stared down at the youngster's naked body, his cute nipples, flat belly, and rearing cock. Scott Harper was made to be loved and fucked, and, although I could scarcely believe it, I was about to do both.

Thirteen

It was one of those rare moments in a relationship, when the two individuals share a sense of union that transcends the mere physical. My cock was hilted in Scott's tight young ass, and his shapely legs were draped over my shoulders, ready to lever his hips up to receive my thrusts. But there was something beautiful and unique in our joining. It was a sensation that was emotional, mental and physical, all rolled into one overwhelming force, and left us feeling as though we could melt and run together on the rumpled sheet.

At first entry, there had been a trace of discomfort in the boy's facial expression, for his anus was still tender, and my only lubrication was the residue of saliva from his oral caresses. Now, there was just the hint of a smile in the sensuous curve of those full lips, and a slight flush in the dimpled cheeks and chin, while the eyes glowed with a light of understanding. Instinctively, we both knew that the other felt the same marvelous thrill that coursed through each of our excited bodies.

We also knew that it might never happen again, regardless of how long we knew each other, or how well. We would never recapture that magical togetherness that swelled my prick and tightened Scott's ass as though seeking to weld the two exactly as they were, keeping my hardness buried in the youngster's belly.

"I . . . I've never felt like this!" Scott murmured, his lips barely moving, as if hesitant to break the spell.

"Enjoy it, Scott,' I whispered. "You'll remember this for a long time."

"UMMMMMMM!" he keened, for I was pulling my cock

back through the sensitive membranes, and they sought to hold it captive, convulsing about the retreating shaft and massaging it with hot undulations.

I could feel the little lump of his prostate as the head of my prick slid past it, and the protesting squeeze of his sphincter when the flare of the plumlike head reached the entrance.

Just as slowly, I eased my cock into him again, burying the full nine inches in the youth's asshole, letting it squeeze and suck as his intestine tried to adjust to the intrusion.

"Oh, Jesus!" Scott gasped, his head rolling back and forth on the pillow, his long hair half obscuring his distorted features. "It feels so good, Jeff! . . . It wasn't this good before! . . . It feels heavenly!"

I didn't have to answer. Looking up into my face with those half closed eyes, the boy could see the pleasure stamped there, pleasure derived from the feeling of his ass about my cock. His long lashes fluttered, and his tongue made a slow circuit of his parted lips. He gave me that strange, wonderful look that was half-smile, half-frown; a look telling me he knew that he was providing me with an equivalent of the pleasure my prick was producing in his belly.

My fingers tightened on his firm thighs, and I began a slow hunching that drove my cock in and out of his responsive asshole almost full-length. When I hilted it, my balls pressed his lower back, and my pubic arch pushed his balls, making his dick jerk and bob above his curled belly.

Looking down, I saw a pearl of jism ooze from the tiny slit in the head of his prick just as my cockhead slid past his prostate on the way into his intestinal depths again.

"Don't ever stop, Jeff!" he moaned. "Just keep fucking me forever!"

The boy echoed my own sentiment. If only we could capture this moment and relive it again and again. Capture that warm, delicious sensation that surged throughout our bodies, making us want to fuck like mad, yet hold back to make it last as long as possible.

I found my hips moving faster, pistoning my cock in and out of Scott's anus like a driving rod, adding a little twist when the head was planted deep inside him. I forced myself to a slower pace, no longer pounding, but dragging my prick through that delightful corridor, savoring every inch.

Scott's intestinal oils had blended with my occasional spurts of pre-come to coat the channel, and it was beginning to feel more and more like a hot wet mouth. It was easier to slide in and out, yet it felt even tighter as the powerful spasms flexed the membranous passageway.

Each time my prick retreated, the intestine tightened behind it, and made it seem as though his ass were sucking my cock. The sum of all this was an intense pleasure that pulled me irresistably toward orgasm.

But, I did not want to come. I was determined to make it last until we had extracted the last possible pulsation of delight from our fusion, and I knew that Scott was feeling the same desire.

I plunged deep into the youngster's ass and held my dick there, throbbing and jerking in reaction to the hot contractions of his colon.

"Let's get on our sides, Scott. I want to fuck you from the back."

"Any way you want it, Jeff!" he gasped. "Just as long as that cock is inside me!"

I began pulling it out, luxuriating in the feel as it slid back through that slippery grip. Just as the head was about to escape the sphincter, I drove it in again, all the way to my balls.

"UUNNGGHH!" Scott cried at the unexpected filling. "OH, GOD!"

"I had to," I murmured, grinding my hips to stir my prick inside him, and making him groan with delight. "This time, I'll pull it all the way out."

Again, I drew back, and it was I who gasped as his asshole released my cock with a slurping sound, and the sphincteral ring snapped over the aroused knob. I rocked back onto my heels, my dick jutting out like a gnarled limb, lifting my balls with its powerful erection.

Scott lowered his legs on either side of me and pushed his upper body erect with extended arms. He stared at my prick.

"God!" he exclaimed, his eyes shining. "That's beautiful!"

He rolled onto his right side, drawing his left leg up toward his chest, and lifting it to expose that inviting asshole. I dropped down onto my side behind him, letting my own left leg slide over his right thigh while I steered my cock into position again, inserting the head into his waiting anus.

"Yessss!" he sighed, his naked body quivering as my prick slipped into the juicy embrace, my balls touching his when I had hilted the shaft. I felt his colon undulate about it, and his hips moved to increase the frictioning of hardness on tender membrane.

His head turned, and he twisted his torso until I could reach his lips without pulling my dick out of his ass. Then, while our tongues swirled in a torrid kiss, I began fucking the boy once more.

Probing the youngster's mouth with my tongue, while my cock drove up into his convulsing ass, was an indescribable delight. My right hand stroked his hair, while my left encircled his narrow waist, pulling his hips back so I could ram full-length into that torrid embrace.

Again and again, I buried my swollen prick in Scott's belly, fucking the lad with slow deliberate strokes that made his body shiver with fulfillment. Repeatedly, between the passionate kisses, he moaned with ecstacy and pushed his ass back against me to make certain he was getting all of that driving prick.

Each time the pleasure became so intense that I knew my orgasm was only a few thrusts away, I drove into him and held my dick there, waiting until I was sure I could fuck him a little longer without coming.

Scott's hands toyed with his own cock and his taut balls. His fingers worked up and down the swollen shaft, matching the thrust and retreat of my prick in his tingling ass. And, when I froze in position, the boy held his own hand motionless, hoping to stay his own climax until I was ready to fill his hungry colon with my come.

Finally, gasping for breath, the youngster cried, "Come in me, Jeff! . . . I can't wait! . . . Fuck me hard! . . . Oh, fuck me!"

That's when I short-stroked him, plunging my prick all the way to the balls, and jabbing the head deep, pulling back just enough to ram it in again, my hips hammering his grinding buttocks.

He squealed with the intense pleasure of the increasingly rapid frictioning of his intestine, and the constant massage of his prostate, that gland pulsating and ready to deliver its part of the load he was building.

I felt the familiar, yet ever-new rush of ecstacy as my balls forced the accumulated semen upward, blending it with my prostatic offering and driving it through my engorged cock.

Scott screamed as the first spurt sprayed his intestine, deep in his belly, and he felt my prick's powerful jerk of ejaculation. His own come shot from his dick and onto his raised thigh, trickling down toward the base of his tool as I poured volley after volley of cream into his hungry ass.

I lost count of the ball-wrenching spasms of delight that sucked my come from the swollen cock, but there were enough to leave me gasping with gratification, and holding the boy in a close embrace as his asshole milked my prick of the last drop before slowly relaxing about it.

"My god, Jeff!" Scott said, almost whimpering. "I thought I was gonna die! . . . never came that hard in my life!"

"You've got good ass, kid!" I assured him, my hand cupping his left pectoral, fingers teasing the strutted nipple. "I could fuck you all night."

"Can you do it again? You're still hard. Can you?"

I brushed my lips against his, and pushed my hips more tightly against his buttocks. "Let's find out," I said, just before claiming his mouth in a long kiss that ended with my cock stroking in and out through its own creamy lubricant, making a wet sucking sound as it slid through the spasming anal sphincter.

This time, we fucked for an hour before I shot my second load into his churning asshole, and he spilled his onto that shapely thigh. Only then, my prick still planted in his tail, I hugged the boy to me until we drifted off to a contented slumber.

Scott's kisses awakened me, his lips and tongue playing over my thighs and lapping at my balls. My cock was hard, and when my fingers tangled in his hair and urged his head into position, he slipped his moist warm lips down about the swollen shaft, beginning a delightful suction that made my hips squirm.

Without losing his oral grip, we managed to turn so that we were lying on our sides, with the boy curled at the foot of the bed, and my hips able to work that prick in and out of his nursing mouth.

With one hand, he fondled my balls, while the other cupped my buttock, urging me to push my dick far back in his throat. Without words, his avid suction and the skillful play of that swirling tongue told me that this was not a prelude to another fuck. Scott wanted to suck me off, and I was equally ready to give the boy what he desired.

When I began hunching, Scott shaped his tongue beneath the soft underbelly of my cock, permitting it to slide between that yielding curvature and his palate, pressing it just enough to provide the slippery friction that sent waves of pleasure through the sliding shaft and into my balls.

He gave a little gurgling moan now and then, to let me know that he was enjoying sucking my prick as much as I was enjoying fucking his warm wet mouth. And I thrust in and out between those soft lips with ever increasing speed, for it was incredibly good, and getting better each time I shoved the head down his gulping throat.

Giving a choked cry, I yanked my dick out of his mouth. "Turn around, boy!" I said, my voice husky with lust. "Let me suck your big dick!"

He told me later that he had not anticipated that. He had intended to suck me until I came, wanting only to give me pleasure, while his ecstacy was in receiving my seminal tribute.

But, he had already learned the joys of sixty-nine, and he wasted no time squirming about to where I could reach his dick, while his lips eagerly reclaimed my cock.

We started out on our sides, but after only a few strokes, I urged the boy to straddle my head, and I used both hands to grip that firm young ass as he fucked my mouth with powerful thrusts.

My own hips pumped my dick up into his nursing embrace, and we both groaned with ecstacy as we tasted and felt the spills of jism. He rode me with vigorous pumping, his balls slapping my nose and his pubic hair tickling my chin with each thrust.

His fingers rolled my nuts about as he sucked my prick, and one finger teased my asshole, making me shove my cock up into his mouth with even greater force. We hit the short rows together, feeding on each other's passion, our hips grinding and jerking, and our tongues wildly swirling about the satin knobs as we sucked.

His body jerked atop me, and he shoved his prick into my mouth just as the first spurt of come erupted from its tip. My own cock jetted its cream into his mouth almost at the same instant, and I heard the muffled sound of his hungry gulping as he claimed his reward.

I swallowed his cum and milked his dick until his balls were drained, just as he carefully nursed my cock to get every drop of the load he had generated.

Still without words, the youngster wriggled about to let me take him in my arms and taste my come on his lips and tongue in a passionate kiss, while our hips moved to rub our spent pricks together between us.

Fourteen

Over the next two days, I spent most of my waking hours at the computer, and resisted the temptation to call one of my young friends over for fun and games. Chris and Billy were the only ones who didn't call me, hinting at their readiness for anything I might suggest. But, in each case, I pleaded a backlog of work, and tried to ignore the erections that arose from just the sound of their voices.

Randy stayed a day longer than he had intended, but phoned me every night. I teased him about his cousins, and he told me that he wanted to screw the boy, but the kid was too young.

"What about the girl?" I asked.

"Not interested," he assured me. "You know what I like."

Mrs. Lonas, he admitted, was just about fed up with her niece and nephew. When she corrected them, one or the other of their parents would step in on the side of the child, and make her task impossible

"She's about ready to come home and let them handle their own problems."

"Can't her sister get a nurse or a maid to handle things until she's well?"

"Sure," he answered. "They've got plenty of money. Mom's

doing this just because she's family."

He promised to be home by four the next afternoon, and then, lowering his voice, told me exactly what he wanted when he got there.

"I'm gonna give you the blowjob of your life, Jeff," he whispered. "All you have to do is just lie back and let me have that cock, those big balls, and that sweet ass."

"I think I can stand about three or four hours of that," I chuckled. My dick was doing pushups in my slacks, and I felt hornier than I had in days.

Friday morning was spent polishing the most recent chapter of my book, and doing a few chores about the house. Since Randy left, I had eaten out more often, and I hadn't bothered to wash the few dishes I had used. Now, I stacked them in the dishwasher, and cleaned up the kitchen. As I did, I thought about how much my mother would have enjoyed this modern kitchen. The several owners of the old house since my parents died had done a superb job of updating.

Not wishing to dwell on the loss of my parents, my mind wandered to the silly card game, and the more serious action that followed, I found myself sporting an enormous hard, one that demanded attention.

I don't hesitate to masturbate when there is no other way to relieve the pressure in my balls, but I much prefer the slender young body of a willing boy, and I had several to choose from.

Considering that Randy would be there in just a few hours, I settled for a cold shower, and after toweling off, slipped on my robe and sat down in front of the television set.

Randy pulled up in the drive at a quarter to four. He left his bag in the car while he hurried in to the house and into my arms.

His lips were deliciously eager, and his young body molded its curves against mine with undisguised hunger. His arms were tight about my neck.

"God!" he breathed. "I've missed you."

"You've just missed being screwed," I said jokingly.

"That, too," he grinned. "Yeah, you're the best at that."

"You know, if I didn't know better, I'd believe you like my cock."

"God, I **love** your cock, Jeff!" he exclaimed, freeing one hand to reach between us and squeeze the bulge he found there. "I told you what I wanted when I got home."

"Why do you think I'm wearing this robe?" I said. "Come on, kid. Let's see if you really meant it."

Holding hands, we entered my room, and I slipped out of the robe, standing naked while Randy's eyes raced up and down my muscular body, dwelling on the jutting shaft of my prick.

"Don't undress," I told him. "Just do what you promised."

I sat down on the bed, then lay back, spreading my legs while Randy knelt on the floor and draped his arms over my thighs.

"Hungry?" I murmured, watching his blond head lower.

"Starved!" he whispered, his tongue flicking the head of my dick, then licking downward to lap at the huge balls.

I lifted my knees and planted my bare feet on his shoulders, pushing my hips up in invitation.

Eagerly, the youngster pushed his face between my thighs and I felt his warm tongue caress my anus, licking the nerve laden circle, then stiffening to bore into the flexing hole.

"Yeah!" I groaned. "That's my boy"

"Ummmm!" was his muffled response as he added suction to his oral attack, and his tongue wriggled up inside my ass.

It was fully ten minutes later that his wet mouth claimed my cock, and fucked it to a powerful and delightful climax that gave him the liquid satisfaction he craved.

Over coffee, in the kitchen, Randy explained that his mother would be flying in on Sunday. The lady had reached the end of her patience, and was coming home. Her sister's family, as she put it, could "root hog or die."

It was an expression I had heard as a child, and it made me smile. "I don't blame her," I observed. "She's done more than enough for them. Anyway, I've got to be leaving real soon."

The boy's face fell. "How soon?"

"Next week," I told him. "I've already stayed longer than I planned. You can blame that on you, Randy."

"I hate to see you go," he frowned. "You will come back, won't you?"

"Damn right. If you promise to give me some more of that ass."

"That's yours anytime you want it, Jeff," he assured me. "You're the best thing that ever happened to me. The other guys are crazy about you, too."

I sipped my coffee. "When do you start college?"

"Maybe not til next year. It's a question of money."

"Have you picked the university yet?"

"No. It's just wishful thinking."

"How about letting me help a little?"

"I couldn't do that. How could I pay you back?"

"You wouldn't have to. I could work it into a tax writeoff. But what I really had in mind was you staying with me while you're going to school. If I'm away, you can look after the apartment."

"You mean, live with you?" His eyes were bright.

"Think you could stand it?"

"There's nothing I'd like better. You know that."

"Good," I said. "Then I'll set it up. You've got a good record, and I know a few people. I think we can fix it so you can start this fall."

"Jesus! I didn't expect all this. Mom'll be tickled to death."

While Randy unpacked and settled back into his usual routine, I drove downtown and spent a couple of hours making a few not so usual purchases. So unusual, in fact, that I drew a few questioning looks from some of the salespeople.

At five o'clock, I pulled into a Burger King lot and parked alongside a Honda Civic. Its occupant and I transferred the packages from my trunk to the Honda's, and we drove off in opposite directions.

That night, I proved to the whimpering Randy just how much I liked that tight little ass, fucking him twice before we slept, and again after waking to find him nibbling on my cock.

On Sunday, we drove to the airport to meet Mrs. Lonas, and she greeted me with a hug almost as fierce as the one she gave Randy. She was disappointed when Randy told her that I was leaving, but elated when he sprang the surprise announcement concerning college.

"You can't do that, honey!" she cried. "Good lord, we've been over this before. We just can't afford it."

"Nonsense! Where there's a will, there's a way. He could come to Nashville and stay with me. And I'll figure out a way to make Uncle Sam pay most of his tuition."

"You're a wonderful man. No wonder Randy thinks the world of you."

"No wonder," I muttered. Then, smiling brightly, I said, "You have a fine son, Mrs. Lonas." I couldn't tell her just *how* fine I had found him to be, but I was certain she knew something of our relationship.

She outdid herself in the preparation of dinner, and I ate entirely too much. Over dessert and coffee, we made plans for my leaving, and Randy's later departure.

"Do you have to leave so soon?" Randy asked. "Can't you wait a while?"

"I've got to get my book to my publisher and I have some loose ends to tie up in Nashville before you get there."

Randy smiled. "Loose ends?"

I returned his smile. I now felt confident enough to say, "Nothing serious."

He spent the next three nights in my room, and his willing response to my demands assured me that having him as a semi-permanent companion would be most pleasant. In the time we had spent together, the youngster had learned to anticipate my wishes, and was usually the first to initiate exactly what I had in mind.

On Wednesday, we loaded my computer and my already packed bags into the car, and Randy followed me back into my room for one last check. Inside, he closed the door and I took the boy into my arms, kissing him long and hard, our hands making one final exploration as our tongues dueled.

Mrs. Lonas followed us to the car, and kissed my cheek. Into my ear she whispered, "Thank you, Jeff, for being so good to Randy."

I gave her a king-sized hug and whispered back, "My dear, thank *you* for Randy."

Fifteen

It was past noon when I finally made it to the post office,

and, with a contented sigh, I sent the floppy discs on their way to New York. Since it was almost seven hundred miles back to Nashville, I stopped in Birmingham for the night. I checked into the Kings Arms, and ate a late dinner in the dining room.

My waiter was named Paul, a red-haired teen with a gorgeous set of buns. He was all smiles, and the way he wiggled that hot little ass told me he wouldn't be angry if I suggested a little fun after his shift. At first I satisfied myself with just looking, and pretending ignorance when he added special emphasis to his "can I do anything else for you, sir?" plea.

As I left the dining room, I turned and saw him standing by the cashier's station. There was such longing in his eyes, I found him utterly irresistible. I walked over to the counter and dropped a ten-dollar bill down in front of him. "I think I forgot the tip."

He was holding my charge receipt in his hand and he stared at it, then looked up into my eyes. "No, but thank you." He stepped over the counter and flashed the receipt at me. "But you did forget to put your room number on the charge."

"Sorry. Five twelve, by the pool."

He nodded and dutifully wrote the number on the charge slip.

"In fact, I think I'll take a swim before I turn in." I winked and stepped away.

"Sounds good. Thanks again."

I was still swimming in the deserted pool when he appeared a little after eleven. "Come in," I told him, "water's fine."

"No suit." He was nervously sucking on a cigarette.

"Nobody'll complain."

"Hey, I work here, you know."

I smiled and, as I climbed out of the pool, his eyes became fixed on my crotch. "Then we'd better get into the room."

"Sounds good to me," he said, smacking his lips.

As much sex as I'd had over the past few weeks seemed to make me want it even more. I couldn't explain it but after a couple of years of arguing over everything to do with sex, it seemed I had died and gone to heaven.

Mercifully, he put his cigarette out before entering the room.

To me, the poisonous habit of smoking says only one thing: "oral fixation." And Paul certainly suffered from this malady. He sucked my nipples until I was dizzy, his excited hands never leaving the swelling in my bathing suit. Finally, he said, "I've got to suck it."

"I know," I said.

He dropped to his knees right there in front of the door and slipped my trunks down to my knees. I let him suck my cock for as long as I could stand it without coming. Then I hauled him up by his fiery hair, his chin slick with saliva, and kissed him full on the mouth.

He undressed hurriedly and propped himself up on the bed. I climbed over him and let him go at it again.

I reached down and took his sex in my hand. It was hardly the biggest I'd ever seen but it was beautifully sculpted. "Now it's my turn," I said. I worked on him with my mouth, bit and kissed the insides of his thighs, sucked his balls, sucked his cock, my hand around the base, my fingers playing in his crimson pubic patch. It had been years since I had dallied with a redhead and I was fascinated anew.

"Good?" I asked, surfacing for air.

He nodded, out of breath. Nothing an oralist likes better than to be treated with the same respect he treats others. I touched his nipples, traced the line of wispy hair down from his navel. I lubed my fingers. "Is this okay?" He nodded. When there was plenty of lube on my fingers, I gently worked one, then two into him.

"Good?"

He didn't answer; merely gasped, then groaned. He was close to orgasm.

I took him in my mouth again and sucked slowly while I fucked his ass with my fingers. Slowly, carefully, so I wouldn't hurt him. Such intimate contact with a virtual stranger has always amazed me. Not three hours before he was serving me my steak.

The boy was now completely vulnerable to hands and teeth. His hands clenched, unclenched. His mouth was open. My tongue traced the tender ridge of his head. A third finger slid in without a struggle. He'd done this before.

"Fuck me, please. Fuck me."

I stopped sucking him and looked up with my fingers still inside him. "You're sure? I'm very large."

"I know. Get on top of me and fuck me."

On all fours I moved up the length of his body, my chest rubbing his belly, chest. I bit his nipple softly and he yelped.

I rubbed the head of my cock into the hole slightly, longing to slam it into him, but enjoying teasing myself as much as I enjoyed teasing him. "Does that feel good? Hmm? Yes? Do you want that?"

"God, please – "

He thrust his hips up, attempted to grab my ass and push me down into him. I moved just out of range and pinned his wrists over his head. His look of frustration was funny.

"Now, don't you move."

He was getting incoherent. I was thoroughly enjoying myself. I just barely shoved in the head, quickly, enough to torture. My muscles were tense, clenched, waiting, ready to come.

"What do you want?" I purred in his ear.

"Stick it in me."

That was what I wanted to hear. I slid into him, all of me inside him, perfect, in one gut-wrenching stab.

He cried out, out of control now, but as the fucking began he calmed down and said, "God, you feel good. I want to stay like this forever." I kissed him, stuck my tongue catlike into his mouth.

"Okay."

We moved in slow motion, drawing it out. I didn't want to come; I was having too much fun. He put his arms around me, his hands on my ass, his breath in my ear. We drifted in there, leisurely fucking, until I felt him jerking beneath me. He had come without touching himself.

I disengaged from him and rolled him over onto his stomach. With one hand on his back I eased my cock back into his ass. He swallowed all of me, forcing breath out of him in a small surprised explosion.

I grabbed his hips. "Now you hold still." I held his hips and fucked him, fucked him hard, the sound of my tight belly slapping his ass, the sound of rough breathing turning into a continuous groan, skin slapping skin, slamming all the way up as far as I could shove it.

His ass in the air slamming back onto me as hard as he could, he began babbling incoherently. My muscles tightened, contracted, hovered for an agonizing moment but I couldn't have stopped it if I'd wanted to. His face buried in the pillow, my fingers dug into either side of his ass as I came. I collapsed, still inside the boy, across his back.

It was a while before we could move.

Seventeen

A good night's sleep left me rested and relaxed, and I was back on the road by seven. The interstate made driving a pleasure, and I pulled into the apartment comlex's parking lot just before eleven.

David Nesbitt, the handyman, barely twenty, was trimming the hedge, and greeted me with a broad smile. "Welcome back. Did you get your book finished?"

"All finished. And it's good to be back." I got out of the car and opened the trunk.

"Want some help with that stuff?"

Dave was a thickly-built lad with piercing blue eyes. He was always ready to help – in any situation. He was a terrible slut and was one of the reasons my last relationship had failed. My ex-lover had happened to come home in the middle of a particularily hot session I was having with Dave. Now there would be no interruptions.

He lugged all of my bags into my apartment in one trip, dropping them in the foyer. I followed him, carrying my briefcase and a duffle bag. As I entered the apartment, he slammed the door behind me.

"God, I've missed you, *Mr.* Archer."

"Prove it," I commanded.

He groped me, and whispered, "I need to be fucked, man. I need it *real* bad."

Two minutes later, we were naked, and lying head to toe, lips and tongues working hungrily on swollen cocks and tightening balls.

From the nightstand, I drew a tube of K-Y Jelly, and let him coat my prick with it while I inserted a well-greased finger in his tight ass.

On his back, his legs raised and spread, he sighed with delight as I eased my cock into his bottom, and began sliding it in and out with slow, full length strokes.

"It seems like a year since the last time," he gasped, his ass grinding to increase the contact of our flesh. "I love that cock, Jeff."

"You know," I grinned down at him, making him grunt with deep thrusts of my cock in his spasming ass. I fucked him faster and harder, making him cry out as I drove my prick deep in his belly again and again, my hands gripping his ankles and holding those muscular legs spread wide.

His lips tightened and quivered, his asshole flexing about my cock. His eyelashes batted furiously as he worked his ass in hungry acceptance of my heated thrusting.

"I'm gonna come, man!" he panted. "It's so fucking good!"

He hadn't touched his own dick. That swollen member was arched over his belly and almost touching his chest. It jerked now with each plunge of my cock.

"Let it go, baby! Daddy's home!" I grunted, ramming deeper and faster, my balls slapping his lower back with each thrust. "Come for me!"

He groaned as his semen spurted up onto his chest, his dick jerking wildly. I felt the echo of those ejaculatory convulsions in his colon, for that heated corridor tightened about my prick with each jet of his cum.

The increased heat and friction toppled me over the edge, and I shot my wad deep in his thirsty asshole, adding to his ecstasy.

Later, as we lay talking, and playing with each other's cock, I told him of my decision concerning Randy. He sat up beside me, his eyes excited, yet sad at the same time. To allay his fears, I said, "I think Randy will like you. I *know* you'll like him."

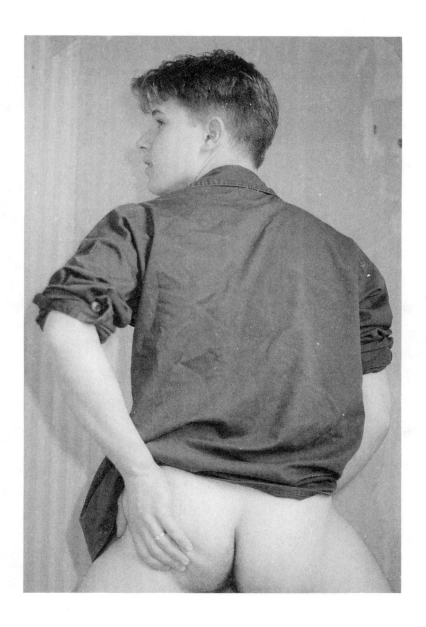

Mad About the Boy

An Erotic Roman a Clef by
JOHN PATRICK

STARbooks Press
Sarasota, FL

Standing in the dock at the Old Bailey in April 1895, Oscar Wilde made a characteristic public display of his inimitable wit, a style upon which his career had flourished for nearly 20 years. Under rigorous crossexamination by Edward Carson, Wilde was asked whether he had "ever adored a young man madly." "No, not madly," Wilde incautiously replied. "I prefer love," he added, "that is a higher form."

What follows is an extraordinary "lost" verse by Noel Coward that was to have been sung by a dapper businessman in formal black coat and striped trousers in a smart office setting in the 1938 New York revue, *Set to Music* (the U.S. version of *Words and Music*). According to Coward's lover and biographer Graham Payn, "It appears to have been written specifically for the New York production but was cut from the show by the management, who found it too daring. One can see their point. After all, it was only 1938!

"Attitudes to homosexuality in the arts were light years away from those of today. In England homosexuality was still illegal and remained so until the late Sixties. America took a more lenient social view but in the theatre or on film it was strictly taboo.

"The Lord Chamberlain was censor and arbiter of what topics could and could not be addressed on stage. Any suggestion of effeminacy was carefully scrutinised. The only way around it was to avoid specific references on the printed page and 'code' it in the performance."

Mad about the boy,
I know it's silly,
But I'm mad about the boy,
And even Doctor Freud cannot explain
Those vexing dreams
I've had about the boy.
When I told my wife,
She said:
'I never heard such nonsense in my life!'
Her lack of empathy
Embarrassed me
And made me frankly glad about the boy.
My doctor can't advise me,
He'd help me if he could;
Three times he's tried to psychoanalyze me
But it's just no good.
People I employ
Have the impertinence
To call me Myrna Loy,
I rise above it,
Frankly love it,
'Cos I'm absolutely
MAD ABOUT THE BOY!

- Noel Coward

Prologue

"You're on the hot seat," Pierce said to Johnny.

Johnny looked at him out of the corner of his eye. He rocked forward and planted his spread hands on the carpet and tried to do a headstand.

"Getting upside down won't help," Pierce said.

Maggie picked a cigarette from a lacquered box on the table. She said, "Johnny, go get Mommy's lighter from the bedroom."

"You send a nine-year-old kid for a cigarette lighter?" Pierce said. He gestured to Johnny to stay where he was. Johnny ignored him.

"I do it all the time," Maggie said. "It never occurred to me."

"Well, when you come home and the apartment is a charred black hole, it will occur to you," Pierce said.

"I just wanted to shoo him off," Maggie said, putting down the cigarette. "I'm going to discuss this stealing thing with him, but not now. He's embarrassed about the scene at supper and on the spot."

"He's always on the spot. He gives Johnny-on-the-spot new meaning."

Johnny was back in a flash. "Aren't you, Johnny?" She leaned over and looked at her son. "Aren't you Johnny-on-the-spot?"

"No," Johnny said.

"What, are you crying? Do I see tears?"

"No," Johnny said. He was biting on his lip.

"Neither do I," Pierce said. "Frankly, Johnny, I could wring your pretty little neck."

Maggie said, "Thank you very much, Pierce. Now I think it's time for Johnny to take a bath."

"I wouldn't know what time it is," Pierce said. "I don't have my watch. Johnny must have stolen it."

"Pierce, please." Maggie refilled her glass and tasted her drink. "My, these are strong," she said. "Excuse me, Pierce." She took the cocktail and Johnny and left the room.

Maggie balanced her drink on the side of the tub in Johnny's bathroom and turned on the gold-plated tub faucets. Johnny came into the room on tiptoes.

"A bath, and then I'm tucking you in," Maggie said.

"Now?" Johnny said. "It's so early. I don't even see the moon."

"What I see is you," Maggie said. "And unless I'm mistaken, you need a bath. Now, get out of those underpants and hop in."

"I'm so hungry," Johnny said, turning his back to his mother and dropping his underpants.

"Didn't we offer you dinner downtown? Would you eat it? No, you wouldn't."

Maggie left Johnny in the bathroom. A few minutes later, she came back carrying a tray with a dish of sliced fruit and cheese and a glass of lemonade on it. She put the tray down on the closed toilet seat. Johnny had poured half the bottle of the bubble bath in the water and had become virtually invisble behind the bubbles. She retrieved her gimlet and stepped over to the tub.

Johnny pushed the bubbles off his face, twisted around and sniffed. "God," he said, "why are you drinking that?"

"Don't say 'God' to me, Johnny Lawrence," Maggie said. "You're in enough trouble. Pierce has had it with you, in case you don't know. He thinks you made off with his watch. And you walked off with Dr. Hanley's paperweight. Then you brought home poor Freddy's baseball glove. And you stole seventy-four dollars from somebody. Think about it."

"I'm sorry," Johnny said.

Maggie finished her drink and submerged her glass in the bathwater. "You've got one last chance, Johnny," she said. "I think you'll agree it's better for us if you stay out of sight and under the blankets tonight. Do I hear a 'yes'?"

Johnny heaved a sigh and nodded.

Maggie's face was flushed. She said, "So you see, if you watch a little TV and go to sleep in a while, or even pretend to go to sleep, I'll buy you a car tomorrow."

"What kind of car?" Johnny said.

"A big Caddy like your Uncle Bennett's. You can drive around town and get some new friends."

"Yeah, sure," Johnny laughed. "What will you *really* buy

me?"

"It depends," Maggie said. "How 'bout tickets to see that cute David Cassidy at the Garden?"

Johnny made a little shiver of pleasure. "I Think I Love You" was his favorite song and he even had a pillowcase with David's picture on it. He had abandoned hope of seeing his idol at Madison Square Garden; the concert had been sold out for months. "Would you *really*?" Johnny asked, eyes shining.

"Really," Maggie said. "Stay out of sight tonight, and tomorrow I'll find us some tickets."

Ordinarily Johnny didn't mind staying out of sight. He was good at it. But tonight he would have preferred being downstairs with Mommy and Pierce. Pierce was the latest, and, at 28, the youngest, in Maggie's never-ending stream of boyfriends. Besides, he was tall, dark and handsome. He just looked like a movie star, which is kind of what he was. Pierce had a featured role in Maggie's last film, a costume epic filmed in Rome, and they carried on a torrid affair off the screen as well as on. Their romance continued even after Maggie returned to New York to prepare for her part in a new William Inge play. Pierce, having no other commitments, stayed on with her in New York.

But Johnny had one consolation: he did steal Pierce's watch. He would wear it tonight as he slept, taking it off before he dressed in the morning, putting it back in the cigar box hidden in his suitcase that contained all his treasures, souvenirs of the men he idolized. He couldn't hide Freddy's glove, however, and when it was reported to the school office Johnny had swiped it, he had to return it. But Johnny did get something out of that as well: After school Freddy jumped him, pushing him to the ground and throttling him until Johnny, reluctantly, was able to squirm out from under the older boy's powerful body and run away. Just thinking about Freddy, sweaty from softball practice, on top of him, slugging him, excited Johnny in his bath and he reached down and began playing with himself. In moments, he was gasping, chest heaving, and then he relaxed, his head on the edge of the tub. He didn't know why these men excited him so, he just knew the minutes spent thinking about them were the most pleasurable of his days.

1

As he had five years before at a different school, Johnny stole something from the boy he liked the most. He stole Luke Maxwell's catcher's mitt. And like Freddy, Luke was pissed. He knew Johnny had taken it, but rather than go to the principal's office as Freddy had, Luke took matters into his own hands. One afternoon as Johnny was walking home from school, he had a feeling he was being followed. He ducked into an alleyway and waited. Sure enough, Luke was behind him. When Luke saw Johnny cowering in the shadows, he began to laugh. "I won't hurt you, squirt. I just want my mitt back."

At first, Johnny denied he was a thief. Luke pressed him against the wall. "Don't lie to me you little fairy. I know what you're up to."

As Luke took the smaller boy in his arms and shook him, Johnny was overcome. He couldn't believe how fixated he had become on Luke. He admired him as a rebel, like the one Marlon Brando played in "The Wild One," a film that had fascinated Johnny. Luke had been set back two grades during his early years because he was continually in trouble and that endeared him to Johnny. And because he was older, Luke was much more developed than his classmates and this turned Johnny on. He had checked Luke out surreptitiously in the showers after Phys Ed. Johnny would sit on the bench nearest the shower room so that he could watch Luke soaping himself, getting a near-erection. Johnny would start to get hard himself and have to turn away.

There was no turning away now. Luke clutched Johnny's arms and began pounding him against the wall. "Please," Johnny begged. "You said you wouldn't hurt me."

"I won't, if you give me my mitt back."

"It's at home. I'll go get it."

"*We'll* go get it."

Johnny agreed to take Luke to the place he called home, the Lawrence's penthouse, which occupied one full floor high in a thirty-two story tower. Johnny smiled at the perfect timing:

Maggie was at a rehearsal for a new play and the maid had the day off.

As they passed through the living room, Luke was awed by the stunning wrap-around view of Central Park – the trees, rocks, and ponds, edged with skyscrapers in the distance, and he stopped just to take it all in.

"Come on," Johnny urged, shaking with anticipation.

No other boy had ever been in his room and Johnny felt a rush of excitement as Luke locked the door behind him. Johnny was glad he had picked everything up.

"Neat," was all Luke said, his eyes wide at the sight of Johnny's huge satinwood-and-mahogany bed, desk and night tables. He picked up a baseball bat that was leaning against the desk. "You steal this, too?"

"No," Johnny said. "One of my mom's boyfriends gave it to me."

"Never been used," Luke said, stroking it lewdly. "Like your dick I'll bet."

Johnny blushed and turned away, dropping to the edge of the bed.

"You ever had anybody suck your dick?"

"No," Johnny mumbled.

"I have. Lots of times. I just go down to Third Avenue and they pay me $50 to suck my dick."

Johnny blinked. "Really?"

"Oh, shit, I shouldn't have told you, you little pervert. You'll go down there and steal all my tricks." He looked at Johnny appraisingly, then chuckled. "Nah, nobody'd want you. You're too puny. Nah, you're no competition. Zero." He shoved Johnny back on the bed and stood over him. He said nothing as he unbuckled his belt and unzipped his chinos.

Johnny's confusion was now giving way to tremendous excietment. He could hardly believe this was actually happening.

"Well?" he said.

Johnny caressed the fine dark pubic hairs, then reached down inside Luke's underwear to feel his nakedness. The head of his dick was oozing with precum, which Johnny smeared down the thick shaft as Luke let his pants drop to the floor. The electricity Johnny felt from Luke's skin touching his was incredible. As Johnny pulled the cock from the briefs, he continued stroking it. He sighed when it was finally completely revealed because it was everything he had hoped for and more. Johnny was dazzled by the incredible thickness, the glowing whiteness, the pinkness, the hugeness of it.

"Kiss it," Luke commanded.

Johnny obeyed.

After a few moments, Luke had shown Johnny exactly what he wanted. And Johnny was getting good at it, nearly taking it all in his mouth, but Luke wanted more. He told Johnny to get undressed. He nonchalantly stroked his cock as he watched Johnny shed his clothes, all but his briefs. Johnny was not about to let the older boy see his cock, which he saw would suffer terribly in comparison.

Luke turned Johnny over and took his underwear completely off, then slid his heavy cock between Johnny's legs.

Johnny giggled. "No way you're going to get that in."

"I only want to tease you." He rubbed a generous wad of his saliva on his cock and the asscrack and for a long time just barely nudged his swollen head in the asshole. Luke pushed the foreskin all the way back, and pressed the hot, sticky tip against the backs of Johnny's legs, then began massaging his ass. His fingers dug deep into the tissue. When three fingers were in him, in a brief moment of panic, Johnny cried out, overwhelmed by the pain. Johnny gradually relaxed and Luke brought his cockhead to the opening.

His pushing became more ardent and the mixture of his saliva and precum loosened his grip. Before Johnny knew it, the entire head was going in and out of him. His breathing became erratic and shallow, his heartbeat completely wild. Luke kept driving in slightly deeper with each thrust. Johnny reached back to feel Luke's balls and realized that Luke was only about halfway in, so he spread his legs apart further and surrendered completely. Luke slowly bore down until his balls were hitting the base of Johnny's. Johnny felt totally saturated. Luke pulled his entire length out and then eased himself back in. Johnny couldn't believe how amazing this felt, both sexually and emotionally. He was delirious with sensation as his orgasm gushed relentlessly from his penis. Luke wrapped his arms tightly around Johnny's chest until the tension in his muscles finally subsided.

"Oh, yeah, little one," Luke moaned, then pulled himself out and pumped ferociously into his hand until Johnny's back was being sprayed with burning semen, then he collapsed on top of Johnny. There they lay, two sweaty, spent bodies.

Luke rolled off Johnny and lay next to him, still panting. Johnny opened Luke's mouth with his tongue and pulled him tightly against him. He hadn't kissed any boys before and he found it delightful. The softness of Luke's mouth contrasted sharply with the hardness of his chest pressing tightly against him. Before long, Johnny was sucking on Luke's chin, nose and ears.

"Hey, I gotta get outta here," Luke said, pushing Johnny off.

Johnny lay still, watching the stud yank on his chinos and pull his T-shirt over his head. He was beautiful, Johnny thought, the most beautiful boy at school. Some boys were more handsome, had even better bodies, but Luke was more beautiful than any of them because he had let his body speak for him in a way Johnny could only envy.

"Going to Third Avenue?" Johnny asked snidely.

"So what if I am?"

"Take me with you."

"Maybe. Some day, when your pecker is bigger."

Johnny pulled a sheet over his lower body. "Don't forget your mitt."

"You can keep the mitt. I got what I wanted."

Luke couldn't seem to make up his mind about the mitt. He would spot Johnny in the halls between classes and ask if there was anyone home. If Johnny said no, then he'd tell Johnny he was coming over to get his mitt.

This went on for weeks. Then one afternoon while Luke was fucking Johnny he suddenly pulled out and rolled the younger boy over. Johnny stopped stroking his dick and it stood high and proud, bending precariously to the left. Luke gently ran his hands over Johnny's hairless chest, then to the navel and beyond. His hands cupped the throbbing cock and he went down on it. The sight of his hero engulfing his erection practically caused Johnny to come. He grabbed Luke's head and stopped him. Luke let go of the prick and tongued his way up to his face, kissing him hard on the lips. As he did, Johnny's legs parted and Luke's sex slipped in. They fucked this way for several minutes, as lovers, locked in each other's arms, until Luke came.

After pulling out, Luke leaned back and took Johnny's cock in his hands. "This isn't a bad dick, you know, squirt. Not bad at all. I think we could do some business with this dick."

He turned Johnny over and slapped his buttocks. "God knows we could do some business with this ass."

And so it secretly began.

2

Johnny discovered he could ask Luke anything. Luke was from the priveleged class, his father worked in Wall Street, but he was street-smart. Johnny had been looking for a friend like Luke all his life.

People asked Johnny, "Who is your girl?" And he said, "I have no girl," and they laughed and his mothcr said, "Johnny doesn't care for girls," and they said, "All that will change," but Maggie knew it wouldn't and she had accepted it.

People said, "Johnny is a good boy," and Johnny knew that was because they didn't really know him. He didn't look or act differently from other boys his age, but he knew he was a bad boy, a misfit, an outcast. Johnny stopped asking questions, though his mind was teeming with them; it was no use. The questions he wanted to ask were the questions grownups and even older boys did not want to answer – until Luke.

When he was younger, Johnny went to the New York Public Library and read Darwin and got a shock: "'...the hair is chiefly retained in the male sex on the chest and face, and in both sexes at the juncture of all four limbs with the trunk....'" There was more, but he heard someone coming and had to replace the book on the shelf. He found another book, called "What Every Boy Should Know" and it told him nothing that he didn't know already. He was a sinner, that much he knew. His mother played them on the screen and as far as he could tell there was little diffeence between the real Maggie and the reel one. Once when Uncle Bennett was in Manhattan, he took Johnny to church. There in his blue serge Sunday suit, Johnny heard the Reverend say solemnly from the pulpit that Johnny was conceived in sin. But afterward, at the church door, in the brilliant sunshine, the Reverend shook hands with Johnny and said he was happy to have the boy with them in their church.

Before Luke, Johnny was sometimes a child, sometimes an adult in an uncomfortable small size. He blushed easily and he had his feelings hurt. His jokes were rarely successful, there point escaping most people – except Luke. Luke even told him it was okay to be homosexual, "Just don't advertise it."

When he was around, which wasn't often, Uncle Bennett would try to discipline the boy, telling him to sit up straight in his chair, to stand with his shoulders back, to pick up his clothes, read in a better light, stop chewing his nails, stop sniffing and go get a Kleenex. Uncle Bennett often teased him about his thinness, his pallor, his poor posture, his moodiness, and concluded that he did not spend enough time out-of-doors. Johnny took that as an admonition to hit the streets.

After weeks of being fucked by Luke, Johnny had his plans made, and his startling green eyes became a facsimile of innocence. He waited for his mother and the maid to be gone from the apartment and then the mirror became his accomplice. He could slip into roles as easily as his mother did, but he soon became stuck in one role: the pretty blond boy hustler.

Even though Maggie had accepted Johnny's homosexuality, little did she know what Johnny was thinking when, on those rare occasions, she would take him out.

One day they were walking through Greenwich Village when they were stopped on the street by a man who invited them into his shop, Ron's Then and Now. The eye contact between Johnny and Ron began immediately. The walls of the shop were covered with posters and photographs of film and theatre stars. Ron brought out a box and began to show Maggie photographs of herself from her early films.

"Look at this one," Ron enthused. "It's from 'The Cattle Queen.' It's my favorite. It was taken in 1960." Maggie looked horrified.

"No it wasn't," she told him. "That's a mistake. It should be 1966." Maggie autographed the picture just the same.

Johnny smiled; he knew all of her films; she had made that horrible western in 1960. It was released in 1961, the year he was born and she had moved to New York to be with his father. She bought Johnny all of the other photographs and they quickly left, but not before Johnny had surreptitiously written, "I'll be back," on one of Ron's business cards. Ron saw the card as they were leaving the shop and raced after them. He stood in the doorway and when Johnny looked around, Ron waved. Johnny winked back.

Johnny went back to the shop a week later. Ron, a slender man in his mid-thirties with wire-rim glasses, was overjoyed to see the boy. The thought that he could spend any time with Maggie Lawrence's son was inconceivable to him. Johnny lingered at a bin of stills of David Cassidy while Ron finished waiting on a customer.

Finally the customer left and Ron came over to Johnny. "May I help you, young man?"

"I think so," Johnny said, turning to face the man, his hand on his crotch.

Ron looked down to where Johnny had brought his hand to rest. He gulped. "You are even more beautiful than your mother."

Johnny smiled. How was it that everyone else was always finding fault with him, but with Luke and these older men he could do no wrong? In fact, all he had to do was stand there and be worshipped. It was the most incredible thing.

"Just a minute," Ron said, stepping to the front of the store. "I've been thinking about you every minute," he said, swinging the sign around to CLOSED and pulling the shades.

Johnny stepped up behind him and tugged at his ponytail; Ron's brown hair fell around his shoulders. When Ron turned around, Johnny stood back, considering him. He found him more attractive than he had first thought, laugh-lines around his eyes the only tell-tale sign of age.

To Ron, Johnny was a luscious temptation. "Such forbidden fruit," he muttered, sinking to his knees before Johnny and cupping the boy's buttocks as he brought his mouth to his groin. He could not get enough of the boy. It was an incredible fantasy come true; he had never had sex with a movie star's son before. A moan of intense longing growled deep within his throat. His tongue explored the growing bulge in Johnny's chinos. Johnny began to breathe fast and hard, chest heaving. Ron went on sucking on the bulge protruding from Johnny's groin. Ron's fingers grappled with the zipper, spreading the pants open, reaching into the white briefs underneath, finally revealing the cock. "Hmmmm," was all Ron could say as he plopped it in his mouth.

"Yes... God, yes," Johnny moaned.

Ron ran his teeth lightly along the entire length of the cock.

His thumb played with the throbbing vein on the underside of the shaft, while the other hand kneaded the lightly-furred balls. Ron felt Johnny tighten up to his body and move restlessly. Soon Ron filled his mouth again with the lovely prick, sucking with relish. It would not take long for Johnny to come, Ron feared, and sure enough, soon an excruciating groan filled the store, Johnny grabbing fistfuls of Ron's hair, holding him fast, plunging his sex into Ron's mouth. Ron accepted the steady stream of cum down his throat as he slid his hands down to undo his own pants and take out his prick. As he jerked himself, his spasms were so intense his whole body ached. Panting, enveloped in Ron's heat, Johnny opened his eyes and began running his fingers gently through Ron's hair.

Even though they both had come, Ron was reluctant to give up Johnny's cock, but finally he did. Johnny zipped up and, a big grin on his face, went back to the David Cassidy bin. He picked three stills that he did not have in his collection.

At the counter, slipping the photos in a brown bag, Ron said, "They're on the house."

Escorting Johnny to the door, Ron rubbed Johnny's shoulders and said, "Your name is Johnny, isn't it?"

"Yeah."

"I finally found it in a story in one of the old magazines. Johnny Lawrence." He said the name as if he was sucking it.

Johnny stopped and put his arm around Ron's waist. "That's not my real name, of course."

"Oh, of course," Ron said, with a giggle.

That night, before they went to dinner, Maggie and Johnny sat in the living room together, the vast panorama of the New York skyline in shadows and neon before them. Johnny had always been captivated, mesmerised by the view: the continuous performance, the scenes, the comings and goings far below them.

Maggie had two martinis and then they went to 21 because Johnny loved their corned beef hash. Lydia Lester, the gossip columnist for the Tribune syndicate, was table-hopping and stopped to chat. Johnny once again found himself revelling in the glamor associated with being a movie star's son. Maggie brought Lydia up-to-date: the play she was going to do in

London, a guest shot on *Kojak*. Then she said, "But the public doesn't care about me anymore. It's always Ryan O'Neal! Always Tatum! Always McQueen, Nicholson, Beatty, Candy B., Sylvia Miles and Andy Warhol...even Tony and Berry for godssakes!"

"Times change," was all Lydia would say.

"But not New York," Maggie said. "The electricity of Manhattan never goes away. The city is always changing and some of the changes are large but they're not distracting. The excitement of the city never ever diminishes – the speed with which it moves and the people, the cab drivers yelling, 'Hey,!' None of that changes. It's such a wonderful place! People feel like they grew up with you or they helped you to get to where you are. They're very supportive; they make me feel terribly welcome." Maggie had her publicist's lines down pat. She could change them to suit whatever city she happened to be in.

"Can I quote you?" Lydia asked, her eyes flashing as she scanned the room for more familiar faces.

"Of course," Maggie said.

They bussed each other's cheeks and Lydia patted Johnny on the head before dashing to a table across the room where Bob Evans was sitting with a starlet whose name Maggie couldn't recall. "The next Maggie Lawrence," she said with a shrug. "God help her."

Before going home they window-shopped along Madison Avenue. When they returned to the penthouse, Maggie was tired and Johnny went with her to her bedroom. Only a few of her things were scattered about the room but it seemed as if she'd always been there. She'd come home, but only temporarily. Now she was taking her young son to California for Christmas.

Johnny stood at the end of her bed watching her get comfortable. When he was sure she was asleep he switched off the light but left the door open in case she called out in the night, then went to his own room. He sat by the window, dialed Luke's number. He wanted to tell him about his encounter in the Village. There was no answer, and holding the telephone, lost in thought, he just let it ring.

When they were in California, Maggie said, "Let's go and

take a look at where I used to live." She slammed on the brakes of the rented baby blue Cadillac convertible and threw the car into reverse. Johnny gripped the leather seat. He couldn't remember a time when he had actually seen her driving, other than in a movie.

They shot across to the other side of the road, managing to miss a truck that appeared from around the bend, and then the car stalled on a small ridge at the entrance to the drive. They slid back down onto the street.

Johnny panicked. The traffic was coming at them from every side. Suddenly they stopped. Then she accelerated. They veered back across the road, bumped up the ridge and ended safely in the driveway of a mansion.

"Mother, why'd you do that?"

"It's not my fault, honey. It's that stupid gateway. It's at the top of a mountain!"

It was wonderful to get out of the car. Johnny thought they were only going on a short trip but it had ended up being a three hour journey. For the first few days of their stay in California the weather had been dreary. It was drizzly and everything looked grey. Now, the sky was a diamond; the buildings and the roads, the cars and the people all glistened. Palm trees, plants and flowers were colors right out of a paintbox. He recalled the names of the roads which had always excited him: Sunset Boulevard, La Cienega, La Brea and Vine. Everything was even more enchanting now than he remembered. And the people all looked beautiful, healthy and clean, dry-cleaned and rich, very rich.

They put the top down at last and as they were driving through Brentwood Maggie spotted the house. It was impressive, owned by Sam Spear, an RKO line producer and Maggie's third husband. Their union lasted for a year. She said once that Spear married her so he could put her in his pictures for free. He was a wealthy purveyor of monster cheapies, drive-in circuit turkeys that raked in considerable cash. Marrying Maggie would, he thought, bring him prestige. Howard Hughes, owner of RKO, had wanted to put her under contract after she left Metro, but Sam had a better idea: he'd marry her.

"What do you think of the house, honey? Do you like it?" Maggie whispered quickly.

They had to peer through the protective screen of tall trees so that Johnny could get a proper look. Maggie didn't want to be "seen" unannounced. Johnny felt that at any moment they would be set upon by a pack of hounds and arrested on suspicion of being robbers.

"Yes. I do like it," Johnny whispered back. "It's so big."

"Sam was a dreadful man, but living there was so much fun in those days." Maggie took his arm and they stood away from the trees. "Betty and Bogey lived right over there," she added, pointing to the mansion across the street.

"It must have been great."

"'Just keep it in the shadows, Maggie,' Bogie used to tell me. 'Let the camera come to you.' Oh, I liked him. We used to go out on his boat, the Santana. And Betty, you know, I still see her when I'm in New York."

"Yes, I know," Johnny said, rolling his eyes.

Maggie clicked her tongue against the roof of her mouth. "Hmm," she winced. "That Betty. She always looks so good."

They sat back in the car and Maggie took a last look.

"Why did you leave?" Johnny asked.

She thought for awhile and then miraculously negotiated a three point turn. "Why to have you, of course." She chuckled. "Sam and I wanted different things from life. Who knows why?" She bumped the car back out of the difficult entrance to the driveway. "I'm sure glad that I got that divorce, honey, 'cause I got you."

The car squealed and tilted to one side as she turned and careered on down the winding roads that led to the coast.

They went to dinner then stopped at the little place Johnny's grandmother owned in Huntington Beach. It had a stunning view of the ocean, but it was small. In the back was a little garden where Grandmother grew tomatoes and flowers. The swimming pool was outside the kitchen window. Johnny thought it idyllic.

Grandma was excited to see them but the conversation soon degenerated into nastiness. Grandma tilted her head at Maggie. "You want to be a good person, but your brother's the real article. Goodness comes to him without any effort at all."

Maggie nodded. Bennett had made a fortune in New York real estate, never married, doted on his beautiful young sister, and said he was devoted to his mother, but lived three thousand miles away, most of the year in splendid semi-retirement in Palm Beach.

"Bennett says you have a new boyfriend."

"He's always a bit behind the times. I used to have one," Maggie snorted. "I'm between enegagements right now."

"Why do people your age always have to find the right person?" Grandma went on. "Why can't you learn to live with the wrong person? Sooner or later everyone's wrong. Love isn't the most important thing. Why can't you see that? I still don't understand why you couldn't live with Jack. He seemed like such a nice young man."

"Come on, Mother," Maggie said, finding some Christmas music on the radio. "Over and done with, gone and gone."

"You live with somebody so that you're living with *somebody*, and then you go out and do the work of the world. I don't understand all this pickiness about lovers. In a pinch anybody'll do, believe me."

On the side table was a picture of Grandfather. Maggie glanced at the picture and let the silence hang between them before asking, "How are you, Mother, really?"

"I'm all right." She leaned back in the sofa, whose springs made a strange, almost human groan. "But I want to get out. I spend too much time in this place. You should expand my horizons. Take me somewhere. Take me back to New York with you."

"I can't. I'm starting a play – in London."

"You should do movies. You're a movie star."

Maggie was growing more agitated by the minute. "Maybe we should go."

"No!" Grandma said, much more loudly than she'd intended. Then more softly, "Please stay awhile. I hardly ever see Johnny, and it's Christmas Eve."

Maggie disappeared into the kitchen while Johnny talked to his grandmother. He told her about New York, then made one-sided small talk about the snowstorm before they left the city for Los Angeles, thinking the idea of "snow" might spark some memories from Grandma. Grandma was well over eighty. Wearing a mauve housedress and a row of beads, with her hair waved and rouge on her cheeks, she reminded Johnny of a little bird, a little operatic songbird. Her voice was high-pitched and seemed to demand great effort. Her accent changed in varying degrees from a lowland Scottish to a proper English pronunciation, but sometimes fell into West Coast American slang.

"Have you ever come across my friend Violet Fairbrother back there in England?" she called to Maggie.

"No, I've never come across her."

Grandma had been called Jean MacDougall. She was born in Scotland but moved to England in her teens where she studied acting at the Royal Academy of Dramatic Art. Along with her best friend Violet Fairbrother, she was, she told Johnny, a star pupil and went on to play Puck at a London theatre before being asked to join the Benson Players, a forerunner of the Royal Shakespeare Company, at Stratford-upon-Avon.

When she married Maggie's father, Michael Lawrence, she gave up the theatre and they emigrated to Canada, where Bennett was born. The family then moved to Pasadena where Jean gave birth to Maggie. When she was divorced by Michael, Jean started teaching acting and elocution at her home to keep the family going. Maggie was her "star" pupil and she was determined that her daughter would become a star in films. After acting in a high school play, Maggie become enamored of the theater. Jean's encouragement and determination for her daughter to succeed were rewarded when Maggie, after leaving high school, began appearing in local productions.

Mother chaperoned her daughter everywhere so when Maggie was asked to understudy Sabina in "The Skin of Our Teeth" at the Plymouth Theatre in New York, Mother went with her. She coached Maggie in the part that turned out to be her first important break. When she was signed to replace the star during the run, she was spotted by an MGM talent scout, taken back to California and put under contract.

"I wish that Maggie would have tried harder," Mother said.

"Oh, Mother," Maggie shouted from the kitchen, agitated by having to listen to her reminiscences.

Mother leaned forward and spoke to Johnny confidentially. "Maggie would never apply herself properly. She'd never talk to the columnists. I used to get them on the phone going crazy. 'That girl's going to ruin her career if she won't talk to me,' they used to say. But Maggie would never talk. She's always hated gossip; even though she created quite a lot. And she'd never dress herself properly. When we used to go over to Zsa Zsa's house, her mother would say, 'Oh that Maggie. She could make something of herself. If she'd only fix herself up a bit.' But that's Maggie. She's impossible. She didn't even wear a new dress when she won her Tony! She just threw on her mink. Maggie likes to do things her way."

"That's enough talking about me," Maggie called out, bringing Grandma a cup of tea and some cookies from the kitchen.

"I like tea," Grandma said with a satisfied smile that made Johnny's eyes get misty.

"All these cards," Johnny said, standing at the mirror and fingering them one by one, flipping them open to read the messages. "So many people love you. Look, here's one from Mrs. Stone. I remember her. She was your crazy old neighbor. She must be in her nineties now."

"Yes, she's in a rest home," Maggie said.

"Hated her," Grandma sighed, lifting the teacup again, letting the last drops slip onto her tongue. "That was good tea."

"Would you like more, Grandma?" Johnny asked, but the question stumped his grandmother, who was busy examining the sugar cookies on the plate. She picked up each one as if considering its shape, turning it over, and replacing it carefully.

"We'd better go now, Johnny," Maggie said finally. "We'll be back tomorrow, take you to dinner."

"I'd like that. I never go out anymore."

Johnny kissed his grandmother's cheek, which was surprisingly smooth and silky. He whispered, "I miss you" into the wisps of white hair that brushed across Grandma's ear. "Merry Christmas."

"Bye bye," Grandma answered, holding up a Santa cookie and waving it at them.

"Let's go for a drive along the coast," Maggie said as they got into the convertible. "It's a beautiful night."

Johnny's face lit up. They stopped in a parking lot on the Pacific and sat on the hood, looking out across the ocean. There were little bonfires burning along the beach where people were having parties and, somewhere, someone was playing a guitar. The sky was a magenta color and seemed to be lit from behind with golden rays. The moon was full and seemed to be sitting on the surface of the ocean. It was a stunning evening sky. Even if there was no snow, Johnny could not imagine a more wonderful Christmas Eve.

"Why don't you like people talking about your career?" Johnny asked. "Don't you like being a movie star?"

"I'm not a movie star anymore, Johnny. I got too old. Now I'm finally an actress. And I like being an actress. That's why I love it when I'm in England. It means something there. I just never liked all that movie star stuff. It's nothing. Sometimes I wish I'd have continued on the New York stage instead of going to Metro. Maybe that might have worked out better. Who knows?" She shrugged and nestled her head on Johnny's shoulder.

It was at times like this that Johnny wished everybody had a mother as wonderful as his.

3

Sooner or later, Luke warned, Johnny would get into trouble. To Johnny, whoring had been a lark because he hadn't needed the money but, after awhile, the men who were picking him up began to bore him. Johnny had become fascinated by the other hustlers on the streets.

Of all the boys he met, it was one named Eric who titillated Johnny the most. But Eric wanted nothing to do with Johnny. Finally Johnny agreed to pay him and the two went off to a place where Eric said he was staying temporarily. It was July and the heat was unrelenting. Johnny paid for a cab.

The neighborhood was vaguely familiar. Johnny had tricked once with a businessman who lived nearby. Johnny waited on the tiny concrete stoop as Eric unlocked the door. Inside, it was too dim to see anything, but Eric seemed to know what he was doing. He immediately stepped into a side room as Johnny stood just inside the door, letting his eyes adjust. There wasn't much to see: a cramped front room with old pictures hung on one wall. Beneath the pictures was a fold-up frame and mattress, stripped of its sheets. The fan was on, humming softly. Eric switched the control setting to maximum cool.

When Eric took off his tight black T-shirt, Johnny saw his broad torso was slick with sweat.

"Lick me," Eric commanded.

Eric guided Johnny's mouth over his hard stomach and pecs, then into his armpits. The stud unbuckled his pants, pulled out a cock even larger than Luke's. Eric pushed Johnny down, to his knees, made him worship the cock until it was fully hard.

"Turn around," Eric ordered, unfolding the bed.

Johnny got on all fours on the bed and the stud pulled down his shorts.

Eric greased Johnny, calling his ass a "boy pussy." He told Johnny to back up on his cock. Johnny pushed his ass against the shaft. It felt like a fist. Johnny pushed hard, but couldn't even slip the head in.

Eric broke a popper under Johnny's nose and pushed. The head slid in. Johnny cried out. A couple of inches of the shaft went in. Johnny wanted it, but he didn't. The pain was too much.

Eric took the belt from his jeans and lashed at Johnny's ass. The crack of the wide belt slapping the flesh sounded fierce and Johnny began trembling.

"Just a little more," Eric demanded, shoving his cock back in.

"No, I can't," Johnny pleaded. "I can't take any more."

Eric broke another popper under the boy's nose and shoved. It was at last all the way in.

"Fuck it," Eric commanded, and Johnny began moving his hips very slowly, sliding the cock in and out. As the lashing continued, Johnny worked harder and harder, riding the stud's shaft.

Johnny, through clenched teeth, began to groan. Eric's eruption was filling him. At last it would be over.

"So what do we have here?"

Johnny turned to see a tall, brutish-looking man standing in the doorway, clad only in a studded leather jockstrap, holding a sweating beer bottle.

"Just having a little fun, Doc."

Doc entered the room. "Save anything for me?"

Eric pulled out. "Plenty to go 'round. Plenty." Eric moved around to Johnny's face while Doc gripped Johnny from behind.

"Did this boy know he was messing with my lover?"

"Of course."

"Well, fair is fair, Eric. You had your fun, now I'll have mine."

His hands clutching Eric's thighs, Johnny took Eric's sopping cock into his mouth, concentrating simply on fellating the monster prick. Then he felt a heavy hand lightly cup first one asscheek, then the other. Then he felt the sting of an open palm land square on his ass. *Thwaaack!* He jerked at the impact. It was followed by another and another and another, a rain of blistering blows. Soon the warmth spread over his ass and he seemed to find the spanking pleasurable for awhile, until Doc changed from his hand to Eric's wide leather belt. Johnny's whimpers became groans, then muffled screams. Tears were flowing down his cheeks before Doc finally eased off, going back to moderate smacks with his hands before changing over into gentle caresses that quickly had Johnny moaning again.

"He's a pretty one, Eric, I'll have to say that," Doc said while his busy fingers stroked and tickled and pinched the boy everywhere he could reach. Johnny began gyrating frantically when he felt Eric was about to come.

"No," Doc ordered, "hold it, Eric. We're just gettin' this one warmed up."

Eric withdrew momentarily, then slammed his cock back into Johnny's gaping mouth.

"Yeah, and now I'm going to stick something in to really give him somethin' to think about."

Johnny felt a cold and greasy finger poke at his hole. Doc shoved it in slowly and moved it around, then pulled it out and paused a moment, then stuck it back, rolling it around inside Johnny, pressing on his prostate. The slowness of the entry started to relax Johnny, and soon his ass was squirming around the invading digit. It was joined by another, and then another, twisting around inside him, opening him up, making him moan from pain turning into pleasure.

"Oh, yeah, give your ass to me...give it up...let go...relax....That's right, you're getting it....I'm going to give you what you need...."

Suddenly a greased cock replaced the fingers and Johnny bucked back to take more of it with each thrust. Doc had a nice-size cock, not small and not terribly large like Eric. He managed to hit his prostate with almost every stroke. Eric came, pulling out, dumping his load, then slamming the prick back in again.

Johnny gave himself over to ecstasy as Doc continued to fuck him and play with his smooth skin. Johnny was moaning and chewing on the semi-hard cock in his mouth, and when Doc finally shouted that he was coming and Johnny's ass spasmed around the thrusting cock, the boy shot his load, too.

Johnny was happily wasted by the time Doc pulled out. Doc stood for awhile with his arms around the boy, gently fondling his nipples. A bell sounded. Doc lifted himself from Johnny and left the room. Dazed, Johnny turned to see what was happening but Eric forced him back down on his cock. Doc entered the room again, accompanied by another man. Again Johnny tried to turn his head to see the visitor but Eric held his head steady, his cock hard again, getting into the suck.

Once more Johnny felt fingers at his asshole. Gently the visitor began to lick and kiss the now-scarlet mounds and the boy moaned and wriggled with excitement.

"My God, what a beauty," the visitor remarked, and his lips pushed towards the boy's throbbing asshole. Very gently he nibbled around the boy's inner cheeks, inhaling the musky scent. Slowly he flicked the open hole with his tongue.

"Aaaaah!" Johnny was sobbing with ecstasy. The visitor began to slowly slip his fingers up and down the shaft of the boy's cock milking it, all the time feeling the lips of the boy's anus moving against his tongue.

"And a pretty cock, too, Joe," Doc said. "Aren't you glad you came by?"

"Hmmmm," groaned Joe, then sank his tongue deep inside Johnny, covering the whole asshole with his mouth. As Johnny tightened his hole instinctively, Joe sucked and nibbled. Johnny writhed and squirmed. He longed for release but his cock was gripped by Joe's powerful, hairy hands.

Joe rose, pulled down his pants. Johnny cried out as Eric came again, pulling the huge dick free and stroking it proudly. Doc now moved towards Johnny's face. Johnny turned to take a look at Joe but Doc held him down, bringing his dick against Johnny's face. The boy's mouth opened and his tongue began to lick the man's heavy balls and then faster and faster it moved up the shaft towards the knob, glistening with cum.

Meanwhile, Joe had put on a pair of thin rubber gloves and he began applying cold cream to the boy's scarlet buttocks. Slowly the fingers moved over the defenseless tender flesh, rubbing and probing at will. Johnny's tongue moved in a frenzy along Doc's cock; sucking, licking, biting. Johnny's sphincter spread for Joe's fingers. The finger-fucking continued for several minutes and at times Johnny thought he would pass out from the pain, but Joe knew exactly when to stop. Then he positioned his dick against Johnny's gaping, juicy hole. Slowly he pushed forward. His cock, about seven inches long and thick, slipped in easily. Reaching beneath him he found Johnny's nipples and he began squeezing them until Johnny cried out. Johnny's buttocks gripped Joe's cock as he drove it in and out. Joe moved his hands down under Johnny's body and grasped the boy's stiff cock. Johnny moved his flanks in time with Joe's fuck-rhythm. His breathing quickened and he thrust his body back, opening his asshole as wide as he could. He couldn't speak because Doc's cock filled his mouth, but he was groaning.

Firmly holding Johnny down, Joe suddenly pulled out and replaced his cock with the gloved fingers of his hand. Johnny rode back more eagerly still, his ass muscles gripping the fingers. Joe's fingers slipped deeper and deeper inside the boy and Johnny suddenly felt his bowels opening at the same time his orgasm exploded uncontrollably. Joe began jacking his cock and soon was spraying his cum across the smooth young cheeks. Slowly, gently, Joe removed his hand and the hot juices dripped from the throbbing, bloated lips. Seeing this, Doc could take no more and began charging into Johnny's mouth, his cum soon blasting down Johnny's throat.

Doc ordered Eric to clean up the mess and to help get Johnny dressed, then he and Joe left the room. Witnessing the scene had turned Eric on again and he began applying more hard licks to Johnny's ass.

"Messy boy," he scolded. "Messy, messy."

Johnny cried out. Eric's hard lashes continued until Johnny was sobbing. Then Eric rolled him over and lifted Johnny's legs over his shoulders. Johnny was now more vulnerable than ever and all Eric had to do was push forward and his erection slid right in all the way. With his hands clasped tightly on Johny's forearms, Eric held Johnny down as he ravaged him. Johnny could hear the other men returning to the room and laughing. "Eric can never get enough boy pussy," Doc said.

"Look at him go – " Joe laughed.

When Johnny returned to the apartment, he went straight to bed. The next morning, the red welts on his buttocks were still hurting him and it was painful for him to sit. Worse still, his anus was bleeding.

The next day, at school, he went to see the nurse, a woman who had been friendly and helpful in the past. He begged her not to tell his mother but the woman betrayed him, calling Maggie with the news that Johnny had been raped.

Johnny refused to tell his mother who had hurt him. Her

reaction was to call Bennett, who was at his summer place in Rhode Island, preparing to return to Florida. He agreed to come into the city and meet Maggie for lunch. His reaction to the rape of Johnny was typically swift. He wanted to take Johnny with him, enroll him in a Christian school in Florida he had helped bankroll.

"I don't want him to go to Florida," Maggie said, shrugging sadly, then lighting a cigarette. "I do not expect you to understand this entirely, but for so many years that boy has been part of everything I've done. I tried to organize my life in order to spend as much time with him as I could. Now that I've done all that and Johnny is just reaching the age where he can fend for himself – "

"What's so hard to understand about that?"

"I know, you're worried about the way I live, you worry about the effect on him."

"You've never spanked him. Well, my feeling is: spare the rod and spoil the child." Bennett loved his sister; he knew that she loved life, loved what she did, offered no apologies, and took responsibility for her actions. Still, he knew the secret about Johnny's father. He went on: "You can't let him grow up to be what his father was. I just hope it's not too late."

Although she had talked with her older brother on the phone many times, she hadn't seen him in a year. Bennett had grown heavier, almost ponderous, and his hair was thinning at the top. He'd always looked younger than he was, he'd always looked to be the youngest man in the room; now he looked older. Her attitude suddenly softened; at least he didn't dye his hair or wear double knits. He'd always been a decisive man, and now his manner was weightier than she remembered.

"You've done very well, Maggie," he said in his careful voice. "And it must be quite a lot of fun, and profitable too, I suppose. Yes, I think you've done damn well. Really damn well in this acting business – "

"To have Johnny in Florida would mean quite a change in my life," she interrupted.

"Mine, too."

"Understand this. For the first time in a long time my life is ordered the way I want it. Johnny is part of it, part and parcel. Perhaps in some ways Johnny is responsible for it – "

He stared at her; she thought he was about to press an advantage. "Well, it's not important." She saw him watching her, a slight smile on his face; the smile irritated her, it was almost a smirk. It was a smile he used when dealing with his tenants.

"Think about *his* life for a moment. Not mine. Not yours. *His* life."

"I am," she said.

"For one thing, he can be troublesome."

"Of course," she said. "He's only a teenager."

Johnny was a teenager whom she provided for. Who was part of her life. He was as happy as any of the other children she knew, those progeny of cheerful, durable marriages. Seeing Bennett looking more and more like her father, she was drawn back against her will into her own childhood. She saw her father sitting in a leather chair. Her big, careless father, who seemed to gulp life like a swimmer perpetually surfacing from under water. He was the source of her energy and her pride and her ambition. He was the source, but not the sustenance. She wished she could ask his advice; he was always very good about advice. She would not be bound to follow it, but at least she would have it. She concentrated, recalling various typical pronouncements of her father's. But there were only the jokes. Her father thought a good dose of humor would solve everything. And perhaps it might. No, she thought, it was impossible for Johnny: Palm Beach would be a death sentence.

That night, she sat in the library at the apartment drinking brandy, surrounded by photos of her family and her eyes welled up. She saw her life in an 8 x 10 photograph: her son had his arm lightly around her waist, they were clowning together. His head was high, her hand rested on his shoulder. They were unconfined, separate centers of gravity, but they were connected, too. They depended, each on the other – not for support alone, but for love. That boy was hers, no one else's.

No, she thought. She would not do it. She knew how to fight and she would fight like hell. She would give in to Bennett only so far; she would agree to move her son to the summer house in Rhode Island, near Newport.

She turned back to the photograph, crying freely now. God,

she loved it. She loved her life and what it meant. In this life you have to take what you want. She turned toward the stairs, momentarily confused. You took what you wanted, when you wanted it badly enough. That was what you had to do. "I will survive," she said aloud, as if she was in a scene from a play she was rehearsing. She said it over and over, differently each time. She raised her voice one last time, putting what she thought was at last the right emphasis on the line.

She hurried up the stairs, stumbling once, then moved down the long hallway to her bedroom, pausing first to look in on Johnny, who was resting peacefully. He'd be fine in Rhode Island, she decided, in a regular school, with ordinary kids and good-hearted, well-meaning teachers.

4

An ass like Johnny's shouldn't have been legal, Steve Parker thought. And then there was the rest of him: the perfect proportions, the flawless skin, the mischievous smile.

Oh, but that ass. Steve often wondered if the other students noticed him watching Johnny every day as he made his way to the same spot: back seat, middle row. Of course, *he* must have known. Just as Johnny passed Steve's desk, he'd dig his hands in his pockets, spreading the fabric tight for his walk to the back.

It was bad enough for Steve to watch him in his classroom and not being able to touch, but then Johnny began showing up during his office hours. *Orifice* hours, he began to think of them, because that's how he wanted to apply his talents on those days when Johnny scooted his chair up close to his. He was always the proper, respectful student, but most of the time his questions were pretty lame; Steve began to think he just wanted attention, and, like most beautiful people, couldn't resist watching the impact he had on others. Steve tried hard to maintain his polite-but-firm classroom persona, but it was rough. All he could think about was locking the door and grabbing that ass and...

But Steve was not amoral; he just lusted for Johnny in silence until one day just before the Thanksgiving holiday recess. Knowing Johnny would be coming in later that afternoon, Steve had been reviewing his file. The report saddened him. After Johnny was thrown out of every private school his mother put him in, it was decided public school was the place for her so-called incorrigible son. He would live with a housekeeper at their "cottage by the sea" and on holidays he would join his mother wherever she happened to be in the world. Of his father, nothing was mentioned.

There was a knock on the office door. Steve put down the report, stood and stretched, taking his time to let the boy in. When he did, Johnny entered slowly and stood by Steve's desk, shifting from foot to foot.

"Yes, Johnny," Steve said, trying to keep his eyes on the latest progress report about Johnny when all he wanted to do was gaze at his crotch, which today was unusually well-packed in his chinos.

"There's something I want to show you," Johnny said.

They piled into the tight quarters of Steve's white Volvo. For a quarter-hour they journeyed up along the highway edging the sea that defined the landscape. Sometimes, while adjusting the clutch, Steve's hand brushed Johnny's knee, causing Steve to feel a sting of intense pleasure. They took a road that seemed somehow familiar, though many of the roads here look alike.

"I live up this way," the boy said, pointing to the left. Suddenly, Steve saw it: the sprawling whitewashed house was framed by a broad stretch of cloudless sky.

Inside, it was fashionably decorated, with white leather chairs and sofas soft as sponges. The mosaic floor was a sea of alternating swirls of blues and yellows. Steve thought a camera crew from *Architectural Digest* could have come right in and started snapping, but it all had a friendly, lived-in air.

The housekeeper, Nell, a small, grandmotherly-type, greeted them. Johnny introduced Steve as his "counselor," ordered by the school administration to get a report on his living conditions.

This was all coming as a shock to Steve; he swallowed hard and continued to glance about the immense living room.

"Is Johnny in trouble again?" Nell asked.

Steve blinked. "Oh, no, not exactly. It's just that – "

"It's just that I'm a transfer," Johnny interjected. "They do this with all the transfers."

Nell seemed to accept this feeble explanation. "Well, make yourself at home," she said. "I have to go to town to do some shopping. I was planning on going when I picked Johnny up at school but now here he is."

"Yeah, here I am," Johnny said, smirking. "Come on, Mr. Parker, I'll show you my room."

Johnny's room was a private suite overlooking the bay. It had the best views of any room in the house. He had every conceivable toy a boy his age could want, most of which looked unused. As soon as Johnny had closed the door and locked it, his impatient hands caressed Steve's crotch. Steve let him revel for a moment in the glory of his swelling, aroused by simply being in forbidden territory: *his* bedroom. Then Steve pulled away. "Whoa! What's going on?"

By now Steve was almost mindless with frustration. By sheer force of will, he kept his arms at his sides as Johnny came to him, pressing against him, warm and hard. Johnny hugged the older man and he hugged him back. Then Johnny kissed Steve. Suddenly generous, Steve relaxed and let the boy continue. As Steve's tongue slid across the boy's full lower lip, savoring the sweetness of him, his cock rose, pressing against Johnny's thighs. Johnny moaned softly, deep in his throat, and closed his eyes as Steve took over, kissing his neck, hearing his quiet breath, and his own, separate amid the crashes of the surf below them. What joy it was to Steve to feel the boy stirring sensuously into him, to imagine this always – two lost souls, cast up on this shore, finding home. He couldn't help himself. In that moment, he loved him madly, entirely.

"Take off your shirt," Johnny commanded.

Steve was stunned by his pleasure in being so direct. He did as he was told. Soon Johnny was covering his skin with kisses and tiny bites, his headful of uncontrollable blond curls adding to the sensation with their tickle. Soon he was unzipping Steve's pants. Steve's penis, dangling free, excited Johnny unbelievably. "Wow!" he cried as he dropped to his knees. Hands or lips, after awhile Steve didn't know which, worked him over; he knew only he was as soaked as a squashed fruit whose skin has burst in the heat. The permission the boy gave freed him to indulge in sensations he had only dreamed about.

Johnny pleaded, in muffled cries, that Steve come in his mouth. At that moment – why, Steve didn't know – he was reminded of his wife, Susan, of how she could never do this for him. And he thought how unfortunate it was that there was only one boy who had – until now.

And how, maybe, finally, he was again allowing this for himself.

As Steve came, Johnny's hands were pressed tightly on his firm, hairy buns. The boy took all Steve had to give; it was the most intense orgasm Steve ever had. Recovering, he reached down and tilted the boy's head. His cock, still spurting, flopped from the boy's mouth.

"Why?"

"You thought I didn't know?"

Steve shrugged. "I don't know how you could know."

Johnny smiled slightly. "How could I *not* know?"

Steve shook his head. "But I hadn't thought of this."

"But you *had* thought of it. From the first day, you've been thinking about it."

Steve raised his eyebrows at him. "But just this once. No more. This is wrong." He used a stern tone.

Johnny stood, slid his underpants down to the floor, bent at the waist and presented the older man with the lightly muscled expanse of his back, his magnificent ass, the sight of which gave Steve's cock a renewed twinge. Straightening and stepping out of the wad of fabric at his feet, Johnny became absolutely bare. He was so astonishingly beautiful that Steve suddenly felt his forehead relax, his worries dissolve. His temptation was to say that he wasn't himself, but he knew this was as true to himself as he'd ever been.

Johnny lay back on the bed, stretched himself lengthwise, putting his hands behind his head on the pillow. He provocatively raised one knee, and studied the ceiling. As he leaned closer to the boy, Steve's eyes consumed his every part. He fondled his nipples until they popped out in sharp, half-inch points. After sucking and flicking them around with his tongue, Steve worked them over with his thumbs and forefingers. Soon Johnny's stiff cock poked straight out. Steve's hand encircled the shaft and gently played with it. Although not unusually large, the cock was in perfect proportion with the rest of him and beautifully cut. Steve knelt between his thighs and started his tongue traveling up and down Johnny's vibrating cock, then worked over his balls with a gentle lapping motion. After a few minutes, he worked his way farther down between his legs, his hands firmly planted on the boy's buttocks.

"Show me your beautiful ass," Steve said, rolling the boy over. Steve sighed; it was the most perfect ass God ever created. He spread his plump buttocks apart with his thumbs. The boy's hole was tight and puckering while Steve gently blew against it, watching it tighten more.

Johnny groaned. Steve began to kiss and nibble on his firm buttocks, first one, then the other. Raising the ass higher, Johnny spread his thighs wider while Steve licked and kissed more urgently, causing the boy to shudder with delight. Steve stuck the tip of his tongue into the narrow, pink opening. Johnny started to protest, but he couldn't find the words. His cock immediately went rigid again when Steve's tongue moved around slowly, conscientiously exploring the sensitive rim.

Johnny began rocking his butt back and forth on Steve's spearing tongue, humping his ass more firmly up into his face. Steve's hands gripped the globes as the tip of his tongue tortured the clenched asshole, flicking around it with feathery strokes.

Soon Johnny was rolling his head from side to side, his asscheeks contracting with pleasure. Steve kept pulling it out and plunging it in, then swirling it around in the tight hole until he knew Johnny was ready. He brought his thick dick up against the frantically squirming butt. Nudging the mushroom head firmly between the writhing globes, he separated the asscheeks. He rubbed his erection smoothly back and forth over the fluttering hole, and the pucker opened like a delicate flower. With steady pressure, he managed to stuff most of his nine inches into the boy's willing hole.

As the boy whimpered beneath him, Steve leaned across his back and began kissing his neck, nibbling on his ear, caressing the back of his head while plunging his cock in and out of him.

The day had been clear and sunny but also windy and cool.

While they made love, the light outside changed from a pale gold to a deep coppery tint. It was so dazzlingly beautiful in Johnny's room, in that bed, that Steve thought he had truly found paradise. Or maybe one thinks like that only if one is an unhappily married man. And a dedicated teacher. He'd heard remarks about certain of his colleagues who were thought to be lecherous, but he was never numbered among them. As an instructor of English, he considered himself sensitive to nuances of dialogue, and innuendo, and had gone out of his way to keep that kind of thing out of his remarks to his students. But with Johnny, although his interest was never verbalized, he caught on. It taught Steve a lesson.

Now Steve came in another glorious rush. He rolled off of Johnny and stretched an arm across his warm back. He turned the boy's face to his. "I hope I didn't hurt you," he panted.

"I love you," Johnny whispered

"Oh, you're just a boy," Steve chuckled.

"Yeah, but I know what I like," he said, groping Steve.

Steve turned away. "So do I."

Steve's torment began the next day. He ached to see the boy, and when he did, it was frustrating not to be able to touch him, hold him, make love to him. School let out early for a faculty meeting. After it was over, for relief, Steve went with a few of his faculty friends to a restaurant for dinner and tried to join in conversation, tried to find interest in things about him, especially one of the cute waiters, but it was no use. All his thoughts would return to the boy. He scowled fiercely and left after coffee was served.

He took the longest possible route home and by the time he reached his house he was more keenly aware of the difficulties of his situation than ever before. He wished over and over that some solution would offer itself, that he could see his way out, but nothing came. He was in a greater quandary than ever. What had he got into? How could things have gotten so out of control, so quickly?

He quietly entered the house and went to the den. At first he got some vague comfort out of a good cigar, but as he sucked on it, it reminded him too much of sucking on Johnny and he put it out. Every once in a while he would clinch his fingers and tap his foot. He fixed a brandy and soda.

He brooded over his situation until long after midnight, when the sheer loneliness of his situation rushed upon him in full. He got up, locked the door to the den. He undid his pants and took out his erection. Leaning against the door, his eyes shut tight, he massaged his balls, then stroked his cock. Visions of Johnny stretched out before him, wiggling his ass at him, consuming him. As he came, all he could hear was Johnny saying, "I love you."

As desperately as he wanted to tell Johnny it was over, that they would never have sex again, when Steve saw the boy, he simply could not.

They invented the need for special tutoring sessions in Johnny's room that lasted three hours. Johnny would greet Steve in his briefs, or sometimes wrapped in a towel, still wet from his shower, his body aroma mingling with that of scented soap and shampoo. Sometimes he was nude, his slender body peeking through the doorway like a forbidden delight tempting the older man.

Steve would close the door with a sigh, all control vanishing, and bury his face in Johnny's crotch, his mouth frantic for his cock, his hands trembling to feel the silken smoothness of his flesh.

Johnny remained in control. There was something predatory about him as he orchestrated the spasms of Steve's pleasure with sure hands, sly murmurs, and words of encouragement that kept Steve utterly off-balance until, with a last little gasp, he begged Steve to come inside him.

Then Johnny would mount Steve and make love to him with such mastery that Steve would climax a second time before Johnny did. Steve realized for the first time in his life his ass had become an organ of sensitivity and yielding, a toy manipulated by a boy's caresses, its spasms ordained by his heated probing.

Sometimes, when he felt Johnny's sex disappear into him, followed by the incredibly energetic thrusting, it seemed as though he finally understood what it meant to be fucked senseless. Steve was astonished. The thought of this had never occurred to him. Still, he did not protest. Johnny's attack on

Steve's ass was savage. It seemed as if he literally intended to impale Steve, tear him apart. His roommate at college, Roger, was the only one who had ever fucked Steve and Johnny was better than Roger ever thought of being. Johnny would thrust hard and slip part way out, then slam into him again with incredible force.

Steve lifted myself up to him and Johnny pressed his cock in all the way. His energetic pumping continued for several minutes, Steve's moans growing more intense with each thrust, until Steve reached down and brought himself off. Hearing Steve's groans of ecstasy, Johnny rammed it into his lover for the final time, his orgasm filling him.

Where did he learn this stuff? Steve asked himself. The kid was far more experienced than he and it showed. In that moment when the boy was finishing, furiously, pressing down on him, Steve only wished he could fuck that well.

As the days passed, he was spending so much time worrying about Johnny, fantasizing about him, and losing himself in the beauty of his body and his ceaseless caresses, that he hadn't really noticed Susan had now taken to spending as much time as she could away from home, leaving a babysitter in charge. She was always out with friends, shopping, playing tennis or bridge, visiting, or going to the movies. She left him dinners to warm up when he chose to come home, and curt notes letting him know where she was.

The few times he spent with her, they got into quarrels. They fought about money, about the kids, about school. Both of them seemed to know what they were really fighting about, but neither wished to address it directly.

. . .

So as not to arouse Nell's suspicion, Johnny suggested they go for a drive. Merely the thought of having sex out in the open turned Steve on. The first time they went for a drive, Steve headed out of the city, past Johnny's house, to a point on the shore where there were no more houses.

As they drove along, Johnny reached over and unbuttoned Steve's shirt. He brushed his fingers across Steve's chest, then dropped his head to Steve's chest and began rooting through the chest hair with his nose, licking all around his nipples with his tongue. He took Steve's right hand off the wheel and placed it on his hard-on. Steve kneaded the bulge in Johnny's pants.

Johnny stretched out flat, undid Steve's belt and pulled down the zipper. He put his hand around his cock to pull it free, up, and out. He blew on it, then began sucking it.

Steve shivered, lifting up his hips and squirming. Johnny slipped his pants down past his hips and dug his balls out, squeezing them, licking them, finally sucking them while he jacked Steve. Steve's hand left Johnny's crotch and grabbed hold of the back of his head. He left the main road and slowly took a rutted path down near the shore. Finally he stopped and turned off the engine. He laid his head back on the top of the seat and lifted Johnny's face from his crotch with both hands. Johnny sat up, wiping the precum from his chin. Johnny pulled down his shorts while Steve watched, then Johnny climbed into the back seat, naked and barefoot, Steve behind him.

"Oh that ass," Steve sighed, sitting back, spreading his thighs. He put a copious load of spit on his cock, stroked it. Johnny got over him and, pressing down, judged his angle and shoved. Steve's cock went all the way in, in one long, incredible thrust. Johnny clamped hard on the prick and started fucking it, jacking himself off. When he came, it was Steve's turn. He pumped and shoved and ground inside him. He began working into the rhythm he knew Johnny loved. Johnny dropped his head and shook it, side to side, sending sweat flying across the front seat. As Steve came, he bit Johnny's shoulders.

Hugging Johnny to him, Steve finally came up for air. Johnny's butthole quivered as Steve removed his cock. Johnny fell back into the seat and took Steve's dripping cock in his hands. He nibbled on the head, then opened wide and swallowed him all the way down. After a few moments, he began fingering Steve's asshole just the way Steve had fingered his, spreading him, massaging the muscle, forcing him to come again.

"Oh, I love you, Johnny," Steve screamed at the height of his orgasm.

As the days passed, they would repeat the scene many times, with variations, sometimes not stopping the car at all. Johnny would blow Steve; they would switch and Steve would suck the boy off.

Steve was playing with fire, but he could not seem to stop himself.

. . .

Finally, with the afternoon sunlight streaming through their living room windows, Susan and Steve had a quiet but definitely unpleasant chat. Marriage is so damned fragile and complicated, Steve thought.

"Steve," she said with her lips tightening, "I know you're seeing somebody. I know these things happen. But I'm not just going to stand by any longer. You make your choice. Either you're in or you're out."

Steve knew he had to stay in. He had his career to think about. They had two young girls. They agreed that he would cease seeing *somebody*. As of immediately. But, Steve knew, *somebody* would have some things to say about it.

5

Driving to school the next morning, Steve knew his situation was impossible. He knew the minute he saw Johnny he would desire him. His goal that day was to avoid him. But Johnny would not be denied. It was the day before the Christmas recess, and Johnny insisted on going for yet another drive.

As they headed to the lonely spot on the shore that had become their favorite, Johnny was not smiling. He announced he would be flying to London to be with his mother, who was performing on stage there in the West End, for the holidays.

Johnny asked Steve to take him to the airport; he had managed to change his reservation so that there would be time for them to rent a motel room. He wanted to make the most of the time remaining. Naked on the bed in the dim light of the motel room, Johnny was intoxicating to Steve. He had never been with anyone so passionate, so inexhaustible. Or so beautiful.

After the initial, obligatory nervousness of being in a strange motel room, Steve surprised himself by managing erection after erection, fucking the boy repeatedly.

"Oh, God," Steve cried, entering the boy for the last time.

"Oh, Jeeezus," Johnny cried as Steve slid it in, began thrusting in and out of him.

"Oh, Johnny," Steve moaned, his body convulsing as he came inside the boy, as if it was the first time, now wanting it to last for eternity. Steve realized this was it, he had done it, he truly had a lover – somebody he could not live without. He could no longer fight the pleasure coursing through his body.

They were speechless for a long time after the orgasm; Steve finally disengaged from Johnny, pulling his now-limp and moist penis from the warmth of the boy's ass. He kissed him on the lips with all the tenderness he could muster, even as he knew that neither gestures nor words could properly express what he had just experienced. The cover of the bed was rumpled, soaked with sweat and sperm; they had not even bothered pulling it down to uncover the sheets.

Steve got up, led the way to the shower. He soaped Johnny, his fingers lingering more than hygiene demanded in the gaping crack of his ass, caressing his erect cock with lather until it shone like a wet jewel. He realized he had been selfish: Johnny had not come a third time, or even a second time. He had come only when Steve was fucking him moments after they entered the room. Johnny rubbed Steve's back and manipulated himself into a position where he could enter the older man. Again, the fuck was astounding. Steve stayed in the shower several minutes after Johnny had left, letting the jets of water soothe his ravaged ass.

"Have you got my shorts?" Steve asked after he emerged from the shower.

"No. What would I do with your baggy old shorts?"

"I don't believe you."

"Tough." Johnny curled himself into a ball on the bed. "If you don't believe me check it out."

Steve flipped the sheet: blond curly hair, bony shoulder blades, vertebrae, then the ass. That incredible ass – more truth, there alone, than was dreamed of in all the philosophy classes he took at the university.

But Johnny wasn't wearing his shorts.

"Turn over. I want to see the rest of you."

"You've seen all you're gonna see today."

Steve kneeled on the floor by the bedside, leaned across, and touched his shoulders. "Come on, give them to me. We have to go."

Johnny rolled over and gazed at Steve's semi-flaccid cock. "Please, no. If we can stay, I'll give 'em back."

Steve said, "No, we have to go. Your plane is leaving."

Steve's underpants flew into his face and Johnny pulled the sheet over his head and now was nowhere to be seen. His voice muffled, he cried, "I don't want to go. I want us to stay here forever."

"Hey, come on. Come on."

"Why? You say you love me, so why won't we stay?"

"We can't. You know why."

"All I know is what you say."

"Please, I do love you, I really do."

Suddenly Steve was ripping the sheet away and was back in bed, where he had left ten minutes before, wrapping the boy tightly in his arms.

"Let me go. I'll scream." Johnny's voice sounded like Christmas morning, the biggest present of all saved for last.

"No. Not until you behave. Stealing my shorts. Playing tricks on me."

"Talk about tricks – what's this supposed to be?" He half-lowered his ass so that it bumped the tip of Steve's now erect cock, then he bumped it a second time. Ten minutes ago, Steve was sure he been fucked-out.

"'Supposed to be?' What do you *think* it is?"

"It's another of your big old nasty hard-ons. You always have a big old nasty hard-on when you're with me."

"So do you," Steve said, grabbing Johnny's cock and kissing him full on the mouth.

Steve twisted them up in the sitting position, Johnny straddling him. They pushed back against the flimsy motel headboard, then humped a little to position Steve's prick for an easy entry. The moment it was in, Johnny fell back on it, impaling himself on it. Johnny fucked himself with it while Steve masturbated him. He jumped up and down on the swollen cock for a few minutes, then slid down and off Steve, onto his back, freeing Steve's prick. "I want to show you how much I love you," Johnny murmured.

A little pre-cum seeped out of the slit of Steve's prick and Johnny licked it off, giving it a generous squeeze with his hand before devouring it. Steve thought he might come again this way but Johnny had other ideas; he slithered his legs around Steve's hips and locked his ankles in the small of Steve's back. Steve entered him again.

Taking him in his arms, Steve looked into his adorable face one last time as he fucked him. He wanted to hold the image in his mind, saying silently: "Remember, there'll never be anything again as beautiful as this."

On the way to the airport, Johnny's hand never left Steve's crotch. The cock was accessible now; Johnny had Steve's underpants in his suitcase.

Steve parked the car in the garage and kissed Johnny one last time. "I love you, Johnny. I'll miss you."

Tears began to flow from Johnny's eyes and Steve wiped them into the boy's smooth, rosy cheeks.

"I'll miss you too, Steve. But I'll be back."

6

When she first appeared on the London stage, it was obvious that most of the audience came just to see Maggie Lawrence. She was inundated with fan mail and her telephone rang constantly. Reporters wanted interviews and photographers started turning up at the house she had rented. The interest shown by the press was surprising. There was a double page spread of photographs of her in one of the Sunday magazines, and a national newspaper ran an article calling her a "legendary floozie." Invitations to cocktail parties, film premieres and first nights at West End theatres arrived in her post. It was as if she had been rediscovered and was now a celebrity around town, mobbed by photographers flashing cameras as soon as she stepped out of the taxi.

Now, after performing in London steadily for almost five years, she could move about without attracting much attention and Johnny was looking forward to Christmas this year. His mother was starring in a revival of Ruth and Augustus Goetz's adaptation of "The Heiress," based on Heny James' "Washington Square," in which a domineering and oppressive father squelches his shy daughter's attempt at romance. Johnny was keenly interested in the young actor who played opposite his mother, Jeffrey Lyndon. Photographs his mother had sent of Jeffrey stirred Johnny's imagination. Jeffrey was an American television actor who had made a success on the London stage in recent years and bore a striking resemblance to Montgomery Clift, who had played the role in the 1949 film version of the play.

But Johnny found things were not happy in London. The play had suspended performances indefinitely because of Maggie's recurrent illnesses. She told Johnny she had a virus she couldn't kick. He asked about Jeffrey. She didn't want to talk about him. He asked about a few of her other beaus. She didn't want to talk about them either. Finally, near tears, Johnny asked about his father.

"You know it hurts me to talk about him," Maggie sniffled, lowering her hands and blotting her face with a linen handkerchief.

"All I did was mention his name. Can't I even mention his name? You never let me talk about him! Never!"

Johnny's mother said something into her brandy snifter that sounded like "It wasn't my fault." Johnny wanted to say he knew that, that no one blamed her, but he was sure Maggie would never believe it. Parents must always think they can save their children, even when they have no control. Johnny put a hand on her shoulder, thinking about the burden she had carried around all these years.

To escape the revolting marriage to Sam Spear, she had married Jack Wilson, a choreographer on the MGM lot. He soon quit the studio and went to New York to stage a show on Broadway. As much as Maggie loved New York, she had her career to think of and she spent more time in California during the first months of their marriage. When she did return to Manhattan, she discovered her husband's secret nature: he was bisexual. She could have lived with that, but her prolonged absences put a severe strain on the marriage. Then she discovered she was pregnant. At first she was going to get an abortion but changed her mind. She had been making one movie after the other and having a child in New York might renew her marriage as well as give her a much-needed rest. But by the time she made this decision, Jack had already become lovers with a young dancer in the show. Still, the thought of having a child so delighted Jack that he agreed to a reconciliation, provided Maggie would permit his lover to live with them. Maggie thought she could deal with it; after all, she was pregnant and at least she would have company. But she found she couldn't deal with seeing her husband with another man and returned to California, where her mother cared for her during her pregnancy.

Shortly after Johnny was born, she went to New York with the baby to see Jack. He was still living with his lover and the quarrels began all over again. Maggie stayed only a month, then returned to California.

Now Johnny was again asking about his father. "Tell me," Johnny kept saying.

She said, "Your father was dancing when he died."

"You told me."

"But now I want you to hear it all. He was rehearsing a show about ballroom dancing..."

And then she went on, to tell Johnny as much as she ever was able to find out about the incident. His father had stayed at the theater after everyone had left and shot himself on stage with a service revolver. They never found out where he had bought it, or when. He was found in his warm-up clothes – a pullover sweater and pleated pants. He was wearing his tap shoes, and he had a short towel folded around his neck. He had aimed the gun barrel down his mouth, so the bullet would not shatter the wall of mirrors behind him. "He was always so considerate of everyone," Maggie said, breaking down.

Johnny sat on the bed and his mother took him in her arms. They didn't stop crying for several minutes.

"Let's go out," Johnny coaxed. "It's Christmas Eve, and it's snowing. Let's go for a walk, okay?"

Maggie dried her eyes with the handkerchief again and blew her nose. Her eyes were red. "I'd like that," she said.

Johnny was left to discover London on his own. He found

that, like New York, it is a great city that reveres its traditions. In the capital's quiet residential corners, wreaths adorned the lacquered doors of row houses, and on street corners everywhere, there was the smoky aroma of hot chestnuts, roasted over open fires and dispensed in warm, steamy paper packets. He shopped with the crowds along Oxford and Regent Streets, becoming especially fond of Hamleys and its seven stories of dolls, games and model trains, and an arcade of video machines and games in the basement. In Leicester Square and Covent Garden, he enjoyed the amusement rides and side-show barkers. And everywhere there was music, and he especially enjoyed the carolers warbling beneath the giant tree in Trafalgar Square. He wanted to show it all to his mother.

After pulling on their coats, they stood at the mirror in the hall. "What do you think I'll look like when I get old?" Johnny asked. The top of his head reached Maggie's nose, but aside from their height difference, they looked remarkably the same. Johnny's body was leaner, but their faces were almost identical, round and pink with deepset green eyes. "I mean, when I'm thirty."

For Johnny it was hard to imagine thirty. Steve was thirty, and on him it looked good, but Johnny never wanted to be thirty.

She ran her hands through Johnny's hair lightly, always surprised at the feel of it, so much like her own. She mumbled that she loved Johnny more than anything in the world, and for some reason was always glad he was a boy, not a girl.

"Maybe someday," Johnny said, "you'll stop getting older and I'll pass you up!"

"Im-possible," Maggie declared. "When elephants fly."

. . .

A couple of days later, Maggie said Jeffrey had returned to London after doing a television show in New York and wanted to take them to dinner at the hotel where he was staying, the Connaught. But later that afternoon, she said she didn't feel up to going out – that Johnny was to go with Jeffrey alone.

Ordinarily, this would have excited Johnny beyound measure but he had become anxious about his mother. "I don't understand what's happened," Johnny said to Jeffrey after the waiter took their order.

"I don't really understand it either," Jeffrey said. "I was staying with her for awhile and one day everything turned strange. She told me she had an appointment with her agent, which I found out afterwards wasn't true. When she returned a few hours later, she closed herself in her room. At first I assumed that she was just 'thinking' and would at some time confront me with some fantastical idea, so I didn't take much notice. Then after a while I started to wonder and thought that, perhaps, she was indulging in one of her childlike, petulant sulks. But it was more than that; she was taken over by these terrible moods.

"We didn't go out that night as we'd planned. We hardly spoke. Maggie just wanted to be left alone; and she smoked. I'd never known her to smoke so much. I remember having to go to the store across the street because she'd finished all the cigarettes. The air was thick with smoke. Maggie was lying in the dark; I couldn't make out the look on her face, but she told me to get out and never come back. But I did. Over the next few weeks she became demanding and possessive, even secretive, taking to disappearing for hours at a time without giving any clue as to where she was going. There were times when we got on well, we had fun and the relationship was like it used to be, but these instances were getting few and far between.

"But Maggie still looked beautiful, radiant, and actually started to take more interest in her appearance. She even stepped up her health regime, going regularly to the gym and becoming even more picky about her food, but still she smoked a lot, which was unusual for her.

"One day, I found myself back on her street and I dialled her number from the callbox across the way and when she picked up the receiver I said, 'It's me,' but she immediately put it back down.

"Eventually she did see me again but it was never the same."

"But why didn't she tell me? Why didn't she tell me she was sick?"

"She didn't want anyone to know. You can't blame yourself

for anything that's happened. Maggie must have had her reasons for not telling us she was ill. What's happened has happened. We can't change that. Things don't always go the way we'd like them to. Something will always go wrong, things will always get fucked up. Life's like that. Maggie just kept this secret, I don't know why. Anyway, let's not get depressed. Let's not get upset." He raised his wine glass. "Let's drink to Maggie, to life."

With her illness, Maggie grew more depressed and her doctor recommended a psychiatrist. She asked the shrink seriously about the boy, what effect would her illness have on him? And what about the way she lived? The psychiatrist shrugged; he didn't know about the boy, Johnny sounded all right to him.

He said, "I'm sure there are dozens of unresolved conflicts, and you've got a pretty good case of guilt about the kid. But I don't believe the conflicts are serious or in any way out of the ordinary, and you know in your heart you're an attentive mother and that the guilties, therefore, are not warranted. You know that. You're not some silly housewife with only her orgasms or her bridge games to worry about. You've lived, you've been around – "

"I appreciate the thought," she said dryly.

Johnny had too much wine with dinner and Jeffrey suggested he spend the night with him at the hotel.

Shock after shock had jolted Johnny into a daze. His mother's strange behavior, her turning Jeffrey away, Jeffrey turning up. It was all too much. As much as he was attracted to Jeffrey, Johnny was dubious about sleeping with a man who had been sleeping with his mother. Jeffrey seemed blase about it all, as if he did this sort of thing every day, which, Johnny decided, perhaps he did. Johnny had noticed that his mother seemed to gravitate toward men who could go one way or another. Perhaps, Johnny mused, that was the *normal* thing. After all, it seemed perfectly natural for Steve to go from being in bed with his wife to being in bed with him. But as eager as Johnny was for sex, he made the conscious decision to let Jeffrey seduce him.

While Jeffrey went to the bathroom, Johnny got naked and slipped into bed and turned out the lamp. Jeffrey, after entering the bedroom, undressed in the dark, but Johnny could see he was extremely well-made. He reminded Johnny a bit of Steve, the nicely-furred chest, the trim body, and he was even handsomer. By the time the older man reached the bed, Johnny had an erection and he exposed it to Jeffrey. Jeffrey said nothing; he simply leaned over Johnny and his tongue darted and licked and stroked Johnny's cock, driving the boy to a shuddering pinnacle, then tethering him there with rapid flicks. It was all so directed, so accurate, so patient that it took Johnny's breath away.

Johnny clutched at Jeffrey's long brown hair as his urgency built, but Jeffrey ignored the boy's demands for harder and wilder sex. And even after Johnny's orgasm, he continued to make love to Johnny.

"Have you ever been – ?" he asked, gently probing Johnny's anus.

"A long time ago," Johnny breathed.

"I'm a big man and you're very small inside," he murmured. "I don't want you to be uncomfortable when I put my cock in."

"I won't," Johnny said, almost giggling.

Johnny rested his heels against Jeffrey's broad shoulders, and Jeffrey pushed against them, forcing Johnny's hips up, his legs awkwardly bent and spread. The boy was vulnerable, helpless.

As Jeffrey began to enter the boy, Johnny shoved his fist to his mouth, stifling the scream that threatened when he began fucking. He rode it through, bucking, begging. Jeffrey dug his fingers into Johnny's ass and held him to him, clearly enjoying the ride.

"Oh, Johnny," he cried, urging Johnny's legs around his neck, and Johnny instinctively tightened the embrace. "That's it, beautiful little boy, hold on tight."

"Please... It's too much..."

"Not nearly."

Jeffrey thrust in and out until he too was a trembling mass of exposed nerves and came.

Johnny started to cry.

"Tell me what I did wrong," Jeffrey said.

Johnny giggled. "Oh, nothing. You were perfect, it's just that I never thought this would happen."

"Me neither," Jeffrey chuckled and untangled Johnny's legs

from around his shoulders, then slid up to cover Johnny's body with his. "You're so soft." He nestled the head of his cock against Johnny's and captured one of the boy's nipples in his mouth. Johnny arched toward his mouth and Jeffrey sucking hungrily on one nipple, then the other.

Before long, Jeffrey was hard again and put the head of his cock at the entrance. "Pull me in," he said.

"I need to rest a minute."

"No, you're ready." He tugged on Johnny's swelling erection.

"Please...wait...." But Johnny's words were choked off as Jeffrey inched the head of his cock into the boy's sweaty body.

"No, now. Oh, yes, see, you want it. Such a greedy little boy." He nudged Johnny's legs wider. "That's it, take it all."

"Wait...oh, please...."

He nipped at Johnny's bottom lip, demanding his acquiescence while he fucked deeper, then, his voice low and dark with emotion. He moaned, "Shit, I've never had a woman drive me this crazy."

"You're so...big."

"Yes. Big enough to take good care of you." The heavy ridge of his cockhead rubbed against the aching anal lips. Then he started jabbing – short and quick, different than before. Johnny dug his fingers into the hard ass, trying to shove him deeper.

"Oh, yes," Jeffrey growled, nearing orgasm once again.

Johnny crushed his body against him and Jeffrey's tongue darted into Johnny's ear as he came.

Jeffrey relaxed, rolled off Johnny and lay on his back gasping. Johnny turned and looked at him. In many ways, he reminded Johnny of Steve, desperate in his need for sexual adventure. He tried to imagine his mother with Jeffrey on top of her but he could not. After Jeffrey was asleep, Johnny let himself out and took a cab back to the apartment.

. . .

"Johnny," Jessie, Maggie's maid, whispered from the bottom of the stairs as Johnny was about to go into his mother's bedroom late the following morning. "Don't go in there. Not just yet. The doctor doesn't want to be disturbed. Come down.

I've made a pot of tea."

Reluctantly he followed Jessie to the kitchen.

"What's going on? What's happened to Mother? Why didn't you wake me up?"

"Nothing's happened. Everything will be fine." Jessie pulled up the flaps of a carton of milk, only from the wrong end. "Oh look what I've gone and done," she said and wiped away the splash. "It's just that the doctor came round again to visit Miss Maggie and we didn't think to wake you. Anyway we thought you needed the sleep. You got in so late."

"How long has he been here?" Johnny asked.

"Oh, not long. It can't be more than half an hour. Don't be so agitated. Sit down and have a drink of tea."

Johnny sat on the edge of a chair, leaning his elbows on the table.

"Oh, I forgot," Jessie said. "You like a mug, don't you? I've gone and poured a cup."

"That doesn't matter, I don't care."

Johnny looked around the kitchen. The sink was piled with dishes, mostly cups and saucers, needing to be washed. The room looked miserable, he thought. "Everything's a bit of a mess," he said.

"Now, eh," Jessie pointed at him with a spoon. "I've been awake all night and your mother's been up since five. Anyway you look a bit of a mess yourself. If I was you I'd have a bath."

"You're right. I think that's what I'll do."

Later, Jessie, sweeping a stray gray hair away from her tired eyes, told Johnny, "The doctor's just gone. We couldn't call you because you were in the bath." Jessie attempted to change the subject. "But he's coming back later today."

"What did he have to say?"

"He's never known anything like it in his life! Hollywood's got nothing on this," she cried and threw her hands in the air. "I feel as though I'm living in a picture - and I've got the lousy part." She began sorting laundry. "And I don't think you should go up to Miss Maggie because she needs to be left alone. The doctor says she needs to be kept quiet and not get too excited. She's losing all her body fluids. There's nothing you can do."

Jessie went to do the laundry, leaving Johnny alone.

7

With Johnny in London, Steve was able to focus his attention on Susan. As her anger subsided, he began remembering what an attractive person he had married – blonde, tall, very thin and willowy. Suddenly he noticed what subtle taste she had in clothes, or perhaps she had bought some new outfits. Whatever, he decided what a pleasure she was to look at. It seemed as if his time with Johnny had revitalized his interest in Susan. And when he had sex with her, although he was thinking of Johnny, and only him, he was very good.

"Things are better, aren't they?" Steve asked her one evening when they were lingering at the table after dinner. The girls were in the basement watching television.

"They're not so bad," she said, turning her head towards the dining room window in a way that he knew meant she was thinking about it, that she would always think about it, wondering who the somebody was who had threatened her. Then she got up and walked around the table, stood behind him and ran her fingers along his shoulders. "In fact," she said, "it's really better than it's ever been."

What Susan did not know was that what had never been better were Steve's sexual fantasies.

He had even begun to fantasize about bringing Johnny into his home, to making it a *menage a trois*.

Some of his fantasies had Susan giving herself to Johnny without hesitation. Others found her flinching and backing pathetically away like a wounded animal, trying to hide her face from the bestial truth of her husband's unnatural desire for the boy. As Steve would leave the house for what she was sure was another tryst with his male lover, she would beg him in clumsy girlish pleas to stay. He instinctively moved toward the door.

Steve's favorite fantasy involved Susan's finally assenting to meet Johnny, but they arrived only to find Susan lying on the kitchen floor, wearing a bikini. She had been drinking and had passed out.

Seeing his wife, despite her condition, aroused Johnny. He desired Steve more greatly than before. But Steve was disgusted with her condition. Steve moved away from Johnny, going to Susan, kneeling next to her as she lay there, her mouth open. Johnny realized now Steve loved his wife, and his hunger for Johnny was somehow wrong. Still, there was the moment to be seized.

"Fuck me," Johnny said, walking toward him.

"What?" Steve said, shocked, not moving from his wife's side.

"Fuck me right now. In front of her. Fuck me," Johnny whispered, smiling a little, feeling the potency of his attraction. He began pulling his clothes away from his body. Steve desperately tried to move Johnny away from her, to lead him out of the kitchen.

"No. I want to do it here. Now." Johnny was naked, his cock hard. Steve put his tongue on the throbbing prick, licking it, then sucking it. Johnny pulled him up, away from it and they kissed.

Steve knelt again in front of Johnny, his face resting on his hard belly, nipping gently at the head of Johnny's cock.

Suddenly Steve pulled Johnny down on him. They fell to the floor, next to his wife, and, as their bodies clashed and sparked, they rolled and tumbled against her inert body. Johnny's ass rested on her ass. He bit Steve on the neck. Steve held him still with his teeth as he sucked the bite hard, forcing him to focus on the pain. Johnny had never known such power between his legs, and he tore at Steve's body, pulled his penis into him.

After a few moments, Johnny looked down to watch with almost clinical detachment Steve's cock disappear into him. Steve opened his eyes and looked at Johnny very hard, fucking him slowly but more forcefully with every thrust. He dug into him as though he was seeking reassurance that with every graceful push of his hips, with every perfected contraction of his ass, of the arch and bend of his tight belly, that he was pleasing the boy. His wife still lay motionless as their bodies fused.

Johnny began coaxing him, holding him together with his

thighs, feeling his body filling more and more with him, with his smell, his sounds, his sex. Steve closed his eyes, close to orgasm. Johnny turned and looked at Susan, still unconscious, and impulsively reached over and touched her.

He touched her skin, her cheek. He put his hand in her hair. Steve opened his eyes and saw that he was touching her, tracing her lips with the tip of his finger.

"Don't do that . . .," Steve said helplessly, knowing that Johnny would do what he pleased, to him and his wife tonight.

Johnny dragged his finger down her chin and over the soft, sexy grotto of her neck. She didn't respond at all. Johnny was excited, filled with limitless possibilities.

Johnny was still holding Steve inside of him, fucking him harder, heading to orgasm.

"Fuck me. He's fucking me," Johnny whispered into Steve's wife's face. He was close enough to smell her boozy breath.

Steve pulled at him, trying to draw his body away from hers. Johnny fell to the side and put his lips over her mouth. He kissed her slowly, letting his tongue caress her lips, feeling the creases of her soft, dead mouth. Steve was holding his flesh hard, reaching for his cock and Johnny could feel his warm breath in his hair. Johnny took her hand and brought it to his mouth, began sucking her fingers as Steve entered him from behind. The more fiercely Steve fucked Johnny, the harder Johnny sucked her fingers. Steve was fucking Johnny into his wife. Steve had one hand on Johnny's cock and the other hand steadied itself on her body.

Johnny tore his mouth from Susan's fingers before he was going to come and Steve pulled him into him, and Johnny braced himself on her and held Steve fast. He came with a scream so violent that it should have awakened her, but it did not.

8

Early on, in telling her story to interviewers, which she was happy to do from time to time, Maggie did not varnish the truth. She spoke of her life with impetuous candor, fully describing both her achievements and her mistakes. She did not neglect her personal life either, because that was what the reporters were most interested in. Questions about her son Johnny usually came at the end of the interview, and were asked out of a sense of politeness. Yes, she had one son, a teenager. No, she was not currently married nor did she believe in marriage any longer. Her personal style was deceptive and tended to conceal her ability.

But since her cancer was diagnosed, she refused interviews and she and Johnny were able to escape London without being detected. As her condition worsened, Bennett insisted she come to Florida to see some specialists. This time, she did not fight with her brother.

Johnny had rarely visited the mansion on North Ocean Boulevard. Bennett had purchased the property at considerably below market value from the estate of a dowager who had let it deteriorate and he was slowly restoring it to its original splendor. It was a two-story Spanish-style house hidden from the street by enormous banyan trees. In the back, an expansive lawn reached to the ocean and was covered with avocado, grapefruit, orange, and coconut palm trees. Pink and salmon bougainvillaea bloomed everywhere along the fences. Under other circumstances, Johnny felt he might actually enjoy living there.

Since retiring to Palm Beach, Bennett got religion in a big way. He became a major contributor to the Good News ministry of James P. Gifford, based in West Palm Beach. The second night Maggie and Johnny were at the mansion, Gifford came to dinner. Maggie said she was too ill to go downstairs. Johnny wanted to have supper with her but Uncle Bennett insisted Johnny meet the man he called The Pastor. Bennett told Johnny to dress for dinner in his Sunday best, while he wore a navy blue blazer; Johnny thought he looked just like Captain

Kangaroo. His skin was deeply tanned from playing golf every day, and although he was nearly bald, a few strands of dark hair crossed the glossy dome of his scalp with precision and order.

Before dinner, they entertained The Pastor in the living room, where ceiling fans revolved slowly. There were two deep-tufted sofas piled high with tapestry pillows, and bookcases along one wall, full of volumes bound in red Moroccan leather with gold lettering.

Johnny couldn't believe the discussion as they ate their filet mignon in the cavernous dining room. Bennett started right out by saying how Johnny was being tempted with evil at every turn in today's society.

"I think most of us lose sight of our goal at times and listen to Satan and his temptations," Gifford said. There was a feverish sparkle in his eyes. "We get in a church and want to love but lose sight of the goal. We have to be so careful to keep the proper goal in mind and not get sidetracked. We have to make sure that we put love first just like Jesus did.

"And, believe me, putting love first isn't always easy. But God has always told us to forgive and not to judge.

"You see, Johnny, Christ stands up to Satan and goes on to carry out His Father's will. He wants to tell the world the 'Good News' that God loves them, and what happens? John 1:11 says, 'He came unto his own, and his own received him not.' He was rejected. Jesus himself was rejected!

"The fear of rejection is one of the biggest fears Satan tries to put on the Christian today. Believe me, I know what rejection means. I live with it daily. People we are trying to love turn on us or misunderstand us. And that hurts. At times it feels like we don't have a friend in the world."

"Johnny doesn't have many friends," Bennett interjected. "He's moved around so much because he's the son of somebody who's in the limelight. He's been hurt a lot – "

"You know, Satan can puff us up to make us think we're somebody, and then he bursts the bubble by making us feel rejected so that we feel like we're a nobody. Satan always is playing his tricks on us."

"Yes, we need to follow Jesus's example," Bennett said. "He got hurt. The religious leaders of His day scoffed and laughed at him. Do you think that didn't hurt? They tried to stone Him and even plotted His death. But did Jesus give up? No. He knew that at the end of everything would be His victory."

"Yes," Gifford said. "I think all of us have experienced rejection at one time or another while we were simply trying to love. I know many people who have been so hurt that they're afraid to get up and try to love again.

"Satan would just love to keep us afraid to expose ourselves to others for fear of being hurt. He wants to keep us separated from each other and feeling all alone. When the devil comes upon us, all we have to say is, 'Go away, Devil, in Jesus' name.' We don't need to have a mad voice, but simply, according to the Word, say, 'Go away, Devil. Go away, right now.'"

"Johnny, you should heed what the Pastor is saying," Bennett said. "I think God wants us to protect our sexual urges from Satan. We know you are constantly bombarded with Satan's sexual traps. And you're not alone. Satan gets housewives to watch soap operas on TV that show broken marriages and sexual fantasies. Satan gets men to hide from admitting that they have strong sexual drives, and he makes them live in fear that they are not normal and that someone might find out that they do not have totally 'pure' minds – "

"Yes, Johnny," Gifford interjected, "girding our loins with truth means we go to the Word for answers instead of going to the TV, the movies, or some magazine to excite us. God will protect us from Satan's sexual urges as we live and walk in truth, as we flood our minds with the Word.

"All through the Bible, God condemns lust. Fornication's a sin and breaks the Seventh Commandment. Homosexuality is condemned in the Bible as sin – sodomites shall not inherit the Kingdom of God! Any use of sex, except as an expression of love in marriage, and, also, for the purpose of procreation in marriage, is a sin, and breaks the Seventh Commandment! Totally refraining from sexual intercourse, masturbation or other sexual outlets does no harm whatsoever. But the self-discipline of continence develops character!"

As he railed on and on, his voice threatening to lose the final consonant of every word, the Pastor's hands punctuated each sentence. At first, Johnny tried to follow the monologue, but soon found himself thinking the man was crazy, deranged, over the line. In appearance, the Pastor reminded Johnny of the evangelist Jimmy Bakker and he wondered if the Pastor had a wife as ugly as Bakker's and was perhaps screwing boys on the side. He couldn't help but think all holy men did the very things they railed against.

Gifford stopped to take a drink of the Ca' Del Bosco Chardonnay Bennett had picked from his extensive wine cave just for the occasion. This gave Johnny an opportunity to say something but he never said a word, just sat there, still as a mouse. He had his eyes closed. Tired as he was, Johnny went to his bathroom before going to bed. A boy couldn't make it through an evening like that just on dinner. What he needed was a drink. Those bastards don't know everything, he thought. He remembered something he'd heard one of his mother's lovers say and changed it to suit the occasion: "Age will be served, but youth has its privileges." He grabbed around under the sink behind the Windex and Comet and came up with the bottle he'd seen Uncle Bennett's maid Millie sneak from and dusted it off.

He poured out a good two fingers in a glass and drank it down. Neat.

. . .

Bennett found Maggie sitting at the dressing table in the suite at the mansion that was always reserved for her. He smiled at her, patiently, serenely. He commented about the weather, about how nice the golf course looked at dawn, how he almost had a hole in one, how nice the dinner was, how attentive Johnny was to the pastor.

"Take care of my little boy," she said, finally interrupting him.

"Don't worry about a thing," he told her.

"I'm not. I have my insurance."

"Insurance?"

"Yes, I wrote it all down. It took me months, but once I was diagnosed I knew I had to do it. To protect Johnny."

"To protect him?"

"From you."

"How can you say that?"

"How could I *not* say that?"

"I've spent thirty years making amends – "

"I know. Well, just so you don't stop, so you don't forget what happened, I wrote it all out and I sent it to someone I trust. I told Johnny if you give him any trouble, he's to call that person. Then the envelope will be opened. That person will know what to do."

"How could you do that? How can you do that to me, to us?"

"You've made my life comfortable for me, Bennett. But that's all."

"I've always been there for you."

"You can say that again." She looked away, growing more frustrated with him with each moment.

Bennett remained silent, listing in his mind all of the things he had done for her in the name of love. She was eight, he was fifteen when it started and it lasted three years.

I was outside, playing. I guess I must have fallen asleep. Suddenly he was over me, his huge eyes staring down. I could feel his eyelashes on my face and they were tickling me... I didn't know what it was but it felt kinda good. He began to run his fingers through my hair. I'd never really had anyone touch me like that before except my mother... I knew there was something wrong but, I don't know, I liked it. He just kept repeating, "You're so beautiful." Then I got nervous and embarrassed, and tried to get up. And he started to laugh, and then he was sort of pulling me down, pinning me to the ground, and I heard this screaming and it was me, and then I started to hear my clothes rip. Now I was scared, and hoped nobody would find us because I was so embarrassed.

Long before being on her deathbed, which approached faster than any of them could have anticipated, Maggie had revealed her biggest secret. If it did not explain everything, at least it illuminated some of it.

To Bennett, their secret was vague, indistinct and shadowy, a half-remembered dream. But he did remember a time when he bought her ice cream and took her to a playground. As they were leaving, he swung her up from the ground and he kissed her cheek and savored her palm against his back, a touch so gentle it made his eyes burn with sudden tears.

"It's so funny, really," she said in a faint voice.

"Funny?"

"Yes, how you were always there. That morning, just before Johnny was born, that last hour or so before it was all over, I thought, if I live through this, I can live through anything; that nothing would ever be as hard as that." She looked into the mirror and up at her brother again, her face puffy with weariness. "I want to know what you were thinking." Her voice grew stronger. "I want to know." What she remembered was the moment of birth; the surprising violence of it, the vividness of color, the blood everywhere, the boy blue-gray looking like something unearthly. What Bennett did remember was being so choked with fear it was as if she was in mortal danger and he might lose her. And now that time had come. Gathering her hair, fine as a baby's now, behind her shoulders, he weighed it delicately in his hands with his eyes closed. Maggie held her breath, waiting for his answer.

He let go of her hair, letting it fall without a sound against her shoulders. "I can't remember what I was thinking," he said, and quietly left the room.

Maggie began combing her hair again. Her brother had become even more contemptible to her. She had never truly hated anyone; this was something remarkable. With a little effort, she could almost feel sorry for him, a man who'd let his whole life slip through his fingers. He devoted himself to making money, as if to prove a point. And now this Good News business. It was pitiful, really. She thought how there had been many women, all dismissed as not being good enough. How sad that there was only one girl good enough for Bennett, and that was his little sister.

9

"I hate this place."

"Johnny, where are you?" Steve held the phone tightly as he got up and quietly shut the door of his study.

"In Palm Beach, at my Uncle Bennett's. I hate Uncle Bennett."

"Palm Beach? I thought you were in London."

"Mom's sick. She's real sick."

"I'm sorry – "

"Uncle Bennett has nurses, everything." He held back a sob. "But I don't think – "

There was a prolonged silence. Finally, Steve asked, "Johnny? What's wrong?"

"Oh Steve, please come down here. Please come get me. I miss you so much."

"I miss you too."

"I hate this place. Come down, please."

"But I can't come right now. There's exams, and – "

The phone went dead. Steve could not call Johnny back, he didn't have the number. He shut his eyes to hold back the tears. What had he done? For weeks he had wanted to call Johnny, to speak to Johnny, to hold him, kiss him, caress him, fuck him. And now he had failed him. Johnny needed him and he refused him. Finally, the tears came. He couldn't help it.

Susan knocked and burst into the room, saw her agonized husband sitting at his desk, still holding the phone. She wanted to know what was wrong.

As usual, Steve remained stoic. "Trouble at school. Kids these days – "

But the kids were not the problem, Susan somehow realized. It was her husband who had the problem. The students were caught up in the frantic stillness of preparation for finals. There was a hushed tension in the corridors, the packed silent libraries, the rooms stunned by collective worry. Many students already suspected their grades could not be saved by final exams, and that their hoped-for grade point average would slump well below what was needed to get any scholarships.

Now among all these struggling, terrified young people, Steve alone walked the corridors with his heart soaring. Spring break would see Susan taking the girls to visit their grandmother and Steve had formed a plan. While ordinarily he would look forward to some peace during the recess, he knew solitude would bring only more thoughts of Johnny. He had still not heard again from the boy. He had gone so far as to check for Bennett Lawrence's number in the Palm Beach phone directory. His phone was unlisted. Then he realized of course the number would be unlisted; Bennett was at one time one of New York's most successful developers. He had retired to Florida but still maintained offices in New York. Steve's plan was to go to into the city, present himself to someone in authority as Johnny's teacher and counselor and have them contact the boy for him.

10

Other than the times when his mother was awake and ready to talk, Palm Beach had become a place of torment for Johnny.

Bennett took it upon himself to set up a rigid schedule for the boy: studies at his school books from nine to noon, then a swim, followed by lunch. By then, Bennett would be back from his round of golf at the country club ready to quiz Johnny on what he had studied earlier. This regimen was to Johnny far worse than actually being in school.

Then Bennett decided that this time would be an ideal one for Johnny to get his driver's license. He took the boy for a drive in the oldest of the two Cadillac Fleetwood Broughams he owned. Johnny couldn't tell the difference between the two huge cars but Bennett assured him the white one was three years older than the yellow one. Once satisfied that Johnny knew how to handle himself behind the wheel, Bennett began coaching the boy for the test. Still, that wasn't enough. There had to be time in driver's education, and every day Johnny would be driven to the school. This was even more frustrating because the instructor was a woman. There was a male instructor at the school, a rather attractive young man, but he was busy.

Johnny's sexual frustration during this period was unprecedented for him. His nights and early mornings were filled with his memories of Jimmy and Steve, with a few memorable bouts with Luke thrown in for good measure. There was one consolation, although it was a meager one. The gardener at the mansion across the street was a beautifully built Latin in his late twenties and Johnny would stand at his second-floor window while the stud pruned the bushes and mowed the lawn in the muggy, eighty-degree heat of the afternoon. He took Bennett's binoculars from the living room and used them to get a better look at the man. His blue work shirt was soaked with sweat and rolled up to his elbows, showing his tanned, muscled forearms and large strong hands. His unbuttoned shirt gaped open, exposing his well-muscled chest beneath curly black hair. His long legs were hugged casually by well-worn Levis. He moved about with consummate grace. The fact that he tended to the yard alone made him even more attractive, as if he was saying he didn't need anybody. But Johnny knew the man needed *somebody* for at least one thing: sex. No man like that would go for long without it, Johnny thought. He put down the binoculars and dropped his shorts to the floor. He often stood there stroking his erection, imagining what it would be like to run his hands across every inch of that tight body, to take that penis in his mouth and suck it to orgasm. The vision of the man standing before him, Johnny on his knees, fucking his face with what had to be a monster dick quickly brought Johnny off.

So desperate was Johnny for closeness to a man that, on occasion, dressed only in his white Speedos, he would go over to the laborer as he was loading his equipment into his rig and ask him some off-the-wall questions. The man, who said his name was Jose, spoke broken English and seemed to be very shy. Up close, Johnny found the stud even more attractive and, one day, Johnny could feel his dark eyes penetrating Johnny's Speedos as Johnny turned to pick up a loose branch, exposing his buttocks. When he handed Jose the branch, Jose was smiling. Johnny looked away, feigning indifference, but felt his cock begin to harden. As he scurried across the street, he turned to look behind him and saw Jose was leaning against his truck, smiling broadly as he broke the fallen branch in half.

. . .

Usually, by late afternoon, Maggie was ready to see Johnny. He would go to her when Millie served tea and quietly sit with his mother and listen to her.

She was his captain, laying out the line of march. "If you don't learn anything else from me, Johnny, learn this."

Drawing herself up, she created a hush into which she let the next words fall. "No matter what happens to you, you *can't afford to let it show*."

Now Johnny was listening hard. He knelt beside the bed and smiled at this beautiful woman. He knew his mother had, for whatever reason, always understood everything.

"Listen," she said, "the worse things are, the better you have to look. You see, it's not what happens to you that makes the difference, it's the way you handle it."

Johnny waited for some more orders. But Maggie had given all she had to give. "That's all," she said. "That's all you have to know."

Johnny dropped his head into his mother's hands and she caressed his hair. "After I change, we're going shopping."

"Shopping," Johnny muttered, holding back the tears. "Of course we will. We'll go shopping."

The next day, when the doctors said the time was at hand, they came and went from her room – Bennett, Johnny, the servants, the Pastor – holding flowers, candy, new bedroom slippers, anything to take her mind off dying. But in her mind she had already left them.

Confused by the suddenness of change, Johnny told Bennett he was going shopping. As he accelerated onto the street from the driveway, he saw Jose's rig pulling away. He had no intention of following it, but that's what he ended up doing, all the way to West Palm Beach and beyond, to a trailer park in a seedy part of town. Jose made no attempt to lose his stalker; rather, he slowed so that the white Cadillac would be able to catch up with him if Johnny had to stop at a traffic signal. By the time the truck stopped at the far end of the trailer park,

Johnny was desperate, pre-cum already staining his tight white walking shorts.

Jose got out of the truck and slammed the door. Johnny pulled up behind the rig and turned off the ignition. Jose passed the Cadillac without saying a word. Johnny followed.

Jose unlocked the door of his trailer and left it open. Johnny tentatively entered the darkened room. The air conditioning was on full blast and Johnny shivered.

"Close the door," Jose instructed. He was standing in the tiny kitchen, opening a can of beer.

Johnny did as he was told.

"Something wrong at the house today?" Jose asked, carrying the beer into the living room where Johnny was still standing by the door. "Many cars."

"Yes, my mother died."

"I sorry. She very sexy. I see her pictures on the TV."

Tears started to flow from Johnny's eyes.

"But you even sexier," Jose said, running his hand down Johnny's arm.

Johnny smiled. He remembered what his mother had said and wiped away the tears. "She's in a better place now."

"And you are here, at Jose's. Why you at Jose's?" The Latin took a long drag on the beer.

Johnny stared at his sneakers. "I just wanted to be with somebody."

Jose put his arm around Johnny's tiny waist. "Well, now you with somebody. You with Jose."

Jose reached over and found Johnny's hand. He brought his hand to his crotch. There was no mistaking that under his jeans Jose had a mammoth dick. He pressed Johnny's hand onto that mound of flesh, then, leaving Johnny's hand to its excited explorations, he peeled off his shirt and let it drop to the floor.

Jose's beefy pecs held coffee-colored nipples that stood erect as Johnny's fingers grazed them. Johnny felt the wisps of damp black hair in the hollow under his arm. He brought his hand back to the ridges that ran across his stomach, then headed down to the heat between his legs.

Jose finished his beer and tossed the can into the kitchen. He let out his breath slowly.

Johnny felt the cock. It was hard. Terribly hard. It was pretty obvious that Jose wanted this just as much as Johnny did.

Johnny roughly jerked Jose's jeans down around his ankles, spread his thighs, and knelt between his legs. Johnny thumped the big dick with his nose and rolled it over his eyes. He pressed soft wet kisses against the thick, fleshy base and ran his tongue flat against it, up and down the sides, as it stretched and jerked about. Jose ran his fingers through Johnny's hair as the boy revelled in the exquisite, satiny texture of Jose's delicate shroud. When Jose's cock was fully extended, the pink glans blossomed out of its sheathing skin. His balls hung close to the base of his dick, one on each side, and the pink and brown skin of his scrotum was tight with expectation. Johnny marvelled at it; he had never seen such a huge prick. It was so large that it was, in fact, pretty ugly, but Johnny loved it.

Johnny put his lips around the massive cock and bathed the entire length of it with his tongue, pausing to lavish extra attention to the cockhead. He sucked hard and fast, savoring the salty taste of the cockhead and milking pre-cum from the slit. Every time he went down on Jose he inhaled deeply the warm and pungent aroma rising from between his legs. He let up just long enough to take the heavy balls in his mouth, bathing them in saliva and coaxing them to release their cum, then licked the soft and tender skin between his scrotum and thighs, until Jose pleaded with him to suck him some more.

Johnny's lips were stretched thin around the cock and he felt its heat on his tongue as he ran rings around his glans, causing Jose to squirm and moan. Johnny felt its heat on the back of his throat as he took him in and buried his lips in his pubic hair.

It didn't take Johnny long to bring him right to the edge. Jose was bucking and moaning, grabbing at his head, pushing Johnny down on his cock. Johnny felt his balls draw up tight against the root of his shaft and heard his gasps become more insistent.

Jose shoved his head into his crotch at the same instant that he thrust his dick deep into Johnny's throat. A strangled moan, then he exploded in the boy's mouth. A torrent of cum spurted out, filling Johnny past overflowing. Cum trickled from the corners of Johnny's mouth as he sucked the last creamy drop from Jose's dick.

Without saying a word, Jose pulled his sopping cock from

Johnny's mouth, hitched up his jeans and walked to the back of the trailer. Johnny leaned against the door, his hand on his own erection, his eyes closed. He could hear water running. He got up and made his way to where Jose was showering. On his right he saw an unkempt double bed that filled the room. He took off his shorts and lay face down on the bed. His hand went to his cock and he played with himself, his head pushed into the pillows. He heard the shower being turned off and then Jose entering the room. Johnny raised up onto his knees. Jose snickered and reached under the bed. He took a tube of Vaseline and squirted some on his cock and began stroking it. Soon it was erect again and Jose climbed on the bed. He dabbed some of the grease on Johnny's puckered hole, then got into position.

Jose began by rubbing his dick up and down Johnny's ass-crack, and Johnny's mind put images to the sensations he felt: the swollen, red head sliding past his hole, and the ridge, adding friction as it slid back. He imagined all the times he had snuck looks at that cock, packed into the dirty work jeans, a tantalizing mound that he never thought he would get to see, let alone touch. Now that thick shaft was grazing his tight, puckered butt, wanting to punch through the ring of muscle and plunge itself deep up inside him. Johnny began to loosen up, and with a long growl of satisfaction, Jose slid into the boy. Johnny cried out, jacking off furiously as first the head then an inch or so of the shaft entered him. "Oh, yeah," he groaned. This was what he had been needing since he came to Florida.

"Easy, baby, easy," Jose cooed.

Johnny could feel the fur on Jose's legs graze his ass-cheeks and thighs as he put his cock in to the hilt. He started pumping faster and his growls became shorter. Johnny felt like he was on fire, like this fuck was the greatest he'd ever had and he just couldn't stand any more. He started to jerk and squirm in spite of Jose's grip on him.

"Oh, yeah. *Oh,* yeah. Uh, huh." Jose's voice was deep and gravelly. He was pounding so violently now that Johnny was nearly hitting the wall with his head. It was more than the boy could stand. Flailing his legs as much as he could in that position, he shot out several long streams of cum. Jose roared and shoved his cock into Johnny with a horrendous jab, and

Johnny felt warm squirts way up in his gut. Jose backed up, and jabbed again. And again.

Everything became a blur for a moment or two; Johnny felt weak and lightheaded. Jose remained inside him, but he was still. All Johnny heard was his heavy breathing.

Finally Jose slid out, and gently laid the bulk of his body across Johnny's back. Jose caressed his shoulders and kissed his neck. "You feel better now?" he whispered.

"Oh, yes," Johnny moaned. "Oh, yes."

11

The hustler's brutal skill was bringing orgasm up from Steve's loins quicker than Steve had expected.

Sensing Steve was near, the hustler murmured encouragement and worked faster at him.

At that instant the phone rang. "Damn."

It was too late. The final spasm had come, but the shock of the sudden noise had ruined his pleasure. Steve cursed himself for not having unplugged the phone. He had not expected it to ring tonight. He had left the number at the Summit Hotel with the secretary at Bennett Lawrence's office, telling her he would be staying overnight, then returning to Rhode Island. He had underestimated the efficiency of a millionaire's secretary.

"Yes?" he said irritably into the receiver, looking down at the young man who had just sucked his cock.

"Steve?"

It was Johnny, calling back at last.

Steve listened for a moment, through the halting breaths of his wasted orgasm.

Then all at once he turned pale.

Johnny was telling him his mother had died and he would be returning to Manhattan with his uncle for the memorial service. Steve went to the desk, took some notes, then hung up the phone. For a moment he seemed lost in thought, his eyes on the night sky outside the window.

Then he glanced back at the bed and the hustler. The young man looked at once resigned and reproachful. He knew his performance was forgotten now. Tragedy had eclipsed pleasure.

"Put your clothes on," Steve said. "Go now." The command in his voice was not without its note of sympathy. The hustler had done his best, after all. And it had started out so right. Earlier, Steve had gotten an irresistible urge to find the gay bar he remembered from years ago. While he was in college and still with Roger, he had wanted to visit one, just to see what it was like. Still it was difficult to get up the nerve to actually enter the place. He walked down the street but kept going right past the door, too nervous to actually open it. Now, tonight, alone in the city, he decided that it was time to stop being silly and to take control of his life. He took a deep breath, and pulled open the door to the bar. When he stepped through it, he felt as if he were moving slowly through water. The blood pounded in his ears and he actually felt dizzy for a moment. Then his eyes adjusted to the dim lights and he looked around. Amazingly, it looked no different from any bars he had been in before, except that all of the patrons and the staff were men.

He ordered a drink. The jukebox was playing "Your Love Is So Good to Me" by Diana Ross; it was so loud he sought a quiet corner. Trying to act as cool as possible, he sat down at a small table. It was difficult; for his stomach was in knots, and he had to take a deep breath and try to stop his hands from shaking. Every time he picked up the glass, he thought he might drop it. He didn't want to be a hunter, but at the same time, he couldn't help but return the glances that came his way.

Eventually a young man came by and looked at the empty stool on the other side of the table. "You waitin' for someone? he asked.

"No, I'm not."

"Mind if I sit down then?"

Hardly believing his own newfound calm, Steve said, "Please do," and watched as his new companion slid onto the stool across from him. The young man seemed eager to please, and after two drinks, Steve was ready to leave.

Now Steve found a hundred-dollar bill in his wallet and threw it on the desk as the hustler pulled his jeans on. Watching him dress, Steve's heart sank. The hustler, who said his name was Ken, was in his early 20s, long-haired, dark-eyed, attractive in a brutish sort of way, and wonderfully skilled at fellatio. But he wasn't Johnny.

Ken opened the door a few inches and turned to Steve, his hand still on the knob.

"I hope everything'll be okay," he said, moving into the hallway.

Steve got up and stood close to him, prepared to watch him go down the corridor to the elevator. The look in Steve's eyes had changed somehow, seeming to hold the hustler back, even as his position urged him to go through the door.

In his white jeans, the hustler was a studly apparition in stark contrast to the dim hallway. Steve stepped towards him. "It wasn't you. It's just that his mother died and he needs me and I'm not there. And I'm so lonely without him."

"Lonely," Ken murmured, a husky note in his voice. "I know what you mean."

Something wise in his words stopped Steve cold. The door opened wider, an inch, then another.

"Life can be awfully cruel sometimes," Steve said. "It can happen to any of us."

Once again Steve was deep under the spell that had taken possession of him earlier in the bar. And again it was simply impossible to resist. He wanted so much to hold someone, to have someone hold him at that moment. But this was just a hustler. Still he did not know where he was going to find the strength to let this quick and easy sex go.

To Steve's enormous relief, Ken came back into the room and the door closed slowly until the lock clicked shut.

Ken's hands slipped to Steve's waist, and with the subtlest of movements he was receding into the room, drawing Steve after him. Steve moved like a sleepwalker, his gaze fixed on the stud's perfectly shaped lips, which were curved in the shape of a smile. He tried to reach out to kiss them, but Ken began moving away. Steve followed him deeper into the room. Ken looked back at him and Steve saw his smile curl a bit more.

At last, in front of the rumpled bed, Ken stopped Steve with two hands on his shoulders and kissed him deeply, hungrily. The smooth inquiring tongue reminded Steve of Johnny's in his mouth, caressing and inflaming. Ken's hands rested on his ribs, his hips shoving the hot bulge of his sex against Steve as he swayed with him in the shadows.

What happened next was the greatest culmination of ecstasy and frustration since that first time with Johnny. Steve remained shy and delicate, slowly letting the hustler kiss him again, and then again, allowing him to touch more and more of him, so that the stud was always the aggressor.

It was his little shrug of acquiescence that allowed Ken's hands once more to enfold and caress his cock, pulling his hips forward onto his sex. And it was Ken's sigh as Steve tore at the buttons of Ken's shirt that told him he would be allowed to bend in worship: to kiss the hard pecs, suck on the nipples. As with Johnny, Steve was being driven mad with excitement.

Every step of the way the hustler was in control, encouraging Steve with a tremor, a returned kiss, a moan, until, despite Steve's fumbling, Ken's clothes had fallen away, his cock slapping hard against his belly.

At last Steve fell before the stud like his slave and, holding him by the backs of his muscular thighs, kissed his hairy stomach, his navel, his hips, and finally became hypnotized by the throbbing cock, oozing precum. He felt a small shudder along the insides of Ken's thighs. A harsh groan came from him, and Steve buried himself against the russet pubic hair before him.

Great sadness was overwhelmed by passion now. Steve was not entirely aware of the sequence of events as Ken pulled him down on the bed beside him and began making love to him. The whole hard length of the stud was caressing Steve all over now, gentle calves on his thighs, their loins pressed together.

And somehow, in all this madness of contact, Steve retained his shyness, yielding with hesitation to the hustler. He did not need to guide the hustler's cock inside his ass. Having Ken entering him was like going into a nether world of unbearable pleasure. Nothing in his life had ever been so perfect as Johnny welcoming his frantic thrusts, and now he was welcoming this virtual stranger. He remembered how much Roger said he had loved it when Steve fucked him. It was so right, somehow.

Steve was chagrined to be doing this at a time when his lover was suffering so greatly. But his shame only made the sexual pleasure all the more maddening. He loved the sensual grace of Ken's kisses, and the touch of his fingers as he became a heedless animal crouched atop him, pushing and groaning and working with all his might. Steve's hands now encouraged him, until at last Ken was torn by the final spasm, and his cum exploded into Steve.

Utterly spent, Ken fell atop Steve. Steve listened to the gasps of his exhaustion as his hands patted his back and shoulders. He lay in the thrall of his touch, his sweaty skin, his robust smell, and of the fresh smile he could even now feel on his lips as Ken once again brought them to Steve's erection. In moments, Steve was coming and Ken held his cock and squeezed the last drops of cum onto Steve's belly.

But Steve's mind again returned to Johnny. Ken was good, but he loved Johnny. He would do anything, risk anything to have him again. Without that hope his future would be death. It was that simple.

Ken got up, a studly, statuesque marvel slipping like a ghost through the darkness, and returned a moment later with a wet towel. He handed it to Steve and then got dressed. Looking in the mirror as he combed his hair, the hustler said, "That'll be another hundred."

12

Steve had told the school he was attending a friend's funeral. But he didn't go to Maggie Lawrence's memorial service. Instead, he again rented a room at the Summit and then got a cab to take him to the Lawrence penthouse on the upper east side. Johnny was waiting in front of the building and came running to the car when he saw Steve.

The half-hour ride to the hotel was agonizing for both of them. They could only hold hands in the cab, and then only discreetly. Once alone in the elevator, they kissed until they reached the seventeenth floor. In the room, Steve pulled the curtains and Johnny went to the bathroom. Over the sound of Johnny peeing, Steve offered the boy a drink.

"I could sure use one," Johnny said.

Steve poured two shots of vodka into two glasses over ice. He added a bit of vermouth to his, a shot of vermouth to

Johnny's. "I only have vodka."

"That's fine," Johnny said, coming from the bathroom. He had left his pants unzipped and sagging. Johnny sipped the martini, pursed his lips. "Wow, I needed that."

Steve had turned shy again, eager for Johnny, but also wanting to take his time, to savor their time together as he was savoring his drink. Johnny went to the bed and, after setting his drink on the nightstand, took off his clothes. Steve stood across the room by the bureau watching the boy. He was again astounded by the youthful beauty before him. And tears came to his eyes at the sight of Johnny's ass. As he sipped his martini, Steve drank in the sight. No matter how many times he had seen Johnny nude, he was still transfixed.

He now gulped his drink and set the empty glass on the bureau. Undressing as he moved, he slowly walked across the room. Johnny got into the bed and Steve cuddled against him for a long while as the liquor warmed his insides. The feel of Johnny's young body against his was so natural and wholesome that some of his fear was assuaged. How could this perfect experience of love, this holy fulfillment be wrong?

He did not know how long they stayed that way, with Johnny's moist lips placing tender kisses on his chest, his fingers stroking his erection softly. He only knew that in what seemed no time at all just the boy's feathery touch was making him come. Johnny's mouth went to the shooting prick, sucking, licking, sucking some more.

"Oh, Steve, I've missed it so much." He brought his cum-slickened lips to Steve's and they kissed. Steve crushed the boy to him. His breath was hot against Johnny's ear, and Steve's silky, dark hairs on his sinewy forearms tickled against the boy's bare skin. All the while, Johnny squirmed against his hard body in agonized horniness, begging Steve to fuck him. Finally Steve could contain himself no longer. He cupped Johnny's ass. His long fingers traced the crack, coming to rest at the puckering asshole. Steve tickled and probed, and when his finger slipped up inside of the boy, Johnny made no protest. Steve flipped him over so that he was on his hands and knees on the bed. Steve began kissing his ass and sticking his tongue inside. Johnny moaned, "I've missed this so much."

At last Steve mounted him and began entering him. Johnny

didn't cry out, despite the sharp pain; he was lost in the purely sensual pleasure of the entry. Soon Steve was bucking and grunting, and his arms tightened around the boy's chest, pulling him back against his heaving body, sending his cock in to the hilt. Johnny jerked himself off, feeling Steve's balls slap against his ass, his vodka-breath on his neck, the hairy bulk of him pressed against his back. Johnny whimpered helplessly as the cum splattered on the hotel's bedcover.

Steve rolled him over and, in a single, gut-wrenching thrust, entered him again. Steve spread the boy's legs apart, baring his asshole to his will. His arms tightened around him. Johnny put his hands on Steve's back and started to trace the curves of bone and muscle slowly, feeling the heat of his skin beneath his hands. He ran his fingers up to where Steve's closely cropped hair had been shaved on his neck, brushing his fingertips along the line where skin met hair. He could feel Steve shiver as he did this.

Leaning down, Steve took one tit between his lips, fluttering his tongue over it lightly and cooling it by blowing on it. He gently moved his mouth over his mound, slipped his tongue into his armpit, licked and sucked at the tiny damp hairs. When he drew away, he saw that Johnny was still looking at him. Gripping him around the waist, Steve kissed him as he slammed into his ass.

Johnny began to whimper almost immediately, and as Steve fucked his ass harder and harder, Johnny let out groan after groan, his voice rolling through the dimly lit hotel room. Johnny took every beat of Steve's prick with another whimper of pleasure. As Steve jacked the boy off, his head was swimming from the heat of it all, and after several more pumps of his cock he started to blast away inside him. Johnny came too, his sphincter tightening around the still-spewing cock as he came, and Steve felt his body convulse. Spent, Steve lay next to Johnny on the bed. Johnny kissed his stomach and began to lick his lover clean.

Suddenly, a whisper of reproach was in Johnny's ear. "You have to go. Your uncle'll be worried."

"And your wife..." Johnny spat. "Don't forget how worried your wife will be."

With shaking hands, Johnny put on his clothes. He was

crying. He did his best in the bathroom to wash Steve's marvelous scent off himself. At the door, he hugged Steve close, intimately close, pelvis pressed to his, arms curled passionately around his back. Steve could feel Johnny's heart beating in his chest. His hands furled his hair, losing themselves in its magic softness as he kissed him goodbye.

He searched for words that would tell him how he felt, but they seemed ugly and insufficient after what had just happened between them. He wiped a tear into Johnny's cheek and Johnny's smile, warm and languid, reappeared. "I have good news, Steve. Uncle Bennett says I can go back to Rhode Island to finish the semester. But then he's selling the place and I'll have to go somewhere else next year."

"It's wonderful that you'll be coming back, even for a little while."

"Yeah, and see if you can fix it so I have to spend the summer there making up all the work I've missed."

"I don't see that as a problem."

Hearing this news lifted Steve above all care or worry. He held in his arms the most beautiful boy in the world – and he was coming back to Rhode Island.

13

So anxious was Steve to see Johnny that he arrived at the shore an hour early, only to find a strange car in the driveway. At first he drove by, then he came back, waited. Finally, he saw Johnny, dressed only in skimpy yellow shorts, leave the house with another boy. The other boy was taller, older, dark, attractive, but mean-looking. He wore blue jeans and a white T-shirt. Johnny and the boy kissed briefly and the older boy got in his car, a sixties vintage Chevy coupe, and started the engine. Steve sped away, waited a few minutes, then went back.

"I saw you down the road. Why didn't you drive in?" Johnny asked when Steve finally rang the bell.
"I think that's obvious."
"Oh, you mean Luke?'
"If that's his name."
Johnny nodded. "He's a friend of mine from when I lived in New York. He's going to a special school in Boston now and was passing through on his way back home. He just stopped to say hello, that's all."
"Oh."
Johnny let Steve into the foyer and closed the door. "Aren't I allowed to have any friends?"
Steve didn't answer as he followed Johnny into the living room. Finally he said, "I'm sorry. I'm being silly."
"Yeah, you are. But there's a lot about me you don't know, Steve."
"Oh?"
"Yeah, I'm a whore. You probably would say slut. Yeah, I'm a *terrible* slut. It runs in the family."
"You're not."
"Oh, yes I am."
"If you say so." Steve wanted a drink desperately. He glanced about the room.
Johnny went on, pacing back and forth. "It's just a fact. I never promised you I'd never *ever* have sex with anyone else."
"No, you never did."

"Then what are you getting so upset about?"

"I'm not upset," he said, clasping his hands behind his back to keep them from shaking.

"Yes, you are. You want me all for yourself."

"No – " He started toward the kitchen. "What I'd like is a drink."

"No booze here, Steve. Nelly sees to that. I can't hide anything from Nelly." He chuckled. "Can you imagine, my uncle has a maid named Nelly?"

Steve stopped and walked back to Johnny. "I better go – "

"You came to fuck. Don't you want to fuck?" Johnny reached out to him. "Luke's fun but you're better."

Steve backed away. "Why are you talking to me like this? I don't want to hear this."

"What do you want to hear, Steve, that you're the only one?"

Steve threw up his hands. "I can't believe I'm having this discussion with one of my students."

Johnny plopped into a chair. "There you go, like all the others. First of all, I'm not just one of your students any longer."

"No, but you're still just a teenager."

"What's age got to do with it? I was born old. Mom always said so."

"Age has a lot to do with it."

"Please don't change on me, Steve. What I have liked about you is that you treat me like I was somebody."

"You are *somebody*. Believe me."

"I mean, you treat me like I was an adult. A real person, not just a kid that has to be bossed around. You treat me like Mom treated me."

Steve slapped his hands together. "Oh, god, Johnny I'm sorry. You miss her terribly. This has all been very difficult for you. That's what it is."

"What *what* is?"

"Why are you acting like this?"

Johnny jumped up, started to go up the stairs. "How am I acting?"

Steve followed the boy. "Like a whore."

"So it's back to that again." Johnny shook his head. "But I

am a whore."

As Johnny bounded up the stairs, his ass was in Steve's face. "Okay, then, whore, let's fuck."

"Let me take a shower first."

"No. I want you with his sweat on you."

"His cum up my ass, you mean."

"All right," Steve said, grabbing him, pulling him down on the landing. He tore Johnny's shorts away and shoved his finger in the boy's ass. It was wet, ready. The kid who had just left had indeed fucked him. Steve hurriedly unzipped his chinos and pulled out his cock. What had attracted him to Johnny in the first place was his sexual aggressiveness. And he had admired more than anything the boy's prowess. The only way to learn how to please a man the way Johnny did was to have many experiences. Steve could deal with the past, but confronting the prospect of competition in the present tense had unnerved him. Still, the boy was saying Luke was good but he was better. And Steve was determined to prove it once again.

"Oh yeah," Johnny murmured, watching intently as Steve parted his thighs and sunk his cock deep into his ass. It was a vigorous fuck for a few minutes, as Steve ran his tongue slowly up Johnny's neck to his earlobe. Already Johnny was responding, begging Steve not to stop. Steve nibbled gently, then darted his tongue in and out in a flurry of probes into the boy's ear. Steve lifted up and took Johnny's pecs in his hands, massaging them, then bringing his lips to the nipples, sucking them, teasing them. Johnny moaned and began writhing uncontrollably.

Slowly, generously Steve licked his way down Johnny's stomach, pausing at his belly-button to tickle it. His cock dropped from the asshole and Johnny lowered his legs. Steve repositioned himself between Johnny's velvety thighs and began flicking, licking, and lashing each inch of Johnny's erection. Johnny started to come, wave after wave of ecstatic bliss now overtaking him completely. He grabbed the head of wavy brown hair and drove Steve's face deeper onto his cock. Steve grabbed the tightened buttocks and plunged three fingers into the gaping asshole.

Finally Steve lifted his face away and was smacking and

licking his lips. Johnny pulled him down on top of him and Steve's erection slid into his asshole again. Johnny clutched at the hard-driving cock, realizing how extraordinary the fuck was, so different from the mechanical fuck Luke had given him that morning. Steve would withdraw most of his cock, then grind back in, building Johnny's desire to a fever pitch. Soon Johnny came again and this time Steve did too.

For a long while, they lay on the landing, Steve cuddling Johnny into his arms, nuzzling his ear and saying, "God, what a whore."

. . .

After the last bell, Johnny went to Steve's office. The door had been left partially open. He closed the door behind him and before he even lifted one box, ruffled through one drawer, he looked around the place for something to take with him. Something small. Something he could slip into his pocket without anyone noticing.

Not that it mattered, he realized, no one would've noticed anyway. And if they had, he didn't think they would've cared. Just as Johnny picked up a freshly sharpened pencil from Steve's desk, the door opened. It was another teacher, Mr. Allen. "What are you doing?"

Being in the office was a dangerous place, Johnny had learned long ago. If he didn't have any business to take care of going in, he got some before he could leave. It always seemed someone would give him something to deliver to someone, or there was an errand that needed to be run, and Johnny was always so trustworthy, they said. The teachers all thought Johnny was "a marvelous boy."

Now, making a big show of rolling back his sleeve to check his watch, Johnny answered he was waiting for Mr. Parker.

"He's gone."

"What?"

"He's gone."

"Really?" Johnny had seen Mr. Allen around the office a lot. He was in his early thirties, slim, good-looking, a nice guy, the kind who always filled the ink bottle in the ditto machine when he was done with it. Johnny wondered what he would be like to fuck. Mr. Allen slipped into the ditto room next to Steve's office. Soon the ditto machine was clunking away. Johnny consulted his watch again, and just for good measure, went to the door and checked the clock above the secretary's desk. He had nowhere to go but Mr. Allen was suspicious.

Mr. Allen came out of the ditto room, holding a sheaf of paper against his chest. "I said, he's gone."

"Oh, yeah, but for how long?"

"The rest of the day. He said he was taking his wife on a long weekend."

"Oh, okay," Johnny said, slipping a pencil from Steve's desk behind his ear and heading for the door.

While Nell drove, Johnny took the pencil from behind his ear and studied it. There was nothing extraordinary about its design. Faber-Castell American No. 2. It was yellow, with an eraser at one end and a fresh point at the other. This wasn't a mitt or anything terribly symbolic. Yet, to Johnny, it was an instrument of creation and was weighted with potential. Of course, like a metaphor, he couldn't actually write with it. Not this pencil. And he carefully stashed it in his notebook.

14

In her dream, they were dancing, but Susan kept stepping on his feet and the music was all wrong. "Wasting away in Margaritaville, looking for..."

"Susan!"

"Umm," she turned in her seat and slowly opened her eyes. His left arm rested on the steering wheel, his right hand caressed her.

"Susan, you're beautiful and I love you."

"I know you do," she said, reaching for his hand. "We've stopped."

"You've been sleeping the last fifty miles."

"I've been dreaming."

"Good dreams I hope."

"Strange!" She looked around her. "Where are we?"

"At the hotel. Finally. I'll go check us in," he said reaching for the door.

"Steve, darling – "

"Huh?"

"I do love you."

"I'll see if they a vacancy," he said planting a kiss on her forehead. He jumped out of the car, his white pants flapping against his bare ankles, taking two steps at a time toward the hotel lobby. Susan settled into the seat and closed her eyes.

After Steve tipped the young bellboy, far too generously Susan thought, they unpacked the liquor from the grocery bag and Steve went to get ice. When he returned to the room, he took off his pants and tossed them over the frayed upholstered chair. She had slipped into a silk negligee. They sipped vodka martinis on the small balcony and watched the sun go down over the lake.

Susan eased into his lap, placing her drink on the table that separated them. "I'm so glad you got this idea for a second honeymoon – "

"It's comfortable, isn't it?" Steve savagely shoved a finger in her cunt. She pushed him away. She wanted to take her time and tried to get up but he held her firmly and kissed her.

She finally pulled away, grabbed her glass and stood at the railing, finishing her drink, went into the room and made another. "You want any more?" she asked.

He followed her and encircled her in his arms kissing her neck. "No, and you've had enough." She set her glass down and turned, pressing herself against him.

"Let's go to bed," he said and lifted her in his arms and kissed her.

It was a short kiss. She pulled away again. Steve was refusing to take his time. Suddenly, the chenille bedspread looked llke she felt, faded and frazzled. Susan reached for the phone, called the babysitter. Everything was fine.

"No one said this was going to be easy. C'mon Susan..." He nuzzled her. He had stripped off his briefs while she had been calling. He had lost his erection. He brought her hand to it.

"No, Steve, I can't," she pulled away from him. "Look at this place. It's a dump. It's nothing like it was. Nothing is!"

"We were lucky to find any room at all."

She started to get up. "I hate it here."

"Don't pout. I hate it when you pout."

"I'm not pouting. I'm... I'm just frustrated."

"What happened? It started out so nice."

"When I see you nude, I can't stop thinking about you with somebody else. I just can't."

"It's always *somebody*." If she only knew, Steve thought. But then, if she did, it would really be over. "Have another drink," Steve offered.

He got up and fixed another martini for himself. Raising the glass, he said, "Cheers!"

"There's nothing cheery in this whole situation." She folded her arms and glared at him. "And getting boozed up won't help, Steve," she scolded.

"Neither will nagging," Steve said, dropping to his side of the bed. The mattress creaked.

"I'm not nagging."

"Methinks she protests too much."

"Oh, get out of your teacher mode."

"Hey, you used to love that. Now that it's a little tough..."

"Steve, it's more than a little tough. It's rotten."

She saw the hurt in his face, the same look when he failed to get tenure at the university, left and joined the public school system. "Why can't I please you?"

"You do."

"No, or you wouldn't be seeing somebody else."

"The somebody I'm seeing has nothing to do with us."

"So you admit it, you are seeing somebody."

"Correction: *was* seeing somebody. And not in the way you think."

"Oh?"

"No."

She got up, stood over him. "I want to leave."

"You're out of control," he said calmly. "I must say I'm surprised. It's a side of you I've never seen before."

"If I'm out of control, it's your fault." She stood over him as he sipped his drink.

"Of course," he smirked. "Everything's always my fault."

"I don't understand this at all."

The martinis finally had their effect. Steve had lost his

patience. "Okay, if you must know, the *somebody* I'm seeing is a man."

At first, Susan stood perfectly still. Then she slapped his face. The last of the vodka sloshed on his crotch. Unruffled, he placed the glass on the bed stand. She stood there, trembling, her hands on her face, sobbing. Steve reached up, grabbed her and tossed her on the bed. Then he mounted her, grinding himself into her, lifting her negligee. She gasped.

"No, I can't. Not now," she said softly, but her protests where smothered by his lips. His hands melted her anger, like always. But it was terrible; Susan cried all the way through it.

They checked out of the hotel early the next morning. Susan waited until they stopped for breakfast before bringing up the inevitable.

"How did it happen?" she asked finally, pushing away a half-eaten plate of eggs and sausage.

"It just did."

Steve knew Susan was fighting down two competing impulses in her gut, the first of total disapproval, the second of total fascination. He watched this conflict translate itself onto Susan's face and said, "It didn't mean anything."

Susan was silent for awhile, trying to understand what this situation meant. She had never been a promiscuous person. Steve, as far as she knew, never had been either. She stared at Steve's face across the table and looked for any perceptible signs of distress. There were none. Then she said, "How could it happen? I simply don't understand you."

He sighed. "Of course I'd never done anything like that before. It was strange – like a compulsion. Inevitable. Dangerous but compulsive. I don't know. I can't understand it myself. There was something explosive about the situation, the confrontation, something strangely...well, strange. Erotic."

Steve looked down at his hands gripping his coffee cup. He had never used the word erotic with Susan before. Using it was fun; he suddenly felt like he was lecturing on D. H. Lawrence.

Susan was devastated. She looked at Steve and he knew she couldn't understand him, couldn't contain what he had done in the relevant compartments of her brain. Her ideas of him had now been so radically altered that any coherent discussion about motivation and intent seemed utterly fruitless. But she wanted to know the details. Eventually, trembling, she asked, "So, how was he?"

Steve looked for a moment like he wasn't going to reply, then said, "Strange." He was silent for a long moment and then added, "How can we even discuss it? How can we talk about it? There's nothing to say."

Susan looked away. "So you won't be seeing him again?"

Steve nodded. He realized that it was as though nothing could be expressed between them which would make sense, which they could both understand. And yet something so incredible had happened. He felt sad, almost bitter, but in his heart he knew that the space that had sprung up between them, the vacuum, had now opened up and it was a positive space that could be filled with so many things; ideas, possibilities. He remembered something he had read once, "Words are like gifts, some people are generous and some frugal," and decided to make himself a present by keeping quiet the rest of the way home.

15

After their weekend away, Susan got Steve to agree to see a marriage counselor. They went to Providence and saw a man highly recommended by one of Steve's former collegues at the university.

Steve liked the rotund Dr. Harris immediately; he appeared to be a thoughtful, kind man, talking to each of them separately, then together. In his session, after some preliminary discussion, Steve relaxed and felt no qualms about recounting his sexual history.

"Tell me about your sex life," Dr. Harris said. "When did you first experience sex?"

"When I was two or three. I actually remember getting this great feeling when I played with myself. I began playing around with girls when I was about eleven or twelve. Nothing heavy but lots of feeling and kissing."

"Did you like it?"

"Yes."

"Did you have anything sexually to do with males at that time?"

"Not unless you count circle jerks at camp, and then there was this kid at school who used to blow everybody."

"Did you like that?"

"Yes, but I didn't admit it, even to myself."

"Why not?"

"I didn't want to be thought of as queer. I didn't want to think of myself that way."

"How old were you when you had your first sexual encounter with a woman?"

"It was a gang-bang. My brother arranged it. He's three years older than me. He became a lawyer like my father. He's married, living in Arizona, and straight as an arrow. I haven't seen him in four or five years. He's been married three times, by the way, whatever that says.

"Anyway, at this party, I must have been tenth in line. I never saw the girl's face. She was kneeling up on a bed and taking it from behind. When I finished, my brother drove me home and told my father I was a man, and that made my father happy."

"But did it make you happy?"

"No. I'm terribly romantic when you get right down to it. The thing is, with a woman I have to *know* her. I have to care about her. Susan was the only one I have ever really cared about. We met in college. Her family has money, she has a good background. She was shy, had never dated much. It took us a long time before we had sex. Like I said, I have to care about a woman."

"Do you see that as a hang-up?"

"Yes, but it's a good one. It means I value sex with women."

"But not with men?"

"It's different with men. I was only with Roger. Except one time, when I was walking the dog in the park at night a couple of years ago. This guy approached me and we went into the bushes. He blew me. It was very exciting. He gave me his phone number, but I didn't call him back, and I stayed away from the park."

"Why?"

"I felt rotten afterwards. Because I enjoyed it I was sure that I must be a homosexual. There was no other way to look at it. Every book on the subject, every expert said that if a man engaged in homosexual acts, no matter how much heterosexual sex he enjoyed, he *was* homosexual. I hate the idea of being homosexual. A closet queen. I didn't feel homosexual. As a matter of fact, I didn't feel heterosexual. I just felt sexual. I wanted sex and I wanted *all* I wanted. It relaxed me. Made me feel better. I now realize that of course I was attracted to men and women from the beginning. Even in camp as a kid during the circle jerks I wanted the other boys, and I wanted them to want me. Of course I never admitted it."

"Until now."

"Yes. Now I can see I am bisexual. I think you have to have areas that are private to each person. It doesn't matter what it is. But you have to have something of your own private to you."

"What does Susan have?"

"I don't know. She has something, though; otherwise she couldn't have kept me so intensely interested all these years."

"Would you like to know what it is?"

"I would and I wouldn't."

. . .

Two days later, Steve went to see the therapist alone.

"Susan appears to be able to cope with this better now," Steve said.

"Yes, she seems to be doing well. But I don't know what she would think if she knew it was really a *boy* you're seeing."

"*Was* seeing."

"All right. But if Susan knew how old he was – "

"He was born old."

"I'm sure of that. But still he's a child and prone to foolishness. And you have your career to consider."

"Yes, this must all appear as if I'm the one who's prone to foolishness."

"And you see no way out of this foolishness, as you call it?"

"That's right. I want him every minute. When I don't see him I miss him terribly."

"Even though you know he is seeing others?"

"I'm afraid the fact of his cheating makes him even more desirable."

It was true. Steve's fantasies when he was masturbating and having sex with Susan now included mental images of Johnny with Luke.

"She wants to meet this man," the therapist said.

Steve shook his head. "What?"

"That's what she said. She wants to meet him. She doesn't look upon him as competition. He is giving you something you can't get from her. If it were another woman, like she thought it was, that would be something else, but *this* – "

"*This* is private."

. . .

"Fuck me in the ass," Susan pleaded that night, "if that's what it is that turns you on now."

"No, that isn't what it is."

Susan told Steve she couldn't even *imagine* two men having sex together, but she had heard that's what they did.

"Then what *is* it?" she asked.

"Stop this. I told you, it's over. You're ruining everything."

Their situation had gone from bad to worse. Steve thought Susan had began obsessing on the man her husband was seeing. At times, Steve was sure he was being followed. Then a colleague at school told him a man, a private investigator, was asking some of his associates questions about Steve. Steve feared Susan was spending her family's money on preparations for a messy divorce that could destroy him.

Finding Steve uncharacteristically moody and reluctant to meet him, Johnny abandoned the pretense of going to summer school altogether and followed Luke to New York. But before leaving, he got Steve to agree to come to the city as soon as he could arrange it.

16

When Johnny arrived at the penthouse, he was surprised to find Uncle Bennett in residence. Johnny made up an excuse for his own sudden appearance, saying he had come to the city to see a friend.

This infuriated Bennett. "It's time we talked," he said. If there was one thing Bennett had learned in the competitive world it was that one could not defeat people by hating them. Hatred brought them too close for one to control. Only by viewing them from afar, like insects surveyed from a great height, could he force their plans and destroy them without putting himself at risk.

Bennett's meddling in his sister's affairs began with her marriage to Jack. His hatred of Jack was so severe that he had gotten careless. He had Jack investigated and presented him with the evidence he had gathered. He also presented him with an ultimatum: either go back to Hollywood to his wife and son or be destroyed. The confrontation with Bennett was more than Jack could bear. No one, least of all Maggie, ever knew of their meeting.

Now Bennett was having Steve Parker investigated. He had been told by Nell about the unusual amount of "tutoring" Johnny was getting and sent detectives to Rhode Island. From the evidence they gathered, Bennett saw Parker as a man whose unnatural passion threatened to ruin him. He felt a mixture of contempt and pity for Steve, but was not about to confront him personally as he had Jack. No, as long as he was Johnny's guardian, he would work subtly by simply removing the temptation that had driven Parker to these acts.

Bennett insisted on meeting Johnny's so-called "friend." Johnny called Luke, who came right over. Bennett made them lunch and seemed satisfied that Johnny was not in New York to meet his older lover. He gave the boys money to go to the movies.

"You still do it?" Johnny asked Luke as they passed a couple of hustlers on the street.

"Sometimes, just to keep my hand in. But I'm too old for the street, man. Now I go to the bar."

The bar, as Luke called it, was Rounds on East 53rd. "You'll get in if you're with me, but for you to go alone, we'll have to get you a fake ID. "

"Okay," Johnny said.

. . .

Luke said the man at the bar was named Chet, but to Johnny it sounded more like "Cheat." Whatever his name, he spoke very little English. Luke seemed to know what the man wanted: two boys. This had never happened before. Luke wasn't sure he wanted to be in the same room with Johnny while the boy was being fucked. But when the man handed him a hundred-dollar bill as his bond, Luke acquiesced.

The man was staying at one of the diplomatic hotels and took them to his suite. In the bedroom, Luke touched Johnny's perfectly up-turned ass and made certain Chet admired it too. Chet sat on the other bed and watched while Luke ate Johnny's ass.

Johnny rubbed his swollen cock against Luke's lips. "Look at this, Chet," Luke gasped. And Luke studied the glistening rod of pleasure. Luke pursed his lips around it and sucked. Johnny looked at Chet while he was being blown. Chet was nodding.

At first Luke thought Chet was going to just watch them fuck, but suddenly he stood and started taking off his clothes. His neck, arms and chest were huge and well-muscled, the skin dark. Hair tufted from both armpits and from his groin and spread in an eagle-shaped design across his chest. His thighs were enormous, knotted with muscle; his uncut cock, which rose out of a mass of wiry black hair, was the size of a baby's arm.

"My, my," Luke said. Johnny was speechless.

Chet made more strange noises deep in his throat, and made a speech in a language that made no sense to them whatsoever. But Luke figured the man wanted Johnny and let Johnny get up. Chet moved up slowly, took Johnny by the waist, and gently pulled him close. He ran his fingers over the blond hair tumbled around his shoulders and smoothed his hands over the small patch of pubic hair, which was as blond as the hair on his head. He stuck a fat finger into Johnny's ass, as Johnny grasped his dick with his hand.

Chet withdrew his finger and smelled it. A smile appeared on his face, and Johnny found herself smiling back. Chet idly continued to stroke his member as the big hairy balls swung back and forth. Then he started to moan a little. He shifted from foot to foot and cupped the boy's ass, giving smart little tweaks to his nipples from time to time. Then the surprisingly smooth hands ran down Johnny's hard belly to his cock, and Chet's fingers went to work on his erection. Johnny began moaning with him and pulled him closer, all the while keeping a tight grip on Chet's enormous prick.

Chet picked him up and tossed him on the bed. Johnny lay down spread-eagle and waited while Chet hovered over him. Johnny began blinking wildly as Chet pulled his legs over his massive shoulders and, with a tongue that felt as wide as a washcloth, he licked and teased Johnny's anus. Pulling him by the hips, he took Johnny's buttocks in his hands and lifted him up to drive his penis right into him. Johnny let out a huge moan. The man was so large that for a moment Johnny thought he would pass out, but he wiggled and struggled to get comfortable. Finally it started to feel good, then damn good. Johnny wrapped his legs around the man's waist and caressed him with both hands.

Chet continued to mumble and moan in his strange language for about ten minutes of the most arduous fucking Johnny had ever experienced. Suddenly, Chet lifted up and pulled out. Johnny sighed. The man motioned to Luke and Luke climbed on, slamming his cock into Johnny.

Then Chet got behind Luke and entered him. It felt as if the man's cock reached right through Luke, and both men were fucking Johnny. Luke was grunting, making animal sounds Johnny had never heard from him before, and Johnny felt his cock stiffen and he gripped it hard with his anal muscles. As Luke shot his load into Johnny, spasms rocked his ass. At the same time, Chet came inside Luke, letting out a loud grunt that was almost a lion's roar, and the three of them shook together as one organism, desperately holding onto each other. Then they collapsed in a sweaty, exhausted heap.

On the street, Luke hailed a cab. Johnny was still shaking. In the cab, Luke handed him two hundreds. "Wow," Johnny said, "to be paid to get fucked like that."

"Only in New York," Luke said.

17

Johnny was desperate. For days, he tried to get Steve to come to New York. Finally he called him and told him he had to come, that he had some news he could only deliver in person. Finally Steve relented. He simply had to see Johnny. They agreed to meet at the Summit Hotel at nine o'clock the next evening.

Johnny told his uncle he was going to spend the night with Luke. So anxious was Steve to see Johnny he caught an earlier train and arrived in mid-town at six. He decided to have a drink before meeting Johnny. Steve entered the bar and saw Johnny immediately, but Johnny was with Luke and they were talking to a well-dressed man with gray hair and didn't see him. Steve stayed in the shadows, finding a stool at one of the little tables. It was seven o'clock and the place was packed.

He moved to the bar to refill his drink. It was then that Johnny finally saw him and left Luke and the other man at the bar. "You're early. You're always early."

"I didn't want to be late."

"I'm surprised to see you here."

"Likewise." Steve lead Johnny to the little table.

"I told you I was a whore."

"But you're also underage."

"Shhh," Johnny said, bringing his forefinger to his lips. "I'm too old for the street and too young for the bars." He placed a firm hand on Steve's thigh, stroking the fabric. "Loosen up, teach."

"Shhh!" Steve mimicked.

"Do you want me to stop?"

"No," Steve replied, so happy to see the boy he could hardly refuse him anything.

Johnny's hand ascended, grazing the hardness concealed below. He pulled Steve's jacket over it discreetly and they giggled over the naughtiness of the situation.

They chatted as Johnny continued stroking Steve. Johnny told Steve about the johns seated across from them, about the hustlers who cruised about. Johnny unsnapped Steve's trousers and eased the zipper down under the cover of his jacket, allowing his fingertips to skate over the head of the stiff cock, rolling a thumb over the creamy drop at its head, his head dropping to Steve's shoulder. Johnny wanted to look at it again. He briefly lifted the jacket and then turned his face up to Steve's. Their eyes locked in a gaze of desperation. Steve felt they were causing a scene. They had to leave.

In the gleaming elevator at the hotel, they were alone. Steve's hands roamed Johnny's body, forcefully, insistently, all the way up to the 17th floor at the Summit. Steve had become crazed, like a beast. Johnny opened Steve's pants and his cock sprung free. He sighed. Johnny's eyes, misty with desire, locked on Steve's. He wrapped his hand around the pulsating cock.

"Oh, God..." Steve moaned as Johnny dropped to his knees and began sucking it. The elevator doors were about to open. Steve pushed the boy away and turned to zip up his pants. No one was in the corridor. Steve circled the boy with his arms and pulled him against his chest. He caressed Johnny's hair, running his hands over his back, sending waves of anticipation shivering through the boy. He tilted his chin up to meet his face and his lips settled on Johnny's. Johnny whimpered and pressed himself even more insistently against his older lover. Steve held Johnny tighter and slipped his tongue into his mouth. The elevator doors shut and Steve broke free, leading the way to his room.

Steve pushed off his shorts and his cock sprang free again. Johnny came form the bathroom with his pants undone and started to undress, but Steve stopped him. "Let me do that." He caressed the nape of Johnny's neck while he removed his shirt. Then he got down on his knees and pulled the jeans down, his tongue flickering over him, tracing the tan line. The jeans fell in a pool at Johnny's feet and he gasped as Steve's fingers softly stroked his cock.

Johnny went to the bed and Steve kneeled over him, smiling gently as he parted the boy's thighs. Johnny arched himself up to meet Steve's embraces. His hands reached out to fondle his hair as Steve continued to explore every part of Johnny's body with his mouth. Trembling, Johnny took Steve's cock in his mouth and, as he flicked his tongue over the balls, he felt Steve's hands on his ears, clutching them as he groaned out his pleasure. Johnny took the cockhead completely in his mouth and as he slid the shaft in, he felt it grow more rigid and fiery. Steve arched to meet Johnny's lips. He let out a howl of pleasure as he got close.

Lying back, Steve gasped as Johnny climbed over him and impaled his ass on Steve's cock. His headlong plunges brought Steve off in moments. Leaving Steve's wilting erection in him, he played with his own cock, his eyes locked on Steve's, and came harder than he had in weeks.

18

Steve slept soundly and it was nearly noon when he awoke. Johnny was in the shower. When he came out, scrubbed and fresh, with an incredible hard-on, Steve blew him. Then they decided to go down to the coffee shop for breakfast.

"So, you never did tell me the news," Steve said after they had ordered. "Why did you have me come down here?"

"I wanted to say goodbye."

"Oh?"

"Uncle Bennett's letting me go live with my grandma."

"Where's that?"

"Los Angeles. Huntington Beach. That was my choice, either live with him and go to that 'Good News' school of his or live with grandma."

"Nice options, Palm Beach or Huntington Beach. Not everyone is so blessed."

"Will you come to see me?"

"I'd love to, you know that. I'll just have to figure out a way."

"You got down here, you can get out there."

"Well, I *am* a married man, remember."

Johnny looked away. "How could I forget?"

"I love my wife, Johnny."

"Yeah, I know. You're a bisexual. You love everything."

"I'll ignore that. Do you like your grandma?"

"She's crazy. I mean, she had my mother and my uncle. She'd have to be crazy, right?"

They took a cab to 42nd Street. New York was baking. Even the nightmare sounds of fire truck sirens were muffled by the heat; cops chewing gum hung around the sidewalks bartering with crime; athletes on skateboards livened up the traffic; narcotics adorned each corner of 42nd Street. New York was on parade.

"I'll miss this," Johnny said.

"You'll be back," Steve said.

They played games at the amusement arcade. Before they left, they went into the Quik Foto booth and had their picture taken. Steve handed the strip of four poses to Johnny. Johnny tore it in half. "Two for you, two for me," he said.

Steve shoved the pictures in his wallet, wondering just where he would hide them when he got home.

"I'd like to have you see me off but Uncle Bennett's taking me. He said he wants to make damn sure I get on that plane. We'll have to make our goodbyes at the hotel."

. . .

Back at the hotel, Steve disappeared momentarily through the bathroom door, then reemerged naked.

He looked at Johnny on the bed, nude, lifting his ass to him. Steve's body flushed again at the always breathtaking sight of him.

Johnny rolled over and looked up at Steve. "Say goodbye to it," Johnny begged, spreading his legs wide apart.

Steve didn't know quite how but he was determined to make this final fuck the very best they had ever enjoyed. He got on the bed between Johnny's thighs, kissing his moist skin, breathing in the smell of him, their earlier sex. Steve ran his hand over the smooth surface of Johnny's cheek. Johnny pulled Steve to him, kissing him passionately, their bodies again alive with the promise of the greatest pleasure either of them had known.

Johnny's eyes were bright, bold, and clear as he looked back into Steve's eyes. Steve smiled, not catching the thoughtfulness on Johnny's face, that he was preparing to say something. Before Johnny had a chance to say what was on his mind, Steve kissed him, and their bodies moved in tight against each other – strong arms, legs entwined.

Steve began gyrating his hips, grinding his cock against Johnny's crotch. Soon Steve began to sink to his knees, his tongue gliding down Johnny's smooth chest and hard abdomen as he went.

Johnny's cock was rigid now. After Steve took his first tentative jab at Johnny's dick, Johnny began to thrust his hips forward, fucking Steve's mouth.

Steve buried his face between Johnny's thighs, burrowing into the lad's ass with his tongue. Johnny's body began to writhe. He placed both hands on Steve's head, pulling him forward.

After a few moments, Steve lifted up and squeezed a large amount of lotion into his hand. He first greased his cock, then reached between Johnny's spread legs and greased his ass. Steve slid his fingers inside Johnny's hole. After Steve loosened him up with his fingers, he entered him, then began to pump slowly, soothing him with a probing kiss, building to an exciting staccato that had Johnny twisting and turning under the weight of his body. Steve came hard, shooting deep inside him over and over again.

Panting, Steve lifted himself up and straddled Johnny. Soon he was clamping his anus around Johnny's stiff prick, oozing pre-cum, sliding up and down on it. Within moments, Johnny was enjoying a thunderous orgasm that seemed to roar through every muscle of his body. Steve lifted up and Johnny's cock plopped out of his ass with an audible pop. Panting, he lay next to Johnny and closed his eyes.

Johnny sat up on an elbow and looked at him, eyes bright, amused, and a little guilty. "I'm sorry," he said, "for getting you in so much trouble with your wife."

"It wasn't your fault," Steve offered, kissing away the crease in the boy's forehead.

Johnny was silent, his face more serious than ever before as he suddenly lost himself in his thoughts. Steve felt the boy pull away from him, felt something shift between them as Johnny announced, "It's time for me to go."

"I know," Steve said, and kissed Johnny deeply, holding him. With a sigh, he hugged Johnny to him. How comfortable he'd become with this boy. "Damn, I'll miss you," he whispered as matter-of-factly as he could, a softness in his voice. He inhaled the smell of their sex still lingering on the boy's young body.

Overcome himself, Johnny covered Steve's face with kisses. They cuddled for a moment on the bed. But neither was really present, both of them having already parted, anticipating the strange emptiness of the times that lay ahead, preparing for it.

Steve watched Johnny dress, his sleek body exposed and still incredibly tempting.

"You're so beautiful, Johnny," he said, sincere, now completely present in the moment.

Johnny was silent, his eyes full of a million feelings and thoughts. Suddenly he moved swiftly back to the bed, leaned down and kissed Steve one last time, soft lips, gentle tongues. Steve leaned up toward the boy, wrapped his arms around him. The kiss finished, they held their faces close.

"Good-bye," Steve said, touching the tip of his finger to Johnny's soft lips as he looked at them, his eyes sad. "You know where to find me."

Johnny stood again, proud and strong at the bedside. "Come down to the lobby with me. See me off."

After Steve hurriedly dressed, Johnny handed him an envelope. "I have a present for you," Johnny said,

Steve opened it. It contained the pencil Johnny had stolen from his desk. "Why, thank you, Johnny. It's what I've always wanted."

"I thought you were going to say you've been wondering what the hell happened to it."

"Oh, you mean you stole it?"

Johnny nodded in mock sheepishness.

"Well, I really hadn't missed it. I mean, I have a whole drawer full of them."

"But there was only one on the desk. And I had to have it."

"You're crazy," Steve laughed. "First my heart, then my shorts, now my pencil."

Johnny snatched the pencil back. "Okay, if you have so many, I'll keep it. It means nothing to you, but to me – "

"Okay, now my heart. Can I have my heart back?"

"No, never." Johnny giggled, clutching the pencil to his chest.

"I was afraid of that."

. . .

Watching Johnny turn and smile at him before he passed through the revolving glass doors to the street, Steve couldn't help thinking about how he had never been to California. How could he arrange it? Nothing came to him. He shrugged. He would think of something.

From a distance, he followed Johnny out onto the street. Johnny hailed a cab. Dusk had begun to settle over Lexington Avenue and, with his hands in his pockets, Steve stood there under the hotel's canopy until he could no longer see the yellow cab that carried Johnny away.

Epilogue

A lot can happen in almost a year.

Steve surveyed Johnny thoroughly. Then he said, "You're looking great, Johnny, do you know that? All that time at the gym has been good for you."

Johnny smiled and nodded. "I know."

Steve was surprised by Johnny's new confidence, this calm assurance. In a year the boy seemed to have changed incalculably. Steve felt rather piqued by this but also attracted. Johnny seemed so happy. He had become a man.

Suddenly it struck Steve that he must have a lover; there was something about him that was so serene and fulfilled. The idea of him incredibly happy with another man made his stomach churn. He said, "Well, I bet you've been having fun?"

Johnny laughed. "Why?"

Steve shrugged. "I dunno. You seem different."

Johnny had picked the restaurant, a vegetarian place with abundant hanging ferns, and offered to meet Steve there. Steve noticed how other men stared at the boy as he walked in. He seemed aloof and oblivious.

They chatted about school and Johnny asked how Steve's wife and kids were. He said everybody was fine. They had stopped in Phoenix to see his brother and then come to Los Angeles. Steve had Susan take the girls to Disneyland. He said he was going to relax by the pool at the hotel.

"Still fuckin' her pussy, eh?"

Steve looked away. "I'll ignore that."

"Oh, I know. Duty calls."

"I love my wife."

"So you've said. Well, I wondered what pussy was like so I had some. I can't say I was impressed."

Johnny had Steve's full attention now. "Oh?"

"Yeah. I fucked a girl. That make you happy?"

"No. I mean, yes, it does. Whatever you want, Johnny."

"I fucked her but I wanted you."

"That happens to me sometimes too. I'll be with Susan but I'll be thinking of you."

"And I'm three thousand miles away."

"Sad, but true."

Now it all felt rather odd and unnatural. He had imagined that Johnny would be tense when he saw him but in fact he seemed perfectly relaxed and at ease. If anything Steve was the one who felt uncomfortable. He knew that Johnny needed someone. Steve felt nosy and jealous but he said nothing.

The nelly young waiter flirted with Johnny as they ordered their meal. Steve noticed their eye contact and it made his stomach churn. After the waiter had left their table with the order, Johnny played with his cutlery, making his finger into a flat, straight scale and trying to balance his knife on the finger so that it didn't tip off, then his fork, then his spoon. Steve watched him with a half-smile flickering around the corners of his lips.

Eventually Steve said, "You said over the phone you were being a good boy – "

"It's a business decision. You know, Uncle Bennett laid it all out for me. It's all mine if I want it."

"If you do as he says."

"No. He agreed I could do as I wished. I just had to graduate, which I have, and go to college, any college, he didn't give a shit, which surprised me, and go back to New York and give real estate management, or whatever it is, a try."

"And you – ?"

Johnny grinned. "Well, I love New York."

"And money. Lots of money."

"I've never known anything else, Steve. I don't think I want to."

Steve sipped his water. "So there's no one special?"

Johnny looked out the window. "I've been seeing some guys, but it's rough. I mean, they're all into drugs, or drinking, or hanging out and I've got my future to think of." He caressed a bicep, flexed.

"You look wonderful. Better than ever."

"Does that mean you'll fuck me after lunch?"

Steve smiled. "Now *that's* my Johnny."

At a motel on Selma near where they had eaten lunch, Steve let Johnny undress him, push him onto the bed. It was the same Johnny, all right. Why the boy wanted him, Steve could never figure out; he did not think of himself as handsome. He was not unattractive, but hardly one to make heads turn the way Johnny did. From the beginning, he had been astounded by Johnny's hunger for him, and today was no exception. Johnny kissed him with deep, passionate, probing strokes of his tongue, delving into Steve's mouth. Steve's tongue met his, entwined in soul kissing in a way he never had experienced before: Johnny sucked Steve's tongue deeply into his mouth as he squiggled his tongue all around it. When he pulled his tongue from the depths of Steve's mouth, he planted tiny kisses on his lips, nose, cheeks and, working his way down his neck, on his pecs. By the time he took the right nipple between his lips, Steve was delirious with lust. When he gently gnawed and bit the hardened bud, Steve was moaning, louder and louder with every delicious bite. Then he went to work on the other, totally disregarding Steve's cock, which was pressing against him for some attention.

Johnny stood and began stripping off his clothes. With the shirt gone, Steve saw the boy had grown some golden hairs on his now-sculpted chest. When Johnny removed his pants and underwear, all Steve could focus on was the incredible fact that the boy's ass was even more delectable than before. His hard-on was just as Steve remembered it, scrumptious-looking and standing up close to his navel.

He came back to the bed, straddled Steve and stuffed Steve's mouth with his cock. The face-fucking, with Johnny reaching behind him occasionally to tease Steve's erection, lasted several minutes until Steve's head was reeling from the pleasure. Johnny was ready to come, but he had just begun. He switched places with Steve and permitted the older man to fuck his mouth with his erection. All the while Johnny's hands were moving, probing, touching, exposing. Steve's face was flushed and he was breathing hard. For a moment Johnny had the full length of him in his mouth; he gave him a smooth, tight suck at the back of his throat before he pulled out. "Fuck me," Johnny begged.

In no time, Steve had mounted Johnny and expertly drew his legs over his shoulders so he could fuck him with the deepest penetration.

"This is what I've been waiting for," Johnny said, as the big head was pressed past the clenching ass muscle. Steve glided into Johnny with ease. As he began to pump, the bed shook.

"Oh, fuck it, man! Everybody out here wants to get fucked," Johnny admitted. "I've needed this for so long."

Steve's eyes glazed over and the passion raged in him, tempering the speed and depth of his thrusts. He grabbed Johnny by the hips and pressed his legs way back as he continued to fill his ass.

"I'm gonna explode," he panted as he fucked. And soon he was rocking, pressing, fucking in shorter, harder, stronger thrusts until Johnny felt his ejaculations shooting through his cock and into him. Steve pressed himself inside Johnny until he could press no more, filling Johnny. Johnny's ass muscles twitched around Steve's cock until the very last drop of jism escaped.

Steve collapsed next to Johnny and brought the boy's cock to his mouth once more. He kissed it, stroked it, adored it. "Will you fuck me with this?"

"If that's what you want."

"Yes, I want it. I guess I'm like all the others," Steve said.

"No, you aren't, or you wouldn't be here."

"What makes me so special anyway?"

"You're just a nice man, Steve. A very nice man. You're the only man who's treated me right. And, besides, you'll always be special to me, *Mr. Parker.*" Johnny mussed Steve's hair. "I mean, you're the only teach I've ever fucked."

As Steve got into position, his legs spread wide, he smiled. "And you're the only student I've ever fucked."

"So," Johnny said, greasing his cock, then sliding it into his former teacher, "that makes us even."

And the thought of being "even" with Johnny Lawrence, the beautiful boy whose cock was inching into him, made Steve shudder with delight.

Footnote

The bisexual 'zine *Logomotive: A Magazine of Sex & Fun from a Bisexual Perspective*, recently offered a page of bisexual lists, including some seventy-five "famous bisexuals," listed alphabetically from (perpetual favorite) Alexander the Great to (perpetual favorite) Virginia Woolf, including Lord Byron, Queen Christina of Sweden, Ram Dass, Freddie Mercury, Sappho, and St. Augustine. A footnote in small type noted, "The list of bisexual figures is arbitrary. These are people who were known to have relationships with people of genders other than their own, as well as their own. , Some have identified as bisexual, others have not labeled themselves, while others still identify with a sexual orientation other than 'bisexual.'" Other "bi lists" were also provided, of bi movies, bi comic books, and bi science-fiction novels, chosen "because they have a bisexual theme, character(s), chapters, story lines or research; or they were written or produced by bisexual(s)." In case the reader was becoming too comfortable with labels, a note from the editor also informs her or him that "we're changing our name." Henceforth the 'zine would be known as *Slippery When Wet*, the editors rather coyly pointed out, still related to "transportation." But the shift to a deliberately erotic double-meaning highlighted another issue relevant to bisexual self-awareness: how to make bisexuality sexy?

As Marjorie Garber states in her book *Vice Versa*, it would seem as if bi-sex might have something for everyone, in terms of fantasy, affection, and desire. Says Garber, "Yet the politics of organized bisexuality in the nineties, with many of its energies coming out of feminism and a discourse of rights, and cognizant also of the popular demonization of the 'bisexual AIDS carrier,' the duplicitous married man who was said to have infected his unsuspecting wife and unborn children, in a way militated against sexiness."

The San Francisco-based *Anything That Moves*, which began publishing in January 1991 and Garber describes as the premier regional magazine of the American "bisexual community," adopted the subtitle "Beyond the Myths of Bisexuality," although its name reflects one of the biggest myths of all.

Under former editor Karla Rossi, every issue began with a standard editorial, "About our name . . . ":

...Our choice to use this title for the magazine has been nothing less than controversial. That we would choose to redefine the stereotype that "bisexuals will fuck anything that moves," to suit our our purposes has created myriad reactions. Those critical of the title feel we are (perpetuating) the stereotype and damaging our images. Those in favor of its use see it as a movement away from the stereotype, toward bisexual empowerment.

...We are challenging people to face their own external and internal biphobia. We are demanding attention, and are re-defining "anything that moves" on our own terms.

READ OUR LIPS: WE WILL WRITE OR PRINT OR SAY ANYTHING THAT MOVES US BEYOND THE LIMITING STEREOTYPES THAT ARE DISPLACED ON TO US.

"The sardonic adoption of a negative stereotype as a proudly worn label," Garber feels, "is consonant with the retrieval of 'queer' among gays, lesbians, and others who describe themselves as 'gay-affirmative,' and also with the insider use of formerly deplored terms like 'nigger' (by African Americans only, as in the rap group N.WA., 'Niggers with Attitude') and 'fag hag,' now occasionally claimed by some women who like hanging out with gay men."

Garber feels that *Anything That Moves*, as the title for a bisexual magazine, not only puts sex on the front burner, it also makes a deliberate gesture of inclusiveness. Not only the "good" bisexuals, who affirm their monogamy and make bisexuality potentially more acceptable to the mainstream, but all persons who are bisexual or interested in bisexuality are, at least in theory, welcome. As bisexual rights activist Lenore Norrgard, herself a founding editor of the Seattle Bisexual Women's Network newsletter *North Bi Northwest*, has argued, bisexuals "should take to heart the hard lesson the gay movement taught us through trying to present gays as 'normal,' that is, by excluding 'drag queens, bulldykes, and gays of color' in favor of an upscale, relatively unthreatening, largely white male image of yuppie professionals and artists.

In 1975, in *Redbook* magazine of all places, Margaret Mead wrote: "The time has come, I think, when we must recognize bisexuality as a normal form of human behavior." Changing traditional attitudes about homosexuality is important, she affirmed, but "we shall not really succeed in discarding the straitjacket of our cultural beliefs about sexual choice if we fail to come to terms with the well-documented, normal human capacity to love members of both sexes."

By "well-documented" Mead meant, Garber feels, "attested to over time." She noted that while homosexual relationships between older and younger men in ancient Greece and Sparta are frequently cited, "it is usually left out of account that the older men also had wives and children."

Contributors
(Other Than the Editor, John Patrick)

"The Mummy" and "Thief of Night's Bounty"
L. Amore

The author is 27 and has been in the book business for ten years. He has lived in upstate New York, Boston and New York City and now resides in Connecticut. He is currently working on his first novel, as yet untitled, and finishing a novella called, "The Night John Preston Flogged Me." The author's stories have appeared in STARbooks' best-selling anthologies *Seduced* and *Insatiable/Unforgettable*.

"Brothers" and "Love in the Bookstore"
Ken Anderson

The Intense Lover, a book of Ken's poetry, was published by STARbooks earlier this year. The author lives in Georgia.

"A Circle of a Thousand Boys"
Antler

The poet lives in Milwaukee when not traveling to perform his poems or wildernessing. His epic poem *Factory* was published by City Lights. His collection of poems *Last Words* was published by Ballantine. Winner of the Whitman Award from the Walt Whitman Society of Camden, New Jersey, and the Witter Bynner prize from the Academy and Institute of Arts & Letters in New York, his poetry has appeared in many periodicals (including *Utne Reader*, *Whole Earth Review* and *American Poetry Review*) and anthologies (including *Gay Roots*, *Erotic by Nature*, and *Gay and Lesbian Poetry of Our Time*).

"Dutch Treat"
Ray Burrell

This story originally appeared in *The Gay Review*, Vol. III, No. 1, Winter 1995.

"Exploring Sam" and "Desert Steam"
David Patrick Beavers

The author's first novel, *Jackal in the Dark*, about Los Angeles in the '70s, and the sequel, *The Jackal Awakens*, were recently published by Millivres Books, London. The author lives in Los Angeles.

"Tonio Joe"
Richie Brooks

The author, who sees nothing wrong with "telling it like it is," resides in Canada.

"A Perfect Summer"
Leo Cardini

Author of the best-selling book, *Mineshaft Nights*, Mr. Cardini's stories and theater-related articles have appeared in a variety of magazines. He is the co-author of a musical now being fine-tuned for Broadway.

"The Blackguard"
William Cozad

The author is a regular contributor to gay magazines and his memoirs are to be published by STARbooks Press in *Lover Boys* and *Boys of the Night*.

"Romancing the Bone"
Griff Davis

The author is a self-proclaimed boy-lover who lives in Tampa. This is his first published work.

"Young & Willing"
John C. Douglas

The author has an enviable track record, having some thirty novels published, and more than twenty screenplays produced. A resident of Alabama, Douglas has a number of works in progress. "Most of the time," he admits, "I don't have a firm plot in mind. I prefer to create the characters and let them do whatever they like. Sometimes, they surprise even me!" A full-length novel, "The Young and the Flawless," appeared in STARbooks Press' most popular anthology of all-time, *Barely Legal*.

"The Rendezvous"
Jarred Goodall

When he is not accepting sabbatical appointments abroad, the author teaches English in a Midwestern university. Born in Wisconsin, he loves back-packing, mountain-climbing, chess and Victorian literature. His favorite color: blue-green; favorite pop-star: Leonard Bernstein; favorite car: WWII Jeep; favorite drink: water, preferably recycled; favorite actor: River Phoenix (alas); favorite hobby: "If you want to know that, read my stories."

"Johnny: Out of Hiding"
Thomas C. Humphrey

The author, who resides in Florida, is working on his first novel, *All the Difference*, and has contributed stories to First Hand publications.

"Practice Pony"
David Laurents

The author is a regular contributor to such publications as *Honcho*, *Overload*, and *The Journal of Erotica* (UK) and has had stories included in the best-selling anthologies *Bizarre Dreams* and *Meltdown!* from BadBoy and *Wired Hard*, *Of Princes and Beauties*, and *The Beast Within* from Circlet Press. He lives in New York City.

"Shorts Weather"
Al Lone

The author's previous story for STARbooks, "What's Your Name?," appeared in the anthology *Insatiable/Unforgettable*. He is temporarily incarcerated in New Jersey.

"Please, Teach Me More"
Bert McKenzie

A free lance writer and drama critic, the Kansan writes a column for a major midwestern newspaper and has contributed erotic fiction to magazines such as *Torso*, *Mandate*, and *Playguy*. He is a frequent contributor to STARbooks' anthologies and an anthology of his work was published by Badboy, *Fringe Benefits*.

"Night Train"
Edmund Miller

Dr. Miller, the author of the legendary poetry book *Fucking Animals* (recently reprinted by STARBooks), is the chairman of the English Department at a large university in the New York area. "Night Train" has been adapted from material originally published by *Playguy*.

"14"
Thom Nickels

The Cliffs of Aries, the author's first novel, was published in 1988 by Aegina Press. His second book, *Two Novellas: Walking Water & After All This*, was published in 1989 by Banned Books and was a Lambda Literary Award finalist in 1990 in the Science Fiction/Fantasy category. A regular columnist for an alternative weekly in Philadelphia, Thom has contributed feature articles, book reviews and celebrity interviews to several gay publications. A collection of his best writing was published by STARbooks Press under the title, *The Boy on the Bicycle*.

"Eddie's Audition"
Peter Z. Pan

A first-generation American of Cuban descent, this twentysomething author calls himself a "quintessential jack-of-all-trades: multimedia writer, theatrical director, and sometime actor-singer." Peter says he resides in Miami, "physically anyway." Spiritually, he says he will always live where Lost Boys forever frolic: "...second star to the right, and straight on till morning."

"The Bet"
Matthew Rettemund

He is the author of the non-fiction Madonna book *Encyclopedia Madonnica* (March '95), the gay novel *Boy Culture* and a book on the pop culture of the '80s, from St. Martin's.

"Rough-boy"
Ian Stewart

The author is another Canadian who sees nothing wrong in "telling it like it is."

"Brother Flesh"
John Terron
The author lives in Paris.

"Milk Run"
Christopher Thomas
The poet has had his work published in many literary journals including *Deviance, The James White Review, Michigan Quarterly Review, Poetry Motel, Chiron Review, Duckabush Review, Evergreen Review, New Voice, RFD* and *Gay Sunshine Review*. He makes his living as a Gentleman Farmer and will soon publish a collection of his best work as *The Smell of Carnal Knowledge*.

ACKNOWLDGEMENTS AND SOURCES

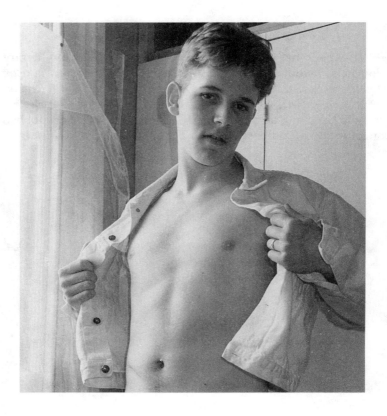

Cover photography by celebrated English photographer David Butt.

Mr. Butt's photographs may be purchased through Suntown, Post Office Box 151, Danbury, Oxfordshire, OX16 8QN, United Kingdom. Ask for a full catalogue.

Sexy, dark-haired Kris, from Solvenia, is the coverboy on *Euroboy* Issue 58, available from STARbooks, and blond babe Lee was one of the most requested models ever in the U.K., appearing on the cover of *Vulcan* and many other magazines.

SPECIAL OFFER

STARbooks Press now offers two very special international gay magazine packages: You can get the hottest American gay magazines, including *GAYME, All-Man, Torso, Advocate Men, Advocate Fresh Men, In Touch,* and *Playguy,* either singly for $6.95, or in a very special deluxe sampler package for only $25 for six big issues.

We also offer the sizzling British and European magazines, including *Euros, Euroboy, Prowl, Vulcan, HUNK,* and *Steam* for $9.95 each or only $49.95 for sampler of six fabulous issues.

Please add $2.75 post per issue or sampler. Order from: STARbooks, P.O. Box 2737-B, Sarasota FL 34230-2737 USA.

ABOUT THE EDITOR

John Patrick is a prolific, prize-winning author of fiction and non-fiction. One of his short stories, "The Well," was honored by PEN American Center as one of the best of 1987. His novels and anthologies, as well as his non-fiction works, including *Legends* and *The Best of the Superstars* series, continue to gain him new fans every day. One of his stories appears in the Badboy collection *Southern Comfort*.

A divorced father of two, the author is a longtime member of the American Booksellers Association, the Florida Publishers' Association, American Civil Liberties Union, and the Adult Video Association. He resides in Florida.